JULIAN COMSTOCK

JULIAN COMSTOCK

A STORY OF 22ND-CENTURY AMERICA

Robert Charles Wilson

TOR®

A TOM DOHERTY ASSOCIATES BOOK

NEW YORK

This is a work of fiction. All of the characters, organizations, and events portrayed in this novel are either products of the author's imagination or are used fictitiously.

JULIAN COMSTOCK: A STORY OF 22ND-CENTURY AMERICA

Copyright © 2009 by Robert Charles Wilson

Edited by Teresa Nielsen Hayden

A Tor Book
Published by Tom Doherty Associates, LLC
175 Fifth Avenue
New York, NY 10010

www.tor-forge.com

Tor® is a registered trademark of Tom Doherty Associates, LLC.

Library of Congress Cataloging-in-Publication Data
Wilson, Robert Charles, 1953–
Julian Comstock : a story of 22nd-century America / Robert Charles Wilson.
      p.   cm.
"A Tom Doherty Associates book."
ISBN-13: 978-0-7653-1971-5
ISBN-10: 0-7653-1971-3
1. United States—Fiction.   2. Political fiction.   I. Title.
PR9199.3.W4987J85   2009
813'.54—dc22
2008053400

First Edition: June 2009

Printed in the United States of America

0   9   8   7   6   5   4   3   2   1

To Mr. William Taylor Adams of Massachusetts,
who might not have approved of it,
this book
is nevertheless respectfully and gratefully dedicated.

We read the past by the light of the present, and the forms vary as the shadows fall, or as the point of vision alters.

—JAMES ANTHONY FROUDE

Look not for roses in Attalus his garden, or wholesome flowers in a venomous plantation. And since there is scarce any one bad, but some others are the worse for him, tempt not contagion by proximity, and hazard not thyself in the shadow of corruption.

—SIR THOMAS BROWNE

Crowns, generally speaking, have thorns.

—ARTHUR E. HERTZLER

JULIAN COMSTOCK

PROLOGUE

I mean to set down here the story of the life and adventures of Julian Comstock, better known as Julian the Agnostic or (after his uncle) Julian Conqueror.

Readers familiar with the name will naturally expect scenes of blood and betrayal, including the War in Labrador and Julian's run-in with the Church of the Dominion. I witnessed all those events firsthand, and at closer proximity than I might have liked, and they are all described in the five "Acts" (as I call them) that follow. In the company of Julian Comstock I traveled from the pine-bark Eden in which I was born all the way to Mascouche, Lake Melville, Manhattan, and stranger places; I saw men and governments rise and fall; and I woke many a morning with death staring me in the face. Some of the memories I mean to set down aren't pleasant ones, or flattering, and I tremble a little at the prospect of reliving them, but I intend to spare no one—we were what we were, and we became what we became, and the facts will ennoble or demean us, as the reader chooses to see it.

But I begin the story the way it began for me—in a town in the boreal west, when Julian was young, and I was young, and neither of us was famous.

A PINE-BARK EDEN;
or,
THE CARIBOU-HORN TRAIN

CHRISTMAS, 2172

And the same fires, which were kindled for Heretics, will serve for the destruction of Philosophers.

—HUME, a Philosopher

1

In October of 2172—the year the Election show came to town—Julian Comstock and I, along with his mentor Sam Godwin, rode to the Tip east of Williams Ford, where I came to possess a book, and Julian tutored me in one of his heresies.

There was a certain resolute promptness to the seasons in Athabaska in those days. Summers were long and hot, December brought snow and sudden freezes, and most years the River Pine ran freely by the first of March. Spring and fall were mere custodial functions, by comparison. Today might be the best we would get of autumn—the air brisk but not cold, the long sunlight unhindered by any cloud. It was a day we ought to have spent under Sam Godwin's tutelage, reading chapters from *The Dominion History of the Union* or Otis's *War and How to Conduct It*. But Sam wasn't a heartless overseer, and the gentle weather suggested the possibility of an outing. So we went to the stables where my father worked, and drew horses, and rode out of the Estate with lunches of black bread and salt ham in our back-satchels.

At first we headed south along the Wire Road, away from the hills and the town. Julian and I rode ahead while Sam paced his mount behind us, his Pittsburgh rifle in the saddle holster at his side. There was no perceptible threat or danger, but Sam Godwin believed in preparedness—if he had a gospel, it was BE PREPARED; also, SHOOT FIRST; and probably, DAMN THE CONSEQUENCES. Sam, who was nearly fifty winters old, wore a dense brown beard stippled with white hairs, and was dressed in what remained presentable of his Army of the Californias uniform. Sam was nearly a father to Julian, Julian's own true father having performed a gallows dance some years before, and lately Sam had been more vigilant than ever, for reasons he hadn't discussed, at least with me.

Julian was my age (seventeen), and we were approximately the same height, but there the resemblance ended. Julian had been born an Aristo, or *Eupatridian*, as they say back east, while my family was of the leasing class. His face was smooth and pale; mine was dark and lunar, scarred by the same Pox that took my sister Flaxie to her grave in '63. His yellow hair was long and almost femininely clean; mine was black and wiry, cut to stubble by my mother with her sewing scissors, and I washed it once a week—more often in summer, when the creek behind the cottage warmed to a pleasant temperature. His clothes were linen and silk, brass-buttoned, cut to fit; my shirt and pants were coarse hempen cloth, sewn to a good approximation but clearly not the work of a New York tailor.

And yet we were friends, and had been friends for three years, ever since we met by chance in the hills west of the Duncan and Crowley Estate. We had gone there to hunt, Julian with his rifle and me with a simple muzzle-loader, and we crossed paths in the forest and got to talking. We both loved books, especially the boys' books written by an author named Charles Curtis Easton.* I had been carrying a copy of Easton's *Against the Brazilians,* illicitly borrowed from the Estate library—Julian recognized the title but vowed not to rat on me for possessing it, since he loved the book as much as I did and longed to discuss it with a fellow enthusiast—in short, he did me an unbegged favor; and we became fast friends despite our differences.

In those early days I hadn't known how fond he was of Philosophy and such petty crimes as that. But I suppose it wouldn't have mattered to me, if I had.

Today Julian turned east from the Wire Road and took us down a lane bordered by split-rail fences on which dense blackberry gnarls had grown up, between fields of wheat and gourds just lately harvested. Before long we passed the rude shacks of the Estate's indentured laborers, whose near-naked children gawked at us from the dusty lane-side, and I deduced that we were headed for the Tip, because where else on this road was there to go?—unless we continued on for many hours more, all the way to the ruins of the old oil towns, left over from the days of the False Tribulation.

The Tip was located a distance from Williams Ford in order to prevent poaching and disorder. There was a strict pecking order to the Tip. It worked this way: professional scavengers hired by the Estate brought their pickings from ruined places to the Tip, which was a pine-fenced enclosure (a sort of stockade) in an open patch of grassland. There the newly-arrived goods were roughly sorted, and riders were dispatched to the Estate to make the high-born aware of the latest discoveries. Then various Aristos (or their trusted servants) rode out to claim the prime gleanings. The next day the leasing class would be allowed to sort through what was left; and after that, if anything remained, indentured laborers could rummage through it, if they calculated it was worthwhile to make the journey.

Every prosperous town had a Tip, though in the East it was sometimes called a Till, a Dump, or an Eebay.

Today we were lucky. A dozen wagonloads of scrounge had just arrived, and riders hadn't yet been sent to notify the Estate. The gate of the enclosure was manned by an armed Reservist, who looked at us suspiciously until Sam announced the name of Julian Comstock. Then the guard briskly stepped aside, and we went inside the fence.

A chubby Tipman, eager to show off his bounty, hurried toward us as we dismounted and moored our horses. "Happy coincidence!" he cried.

---

* Whom I would meet when he was sixty years old, and I was a newcomer to the book trade—but I anticipate myself.

"Gentlemen!" Addressing mostly Sam by this remark, with a cautious smile for Julian and a disdainful sidelong glance at me. "Anything in particular you're looking for?"

"Books," said Julian, before Sam or I could answer.

"Books! Well—ordinarily, I set aside books for the Dominion Conservator . . ."

"This boy is a Comstock," Sam said. "I don't suppose you mean to balk him."

The Tipman promptly reddened. "No, not at all—in fact we came across something in our digging—a sort of *library in miniature*—I'll show you, if you like."

That was intriguing, especially to Julian, who beamed as if he had been invited to a Christmas party; and we followed the stout Tipman to a freshly-arrived canvasback wagon, from which a shirtless laborer was tossing bundles into a stack beside a tent.

The twine-wrapped bales contained books—ancient books, wholly free of the Dominion Stamp of Approval. They must have been more than a century old, for although they were faded it was obvious that they had once been colorful and expensively printed, not made of stiff brown paper like the Charles Curtis Easton books of modern times. They had not even rotted much. Their smell, under the cleansing Athabaska sunlight, was inoffensive.

"Sam!" Julian whispered ecstatically. He had already drawn his knife, and he began slicing through the twine.

"Calm down," said Sam, who wasn't an enthusiast like Julian.

"Oh, but—*Sam!* We should have brought a cart!"

"We can't carry away armloads, Julian, nor would we ever be allowed to. The Dominion scholars will have all this, and most of it will be locked up in their Archive in New York City, if it isn't burned. Though I expect you can get away with a volume or two if you're discreet about it."

The Tipman said, "These are from Lundsford." Lundsford was the name of a ruined town twenty miles or so to the southeast. The Tipman leaned toward Sam Godwin and said: "We thought Lundsford had been mined out a decade ago. But even a dry well may freshen. One of my workers spotted a low place off the main excavation—a sort of *sink-hole*: the recent rain had cut it through. Once a basement or warehouse of some kind. Oh, sir, we found good china there, and glasswork, and many more books than this . . . most hopelessly mildewed, but some had been wrapped in a kind of oilcoth, and were lodged under a fallen ceiling . . . there had been a fire, but they survived it . . ."

"Good work, Tipman," Sam Godwin said with palpable disinterest.

"Thank you, sir! Perhaps you could remember me to the men of the Estate?" And he gave his name (which I have forgotten).

Julian knelt amidst the compacted clay and rubble of the Tip, lifting up each book in turn and examining it with wide eyes. I joined him in his exploration, though I had never much liked the Tip. It had always seemed to me a haunted place. And of course it *was* haunted—it existed in order to be haunted—that is, to house the revenants of the past, ghosts of the False Tribulation startled out of their century-long slumber. Here was evidence of the best and worst of the people who had inhabited the Years of Vice and Profligacy. Their fine things were very fine, their glassware especially, and it was a straitened Aristo indeed who did not sit down to an antique table-setting rescued from some ruin or other. Sometimes you might find useful knives or other tools at the Tip. Coins were common. The coins were never gold or silver, and were too plentiful to be worth much, individually, but they could be worked into buttons and such adornments. One of the high-born back at the Estate owned a saddle studded with copper pennies all from the year 2032—I had often been enlisted to polish it, and disliked it for that reason.

Here too was the trash and inexplicable detritus of the old times: "plastic," gone brittle with sunlight or soft with the juices of the earth; bits of metal blooming with rust; electronic devices blackened by time and imbued with the sad inutility of a tensionless spring; engine parts, corroded; copper wire rotten with verdigris; aluminum cans and steel barrels eaten through by the poisonous fluids they had once contained—and so on, almost *ad infinitum.*

Here as well were the in-between things, the curiosities, as intriguing and as useless as seashells. ("Put down that rusty trumpet, Adam, you'll cut your lip and poison your blood!"—my mother, when we had visited the Tip many years before I met Julian. There had been no music in the trumpet anyway—its bell was bent and corroded through.)

More than that, though, there hovered above the Tip (*any* Tip) the uneasy knowledge that all these things, fine or corrupt, had outlived their makers—had proved more imperishable, in the long run, than flesh or spirit; for the souls of the Secular Ancients are almost certainly not first in line for Resurrection.

And yet, these books . . . they tempted eye and mind alike. Some were decorated with beautiful women in various degrees of undress. I had already sacrificed my claim to spotless virtue with certain young women at the Estate, whom I had recklessly kissed; at the age of seventeen I considered myself a jade, or something like one; but these images were so frank and impudent they made me blush and look away.

Julian ignored them, as he had always been invulnerable to the charms of women. He preferred the more densely-written material. He had already set aside a spotted and discolored Textbook of Biology. He found another volume almost as large, and handed it to me, saying, "Here, Adam, try this—you might find it enlightening."

I inspected it skeptically. The book was called *A History of Mankind in Space.*

"The moon again," I said.

"Read it for yourself."

"Tissue of lies, I'm sure."

"With photographs."

"Photographs prove nothing. Those people could do anything with photographs."

"Well, read it anyway," said Julian.

In truth the idea excited me. We had had this argument many times, especially on autumn nights when the moon hung low and ponderous on the horizon. *People have walked there*, Julian would say, pointing at that celestial body. The first time he made the claim I laughed at him; the second time I said, "Yes, certainly: I once climbed there myself, on a greased rainbow—" But he had been serious.

Oh, I had heard these stories. Who hadn't? Men on the moon. What surprised me was that someone as well-educated as Julian would believe them.

"Just take the book," he insisted.

"What: to keep?"

"Certainly to keep."

"Believe I will," I muttered, and I stuck the object in my back-satchel and felt both proud and guilty. What would my father say, if he knew I was reading literature without a Dominion Stamp? What would my mother make of it? (Of course I wouldn't tell them.)

At this point I backed off and found a grassy patch a little away from the rubble, where I could sit and eat lunch while Julian went on sorting through the old texts. Sam Godwin came and joined me, brushing a spot on a charred timber so he could sit without soiling his uniform, such as it was.

"He loves those musty old books," I said, making conversation.

Sam was often taciturn—the very picture of an old veteran—but today he nodded and spoke familiarly. "He's learned to love them, and I helped to teach him. His father wanted him to know more of the world than the Dominion histories of it. But I wonder if that was wise, in the long run. He loves his books too dearly, I think, or gives them too much credence. It might be they'll kill him one of these days."

"How, Sam? By the apostasy of them?"

"He debates with the Dominion clergy. Just last week I found him arguing with Ben Kreel* about God, and history, and such abstractions. Which is precisely what he must *not* do, if he means to survive the next few years."

"Why? What threatens him?"

"The jealousy of the powerful," said Sam.

But he would say no more on the subject, only stroked his graying beard, and glanced occasionally and uneasily to the east.

---

* Our local representative of the Council of the Dominion; in effect, the Mayor of the town.

Eventually Julian had to drag himself from his nest of books with only a pair of prizes: the *Introduction to Biology* and another volume called *Geology of North America.* Time to go, Sam insisted; better to be back at the Estate by supper, so we wouldn't be missed; soon enough the official pickers would arrive to cull what we had left.

But I have said that Julian tutored me in one of his apostasies. This is how it happened. As we headed home we stopped at the height of a hill overlooking the town of Williams Ford and the River Pine as it cut through the low places on its way from the mountains of the West. From here we had a fine view of the steeple of the Dominion Hall, and the revolving waterwheels of the grist mill and the lumber mill, all blue in the long light and hazy with coal-smoke, and far to the south a railway bridge spanning the gorge of the Pine like a suspended thread. *Go inside,* the weather seemed to proclaim; *it's fair but it won't be fair for long; bolt the window, stoke the fire, boil the apples; winter's due.* We rested our horses on that windy hilltop as the afternoon softened toward evening, and Julian found a blackberry bramble where the berries were still plump and dark, and we plucked some of these and ate them.

That was the world I had been born into. It was an autumn like every autumn I could remember, drowsy in its familiarity. But I couldn't help thinking of the Tip and its ghosts. Maybe those people, the people who had lived through the Efflorescence of Oil and the False Tribulation, had felt about their homes and neighborhoods just as I felt about Williams Ford. They were ghosts to me, but they must have seemed real enough to themselves—must have *been* real; had not realized they were ghosts; and did that mean I was also a ghost, a revenant to haunt some future generation?

Julian saw my expression and asked what was troubling me. I told him my thoughts.

"Now you're thinking like a Philosopher," he said, grinning.

"No wonder they're such a miserable brigade, then."

"Unfair, Adam—you've never seen a Philosopher in your life." Julian believed in Philosophers, and claimed to have met one or two.

"Well, I *imagine* they're miserable, if they go around thinking of themselves as ghosts and such."

"It's the condition of all things," Julian said. "This blackberry, for example." He plucked one and held it in the pale palm of his hand. "Has it always looked like this?"

"Obviously not," I said, impatiently.

"Once it was a tiny green bud of a thing, and before that it was part of the substance of the bramble, which before that was a seed inside a blackberry—"

"And round and round for all eternity."

"But no, Adam, that's the point. The bramble, and that tree over there, and the gourds in the field, and the crow circling over them—they're all descended from ancestors that didn't quite resemble them. A blackberry or a crow is a *form*, and forms change over time, the way clouds change shape as they travel across the sky."

"Forms of what?"

"Of DNA," Julian said earnestly. (The *Biology* he had picked out of the Tip was not the first *Biology* he had read.)

"Julian," Sam said, "I once promised this boy's parents you wouldn't corrupt him."

"I've heard of DNA," I said. "It's the life force of the secular ancients. And it's a myth."

"Like men walking on the moon?"

"Exactly like."

"And who's your authority on this? Ben Kreel? *The Dominion History of the Union*?"

"Everything changes except DNA? That's a peculiar argument even from you, Julian."

"It would be, if I were making it. But DNA *isn't* changeless. It struggles to remember itself, but it never remembers itself perfectly. Remembering a fish, it imagines a lizard. Remembering a horse, it imagines a hippopotamus. Remembering an ape, it imagines a man."

"Julian!" Sam was insistent now. "That's enough."

"You sound like a Darwinist," I said.

"Yes," Julian admitted, smiling in spite of his unorthodoxy, the autumn sun turning his face the color of penny copper. "I suppose I do."

That night I lay in bed until I was reasonably certain both my parents were asleep. Then I rose, lit a lamp, and took the new (or rather very old) *History of Mankind in Space* from where I had hidden it behind a pinewood chest.

I leafed through the brittle pages of it. I didn't read the book. I *would* read it, but tonight I was too weary to pay close attention, and in any case I wanted to savor the words (lies and fictions though they might be), not rush through them like a glutton. Tonight I meant only to sample it—to look at the pictures, in other words.

There were dozens of photographs, and each one captured my attention with fresh marvels and implausibilities. One of them showed, or purported to show, men standing on the surface of the moon, just as Julian had described.

The men in the picture were Americans. They wore flags stitched to the shoulders of their moon clothing, an archaic version of our own flag, with something less than the customary sixty stars. Their clothing was white and ridiculously bulky, like the winter clothes of the Inuit, and they wore helmets with golden visors that hid their faces. I supposed it must be very cold on the moon, if explorers required such cumbersome protection. They must have arrived in winter. However, there was no ice or snow in the neighborhood. The moon seemed to be little more than a desert—dry as a stick and dusty as a Tipman's wardrobe.

I cannot say how long I stared at this picture, puzzling over it. It might have been an hour or more. Nor can I accurately describe how it made me feel—larger than myself, but lonely, too, as if I had grown as tall as the clouds and lost sight of every familiar thing. By the time I closed the book I saw that the moon had risen outside my window—the real moon, I mean; a harvest moon, fat and orange, half-hidden behind wind-tattered clouds.

I found myself wondering whether it was truly possible that men had visited that celestial orb. Whether, as the pictures implied, they had ridden there on rockets, rockets a thousand times larger than our familiar Independence Day fireworks. But if men had visited the moon, why hadn't they stayed there? Was it so inhospitable a place that no one wanted to remain?

Or perhaps they *had* stayed, and were living there still. If the moon was such a cold place, I reasoned, people living on its surface would be forced to build fires to keep warm. There seemed to be no wood on the moon, judging by the photographs, so they must have resorted to coal or peat. I went to the window and examined the moon minutely for any sign of campfires, pit mining, or other lunar industry. But I could see none. It was only the moon, mottled and changeless. I blushed at my own gullibility, replaced the book in its hiding place, chased all these recreant thoughts from my mind with a hasty prayer, and eventually fell asleep.

2

It falls to me to explain something of Williams Ford, and of my family's place in it, and Julian's, before I describe the threat Sam Godwin feared, which materialized in our village not long before Christmas.*

Situated at the head of the valley was the font of our prosperity, the Duncan and Crowley Estate. It was a country Estate, owned by two New York mercantile families with hereditary Senate seats, who maintained their villa not only as a source of income but as a resort, safely distant (several days' journey by train) from the intrigues and pestilences of the Eastern cities. It was inhabited—ruled, I might say—not only by the Duncan and Crowley patriarchs but by a whole legion of cousins, nephews, relations by marriage, and distinguished guests in search of clean air and rural views. Our corner of Athabaska was blessed with a benign climate and pleasant scenery, according to the season, and these things attract idle Aristos the way strong butter attracts flies.

It remains unrecorded whether the town existed before the Estate or vice versa; but certainly the town depended on the Estate for its prosperity. In Williams Ford there were essentially three classes: the Owners, or Aristos; below them the leasing class, who worked as smiths, carpenters, coopers, overseers, gardeners, beekeepers, etc., and whose leases were repaid in service; and finally the indentured laborers, who worked as field hands, inhabited rude shacks east of the River Pine, and received no compensation beyond bad food and worse lodging.

My family occupied an ambivalent place in this hierarchy. My mother was a seamstress. She worked at the Estate, as had her mother before her. My father, however, had arrived in Williams Ford as a bondless transient, and his marriage to my mother had been controversial. He had "married a lease," as the saying goes, and had been taken on as a stablehand at the Estate in lieu of a dowry. The law in Athabaska allowed such unions, but popular opinion frowned on them. My mother had retained only a few friends of her own class after the wedding, her blood relations had since died (perhaps of embarrassment), and as a child I was often mocked and derided for my father's low origins.

On top of that was the thorny issue of our religion. We were—because my father was—Church of Signs, which is a marginal Church. Every Christian church in America was required to secure formal approval from the Council of Registrars of the Dominion of Jesus Christ on Earth, if it wanted

---

* I beg the reader's patience if I detail matters that seem well-known. I indulge the possibility of a foreign audience, or a posterity to whom our present arrangements are not self-evident.

to operate without the imposition of crippling federal taxes. (The Dominion is sometimes called "the Church of the Dominion," but that's a misnomer, since every church is a Dominion Church as long as it's recognized by the Council. Dominion Episcopal, Dominion Presbyterian, Dominion Baptist—even the Catholic Church of America since it renounced its fealty to the Pope of Rome in 2112—all are included under the Dominionist umbrella, since the purpose of the Dominion is not to *be* a church but to *certify* churches. In America we're entitled by the Constitution to worship at any church we please, as long as it's a genuine Christian congregation and not some fraudulent or satanistic sect. The Dominion exists to make that distinction. Also to collect fees and tithes to further its important work.)

We were, as I said, Church of Signs, a denomination shunned by the leasing class and grudgingly recognized (but never fully endorsed) by the Dominion. It was popular mostly with the illiterate transient workers among whom my father had been raised. Our faith took for its master text that passage in Mark which proclaims, "In my Name they will cast out devils, and speak in new tongues; they will handle serpents, and if they drink poison they will not be sickened by it." We were snake-handlers, in other words, and famous beyond our modest numbers for it. Our congregation consisted of a dozen farmhands, most of them lately arrived from the Southern states. My father was its deacon (though we didn't use that title), and we kept snakes, for ritual purposes, in wire cages on our back acre, a practice that contributed very little to our social standing.

That had been the situation of our family when Julian Comstock arrived in Williams Ford as a guest of the Duncan and Crowley families, along with his mentor Sam Godwin, and when Julian and I met while hunting.

At that time I had been apprenticed to my father, who had risen to the rank of an overseer at the Estate's lavish and extensive stables. My father loved and understood animals, especially horses. Unfortunately I was not made in the same mold, and my relations with the stable's equine inhabitants rarely extended beyond a brisk mutual tolerance. I didn't love my job—which consisted of sweeping straw, shoveling ordure, and in general doing those chores the older stablehands felt to be beneath their dignity—so I was pleased when my friendship with Julian deepened, and it became customary for a household amanuensis to arrive unannounced and request my presence at the House. Since the request emanated from a Comstock it couldn't be overruled, no matter how fiercely the grooms and saddlers gnashed their teeth to see me escape their autocracy.

At first we met to read and discuss books, or hunt together. Later Sam Godwin invited me to audit Julian's lessons, for he had been charged with Julian's education as well as his general welfare. (Fortunately I had already been taught the rudiments of reading and writing at the Dominion school, and refined these skills under the tutelage of my mother, who believed in the power of literacy as an improving force. My father could neither read nor write.) And it was not more than a year after our first acquaintance that Sam presented himself one evening at my parents' cottage with an extraordinary proposal.

"Mr. and Mrs. Hazzard," Sam had said, putting his hand up to touch his Army cap (which he had removed when he entered the cottage, so that the gesture looked like an aborted salute), "you know of course about the friendship between your son and Julian Comstock."

"Yes," my mother said. "And worry over it often enough—matters at the Estate being what they are."

My mother was a small woman, delicate in stature but forceful, with ideas of her own. My father, who spoke seldom, on this occasion spoke not at all, only sat in his chair gripping a laurel-root pipe, which he did not light.

"Matters at the Estate are exactly the crux of the issue," Sam Godwin said. "I'm not sure how much Adam has told you about our situation there. Julian's father, General Bryce Comstock, who was my friend as well as my commanding officer, shortly before his death charged me with Julian's care and well-being—"

"Before his death," my mother pointed out, "at the *gallows,* for *treason.*"

Sam winced. "That's true, Mrs. Hazzard—I can't deny it—but I assert my belief that the trial was unfair and the verdict unjust. Just or not, however, it doesn't alter my obligation as far as the son is concerned. I promised to care for the boy, and I mean to keep my promise."

"A Christian sentiment," my mother said, not entirely disguising her skepticism.

"As for your implication about the Estate, and the practices of the young Eupatridians there, I agree with you entirely. Which is why I approved and encouraged Julian's friendship with your son. Apart from Adam, Julian has no reliable friends. The Estate is such a den of venomous snakes—no offense," he added, remembering our religious affiliation, and making the common but mistaken assumption that congregants of the Church of Signs necessarily *like* snakes, or feel some kinship with them—"no offense, but I would sooner allow Julian to associate with, uh, scorpions," striking for a more palatable simile, "than abandon him to the sneers, machinations, ruses, and ruinous habits of his peers. That makes me not only his teacher but his constant companion. But I'm more than twice his age, Mrs. Hazzard, and he needs a friend more nearly of his own growth."

"What do you propose, exactly, Mr. Godwin?"

"I propose to take on Adam as a second student, to the ultimate benefit of both boys."

Sam was ordinarily a man of few words—even as a teacher—and he seemed as exhausted by this oration as if he had lifted some great weight.

"As a student of *what,* Mr. Godwin?"

"Mechanics. History. Grammar and composition. Martial skills—"

"Adam already knows how to fire a rifle."

"Pistolwork, sabrework, fist-fighting—but that's only a fraction of it," Sam added hastily. "Julian's father asked me to cultivate the boy's mind as well as his reflexes."

My mother had more to say on the subject, chiefly about how my work at the stables helped offset the family's leases, and how difficult it would be to get along without those extra vouchers at the Estate store. But Sam had anticipated the point. He had been entrusted by Julian's mother—that is to say, the sister-in-law of the President—with a discretionary fund for Julian's education, which could be tapped to compensate for my absence from the stables. And at a handsome rate. He quoted a number, and the objections from my parents grew less strenuous, and were finally whittled away to nothing. (I observed all this from a room away, through a gap in the door.)

Which is not to say there were no misgivings. Before I set off for the Estate the next day, this time to visit one of the Great Houses rather than to shovel ordure in the stables, my mother warned me not to entangle myself in the affairs of the high-born. I promised her I would cling to my Christian virtues—a hasty promise, less easily kept than I imagined.*

"It may not be your morals that are at risk," she said. "The high-born conduct themselves by their own rules, and the games they play have mortal stakes. You do know that Julian's father was hanged?"

Julian had never spoken of it, and I had never pressed him, but it was a matter of public record. I repeated Sam's assertion that Bryce Comstock had been innocent.

"He may well have been. That's exactly the point. There has been a Comstock in the Presidency for the past thirty years, and the current Comstock is said to be jealous of his power. The only real threat to the reign of Julian's uncle was the ascendancy of his brother, who made himself dangerously popular in the war with the Brazilians. I suspect Mr. Godwin is correct—Bryce Comstock was hanged not because he was a *bad* General but because he was a *successful* one."

No doubt such scandals were possible. I had heard stories about life in New York City, where the President resided, that would curl a Cynic's hair. But what could these things possibly have to do with me? Or even Julian? We were only boys.

Such was my naïveté.

---

* Julian's somewhat feminine nature had won him a reputation among the other young Aristos as a sodomite. That they could believe this of him without evidence is testimony to the tenor of their thoughts, as a class. But it had occasionally redounded to my benefit. On more than one occasion his female acquaintances—sophisticated girls of my own age, or older—made the assumption that I was Julian's intimate companion, in a physical sense. Whereupon they undertook to cure me of my deviant habits, in the most direct fashion. I was happy to cooperate with these "cures," and they were successful, every time.

3

The days had grown short, and Thanksgiving had come and gone, and so had November, and snow was in the air—the tang of it, anyway—when fifty cavalrymen of the Athabaska Reserve rode into Williams Ford, escorting an equal number of Campaigners and Poll-Takers.

Most people in Williams Ford despised the Athabaskan winter. I wasn't one of them. I didn't mind the cold and the darkness, not so long as there was a hard-coal heater in the kitchen, a spirit lamp to read by on long nights, and the chance of wheat-cakes or head-cheese for breakfast. And Christmas was coming up fast—one of the four Universal Christian Holidays recognized by the Dominion (the others being Thanksgiving, Easter, and Independence Day). My favorite of these had always been Christmas. It was not so much the gifts, which were generally meager—though last year I had received from my parents the lease of a muzzle-loading rifle, mine to carry, of which I was exceptionally proud—nor was it entirely the spiritual substance of the holiday, which I'm ashamed to say seldom entered my mind except when it was thrust upon me at religious services. What I loved was the combined effect of brisk air, frost-whitened mornings, pine and holly wreaths nailed to doorways, cranberry-red banners draped across the main street to flap cheerfully in the cold wind, carols and hymns chanted or sung. I liked the clockwork regularity of it, as if a particular cog on the wheel of time had engaged with neat precision.

But this year it was an ill-omened season.

The body of Reserve troops rode into town on the fifteenth of December. Ostensibly they had come to conduct the Presidential Election. National elections were a formality in Williams Ford, and in all such places distant from the national capital. By the time our citizens were polled the outcome was a foregone conclusion, already decided in the populous Eastern states—that is, when there was more than one candidate, which was very seldom. For the last six electoral years no individual or party had contested the federal election, and we had been ruled by one Comstock or another for three decades. *Election* had become indistinguishable from *acclamation*.

But that was all right, because an election was still a momentous event, almost a kind of circus, involving the arrival of Poll-Takers and Campaigners, who always had a fine show to put on.

And this year—the rumor emanated from high chambers of the Estate, and had been whispered everywhere—there would be a movie shown in the Dominion Hall.

I had never seen any movies, though Julian had described them to me. He had seen them often in New York City when he was younger, and whenever he grew nostalgic—for life in Williams Ford was sometimes too sedate for Julian's taste—it was the movies he was provoked to mention. And so, when the showing of a movie was announced as part of the electoral process, both of us were excited, and we agreed to meet behind the Dominion Hall at the appointed hour.

Neither of us had any legitimate reason to be there. I was too young to vote, and Julian would have been conspicuous and perhaps unwelcome as the only Aristo at a gathering of the leasing class. (The high-born had been polled independently at the Estate, and had already voted proxies on behalf of their indentured labor.) So I let my parents leave for the Hall early in the evening, and I followed surreptitiously, taking one of my father's horses, and arrived just before the event was scheduled to begin. I waited behind the meeting hall where a dozen lease-horses were tethered, until Julian arrived on a much finer animal borrowed from the Estate stables. He was dressed in his best approximation of a leaser's clothing: hempen shirt and trousers of a dark color, and a black felt hat with its brim pulled low to disguise his face.

He dismounted, looking troubled, and I asked him what was wrong. Julian shook his head. "Nothing, Adam—or nothing yet—but Sam says there's trouble brewing." And here he regarded me with an expression verging on pity. "War," he said.

"War! There's always war—"

"A new offensive."

"Well, what of it? Labrador's a million miles away."

"Obviously your sense of geography hasn't been much improved by Sam's classes. And we might be *physically* a long distance from the front, but we're *operationally* far too close for comfort."

I didn't know what that meant, and so I dismissed it. "We can worry about that after the movie, Julian."

He forced a grin and said, "Yes, I suppose so. As well after as before."

So we entered the Dominion Hall just as the torches were being extinguished, and slouched into the last row of crowded pews, and waited for the show to start.

There was a broad wooden stage at the front of the Hall. All religious appurtenances had been removed from it, and a square white screen had been erected in place of the usual pulpit or dais. On each side of the screen was a kind of tent, in which the Players sat with their scripts and dramatic gear: speaking-horns, bells, blocks, a drum, a pennywhistle, and so forth. This, Julian said, was a stripped-down edition of what one might find in a fashionable Manhattan movie theater. In the city, the screen (and therefore the images projected on it) would be larger; the Players would be more professional, for script-reading and noise-making were considered fashionable arts, and attracted talented artists; and there might be additional Players stationed behind the screen for dramatic narration or particular "sound effects." There might even be an orchestra, with music written for each individual production.

The Players provided voices for the actors and actresses who appeared in the photographed, but silent, images. As the movie was shown, the Players observed it by a system of mirrors, and could follow scripts illuminated by a kind of binnacle lamp (so as not to cast a distracting light), and they spoke their lines as the photographed actors spoke, so that their voices seemed to emanate from the screen. Likewise, their drumming and bell-ringing and such corresponded to events within the movie.*

"Of course, they did it better in the secular era," Julian whispered, and I prayed no one had overheard this indelicate comment. By all reports, movies had surely been very spectacular during the Efflorescence of Oil—with recorded sound, natural color rather than black-and-gray, etc. But they were also, by the same reports, hideously impious and often pornographic. Fortunately (or *unfortunately*, from Julian's point of view) no examples were believed to have survived; the film stock had long since rotted, and "digital" copies were wholly undecodable. These movies belonged to the twentieth and early twenty-first centuries—that period of great, unsustainable, and hedonistic prosperity, driven by the burning of Earth's reserves of perishable oil, which culminated in the False Tribulation, and the wars, and the plagues, and the painful dwindling of inflated populations to more reasonable numbers.

Our truest and best American antiquity, as the *Dominion History of the Union* insisted, was the nineteenth century, whose household virtues and modest industries we had been forced by circumstance to imperfectly restore, whose skills were unfailingly practical, and whose literature was often useful and improving.

But I have to confess that some of Julian's apostasy had infected me. I was troubled by unhappy thoughts even as the hall torches were pinched out and Ben Kreel (our Dominion pastor, pacing in front of the movie screen) delivered a lecture on Nation, Piety, and Duty. *War*, Julian had said, implying not just the everlasting War in Labrador but a new phase of it, one that might reach its skeletal hand right into Williams Ford—and then what of me, and what of my family?

"We're here to cast our ballots," Ben Kreel said in his eventual summation, "a sacred duty at once to our faith and to our country, a country so successfully and benevolently stewarded by its leader, President Deklan Comstock, whose Campaigners, I see by the motions of their hands, are anxious to get on with the events of the night; and so, without further ado, etc., please direct your attention to the presentation of their moving picture, *First Under Heaven*, which they have prepared for our enjoyment—"

---

* The illusion was quite striking when the Players were professional, but their lapses could be equally astonishing. Julian once recounted to me a New York movie production of Wm. Shakespeare's *Hamlet*, in which a Player had come to the theater intoxicated with drink, causing the unhappy Denmark to seem to exclaim "Sea of troubles—(an unprintable oath)—I have troubles of my own," with more obscenities, and much inappropriate bell-ringing and vulgar whistling, until an understudy could be hurried out to replace him.

The necessary gear had been hauled into Williams Ford under a canvas-top wagon: a projection apparatus and a portable Swiss dynamo (probably captured from the Dutch in Labrador), powered by distilled spirits. The dynamo had been installed in a trench freshly dug behind the church, in order to muffle its sound, which nevertheless came up through the plank floor like the aggravated growling of a huge, buried dog. That vibration only added to the sense of moment, as the last illuminating flame was extinguished and the electric bulb within the mechanical projector flared up.

The movie began. As it was the first I had ever seen, my astonishment was complete. I was so entranced by the illusion of photographs "come to life" that the substance of it almost escaped me . . . but I remember an ornate title card, and scenes of the Second Battle of Quebec, re-created by actors but utterly real to me, accompanied by drum-banging and shrill pennywhistling to represent the reports of shot and shell. Those at the front of the auditorium flinched instinctively, while several of the village's prominent women came near to fainting, and grabbed up the hands or arms of their male companions, who might be as bruised, come morning, as if they had participated in the battle itself.

Soon enough, however, the Dutchmen under their cross-and-laurel flag began to retreat from the American forces, and an actor representing the young Deklan Comstock came to the fore, reciting his Vows of Inauguration (a bit prematurely, but history was here truncated for the purposes of art)—that's the one in which he mentions both the Continental Imperative and the Debt to the Past. He was voiced, of course, by one of the Players, a *basso profundo* whose tones emerged from his speaking-bell with ponderous gravity. (Which was also a slight revision of the truth, for the genuine Deklan Comstock possessed a high-pitched voice, and was prone to petulance.)

The movie then proceeded to more decorous episodes and scenic views representing the glories of the reign of Deklan Conqueror, as he was known to the Army of the Laurentians, which had marched him to his ascendancy in New York City. Here was the reconstruction of Washington, DC (a project never completed, always in progress, hindered by a swampy climate and insect-borne diseases); here was the Illumination of Manhattan, whereby electric streetlights were powered by a hydroelectric dynamo, four hours every day between 6 and 10 p.m.; here was the military shipyard at Boston Harbor, the coal mines and re-rolling mills of Pennsylvania, the newest and shiniest steam engines to pull the newest and shiniest trains, etc., etc.

I had to wonder at Julian's reaction to all this. This entire show, after all, had been concocted to extoll the virtues of the man who had executed his father. I couldn't forget—and Julian must be constantly aware—that the incumbent President here praised was in fact a fratricidal tyrant. But Julian's eyes were riveted on the screen. This reflected (I later learned) not his opinion of current events but his fascination with what he preferred to call "cinema." This making of illusions in two dimensions was never far from his mind—it was, perhaps, his "true calling," and would eventually culminate in the creation of Julian's suppressed cinematic masterwork, *The Life and Adventures of the Great Naturalist Charles Darwin* . . . but I anticipate myself.

The present movie went on to mention the successful forays against the Brazilians at Panama during Deklan Conqueror's reign, which may have struck closer to home, for I saw Julian flinch once or twice.

As exciting as the movie was, I found my attention wandering from the screen. Perhaps it was the strangeness of the event, coming so close to Christmas. Or perhaps it was the influence of the *History of Mankind in Space*, which I had been reading in bed, a page or two a night, ever since our journey to the Tip. Whatever the cause, I was beset by a sudden sense of melancholy. Here I was in the midst of everything that was familiar and ought to be comforting—the crowd of the leasing class, the enclosing benevolence of the Dominion Hall, the banners and tokens of the Christmas season—and it all felt suddenly *thin*, as if the world were a bucket from which the bottom had dropped out.

I supposed this was what Julian had called "the Philosopher's perspective." If so, I wondered how the Philosophers endured it. I had learned a little from Sam Godwin—and more from Julian, who read books of which even Sam disapproved—about the discredited ideas of the Secular Era. I thought of Einstein, and his insistence that no particular point of view was more privileged than any other: in other words his "general relativity," and its claim that the answer to the question "What is real?" begins with the question "Where are you standing?" Was that all I was, I wondered, here in the cocoon of Williams Ford—a Point of View? Or was I an incarnation of a molecule of DNA, "imperfectly remembering," as Julian had said, an ape, a fish, and an amoeba?

Maybe even the Nation that Ben Kreel praised so extravagantly was only an example of the same trend in nature—an imperfect memory of another Nation, which had itself been an imperfect memory of all the Nations before it, all the way back to the dawn of Man (in Eden, or in Africa, as Julian believed).

The movie ended with a stirring view of an American flag, its thirteen stripes and sixty stars rippling in sunlight—betokening, the narrator insisted, another four years of the prosperity and benevolence engendered by the rule of Deklan Conqueror, for whom the audience's votes were solicited, not that there was any competing candidate known or rumored. The completed film flapped against its reel; the electric bulb was quickly extinguished; the Poll-Takers began to reignite the wall torches. Several of the lease-men in the audience had lit pipes during the display, and their smoke mingled with the smudge of the torches to make a blue-gray thundercloud that brooded under the high arches of the ceiling.

Julian seemed distracted, and slumped in his pew with his hat pulled low. "Adam," he whispered, "we have to find a way out of here."

"I believe I see one," I said, "it's called the door—but what's the hurry?"

"Look at the door more closely. Two men of the Reserve have been posted there."

I looked again, and what he said was true. "But isn't that just to protect the balloting?" For Ben Kreel had retaken the stage, and was getting ready to ask for a formal show of hands.

"Tom Shearney, the barber with a bladder complaint, just tried to leave to use the jakes. He was turned back."

Tom Shearney was seated less than a yard away from us, squirming unhappily and casting resentful glances at the Reserve men.

"But after the balloting—"

"This isn't about balloting. This is about conscription."

"Conscription!"

"Quiet! You'll start a stampede. I didn't think it would begin so soon . . . but we've had telegrams from New York about a defeat in Labrador and a call for new divisions. Once the balloting is finished the Campaigners will probably announce a recruitment drive, and take the names of everyone present, and survey them for the names and ages of their children."

"We're too young to be drafted," I said, for we were both just seventeen.

"Not according to what I've heard. The rules have been changed to draw in more men. Oh, you can probably find a way to hide out when the culling begins. But my presence here is well-known. I don't have a mob to melt away into. In fact it's probably not a coincidence that so many Reservists have been sent to such a little town as Williams Ford."

"What do you mean, not a coincidence?"

"My uncle has never been happy about my existence. He has no children of his own. No heirs, and he sees me as a possible competitor for the Executive."

"But that's absurd. You don't *want* to be President—do you?"

"I would sooner shoot myself. But Uncle Deklan has a jealous bent, and he distrusts the motives of my mother in protecting me."

"How does a draft help him?"

"The entire draft isn't aimed at me, but I'm sure he finds it a useful tool. If I'm drafted, no one can complain that he's exempting his own family from the conscription. And when he has me in the infantry he can make sure I find myself on the front lines in Labrador—performing some noble but suicidal trench attack."

"But—Julian! Can't Sam protect you?"

"Sam is a retired soldier and has no power except what arises from the patronage of my mother. Which isn't worth much in the coin of the present realm. Adam, is there another way out of this building?"

"Only the door, unless you mean to break a pane of that colored glass that fills the windows."

"Somewhere to hide, then?"

I thought about it. "Maybe," I said. "There's a room behind the stage where the religious gear is stored. You can enter it from the wings. We could hide there, but it has no exit of its own."

"It'll do. As long as we can get there without attracting attention."

That wasn't too difficult, for the torches had not all been re-lit, much of the hall was still in shadow, and the audience was milling about and stretching while the Campaigners got ready to record the vote that was to follow—the Campaigners were meticulous accountants even though the final tally was a foregone conclusion and the ballrooms were already booked for Deklan Conqueror's latest inauguration. Julian and I shuffled from one shadow to another, giving no appearance of haste, until we were close to the foot of the stage. We loitered near the entrance to the storage room until a goonish Reserve man, who had been eyeing us, was called away to dismantle the projecting equipment—that was our chance. We ducked through the curtained door into near-absolute darkness. Julian stumbled over some obstruction (a piece of the church's tack piano, which had been taken apart for cleaning by a traveling piano-mechanic who died of a seizure before finishing the job), the result being a woody "clang!" that seemed loud enough to alert the whole occupancy of the church—but didn't.

What little light there was came through a high glazed window that was hinged so that it could be opened in summer for ventilation. It gave a weak sort of illumination, for the night was cloudy, and only the torches along the main street were shining. But the window became a beacon as soon as our eyes adjusted to the dimness. "Perhaps we can get out that way," Julian said.

"Not without a ladder. Although—"

"What? Speak up, Adam, if you have an idea."

"This is where they store the risers—the long wooden blocks the choir stands on when they're racked up for a performance. Maybe those would do."

Julian understood the plan at once, and began to survey the shadowy contents of the storage room as intently as he had surveyed the Tip for books. We found the raw pine risers, and managed to stack them to a useful height without causing too much noise. (In the church hall the Campaigners registered a unanimous vote for Deklan Comstock, and then began to break the news about the conscription drive, just as Julian had surmised. Some few voices were raised in futile objection; Ben Kreel called loudly for calm—no one heard us rearranging the furniture.)

The window was at least ten feet high, and painfully narrow, and when we emerged on the other side we had to hang by our fingertips before dropping to the ground. I bent my right ankle as I landed, though no lasting harm was done.

The night, already cold, had turned colder. We had dropped just near the hitching posts, and the horses whinnied at our unexpected arrival and blew steam from their nostrils. A fine, gritty snow had begun to fall. There was not much wind, however, and Christmas banners hung limply in the brittle air.

Julian made straight for his horse and loosed its reins from the post. "What do we do now?" I asked.

"You, Adam, will do nothing but protect your own existence, while I—"

But he balked at pronouncing his plans, and a shadow of anxiety passed over his face.

"We can wait this crisis out," I insisted, a little desperately. "The Reserves can't stay in Williams Ford forever."

"No. Unfortunately neither can I, for Deklan Conqueror knows where to find me."

"Where will you go, though?"

He put a finger to his mouth. There was a noise from the front of the Dominion Hall. The doors had been thrown open and the congregants were beginning to emerge. "Ride after me," Julian said. "Quick, now!"

I did as he asked. We didn't follow the main street, but caught a path that turned behind the blacksmith's barn and through the wooded border of the River Pine, north in the direction of the Estate. The night was dark, and the horses stepped slowly; but they knew the path almost by instinct, and some light from the town still filtered through the thinly falling snow that touched my face like a hundred small cold fingers.

"It was never possible that I could stay at Williams Ford," Julian said. "You ought to have known that, Adam."

Truly, I should have. It was Julian's constant theme, after all: the impermanence of things. He preached it like a sermon. I had always put this down to the circumstances of his childhood—the death of his father, the separation from his mother, the kind but impersonal tutelage of Sam Godwin.

But I couldn't help thinking once more of the *History of Mankind in Space* and of the photographs in it—not of the First Men on the Moon, who were Americans, but of the Last Visitors to that celestial sphere, who had been Chinamen, and whose "space suits" had been firecracker-red. Like the Americans, they had planted their flag in expectation of more visitations to come; but the End of Oil and the False Tribulation had put paid to those plans.

Then I thought of the even lonelier Plains of Mars, photographed by machines, or so the book alleged, but never touched by human feet. The universe, it seemed, was full to brimming with lonesome places. Somehow I had stumbled into one. The snow squall ended. The uninhabited moon peeked through the clouds, and the winter fields of Williams Ford glowed with an unearthly luminescence.

"If you have to leave," I said, "let me come with you."

"No," said Julian. He had pulled his hat down around his ears to protect himself from the cold, and I couldn't see much of his face, but his eyes shone when he glanced in my direction. "Thank you, Adam. I wish it were possible.

But it isn't. You must stay here, and dodge the draft, if possible, and polish your literary skills, and one day write books, like Mr. Charles Curtis Easton."

That was my ambition, which had grown over the last year, nourished by our mutual love of books and by Sam Godwin's exercises in English Composition, for which I had discovered an unexpected talent.* At the moment it seemed a petty dream. "None of that matters," I said.

"That's where you're wrong," Julian said. "You must not make the mistake of thinking that because nothing lasts, nothing matters."

"Isn't that the Philosophical point of view?"

"Not if the Philosopher knows what he's talking about." Julian reined up his horse and turned to face me, something of the imperiousness of his famous family entering into his mien. "Listen, Adam, there's something important you can do for me—at some personal risk. Are you willing?"

"Yes," I said immediately.

"Then listen closely. Before long the Reservists will be watching the roads out of Williams Ford, if they aren't already. I have to leave, and I have to leave tonight. I won't be missed until morning, and then, at least at first, only by Sam. What I want you to do is this: go home—your parents will be worried about the conscription, and you can try to calm them down, but don't allude to any of what happened tonight—and first thing in the morning make your way to the Estate and find Sam. Tell him what happened at the Dominion Hall, and tell him to ride out of town as soon as he can do so without being caught. Tell him he can find me at Lundsford. That's the message."

"Lundsford! There's nothing at Lundsford."

"Precisely—nothing important enough that the Reservists would think to look for us there. You remember what the Tipman said last fall, about the place he found those books? 'A low place near the main excavations.' Tell Sam he can look for me there."

"I will," I promised, blinking against the cold wind, which irritated my eyes.

"Thank you," he said gravely. "For everything." Then he forced a smile, and for a moment he was no longer the President's nephew, but just Julian, the friend with whom I had hunted squirrels and gazed at the moon. "Merry Christmas, Adam," he said. "And all the Christmases to come."

Then he wheeled his horse about and rode away.

---

* Not a talent that was born fully-formed, however. Only two years previously I had presented to Sam Godwin my first finished story, which I had called "A Western Boy: His Adventures in Enemy Europe." Sam had praised its style and ambition, but called attention to a number of flaws: elephants, for instance, are not native to Brussels, and are generally too massive to be wrestled to the ground by American lads; a journey from London to Rome can't be accomplished in a matter of hours, even on "a very fast horse"—and Sam might have continued in that vein, had I not found an excuse to leave the room.

4

There is a Dominion cemetery in Williams Ford, and I passed it on the ride back home, but my sister Flaxie wasn't buried there.

As congregants of the Church of Signs we weren't entitled to plots in the Dominion yard. Flaxie had a place in the acreage behind our cottage, marked by a modest wooden cross; but the cemetery put the thought of Flaxie in my mind, and after I returned the horse to the barn I stopped by her grave, despite the shivery cold, and tipped my hat to her, the way I had always tipped my hat to her in life.

Flaxie had been a bright, impudent, mischievous small thing—as golden-haired as her nickname implied. Her given name was Dolores, but she was always Flaxie to me. The Pox had taken her very suddenly and, as these things go, mercifully. I didn't remember her death—I had been down with the same Pox, though I had survived it. What I remembered was waking up from my fever into a house gone strangely quiet. No one had wanted to tell me about Flaxie, but I had seen my mother's tormented eyes, and I knew the truth without having to be told. Death had played lottery with us, and Flaxie had drawn the short straw.

(It is, I think, for the likes of Flaxie that we keep up a belief in Heaven. I have met relatively few adults, outside the enthusiasts of the established Church, who believe very fervently in Heaven; and Heaven was scant consolation for my grieving mother. But Flaxie, who was five, had believed in it wholeheartedly—imagined it was something like a summer meadow, with wildflowers blooming, and a picnic eternally under way—and if that childish belief soothed her in her extremity then it served a purpose more noble than truth.)

Tonight the cottage was almost as quiet as it had been on the morning af- ter Flaxie's death. I came through the door to find my mother dabbing her eyes with a handkerchief, and my father frowning into the bowl of his pipe as if it had posed a question he couldn't answer. "The draft," he said, as if this explained everything, which in fact it did.

"I know," I said. "I heard all about it."

My mother was too distraught to speak. My father said, "We'll do what we can to protect you, Adam. But—"

"I'm not afraid to serve my country."

"Well, that's a praiseworthy attitude," he said, and my mother wept even harder. "But we don't know what's necessary. It might be the situation in Labrador isn't as bad as it seems."

Scant of words though my father was, I had often enough relied on him for advice, which he had freely given. He was aware, for instance, of my dis- taste for snakes; for which reason, abetted by my mother, I had been allowed to avoid the sacraments of our faith, and the venomous swellings and occasional amputations that sometimes followed. And although that aversion disappointed him, he had nevertheless taught me the practical aspects of snake-handling, including how to grasp a serpent in such a way as to avoid its bite, and how to kill one, should the necessity arise.* He was a practical man despite his unusual beliefs.

But on this occasion his well of advice had run dry. He looked like a hunted man who has come to the end of a cul-de-sac, and can neither go forward nor safely turn back.

I went to my bedroom, but not to sleep. Instead I bundled a few of my possessions for easy carrying—my squirrel gun, chiefly, and some notes and writing, and the *History of Mankind in Space*. I thought I should add some salted pork, or something of that nature, but I resolved to wait a while, so my mother wouldn't see me packing.

Before dawn I put on several layers of clothing and rolled down the rim of my packle hat until the wool covered my ears. I opened the window of my room and clambered over the sill, and closed the glass behind me after I had retrieved my rifle and gear. Then I crept across the open yard to the barn, where I saddled a horse (a gelding named Rapture, who was fast and strong), and rode out under a sky that had just begun to show first light.

Last night's snowfall still covered the ground. I was not the first up this winter morning, and the cold air already smelled of Christmas. The bakery in Williams Ford was making Nativity cakes and cinnamon buns, and the yeasty smell from the ovens covered the northwest end of town like an intoxicating fog, for there was no wind to carry it away. The day was dawning blue and still.

Signs of Christmas were everywhere—as they ought to be, for today was the Eve of that universal holiday—but so was evidence of the conscription drive. The Reservists were already awake, passing like shadows in their scruffy uniforms, and a crowd of them had gathered by the hardware store. They had hung out a faded flag and posted a sign, which I couldn't read, because I was determined to keep a distance between myself and the soldiers; but I knew a recruiting-post when I saw one. I didn't doubt that the main ways in and out of town had been put under close observation.

I took a back road to the Estate, the same riverside road Julian and I had traveled the night before. In the calm air our tracks had remained undisturbed, and I could see that no one else had recently passed this way. When I

---

* *"Grasp it where its neck ought to be, behind the head; ignore the tail, however it may thrash; and crack its skull, hard and often enough to subdue it."* I had recounted these instructions to Julian, whose horror of serpents far exceeded my own: "I could never do such a thing!" he had exclaimed. This surfeit of timidity may surprise readers familiar with his later career.

came close to the Estate I lashed Rapture to a tree in a concealing grove of pines and proceeded on foot.

The Duncan-Crowley Estate was not fenced, nor was there any real demarcation of its boundaries, for under the Leasing System everything in Williams Ford was owned (in the legal sense) by the two great families. I approached the Estate from the western side, which was wooded and used by the Aristos for casual riding and hunting. This morning the copse was not inhabited, and I saw no one until I had passed the snow-mounded hedges where the formal gardens were planted. Here, in summer, apple and cherry trees blossomed and produced fruit, flowers bloomed, bees nursed in languid ecstasies. But now the garden was barren, its paths were quilted with snow, and there was no one visible except the senior groundskeeper, sweeping the portico of the nearest of the several Great Houses.

The Houses were dressed for Christmas. Christmas was an even grander event at the Estate than in the town proper, as might be expected. The winter population of the Duncan-Crowley Estate wasn't as large as its summer population, but a number of both families resided here year-round, along with their retinues, and any cousins and hangers-on who felt like hibernating over the cold season. Sam Godwin, as Julian's tutor, wasn't permitted to sleep in either of the two most luxurious buildings, but bunked among the staff in a white-pillared house which was smaller than its neighbors but would have passed for a tolerable mansion among the leasing class. This was where he had conducted lessons for Julian and me, and I knew the building intimately. It, too, was dressed for Christmas; pine boughs were suspended over the lintels, and a red and white Banner of the Cross dangled from the eaves. The door wasn't locked—I let myself in.

It was still early in the morning, as the Aristos calculate time. The tiled entranceway was empty and silent. I went directly to the room where Sam Godwin slept and conducted his classes, down an oaken corridor lit only by the early sun shining through a single window. The floor was carpeted and gave out no sound, though my shoes left damp footprints in the weft of it.

At Sam's particular door I was confronted with a dilemma. I was afraid to knock, for fear of alerting others. My mission as I saw it was to deliver Julian's message as discreetly as possible. But I couldn't walk in unannounced on a sleeping man—could I?

I tried the handle of the door. It moved freely. I opened the door a fraction of an inch, meaning to whisper "Sam?" and give him some warning.

But I heard Sam's voice, low and muttering, as if he were talking to himself, and I stopped and listened more closely. The words were strange to me. He was speaking a guttural language, not English. Perhaps he wasn't alone. It was too late to back away, however, so I decided to brazen it out. I opened the door entirely and stepped inside, saying, "Sam! It's me, Adam. I have a message from Julian—"

I stopped short, startled by what I saw. Sam Godwin—the same gruff but familiar Sam who had taught me the rudiments of History and Geography—was practicing *black magic,* or some other form of witchcraft—and on Christmas Eve! He wore a striped cowl about his shoulders, and leather lacings on his arm, and a boxlike implement strapped to his forehead, and his hands were upraised over an arrangement of candles mounted in a brass holder that appeared to have been scavenged from some ancient Tip. The invocation he was murmuring hung like a fading echo in the still air of the room: *Bah-rook a-tah atten-eye hello hey-noo . . .*

My jaw dropped.

"Adam!" Sam was nearly as startled as I was, and he hurriedly pulled the shawl off his back and began to unlace his various unholy riggings.

This was so irregular I could barely comprehend it.

Then I was afraid I *did* comprehend it. Often enough in Dominion school I had heard Ben Kreel talk about the vices and wickedness of the Secular Era, some of which still lingered, he said, in the cities of the East—irreligiosity, skepticism, occultism, depravity. And I thought of the ideas I had so casually imbibed from Julian and (indirectly) from Sam, some of which I had even begun to believe: Einsteinism, Darwinism, space travel. . . . Had I been seduced by the outrunners of some fashionable paganism, borne into Williams Ford from the gutters and alleys of Manhattan? Had I been duped, that is, by Philosophy?

"A message," Sam said, concealing his heathen gear, "what message? Where is Julian?"

But I couldn't stay. I fled the room.

Sam barreled out of the house after me. I was fast, but he was long-legged and strong for all his forty-odd years, and he caught me up in the winter gardens—tackled me from behind. I kicked, and tried to pull away, but he pinned my shoulders securely.

"Adam, for God's sake, settle down!" he cried. That was impudent, I thought, invoking God, *him*—but then he said, "Don't you understand what you saw? I am a Jew!"

A Jew!

Of course, I had heard of Jews. They lived in the Bible, and in New York City. Their equivocal relationship with Our Savior had won them opprobrium down the ages, and they were not approved of by the Dominion. But I had never seen a living Jew in the flesh, and I was astonished by the idea that Sam had been one all along: *invisibly,* so to speak.

"You deceived everyone, then!" I said.

"I never claimed to be a Christian! I never spoke of it at all. But what does it matter? You said you had a message from Julian—give it to me, damn you! Where is he?"

I wondered what I should say, or who I might betray if I said it. The world had turned upside-down. All Ben Kreel's lectures on patriotism and fidelity came back to me in one great flood of shame. Had I been a party to treason as well as atheism?

But I felt I owed this last favor to Julian, who would surely have wanted me to deliver his intelligence whether Sam was a Jew or a Mohammedan: "There are soldiers on all the roads out of town," I said sullenly. "Julian went for Lundsford last night. He says he'll meet you there. Now *get off of me!*"

Sam did so, sitting back on his heels, anxiety inscribed upon his face. "Has it begun so soon? I thought they might wait for the New Year . . ."

"I don't know *what* has begun. I don't think I know anything at all!" And so saying I leapt to my feet and ran out of the lifeless garden. I fled back to Rapture, who was tied to the tree where I had left him, nosing unproductively in the soft white snow.

I had traveled perhaps an eighth of a mile back toward Williams Ford when another rider came up on my flank from behind.

It was Ben Kreel himself. He touched his cap and said, "Do you mind if I ride with you a ways, Adam Hazzard?"

I could hardly say no.

Ben Kreel wasn't a pastor—we had plenty of those in Williams Ford, each catering to his own denomination—but he was the appointed representative of the Athabaska branch of the Dominion of Jesus Christ on Earth, almost as powerful in his way as the men who owned the Estate. And if he wasn't technically a pastor, he was at least a sort of moral shepherd to the towns-people. He had been born right here in Williams Ford, son of a saddler; had been educated, at the Estate's expense, at the Dominion College in Colorado Springs; and for the last twenty years he had taught elementary school five days a week and General Christianity on Sundays. I had marked my first let-ters on a slate board under Ben Kreel's tutelage. Every Independence Day he addressed the townsfolk and reminded them of the symbolism and signifi-cance of the Thirteen Stripes and the Sixty Stars, and every Christmas he led the Ecumenical Service at the Dominion Hall.

He was stout and gray at the temples, clean-shaven. He wore a woolen jacket, deerskin boots, and a packle hat not much grander than my own. But he carried himself with an immense dignity, as much in the saddle as on foot. The expression on his face was kindly, but that was no surprise; his expression was almost always kindly. "You're out early, Adam," he said. "What are you doing abroad at this hour?"

I blushed down to my hair-roots. "Nothing," I said. Is there any other word that so spectacularly represents everything it wants to deny? Under the circumstances, "nothing" amounted to a confession of bad intent. "Couldn't sleep," I added hastily. "Thought I might shoot a squirrel or so." That would explain the rifle knotted across my saddlehorn, and it was at least remotely plausible, for the squirrels were still active, doing the last of their scrounging before settling in for the cold months.

"On the day before Christmas?" Ben Kreel asked. "And in the copse on the grounds of the Estate? I hope the Duncans and Crowleys don't hear about it! They're jealous of their trees. And I'm sure gunfire would disturb them at this hour. Wealthy men and Easterners prefer to sleep past dawn, as a rule."

"I didn't fire," I muttered. "I thought better of it."

"Well, good. Wisdom prevails. You're headed back to town?"

"Yes, sir."

"Let me keep you company, then."

"Please do." I could hardly say otherwise, no matter how I longed to be alone with my thoughts.

Our horses moved slowly—the snow made for awkward footing—and Ben Kreel was silent for a while. Then he said, "You needn't conceal your fears, Adam. I think I know what's troubling you."

For a moment I had the terrible idea that Ben Kreel had been behind me in the hallway at the Estate, and that he had glimpsed Sam Godwin in his Old Testament paraphernalia. Wouldn't that create a scandal! (And then I thought it was exactly such a scandal Sam must have feared all his life: it was worse even than being Church of Signs, for in some states a Jew can be fined or even imprisoned for practicing his faith. I didn't know where Athabaska stood on the issue, but I feared the worst.)

But Ben Kreel was talking about conscription, not about Sam.

"I've already discussed this with some of the other boys in town," he said. "You're not alone, Adam, if you're wondering what it all means, this military excitement, and what might happen as a result of it. And you're something of a special case. I've been keeping an eye on you. From a distance, as it were. Here, stop a moment."

We had come to a bluff above the River Pine, looking south toward Williams Ford from a little height.

"Gaze at that," Ben Kreel said contemplatively. He stretched his arm out in an arc, as if to include not just the cluster of buildings that was the town but the empty fields as well, and the murky flow of the river, and the wheels of the mills, and even the shacks of the indentured laborers down in the low country. The valley seemed at once a living thing, inhaling the crisp atmosphere of the season and breathing out its steams, and a portrait, static in the still blue winter air. As deeply rooted as an oak and as fragile as a ball of Nativity glass.

"Gaze at that," Ben Kreel repeated. "Look at Williams Ford, laid out pretty there. What is it, Adam? More than a place, I think. It's a way of life. It's the sum of all our labors. It's what our fathers gave us and it's what we give our sons. It's where we bury our mothers and where our daughters will be buried." Here was more Philosophy, then, and after the turmoil of the morning I wasn't sure I wanted any. But Ben Kreel's voice ran on like the soothing syrup my mother used to administer whenever Flaxie or I came down with a cough. "Every boy in Williams Ford—every boy old enough to submit himself for national service—is just now discovering how reluctant he is to leave the only place he truly knows and loves. Even you, I suspect."

"I'm no more or less willing than anyone else."

"I'm not questioning your courage or your loyalty. It's just that you've had a little taste of what life might be like elsewhere—or so I imagine, given how closely you associated yourself with Julian Comstock. Now, I'm sure Julian's a fine young man and an excellent Christian. He could hardly be otherwise, could he, as the nephew of the man who holds the nation in his palm. But his experience has been very different from yours. He's accustomed to cities—to movies like the one we saw at the Hall last night (and I glimpsed you there, didn't I, sitting in the back pews?)—to books and ideas that might strike a youth of your background as exciting and, well, *different*. Am I wrong?"

"I could hardly say you are, sir."

"And much of what Julian may have described to you is no doubt true. I've traveled some myself, you know, Adam. I've seen Colorado Springs, Pittsburgh—even New York City. Our Eastern cities are great, proud metropolises—some of the biggest and most productive in the world—and they're worth defending, which is one reason we're trying so hard to drive the Dutch out of Labrador."

"Surely you're right."

"I'm glad you agree. Because there's a trap certain young people are prey to. I've seen it before. A boy might think one of those great cities is a place he can *run away to*—a place where he can escape all the duties and obligations he learned at his mother's knee. Simple things like faith and patriotism can feel to a young man like burdens, which might be shrugged off when they become too weighty."

"I'm not like that, sir," I said, though every word he spoke seemed to have my name written all over it.

"And there's yet another element in the calculation. The conscription threatens to carry you out of Williams Ford; and the thought that runs through many boys' minds is, if I *must* leave, then maybe I ought to leave on my own hook, and find my destiny on a city's streets rather than in a battalion of the Athabaska Brigade . . . and you're good to deny it, Adam, but you wouldn't be human if such ideas didn't occur to you."

"No, sir," I muttered, and I felt my guilt increasing, for I had in fact been a little seduced by Julian's tales of city life, and Sam's dubious lessons, and the *History of Mankind in Space*—perhaps it was true that I had neglected my obligations to the village that lay so still and so inviting in the blue near distance.

"I know," Ben Kreel said, "things haven't been easy for your family. Your father's faith, in particular, has been a trial, and we haven't always been good neighbors to you—speaking on behalf of the village as a whole. Perhaps

you've been left out of activities other boys enjoy as a matter of course: picnics, games, friendships. . . . Well, even Williams Ford isn't Paradise. But I
promise you, Adam: if you find yourself in the Brigades, and especially if you
find yourself tested in time of war, you'll discover that the same boys who
shunned you in the dusty streets of your home town become your best friends
and bravest allies, and you theirs. For our common heritage knits us together
in ways that may seem obscure, but become obvious under the harsh light of
combat."

I had spent so much time smarting under the remarks of other boys (that
my father "raised vipers the way other folks raise chickens," for example) that
I could hardly credit Ben Kreel's assertion. But I knew very little of modern
warfare, except what I had read in the novels of Mr. Charles Curtis Easton, so
it might be true. And the prospect (as was intended) made me feel even more
shame-faced.

"There!" Ben Kreel said. "Do you hear that, Adam?"

I did. I could hardly avoid it. The bell was clanging in the Dominion
church steeple, announcing the early Ecumenical Service. It was a silvery
sound on the winter air, at once lonesome and consoling, and I wanted almost
to run toward it—to shelter in it, as if I were a child again.

"They'll be wanting me," Ben Kreel said. "Will you excuse me if I ride
ahead?"

"No, sir. Please don't mind about me."

"As long as we understand each other. Don't look so downcast, Adam!
The future may be brighter than you expect."

"Thank you for saying so, sir."

I stayed a while longer on the low bluff, watching as Ben Kreel's horse carried
him toward town. Even in the sunlight I felt the cold, and I shivered some,
perhaps more because of the conflict in my mind than because of the weather.
The Dominion man had made me ashamed of myself, and had put into perspective my loose ways of the last few years, and pointed up how many of my
native beliefs I had abandoned before the seductive Philosophy of an agnostic
Aristo and an aging Jew.

Then I sighed and urged Rapture back along the path toward Williams
Ford, meaning to explain to my parents where I had been, and to reassure
them that I wouldn't suffer too much in the coming conscription, to which I
would willingly submit.

I was so disheartened by the morning's events that my eyes drifted toward
the ground even as Rapture retraced his steps. As I have said, the snows of the
night before lay largely undisturbed on this back trail between the town and
the Estate. I could see where I had come through this morning, Rapture's
hoofprints having recorded the passage as clearly as figures in a book. Then I

reached the place where Julian and I had parted the night before. There were more hoofprints here, in fact a crowd of them.

And I saw something else written (in effect) on the snowy ground— something which alarmed me.

I reined up at once.

I looked south, toward Williams Ford. I looked east, the way Julian had gone last night.

Then I took a bracing inhalation of icy air, and followed the trail that seemed to me most urgent.

5

The east-west road through Williams Ford was not heavily traveled, especially in winter.

The southern road, which was called the "Wire Road" because the telegraph line runs alongside it, connected Williams Ford to the railhead at Connaught, and sustained a great deal of traffic. But the east-west road went essentially nowhere: it was a remnant of a road of the Secular Ancients, traversed mainly by Tipmen and freelance antiquarians, and then only in the warmer months. I suppose, if you followed the old road as far as it would take you, you might reach the Great Lakes, or somewhere farther east, in that direction; or you could ride the opposite way, and get yourself lost among washouts and landslips in the Rocky Mountains. But the railroad—and a parallel turnpike farther south—had obviated the need for all that trouble.

Still, the east-west road was closely watched where it left the outskirts of Williams Ford. The Reserves had posted a man on a hill overlooking it, the same hill where Julian and Sam and I had paused for blackberries on our way from the Tip last October. But it was a fact that the Reserve troops were held in Reserve, and not sent to the front lines, mainly because of a disabling flaw of body or mind—some were wounded veterans, missing a hand or an arm; some were elderly; some were too simple or sullen to function in a disciplined body of men. I can't say anything for certain about the soldier posted as lookout on the hill, but if he wasn't a fool he was at least utterly unconcerned about concealment, for his silhouette (and the silhouette of his rifle) stood etched against the bright eastern sky for all to see. But maybe that was intentional, to let prospective fugitives know their way was barred.

Not *every* way was barred, however, not for someone who had grown up in Williams Ford and hunted everywhere on its perimeter. Instead of following Julian directly I rode north a distance, and then through an encampment of indentured laborers, whose ragged children gaped at me from the glassless windows of their shanties, and whose soft-coal fires made a smoky gauze of the motionless air. This route connected with lanes cut through the wheat fields for the transportation of harvests and field-hands—lanes that had been deepened by years of use, so that I rode behind a berm of earth and snake rail fences, hidden from the distant sentinel. When I was safely east I came down a cattle-trail that reconnected me with the east-leading road, on which I was able to read the same signs that had alerted me back at Williams Ford, thanks to a fine layer of snow still undisturbed by any wind.

Julian had come this way. He had done as he said he would, and ridden toward Lundsford before midnight. The snow had stopped soon after, leaving his horse's prints clearly visible, though softened and half-covered.

But his were not the only tracks. There was a second set, more crisply defined and hence more recent, probably set down during the night. This was what had caught my attention at the crossroads in Williams Ford: clear evidence of pursuit. Someone had followed Julian, without Julian's knowledge. That had dire implications, the only redeeming circumstance being the fact of a single pursuer rather than a company of men. If the powerful people of the Estate had known it was Julian Comstock who had fled they would have sent an entire battalion to haul him back. I supposed Julian had been mistaken for an indentured fugitive or a lease-boy fleeing the conscription, and that he had been followed by some ambitious Reservist acting on his own initiative. Otherwise that whole imagined battalion might be right behind me—or perhaps soon would be, since Julian's absence must have been noticed by now.

I rode east, adding my own track to the previous set.

It was a long ride. Noon came, and noon went, and more hours passed, and I began to have second thoughts as the sun angled toward its rendezvous with the southwestern horizon. What exactly did I hope to accomplish? To warn Julian? If so, I was a little late off the mark . . . though I hoped that at some point Julian had covered his tracks, or otherwise misled his pursuer, who didn't have the advantage I had, of knowing where Julian meant to stay until Sam Godwin arrived. Failing that, I half-imagined *rescuing* Julian from capture, even though I had but a squirrel rifle and a few rounds of ammunition (plus a knife and my own wits, both feeble enough weapons) against whatever a Reservist might carry. In any case these were more wishes and anxieties than calculations or plans. I had no fully-formed plan beyond riding to Julian's aid and telling him that I had delivered my message to Sam, who would follow along as soon as he could discreetly leave the Estate.

And then what? It was a question I dared not ask—not out on this lonely road, well past the Tip now, farther than I had ever been from Williams Ford; not out here where the flatlands stretched away on every side like the frosty Plains of Mars, and the wind, which had been absent all morning, began to pluck at the fringes of my coat; not when my own shadow was drawn out before me like a scarecrow gone riding. It was cold and getting colder, and soon the winter moon would be aloft, and me with only a few ounces of salt pork in my saddlebag and a dozen matches to make a fire, if I was able to secure any kindling by nightfall. I began to wonder if I had gone insane. I told myself that I could go back; that I hadn't yet been missed; that it wasn't too late to sit down to a Christmas Eve supper, and wake in time to hear the ringing-in of the Holiday and smell the goodness of Nativity apples drenched in cinnamon and brown sugar. I mused on it repeatedly, sometimes with tears in my eyes; but I let Rapture keep on carrying me toward the darkest part of the horizon.

Then, after what seemed endless hours of dusk, with only a brief pause when both Rapture and I drank from a creek which had a skin of ice on it, I began to come among the ruins of the Secular Ancients.

Not that there was anything spectacular about them. Fanciful drawings often portray the ruins of the last century as tall buildings, ragged and hollow as broken teeth, forming vine-encrusted canyons and shadowy cul-de-sacs.* No doubt such places exist—most of them in the uninhabitable Southwest, however, where "famine sits enthroned, and waves his scepter over a dominion expressly made for him," which would rule out vines and such tropical items†—but most ruins were like the ones I now passed, mere irregularities (or more precisely, *regularities*) in the landscape, which indicated the former presence of foundations. These terrains were treacherous, often concealing deep basements that could open like hungry mouths on unwary travelers, and only Tipmen loved them. I was careful to keep to the path, though I began to wonder whether Julian would be as easy to find as I had imagined—"Lundsford" was a big locality, and the wind had begun to scour away the hoofprints I relied on for navigation.

I was haunted, too, by thoughts of the False Tribulation of the last century. It wasn't unusual to come across desiccated old bones in localities like this. Millions had died in the worst dislocations of the End of Oil—of disease, of fighting, but mostly of starvation. The Age of Oil had allowed a fierce intensity of fertilization and irrigation, which had fed more people than a humbler agriculture could support. I had seen photographs of Americans from that blighted age, thin as sticks, their children with distended bellies, crowded into "relief camps" that would soon enough become communal graves when the imagined "relief" failed to materialize. No wonder, then, that our ancestors had mistaken those decades for the Tribulation of Biblical prophecy. What was astonishing was how many of our current institutions—the Church, the Army, the Federal Government—had survived more or less intact. There was a passage in the Dominion Bible that Ben Kreel read to us whenever the subject of the False Tribulation arose in school, and which I had committed to memory: *The field is wasted, the land mourns; for the corn is shriveled, the wine is dry, the oil languishes. Be ashamed, farmers; howl, vinekeepers; howl for the wheat and the barley, for the harvest of the field has perished . . .*

It had made me shiver then, and it made me shiver now, in these barrens that had been stripped of all their utility by a century of scavenging. Where in this rubble was Julian, and where was his pursuer?

It was by his fire I found him. But I wasn't the first to arrive.

The sun was altogether down, and a filmy Aurora played about the northern sky, dimmed by a fingernail moon, when I came to the most recently excavated

---

* Or "culs-de-sac"? My French is rudimentary.
† Though Old Miami or Orlando might begin to fit the bill.

part of Lundsford. The temporary dwellings of the Tipmen—rude huts of scavenged timber—had been abandoned here for the season, and corduroy ramps led down into the empty digs.

The snow here had been blown into windrows and dunes, and all evidence of hoofprints had been erased. But I rode slowly and paid close attention to the environs, knowing I was close to my goal. I was buoyed by the observation that Julian's pursuer, whoever he was, hadn't returned this way from his mission: had not, that is, taken Julian captive, or at least hadn't gone back to Williams Ford with his prisoner in tow. Perhaps the pursuit had been suspended for the night.

A little while later—though it seemed an eternity, as Rapture short-stepped down the frozen road, dodging pitfalls—I heard the whicker of another horse, and saw a plume of smoke curl into the moon-bright sky.

Quickly I turned Rapture off the road, and tied his reins to the stump of a concrete pillar. I took my squirrel rifle from the saddle holster and moved on foot toward the source of the smoke, until I was able to discern that the fumes emerged from a fissure in the landscape, perhaps the very dig from which the Tipmen had extracted *A History of Mankind in Space* months ago. Surely this was where Julian had gone to wait for Sam's arrival. I crept a little farther on and saw Julian's horse, unmistakably a fine Estate horse (worth more, I'm sure, in the eyes of its owner, than a hundred Julian Comstocks), moored to an outcrop—and, alarmingly, here was another horse as well, not far away. The second animal was a stranger to me; it was slat-ribbed and elderly in appearance, but it wore a military bridle and the sort of cloth bib—blue, with a red star in it—that marked a mount belonging to the Reserves.

I studied the situation from behind the moon-shadow of a fractured abutment.

The smoke suggested that Julian had gone down into the hollow of the Tipmen's dig, to shelter from the cold and bank his fire for the night. The presence of the second horse suggested that he had been discovered, and that his pursuer must already have confronted him.

More than that I could not deduce. It remained only to approach the contested grounds as closely as possible, and see what more I could learn.

I inched another yard forward. The dig was revealed by moonlight as a deep but narrow excavation, covered in part with boards, with a sloping entrance framed in old timber. The glow of the fire within was just visible, as was the chimney-hole that had cut through the planking some distance south. There was, as far as I could discern, only the single way in or out. I decided to proceed as far as I could without being seen, and to that end I lowered myself down the slope, sliding by the seat of my pants over ground that was as cold, it seemed to me, as the wastelands of the arctic North.

I was slow, I was cautious, and I was quiet. But I was not slow, cautious, or quiet *enough*; for I had just got far enough to glimpse an excavated chamber, in which the firelight cast a kaleidoscopic flux of shadows, when I felt a pressure behind my ear—the barrel of a gun—and a voice said, "Keep moving, mister, and join your friend below."

I kept silent until I could comprehend more of the situation than I presently understood.

My captor marched me down into the low part of the dig. Here the air was noticeably warmer, and we were screened from the wind, though not from the stagnant reek of what once had been a basement or cellar in some establishment of the Secular Ancients.

The Tipmen hadn't left much behind at the end of the season: only a rubble of broken bits of things, indistinguishable under layers of dust and dirt. The far wall was of concrete, and the fire had been banked against it, under a chimney-hole that must have been cut by antiquarians in the course of their labors. A circle of stones hedged the fiercely-burning fire, and the damp planks and splinters in it crackled with a deceptive cheerfulness. Deeper parts of the excavation, with ceilings lower than a man standing erect, opened in several directions.

Julian sat near the fire with his back to the wall and his knees drawn up under his chin. His clothes had been made filthy by the grime of the place. He frowned, and when he caught sight of me his frown deepened into a scowl.

"Go over there and get beside him," my captor said, "but give me that little bird rifle first."

I surrendered my weapon, modest as it was, and joined Julian. Thus I was able to get my first clear look at the man who had captured me. He appeared not much older than myself, but he was dressed in the blue and yellow uniform of the Reserves. His Reserve cap was pulled low over his eyes, which twitched left and right as though he feared an ambush. In short he appeared both inexperienced and nervous—and maybe a little dim, for his jaw was slack, and he seemed unaware of the dribble of mucus that had escaped his nostrils as a result of the cold weather.

His weapon, however, was very much in earnest, and not to be trifled with. It was a Pittsburgh rifle manufactured by the famous Porter & Earle Works, which loaded at the breech from a cassette and could fire five rounds in succession without any more attention from its owner than a twitch of the index finger. Julian had carried a similar weapon but had been disarmed of it; it rested against a stack of small staved barrels, well out of reach; and the Reservist put my squirrel rifle beside it.

I began to feel sorry for myself, and to think what a poor way of spending Christmas Eve I had chosen. I didn't resent the action of the Reservist nearly as much as I regretted my own stupidity and lapse of judgment.

"I don't know who you are," the Reservist said, "and I don't care—one draft dodger is as good as the next, in my opinion—but I was given the job of collecting runaways, and my bag is getting full. I hope you'll both keep till morning, when I can ride you back into Williams Ford. Anyhow, none of us will sleep tonight. I won't, in any case, so you might as well resign yourself to captivity. If you're hungry, there's a hank of old pork for you."

I was never less hungry in my life, and I began to say so, but Julian interrupted: "It's true, Adam," he said, "we're fairly caught. I wish you hadn't come after me."

"I'm beginning to feel the same way," I said.

He gave me a meaningful look, and said in a lower voice, "Is Sam—?"

"No whispering there," our captor barked.

But I divined the intent of the question, and nodded to indicate that I had communicated Julian's message, though that was by no means a guarantee of our deliverance. Not only were the exits from Williams Ford under close watch, but Sam couldn't slip away as easily as I had, and if Julian's absence had been noted there would have been a redoubling of the guard, and probably an expedition sent out to hunt us. The man who had captured Julian was evidently an outrider, assigned to patrol the roads for runaways, and he had been diligent in his work; but didn't know the significance of the trophies he had bagged.

He was less diligent now that he had us cornered, however, for he took a soapstone pipe from his pocket and proceeded to fill it, making himself comfortable on a wooden crate. His gestures were nervous, and I supposed the pipe was meant to relax him, for it was not tobacco he put into it.

Perhaps the Reservist was a Kentuckian, for I understand the less respectable people of that State often form the habit of smoking the silk of the female hemp plant, which is cultivated prodigiously there. Kentucky hemp is grown for cordage and cloth and paper, and as a drug is less intoxicating than the Indian Hemp of lore; but its mild smoke is said to be pleasant for those who indulge in it, though too much can result in sleepiness and great thirst.

Julian evidently thought those symptoms would be a welcome distraction in our captor, and he gestured at me to remain silent, so as not to interrupt the Reservist in his vice. The Reservist packed his bowl from an oilcloth envelope until it was full, and soon the substance was alight, and a more fragrant smoke joined the effluvia of the campfire as it swirled toward the ragged gap in the ceiling.

Clearly the night would be a long one; and I tried to be patient in my captivity, and not think too much of Christmas, or the yellow light of my parents' cottage on dark winter mornings, or the soft bed where I might have been sleeping if I had been less rash in my deliberations.

6

I began by saying this was a story about Julian Comstock, and I don't mean to turn it into a story about myself. Perhaps it seems so; but there's a reason for it, beyond the obvious temptations of vanity and self-regard. I did not at the time know Julian nearly as well as I thought I did.

Our friendship was a boys' friendship. I couldn't help reviewing, as we sat in silent captivity in the ruins of Lundsford, all the things we had done together: reading books, hunting in the foothills west of Williams Ford, arguing amiably over everything from Philosophy and Moon-Visiting to the best way to bait a hook or cinch a bridle. It had been too easy, during our time together, to forget that Julian was an Aristo with close connections to men of power, or that his father had been famous both as a hero and as a traitor, or that his uncle Deklan Comstock—Deklan Conqueror—might not have Julian's best interests at heart.

All that seemed far away, and distant from the nature of Julian's true spirit, which was gentle and inquisitive—a naturalist's disposition, not a politician's or a general's. When I pictured Julian as an adult I imagined him pursuing some scholarly or artistic adventure: digging the bones of pre-Adamite monsters out of the Athabaska shale, perhaps, or making an improved kind of movie. He was not a warlike person, and the thoughts of the great men of the day were almost exclusively concerned with war.

So I had let myself forget that he was also everything he had been before he came to Williams Ford. He was the heir of a brave, determined, and ultimately betrayed father, who had conquered an army of Brazilians but had been crushed by the millstone of political intrigue. He was the son of a wealthy woman, born to a powerful family of her own—not powerful enough to save Bryce Comstock from the gallows, but powerful enough to protect Julian, at least temporarily, from the mad calculations of his uncle. He was both a pawn and a player in the great games of the Aristos. And while I might have forgotten all this, Julian hadn't—those were the people who had made him, and if he chose not to speak of them, they nevertheless must have haunted his thoughts.

It's true that he was often frightened of small things—I remember his disquiet when I described the rituals of the Church of Signs to him, and he would sometimes shriek at the distress of animals when our hunting failed to result in a clean kill. But tonight, here in the ruins, I was the one who half-dozed in a morose funk, fighting tears; while it was Julian who sat intently still, as coolly calculating as a bank clerk, gazing with resolve from beneath the strands of dusty hair that straggled over his brows.

When we hunted he often gave me the rifle and begged me to fire the last lethal shot, distrusting his own resolve. Tonight—had the opportunity presented itself—I would have given the rifle to him.

I half-dozed, as I said, and from time to time woke to see the Reservist still sitting guard. His eyelids were at half-mast, but I put that down to the effect of the hemp flowers he had smoked. Periodically he would start, as if at a sound inaudible to others, then settle back into place.

He had boiled a copious amount of coffee in a tin pan, and he warmed it whenever he renewed the fire, and drank sufficiently to keep himself from falling asleep. That obliged him periodically to retreat to a distant part of the dig and attend to his physical needs in relative privacy. We couldn't take any advantage from it, however, since he carried his Pittsburgh rifle with him; but it allowed a moment or two in which Julian and I were able to whisper without being overheard.

"The man is no mental giant," Julian said. "We may yet get out of here with our freedom."

"It's not his *brains* so much as his *artillery* that's stopping us," I said.

"Perhaps we can separate the one from the other. Look there, Adam. Beyond the fire I mean—back in the rubble."

I looked at the place he indicated. There was motion in the shadows—a particular sort of motion, which I began to recognize.

"The distraction may suit our purposes," Julian said, "unless it becomes fatal." And I saw the sweat that had begun to stand out on his forehead. "But I need your help," he added.

I have said that I didn't partake of the particular rites of my father's church, and that snakes were not my favorite creatures. As much as I had heard about surrendering one's volition to God—and I had seen my father with a Massassauga Rattler in each hand, trembling with devotion, speaking in a tongue not only foreign but utterly unknown (though it favored long vowels and stuttered consonants, much like the sounds he made when he burned his fingers on the coal stove)—I could never entirely convince myself that I was protected from the serpent's bite. Some in the congregation obviously had not been: there was Sarah Prestley, for instance, whose right arm had swollen up black with venom until it had to be amputated by Williams Ford's physician . . . but I won't dwell on that. The point is, that while I *disliked* snakes, I was not especially *afraid* of them, as Julian was. And I couldn't help admiring his restraint: for what was writhing in the shadows nearby was a nest of snakes, scorched out of hibernation by the heat of the fire right nearby.

I should add that it wasn't uncommon for these collapsed ruins to be infested with snakes, mice, spiders, and poisonous insects. Death by bite or sting

was one of the routine hazards faced by professional Tipmen, including concussion, blood poisoning, and accidental burial. The snakes, after the Tipmen
ceased work for the winter, must have crept into this chasm anticipating an
undisturbed sleep, of which we and the Reservist had unfortunately deprived
them.

The Reservist—who came back a little unsteadily from his necessaries—
had not yet noticed the dig's prior tenants. He seated himself on his crate, and
scowled at us, and studiously refilled his pipe.

"If he discharges all five shots from his rifle," Julian whispered tremu-
lously, "then we have a chance of overcoming him, or of recovering our own
weapons. But, Adam—"

"No talking there," the Reservist mumbled.

"—you must remember your father's advice," Julian finished.

"I said keep quiet!"

Julian cleared his throat and addressed the Reservist directly, since the
time for action had obviously arrived: "Sir, I have to draw your attention to
something."

"What would that be, my little draft dodger?"

"I'm afraid we're not alone in this place."

"Not alone!" the Reservist said, casting his eyes about him nervously.
Then he recovered and squinted at Julian. "I don't see any other persons."

"I don't mean persons, but vipers," said Julian.

"Vipers!"

"In other words—snakes."

At this the Reservist started again, his mind perhaps still confused by the
effects of the hemp smoke; then he sneered and said, "Go on, you can't pull
that one on me."

"I'm sorry if you think I'm joking, for there are at least a dozen snakes
advancing from the shadows, and one of them is about to achieve intimacy
with your right boot."*

"Hah," the Reservist said, but he couldn't help glancing in the indicated
direction, where one of the serpents—a fat and lengthy example—had lifted
its head and was sampling the air above his bootlace.

The effect was immediate, and left no more time for planning. The Reservist leapt from his seat on the wooden crate, uttering oaths, and danced
backward, at the same time attempting to bring his rifle to his shoulder and
confront the threat. He discovered to his dismay that it wasn't a question of
one snake but of *dozens,* and he compressed the trigger of the weapon. The resulting shot went wild. The bullet impacted near the main nest of the creatures, causing them to scatter with astonishing speed, like a box of loaded
springs, unfortunately for the hapless Reservist, who was directly in their

---

* Julian's sense of timing was exquisite, perhaps as a result of his theatrical inclinations.

path. He cursed and fired four more times. Most of the shots careened harm-lessly; one obliterated the midsection of the lead serpent, which knotted around its own wound like a bloody rope.

"Now, Adam!" Julian shouted, and I stood up, thinking: My father's advice?

My father was a taciturn man, and most of his advice had involved the practical matter of running the Estate's stables. I hesitated a moment in confusion while Julian advanced toward the captive rifles, dancing among the surviving snakes like a dervish. The Reservist, recovering somewhat, raced in the same direction; and then I recalled the only advice of my father's that I had ever shared with Julian:

Grasp it where its neck ought to be, behind the head; ignore the tail, however it may thrash; and crack its skull, hard and often enough to subdue it.

And so I did just that—until the threat was neutralized.

Julian, meanwhile, recovered the weapons, and came away from the infested area of the dig.

He looked with some astonishment at the Reservist, who was slumped at my feet, bleeding from his scalp, which I had "cracked, hard and often" against a concrete pillar.

"Adam," he said. "When I spoke of your father's advice—I meant the snakes."

"The snakes?" Several of them still twined about the dig. But I reminded myself that Julian knew very little about the nature and variety of reptiles. "They're only corn snakes," I explained.* "They're big, but they're not venomous."

Julian, his eyes gone large, absorbed this information.

Then he looked at the crumpled form of the Reservist again.

"Have you killed him?"

"Well, I hope not," I said.

---

* Once confined to the Southeast, corn snakes have spread north with the warming climate. I have read that certain of the Secular Ancients once kept them as pets—yet another instance of our ancestors' willful perversity.

7

We made a new camp in a less populated part of the ruins, and kept a watch on the road, and at dawn we saw a single horse and rider approaching from the west. It was Sam Godwin.

Julian hailed him, waving his arms. Sam came closer, and looked with some relief at Julian, and then speculatively at me. I blushed, thinking of how I had interrupted him at his prayers (however unorthodox those prayers might have been, from a purely Christian perspective), and how poorly I had reacted to my discovery of his true religion. But I said nothing, and Sam said nothing, and relations between us seemed to have been regularized, since I had demonstrated my loyalty (or patent foolishness) by riding to Julian's aid.

It was Christmas morning. I supposed that didn't mean anything in particular to Julian or Sam, but I was poignantly aware of the date. The sky was blue again, but a squall had passed during the dark hours of the morning, and the snow "lay round about, deep and crisp and even." Even the ruins of Lundsford were transformed into something soft-edged and oddly beautiful; and I was amazed at how simple it was for nature to cloak corruption in the garb of purity and make it peaceful.

But it wouldn't be peaceful for long, and Sam said so. "There are troops behind me as we speak. Word came by wire from New York not to let Julian escape. We can't linger here more than a moment."

"Where will we go?" Julian asked.

"It's impossible to ride much farther east. There's no forage for the animals and precious little water. Sooner or later we'll have to turn south and make a connection with the railroad or the turnpike. It's going to be short rations and hard riding, I'm afraid, and if we want to make good our escape we'll need to assume false names. We'll be little better than draft dodgers or labor refugees, and I expect we'll have to pass some time among that hard crew, at least until we reach New York City. We can find friends in New York."

It was a plan, but it was a large and lonesome one, and my heart sank at the prospect of it.

"We have a prisoner," Julian told his mentor, and we escorted Sam back into the excavated ruins to explain how we had spent the night.

The Reservist was there, his hands tied behind his back, still groggy from the punishment I had inflicted on him but well enough to open his eyes and scowl. Julian and Sam spent a little time debating how to deal with this encumbrance. We could not, of course, take him with us; the question was how to send him home without endangering ourselves needlessly.

It was a debate to which I could contribute nothing, so I took a little slip of paper from my back-satchel, and a pencil, and wrote a letter.

It was addressed to my mother, since my father was without the art of literacy.

You will no doubt have noticed my absence, I wrote. *It saddens me to be away from home, especially at this time (I write on Christmas Day). But I hope you will be consoled with the knowledge that I am all right, and not in any immediate danger.*

(That was a lie, depending on how you defined "immediate," but a kindly one, I reasoned.)

In any case I would not have been able to remain in Williams Ford, since I could not have escaped the draft for long even if I postponed my military service for some few more months. The conscription drive is in earnest; I expect the War in Labrador is going badly. It was inevitable that we should be separated, as much as I mourn for my home and all its comforts.

(And it was all I could do not to decorate the page with a vagrant tear.)

Please accept my best wishes and my gratitude for everything you and Father have done for me. I will write again as soon as it is practicable, which may not be immediately. Trust in the knowledge that I will pursue my destiny faithfully and with every Christian virtue you have taught me. God bless you in the coming and every year.

That wasn't enough to say, but I couldn't spare time for more. Julian and Sam were calling for me. I signed my name, and added, as a postscript:

Please tell Father that I value his advice, and that it has already served me usefully. Yrs. etc. once again, Adam.

"You've written a letter," Sam observed as he came to rush me to my horse. "But have you given any thought to how you might mail it?"

I confessed I had not.

"The Reservist can carry it," said Julian, who had already mounted his horse.

The Reservist was also mounted, but with his hands tied behind him, as it was Sam's final conclusion that we should set him loose with the horse headed west, where he would encounter more troops before very long. He was awake but, as I have said, sullen; and he barked, "I'm nobody's damned mailman!"

I addressed the message, and Julian took it and tucked it into the Reservist's saddlebag. Despite his youth, and despite the slightly dilapidated condition of his hair and clothing, Julian sat tall in the saddle. He was, of course, an Aristo of the highest order, but I had never really thought of him as high-born until that moment, when he took on the aspect of command with a startling ease and familiarity. He said to the Reservist, "We treated you kindly—"

The Reservist uttered an oath.

"Be quiet. You were injured in the conflict, but we took you prisoner, and we treated you more gently than you treated us when the conditions were reversed. I am a Comstock, and I won't be spoken to crudely by an infantryman, at any price. You'll deliver this boy's message and you'll do it gratefully."

The Reservist was clearly startled by the assertion that Julian was a Comstock—he had been laboring under the assumption that we were mere village runaways—but he screwed up his courage and said, "Why should I?"

"Because it's the Christian thing to do," Julian said, "and because, if this argument with my uncle is ever settled, the power to remove your head from your shoulders may well reside in my hands. Does that make sense to you, soldier?"

The Reservist allowed that it did.

And so we rode out that Christmas morning from the ruins where the Tip-men had discovered *A History of Mankind in Space,* which I had tucked into my back-satchel like a vagrant memory.

My mind was a confusion of ideas and anxieties; but I found myself recalling what Julian had said, long ago it now seemed, about DNA, and how it aspired to perfect replication but progressed by remembering itself imperfectly. It might be true, I thought, because our lives were like that—*time itself* was like that, every moment dying and pregnant with its own distorted reflection. Today was Christmas: which Julian claimed had once been a pagan holiday, dedicated to Sol Invictus or some such Roman god; but which had evolved into the familiar celebration of the present, and was no less dear because of it.

(I imagined I heard the Christmas bells ringing from the Dominion Hall at Williams Ford, though that was impossible, for we were miles away, and not even the sound of a cannon shot could carry so far across the prairie. It was only memory speaking.)

Maybe that logic was true of people, too—maybe I was already an inexact echo of what I had been just days before. And maybe the same was true of Julian. Already something hard and uncompromising had begun to emerge from his gentle features—the first manifestation of a *freshly evolved* Julian, called forth, perhaps, by his violent departure from Williams Ford. Evolution can't be predicted, Julian used to tell me; it's a scattershot business; it fires, but it doesn't aim. Perhaps we couldn't know what we were becoming.

But that was all Philosophy, and not much use; and I kept quiet about it as we spurred our horses toward the railroad, the distant East, and the whole onrushing future.

8

By leaving Williams Ford in search of the safety and anonymity of a distant city, I began to learn something of the imponderable vastness of the Nation in which I lived, and the surprising variety of its people. That useful knowledge was obtained at considerable risk, however, since we were still pursued by the horsemen of the Reserve, who considered us less Tourists than Fugitives.

After we left the digs at Lundsford we found ourselves once more in open country, a drear treeless fiefdom unrelieved by the vertical works of man or nature. Clouds gathered and darkened the wintry sky, and by the afternoon we were riding through curtains of squalling snow. Our horses, already tired, quickly became exhausted—my own mount Rapture perhaps more than the other two animals, for both Sam and Julian had taken young geldings from the Estate's stables, while Rapture was just a working horse, thin at the shanks and of an appreciable age. Indifferent as I generally was to the wants of animals—not a few of the Estate's horses and mules had attempted to plant their heels on my skull as I shoveled out their stalls, thus alienating my natural sympathy—I did begin to feel sorry for Rapture, and for myself as well, as the discomfort of the journey settled into my legs, thighs, and spine. I was relieved when darkness began to gather, since it meant we would be obliged to stop and rest.

But that wasn't a simple matter in the snowy wastes of Athabaska. There was no natural shelter at hand, only a landscape so nearly flat that I could credit Julian's assertion that it had once seen service as the bottom of a primordial ocean. Sam halted, and stared into the gloomy and snow-shrouded distance as if listening for pursuers. Then he beckoned us off the road a ways. This seemed to me a dubious choice, since the true path of even the main road was increasingly obscured by blowing snow. But Sam had long anticipated the need for an eventual escape from Williams Ford, and he had scouted this route in advance. We followed the remains of a rail fence, the posts of which were blunted protuberances from the whitened prairie, until we reached the ruin of a fieldstone farmhouse, degraded by time and weather but stout enough to provide shelter and a place for a modest fire.

Thus the snow became an ally, concealing any trail we might have left. Sam had laid in a cord of wood (chopped from the spindly willows that grew along a nearby creek) and had even provided fodder for the horses. Sam and Julian set about preparing a meal while I dried and curried the horses, and I made sure Rapture got his ration of hay without interference from the high-born animals.

I was wet and cold myself, and the farmhouse was gloomy and admitted the wind through every hollow window and dropped board; and I didn't like the dangerously fractured and weakened plank floors, or the walls and rafters that seemed made more of mildew than of anything substantial enough to support a roof. But Sam selected the most sheltered corner of the building, and reinforced its gaps with a tarpaulin from his kit; and he built the fire in a galvanized washtub suspended on massive rocks, so we could stoke its heat without fear of setting the entire house aflame. And because Sam had equipped himself like a soldier embarking on a long march, we enjoyed cornmeal and bacon and coffee, in addition to the salt pork and stale bread I had hastily packed.

We talked among ourselves while the fire crackled and the night wind stabbed its knives about. I was uneasy with Sam, whose unusual religious inclinations I had so recently discovered. And perhaps he was as uneasy with me, for he turned to me as we finished our corn-cakes and said, "I never meant for you to come with us, Adam. You would have been safer in Williams Ford, despite the conscription."

I told him I knew the choice I had made, and what it meant; and I thanked him for his help, and promised to make myself as useful as possible on the journey.

"Since you've cast your lot with us I'll do my best to protect you from any risk—I promise you that, Adam. But my first obligation is to Julian's safety, only secondarily to yours. Do you understand?"

It wasn't a reassuring statement, but it was honest and, within its scope, generous. I acknowledged it with a nod. Then I took a breath and apologized for my shock at the discovery that he was a Jew.

"It's a matter best left undiscussed," he said, "especially in public."

No doubt that was true; but my curiosity had gotten the better of me, and since the present situation was very far from "public" I ventured to ask how long he had been a Jew, and what had led him to choose that venerable if problematic faith out of the many possibilities at hand.

Sam frowned, in so far as I could detect any expression beneath his beard. "Adam . . . those are personal questions. . . ."

"Yes, and I'm sorry, please excuse me, I only wondered—"

"No—stop. If we're going to be traveling together I suppose you're entitled to ask. What embarrasses me is that I can't supply a whole answer." He stirred the fire contemplatively while the wind howled in the crevices of the darkened ruin. "My parents were Jews, though they kept their practices clandestine. They died when I was very young. I was raised by a charitable Christian family until I was old enough to enter the military."

I guessed that was how he had acquired the skills necessary for passing undetected in a Christian majority. "But the rituals you were enacting—"

"That's all I have of Judaism, Adam. A few prayers for special occasions, poorly remembered. I've met a number of Jews in my career and to some degree refreshed my understanding of the religion's rites and doctrines. But I can't claim to be either knowledgeable or observant."

"Then why do you light the candles and say the prayers?"

"It honors my parents, and their parents before them, and so on."

"Is that enough to make a man a Jew?"

"In my case it is. I'm sure the Dominion would say so."

"But you disguise yourself very successfully," I said, meaning to compliment him.

"Thank you," he said, somewhat acidly, adding, "We'll all three have to disguise ourselves very soon. Ultimately I mean to get us aboard a train bound for the east. But we can't travel among respectable people—the news of Julian's disappearance will have been disseminated among that class. We'll have to present ourselves as landless. You in particular, Julian, will have to suppress your manners and vocabulary, and you, Adam," and here he cocked his eye at me with an earnestness I found disquieting, "you'll have to forgo some of the gentility of the leasing class, if we're not to be discovered."

I told him I had met many examples of indentured or transient laborers through my father's activities in the Church of Signs. I knew how to say "don't" for "doesn't," and how to spit, should the necessity arise, and how to swear, though I didn't like to.

"Even so," Sam instructed me, "the men and women who follow your father's faith have already distinguished themselves from the lowest types by their urge to attend a church. In a few days we'll be surrounded by thieves, fugitives, adulterers, and worse, and not one of them interested in repentance. I can make you look low-born easily enough, but it will take some study before you can act and speak the part. Until then my urgent advice is to keep your mouths shut whenever possible—both of you."

As if to set a tutelary example, he lapsed into a brooding silence.

In any case we were too exhausted for further talk; and despite the crude circumstances, the keening of the wind, the thinness of the old Army blanket Sam had given me, and the daunting prospects before us, I was asleep before very long.

In the morning Sam ordered Julian and me to scout the east-west road from a prudent distance and alert him if we saw any military traffic there.

Our horses would have made us conspicuous, so we left them behind and hiked to the verge of the main road, where we concealed ourselves behind hummocks of snow. We had put on as many layers of clothing as we could get our hands on, and taken all the cold-weather precautions we had learned from Sam and gleaned from the military romances of Mr. Charles Curtis Easton. None of it was especially effective, however, so we spent much of the afternoon stomping our feet and breathing into our hands. The snowfall had ended and the wind had passed, but the temperature hovered near the freezing point, causing a sort of wraithy mist to rise from the landscape, and making everything chill and drear.

Late in the afternoon we heard a group of cavalry moving through the fog. Quickly we hid ourselves. Peeping through an embrasure in the mounded snow, I counted five men of the Athabaska Reserve coming down the road. They were the usual back-country soldiers, with the exception of the man who rode at the head of the troop. That man was a long-haired veteran of stern demeanor. His uniform was in impeccable order, but he rode at a curious angle; which was explained when I saw that he had been strapped to the saddle by an arrangement of belts, on account of the fact that he was missing his right leg. He was, in other words, a different kind of Reservist, one whose inventory of bodily parts had been whittled by the war but whose military skill and professional instincts remained fully intact.

When he came abreast of our position he reined up and turned his head this way and that, seeming almost to scent the air. Julian kept utterly still, while I resisted an impulse to flee with all the speed in my legs. During this interval I was scarcely able to breathe, though my heart raced like a mouse in a tithe-box, and the silence was broken only by the wheezing of the horses and the creak of leather saddles.

Then one of the Reservists cleared his throat, and another pronounced some witticism, which caused a third to laugh; and the one-legged man sighed as if in resignation, and spurred his horse, and the cavalrymen rode on.

We hurried back to deliver our intelligence to Sam.

Sam, as a result of his past service in the Army of the Californias, was comfortable in the company of military men, and he had made the acquaintance of several Reservists during their visits to Williams Ford and his travels to Connaught. When Julian described the man who led the small company we had seen, Sam shook his head in dismay. "That must be One-Leg Willy Bass," he said. "An excellent tracker. But your report's incomplete, Julian. Finish it, please."

I didn't know what he meant. Julian had described the cavalry detachment in minute detail, I thought, very nearly to brand of polish Mr. Willy Bass used on his pommel, and I couldn't imagine what he had left out. Julian, too, seemed nonplused, until the critical datum came to mind. Then he smiled.

"West," he said.

"In full, please, Julian?"

"The detachment was traveling from the east to the west."

"Good. Now draw a conclusion from that."

"Well . . . since they must have ridden out of Williams Ford in the first place, I guess they were returning home."

"Yes. I know One-Leg Willy well enough that I doubt he's finished with us. Most of his virtue as a tracker is in his obstinacy—the rest is guile. But if he's ranged to the east of us and turned back, he must not have our scent exactly. I calculate this would be a good time for us to make for the railroad."

I ventured to ask more exactly where we were headed. Sam said, "A coaling station called Bad Jump. It has a poor reputation, and the businesses that operate there aren't the kind that keep honest ledgers. But that suits our purposes entirely."

Bad Jump may have been our likeliest destination, but it was nowhere close, and we had to ride all that day and through the night nearly without rest. That was hard on us, and even harder on the horses. But the animals weren't our main concern, Sam said; in Bad Jump we would have to sell them, in any case, or rid ourselves of them some other way. By this time I had become almost affectionate toward Rapture, who hadn't attempted to kick me even once, and I was reluctant to abandon him. I couldn't argue with Sam's logic, however, for horses are cumbersome baggage on a train, and the quality of the animals (Sam's and Julian's, at least) would instantly incriminate them as Estate horses.

We rode for three days and "camped rough" three nights. The end of December was raw and cold, and I couldn't sleep for shivering, even in the ingenious shelters Sam contrived for us along the route. Because of the clear skies our fires would have been easy to detect, and Sam was quick to quench them. He had considerable respect for the tracking skill of One-Leg Willy Bass, and often scanned the horizon behind us; and his nervousness spurred us to a greater exertion, in so far as we were capable of it.

Early on one of those cold mornings, long before dawn, I crawled out from our makeshift tent under a sky in which the Aurora Borealis burned and trembled with unusual vividness and clarity. Meaning only to attend to a call of nature, I found myself staring upward. The air was as clear as freshwater ice, and the shifting lights in the zenith looked to my weary eyes like the green-shaded alleys, gilded walls, and glacial parapets of some vast Celestial City. *Heaven,* Flaxie might have said, though it was surely a more austere and indifferent Heaven than the one she used to imagine. According to the *Dominion Reader for Young Persons,* from which my mother had liked to quote, Heaven was a New Jerusalem: a City, that is, with many Gates, one by which Presbyterians might enter, another for Baptists, and so forth—but none for Jews or Atheists.* It occurred to me that I was bound for a different City, however, more substantial if less desirable, and that this glowing intimation of Heaven might be as close to divinity as I was likely to get.

I might have stood there indefinitely, bound up in these thoughts, if Rapture had not snorted, and by that homely noise recalled me to the material world.

---

* And probably not much more than a mousehole for the Church of Signs, though that codicil was not explicit.

9

By the time we sighted Bad Jump, a smudge of soot against the thin line of the railroad, poor Rapture was nearly halt, having turned his hoof in a gopher-hole; and I wasn't feeling much better, though I was glad we had escaped the attention of One-Leg Willy Bass.

"Be aware that we're entering a kingdom of larceny," Sam advised us. "Commerce in these coaling towns is conducted by rougher rules than the ones that prevail in Williams Ford. We'll have to give up much to get the little we really need, and if the bargain seems unfair, please stifle your objections. In fact speak as little as possible. Keep your hats pulled low, for that matter. Our first stop will be at the stables of a horse-trader, and then, with luck, we'll board a train."

Julian might have been the most conspicuous of us, had his hands and face not been grimed with soot, for he was the most fair-skinned. (It isn't a hard rule that Aristos *must* be lighter-skinned than the leasing or indentured classes—there are plenty of dark-skinned Aristos, and no shortage of light-skinned laborers—but the tendency is unmistakable. This has to do, I've been told, with the way populations were dispersed during the Fall of the Cities in the last century, and how the vagrant urban masses were taken up as corvée labor by propertied interests.) In my case my skin wasn't a problem, but my vocabulary and manners might be. Sam had turned his old Army jacket inside out, by way of disguise, and this morning he had boiled a pan of water and shaved off his beard—a shocking transformation. With his beard he had always seemed the perfect exemplar of an aged military scholar. Without it he looked dismayingly young and vulnerable. The blade revealed a stern jaw, scratched and bleeding in places, and a wider and more mobile mouth than had ever been perceptible through his whiskers.

(I joked to Julian that this couldn't be an "evolution," since it had happened so suddenly; but in Darwinian philosophy, Julian said, such drastic changes were allowed for—they were called "catastrophic." Thenceforth Julian often made remarks about Sam's "catastrophic razor," and described the cuts and scrapes as Sam's "punctuated equilibrium," a witticism the significance of which escaped me.)

We rode down a gentle slope toward the corrals and stables of the horse-trader. Bad Jump came into closer focus as a conglomeration of board sheds and tin shacks, attached to the general area of the coaling tower like a barnacle on the hull of a ship, and I asked Sam how such a rude town could have come to exist in the midst of the prairie, with no visible agriculture to sustain it.

"It's a product of the rail fees," Sam said, "which are fixed by the landed aristocracy of the coastal ports."

"How can a rail fee create a town, though?"

"A fixed price invites a black market. It means a profit can be taken invisibly by stationmasters and their collaborators in the Rail Trust. Labor refugees, for instance, would never be allowed to buy passage on a respectable passenger car. But there are 'phantom cars'—freight cars rigged with a few crude amenities—that move about the country almost by stealth, and they can be hired for a price. And where one kind of illicit commerce flourishes, others are inevitably attracted. This trader," he said, as we passed through an iron gate enclosing an immense property of sheds, stables, and corrals, "deals mainly in stolen horses, for instance. From time to time a Reservist might want to exchange his Federal mount for specie and flee the State by train. No licensed dealer would conduct such a business, but other men are willing to assume the risk of prison or worse, if the price is attractive enough."

The trade was less brisk in the winter, Sam said, but it didn't cease entirely. That it did not was evidenced by the trader's well-populated stables and stock yards, and by the number of hands who worked about the place. We rode up to the main house or office, which was a slightly grander building than the general run of rude shacks in the neighborhood. We were ignored by a score of indifferent stablehands, until an unkempt woman appeared at the door of the house. Sam inquired for the owner, and without speaking a word the woman turned and went inside, and a large and brutish individual returned in her place.

He gave his name as Winslow, but he didn't offer his hand. Instead he stared at us with a feigned disinterest and asked why we were bothering him on a peaceful Sunday morning.

"Certain items to sell," said Sam.

"Well, I'm not buying right at the moment." But Mr. Winslow's eyes lingered on the Estate horses.

"Perhaps we can talk it over privately," said Sam; and Mr. Winslow sighed, and made theatrical gestures of impatience and disdain, but finally invited Sam indoors to dicker, while Julian and I stayed with the horses.

We passed the time by surveying our surroundings. The animals in the stables were only cursorily tended, so far as we could judge. I was reluctant to release Rapture into this company, though I had been convinced of the necessity of it. "It'll come by all right in the long term," I whispered to my spavined but loyal mount; and I stroked his mane, and pronounced the words as if I believed them.

Beyond the trading post of Mr. Winslow stood the towers of the coaling silo, where the railway tracks bisected the snowy plain. The sight of the tracks excited me a little. I had been once or twice to Connaught, the railhead that served Williams Ford, but I had never been aboard a train. Trains, and the rails and bridges they ran on, had always seemed marvelous to me. I wondered what it would be like to ride one—to feel the miles slip away under me like clouds under the wings of a bird, and to be borne off at flying speed to the fabled cities and harbors of the East.

When Sam emerged from Mr. Winslow's hovel his expression was grim. He instructed us to dismount and fill our satchels with food from the saddlebags, for everything else had been sold: mounts, saddles, rifles. I protested at this last—wouldn't we need weapons to protect ourselves? But Sam pointed out that a rifle is a cumbersome object, difficult to disguise, and that none of our fellow travelers would have one. Then Winslow emerged from his cabin and inspected the horses with a critical eye, clucking his tongue at invisible defects; but he couldn't entirely mask his pleasure at the quality of the Estate-bred mounts.

"And Mr. Winslow has been kind enough to let us sleep in his hayloft tonight," Sam said. "A train is scheduled to come through tomorrow morning, if it hasn't been delayed by snow in the mountain passes. With any luck we'll be on it, though we still have to buy passage."

I said a final goodbye to Rapture, who rewarded me with a disdainful stare, and tried to fix my mind on the exciting prospect of train travel.

Sam walked ahead of us toward the crowd of would-be refugees who had camped by the coaling station in anticipation of tomorrow's train. These landless people circulated among huts and colorful tents, where vendors bartered hot meals, hand weapons, piecemeal salvage, and lucky trinkets. Most of these travelers, vendors and customers alike, were men, but there were a few families among the crowd, including a few children. I asked Sam in a whisper how these people had come to be here.

Some were labor refugees from the great western Estates, he said, fleeing indenture and the law. Some were migrant farmworkers or free factory hands, stranded by the exigencies of black-market travel. Some were smallholders displaced by expanding Estates. Many were criminals of the commonest sort. Most were expecting to catch the next train east.

I was afraid we would have to fight them for a berth, or perhaps be left behind—not a pleasant prospect, with One-Leg Willy Bass still hunting us—but Sam said not to worry, that he had held back more than enough scrip to guarantee us a ready place.

We waited while Sam went inside the timber building which housed the offices of the Rail Trust. Sam spent a considerable time in there, and Julian and I wandered a little among the vendors' stalls, inspecting dyed blankets and alcohol stoves, pocket knives and lucky pig's-knuckles. I was tempted by a vendor who sold morsels of skewered meat grilled over a charcoal fire—the smell, after days of trail food, was intoxicating—but Julian reminded me that the quality of the meat might not be good, given that it was almost certainly derived from animals Mr. Winslow couldn't profitably ship east: elderly mules and tubercular cattle. My appetite, powerful as it was, retreated before the suggestion.

Then Sam came out of the Rail Trust office looking grimly satisfied. He had bought us a place on the very next train, he said, and we would only have to spend one more night in Bad Jump, with any luck.

We passed the night in the loft of one of Mr. Winslow's barns, a crude accommodation. Sam divided the hours of darkness into three watches. Julian took the first, Sam the second, and I the last—the early-morning watch, which was the coldest. When Sam woke me to attend to these duties I wrapped my blanket around myself and took his place at the loft door, which was open to the wind, and heaped loose hay about myself until I was little more than a pair of eyes contained in a haybale.

An eventless three hours passed in which I struggled against cold and the temptation of sleep. Then the sky lightened with the pearlescent glow that announces the dawn. The western horizon revealed itself in a wintry silhouette, and I saw something that interested me deeply: an inky column of smoke, distant but steadily approaching. It was the train. (Most trains in those days burned soft coal rather than anthracite, and on a clear day their smudgy signatures were unmistakable.)

I climbed out of the hay meaning to wake the others, but I was preempted by the appearance of Mr. Winslow's wife, who came up a ladder from the barn below and said briskly, "Train from the west, boys! Cavalry from the north! Best be on your way!"

The news of approaching cavalry seemed to have spread widely in Bad Jump, for by the time we had packed our possessions and left the barn the whole town was in turmoil.

We hurried down to the vicinity of the tracks, where we stood as the train approached.

Anxious as I was about the threat from the north, I was captivated by the arrival of the engine and its immense chain of freight cars. Some of the cars were labeled SULFUR or BAUXITE or NITRE, and must have come by way of California, Cascadia, or the fearful mines of the Desert Southwest. Some bore goods imported from Asia to our Pacific ports, and were inscribed with Chinese characters like arrangements of tumbled sticks. There were cars that stank of cattle, goats, and sheep, followed by cars that smelled of wood and cold iron. The engine at the head of it all was a very fine one, in my estimation—what the lease-boys back in Williams Ford would have called a "prime charger." Its iron and brass and steel parts shone as if freshly polished. The crew had attached a rack of caribou antlers to the span between the headlight and the smokestack, giving it a fierce appearance; and it arrived at the coaling station with such a hissing of steam and clanging of muscular metal parts that I was almost paralyzed with awe. Its shadow fell over the prairie like a giant's fist.

Sam and Julian, who had seen more trains than I had, hauled me out of my trance by the collar of my coat, as the flood of would-be pilgrims rushed to the "Phantom Cars." These cars were manned by Travel Agents, as they were called—minor employees of the Rail Trust who supplemented their incomes by riding herd over black-market passengers.

Not all of the transients at Bad Jump had bought passage, but all of them were eager to escape the threat of approaching horsemen. Many of these people were indentured laborers fleeing their Estates, who dreaded the punishment that would be inflicted on them should they be returned to their rightful employers; others had committed crimes even graver than Theft of Due Service, or were afraid of the new conscription; and their panic created an unexpected crush. Travel Agents shouted from the open doors of the Phantom Cars, demanding the presentation of paid tickets and fending off desperate stragglers. They made their rifles conspicuous, and a shot was fired within our hearing, which only aroused the mob to more frenzied exertions.

"Stay close!" Sam ordered as we pushed our way through that gauntlet of elbows and knees. The car on which we had bought passage was Number Thirty-Two, last in a line of six such cars. The Travel Agent in charge of it was a burly man in a tattered Trust jacket, with two pistols strapped to his hip and a rifle in his left hand. He discharged the rifle into the air twice while I watched; but still the mob pressed him, and he began to look uneasy.

"The train won't be stopped long," Sam said. It was taking on coal and water with obvious haste. "But look there."

On a low ridge to the northwest a group of riders had appeared. They were too far away to be individually distinguished, but I didn't doubt that their leader was the persistent One-Leg Willy Bass.

"Paid passage only!" the Travel Agent shouted as we pressed through the mass of ill-dressed refugees. "Show papers or be shot! No passage without papers!"

The car was filling quickly. I glanced back at the cavalrymen, who had begun to approach the train at a steady gallop. Sam waved our credentials like a flag in the air. "Come on, then!" the Agent said, and we were lofted aboard like so many sacks of mail. Then the Travel Agent fired his rifle at the sky and announced that the next unticketed man within three feet of him would be shot dead.

The cavalry rode down on us at a gallop, closing the distance. Just then the train gave a lurch and began to move, and the Agent turned to the nearest of his passengers and said, "Secure that door!"

The ticketless mob shrieked to see their hopes thus extinguished, and the door as it slid closed encountered many scrabbling hands and fingers. I was able to catch a last glimpse of the horsemen under the command of One-Leg Willy Bass as they charged through the tents and shacks of Bad Jump, the cavalrymen shouting and gesticulating in an attempt to delay the train's departure. Then the door clanged fully shut; and only by putting my eye to a crack in the boards could I see blue sky, a few pearly clouds, and the prairie seeming to move with ponderous grace as the Caribou-Horn Train began to gather speed.

10

A book could be written about the events that transpired aboard the Phantom Car, but it would a sad and often obscene volume. I mean to chronicle only the adventures that affected us most directly.

The car was a converted freight-box that ought to have been retired from service years ago. It was essentially a single room, long and narrow, with loose straw scattered at one end of it, and a few bound bales on which passengers might sit or lie, and at the other end a stove, vented through the roof, and a chair on which the Travel Agent sat vigilantly, his rifle in his lap. Of other furniture there was a water barrel, a whiskey barrel, and a barrel of salt meat, probably horse. The walls of the car were poorly-joined planks through which the wind came rushing in. The skimpy daylight admitted by these cracked boards was supplemented by the glow of the stove and glimmer of three or four hanging lamps.

Our fellow passengers were among the best and worst men I have ever met, the latter outnumbering the former by a fair throw.

We introduced ourselves to a few of them as Bad Jump receded behind us. I "kept my mouth shut," for the most part, as Sam had suggested, speaking only the polite minimum; but I was tempted to curiosity now and then. I had never seen such folks as these. There were a dozen indentured men from a cruelly-managed California Estate, for instance, who spoke the Spanish language, and wore tattoos in the shape of weeping roses on their arms. There were cattle-herders and shepherds who were evasive about their origins. There were manual laborers aiming for work in the East, and many single sullen men who growled insults when spoken to, or confined their sociability to the card games that sprang up as soon as the train left Bad Jump.

There was at least one well-spoken and literate man aboard. His name was Langers, and he described himself as a "colporteur," that is, a salesman of religious tracts. As soon as the train was in motion Langers opened the large sample case he carried and began to offer his wares at what he called "discount prices." At first I was astonished that he would bother attempting such sales, since the great majority of the passengers was almost certainly illiterate. But on closer examination his pamphlets proved to be little more than picture-books got up to resemble sacred literature.* These were offensive, and I put a distance between myself and the colporteur; but he did a brisk trade among the laborers and refugees, whose appetite for religious instruction seemed nearly insatiable.

---

* *The Song of Solomon, Frankly Illustrated,* was one title; another was *Acts Condemned by Leviticus, Explained and Described, with Diagrams.* They did not bear the Dominion Stamp of Approval.

Many of the men had been wage-workers, and during the afternoon we were treated to massed choruses of *Piston, Loom, and Anvil,* the popular anthem of the industrial laborer. This was the first time I had heard the chorus of that song:

> By Piston, Loom, and Anvil, boys,
> We clothe and arm the nation,
> And sweat all day for a pauper's pay,
> And half a soldier's ration

(though I have heard it many times since), and it struck me as awkwardly rhymed and, in its later verses, seditious. I asked Julian about the bellicosity of the song, and he explained that the ongoing War in Labrador had engendered new industries that employed mechanics and wage-laborers in large number. The complaints of that emerging class had lately become vocal; and these discontents, Julian said, might eventually transform the traditional rural economy of Estate and Indenture.

I was feeling homesick, however, and I didn't much relish the company of militant mechanics anxious to overturn the existing order. Williams Ford, for all its inequities, had been a less raucous place than Bad Jump or the Phantom Car, and I wished I had not been forced to leave it.

That feeling deepened as the afternoon passed into evening. Passengers lined up to take a hot meal from the bubbling pot atop the stove, while the Travel Agent doled out rations from the whiskey barrel* to anyone who could pay. I sat at the rear of the car sipping snowmelt water from a canteen and nursing my unhappiness.

After a time Julian came to sit with me.

Much of his Eupatridian softness had been worked out of him over the last few days, and he was beginning to grow the sparse beard that would eventually become his trademark. His hands and face were dirty—shockingly so, given his fondness for bathing. He had endured all the same trials I had lately endured; and yet he was able to smile and ask what it was that had got the worse of me.

"Do you have to ask?" I waved my hand at the raucous passengers, the smoky stove, the grim Travel Agent, and the noisome hole in the floor that served as a privy. "We're in a terrible place, among terrible men."

"Temporary companions," Julian said carelessly, "all bound for a better life."†

"It wouldn't be so bad if they would conduct themselves like Christians."

"Perhaps it would or perhaps it wouldn't. My father served among men just like these, and led them into battle, where their manners mattered less

---

* Whiskey was the word he used, but experienced drinkers, of whom there were many in the crowd, expressed the opinion that the fiery fluid was in fact "Idaho Velvet," or Potato-Jack.

† A statement too optimistic by half, as it turned out.

than their courage. And that's a quality not apportioned by one's station in life—it exists or not, to the same proportion, among all men, regardless of origin. In Panama my father's life was often enough saved by men who used to be called beggars or thieves, and he took that lesson to heart."

It was a sentiment I had also encountered in the literary works of Mr. Charles Curtis Easton, where (admittedly) I had liked it better. "Do I have to tolerate vulgarity, though, on the chance that a hooligan might save my life?"

"True vulgarity is obviously not to be tolerated. But the point, Adam, is that the standards by which we judge these things are pliable, or ought to be, and they expand or contract from place to place and time to time."

"I suppose they *evolve*," I said, grimly.

"In fact they do, and if you want to make a success of your travels you'd do well to remember that fact."

I said I would try, though my heart wasn't in it. But an incident that evening served as a painful illustration of the truth of Julian's lesson. The Caribou-Horn Train stopped at a coaling station, and two more Travel Agents came aboard to relieve the one who had guarded us through the day's journey. During that exchange I caught a glimpse of the world outside, which in the darkness looked just like Bad Jump: tin-roofed shacks and a prairie horizon. A few flakes of snow swirled into the Phantom Car along with the two Agents in hide coats, who carried battered rifles and wore ammunition belts over their shoulders. Then the door was closed again, and the stove stoked up to a simmering redness. Our new overseers took their place at the front of the car, and we were docile under their surveillance, until it became obvious that the Agents had no especial interest in our behavior beyond preventing a full-scale riot. Then the revelries resumed.

Sam and Julian called me forward to join a circle of men around the stove. I did so reluctantly. There was a song in progress, which Julian accompanied on the choruses. Perhaps I should have joined in, too, just to be companionable. But it wasn't a suitable song. It was about a young woman who lost her shawl on the way to church—but that was only the beginning of her misfortune, for on each succeeding day the unlucky female lost yet another article of clothing, culminating on a Saturday night on which she lost "that which a virtuous woman values above all else," her downfall being minutely described. The song provoked much laughter and gaiety, but I failed to find the humor in it.

Then a flask was passed around the circle. It came eventually to the person on my left, who swilled from it enthusiastically and offered it to me.

"No thank you," I said.

The man who made the offer wasn't much older than myself. He was tall, and raggedly dressed, and he wore a threadbare woolen cap pulled down around his ears. His face was ruddy, and he had seemed genial enough during the singing, but my refusal of the liquor caused him to squint in bewilderment. "What's that mean, no thank you?"

"Pass your bottle to the next man; I'm not a drinker."

"Not a drinker!"

"Nor ever have been."

"You won't drink! Why not?"

He seemed genuinely curious, and I cast about for a suitable answer. Unfortunately what came to mind was the *Dominion Reader for Young Persons*, a volume from which my mother used to read aloud on Sundays. That book was filled with proverbs and commonplace wisdom, and I had learned much of it by heart. In the past, when I particularly wanted to irritate Julian (or when his arguments about Moon-Visiting began to pall), I would cite one of the quotations from it: *To discuss the nature and position of the Earth does not help us in our hope of the life to come.** That would send him into paroxysms of indignation—an entertaining spectacle, if you were in the mood for it.

Tonight, however, the quotation that came to mind was from the chapter on Temperance. I turned to the man with the flask and said, "I would not put a thief in my mouth to steal my brains."

He blinked at me. "Say that again."

I had assumed this homily about the evils of drink was universally familiar, and I began to repeat it: "I would not put a thief in my mouth—"

But I was interrupted by his fist.

What I didn't understand was that Lymon Pugh (as he called himself) was a simple man, not accustomed to metaphor or simile, and he thought I had accused him of being a thief, or made an implication about what he might be willing to put in his mouth.

"I'll fight the man who says that twice," he declared. "Stand up!"

It was a fight from which I couldn't honorably back away. But Mr. Pugh was a daunting opponent. He squared his shoulders and rolled up the sleeves of his shirt to reveal muscular forearms crossed with numerous scars. His big hands, clenched into rocklike fists, were similarly scarred, and he possessed only a stump where his right-hand pinkie finger ought to have been.

I had been trained in fighting by Sam Godwin, however, so I raised my own fists, and set one foot ahead of the other, and made clear my determination not to back down.

The crowd moved back to give us room. The card players abandoned their games, and some began to place bets on the impending combat. "Go on," my assailant jeered, "strike a blow, or try to!"

He had had no formal training and took a loose-limbed approach to the battle. My cheek was still smarting from his first blow, and I meant to erase his smugness, and I did this by feigning a punch with my left hand and striking him squarely with the right. The blow was telling, and his eyes widened as the breath went out of him, and the crowd murmured its appreciation.

* Attributed to Saint Ambrose by some scholars, by others to Timothy LeHaye.

"Good one!" I heard Julian cry.

Lymon Pugh was surprised but not deterred. As soon as he recovered he swung into me with a will, his big arms flailing.

Had he fought decently, with a sense of style and grace, as I did, I'm sure I would have defeated him. But Lymon Pugh wasn't educated in the art, and he used his scarred hands and arms as if they were clubs. I had countered only a few of these windmill punches before my own arms began to numb with the impacts. Pugh's arms were as insensible as salted hams, however, and he used them to advantage, getting through my guard twice and finally rendering a blow so ferocious that my head filled with fireworks and my legs lost all direction.

Before I could regain my senses the fight was declared a victory for Mr. Pugh, who danced in circles, and waved his hat, and hooted like an ape in his triumph.

Sam and Julian helped me to a haybale at the rear of the car, where Sam applied a handkerchief to my bleeding face.

"I let my guard down," I said thickly. "I'm sorry you had to see that."

"On the contrary," Sam said. "Whether you know it or not, you did exactly the right thing. As far as these people are concerned, the haughtiness has been knocked out of you—you're no better or worse than any of them now."

That was a bitter consolation, however, and it provided little comfort as the raucous night roared on.

11

The reveling stopped at last, once the liquor began to tell on the revelers, who slumped and dozed under the indifferent gaze of the Travel Agents. I was eventually able to sleep, although my injuries, and the cold air keening through the cracks in the car, woke me from time to time.

There is something mournful and uneasy about waking up late at night on a moving train. The wheels clicked a bony rhythm, the engine growled like a distant Leviathan, and from time to time the whistle sounded a cry so lonesome it seemed to speak for the whole wide moonless night.

But there was an exception to this monotony of sound, and I should have paid greater attention to it. I was dreaming in a disjointed fashion of Williams Ford, and of Flaxie playing by the stream on a summer afternoon, when I felt the Phantom Car lurch to a slow stop.

There followed a clanking and a rumbling, and a silence, and more clanking, until the train started up again. I wondered if I should wake Sam, who was snoring nearby, and tell him about these events. But I was afraid of seeming naive. Sam had ridden trains often before in his career, and this was probably only another coaling stop or a pause in some switching yard where a branch road intersected the main line. The Travel Agents huddling in the glow of the stove seemed unalarmed, so I put the matter out of my mind.

The next day passed as the previous one had, though the men were sullen after their indulgence of the night before, and the smell of sickness hung about the privy hole and interfered with everyone's appetite.

I was still smarting from yesterday's battle. I spent the morning by myself, perched on a haybale and composing a letter to my parents, though the jarring of the railroad car made my handwriting childish.

I worked at it without interruption until Lymon Pugh came and stood in front of me, his legs planted like trees in the scattered straw. I didn't like to see him there—I feared some fresh confrontation—but all he said was, "What are you doing?"

"Writing a letter," I said.

He lifted his hat and smoothed the unruly knot of black hair beneath it. "Well, then," he said. "A letter."

This wasn't much of a conversation, and I returned my attention to the page.

Lymon Pugh cleared his throat. "Listen here . . . do you take back what you said last night?"

I considered my response carefully, for I was not anxious to provoke him into another battle. "I meant no insult by it."

"You called me a thief, though."

"No—you misunderstood me. I only meant to explain my abstinence. The 'thief' is liquor, do you see? I don't drink liquor, because it steals my sensibility."

"Your sensibility!"

"My capacity for reason. It makes me drunk, in other words."

"That's all you were trying to say—that liquor makes you drunk?"

"That's it exactly."

He gave me a scornful look. "Of course liquor makes you drunk! I learned *that* at an early age. You don't need to tell me anything about it, much less make a riddle of it. What's your name?"

"Adam Hazzard."

"Lymon Pugh," he said, and put out his big scarred hand, which I cautiously shook. "Where are you from, Adam Hazzard?"

"Athabaska."

"Cascadia, me," he said. A true Westerner—Cascadia is as far west as you can go without wetting your feet in the ocean. "What do you call that hat you're wearing?"

"A packle hat." (A packle hat, for readers who haven't seen one, has a disk of stiffened wool or hemp for the crown, attached to a tube of the same fabric, the tube being rolled up to form a brim, tied in place with threads.)

"That's a strange kind of hat," he said, though his own hat, which resembled a sailor's watch-cap picked over by moths, was nothing to brag about. "I guess it keeps you warm?"

"Warm enough. How did you come by all those scars on your arms?"

"I was a boner," he said; and to my blank expression he added, "In a packing plant, in the Valley—the Willamette Valley. I boned beeves. That was my job—haven't you ever worked in a slaughterhouse?"

"No; I missed that opportunity, somehow."

"The beeves come along a line on hooks, and the boner cuts the muscle from the bone. You have to work close and fast, for a dozen other men are doing the same job on all sides of you, and the overseer brooks no slacking. But it gets hot in the boning room, and on wet days the air fogs, and the blood slicks your grip, so the knife is bound to go wrong sooner or later. Nobody lasts too long in that trade. Blood poisoning takes 'em, or they whittle themselves down so far they can't hold a haft any longer."

Ben Kreel, back in Williams Ford, had occasionally lectured us about the evils of Wage Labor, as opposed to the system of Leasing and Private Indenture. He might have cited this as an example, had he ever ventured near a packing plant in the Willamette Valley. "I suppose that's why you left?"

"Yes; but it pains me," Lymon Pugh said.

"The job, or the leaving of it?"

"I supported my mother there. I might have stayed, but I hear the packing industry out east has boomed just recently. My idea was to get a bigger wage and send part of it home."

"That seems sensible enough, though your fingers might be whittled off as quickly in New York as in Cascadia."

"I might get better work than boning, with luck. Canning, say, or even overseeing. But I had to leave in a hurry, is what galls me. I had an argument with the shift boss, which left him with a broken rib, and he would have had me arrested if I hadn't collected what I found in his pockets and bought passage east. I didn't have time to tell my plans to my mother—for all I know she thinks I'm dead." He shuffled his feet. "Though I guess I could write her a letter."

"Yes; you should—that's exactly what you should do."

"Except but that I can't write."

I told him he wasn't alone in that regard, and that it was nothing to be ashamed of; but he wasn't consoled. He shuffled his feet again and said, "Unless I can get a person to write it out for me."

Now I understood his object in approaching me, and it seemed a reasonable enough request—better than risking another controversy, anyhow. So I offered to take his dictation; and Lymon Pugh grinned hugely, and insisted on shaking my hand again—a habit he ought to refrain from, I told him, for his grip almost crushed my fingers, and made it difficult for me to grasp the pencil.

Then the obligation of actually composing his thoughts fell upon him, and he stomped about for a few minutes, muttering to himself.

"Just say what you'd say if your mother was here in front of you," I suggested.

"That's no help—if she was here, I wouldn't need to write a letter."

"Well, then, make any beginning you want. You might start with *Dear Mother*, for example."

He liked that idea, and repeated the phrase several times, and I made a show of writing it on a fresh page in my notebook, and he looked at the marks with admiration. Then he frowned again. "No, it's no good. A letter won't work. My mother can't read, any more than I can."

"Well, in that case . . . do you know anyone who *can* read? A cousin, a friend of the family?"

"No. Except the man who runs the company store. *He* can read—I've seen him lettering signs—and he was always friendly enough when we came in."

"Does he have a name?"

"Mr. Harking."

"Then we can ask him to carry the message to your mother on your behalf. I'll cross out *Dear Mother*, and write in *Dear Mr. Harking—*"

"No, sir!" Lymon Pugh exclaimed.

"What?"

"That would be an impertinence, if not something worse! I never called him 'dear' in my life, and I don't propose to begin now!"

"It's just a salutation."

"Call it whatever you want—maybe that's how they do things in Athabaska—but in the Valley a man don't call the grocer 'dear'—it's not suitable!"

"Look," I said, "this project is poorly thought-out. Why don't you consider what you want Mr. Harking to say to your mother on your behalf—sleep on the question—and in the morning we'll start again: how about that?"

"I hate to postpone it," he said, "but—well, it feels like the train's stopping anyhow. Are we in New York already, do you suppose, or is it just another watering hole?"

Neither, as it turned out. The Travel Agents stood up briskly and hoisted their rifles. They shouted the train awake, and when the passengers were all standing and blinking the foremost of the two men called out, "You two! Crack that door."

Lymon Pugh and I unbolted the long door and slid it open. What we saw outside was no coaling station. Instead we faced a crowd of uniformed soldiers, and beyond them a sea of tents, and an open space in which men marched to orders, counting cadences.

"A soldier camp!" Lymon Pugh exclaimed.

The Travel Agent directed us to climb down from the Phantom Car, and the other passengers followed behind. I waited with the milling crowd in the sunlight until I could sidle closer to Sam and Julian.

"Are we caught?" I whispered.

"Not caught," Sam said in disgust, "just sold. The Trust took our money and sold us to recruiters, a double sale. I should have guessed something was up when the ticket-seller at Bad Jump inquired so closely about your ages. I was foolish," he said bitterly, "and now we're in the infantry, or will be soon enough, and bound for Labrador by summer."

I wanted to question him more closely, but a man in sergeant's stripes formed us up into two lines and marched us off to be deloused.

THE INVENTION OF
CAPTAIN COMMONGOLD

EASTER, 2173–EASTER, 2174

Happy is the bride that the sun shines on,
And blessed is the corpse that the rain rains on.

—Saxon proverb

—

1

Here begins that portion of the narrative with which my readers may already be somewhat familiar, that is, the passage of Julian Comstock into the person of Julian Conqueror; but that transformation, and its consequences, have been so often misrepresented that even a scholar of Recent History may be surprised by the story as I saw and experienced it—and by my part in it, for that matter.

Certainly Julian was no Conqueror as we arrived at the mustering camp, though he soon enough ceased to be a Comstock.

"Give a false name," Sam told Julian when, as a part of a line of sullen men from the Phantom Car, we approached a tent in which Army physicians waited to examine us and Army clerks stood ready to enter us into the rolls. "Do that, and we'll be safe from the inquiries of your uncle—if not 'safe' in any other sense of the word."

"What name should I give?"

Sam shrugged. "Anything that appeals to you. 'Smith' is a popular choice." (Though I couldn't picture Julian as a Smith, a Jones, a Wilson, or any of those penny-a-bushel names: they didn't just suit him, somehow.) I asked Sam if it would be all right for me to continue as Adam Hazzard, and Sam said he supposed so, much to my relief. My family name may not have been aristocratic, but my father would have been ashamed if I had altered it.

But before we were set down on paper we had to be evaluated by the medical faculty: two bald men whose stained cotton smocks might once have been white, who listened to our hearts, and thumped our backs, and generally made quick work of their observations—though they did turn away seven men.*

I don't know what happened to the rejected men. I believe they were put back aboard the Phantom Car, perhaps to be abandoned at some switching station along the main line, and probably robbed in the process.

Sam himself was the object of considerable scrutiny because of his age. He told the examining physician he was thirty-two; but we were required to disrobe, and Sam's body betrayed the lie in its wrinkled and leathery flesh. But he was also strong, and lean, and sound of breath; and after only a little discussion the doctors gave him their approval. Julian and I were ushered through more quickly.

---

* One of the men was clearly tubercular, while two others showed evidence of active Pox about their wrists and throats. Five more were turned back simply because they had lost a great number of teeth, or their teeth were too loose in the jaw to be useful. A toothless man could not bite or chew Army hardtack, and such men had been known to starve to death on a long march.

Then we were made to line up beside a trench into which we dropped our familiar clothing, retaining only a few possessions in satchels or "ditty-bags" provided by the Quartermaster, while a scrawny recruit doused our naked bodies with yellow powder from a bucket—an insecticide, intended to kill lice, fleas, and other vermin.

The dust was noxious, and it coated our hair, our skin, our throats, and our lungs. It burned our eyes so badly that we were soon weeping as helplessly as infants, and we coughed and gagged like consumptive patients in the final stages of that disorder. We were nearly murdered by it, in other words; and I suppose even the lice among us must have been badly inconvenienced, though at the end of a week they had rallied and staged a come-back.

As soon as we had recovered our breath we were lined up in front of a Company Clerk, who marked our names on a list of inductees. Sam gave his name as Sam Samson, which drew a skeptical look. I registered as Adam Hazzard, and pronounced my name proudly despite the fact that I was shivering, and clad mainly in a coating of insecticidal dust. Then Julian stepped up. He was still dizzy under the influence of the yellow powder, and when asked his name he began, "Julian, Julian Com—" at which point Sam delivered a kick to his shins. "*Commongold,*" Julian finished, adding a little cough.

It was a striking pseudonym, I thought, and entirely appropriate: Julian Commongold, gilded in lice powder and abandoned among the common folk; but a noble name for all that, rich with dignity. "It suits you," I whispered.

"Little else does, today," he whispered back.

Then we were administered an Oath—a pledge of loyalty to Flag and Savior, to the worldly power of the Executive Branch, the wisdom of the Senate, and the spiritual majesty of the Dominion. That was a solemn moment, in spite of our nakedness and uncontrollable shivering.* Then we lined up for uniforms, which were handed out with only cursory attention to size and fit, so that we spent another half-hour bartering coats and pants among ourselves, and warming ourselves at the trench in which our civilian rags had been soaked in spirits and set aflame. At the end of that time a sergeant escorted us to a mess tent in which we were given a hot meal of beef stew, much to the delight of the vagabond men among us, for whom this simple but reliable bill of fare was and would continue to be the Infantry's great redeeming virtue.

At last we were assigned to cots, which were arranged in rows under a canvas tent large enough to house a circus (as I imagined), and we had a few moments to ourselves, to smoke or talk as we preferred, by the light of scattered lamps, before "all dark" was sounded on a trumpet. During this time Julian reminded me that New Year's Day must have come and gone while we

---

* The Oath, though we swore to it under a sort of compulsion, was not meaningless to me. I held those Institutions of Liberty in awe, and I had been feeling guilty about my draft-dodging, necessary though it seemed at the time. By swearing fealty I felt *washed clean*—despite the bug powder clinging to my mortal fraction.

were aboard the Caribou-Horn Train. The year 2172 had exhausted itself, and passed into that haunted sepulcher we call the Past; and now it was 2173, a year in which Julian's uncle Deklan would be inaugurated into yet another term as the uncontested President of the United States, sea-to-sea and equator-to-pole; and I reminded myself that I was now a warrior in that cause, and would remain one for some time to come. By Spring I might be fighting to drive the Dutch from the sacred precincts of Labrador, to reclaim our right to the wood, water, and minerals of that contested State, and to assert our God-granted master of the Northwest Passage. I was, in short, and irrevocably, an American Soldier.

"You have fallen out of obscurity, Adam, and into history," Julian said, with only a little of his customary cynicism.

It was a daunting thought, but exciting, and I was still dwelling on it when my fatigue overcame me and I fell asleep.

I will not narrate every trivial detail of camp life, or postpone indefinitely my attention to the battles and conflicts in which Julian and I participated. In any event we did not long remain in that crude camp on the winter prairie. We were kept there only for the most basic kind of training, and to weed out men with hidden epilepsy or pox-gaunt, or who were prone to fits of madness or mad-melancholy. By Easter all such draftees would be mustered out, or put to such simple duties as suited them.

Those of us who remained were naturally curious about our future. Some of the formerly indentured men were ignorant of the nature and purpose of the War in Labrador, an ignorance that made them more fearful than they needed to be. In the great cities there were newspapers to recount the course and outcome of this or that battle, and to chart the overall progress of the War, so that even clerks and wage-laborers might be reasonably well-informed; but the majority of the draftees were landless men and deaf to such sources of information. They took their intelligence where they could find it: from Sunday All-Camp Service or from rumor and hearsay. And some of them took Julian's counsel on the subject.

It must not be assumed that our time at the mustering camp was one long round of historical and philosophical debate—of course it was not. We were up early in the morning for reveille, roll call, sick call, mess call, followed by squad and company drill (as soon as we had been assigned to squads and companies), guard mound, adjutant's call, policing camp (which meant picking up trash); then it was battalion drill until noon, another mess call, regimental drill until the five o'clock mess, general parade, tattoo, and taps—six days out of seven. On Sundays there was no drill, and nothing more formal than a morning All-Camp Service, which allowed for restorative rest and conversation.

We learned the presentation of arms and the intricacies of parade, and we were introduced to the Pittsburgh rifles that would accompany us into battle. We learned to take our weapons apart and put them together, to keep them clean, dry, and oiled, and in general to treat them with all the tender feeling a young mother might attach to a firstborn infant. As the winter became less severe, and the month of February ended, we were taken on marches across the damp patch of prairie where the camp was situated, allowing our boots to make accommodation with our blisters and vice versa; and we were ordered into mock battles, and tutored in the digging of entrenchments, and taught how to negotiate a cutwire fence, how to attack an enemy's lunette, and how to follow a regimental flag. We refined our marksmanship on the firing range. We learned to call out marching cadences without blushing at the obscenities in the chants—toughening us against moral as well as physical hardship. In short, we were worked hard and fed well, until we felt proud of ourselves for having survived the ordeal, and considered ourselves superior to the general run of civilian clerks and laborers. We suspected we could not be bested in genuine warfare, and certainly not by the Dutch (as we called the Mitteleuropan forces).

Julian and I benefited from Sam's prior tutelage, and we were among the more skillful recruits for that reason—though Sam warned us not to make ourselves too conspicuous. Julian in particular had to feign a certain clumsiness during our drills with horses, otherwise he might have been taken up into the cavalry and out of Sam's sphere of protection. Sam himself (by design or because of his age) put in a mediocre performance on the endurance exercises, but he was steadily and expertly working up another line of influence. He made a friend of the camp's Quartermaster, who was also a veteran of the Isthmian War. The rivalry between the Army of the Californias and the Army of the Laurentians meant that neither Sam nor the Quartermaster could expect any favoritism because of their prior experience; and for reasons of anonymity Sam could confess to nothing more than a short "stint" as a foot soldier. But the two men supported each other in extra-curricular ways, and did each other collegial favors; and Sam was soon adopted into the small circle of Isthmian veterans who had found their way into the Eastern forces, including officers. Sam used his influence to keep Julian and me within arm's length, and to guarantee that the three of us would stay together even after we were dispatched to Labrador.

Labrador was the subject of many Sunday sermons. Sunday Service was conducted by Dominion Officers, and for that reason, the conflict was cast mainly in spiritual terms. That is to say, the war was presented as a battle between Good and Evil. What was good was full ownership of North America by its natural masters; and what was evil was the claim of "territorial interest" advanced by that ungodly commonwealth of nations known as Mitteleuropa.

We listened with due attention to these sermons, often delivered at white heat, and we took them to heart. But in the free hours after All-Camp Meeting many of the inductees (including Lymon Pugh and myself) gathered around Julian "Commongold," to hear him air a more pragmatic version of War History.

Those talks took place over consecutive Sundays. What Julian told us, in brief, was that the possession of Labrador had been contested, in principle or in fact, ever since the False Tribulation of the last century. The allied nations of Mitteleuropa, while America was still in the grip of civil unrest, had recognized the significance of the Northwest Passage (opened to shipping by a warming climate) and coveted its rich natural resources. They asserted what some call the Stepping-Stone Theory of International Entitlement: that because Europe controlled Iceland and Greenland—and because Greenland was just adjacent to Baffin Island—and Baffin Island to the Hudson Strait—hence Hudson Bay—hence Labrador and Newfoundland—therefore all this territory ought to be administered by Mitteleuropa from its bureaucratic palaces at Munich.*

By the time the Union had rallied and was ready to dispute that claim there were Mitteleuropan coaling stations from Devon Island to Kangiqsujuaq, Mitteleuropan trawlers plying the rich waters of the Foxe Basin, Mitteleuropan warships patrolling off Belcher Island, and Mitteleuropan troops and colonists ashore at Battle Harbor and Goose Bay.

America fought back, of course. This all happened in the reign of President Otis, who consolidated much of North America under his own unitary rule. It was Otis who gained us such boreal states as Athabaska and Nunavut, and added immense territories to the Union. But Otis's campaign against the forces of centralized Europe was less successful, and is passed over lightly in the official texts. Suffice to say that at the end of President Otis's thirty-year term of office the Dutch had secured a permanent foothold in Labrador, occupied rebellious Newfoundland, and taken control of the northern bank of the St. Lawrence all the way from the sea to Baie Comeau.†

There the matter had rested—or *festered*; for what followed was decades of clashes between American and Mitteleuropan warships, accusations of piracy, skirmishes along the Laurentians, stern diplomatic notes sent and received, etc. Nevertheless a sort of *modus vivendi* had prevailed, in which the continuity of commerce took precedence over national pride. The so-called Pious Presidents, who ruled during this interlude, were more concerned with entrenching the power of the Dominion of Jesus Christ, and regulating land use in the prairie West, than with battling foreigners.

The Union grew in power and prosperity during the long and sunny reigns of the Pious. Our great rail network was perfected and enlarged, while

---

* Airier justifications were sometimes cited, including the theorized ancient landing of Vikings on the eastern shores of North America; but Julian assayed the tolerance of his listeners, and confined his argument to the most pertinent points.

† Even this thumbnail sketch of history taxed the geographical understanding of his auditors, and Julian was reduced to scratching maps in the dirt with the point of his bayonet.

the Estate System imposed legal regularity on the patchwork of land and indenture customs that prevailed prior to that time. Food was reasonably plentiful, the population began growing after the catastrophic mass deaths of the False Tribulation, the Pox took fewer children during those years, and international trade turned our ports into respectable cities harboring tens of thousands of inhabitants.

That was the State of the Nation when Julian's grandfather Emmanuel Comstock assumed the presidency. (Julian's narrative, as I have said, was not as dry and abbreviated as mine, or he would never have held an audience. In fact his theatrical instincts served him admirably on these slow Sunday afternoons. He spoke in lilting cadences, adopted comic voices or postures to suit his subject, stroked his wispy beard to imitate the Pious Presidents, etc. And when he discussed the Comstock dynasty Julian's impersonations became sharper and more cutting—though I doubt any of his listeners noticed.)

Emmanuel Comstock, the first of the imperial Comstocks, was a brutal but far-sighted President who made it his business to modernize the Armies and bring them under the discipline of the Church of the Dominion. His work was successful, and before long the Nation possessed a fighting force to be reckoned with—a force Emmanuel Comstock wasted no time in exercising. The newly-reformed Army of the Laurentians attacked the Dutch north of the St. Lawrence, while Admiral Finch's Red-and-White Fleet inflicted dramatic losses on the Mitteleuropans off Groswater Bay.

During the course of these conflicts Emmanuel Comstock took for his wife a Senator's daughter, and in the fifth and sixth year of his reign the union produced two sons: Deklan, the eldest, and Bryce Comstock. Emmanuel Comstock was determined that his sons would not be aristocratic idlers, so the brothers were trained from infancy as warriors and statesmen, and as soon as they reached maturity they were given military commissions in order to hone their command skills: Deklan was made a Major General in the Army of the Laurentians, and the younger Bryce received a comparable rank in the Army of the Californias.

Different as the brothers were—the kindly, happily married Bryce and the brooding, solitary Deklan—both proved able-enough commanders. The first Comstock's victories had pushed back the Mitteleuropans but had not driven them from North America: the *Stadhouders*, or Dutch Governors, were too firmly entrenched in the vast tracts of northeastern land they had ruled and exploited for so many years. But the Army of the Laurentians, under Deklan Comstock, captured and occupied all of Newfoundland, and the rail link between Sept-Iles and Schefferville passed into American hands.

That was the famous Summer Campaign of 2160.* In its wake, core elements of the Army of the Laurentians marched to New York City for a

---

* Described in the novel *The Boys of '60* by Mr. Charles Curtis Easton.

Victory Parade. Soon afterward* Emmanuel Comstock died of a fall from his horse while hunting on the grounds of the Executive Palace; and Deklan, by the consent of a passive Senate, assumed the Presidency.

(Here Julian called his listeners into a closer circle, so that his impersonation of Deklan Comstock's shrill voice and petulant manner would not be overheard by passing officers. Sam was not present, or else he would have put a stop to the proceedings. Sam had already warned Julian against displays of Atheism or Sedition; but Julian saw no reason why his induction into the military should interfere with those interesting hobbies.)

Deklan had been competent enough as a figurehead General, but he proved to be a jealous and suspicious President. He was especially jealous of his younger brother Bryce, whom he saw as a potential rival, and it was partly to put Bryce in harm's way that Deklan conjured up the Isthmian War.† An American warship, the *Maude,* had exploded while passing out of the Panama Canal—probably due to a faulty boiler; but Deklan Comstock declared it an act of sabotage and blamed the canal's Brazilian custodians. He wanted the Canal in American hands; and after a keenly-managed campaign the Army of the Californias—under the command of Bryce Comstock—gave it to him.

Panama should have been a fine gem in Deklan's diadem. But the younger Bryce had frustrated his brother's dark hopes simply by surviving, and aroused further jealousy by the much-discussed brilliance of his military career.

The Western armies could not march all the way to New York for their celebrations. Bryce was called back to that city alone, ostensibly to have the Order of Merit bestowed upon him. But no sooner had Bryce Comstock left the train than he was surrounded by Eastern soldiers and taken up on charges of treason.

(I will not weary the reader with a description of that "trumped-up" charge, as Julian called it, or the fratricidal logic that transformed a victorious officer into an enemy of the Nation. Suffice to say that the trophy to be placed around the neck of Bryce Comstock went from Gold to Hemp, and that his true reward was a place at the throne of a Ruler more majestic than the reigning Commander in Chief.)

And so matters had stood, Julian told his eager listeners, for the last decade—a stalemate in Labrador, a victory on the Isthmus of Panama, and Deklan Comstock growing ever more brooding and self-absorbed in the marbled corridors of the Presidential Palace. At least until last year. America's acquisition of the Canal had alarmed the Mitteleuropan powers, who were forced to depend ever more heavily on the Northwest Passage for their trade into the Pacific, and they feared American dominance there. So they had fortified their remaining American possessions, enhanced their military and

---

* Coincidentally—or so the textbooks say.
† See Mr. Easton's *Against the Brazilians.*

naval forces, and soon enough launched a massive counterattack against the Army of the Laurentians.

"This is the war *we* are to fight?" asked Lymon Pugh, whose attention had been strained by Julian's narrative.

"That's exactly the war we are to fight, and it isn't going well for us. The Dutch are arrayed in force, we've already lost the railroad to Schefferville, and both Quebec City and Montreal are threatened by the enemy. The Army of the Laurentians took heavy casualties last summer, which is why the draft was doubled up."

"Sounds like we have the short end of the stick, then," another soldier remarked.

"Perhaps not," said Julian, for he was not a defeatist, or a friend of the Dutch. "The enemy are well-provisioned, but their supply lines stretch all the way across the Atlantic Ocean, and our Navy is making things hot for Dutch shipping. Their army is of a fixed number, while ours is growing. And," Julian added, grinning broadly, "we're Americans, and they are not, which makes all the difference."

There followed a cheer for the Union, and much chest-thumping, and the crowd of draftees went off bragging about how they would rout the enemy, and show the Dutch what American soldiers were truly made of. It was Lymon Pugh, lingering behind, who asked, "How do you know all these things, Julian Commongold? Are you some kind of scholar? You talk like one."

Julian deflected the question with a shrug. "I'm from New York City—I read the newspapers."

This put Lymon Pugh's mind back on the subject of reading, and literacy in general, and he grew thoughtful as we broke for mess.

Of course Julian's tutorials on the state of the war did not escape the attention of the camp's ranking officers for long. Word spread, and (according to Sam, who kept his ear to the ground) the Dominion men on the staff were unhappy with Julian for his editorializing, and wanted him to receive a reprimand. But the camp's military commander vetoed that idea, for Julian was a promising soldier, and his blunt talk had braced the men more effectively than a dozen fire-breathing Sunday sermons.

Sam was not bound by such scruples, and chastised Julian roundly for his loose talk—reminding him that in the long run *notoriety* might be as dangerous as *combat*—but Julian paid little attention.

"I suppose I shouldn't be surprised," Sam said to me after one of these confrontations. "It's the Comstock in him."

"He'll make a fine soldier, then," I said.

"Or a famous corpse," said Sam.

We were scheduled to be shipped east for the spring campaign; but before then, on another Sunday afternoon, Lymon Pugh approached me once again on the subject of reading and writing.

"Thought perhaps I could learn all about it," he said sheepishly. "Unless I left it too late. What about that, Adam Hazzard? Is it something only children can learn?"

"No," I said, for I considered myself, in this community, a sort of Evangelist of Literacy. My writing skills had been mooted about, and many of the men came to me to help them read or compose letters. "Anyone can learn it at any time. It's not especially difficult."

"Could I learn, then?"

"I expect you could."

"And will you teach me?"

I was feeling magnanimous—the day was bright, the air had a delicate warmth, and a general languor had descended over the camp (along with the swampy smell of the thawing prairie and an unfortunate breeze from the latrines). I reclined on my cot with my boots off and my toes exposed to the air. Lymon Pugh sat on the cot adjoining, where he greased his rifle in a distracted way, his scarred hands moving almost of their own volition. A charitable act did not seem out of order. "But I can't do it in one lesson, mind. We'll have to begin from first principles."

"I expect we'll have plenty of time, if neither of us is killed in the war. You can give it to me piecemeal, Adam."

"In that case we'll begin with the letters of the Alphabet. The Alphabet is a collection of all the letters there are, and once you learn them no unexpected letters will come along to confuse you."

"How many of these letters are there?"

"Twenty-six altogether."

He looked crestfallen. "That's a large number."

"It only seems so. Here, I'll write them out for you, and you can keep this paper and study it." I took a page from my notebook and copied down all the letters in their large and small incarnations, thus:

Aa—Bb—Cc—(etc.)

"Seems like you're wrong on the count," Lymon Pugh observed when I had finished. "That's at least fifty, I estimate."

"No, only twenty-six, but each one comes in a greater or lesser variety, the larger being called a *capital* letter."

He studied the page uncomprehendingly. "Maybe we should call this off . . . it don't seem like anything I could ever commit to memory."

"You underestimate yourself. Suppose, while you were wandering east from the Willamette Valley, you came upon a village with just twenty-six people in it, and decided to stay there. You'd learn the names of the whole tribe soon enough, wouldn't you? And many other things about them."

"People aren't scratches on a page, though. People walk about, and talk, and such."

"Letters may not walk about, but they do talk, for each one represents a sound. Look, we don't have to introduce you to all twenty-six at once. That would make you like a stranger at a crowded social event, which is always an uneasy experience. Take the first three by themselves, as if they were sitting around a campfire and invited you to join them."

"This is fanciful."

"Bear with me. Here is **A**, and his companion the lesser **a**," and I pronounced the sound of the letter and its variations, and instructed Lymon Pugh to repeat them, and to associate the sounds with the letter's shape, the way he might connect a face with a name. When he had done this satisfactorily we proceeded to blunt, simple **Bb** and the more elusive and chameleonic **Cc**. By the time he mastered these three letters nearly an hour had passed, and it seemed to me that Lymon Pugh, like a sponge, had absorbed all the knowledge he had room for at the moment, and any more of it would simply leak out around the edges.

He agreed to defer further instruction until the next lesson—perhaps the following Sunday—but observed, "These are only sounds, and I don't see how they connect to writing or reading."

"You can stack and arrange them to make words, ultimately. But don't get ahead of yourself."

"Is there a word I might make with just these three?"

The only one I could think of was the word **CAB**, so I wrote that out for him, and he was delighted by it. "Damn if my uncle didn't drive a cab in Portland some years back, and it was a fine rig, with a four-horse team. I wish I could have written out that word for him! He would have thought I was a Dominion scholar, or an Aristo in disguise."

"Practice the letters in your spare time," I said, giving him a blank page to work with, and an extra pencil I had stolen from the Quartermaster's tent last week previously (because I like to keep a stock of pencils on hand: they're perishable, and often hard to come by). "You can write **CAB**," I said, and showed him, "or **cab**—they mean the same—but you should practice both."

"I will," he said, and after a moment's pondering added, "But this is too generous, Adam Hazzard. I ought to pay you for all this work."

I was happy enough that he had got out of the habit of striking me with his fists, and that was all the payment I wished for; but to smooth the awkwardness I said, "There must be many things you know about that I don't. Someday you can teach me one or two of them."

He frowned over this idea, taking up his rifle again and finishing its assembly. Then, as he set aside the last oiled rag, he brightened. "I guess I can tell you how to make a fine Knocker."

"That might be a good example, since I don't know what a Knocker is."

"Oh, well," (warming to his subject), "I guess anyone can make a *crude* sort of Knocker—you've probably done it yourself, though maybe they call it by some other name in Athabaska. A *Knocker*, Adam, you know: the thing you use when you want to knock someone about the head."

"Perhaps if you described it."

"Put a stone in the end of a sock and you have one. Swing it in a circle and bring it down on the skull of your enemy: *bang!*"

I was startled by his violent exclamation. "Do you *need* to do this—very often?"

"Did in the Valley. Most of us boys did, if we wanted to make any money outside of the slaughterhouse, by taking it from drunks, for instance, or when we set to fighting each other. But a stone in a sock is a poor sort of Knocker, the very worst."

Here Lymon Pugh launched into an exposition of the way to make a superior Knocker, of which the owner might justly be proud. You begin, he said, by cracking a chicken egg, "only not in the usual style: you must crack it very fine at the narrow end, to make a small hole, and then empty out the soft parts and let the shell dry. Then you melt some lead—an old candlestick, a handful of bullets, or some such thing. Bury the shell up to its hole in sand and pour the molten lead inside. You let it settle overnight; then you dig it out and peel away the shell, and what's inside is a good smooth heavy slug in the shape of an egg. Then you make a sling for it—an old sock won't do for a respectable man—of pressed leather or strong hemp, and tie it with a leather thatch, and stitch on a bead or a brass button if you're feeling artistic. The whole assembly tucks into your pocket real neat—it's not bulky—but a Knocker like that will crack a man's head just like an egg."

"Thus bringing the process *full circle*," I said, slightly appalled.

"How's that?"

"Never mind. That's a fine piece of knowledge, Lymon, and I thank you for it, and I consider myself paid in full, though I don't have any use for a Knocker right at the moment."

"That's all right," said Lymon Pugh, grinning. "I don't have anyone to write to, either, except maybe the grocer, or any books to read. But you never know when the Alphabet might come in handy."

"Or a Knocker," I said; and then the mess call sounded.

It must not be assumed that our adjustment to the military life was easily made. Many were the nights in that camp on the prairie when I fell asleep with tears trembling in my eyes, thinking of what seemed like a carefree existence back in

Williams Ford. If I had been scorned by other boys, or treated roughly in the stables, or nipped by a brood mare now and then, those memories receded, so that all my previous life appeared as one lazy summer on the banks of the River Pine, where squirrels fell from the trees like tropical fruit, and I was forever a-doze in a sun-dappled glade, with a book open on my chest, dreaming of pleasanter wars than this one.

My thoughts turned, too, to the gentler sex, who were in scant supply at the moment, and I wondered if I would ever again be allowed to gaze on a smiling face or examine a pair of feminine eyes from close proximity. The male urge was not dormant in me, and I was afraid I might grow as lonely and desperate as some of my fellow soldiers, who dispelled their lusts in obscene and indescribable pursuits. A copy of *Acts Condemned by Leviticus* circulated furtively among the men, and I confess I glanced at it once or twice, out of curiosity.

But in general we were kept too busy to feel sorry for ourselves. For many of these men the Army was a marked improvement on the lives they used to live, and had its compensations in regular meals and the small but dependable pay.

We were paid for the first time shortly before we were due to ship east, where there might be an opportunity to spend some of our geld, especially if we were stationed near Montreal or Quebec—or so the speculation ran. In any case it was a novelty to hold cash in our hands. Many of the soldiers promptly sewed the scrip and coin into secret pockets in their ditty-bags, or hid it in their clothing or in makeshift belts tied about their waists. But because the money was a new thing to me—all I had seen of money in Williams Ford was lease-chits and antique pennies—I repaired right away to the dormitory tent to handle and examine it, where Sam and Julian joined me.

"We're off in the morning," Sam said as he came in, "for better or worse. Celebrating Easter in Montreal I think. And then battle—the real thing. . . . What are you staring at so steadfastly, Adam Hazzard?"

"These coins."

Of the coins I especially liked the largest, the One Dollar coin. It was not as finely wrought as the coinage of the Secular Ancients, but still very neatly pressed and stamped. The dollar contained a measurable amount of real silver, and had milled edges, and vine stalks engraved around the face, and the words *In God We Trust* written in letters so ornate as to be all but illegible, and in the middle of all this a relief portrait of a stern-looking man with small eyes and a pointed nose. There were silhouettes on the coins of smaller denomination, too, some of which I recognized from illustrations in *The Dominion History of the Union* as the historic patriots Washington, Hamilton, and Otis; but the face on the Dollar was unfamiliar to me, and when I showed it to Julian he laughed. "So the old villain's vanity finds yet another expression! That's my uncle, Adam—Deklan Comstock, or a flattering facsimile of him."

"He's on a coin now?"

"A new coin for a new year. And plenty of them, I imagine. The Mint must be working overtime to pay for the war effort." Julian directed my attention to the obverse of the Dollar, on which was written *DEKLAN COMSTOCK POTUS,** and the year 2173, with a representation of two Clasped Hands, signifying the concord of the Armies of the East and West, alongside the stamp of the Boston Mint, and the ambiguous but vaguely threatening legend *NOW AND FOREVER.*

"Let me see that," Sam said, and on examining the coin he remarked, "Yes, that's him, a flattering-enough likeness. He could drill holes in wood with that nose of his. It was Bryce who got all the looks in the family."

Here we approached territory which I had not dared to explore—that is, the subject of Julian's family. But I was not a stable-boy right at the moment, and Julian was not an Aristo. We were both soldiers, and would so remain, at least for the duration of our involuntary enlistment. So I dared to ask, "What was your father like, Julian? Did you know him well before he died?"

Sam and Julian exchanged glances.

"I knew him well enough," Julian said in a softer voice. "I was but eight years old when he died, and he went to war two years before that. To be honest, Adam, he's more an impression in my mind than a solid memory. He was always kind to me. He never condescended to me, though I was a child, and he was patient enough to explain what I didn't understand."

"And your mother?"

To my surprise it was Sam who answered. "Emily Baines Comstock is as fine a woman as you'll ever meet," he declared, "and perhaps you will meet her, someday. She's exactly the kind of woman a man like Bryce Comstock deserved to have at his side, and she loved him dearly, and was inconsolable for a long time after his death. Emily's more than just beautiful—she's clever and resourceful." And here he reddened, and cleared his throat.

"Does she live in the Executive Palace?" I asked.

"There's a cottage reserved for her on the Palace grounds," said Sam, "but she keeps a row-house in Manhattan where she prefers to stay. Emily doesn't care for the rivalries and jealousies of the high-born. She's happier with artists, actors, scholars—that type of person, from whom she has little to fear."

"My mother's a cultured woman," Julian added, "and doesn't care to be in the presence of Deklan Conqueror, who is as ignorant as he is villainous."

That was how Julian had come to be raised in Manhattan, which was where he had seen so many plays and movies, and spoken with Philosophers, and picked up his heretical ideas. "But you must have met your uncle face-to-face," I said.

---

* President of the United States.

"Too often. After my father's death it was all I could do to restrain myself from calling him a murderer. Oh, those holiday dinners at the Executive Palace! You have no idea, Adam. My mother and I pressed in with Deklan and his crowd of sycophants, while the craven agents of the Dominion blessed his every whim and impulse. We were on display, I think—Deklan's way of announcing that he could command the loyalty even of his murdered brother's widow and son. We were powerless against him. He could have snuffed us out at any time. He tolerated my mother because she was a woman, and me because I was a child, and both of us because we were a perverse emblem of his supposed generosity."

I had touched a hostility that ran deep in Julian, and the edge in his voice was impossible to ignore. The way he spoke of those Palace dinners, and the clergy who presided at them, made me wonder if this humiliation might be the ultimate source of his apostasy. But such speculation was not useful, and I dropped the subject because it made Julian so conspicuously unhappy.

"There!" Sam said. "Do you hear that?"

It was the sound of a train whistle wind-borne over the thawing prairie— not the Caribou-Horn Train that had brought us here from Bad Jump but an Army train, which we would board first thing in the morning, and which would carry us to the battle-front in the East.

"Pack away those Comstock dollars," Sam said, "or you'll have nothing to spend on women and liquor by the time we get to Montreal."

I blushed at his joke, and tried to laugh, though there was more truth in it, ultimately, than I like to admit.

2

The social atmosphere aboard the troop train to Montreal differed in instructive ways from that aboard the Phantom Car. Months had passed since we left Bad Jump, and those of us who had been strangers then had since become, if not friends, at least confederates—intimately known to one another, for better or worse. If we were afraid of the war to which we were being delivered, we kept that tender feeling to ourselves. We sang a great deal, to maintain high spirits, and I was not the prude and child I once had been, and I joined in on the less obscene choruses of *Those Two-Dollar Shoes Hurt My Feet*. Not because vulgarity had become especially desirable, but because merriment is an antidote to dread.

I noticed, too, how the soldiers often appealed to "Julian Commongold" for an opinion or a verdict in some dispute, and accepted his judgment as settled law. This despite Julian's evident youth, unsuccessfully disguised by his sparse yellow beard. It was as if he carried around with him an invisible but perceptible *aura of authority*, which perhaps was what Sam had called "the Comstock in him." It manifested in his square-set shoulders, his careful grooming, and the easy way he wore the blue-and-yellow uniform of the Infantry. But it was a comradely authority, too, coexistent with his confident sense of himself and the evident pleasure he took in socializing even with those beneath his original station in life. He smiled often, and it was a smile only the most truculent among us could fail to give back.

The train carried us out of the prairie and into a land of forest and lakes. Rain beat down steadily most of the day, but it made no difference to us, for we were inside a fully-equipped passenger car, with protection from the weather. This was train travel as I had always imagined it. I sat at a window watching raindrops glide sideways as we passed in and out of cavernous pine forests and followed the smoky shore of a great gray lake. To the pagans of ancient Rome, Julian once told me, the Easter season had represented Death and Rebirth. Certainly there was no lack of Rebirth in the countryside through which we passed. Ferns unrolled in shady glens, the sodden limbs of trees were budding afresh, and cattails poked through ponded winter marshes. And there was Death, too, if you looked for it, in the occasional ruins we passed—not just old settled basements, as in Lundsford, but whole stone buildings, mossy-green, and once or twice the remains of entire towns, slouching brick boxes that shed raindrops as we rattled past them at thirty miles to the hour. Crows nested in those old buildings, and their eaves were crowned with chalky dung, and the only visitors were the local deer, or an occasional wolf or bear, as might be.

I gazed on many more such overgrown ruins until night fell. It was wholly dark when we approached the outskirts of Montreal, where campfires smoldered in the rainy distance. We heard an occasional growl of thunder (or perhaps it was cannonade), and it was at this point that the singing stopped, and a wary silence replaced it, and we fell into less pleasant reveries about the future and what it might hold for us.

An entire Regiment of draftees had been packed into the train—a big body of men, but it was nothing compared to the great Army assembled by General Galligasken outside of the City of Montreal. Our company was, in the common phrase, "a drop in the bucket"—and it was a large, ungainly bucket, uninterested in welcoming new drips. As soon as we collected our gear and left the train we were conducted to a muddy field in which we were invited to make our own contribution to a sea of tents—nothing but mud and canvas as far (in the rain and the night) as the eye could see. After much flailing about, during which we repeatedly slipped and stumbled in the glutinous muck, and cursed, and were cursed in turn by the soldiers trying to sleep in adjoining quarters, we had erected our own rough sleeping-places, and we tumbled into them fully-dressed, and woke a few hours later when reveille sounded, our uniforms all scabbed with mud.

I could not help looking about curiously as we formed up in companies for roll call. The rain had ceased during the night. The morning was brisk and bright, and high clouds careened across the sky like runaway melon-carts. Everywhere, in every direction, men were being bugled out of bed and mustered up, and regimental flags popped in the breeze with a sound like knots bursting in a pinewood fire. The vast flat field in which we stood was cross-cut with muddy roads, and already horses and mules crowded these paths, straining to pull provision wagons or caissons; and I discerned in the distance the grander tents of regimental and battalion commanders. Otherwise there was nothing but an ocean of soldiers on all sides—infantry, cavalry, artillery. The nearest thing I could see that was not a part of the Army of the Laurentians was a line of low trees, as far away as a cloud seems when it sits upon the horizon.

"Is this Montreal?" I asked Sam. If so, the city was considerably less grand than I had imagined it, though still very large.

"Don't be idiotic," Sam said. "The City of Montreal is some miles distant, most of it on an island in the St. Lawrence River. Do you think they would muster so many men in the midst of a modern city? Half of them would be drunk by noon, if that was the case—the other half having absconded to the whorehouses. And don't blush like that, Adam: you're a soldier now, you ought to be hardened to such things."*

* The sensitive reader, not so hardened, may dislike to see rough talk set down verbatim on the innocent page. I apologize, and rest my defense on the cold grounds of veracity.

It has been said, I forget by whom, that you can't throw a stone in the City of Montreal without hitting either a church or a whorehouse. I would soon enough find out for myself the truth of that statement, for it was announced at noon mess that our regiment was to be allowed a supervised leave, and we would be escorted to the city for Easter services in one of the grand ancient Dominion churches there.

"**Do** Jews celebrate Easter?" I asked Sam as we marched to the outskirts of Montreal. "I don't suppose they do."

"It would be surprising if they did," Sam agreed, "though we have our own holiday about this time of year, which is called Pass-Over."

"What event does it mark, if not the Crucifixion and Resurrection?"

"The fact that the Jews were exempted from the plagues that fell upon Egypt."

"Well," I said, "that's something to be grateful for," recalling my Bible studies under Ben Kreel. "Those were unpleasant plagues, and not to be taken lightly."

"More than unpleasant," Julian chimed in, and I was glad that the sound of tramping feet, though muffled by the damp ground, was loud enough to prevent anyone eavesdropping while Julian dilated on this delicate subject. "*Inventive,* I would say, almost to the point of madness. Insects—boils—the butchery of children—such work by any other agency would be considered an example of unexcelled sadism rather than celestial justice."

I was quietly shocked (though hardly surprised) by this fresh apostasy. "God is jealous by nature, Julian," I reminded him. "It says so in the text."

"Oh yes," Julian agreed, "*jealous,* certainly, but also *forgiving; merciful,* but *vengeful; wrathful,* but *loving*—in fact just about anything we can imagine Him to be. That's the *Paradox of Monotheism,* as I call it. Contrast a Christian with a nature-worshipping pagan: if the pagan's cornfield is ravaged by a windstorm he can blame the bad manners of the Cyclone-God; and if the weather is kind he addresses his thanks to Mother Sunshine, or some such; and all this, though not sensible, has a kind of rude logic to it. But with the invention of monotheism a single Deity is forced to take responsibility for every contradictory joy and tragedy that comes down the turnpike. He is obliged to be the God of the hurricane and the gentle breeze together, present in every act of love or violence, in every welcome birth or untimely death."

"I could do with a little less Mother Sunshine at the moment," remarked Sam, applying a handkerchief to his brow, for the day had grown warm, and the march was tiring.

"But you can't blame the Jews for celebrating their exemption from His wrath," I protested.

"No," Julian said, "no more than I can blame the sole survivor of a train wreck for crying out a heartfelt, 'Thank God I was allowed to live!'—though the same God who spared him must therefore have abstained from *preventing* the wreck, or rescuing any other person from it. The impulse to gratitude on the part of the survivor is understandable, but shortsighted."

"I don't see how monotheism makes it any worse, though. It seems to me, once you start multiplying your gods, you might not know just where to stop. A crowd of gods so numerous you can't recognize most of them seems hardly better than no god at all. Especially once they begin to bicker among themselves. Don't you often tell me to seek out the simplest explanation for a thing?"

"One is a simpler number than a dozen," Julian admitted. "But *none* is simpler than *one*."

"That's enough of this, thank you," said Sam.

"Why Sam," said Julian, grinning mischievously, "are you afraid of a little Philosophical Conversation?"

"This is Theology, not Philosophy—an altogether more dangerous subject, Julian; and I'm not so much afraid of the loose talk as I am of the loose tongue behind it."

"Where is the Dominion that we should censor ourselves?"

"Where is the Dominion? The Dominion is everywhere—you know that! The Dominion is at the head of this very march," referring to our newly-installed Dominion Officer, one Major Lampret, who strode before us, a handsome man in a handsome uniform.*

Julian might have insisted on continuing the conversation, if only for the purpose of aggravating Sam, but by this time we had come upon a great iron bridge, by which we crossed a body of water so immense that I could hardly credit its christening as a River. Vessels from many nations moved beneath that bridge, some with immense white sails and some powered by boilers, some warping toward the Port of Montreal and others bound for the inland Great Lakes trade or for the wide ocean far to the east; and beyond this bridge lay the astonishing City of Montreal, and it was the City that finally drew all of our attention—all of mine, at least.

I would see bigger cities in my life, and travel farther from home; but as Montreal was the first true City I had seen I could not help but contrast it with Williams Ford. By that measure, it was immense. And it had once been even larger, Julian reminded me, for we had all morning passed through a landscape that was essentially one vast Tip, played-out and burned-over, with scrub brush and low trees overlying what must once have been zones of in-

---

* A Dominion Officer, who is by definition a commissioned officer trained at the Dominion Academy in Colorado Springs, wears the standard uniform of an Infantryman of his rank, but adorned with red-and-purple pipings and blazons, and a pair of silver Angel's Wings pinned to the chest, and the soft wide-brimmed hat sometimes called a "chaplain's crown."

dustry or sprawling suburbs. What remained was only the core of the city as it was known to the Secular Ancients, all its rind and peelings having been stripped away.

But that central core preserved many wonderful antique structures. "The buildings are so tall!" I could not help exclaiming, and Julian said, "Though once much taller. Even these buildings have been scavenged, Adam." He drew my attention from the stark concrete walls, complexly chambered, to the crude peaked roofs above them with their fluted red-clay tiles and slumping chimneys: "You see how the roof is less sturdy than the building under it, though considerably newer? There's nothing much over four or five stories tall here (yes, yes, 'tall enough,' and stop gawking, Adam, you'll embarrass yourself), but some of these buildings were once almost *ten times higher,* the greater part of them having been taken down by inches for their wood, wire, and aluminum. Even their steel frames were eventually whittled down and sent to the re-rolling mills, leaving only the subdivided stumps for people to inhabit. If you think this city is magnificent, Adam, conjure up in your mind's eye the city it once was. Run the decades back and you'd see marvels of steel and glass—man-made mountains—a city halfway to infiltrating the sky itself. New York City is the same," he added with evident pride, "only larger."

I was not daunted by his comparisons, however, for modern-day Montreal seemed quite astonishing enough, with its bricked or cobbled streets and busy occupants. Let Julian dwell on the glories of the past—there was enough here to occupy the inquisitive mind.

The people were almost as surprising as the city in which they resided. Because we marched in a unit our regiment made a kind of martial parade, and the inhabitants of the city stood back (not always graciously) to accommodate our passage, while horses and wagons took alternative routes at the sound of our approach. The women of the city wore colorful clothes, dyed all the colors of the rainbow, and seemed both aloof and alluring as they strolled through the vernal sunshine and passed in and out of the innumerable shops and markets. The men dressed more conservatively—more *peahen* than *peacock*—but their trousers and shirts and coats were clean and pressed. Even the children were well-dressed, and only a few of them went barefoot. I asked Julian, "Are these folks Aristos?"

"Some, but mostly not. The eastern cities are not Estates, with a tightly-controlled leasing class. The business of the city requires artisans and laborers to be able to move freely between various jobs, and managers and petty owners can negotiate loans and establish factories or shops as they please, and profit from them. The cumulative effect is a population some of whom are prosperous enough to dress extravagantly—at least at Easter—even though they aren't *propertied* in the full sense of that word."

"Hasn't the war harmed the city?"

"It's been a mixed blessing, I gather. In the recent past the city has been exclusively in American hands, and the presence of garrisoned troops has created an economic boom, along with a bumper crop of larceny and vice. Look there, Adam, that should impress you—I believe that's the cathedral in which we're supposed to worship."

After this sarcastic comment I could not admit how astonished I truly was, though Julian laughed once more at my gawking. We had come up a low rise and around a corner into the neighborhood of a huge church. It was the largest I had ever seen—not the largest *church* but the largest *thing* I had ever seen, meaning a man-made thing and not an act of nature.* Its spires were tall enough to snag clouds, and I could hardly catch my breath as we marched under its shadow and through the enormous and ornate wooden doors. We paused in the dimness of the foyer, under the direction of Major Lampret, and took off our caps and stuffed them in our pockets, out of respect. Then we passed through a second set of doors into the body of the "cathedral," as Julian called it, which was like the Dominion Hall back in Williams Ford, if the Dominion Hall had been inflated to monstrous size, its modest walls exchanged for vaulted granite, and its woodwork shaped and polished by an army of imaginative and slightly mad carpenters. Everywhere, in every direction, was *filigree,* down to the finest scale, and alcoves and cubbies in which more filigree was on display, and candles more numerous than stars in the sky, creating a miasmic odor of smoky wax, and above all this were several great Stained Glass Windows, as tall as the pines of Athabaska, illustrating ecclesiastical themes, and of sun-shot colors so radiant as to seem Edenic.

There was some awed commentary among the troops, few of whom had ever been inside a Cathedral, and several of the men hooted loudly in order to hear their voices come echoing back from the high arched ceiling, until Major Lampret cuffed them into a respectful silence. Then we took our places in the pews.

"Does it gall you," I whispered to Sam, "to be in such a place for a Christian religious service?"

"I was raised by Christians after the death of my true parents," he reminded me, "and I've been inside many churches on many Easters, and on other occasions too, and I try to conduct myself as a well-mannered guest, if not a genuine devotee. Now be quiet, Adam Hazzard, and listen to the singing."

As it happened, we were stationed near the choir. At first the choir seemed only a vague crowd dressed all in white. Then, as my eyes adjusted to the dimness, I realized the choristers were female, and most of them young, and I am ashamed to say that I was pleased by that discovery, for the city women possessed a beauty just as striking (it seemed to me right then) as all the stained glass saints and marble martyrs in Christendom.

* Railroad bridges aside. But even the airy trestle at Connaught, which crosses the River Pine, might have fit inside this cathedral, if properly folded.

Skeptics will put that down to the deprivations of Army life—and there is, of course, some truth to that—but I am convinced there was also an element of Destiny in my fascination, for standing in the front rank of the choir was the most beautiful woman I had ever seen.

I won't attempt to set down here the emotions this anonymous woman stirred in me, for the superlatives would embarrass the mature writer. Summoning all my powers of objectivity, then, this is what I saw: a short female person of approximately my own age, in a cloud-white surplice, her body what some might call *stout* and others would call *healthy*, with a pink and radiant face, and large eyes whose color I could not at this distance discern, although I imagined them (correctly, as it turned out) to be a handsome chestnut-brown; and a crown of hair that coiled like a vast collation of ebony springs, the light behind her making a spectacular Halo of it. If she noticed me staring at her, she showed no sign.

I could not distinguish her voice from the voices of the other female choristers, but I was sure it was at least as pure and angelic as the rest. They sang a hymn that was unfamiliar to me, with references to the Fortress of Virtue, the Armory of Faith, and other metaphorical architecture. Then—unhappily, for I was transported by the sound—the singing stopped, and Major Lampret himself stepped up to the pulpit. All eyes were suddenly on him, including those of the choir, and I found myself resenting the trim figure he cut in his Dominion uniform, its angel-wing breast pin glinting in the multicolored light.

Major Lampret, employing his parade-ground voice so as to reach the back pews, explained that the Cathedral, though nominally a Catholic church, had agreed to allow its premises to be used for nondenominational Christian services, Dominion-contrived and Dominion-approved, for the spiritual benefit of such divisions as the Army could spare from duty at the front. He thanked the local clergy for their generosity; then he admonished us all to keep silent, and refrain from eating any food we might have concealed about ourselves, and not to interrupt the service with cries of "That's so!" or "Go on!" or other vulgar ejaculations, nor to clap and whistle at the end of the sermon, but rather to sit tight and think of Redemption.

Then a local clergyman—a priest, I suppose, for Catholic clergy are so called—mounted the podium and began to read the sermon that had been prepared for him by the Dominion scholars. The lesson bid fair to be a long one—it began with palm leaves, and promised a leisurely route to the Resurrection (which for me was the highlight of the story, for I had always enjoyed picturing the astonishment of observers at the discovery of the Empty Tomb)—and the clergyman had mastered that peculiar ecclesiastical drone which, in combination with the heat, and the fatigue of the march, and the smoky air, caused more than a few nodding heads among his temporary parishioners. Julian, sitting next to me, seemed deeply attentive, but I knew better than to believe the appearance, for Julian had once told me what he did during church services (an Atheist being as much a foreigner in church as a Jew): he passed the time, he said, by imagining the movie he would one day make, *The Life and Adventures of the Great Naturalist Charles Darwin*, rehearsing in his mind the individual scenes, and the dialogue, and how he might decorate the sets, or work out the plot for maximum drama.

I fought off my own drowsiness by occasionally glancing back at the choir, where the woman who had captivated me stood patiently. She betrayed no boredom with the sermon, though she occasionally cast a glance heavenward, more in exasperation (it seemed) than in prayer, and twice raised her left foot to scratch the calf of her right leg. As the day grew warmer a bead of sweat formed on her forehead and trickled down her cheek, absorbing and reflecting the colorful light. It fascinated me.

An hour passed. The clergyman was halfway through his oration (or so I deduced, since we had got past Judas and were about to embark on the nasty business with Pontius Pilate) when there was a distant crack as of thunder, followed by a low rumbling that traveled up the wooden pews and into our spines. This caused some muttering in the ranks; but the priest carried on regardless, and Sam whispered, "Artillery fire—no danger to us; the Dutch don't have a cannon capable of reaching Montreal from their trenches."

That reassured me. A few more minutes passed—the Stations of the Cross were painstakingly negotiated—then came another explosion, nearer this time, causing the clergyman to hesitate and a rain of dust to sift down from the ceiling. "That was close!" I exclaimed to Sam.

He was frowning. "It shouldn't be possible . . ."

Major Lampret hushed us. But it came again: a sharp report and a rolling boom, so loud that it seemed to be—perhaps *was*—right next door. I heard the distant clangor of fire bells, and someone in the city began to crank a hand siren—a dolorous and eerie sound, which I had not heard before.

Now the regiment stood up in alarm, and the clergyman at the pulpit waved his hands in an urgent but indecipherable gesture, and Major Lampret shouted, "*Form up!* Form up and march out, boys, we're wanted elsewhere, but don't run, you'll clog the doors—"

Then a shell struck a deafening blow to the cathedral itself, causing the illustrated windows to shatter and fly inward from their frames. Shards of glass, brightly colored and razor-sharp, cascaded down around us. I saw a man near the pulpit pierced by some crystalline splinter from a glass saint—the wound was almost certainly mortal—and then a general panic began in earnest, despite Major Lampret's shouted orders. At first I joined the rush for the door. Then I turned back to see what had happened to the fascinating chorister. But she was gone—just a flash of white among a flock of billowing surplices as the choir hurried into an adjoining chamber.

I followed behind Sam and Julian, and had almost achieved the exit, when some force from behind (probably an overeager infantryman) pushed me off-balance, so that I fell, and struck my head on the exquisitely carved backboard of a pew, knocking myself quite unconscious.

I was not out of my senses for long—just long enough to become separated from my regiment.

I raised my head in confusion, aware of the pain in my temple and little more. The great cathedral was still intact, except for the shattered windows, and the stampede had left it almost deserted, save for the priest and a few other clergymen who were attending the wounded man down front. I touched my scalp where it had impacted the pew, and my fingers came back stained with blood. I looked around for Sam, or Julian, or even Lymon Pugh, but they were gone with all the rest—gone back to camp, I guessed, to prepare some response to this fresh Dutch outrage. I was sure they would have taken me with them, except that I had fallen between the rows of pews, and would have been easily missed in the rush. I reasoned that I ought to rejoin my regiment as soon as possible, lest I be set down as Absent Without Leave or marked as a deserter.

But when I stumbled out of the cathedral I was immediately lost. The shelling had caused no little damage in the neighborhood, and the street by which I had arrived here was blocked with debris and partially aflame. City folk rushed about haphazardly, some wounded or burned, and red-painted fire-reels drawn by panting dray horses clattered down the open roadways with their brass bells fiercely clanging. But only certain areas of this vast City had been damaged—it was so large that most of it seemed untouched—and after a brief thought I resolved to work my way north until I came within sight of the iron bridge my regiment had originally crossed. It was with this purpose in mind that I set out along a side street undamaged in the attack, where the four- and five-story concrete buildings had been divided into shops, and the floors above were balconied and iron-railed and decorated with spring flowers. The picturesque alley was not straight, however; it twined like a serpent, and when I reached the next intersection I couldn't tell which way to go.

In the meantime crowds of city people continued to brush past me. Not a few of them were fleeing the artillery attack in the cathedral district, and they were too absorbed in their own misfortune to notice one dislocated infantryman. I stood helpless in my confusion, until my eyes were drawn by a flourish of white across the way—a *surplice robe,* as you may have guessed, and it was worn by none other than the woman with the spring-loaded hair and lustrous eyes. I dashed across the street, heedless of the many passing carriages.

"You were in the church!" I said when I reached her; and she turned to squint at me, her small fists clenched in case I proved hostile.

"Yes?" she said brusquely.

"Were you—ah—were you hurt?"

"Obviously I was not," she replied, in a tone so cool that I supposed she must have grown accustomed to being shelled by the Dutch from time to time, the event being no more surprising to her than a summer squall.

"I was!" I managed to say. "I injured my head!"

"How unfortunate. I hope you recover."

She turned away.

"Wait!" I said, and gestured back toward the billowing smoke. "What's happening here?"

"It's called *war*," she said as if she were addressing an idiot who had inquired about the color of the sky (and in her defense, that must have been how I sounded). "The Dutch have launched an artillery barrage. Though it seems to be finished for the moment. Shouldn't you be with your regiment, Soldier?"

"I should be; and I would be, if I could find it. Which way is the big iron bridge?"

"There are several, but the one you want is just down that direction."

I thanked her and added, "May I see you safely home?"

"Of course not," she said

"My name is Adam Hazzard," I said, remembering the importance of a polite introduction.

"Calyxa," she said grudgingly—the first time I had heard that interesting name. "Go back to your regiment, Adam Hazzard, and put a bandage on your head. It's bleeding."

"You sing very beautifully."

"Huh," said she, and walked off without looking back.

It was a brief meeting but a pleasant one, even under these extraordinary circumstances, and as I hurried to the bridge, despite my anxiety, and the blood trickling down my face, and the smoke rising from the city behind me, I thanked Providence, or Fate, or Fortune, or one of those other pagan deities, for having brought the two of us together.

3

"They have a Chinese Cannon," said Sam.

I had caught up with my regiment, and both Sam and Julian had apologized for not rescuing me, or even noticing that I was missing until after the cathedral was evacuated. I took this as a commentary on the chaos that followed the attack rather than on my own insignificance, and a hearty welcome dispelled any lingering resentment on my part.

I expected we would be thrust into immediate battle, in order to punish the Dutch for their impudence. But a modern Army is a sedentary beast and slow to move. General Galligasken, who commanded the Army in total, was a notoriously cautious leader, reluctant to unleash his forces until every contingency had been accounted for and all preparations were fully in place. It was a tendency that frustrated the Executive Branch, Julian said, but it made Galligasken a popular figure with the troops, who were well-fed under his regime, and whose lives were not recklessly squandered. (The veterans among us had shared stories of the harsh rule of Galligasken's predecessor, General Stratemeyer, a disciplinarian who squandered thousands of lives in futile and unproductive trench attacks. General Stratemeyer had been killed early last year, when he rode away from his camp to consult a cavalry commander but took a wrong turn, placing him athwart a line of Dutch skirmishers, who were pleased to employ him for target practice.)

For these reasons we did not march into battle at once, but sat in camp while scouts and pickets probed the opposing lines, and brought back captives who disgorged useful intelligence about the enemy's capabilities and intentions. Sam, though still a mere private, worked his connections until he was well-educated about the current state of military affairs. A week after the attack on Montreal the three of us huddled in our tent against another interval of rain, and Sam told us about the Chinese Cannon, while a springtime zephyr whipped the canvas above our heads.

I asked him what made a cannon Chinese, and why it was to be particularly feared.

"The Chinese," he said, "have been waging wars of their own for many years, and they're cunning in the production of field artillery, especially long-bore cannonry. Some of these weapons they sell abroad, to help finance their own military expeditions. Chinese Cannons are formidable but very expensive. The Mitteleuropans must have bought one, or are using their own factories to mimic the design."

"We have artillery pieces aplenty," I protested, for I had seen them about the camp.

"Many, and well-made," Sam agreed. "But the Chinese Cannon has a greater range than anything of ours. It can deliver shells and canister deep into an opponent's territory. I suppose we could build a similar cannon along traditional lines, but it would be clumsy to transport. The genius of the Chinese Cannon is that it quickly breaks down into what are called 'sub-assemblies,' which can be moved by horse or rail as easily as a conventional artillery piece."

"We need to capture or decommission this cannon," I said firmly.

"Probably General Galligasken has thought of that," said Julian, "though your reasoning, as far as it goes, is flawless, Adam."

Sam ignored Julian's sarcasm and said, "We will do so, or at least make the attempt, but it needs forethought and careful planning. I expect we'll see action before the week is out. Curb your impatience, Adam—the Dutch are just as eager to get you in their sights as you are to punish them."

I would punish them grandly, I declared, for it was cowardly of them to have attacked helpless civilians at Montreal (putting Calyxa, among others, at risk). "You'll see worse things before the Army is done with us," said Sam; and in that, as in most of his prophecies, he was entirely correct.

The next day the rain stopped, and a few days after that the roads had dried, and General Galligasken himself rode through camp, which we took to be the signal of an impending attack.

I caught a brief glimpse of the General. One wide dirt lane cut through the entirety of the Army encampment, connecting several parade grounds, and it was down this route that General Galligasken rode. Infantrymen pressed the margins of the road on all sides, waving their caps and shouting as the General passed by. I was determined not to miss such a spectacle, and by a determined use of my elbows I made my way to the front of the crowd, or close enough that by some well-timed jumping I could see the whole of the procession.

What surprised me was the General's relative youth. He was not a young man, especially, but neither was he a grizzled veteran—last year's campaigns had been a success for the Dutch, Sam had explained, and there were fewer grizzled veterans extant than there ought to have been. Many younger men had been catapulted up the ranks. General Bernard W. Galligasken was one of these, and he cut a sprightly figure in the saddle, smiling serenely at the lapping ocean of infantrymen that surrounded him. He was vain, some said, about his appearance, and certainly his uniform was tailored to within a fine inch, and bright in all its colors. The blue-and-yellow costume suited him, however, and his long hair brushed his stiff starched collar in a jaunty fashion. The alabaster handle of his Porter & Earle pistol glinted from the supple leather holster at his hip, and there was a great deal of stamped metal on his chest, to mark the battles he had endured and the bravery he had displayed in them. His hat was a broad-brimmed extravagance with a turkey feather attached.

(The Chinese Cannon spoke twice during this display, and one of the shells burst less than a quarter of a mile from our camp; but the Dutch did not exactly have our range, because of the great distance from which they aimed and their inability to spot the impacts. It was a haphazard affair, which we all ignored.)*

This procession of General Galligasken with his train of subordinates and standard-bearers was a little more "fuss and feathers" than would have been deemed proper back in Williams Ford; but the General was not in camp solely to make a show. He met with his battalion commanders that night in a Council of War. Final plans were laid, and we were instructed by our superiors to "sleep on our arms," and be ready to move before dawn.

The next morning we marched to battle.

At first it was "route march," in which we were not held to a strict formation; though our Regiment, aware of its unblooded status, kept up in dignified lines-of-four. Things went slowly in the darkness of the early morning, and the roads were still damp, so that mule trains and horse-drawn wagons struggled in the soft spots. As dawn pearled the horizon the sound of marching feet, creaking leather, rattling canteens and tinkling spurs was joined by an incongruously joyful chorus of bird song. It was spring, and the birds were nesting, unaware that their homes might be destroyed by cannonade or rifle fire before the day or the season was out.

The territory through which we passed had been overbuilt in the days of the Secular Ancients, but only a few traces of that exuberant time remained, and a whole forest had grown up since then, maple and birch and pine, its woody roots no doubt entwined with artifacts from the Efflorescence of Oil and with the bones of the artifacts' owners. What is the modern world, Julian once asked, but a vast Cemetery, reclaimed by nature? Every step we took reverberated in the skulls of our ancestors, and I felt as if there were centuries rather than soil beneath my feet.

The skirmishing began as soon as the sun cleared the horizon, or perhaps it had begun sooner, since we were in the rear of the advance and the hilly terrain around us obscured the sounds of battle. In fact the battle announced itself like a coming storm, by a series of ominous signs: first, the pall of smoke over the hilly ground ahead of us; second, the low growl of artillery; third, the crackle of small-arms fire; fourth, the acrid smell of gunpowder. These tokens of conflict increased in volume and intensity as the sun rose, and then we be-

---

* The Cannon, Sam said, used particular and expensive ammunition, which the Dutch were probably hoarding for the more intense fighting to come.

gan to see a sight that disheartens any soldier: wagonloads of casualties being carried to the rear. "It must be fierce fighting," I said in a low voice, as a canvas-back Dominion wagon (as these makeshift ambulances were called) jounced past, its passengers concealed but their groans and screams all too audible on the morning air.

Then we topped another hill, and the battlefield was briefly laid out before us like a game board—much of it, however, masked by smoke. I thought I saw General Galligasken observing from this same ridge, and our longest-range cannons were here arrayed, banging and recoiling repetitively. Down below were the nearest of the enemy's trenches.

It was my first glimpse of the Dutch.*

I could hardly contain myself at the sight of their massed army. All my life I had heard of the vicious and aggressive Mitteleuropans, until they became a kind of legend to me, often *cited* but never *seen*. But here they were in the flesh, and even at this great distance, through the coiling smoke and the air hot with gunfire, I caught glimpses of their characteristic black uniforms and blue helmets, and their curious cross-and-laurel flags.

They seemed from this height to be in well-defended positions, with their trenches arranged in a broad semicircle dotted with lunettes and redoubts and abatisses, each end anchored against a riverbank firmly controlled by enemy artillery. Currently an American division was making a brazen frontal attack, with some diversionary skirmishing at the sides. The attack was not going well, however, to judge by the numerous corpses already littering the ground before the Dutch entrenchments.

Sam leaned close to Julian and asked, in his tutelary voice, "What do you see?"

"A battle," Julian said. His voice was unsteady, and I had seldom seen his face so bloodless, though he was pale by nature.

"You can do better than that! Keep your wits about you, and *tell me what you see!*"

Julian suppressed his fear with a visible effort. "I see . . . well, a conventional attack . . . boldly conducted, but I can't imagine why the General is wasting so many troops this way . . . there seems to be no strategy about it, only brute force."

"Galligasken is a cannier officer than that. What do you *not* see, Julian?"

Julian gazed a little longer, then nodded. "The cavalry."

"And why would Galligasken not put his cavalry into battle?"

"Because they're elsewhere. You're implying that he *does* have a strategy, and that it involves our mounted forces."

---

* Or "Deutsche," as they are more properly called, for Germany is the heart and brain of Mitteleuropa, and "Deutsche" is another name for the German language. But many of the foreign soldiers in Labrador, and most of the foreign settlers, were former residents of the Netherlands, which had lost much of its land to the sea in recent times.

"That, at least, is what I'm hoping."

It was true that the fight seemed bold but ineffective. The American attack began to buckle as we watched—one of our veteran divisions had come under especially galling fire, and the commander failed to rally his troops. A standard-bearer fell; his flag was not recovered. Terrified men lay motionless or turned and dashed for the rear, and it might have been the beginning of a rout, except that our regiment was sent into the fray as reinforcements.

A soldier whose arm had been shattered walked past me as we advanced into the smoke and noise. His left forearm was all but detached—connected to its elbow by a few mucilaginous strings—and he clasped it against his belly with his right hand as a child might clutch a bag of candy to protect it from thieving playmates. His uniform was thoroughly doused with blood. He seemed not to see us, and although he opened his mouth repeatedly no sound emerged from it.

"Don't look at that man!" Sam scolded me. "Eyes ahead, Adam!"

Sam was the only soldierly one among us. He advanced in a crouch with his Pittsburgh rifle held steadily. The rest of us moved across this scarred meadow like cattle up a slaughterhouse chute (a process Lymon Pugh had described to me). Our company commander shouted at us to stop bunching together or be killed like geese, and we separated, but reluctantly. At such a time any normal person craves the presence of another human being, if only to have something to hide behind.

We were protected for a time by the thick pall of smoke, stinking of cordite and blood, that lay over the battlefield, though shells from enemy artillery exploded around us at intervals and some in our company were wounded by the shrapnel. But as we approached the enemy's lines volleys of bullets flew past at close proximity, and our company was not exempt from casualties. I saw two men fall, one wounded in the face, and one of our men who had been in the vanguard we re-encountered as a corpse in a bomb-crater, his vitals so widely scattered over the bloody earth that we had to step carefully to avoid treading on his steaming viscera. This was so irregular that I became convinced that I was mad, or that the world had suddenly become so. War, in the novels of Mr. Charles Curtis Easton, was not conducted with such savagery. Mr. Easton's wars allowed for bravery, pluck, patriotism, and all that tribe of reassuring virtues. The present war seemed to make no such allowances; it was purely a matter of killing, or being killed, as chance and circumstance would have it. I kept my rifle at the ready, and twice fired at wraiths in the smoke, without any way to determine whether the shot went home.

Among my swirling thoughts was a passing concern for Julian. I could not help thinking of the time we had spent hunting squirrels and other game back at Williams Ford, and how Julian had enjoyed every part of those expeditions except the killing. He was one of those gentle souls who instinctively recoil from death and who dread inflicting it on others. This was not Cowardice but a species of Innocence—an admirable if innate *tenderness of feeling,* which I suspected was about to get him killed.

At that moment a wind sprang up, clearing some of the haze from the becalmed, though savagely active, battlefield. With the next gust the nearest lines of the Dutch defenders were revealed to us in stark clarity, as if a curtain had been drawn. A line of rifle-barrels protruded from earthen breastworks like quilly spines from a porcupine, and these were hastily leveled at us, now that visibility permitted careful aiming; and smoke erupted from their barrels.

"Down!" Sam shouted—forgetting for the moment that he was not the company commander, but only an ordinary soldier. Nevertheless it was sturdy advice, which we all obeyed. We dropped: most of us voluntarily, though several fell in a fashion that indicated they might not rise again. The Dutch bullets whined past us with maddening insectile noises, "mosquito-voiced but deadly in their flight," as Mr. Easton once wrote, in this case correctly. We hugged the ground as if the familiar metaphor of Mother Earth had become a fact—suckling pigs could not have been more intimately connected to their maternal sow.

All of us except Julian. As soon as I dared to look up, I was shocked to find him still standing.

That image of Julian has been so deeply impressed upon me that, to this day, I see it from time to time in dreams. He had washed and dried his uniform just yesterday, anticipating battle as if it were a social soiree, and despite the rigors of the march he seemed as clean and unspoiled as a stage-soldier in some New York operetta. He frowned as if what confronted him was not the barbarous enemy but an especially perplexing puzzle, which required deep thought to work out. He held his rifle at ready but didn't aim or fire it.

"*Julian!*" cried Sam. "For the love of God! *Down!*"

The love of God did not add any weight to the admonition—Julian had always been impermeable to God, and just now it seemed he might also be impermeable to bullets. The volleys surged around, and kicked up dirt at his feet, without interfering with his person. By this time nearby soldiers had noticed him standing like a sentinel in the rain of sizzling lead; and we waited for what seemed an inevitable lethal impact, already impossibly postponed.

For the Dutch shooters were finding their range as the air cleared. A bullet like a flicking finger tugged at the collar of Julian's uniform. Another doffed his cap for him. Still he didn't move. The spectacle entranced us all, and small appreciative or despairing cries of "Julian Commongold!" began to sound above the clamor of battle. He stood and kept standing—it was as if an angel had dropped down to Earth in the guise of a foot soldier—the crude material world couldn't touch him, and he was as immune to bloodshed as an elephant to flea-bites.

Then a bullet creased his ear. I saw it happen. There was no impact, since the bullet passed through the fleshy part of the lobe, spraying just a little blood; but Julian turned his head as if he had been tapped on the shoulder by an invisible adjutant.

The contact shook him into a fresh awareness of his situation. He did not drop to the ground, however. It was only that his puzzled frown evolved into a grimace of anger and disdain. He lifted his rifle with grave deliberation, sighted it on the enemy breastworks, and fired.

Though Julian had said nothing, the men around him reacted as if he had given an order to advance. Our standard-bearer, who was hardly more than a dozen years old, leapt up and ran forward with the regimental flag in his hands. The rest of us fired our weapons almost in unison, and then joined the charge, whooping.

The smoke of battle provided cover enough that we came close to the Dutch entrenchments without being decimated, and our reckless charge had a greater than anticipated effect. Only a moment seemed to pass before we were athwart the Mitteleuropan trenches, firing our Pittsburgh rifles with abandon or dropping to reload them with fresh cassettes. The Dutch at close proximity looked much like Americans, apart from their peculiar uniforms, and so it was their uniforms I fired at, half convinced that I was killing, not human beings, but *enemy costumes,* which had borne their contents here from a distant land; and if some living man suffered for his enslavement to the uniform, or was penetrated by the bullets aimed at it—well, that was unavoidable, and the fault couldn't be placed at my feet.

This private charade was not equivalent to Courage, but it enabled a Callousness that served a similar purpose.

I lost sight of Julian in the melee, and in truth I could not spare much thought for him at this chaotic moment. Even today the memory is little more than a collage of noise and ugly incidents. The battle evolved quickly, or took forever—in all honesty I cannot say which—and then we heard a new and alarming sound. It was a sort of gunfire: not the sharp report of a Pittsburgh rifle but a staccato *chain* of gunshots, sustained for seconds and then repeated.

Sam explained later what had happened. General Galligasken had sent his cavalry out on a flank attack against the Dutch positions—hardly an unusual maneuver; but the cavalry had been training in secret with a new weapon, which was our answer to the Chinese Cannon.

This weapon, which came to be called the Trench Sweeper, was a heavy rifle with an enormous cassette the size and shape of a pie-plate, which fed bullets to its chamber and fired them in rapid succession—a volley of gunshots continuing for as long a time as the trigger was depressed. The Porter & Earle

Works had produced relatively few of these guns, but a number of them had been distributed to Galligasken's cavalry division for occasions such as this.

The cavalry, riding into the Dutch at their flanks, encountered a fierce resistance; but the Dutch commander had been fooled by Galligasken's frontal attack, and he had weakened his left and right in order to shore up the center. A good many American cavalrymen were killed before the Dutch defenses were penetrated, but eventually the Trench Sweepers were brought to bear, and the resultant rain of fire caused enemy troops to panic and abandon their positions in increasing numbers. Before long they were fleeing across the river at which they had made their stand. Scores of them were drowned in the process, and their bodies littered the shore like branches from a thunderstruck tree.

It was a rout, ultimately. More than a thousand of the enemy were killed, and twice that number were taken prisoner. Our own corpses numbered just a little over five hundred.

General Galligasken ordered a pursuit of the fleeing Dutch army, and captured a few stragglers and some supply wagons and horses; but the main column disappeared into the hills and forests, and Galligasken wisely held back, fearing an ambush, and was content with the spoils of the day. This was eventually called the *Battle of Mascouche* ("Mascouche" being the name of a nearby Tip). It was a stirring victory, all in all, except that we did not capture the Chinese Cannon; it had been kept to the rear of the action, and was dismantled and spirited away before we could reach it.

In the aftermath of the battle I found Sam and Julian, both more or less unhurt, and we made a new camp on the riverside as supplies were trucked forward and field hospitals established for the wounded. By nightfall we had been fed, and were resting in our tents. It was an incongruously warm, benevolent evening, sweet as April butter, and the moon was bright and cheerfully indifferent to the shed blood congealing beneath it.

Julian said very little that evening. In truth, although he had survived the fight with only a nick to his earlobe, I was afraid for him. It seemed that something just as vital as blood had drained out of him during the exciting events of the day.

As we were getting ready to sleep he leaned from his bedroll and whispered, "I don't know how many men I killed today, Adam."

"Enough to help ensure a victory," I said.

"Is it really a victory? What we saw today? It more closely resembled a fire in a charnel house." He added, "It's a bitter thing to kill a stranger—worse to kill strangers beyond counting."

He was speaking hyperbole; but the very flatness of his voice suggested a grievance too deep for words. And to a degree I shared it. To fire a bullet into the heart or brains of one's fellow man—even a fellow man striving to do the same to you—creates what might be called an *unassimilable memory*: a memory that floats on daily life the way an oil stain floats on rainwater. Stir the rain barrel, scatter the oil into countless drops, disperse it all you like, but it will not mix; and eventually the slick comes back, as loathsomely intact as it ever was.

"We can never again be what we once were," Julian whispered.

I sat up indignantly. "I'm still just Adam Hazzard. Adam Hazzard from Williams Ford hasn't gone away, Julian. He just went to war. Someday he'll go somewhere else. New York City, perhaps."

Julian evidently took some comfort from my crude philosophizing, for he grasped my hand warmly, and said in a trembling voice, "Thank you for saying so."

"Sleep on it," I suggested. "Perhaps we won't have to kill anyone tomorrow, and you can get some useful rest."

But I couldn't take my own advice—couldn't sleep, despite my exhaustion, any more than Julian could; so we lay awake while the moon shone down on the battlefield where we had driven back the Dutch, and on the hospital tents with their detritus of severed limbs, and on the river that flowed somewhat bloodstained to the mighty St. Lawrence and all the way to the shoreless sea.

4

Because of General Galligasken's humanitarian concern for the Army of the Laurentians we were not obliged to fight the following day, nor did we march in pursuit of the enemy, but stayed where we were, and buried our dead, and consolidated our defenses in case the Dutch attempted a counterattack.

In another month or less this land would be a steaming Gehenna, hospitable only to the mosquitos and the horseflies that feed on human and animal flesh; and our marches, should we make any, would be mortal contests of endurance. Already the hospital tents, where they were not wholly preoccupied with wounded men, hosted a number of invalids down with "the summer complaint," and there was the ever-present danger of an outbreak of cholera or some other communicable disease. We drew water from local streams to drink, for the Army barrel-water was stagnant and fusty; and we hoped for the best.

But the weather held calm and pleasant for a few days more. On Sunday afternoon after Dominion services a general lassitude fell over the camp, and I wandered among the tents like an Aristo strolling through his garden (though aristocratic gardens are generally more pleasing to the nose than military encampments).

It was while I was strolling, and sampling the sunshine, and humming tunes to myself, that I heard a noise which puzzled and interested me.

There are all sorts of noises around an army camp: army engineers banging wood for inscrutable purposes, army blacksmiths bending horseshoes on an anvil, infantrymen at target practice, and any number of other clattery pursuits. But most of those sounds had abated on account of the Sabbath. What I heard was a sound that could be mistaken, at a distance, for the irregular knocking of a woodpecker on a tree, or a boy drummer unsuccessfully attempting some novel rhythm. But the sound had a brittler, more mechanical quality than that; and once my curiosity was engaged I could think of nothing else but to track the noise to its source.

Its *approximate* source, I soon discerned, was a square canvas tent situated up a sloping meadow that became, farther east, a respectable hill. The tent's flaps were open so I wandered past it, hands clasped behind my back, feigning indifference but sparing a subtle glance or two inside. But it was difficult to see inside in any meaningful way—my vision was hampered not just by the shade of the canvas but by an obscuring miasma of tobacco and hemp smoke, which wafted into the sunshine in coiling exhalations as if the tent itself were alive and breathing—and I had to make several passes before I could discern the agency responsible for so much smoke and noise: it was a man seated at a flimsy wooden table, working a machine.

My effort to remain inconspicuous was apparently not successful, for on my seventh or eighth pass the mysterious man called out, "Stop hovering there, whoever you are!" His voice was rough, and he spoke with a nasal accent not unlike Julian's. "Come in or go out—I don't care which—but choose one."

"I'm sorry if I disturbed you," I said hastily.

"I was disturbed before you came along; don't take all the credit . . . What are you staring at?"

"That machine," I admitted, taking an uninvited step into the shade, and resisting the temptation to hold my breath. As my vision adapted to the dim light I could see that the man had equipped himself with an ashtray, pipe, leather poke-bag, and a flask that added the astringent odor of alcohol to the already dizzying assortment of musks in the air. He was not dressed as an infantryman, and in fact he seemed to be a civilian. His clothes were thread-bare and patched but must have been respectable at one time. He wore a nar-row hat slouched over his eyes.

But this was only a sparing assay of the *man*, for I was much more in-terested in the *machine*. The machine, though not much larger than a generously-proportioned bread box, was as intricate as a pocket watch turned inside-out, finished in black enamel and studded with round ridged buttons on which letters were etched, one per key. A sheet of paper was squeezed around a cylinder like a rolling pin set behind all this, and words were printed on the page.

"It's a typewriter," the man said. "I suppose they don't have typewriters in whatever hamlet you hail from."

I ignored this implied insult to Williams Ford and said, "You mean it's a printing press? Are you making a book?" (For I had not yet inquired into the mechanics of book-making, and I guessed this might be the way books were manufactured: by grubby men copying them one letter at a time.)

"Do I look like a *publisher* to you? You ought not to impose on my hospi-tality and then insult me."

"My name is Adam Hazzard," I said.

"Theodore Dornwood," he muttered, and returned his attention to the business before him.

"That's an admirable machine," I persisted, "even if it's not a printing press. What do you do with it? Do you make signs or notices?"

"I'm not a publisher, I'm not a sign-maker, and I'm not even a company clerk. My station in life is below all those. I'm a writer."

That startled me—I had never seen a writer before, nor met anyone who described himself as one. My eyes widened; and I exclaimed without much in the way of forethought, "So am I!"

Mr. Dornwood caught the smoke from his pipe the wrong way and began to cough.

"At least," I added, "that's my ambition. I mean one day to write books such as the ones by Mr. Charles Curtis Easton—I assume you've heard of him?"

"Of course I've heard of him. His books litter all the stalls in Hudson Street."

"Where is Hudson Street, then?" (Thinking that if this street were in Montreal I might be willing to part with some of my Army pay in order to catch up with Mr. Easton's recent work.)

"Manhattan," Mr. Theodore Dornwood said, casting a glance at the page in his typewriter with a certain rueful longing.

"You're a New York writer, then?"

"I correspond for the *Spark*."

The *Spark* was a New York City newspaper. I had never seen a copy—of the *Spark*, or any other newspaper—but Julian had mentioned it once or twice as a popular if vulgar daily journal.

"Is that what you're doing now—corresponding?"

"No! Just at the moment I'm passing the time with every idle infantryman who happens to wander by; but I *was* working, curiously enough, before you began hovering at the tent-flap."

Since Theodore Dornwood came from Manhattan I was tempted to ask whether he had met Julian Comstock there, or passed him on the streets; but I remembered that any careless identification of Julian as a Comstock might attract the attention of Julian's murderous uncle.* Therefore I left Julian's name out of the discussion and said, "Well, I wish I had a machine as fine as that one. Do all New York writers own one?"

"The privileged few."

"How does it work?"

"You push the keys—like this, see?—and the letters are impressed on the paper—at least when the operator is allowed sufficient privacy in which to work."

"Isn't it a slow process, compared to handwriting?"

"Faster, if you're trained to it, and the finished manuscript is easier to set as copy . . . *Hazzard*, you said your name was? Are you the soldier who's been teaching these country boys their letters?"

The lessons I gave Lymon Pugh had been so successful that a few other infantrymen had begged to be included. I was pleased that Mr. Dornwood had heard of me. "I'm the one."

"And you write, too?" He inhaled from his pipe and gave out a Vesuvius-load of smoke. The pungent air in the tent was beginning to make me feel light-headed, though it seemed to have no such effect on Dornwood, who

---

* And Deklan Conqueror must be uniquely sinister, I had lately thought, if he was more dangerous to confront than a legion of armed and angry Dutchmen. The difference, Sam explained, was that our enlistment would only last a year or so, while the threat from Julian's uncle would persist throughout his reign.

must have saturated himself in his vices so long that he had acquired an immunity to them. (He wasn't old, in the sense that Sam Godwin was old, but he was at least ten years older than myself—old enough to be hardened to his own bad habits.) "What are you working on at the moment, Adam Hazzard?"

I blushed at the question and said, "Well, I do keep paper and pencils handy . . . though I don't have a writing-machine with springs and levers . . . I mark down a word or two from time to time . . ."

"No modesty between scribblers," said Dornwood. "Fiction, is it?"

"Yes—a story about a Western boy kidnapped by Chinese traders, and taken to sea against his will, and when he escapes his captors he falls in with pirates, but what they don't know is—"

"I see. And how many pirates have you met, Adam Hazzard?"

The question took me by surprise. "In life? Well—none."

"But you must have studied them extensively, from a distance?"

"Not exactly—"

"Well, are you absolutely sure pirates *exist*—since they're so foreign to your experience? No, don't answer that; I'm making a point. Why write about pirates, Adam, when you're embedded in an adventure at least as momentous as anything C. C. Easton ever imagined?"

"What are you saying—that I should write about the war? But I've only seen a little of it."

"No matter! *Write what you know*: it's one of the abiding principles of the trade."

"The worse for me, then," I said ruefully, "for I don't know much at all, when you come down to it."

"Surely everybody knows something. The Battle of Mascouche, for instance. Weren't you in the thick of it?"

"Yes, but it was my first."

"Wouldn't it be a sensible exercise to set down in pencil what happened on that day? Not what happened to the Army of the Laurentians—leave that to the historians—I mean what happened *to you*—your *personal* experience."

"Who would be interested?"

"It would be an exercise in writing, if nothing else. Adam," he exclaimed, standing up from his desk, and flinging an arm around my shoulders in a surprising display of conviviality, "why are you wasting your time here? A writer must *write*, first and last! Don't squander precious minutes gazing at my typewriter—or worse, touching it—now is the time to hone your literary skills, while the Dutch are quiet and the weather's fair! Take up your humble pencil, Adam Hazzard, and set down in all the detail you can remember the events of a few days past."

This made immediate sense to me—in fact I was excited by his suggestion, and reproached myself for not having thought of such an exercise before. "And when it's done, shall I show it to you?"

He sat back down as if the wind had gone out of him. "Show it to me?"

"My account of the battle. So that you can point out what an experienced writer might have done differently."

Mr. Dornwood knotted his brows and looked uncomfortable; then he said, "Well, all right . . . I suppose you can bring it to me next Sunday, if neither of us is killed by then."

"That's very generous!"

"I'm a well-known saint," said Dornwood.

I meant to go straight to my tent and practice my literary skills as Dornwood had suggested, but on the way back I was distracted by a crowd of men who had gathered around the tent of Private Langers.

Langers, the reader will remember, was a passenger on the Caribou-Horn Train: a *colporteur*, as he pleased to call himself, who had been in the business of selling religious pamphlets on delicate topics to lonely men, who enjoyed the printed illustrations for reasons not necessarily allied to piety or faith. Private Langers had been put out of that trade by conscription, and he was just another infantryman now. But his entrepreneurial instincts had survived the transformation, and it seemed like he was back in business—some kind of business—judging by the eager crowd around him.

I asked another soldier what was going on.

"Langers was on burial duty," the man said.

"Surprising that *that* should have made him so popular."

"He collected all sorts of things from the bodies of dead Dutchmen. Jackets and hats, badges and wallets, eyeglasses and glass eyes, brass buckles and leather holsters . . ."

Enemy armaments had to be handed over to the Quartermaster, but everything else, I gathered, was fair game for the burial detail. I knew that men were often tempted to take a souvenir or two from their fallen foes, if their stomachs were strong enough for the treasure-hunt. But he had gone far beyond that modest impulse. He had harvested the fields of the fallen with a bushel basket, and put the culled trinkets on display. Dozens of Dutch prizes were arrayed on a blanket in front of his tent, under a sign which read: EVERYTHING $1.

It seemed to me an odd price. A few of the objects were obviously worth more than that, such as the collections of Dutch coins, which could be traded in Montreal for legal tender. But most were worth much less. The jackets almost all had bullet-holes in them, for instance; and even the glass eye, though lifelike, was cracked. But there was a trick to it, the soldier next to me explained.

"It don't mean you pay a dollar and take what you like. Everything has a number beside it, written on those scraps of paper. And Langers has a jar, with similar scraps inside it. When you pay your dollar he says, 'Reach into the jar,' and you do so, and you pull out a number and find out just what it was you bought. It might be something good, like that mermaid buckle there. But it might be a sad little leather bag, or a shoe with a hole in it."

"Isn't that Gambling?"

"Hell no," the soldier said, "it's not half as much fun."

I had been warned against gambling all my life, both by my mother and by the *Dominion Reader for Young Persons,* though the only gambling I had ever seen first-hand was the kind the indentured folks indulged in, betting tobacco or alcohol on dice or cards. Most of those games ended in fist fights, and I was never tempted by them. But Private Langers's pick-a-number enterprise was more difficult to resist. I was curious about the Dutch, and felt that I ought to know a thing or two about the people I had been shooting at and, occasionally, killing. To own one of their possessions seemed almost a religious act (if I can be excused that small apostasy), like the custom primitive peoples have of eating their enemy's hearts—a more Christian enactment of the same urge.

So I pushed to the front of the crowd, and took a Comstock dollar from my pocket, and paid it over for the privilege of reaching into Private Langers's Lucky Mug. The number I retrieved was *32,* which corresponded to a small leather satchel, much-scuffed and disappointingly slender. This was not, by any standards, a *valuable* thing to have bought—and Langers smiled with satisfaction as he tucked away my dollar and handed over the satchel. But my disappointment didn't last; for the satchel, when I opened it, contained a letter, apparently written by a Dutch soldier shortly before his death. Again, this had no monetary value, and Langers had every reason to crow over the bargain; but as a souvenir of a man's life, and a glimpse into the habits of the Mitteleuropan infantry, the letter interested me terrifically.

I unfolded the two closely-written pages I had bought, and thought about that deceased Dutchman putting his pen to paper, little suspecting that his words would become the property of a Williams Ford lease-boy (much less the booty of a corpse-looting colporteur). I took the letter to my tent and stared at it for nearly an hour, thinking about fate, and death, and other weighty and Philosophical subjects.

Lymon Pugh came by as I was deep in these reveries, and I showed him the letter.

He puzzled over it a moment. "My lessons in reading don't seem to have advanced this far," he said.

"Of course you can't read it. It's written in Dutch."

"Dutch? They don't just speak that noise, they also write it down?"

"That's their habit, yes."

"But you know all your letters, Adam: can't you decipher it?"

"Oh, I can read the *letters* all right—so can you, though you might not be accustomed to cursive script. This word here, for example: L-I-E-F-S-T-E— those are all familiar letters."

"I can't make out what they spell, though."

"It looks like it might be pronounced *leafst*. Or *leaf-stee*, depending on how they use their terminal vowels."

Lymon Pugh looked scornful. "That's not a word."

"It's certainly not a word in English; but in Dutch—"

"If they're going to write out letters, why can't they do it decently? No wonder we have to fight them. But I suppose it's not meant to be understood. Not by the likes of us, at least. Perhaps it's a code. Maybe what you have there is a plan of action, written from one Dutch General to another."

That had not occurred to me. The suggestion was troubling, and I determined to show the letter to Major Ramsden of our regiment. Major Ramsden spoke a little Dutch, since his father had been a stranded Dutch sailor, and it was Ramsden who interrogated captured prisoners in their own language.

I found him dozing in his tent, taking advantage of the Sabbath calm, and he was not delighted to see me; but he agreed to look at what I'd brought him.

When I handed him the letter he turned it half-sideways, and squinted at it, and ran his fingers over it, and hummed to himself at length. He was so reluctant to render a translation that I wondered whether he might be illiterate— able to speak Dutch but not read it. But when I hinted at that possibility he gave me a venomous look, and I let the matter drop.

I have preserved the letter through many years, and it sits beside me as I write, and this is how it looked, though the ink is faded now and some of the letters are uncertain:

Liefste Hannie (it began),

Ik hoop dat je deze brief krijgt. Ik probeer hem met de postboot vanuit Goose Bay te versturen.

Ik mis je heel erg. Dit is een afschuwelijke oorlog in een vreselijk land—ijzig koud in de winter en walgelijk heet en vochtig in de zomer. De vliegen eten je levend, en de bestuurders hier zijn tirannen. Ik verlang er zo naar om je in mijn armen te houden!

"What does that mean?" I asked.

Major Ramsden frowned some more, and looked at me resentfully; then he said, "It's all about how he hates America."

"He hates America?"

"They all do—the Dutch."

"What does he hate us for?"

Major Ramsden squinted at the text.

"For our freedoms," he said.

This had been the subject of today's Dominion Service, by coincidence: our God-given freedoms, enumerated, and the enemy's instinctive hatred for them. "Does he say *which* freedoms upset him so? Is it the Freedom of Pious Assembly? The Freedom of Acceptable Speech?"

"All those."

"And what about this?"

I pointed out the second sheet of the letter, on which the Dutchman had committed a drawing. The pen sketch was ambiguous: it appeared to show some sort of animal, or perhaps a sweet potato, with spots and a tail. Under it was written:

Fikkie mis ik ook!

"It says, 'All Americans are dogs,'" the Major explained.

I could only marvel at the fanaticism of the Mitteleuropans, and at the unreasoning hatred their rulers had instilled in them.

5

For the next few months our Regiment was largely exempted from the war, though not from its consequences. It was explained to us in a series of general camp meetings that the Dutch attack on Montreal, as it turned out, had been little more than a feint by a few divisions of the Mitteleuropan army. The real action was at the Saguenay River where it entered the St. Lawrence east of Quebec City. That was where our freshwater navy under Admiral Bolen fought a pitched battle with a fleet of heavily-armored enemy gunboats, which had been assembled in Lake St. John by the stealthy Dutch. We had lost many a vessel in that encounter; and the burning wrecks, some still flying the Thirteen Stripes and Sixty Stars, had been seen floating down the St. Lawrence like the candled boats the Japanese launch in honor of their dead.* The Dutch proceeded to build fortifications near Tadoussac overlooking the river, and brought up their best artillery, including a Chinese Cannon, to harass Union traffic and strangle American trade, and it quickly became apparent that the purpose of the Campaign of 2173 would be to reduce these fortifications while maintaining a protective cordon around both Montreal and Quebec City.

Much of the Army of the Laurentians, therefore, was put aboard boats and shipped east to participate in the land battle. But Montreal itself must still be garrisoned, and that responsibility fell to the less seasoned troops, which included our Regiment of western conscripts.

I was sad not to be included in the summer action, but Julian scoffed at that sentiment, and said we were lucky, and that if our luck held we might be released from the military without seeing more bloodshed than the Battle of Mascouche, and that would be a fine thing. But my patriotism, or naïveté, burned more brightly than Julian's, and I was occasionally distraught to think of all the Dutchmen being killed by other soldiers, creating a shortage for the rest of us.

And yet it was not all bad news, for we would be allowed many recreational leaves in the City of Montreal that summer, and I was eager for another chance to meet with Calyxa, and perhaps even to learn her last name.

Our first leave was nearly canceled, however, because of an event which involved Julian and cast a pall over the entire camp.

A new-fashioned Colonel, lately assigned from New York City, had

* Mr. Easton describes this poignant custom in his novel of 2168, *A Union Sailor in the Orient*.

decided our encampment ran too close to our breastworks, and I was assigned to help relocate the offending tents. The tents by this time had taken on all the qualities of Homesteads, however, with rude cooking-pits, flues made of mud, lines strung to dry laundry, and all such small domestic entanglements; thus the work had lasted well into the night, and I had not had very much sleep when I was awakened by Sam Godwin's hand on my shoulder the following morning.

"Wake up, Adam," he said. "Julian needs your help."

"What's he done now?" I asked, rubbing my eyes with hands still gritty from the night's work.

"Only the usual intemperate talk. But Lampret has got wind of it, and Julian has been called to the Major's headquarters for what Lampret calls 'a discussion.'"

"Surely Julian can handle a *discussion* all by himself? I would like to sleep an hour longer, and then go down to the river to bathe, if it's all the same."

"Bathe later! I'm not asking you to go with Julian and hold his hand. I want you to conceal yourself outside Lampret's tent and listen to their conversation. Take notes, if necessary, or just apply your memory. Then come and tell me what transpired."

"Can't you just ask Julian about it, after the thing's done?"

"Major Lampret is a Dominion officer. He has the power to assign Julian to some other company, or even send him off to the front, at any time he chooses. If Lampret is angry enough he might not give Julian time to pack— we might not see Julian again, in the worst case, or discover where he's been sent."

That made sense, and was alarming. I said (as a last wistful defense), "Can't you listen in on their conversation as well as I can?"

"A muddy young private who's been on work detail all night might be excused for dozing off among the ropes and barrels outside Lampret's tent. I have no such excuse, and my age makes me conspicuous. Go on, Adam: there's no time to lose!"

So I roused myself, and drank a little tepid water from a canteen to bring myself fully awake. Then I walked over to Major Lampret's headquarters, which was just a big square tent pitched next to the Quartermaster's warren of fresh supplies. It was this surplus of barrels, boxes, ropes, and loose equipment that provided my cover, as Sam had suggested. Three convoys had unloaded just yesterday, and our Quartermaster was overworked trying to distribute, store, and apportion the bounty. As a result I was able to saunter into a labyrinth of stacked goods and negotiate my way to the layer of provisions which happened to abut Major Lampret's tent. By some quiet and artful shifting I created a blind, and I curled up in it just adjacent to Lampret's canvas.

Sam had not told me when the meeting between Julian and Lampret was set to take place, however, and as I waited I was tempted again by sleep, for the day was warm, and so was my uniform, and a barrel of salt pork nearby had drawn a crowd of flies whose droning became a kind of lullaby, and the resinous boxboards sweating in the sunlight gave off a dolorous perfume. My chin dipped from time to time; and I was afraid I would be found here, hours later, dreaming contentedly, only to discover on waking that Julian had been shipped off to Schefferville or points north. I used this unpleasant prospect to torture myself into alertness; nevertheless I was relieved when I caught sight of Julian approaching across the parade ground, his head erect and his uniform clean and square.

"Reporting as ordered," Julian said when he arrived, and although I could no longer see him his voice was as crisply audible as if he had spoken into my ear.

"Julian Commongold," said Major Lampret said. "Private Commongold—or should I call you *Pastor* Commongold?"

"Sir?" Julian asked.

"I understand you've been lecturing the troops on religious subjects."

Since I was unable to see either party to this conversation I mean to transcribe it as if it were dialogue in a Play: that is, without benefit of observation, for that is how I experienced it, thus:

JULIAN: "I'm not sure I know what you mean, sir."

LAMPRET: "Let's be straightforward with one another. I've had my eye on you for a while now. You're not like the other men, are you?"

JULIAN (hesitating): "No two of us are alike, as far as I can see."

LAMPRET: "You're literate, for one thing, and obviously well-read. You have opinions on current events. And I've been a few places, Private Commongold, and I know a Manhattan accent when I hear one."

JULIAN: "Is that so uncommon?"

LAMPRET: "Quite the opposite. One of your type turns up in every regiment sooner or later—if not a Manhattan cynic, then a barracks lawyer from Boston or a would-be Senator with a rural address. I'm just trying to sort out which kind of problem you are. Raised in New York, and you had a comfortable life there, by the look and bearing of you . . . Who was your father, Julian Commongold? Some up-and-coming rag merchant? A mechanic with enough money to buy the illusion of prosperity and a storefront education for his son? Toadying before his betters by day and cursing them at night in the privacy of his kitchen? Is that why you decided to leave your family and join the Army? Or did you just get drunk and end up on the wrong train, like a lost schoolboy?"

JULIAN (coolly): "The Major is very perceptive."

LAMPRET: "Or if not that, something similar . . . I suppose you were the sort of boy who always had his way on the playground? A few impressive words and everyone wants to be your friend?"

JULIAN: "No, sir—not everyone."

LAMPRET: "No—there's always the inconvenient few who see through the charade."

JULIAN: "The Major is surprisingly well-informed about life in New York City. I was under the impression that he had spent most of his time in Colorado Springs."

That was a daring and dangerous thing for Julian to say. The Dominion Academy in Colorado Springs had produced some fine Strategists and Tacticians; it had also produced, and in greater abundance, a legion of spies and informers. According to Sam the Dominion Military College was once an authentic Military Academy, back when the Union still operated an Air Force— that is, a battalion of Airplanes, and Air-Men to fly them.* But that institution declined with the End of Oil, although strategic stockpiles, it's said, kept the Air Force flying a few years into the False Tribulation. After that the Air Force Academy came increasingly under the sway of the Dominionist center of power at Colorado Springs—became, ultimately, a sort of institutional liaison between the Dominion and the Generals.

Dominion men are full officers, and entitled to issue orders. But their real power is disciplinary. Unlike other COs, a Dominion Officer can bring up a man on charges of Impiety or Sedition. A soldier convicted of those crimes might face anything from Dismissal with Prejudice to ten years in a stockade.

It was a power seldom exercised, for the relationship between the Army and the Dominion had always been a delicate one. Dominion Officers were generally not well-liked, and were often regarded as priggish and potentially dangerous interlopers. A good Dominion Officer, from the point of view of the men of the line, was one who would do his share of the work, who would foster piety by example rather than punishing its absence, and whose Sunday sermons were brief and to the point. Major Lampret was well-enough liked by the men, for he seldom threatened them. But he was aloof in their company, and watched them carefully from a distance. There was about Major Lampret something of the aspect of a well-fed Colorado Mountain Lion: lethargic, but muscular, and ready to pounce the moment his appetite revived.

Had Julian whetted Major Lampret's appetite for apostates and contrarians? That was the question I asked myself as I listened from my nest of ropes and boxes.

LAMPRET: "You might want to consider your tone of voice, Private Commongold. May I offer you a lesson in Civics? There are three centers of power in the modern Union, and *only* three. One is the Executive Branch, with its supporting host of Owners and Senators. One is the Military. And the last is the Dominion of Jesus Christ on Earth. They're like the tripod feet

* This is the sort of thing I would once have dismissed as another of Julian's historical fantasies, except that the *Dominion History of the Union* made passing reference to it. War in the Air!—another of the unimaginable pastimes of the Secular Ancients.

of a stool: each supports the other, and they work best when they're equal in reach. But you're not a propertied person, Mr. Commongold, as far as I know; and you're certainly not a Clergyman; and the Army in its wisdom has put you in the lowest possible rank. Your position doesn't entitle you to an opinion, much less the loose expression of it."

JULIAN: "There is proverb, sir, that opinions are like—like—"

LAMPRET: "Say noses."

JULIAN: "*Noses,* in the sense that everyone has one."

LAMPRET: "Yes, and like *noses,* some opinions are less noble than others, and some are thrust in where they don't belong. You may have all the opinions you want, Mr. Commongold, but you may not share them if they undermine the piety or preparedness of American troops."

JULIAN: "I have no love for the Dutch, sir, or any intention of undermining American soldiers."

LAMPRET: "That's a guarded denial! Do you think I'm a bully, Private Commongold, looking for an excuse to exercise my authority? On the contrary. I'm a realist. By and large, the men under my command are untutored and ignorant. I understand that and I accept it. For these men religion is little more than their mothers' half-forgotten admonitions and the promise of a better world to come. But that's what serves them, and I expect that's how the Lord intended it. I don't want my men to go into battle harboring doubts about their personal immortality—it makes them poorer soldiers."

JULIAN: "Not in my experience. I fought beside those men, and they gave exemplary service. The Major may not have noticed, since he wasn't there."

That was a gauntlet thrown at Lampret's feet, and my concern for Julian escalated to real fear. It was one thing to argue with the Major, it was another thing to bait him. Dominion Officers were traditionally excused from combat. They carried pistols, not rifles, and they were more useful behind the lines, where they ministered to the spiritual needs of the troops. The commonest slur made against Dominion men was that they were cowards, hiding behind their angel's-wing badges and their big felt hats. I could not, of course, *see* the Major's reaction to Julian's statement; but a kind of steely silence radiated from the tent like the heat from a smoldering coal-pile.

Then there was a sound of rustling paper. Major Lampret spoke next, evidently quoting from a document.

LAMPRET: "'On consecutive Sundays Private Commongold was observed speaking to soldiers on the parade ground behind the Meeting Tent. On these occasions he talked without restraint or decency about the Holy Bible and other matters that fall within the purview of the Dominion.' Is that correct?"

JULIAN (less audibly, no doubt surprised by the written evidence): "In so far as it goes, I suppose it is; but—"

LAMPRET: "Did you, for instance, suggest to these men that there's no evidence of Divine Creation, and that Eden is a mythical place?"

JULIAN (after a lengthy pause): "Perhaps I compared the Biblical account of Genesis to other mythologies—"

LAMPRET: "To other *mythologies*—suggesting that it *is* one."

JULIAN: "Sir, if my remarks are to be taken out of context—"

LAMPRET (reading again): "'Private Commongold went on to assert that the story of the expulsion of the first man and woman from Eden might be understood in unorthodox ways. He claimed that, as it seemed to him, the chief virtue of Eden was the relative absence from it of God, Who created the First Couple in His image and then left them undisturbed in their innocent revels. Private Commongold also suggested that the Tree of Knowledge and its forbidden fruit was a hoax worked up by the Serpent, who wanted the Garden all to himself; and that Adam and Eve had probably been expelled by trickery when God wasn't looking, since God, the Private said, was an incorrigibly inattentive Deity, judging by the sins and enormities He habitually leaves unpunished.'"

JULIAN (in an even quieter voice, since he must have realized by now that Lampret had a spy among the troops, and that he was at risk of more than an upbraiding): "It was only a sort of joke, Major. Really nothing but a pleasing paradox."

LAMPRET: "Pleasing to whom, though?" (clearing his throat): "'Private Commongold further hinted that the Dominion, though it claimed to speak with the authority of Holy Writ, was more akin to the voice of that Serpent, sowing fear and shame where there was none before, and no pressing need for it.' *Did you in fact say this?*"

JULIAN: "I suppose I must have . . . or words that might be mistaken for it."

LAMPRET: "The report is lengthy and detailed. It cites apostasies too grotesque and numerous to mention, capped with your enthusiastic endorsement of the ancient and discredited creed of Biological Evolution. Need I go on?"

JULIAN: "Not on my account."

LAMPRET: "Is there any doubt in your mind that these remarks constitute a breach not just of decency but of explicit regulations for the conduct of enlisted men?"

JULIAN: "No doubt whatsoever."

LAMPRET: "Do you understand that one of the fundamental services the Dominion of Jesus Christ performs is to prevent harmful or mistaken religious ideas from circulating among the gullible classes?"

JULIAN: "I do understand."

LAMPRET (lightening his tone abruptly): "I'm not in the business of harassing infantrymen without cause. I've spoken to your commanding officers, and they all say you're a competent soldier, and useful in battle, in so far as you've been tested. Some even think you might have command potential, when your greenness and arrogance begin to rub off. And the rank and file seem to approve of you—if they scorned your apostasies we wouldn't need to have this discussion, would we?"

JULIAN: "I don't suppose so."

LAMPRET: "Then let's get to the meat of the matter. These atheistic lectures must stop. Is that understood?"

JULIAN: "Sir, yes, sir."

LAMPRET: "They must stop *completely*, along with any denigrating mention of the Dominion of Jesus Christ on Earth, or any other duly constituted arm of the government. Do you understand?"

JULIAN (a whisper): "Yes."

LAMPRET: "I hope you're sincere about that—I won't be so generous in the case of a second offense. Remember, Private Commongold, it's not *your* soul I'm worried about. I can't control your thoughts—those are between you and your maker. You can absorb heresies until they bleed out your pores, for all I have to do with it. But I can, and will, stand between your vulgar jokes and the integrity of the Army of the Laurentians. Is that clear? Innocent men must not be sent into battle with their immortal souls at risk, just because Julian Commongold is bound and determined to go to Hell."

JULIAN: "I understand, sir. And I expect I'll see you there." (a pause): "In battle, I mean, of course."

I have been asked many times whether Julian when I first knew him was an Atheist or an Agnostic.

I'm not a Philosopher, much less a Theologian, and I don't understand the distinction between those two species of nonbelievers. In so far as I have an image in my mind, I picture the *Agnostic* as a modest man, politely refusing to kneel before any Gods or Icons in which he does not place his complete confidence; while the *Atheist*, although operating from the same principles, brings a hammer to the event.

Readers may draw their own conclusions about Julian's later career and the convictions he carried into it. As for his Biblical heresies, these must have seemed novel and alarming to Major Lampret; but I had heard them all before—I was an old customer, and jaded. I thought his stories were, in a way, testimony to the close attention with which Julian had read the Bible, even if his interpretations of it were too imaginative by half. I'm an indifferent student of Scripture, myself, and I prefer the sensible parts of that Book, such as the Sermon on the Mount, while I leave the more perplexing passages—the ones that mention seven-headed dragons, the Whore of Babylon, or any of that crew—to scholars, who relish such conundrums. But Julian read the Bible as if it were a work of contemporary fiction, open to criticism or even revision. Once, when I queried him about the purpose of his unusual reinterpretations, he said to me,

"I want a *better* Bible, Adam. I want a Bible in which the Fruit of Knowledge contains the Seeds of Wisdom, and makes life more pleasurable for mankind, not worse. I want a Bible in which Isaac leaps up from the sacrificial stone and chokes the life out of Abraham, to punish him for the abject and bloody sin of Obedience. I want a Bible in which Lazarus is dead and stubborn about it, rather than standing to attention at the beck and call of every passing Messiah."

That was appalling enough that I hastily dropped the subject; but it hinted at some of the motives behind Julian's early apostasies.

I made my way out of the maze of boxed and barreled supplies shortly after Julian left Major Lampret's tent. Since Julian hadn't been sent off to Schefferville, I felt no pressing need to add my penny's-worth to the dialogue Sam and Julian must already be having. But I wanted Sam to know I had done what he asked of me, so I slow-walked back to our encampment, and came in on the end of an argument.

Their raised voices stopped me from interrupting. I gathered Sam had begun to lecture Julian on the importance of not attracting undue attention, or creating any controversy that might snag the attention of the Executive Branch. "We're a fair distance from the Presidential Palace," Julian retorted as I entered the tent.

"Not as far as you think," Sam said angrily. "And the very *last* thing you need is to become prominent in the eyes of the Dominion. Major Lampret is no Deklan Comstock, but he could have you sent to the trenches just by snapping his fingers—especially now that General Galligasken is fighting battles up the Saguenay. You don't act as if you realize that."

"But I do realize it!" said Julian, returning Sam's anger ounce-for-ounce. "I'm bitterly aware of it! I just stood in the presence of a man not fit to polish my boots, and listened without objection to his insinuations and his sneers! I looked him in the eye, Sam, and as he barked and whined I thought how little he suspected what *I* could do to *him*, and how quickly he would genuflect if *that* truth came out! I wasn't raised to grovel before an Army parson! And yet I did it—I swallowed my pride, and I did it—but that's not enough for you!"

"You might have swallowed your pride a little sooner, and thought twice about holding classes in sedition for the enlisted men! In fact I recall forbidding you to do any such thing."

"Forbidding me!"

Julian stood up so stiff-spined he seemed an inch taller than he really was.

"I was entrusted by your father with the duty of protecting you," Sam said.

"Do it, then! Do as you were told, and protect me! But don't *mother* me, or *censor* me, or question my judgment! That was never your province! Do what you were asked to do, and do it like any other sensible servant!"

The words struck Sam as if they had real weight and momentum. His face contorted, then stiffened into a soldierly mask. He seemed full of words, unspoken or unspeakable; but what he said, in the end, was, "All right, Julian—as you prefer."

It was a servile response, and Julian was quite undone by it. All the rage went out of him in a rush. "Sam, I'm sorry! I was just—well, the words came without thinking. You know I don't think of you as a servant!"

"I wouldn't have said so, until now."

"Then forgive me! It isn't you I'm unhappy with—never you!"

"Of course I forgive you," said Sam.

Julian seemed ashamed of himself, and he hurried away without acknowledging me.

Sam was a silent a long while, and I began to wonder if I had become altogether invisible; but just as I was about to clear my throat to signal my presence he looked at me and shook his head. "He's a Comstock, Adam. A Comstock heart and soul, for better or for worse. I let myself forget that. Don't make the same mistake."

"I won't," I said—but only to reassure him.

Major Lampret made a display of singling out Julian at the next Sunday meeting, in a sermon on Unhelpful Thinking. He denounced Julian's apostasies, and mocked them, and ridiculed the idea of an Army private giving out opinions on theological matters. Then he told us weekend leave was canceled, not just for Julian but for all the men of our company, to punish Julian for treading on the angels' coat-tails and us for being foolish enough to listen to him. It was tactic meant to make Julian unpopular among his peers, and undo some of the goodwill the other soldiers felt toward him. And the ploy was successful, at least for a time. Disparaging remarks were made in Julian's presence by men cruelly deprived of the opportunity to squander their pay in Montreal whorehouses; and Julian was cut by these barbed comments, though he was careful to say nothing in return.

But that wasn't the end of the matter. Just about then—and for weeks thereafter, in a steady crescendo—a certain libel about Major Lampret began to circulate and gain currency: that the Major was a Colorado Springs cloud salesman who was careful never to get in the line of fire, because of all the immortal souls entrusted to his care his own took first place, and was too precious to be exposed to flying lead—in other words, that he was a coward who reveled in his noncombatant status.

There was no discernible source for this talk; it passed like a fog from one group of soldiers to another, never adhering to anyone in particular; but I noticed Julian always smiled when he heard it.

I was as upset as anyone else over missing my first opportunity to return to Montreal, for I wanted to seek out Calyxa and make myself better known to her. But I consoled myself with the hope that I might get another chance, and I used the empty time to finish my report about the Battle of Mascouche, and deliver it to Mr. Theodore Dornwood, the journalist.

Dornwood had forgotten his agreement to read my work, and I had to remind him of it; but at last he relented and took the papers from me. While he read them I admired his typewriter once more. I took my time looking over the mechanical device, and even fingered the keys, in a gingerly manner, and watched the greased levers rise and fall, and felt the intoxicating power to make Letters—solid *booklike* letters, not pencil scratches—appear on a blank white page. I was determined to get one of these machines for myself. No doubt they were expensive. But I would save my pay, and eventually I would buy a typewriter, even if I had to go all the way to Manhattan to acquire one. This I solemnly resolved.

"Not actually bad," Dornwood said, in a thoughtful tone, when he had finished reading my work.

It was as much praise as I had expected from him—more, in fact. "It's all right, then?"

"Oh, yes."

"Would you say you liked it?"

"I'd go that far."

"You might even call it good?"

"I suppose so—in its way, quite good, actually."

I savored that word, *good*, coming as it did from a genuine New York City newspaper correspondent, even at the expense of a little prodding. And not just good, but *quite* good. I was beside myself with pride.

"Not that you haven't got a thing or two to learn," Dornwood added, deflating me.

"How's that?" I asked. "I tried to write it as truthfully as possible. I didn't include elephants, or anything of that nature."

"Your restraint is admirable—perhaps even excessive." Dornwood paused to gather his thoughts, which could not have been a trivial task, given how much liquor he had consumed (judging by the empty flasks scattered about the place) and how the aroma of hemp smoke still suffused the air. "As much as I like what you've written—it's clear, grammatical, and orderly—this piece would have to be 'punched up' if it were submitted for newspaper publication."

"How so?"

"Well, for instance, here. You say, 'Private Commongold walked ahead of me, very steadily, toward the fighting.' "

"That's how it happened. I was careful about the phrase."

"Too careful. A reader doesn't want to hear about someone walking steadily. It's not dramatic. You might say, instead, 'Private Commongold ignored the shot and shell exploding all around him to such devastating effect, and strode with fierce determination straight into the beating heart of the battle.' You see how that livens it up?"

"I guess it does, though at the expense of a degree of accuracy."

"Accuracy and drama are the Scylla and Charybdis of journalism, Adam.* Steer between them, is my advice, but list toward drama, if you want a successful career. In fact, 'Private Commongold' is a little tepid, regarding rank, though the name itself is good—so let's promote him. Captain Commongold! Doesn't that have a ring to it?"

"I suppose so."

"Leave these papers with me," Dornwood said, casting a glance at his typewriter, which had been silent lately, perhaps due to his consumption of fiery spirits. "I'll give the subject further thought, and render you more useful advice next week. In the meantime, Adam, in the event of further military action, please repeat the exercise: write it up, as dramatically as the facts allow, and bring it to me. If you do that, I may be willing to show you how to work that typewriter you love to stare at, since you're an aspiring writer of some talent. How does that sound?"

"Excellent, Mr. Dornwood," I said, all unsuspecting.

---

* At the time I took "Scylla and Charybdis" to be New York City editors with whom Dornwood had dealt, or perhaps a publishing firm. In fact they were two great Nautical Rocks, in Greek mythology, which had the unusual ability to move about under their own steam, and had formed the bad habit of crushing sailors.

6

The fighting continued up the Saguenay, and things were mainly quiet around Montreal. There was occasional skirmishing, of course, for Mitteleuropan forces remained scattered through the Laurentians, and they would sally forth now and then for a little fun and distraction. I duly wrote up these exchanges for Theodore Dornwood, in return for literary advice; but there was very little to it. During this time Julian distinguished himself by holding a vital artillery position when it came under heavy fire from the Dutch; and his reputation among the men steadily improved—while Major Lampret's continued to decline.

But what mattered most to me that summer took place in the City of Montreal, during the weekends on which, after Lampret lifted the ban, we were offered leave.

"**So,**" Lymon Pugh said, his sleeves rolled up to expose his hideously scarred and muscular forearms, which often frightened strangers, and of which he was very proud, "only the two of us left."

We were in Montreal, and we had just entered a tavern on Guy Street. Lymon was there to get drunk; but it was the sort of establishment that served food as well as liquor, and I meant to smother my sorrows in a beef-steak, while Lymon drowned his in a bucket of beer. (As for drink, I took a dipperful of plain water from the ceramic jug by the door as we entered. The water was brackish and tasted of tobacco—perhaps one of the previous customers had mistaken the jug for a spittoon.)

"Only the two of us left," Lymon repeated—by which he meant that Sam and Julian had gone off to separate entertainments this Friday night.

Summer was a fearfully hot and humid time around the City of Montreal. The horseflies, which the locals called Black Flies, had lately come into season, and they patrolled the streets in brigade strength, alert for human flesh. The day had been overcast, and the air was thick as butter, and although we were fresh from camp our shirts were already sodden. We wore what scraps of civilian clothing we still possessed or had recently purchased, so that we would not be mistaken for men on active duty, and would blend in more closely with the local population.

But as I had learned on previous expeditions into the city, a soldier is never quite at home in Montreal. The local citizens did not hate us exactly—at one time they had been under garrison by the Dutch, and the memory of that unhappy time persisted, and the Army of the Laurentians was a more comfortable master than Mitteleuropa had been, taken all in all. But we *were* their masters, at least nominally, for Montreal was under military law, and many of its citizens chafed at the constraints imposed upon them. The Catholic clergy were especially volatile, still smarting over the Dominion's interference in their affairs; and local men of Cree descent had been known to challenge soldiers on the street, out of some grievance never fully explained to me.

But it was not difficult to avoid the worst of such unpleasantness, and the obverse side of that coin was the generous hospitality of the less political residents of Montreal, including restaurant-owners and barkeepers. We had been given a good table in this tavern, which was called the Thirsty Boot, and we ordered what we wanted from a pleasant woman in an apron, and we were otherwise left to ourselves.

"I swear I don't know what those two do with their time," Lymon Pugh was saying. "For instance, what on Earth does Sam want with all those damned Amish?"

"Amish?"

"You know—those black-hatted and bearded men he consorts with whenever we come into the city."

Lymon was laboring under a misapprehension. Judaism was legal in Montreal, and the city had a substantial community of very devout Jews, with whom Sam had begun taking religious services. It was true that the men in that part of town often sported beards, and wore wide black hats, or small ones that sat on their scalps as if glued there. But they weren't Amish. "I think the Amish live in Pennsylvania, or Ohio, or somewhere like that," I said.

"You mean to say those men aren't Amish? They fit every description I ever heard."

"I think they're Jews."

"Oh! Then is Sam a Jew of some kind? He don't resemble them in his dress."

Sam had not made any public announcement about his unusual religion (though neither had he gone to any lengths to disguise his association with the Jews of Montreal), and I could not bring myself to indict him quite so frankly. "Perhaps he's fond of their cuisine. The Jews have their own special menu of foods, just as Chinamen do."

"The sight of all those beards might inhibit my appetite, if it was me," said Lymon, who was religious (figuratively) about shaving his chin, "whatever they eat for dinner. But to each his own."

"Julian wears a beard," I pointed out.

"What, that fringe of his? Yellow as a female's wig, and just about as ridiculous. Speaking of Julian Commongold, I'm confused about *his* habits, too. Once again he's gone to that *coffee-shop*, or whatever they call it, down in the narrow streets by the riverside. Did you get a look at the other customers there, Adam? Frail, loose-limbed types—I don't know what he sees in them.

The place is called Dorothy's, and I'm sure I don't know who Dorothy is—perhaps the only *woman* ever to visit the establishment."

"Philosophers," I said.

"What?"

"Julian has made friends among the city's Philosophers, just as Sam has made friends among the Jews."

"Those are Philosophers? I suppose that means Philosophers also have their own particular foods, and that Julian is partial to Philosophical dinners?"

"Yes, in a sense, though it's more likely the *conversation* than the *food* that attracts him. Philosophers discuss Time, and Space, and the Purpose of Humanity, and such topics as that, in which Julian is deeply interested."

"They have enough to say about those subjects to carry over more than a few minutes? I doubt I could talk about Space any longer than a second or two before I ran out of thoughts altogether. In any case, I overheard two of those Philosophers who followed Julian into the coffee-shop, and their discussion was all about some musical review that opened here in town."

"I don't know all the details," I confessed, "but Julian says there are Aesthetes among the Philosophers, who are more concerned with Art than with human destiny."

"They seemed more concerned with the fellow who played the romantic lead in the piece."

"I imagine that's a legitimate subject of debate among Aesthetes."

"Well, it's all beyond me," said Lymon Pugh, and he called for another pitcher of beer. "You, too, Adam, if you don't mind me saying so—*you're* a mystery! You come into a city as fine as this one, with all its sinful opportunities, and you wander from church to church like a Godstruck pilgrim, though it's not even Sunday."

This wasn't a topic I cared to discuss. "I was looking for someone," I said. Of course the person I had been looking for since Easter was Calyxa. But I had not been able to find her. When I approached the choirmaster at the Cathedral where I had first seen her, he explained that the Easter chorus had been put together specifically to sing to the troops. The Church's own choristers refused to entertain "occupying forces," as they called us; and the choirmaster had been forced to hire substitute singers at fifty cents an hour plus a free lunch. But the names of these women had not been recorded. That led me to make inquiries at several other grand Churches, of which the city possessed a dizzying number—all without success. "What about you, Lymon? Since you find our pursuits so unrewarding, what are your plans for the weekend?"

"Well, to get drunk, first of all . . ."

"That's a noble ambition—or at least easily achieved."

"But not *stinking* drunk. Not so drunk I can't navigate. Then it's off to the Shade Tree Hotel." The Shade Tree was one of those establishments in which "women sell their virtue for money, and throw in their diseases free of charge," as Major Lampret had put it in one of his sermons. I asked Lymon whether he was not afraid, as Lampret had also put it, that he would come back "absent those three essential possessions of any decent man: his health, his savings, and his hope of salvation."

"The women at the Shade Tree are pretty clean," Lymon said earnestly. "And what I'm *afraid* of is that I'll come back absent what I came to *get*, which is the satisfaction of a man's deepest need, the *unsatisfaction* of which can *also* make him sick, or at least surly."

He clenched his scarred fists as he said this, and I told him he was probably correct in wanting to avoid any condition that left him surly. "But shouldn't you brace yourself up before you begin such an adventure? And I don't mean with liquor. Have something to eat."

"I am a little hungry," he admitted, and I watched with a quiet pride as he puzzled out the items on the menu board. He was surprised that the word "eggs" did not begin with **A**, as it was pronounced—but by this time he had become resigned to the inevitable inconsistencies of the written language, and accepted them without rancor.

Both of us ordered meals, and we enjoyed them as the tavern grew busier around us. Lymon had just made quick work of a plate of boiled eggs and stewed onions when he detected an expression of astonishment on my face and said, "You look like you've been ambushed."

And, in a sense, I had.

She didn't recognize me; but—of course—I recognized her.

She had been sitting just yards away, hidden by the crowd of coarsely-attired men and women who shared her table. It would have been easy to miss her altogether. But right now she stood up, and strode through billowing pipe smoke light and humid air to the tavern's small stage; and I knew her at once—Calyxa!

She wasn't dressed as she had been at the Cathedral. If that Calyxa had seemed unworldly in her white surplice, this Calyxa was entirely earthbound, in a man's black shirt a size too big for her and stiff denim trousers.* The easy confidence of her walk suggested that she was at home in this place, and as she took the stage to genial applause I was sure of it.

"Look at that! That one's a fireplug," Lymon Pugh said. "Do you suppose she means to sing to us?"

---

* At first I had been shocked by the sight of Montreal women wearing trousers rather than skirts—in Williams Ford no respectable female wore trousers past the age of ten—but social customs vary by location, as Julian had taught me, and clothes signify differently in different parts of the world. I had lately begun to take pride in my ability to accept such unusual behavior as female trouser-wearing, and I considered myself a sophisticate, far in advance of my old crowd of Williams Ford lease-boys.

"I hope so," I said, annoyed.

"Her pants are cut too short, though. Pretty enough face, but look at the thick ankles on her."

"I'm sure I don't need to hear your opinion of her ankles! Her ankles are her own business."

"They're right there hanging off the ends of her legs—as much my business as anyone's, I'd say!"

"No one's business, then! Please be quiet."

"What bit you?" Lymon asked; but he subsided, for which I was grateful.

Calyxa did begin to sing, then, in a voice that was pure but also precise and pleasingly workmanlike. She did not adopt trills, tremolos, theatrical asides, illustrative whistles, or any of those musical furbelows so common among contemporary singers. Instead she sang the songs as they had been composed: plainly, that is, deriving all her nuance from the words and melodies, and not their decorations.

Nor was she wildly demonstrative in her singing. She just clasped her hands, cleared her throat, and went at it. This was too subtle for some of the audience, judging by the occasional cries of drunken critics; but I took it as an expression of her natural modesty—a striking contrast to the songs themselves.

She performed five songs before she was finished, most of which had verses that would not have been out of place aboard the Caribou-Horn Train, or wherever less respectable people gather. At first I was dismayed by this. But I was reminded—perhaps for the first time truly convinced—of Julian's doctrine of *cultural relativism*, so-called. For these songs, which had sounded so corrupt in other voices, were purified in hers. I reflected that Calyxa must have been raised among people for whom such songs and sentiments were, in effect, their daily bread, and not counted as obscene or irregular in any way. In other words her innocence was *innate*, and not compromised by the vulgarity of her upbringing—it was a kind of indestructible *primal innocence*, as I came to think of it.

Two of the songs she sang were not in English, which astonished Lymon Pugh. "That's some nerve on her part, to sing a song in Dutch!"

"Not Dutch, Lymon, but French. The language was spoken here for centuries, and still is, in places."

Apparently Lymon had believed there were only two kinds of human speech, American and Foreign, and he was dismayed by the news that languages were prolific, often coming packaged one per country. "Just when I learn to write a language they begin to multiply like rabbits! I tell you, Adam, there's a catch to everything. The world is as meanly rigged as that Lucky Mug of Private Langers."

"English will suit in most circumstances, unless you travel abroad."

"I've traveled far enough, I thank you—this is as foreign a country as I care to see, even if it is America."

I begged him once more to be quiet, as Calyxa finished her singing. She ignored the applause, stepped down from the stage with an air of calm satisfaction, and headed back to her table. I was consumed by the need to attract her attention, and I did this by standing up abruptly as she passed, nearly knocking my dinner plate onto the floor, and exclaiming in a choked voice, "Calyxa!"

I may have spoken too loudly; for she flinched, and there was a lull in the conversation in the tavern, as if some of the patrons expected violence to follow.

"Do I know you?" she asked, when she had recovered her composure.

"We met at Easter. I was in the Cathedral where you performed, before Dutch artillery closed it up. Don't you remember? I hurt my head!"

"Oh," she said, smiling faintly, and by this reaction causing the other customers to relax their vigilance, "the soldier with the small injury. Did you find your regiment?"

"Yes, I did—thank you very much."

"You're welcome," she said, and walked on.

Naturally I had not expected her to prolong the conversation, or to ignore her friends on my behalf. Nevertheless this response was a disappointment.

"She blew you off pretty quick," Lymon Pugh said, laughing to himself. "You're wasting your time here, Adam. That type of woman don't make herself available on a moment's notice. Come to the Shade Tree, and your luck will change."

"I won't." Not when my quarry was so close.

"Well, suit yourself. I have a schedule to keep."

Lymon Pugh stood up, not as steadily as he might have, and after some exploration found the door of the tavern, and left.

I felt conspicuous sitting alone at a table when everyone else in the tavern seemed to have arrived with a party of friends; but I suppressed my uneasiness, and ordered an entire second meal, which I did not plan to eat, simply to keep the waitress from frowning at me.

Calyxa continued to sit with her companions. Other singers or musicians took the stage from time to time, apparently by arrangement with the management. None was as talented as Calyxa, and the vulgarity of their singing was not adulterated with any kind of Innocence, Primal or otherwise. She herself talked amiably, as it seemed to me, with her friends, who were a mixed group of men and women, all as young as Calyxa herself—my age, that is, or only slightly older. The females among them shared Calyxa's simple taste in clothing, along with a certain inattention to the finer points of hairdressing and such feminine arts. The men of the group took this charming roughness to another level entirely, seeming to pride themselves on their tattered pants and hempen shirts. Several of them wore woolen caps, despite the heat of the evening, as if they needed something available to tug or pull low at dramatic moments in the conversation. Their gestures were dramatic, their voices were curt and insistent, and their opinions, though I could make out only a few words, were vehement and complex, almost to the point of Philosophy.

It occurred to me in a dismaying moment that Calyxa might have a male friend or even a husband among the crowd. Tragically, I knew so little about her! I set about studying her, in the hope that I could glean a few facts by observation.

I noticed that she glanced occasionally at the tavern's door, and that whenever she did this an expression of anxiety darkened her features. But that was all that happened for an hour or so, and I could make no sense of it, and I had begun to despair of ever passing another word with her, when a series of unexpected events brought us together in a surprising way.

The waitress who served my table appeared to be on friendly terms with Calyxa. They put their heads together now and then to exchange words. After one of these exchanges an expression of profound concern once more overcame Calyxa, and she nodded solemnly at whatever news the waitress had delivered.

And dire news it must have been; for Calyxa, although she remained at the table, dropped out of the conversation swirling around her, and seemed lost in the most sobering kind of thoughts. Several times she called the waitress back, and they conferred again; and on one of these occasions they both looked at me in a pointed fashion. But I couldn't deduce the significance of any of these maneuvers.

That they had *some* significance I did not doubt, for before long the same waitress returned to my table, and she pulled out the chair Lymon Pugh had left vacant, and sat in it.

I was surprised by this bold move on her part. Fortunately the waitress took the commanding role in the talk that followed. "You're a soldier," she said, in a tone that was brisk but not unfriendly.

I agreed that I was.

"And you have some interest in Calyxa Blake?"

Finally I had learned her surname!—admittedly, at second hand. I wondered if Calyxa Blake had mistaken my intentions, and had communicated her apprehension to the waitress. "Only the most benevolent interest," I said sincerely. "I was impressed with her singing, when she sang at one of the enormous churches of this city, last Easter. After that I spoke to her, but only briefly. I was injured at the time. But she was kind to me. I want to thank her for that—well, I *have* thanked her for it, in fact—and as much as I would like to speak further with, uh, Miss Blake," hoping I was right about the *Miss*, "I would never force my attention on her. If I upset her with my clumsy greeting, please tell her I meant nothing by it, except to mark my pleasurable surprise at recognizing her."

That was a pretty speech, though extemporaneous, and I was proud of it.

The waitress sat and examined me with her eyes, displaying no reaction. Then she asked for the second time, "You're a soldier?"

"Yes, a soldier. I was drafted away from my home, which is in Athabaska—"

"Does that mean you carry a pistol? They say all you soldiers do."

I was off-duty, and not in uniform, but it was standard practice for an American soldier in these parts to keep his pistol with him at all times. My pistol was strapped under the waist of my shirt, where it wasn't easily visible, because I didn't want to alarm anyone, or provoke any unnecessary confrontation; but it was within easy reach. I nodded. "Does that frighten her?"

"No."

"Does it frighten you, then?"

She almost smiled. "A pistol in hands such as yours doesn't frighten me, no. What did you say your name was?"

"Adam Hazzard."

"Stay here, Adam Hazzard."

I nodded in mute if bewildered consent. After servicing the handful of customers who had begun to shout in an aggrieved manner for her attention, the friendly waitress returned to Calyxa's table, and there was more fervid whispering between the two of them, and I tried not to blush at the unusual attention they paid me.

Not fifteen minutes passed, during which Calyxa stared at the door as if she expected the devil himself to burst in, before the waitress came to my table and whispered, "She'll meet you upstairs, Adam Hazzard."

I was afraid that my interest in Calyxa had been too broadly interpreted, and that an assignation had been set up—but of course Calyxa was not the type of female who would "make herself available at a moment's notice." So I was confused by the suggested arrangement; but the waitress evinced some urgency about the matter, and the grave expression on Calyxa's face seemed to confirm the need for haste; and I nodded and said, "Whereabouts, upstairs?"

"Second landing. Third door to the right. Don't run right up there, though. Wait a moment or two after I leave. Don't be conspicuous about it."

I agreed to all these conditions. The next few minutes passed slowly; then I stood up, affecting a nonchalance that might have been a shade too theatrical, judging by the way Calyxa rolled her eyes from her place at the adjoining table. But that couldn't be helped. Shortly thereafter I was up the dimly-lit stairs, and I found the appointed room and let myself inside.

It was a small room, containing only a chair, a few boxes loosely stuffed with straw packing, a barrel marked SALT FISH (empty), and a rusty hurricane lamp, which I lit up. The room smelled of moist, mildewed wood. A single grimy window overlooked the crowded stalls and torch-lit shops of Guy Street. From the window I could see a little of the night sky, which was very dark and shot through with distant flashes of lightning; the wind had a gustiness that flapped all the Guy Street awnings, and I guessed a storm was imminent. Certainly the air in the city was humid enough for it—and sweleringly hot, especially in this upstairs chamber. I perched on one of the boxes, thinking Calyxa might prefer the chair, and waited for her to arrive, trying not to perspire.

She opened the door not ten minutes later. The reader may imagine the excitement and the curiosity her visit aroused in me. Her hair was a skein of ebony knitwork in the light from the hall. She put her hands on her hips and regarded me.

"Evangelica thinks you're harmless," she said. "*Are* you harmless?"

I guessed "Evangelica" was the name of the waitress. "Well, I'm not dangerous, if that's what you mean."

"Adam Hazzard—that's your name?"

I nodded. "And you're Calyxa Blake."

"Adam Hazzard, I don't know who you are—you're only a loose soldier to me—but I need a favor, and Evangelica thinks you might be willing to help, without wanting too much in return."

"Of course I'll help, whatever your situation, and without demanding anything at all in return."

"Western boy. Just as Evangelica said. How old are you?"

"Nineteen," I said, exaggerating by less than a month.

"Do you know how to use the pistol you carry around with you?"

"As a soldier I'm supposed to, and I do."

"Have you ever used it? To shoot at someone, I mean?"

"I've shot at many people, Miss Blake, all of them Dutchmen, with my Pittsburgh rifle; and hit some of them, I don't doubt. As for my pistol, it's only shot targets to date, but I understand the principle and I'm not a stranger to the practice. Do you mean for me to shoot someone? That's a tall order . . . not that I'm backing down . . . but an explanation would be welcome."

"You can have one, if there's time." She glanced around the narrow room.

"Take the chair," I suggested, "if you want to sit."

"I do want to sit, but I want to look out the window while I do it." She dragged the chair in that direction. She didn't need help—Calyxa was a sturdy girl, evidently accustomed to performing such tasks on her own hook. She sat with her head turned, so that she could watch the window while we talked, putting her neck in profile. "This is awkward," she said.

"You can sit on a box if you'd prefer it."

"I mean the conversation."

"Well, that's because we hardly know each other . . . though I've thought of you often since Easter."

"Have you? Why me?"

"What do you mean?"

"Of all the women in the choir, what set you onto me? Most of the soldiers I've met are more interested in whores than choristers."

"To be honest, I can't say. You seemed—exceptional." I could hardly speak for blushing.

"How childish. But never mind." She scanned the street again. "I don't see them . . . though in this murkiness it's hard to tell. . . ."

"Who are you expecting?"

"Some men who mean to harm me."

"In that case I guarantee you every protection in my power! Who are these villains?"

"My brothers," she said.

We talked for most of an hour more, alone in that airless chamber. What she told me—with a frankness I found admirable, if surprising—was that her parents had died when she was just three years old, and that she had been raised by her brothers, Job and Utty (Uther) Blake, who were bush runners.*

Calyxa was not of much use to them, as a female, and her brothers had never been patient or kind toward her. Her only relief from their autocracy was a four-year period when Job and Utty were sent to prison, and she was installed in a charitable Church School in Quebec City, where she learned to read and write. The school was not a paradise, but she had thrived on three regular meals a day and had enjoyed at least some access to the world of learning. Her innate curiosity and liveliness had been engaged, and she had fought bitterly against her return to the custody of her paroled siblings.

But the law was stern, and she was eventually given back to them. To her horror, they no longer considered her a useless encumbrance, but had worked out a scheme by which she could be sold to a Montreal brothel, or, failing that, bartered to some other guerilla band in exchange for considerations.

That did not suit her plans, and she resolved to escape before the transaction could be consummated. Fortunately her brothers still thought of her as a child, at least in her mental and spiritual faculties, and assumed they could bully her into submission. They were wrong. Calyxa had grown up considerably during the time they languished in prison. She was not just clever enough to outwit them, she was wise enough to disguise herself as meek, and lull her captors into equanimity, until an opportunity for escape presented itself. When Job and Utty left her alone in the wilderness cabin from which they ran their autumn trap lines—trusting in the isolation of the place, and a few stern threats, to keep her docile in their absence—she recognized an opportunity and took it.

---

* "Bush runners" are men who operate in the wilds of the Laurentians and up into the rocky wastelands of Labrador, living on the margins of the law. Some of them form guerilla bands, and might align themselves temporarily with the Americans or the Mitteleuropans; but their main business is horse thievery, smuggling, and opportunistic pillage.

She packed up what little food was available, along with a compass she had stolen from Utty, and set out for Montreal. She spoke reluctantly of that grueling, lonely journey, and would only say that she had arrived in the city exhausted and starving. A few nights spent on the streets convinced her she needed to support herself in better style, and that was when she took up singing—at first on sidewalks, for pennies, and then in establishments such as the Thirsty Boot. She had learned singing from the clerics at the residential school, and she had a natural aptitude for the work.

Since then she had got along all right, and had fallen in with better company than Job and Utty Blake. But her escape from her brothers would never be complete as long as they lived, for they were angry at the loss they had suffered. In their eyes she had stolen herself from them; and they meant to have her back, and to punish her for the crime of self-theft.

Calyxa was determined not to let that happen. During the winter months there was little to fear, for the Blake brothers wintered on land held by the Dutch Governor of the Saguenay Region, poaching and drinking and hiring themselves to the Mitteleuropans as spies. But in summer the brothers became more ambitious, and often came into Montreal with furs to trade or money to gamble away. For three years now Calyxa had spent the summer months dreading the chance that her brothers would discover her whereabouts. She relied on friends, who were sympathetic to her cause, to keep their eyes and ears open; and so far, though the brothers had twice come to the city, they hadn't found her, or heard anything about her, and she always had sufficient warning to keep herself out of their view.

Tonight, however, Calyxa had received the worst possible news. Job and Utty were back in town, and they had picked up hints of her presence and were actively hunting her. In fact—so Evangelica had heard from a friend—the Blakes had learned that she frequented the Thirsty Boot, and they were hastening this way even now.

"You ought to go home, then," I said, "and hide. I'll escort you, if that's what you need."

"That would be exactly the wrong thing to do. Job and Utty—especially Job, he's the smart one—probably formed a plan to watch the tavern rather than barge inside to make trouble. They're hunters, Adam Hazzard, and they know how to stalk prey even when the prey has got wind of them. It's true—I hope it's true—they don't know where I live. But if I leave now there's every chance they'll follow me, and break in when there are no witnesses present."

"You live alone, then?"

"I do."

"No male companion right at the moment?"

"No, but what does that matter?"

"Well, it increases the risk. What *will* you do, if you can't go home?"

"All I can do is hide here. Evangelica will warn me if Job and Utty come inside. Even then I should be all right, unless my brothers search the building. That's why I wanted you here with me—specifically, that's why I wanted your *pistol* here with me."

"Are your brothers armed?"

It wasn't legal for citizens to go about armed within city limits, and the majority adhered to the rule. Her brothers weren't among that majority, Calyxa explained. Both were experienced pistol-fighters, and unabashed about advertising the number of men they had killed. That brought home to me the severity of her crisis, and I advised her to check the street once more, to make sure the brothers hadn't crept up on us unannounced.

Enough time passed, however, that we eventually began to let down our guard; and I was admiring her clockspring hair by lamplight, and beginning to feel brave again, when she stood up from her chair at the window and said, "Oh, Hell!"*

"They're coming?"

She nodded. I hurried to the window, and caught a glimpse of two burly men, one in a patched wool coat and one in what looked like a sailor's peajacket, as they strode across the torch-lit street to the entrance of the Thirsty Boot directly below us.

"Put out the light!" Calyxa said. "But before you do, *unlatch the window.*"

"Why, what for?"

"In case we need a quick escape."

"There's nothing outside but the street, and that's two stories down," I said.

"Consider it a last resort," she said.

We huddled in the darkened room, anticipating disaster. The heat was oppressive. I could smell the approaching storm—a heavy, salty odor—and I wasn't very fresh myself, though I had bathed that very morning. Perhaps Calyxa was equally conscious of her own scent—I was aware of it, but it wasn't offensive to me—to me she smelled steamy and utterly distracting—but I won't dwell on the matter.

Her brothers kept themselves downstairs for a great length of time, perhaps drinking and evaluating the tavern. But they were here for a purpose, and it was not to be indefinitely postponed. We heard footsteps on the stairs . . . it was Evangelica, the friendly waitress, come in stealth to warn us.

She knocked very faintly at the door of the room. "*They're coming up!*" she whispered. "Arnaud and the bartender threatened them, but the Blakes showed their pistols and everyone is cowed. They mean to search all the rooms in the building—I have to go back! Be prepared."

* Or an even stronger word, best understood under the generous allowances of Cultural Relativism, and not printable here.

"Is your weapon loaded, Adam Hazzard?" Calyxa asked in a firm voice.

I took it out and made sure it was ready to fire.

"Give it to me, then," she said.

"Give it to you!"

"I don't want to burden you with the work of killing my brothers."

"It's not a burden—I only hope it doesn't become a necessity."

"Not a burden for you, but a positive pleasure for me." (She was pretending to be bloodthirsty in order to spare my feelings, and my heart melted a little at her generosity.) "Give me the gun," she said.

"I won't."

"Well, then, will you shoot them? Shoot them dead? Do you *promise* to shoot them?"

"At the first hint of a threat—"

"The hint has been given! Adam, they're *experienced murderers*! You *must* shoot them, as soon as you see their shadows—and shoot to *kill*, not to *wound*—or we're already lost!"

"They can't be as ferocious as all that."

"Dear God! Give me the gun, I beg you."

"No—if there must be bloodshed, I want it on my conscience, not yours."

"Conscience!" She pronounced the word as if it were a lament. "*A quel genre d'idiot j'ai affaire?** Maybe the window is the better option, if you won't hand over the pistol . . ."

"Surely we needn't jump to our doom!"

"I'm not suggesting we jump! The only danger is that we might fall. Quickly, Adam, I hear them on the stairs . . . take off your shoes!"

I obeyed without question, because she seemed to have some plan in mind, though I was not pleased that it involved the window. "Why am I taking off my shoes, though?"

"Leather doesn't grip like flesh. Holster your pistol, to keep your hands available. Now follow me."

I followed her as closely as I could through the darkened room, though not without stubbing my toe on a barrel-rim. Then she threw open the hinged window, admitting a gust of rain and a lightning-flash. The storm, which had threatened all day, was upon us. The rattle of thunder was continuous, and the wind howled mercilessly. I watched with disbelief as Calyxa put her upper body through the open window and squirmed until she was standing outside of it, her toes clasping the narrow sill. Then she grabbed a gable on the roof above and hauled herself up.

---

* Calyxa, unlike myself, was fluent in French, and sometimes fell into that language at odd moments. French has always been a mystery to me, and remains so; but I have taken pains to make sure her words are accurately transcribed.

At last her pleasant face appeared again, upside down in the high end of the window frame. "Hurry, Adam! Take my hand."

It was embarrassing to be assisted by a girl at such a time, but it would have been more embarrassing to be trapped by a Blake brother and shot, or to tumble to my death; so I took her hand, and put my bare feet on the rain-drenched sill, and tried not to think of the hard surface of the street below, or of the lightning that forked about the sky and fingered the lightning-rods of the city's countless steeples.

"Now grasp the rim of the roof and pull yourself up!"

I doubted I could do so—I was convinced I could not—but a few breaths later I was lying beside Calyxa on the half-pipe ceramic tiles that capped the Thirsty Boot. We were inclined at a reckless angle, and in danger of sliding into the void. Rainwater sluiced over us freely. But we were, for this fraction of a moment, more or less safe—if that word can be stretched to cover the situation.

I turned to speak to Calyxa—her face was only inches from mine—but she put a finger to her lips and hushed me. "Your pistol?"

I took it from where I had secured it. It was a Porter & Earle military revolver of modern design, and I was almost certain it wouldn't be badly affected by the weather.

"Point it," she said.

"At what?"

"Between your feet!" Where the roof ended, she meant: at the eaves-gutters, where we had just lofted ourselves up. I obliged her whim, steadying my right hand by bracing it with my left, and pressing the tiles with my feet to keep from falling. As warm as the day had been, the rain was plummeting down from some glacial height of the atmosphere, and I had to clench my teeth to keep from shivering. "Probably it won't occur to them to look for us here," said Calyxa. "But if they do, you must shoot the first person who attempts to cross the margin of the roof. In other words, if you see a *head*, put a *hole* in it. Now be quiet!"

I had no difficulty keeping quiet, and in any case it was a noisy night. The rain had the velocity of artillery fire, and it burst upon the roof with a similar impact. The roofs of these Montreal City buildings were irregular—they didn't bear the stamp of the work of the Secular Ancients, which is an exacting symmetry; rather, they had been built over the dismantled remnants of older buildings, with haphazard attention to detail and no coherent plan. Water gushed down labyrinthine flues and runways, cascaded into bricked cisterns and holding tanks, and ran across the tiles in glistening washes. We might have been inside a flooding river, for all the noise we could contribute to it.

But Calyxa was listening intently for sounds from inside the room we had recently left, below us. She cupped her ear in that direction, and I tried to

listen as well, though without success—or with *too much* success, for I imagined I heard innumerable thumps and rattles, any one of which might have signaled the approach of an angry Blake Brother. Suddenly Calyxa stiffened, and her eyes went wide. "Be ready, Adam!" she said.

I put all my attention on the eaves of the roof, though my heart was beating a military tempo. Rainwater in my eyes gave the scene a liquid inconstancy. I saw the tile-ends, and the edge of the eaves-gutter, and the high building across Guy Street, and a section of the street far below. There was a sound that might have been a window swinging wide and bouncing on its hinge-stops. Calyxa inhaled fearfully, and I reminded myself to continue breathing.

Seconds passed. Rain fell; thunder cracked; lightning crazed the tumbled clouds.

Then there was motion at the gutter by my feet. Two sets of knuckles, left and right, gripped the eaves-trough. That was the Horizon of the Roof, as I suddenly thought of it; and now a hairy Moon began to rise.

The lunar object was a Blake Brother, investigating what he must have deduced was his sister's escape route. Perhaps the brothers' opinion of Calyxa's mental and physical capabilities had improved since her last encounter with them. I did not doubt that this was one of her brothers, for there was a family resemblance about the hair: the hair on this unwelcome Rising Moon curled like Calyxa's, but it was unkempt, and washed only by the gusty rain, and so oily that it gave back the lightning-flashes in an inky blue reflection. The hair was followed by a forehead even more uncannily lunar in its scarped and pitted aspect; then rose a pair of eyes, yellow-rimmed and threaded with blood. Those eyes met mine and narrowed, as I imagine the eyes of a savage cat narrow when it spies its next meal a-hoof.

"Fire!" shouted Calyxa.

I don't know that I could have brought myself to do as she asked—to fire on an apparently unarmed man, even a hostile one, when he was in a position of such vulnerability—except that her voice startled me, and caused my finger to compress the trigger of the pistol. The result was instantaneous. The pistol kicked in my hand. The sound of the concussion joined the rattle of thunder. There was a flash of red and white (of *bone* and *blood*, I supposed) where the head of the Blake Brother had been; then a rending screech, and terrible thumps as the injured man was pulled back inside the window, presumably by his outraged sibling.

I was too dazed to think of what to do next—this wasn't much like shooting Dutch uniforms across an earthworks—but Calyxa had retained all her presence of mind. She grabbed my free hand and yanked on it. "Now run!" she said.

She set an example for me, scrabbling up the slope of the roof, her bare feet sliding back an inch for every two they gained. I lurched after her. Eventually

we achieved the peak of the roof, where a series of crude chimneys leaned into one another like arthritic pickets on a ridge top. I glanced back at the eaves-gutters, and I saw a hand waving a pistol and shooting it blindly. A bullet clipped a chimney-brick just adjacent to my head, and Calyxa tugged me forward, so that we slid down the opposite angle of the roof—to our doom, I expected; but this slope conjoined another one next to it, so that we found ourselves in a sort of clay-tile riverbed, through which we splashed a few yards more. Then Calyxa leapt across a narrow gap between two buildings, ignoring the empty air below her, and again I followed her example. There was no bravery in this—I felt every raindrop as if it were a shot between the shoulder-blades.

I will not record all the arduous climbs, giddy descents, perilous slides, and painful near-disasters that befell us as we fled across the darkened roofs of Montreal City that stormy night. After a time we slowed, and began to move more cautiously. It did not seem that we were being followed—understandably, perhaps, for I had killed or severely wounded one of the Blake Brothers, and the other might not be willing to leave his wounded sibling and chase us about the tiled slopes of the city, especially in weather so severe that funnel-clouds were seen spinning down the St. Lawrence River. It's enough to say that we arrived at last at an iron fire-escape more than a mile from the Thirsty Boot in some direction that was incalculable to me, and that when I descended to street level my bare feet left bloody prints on the rusty ladder rungs. "Do you live near here?" I asked Calyxa hopefully, once I had gathered breath enough to speak.

The rain had drenched her—every part of her was slicked or drooped by it except her hair, which, amazingly, kept its all curly depth. Her mannish shirt clung to her body in a way that might have been indelicate if I had allowed my attention to linger on it. She had laced her shoelaces together and carried her shoes looped around her neck like clumsy pendants. She put them back on her feet, bending over to tie them. I had no such option—my own boots had been abandoned at the tavern.

"Not far," she said, standing up.

"Then, this time, please let me walk you there."

She managed to smile, despite the horrifying circumstances. "I won't leave you barefoot in the rain, Adam Hazzard," she said. "Not on a night like this."

There is a kind of urban living, I have discovered, in which poverty and luxury mix together, and become indistinguishable. That was the case with the rooms in which Calyxa Blake lived. She occupied several chambers in a building that had been divided up into dark but rentable spaces by some absent and inattentive Owner. The rooms were confining, the windows minuscule, the

ceilings perilously low. She could not have spent much money on the furnishings, which were shabby, threadbare, nicked, and splintered—I had seen better furniture abandoned at Montreal curbsides.

But if her book-cases were humble, they were bowed under the weight of surprisingly many books—almost as many as there had been in the library of the Duncan and Crowley Estate back in Williams Ford. It seemed to me a treasure more estimable than any fine sofa or plush footstool, and worth all the rough economies surrounding it.

We entered dripping from the effects of the storm, which continued to beat its wings against the windows of Calyxa's snug if threadbare retreat. As soon as she had thrown the several latches behind her and lit the nearest lamp she began unselfconsciously to strip off her sodden clothes. I looked away, blushing. "You too," she said. "No exceptions for Western prudishness—you're dripping all over everything."

"I have nothing else to wear!"

"I'll find you something. Undress yourself—those pants won't dry while you're wearing them."

That extraordinary statement was inarguably true; and I did as she suggested, while she went to another room in search of something to cover herself, and me. She came back wearing a kind of Chinese robe, with fanciful Dragons embroidered on it, and carrying a similar garment, along with a towel, which she handed to me.

I dried myself willingly but balked at the robe. "I think this is a woman's item."

"It's a silk robe. All the better Chinese persons wear them, men included. You can buy them down at the dockside—cheap, when the boats come in, if you know the right vendor. Put it on, please."

I obeyed, though not without feeling slightly ridiculous. But the robe was comfortable, and supplied just the right degree of warmth and concealment. I was content with it, I decided, as long as some Blake brother didn't break down the door and shoot me, for dying in such a garment might provoke awkward questions.

Calyxa started a fire in the kitchen stove and put a kettle on to boil. While she worked I examined her book-cases more closely. I hoped to find an unfamiliar title by Mr. Charles Curtis Easton, which I could borrow. But Calyxa's taste didn't run in that direction. Few of the books were fiction, and even fewer bore the Dominion Stamp of Approval. I guessed the authority of the Dominion was more powerful out West than in these border lands, which had so often changed hands with the Dutch. Here were titles and authors altogether unfamiliar to me. Some were in French, and could not be decrypted. Of the English titles, I selected one called *American History Since the Fall of the Cities*, by Arwal Parmentier. It had been published in England—a country which, though sparsely inhabited, had a long history of its own, and whose allegiance to Mitteleuropa was more formal than devotional. I took the volume closer to a lamp, opened it at random, and read this paragraph:

> The ascent of the Aristocracy should not be understood solely as a response to the near-exhaustion of oil, platinum, iridium, and other essential resources of the Technological Efflorescence. The trend to oligarchy predated that crisis and contributed to it. Even before the Fall of the Cities the global economy had become what our farmers call a "Monoculture," streamlined and relatively efficient, but without the useful diversity fostered in prior times by the existence of National Borders and Local Regulation of Business. Long before plague, starvation, and childlessness reduced the population so dramatically, wealth had already begun to concentrate in the hands of a minority of powerful Owners. The Crisis of Scarcity, therefore, when it came, was met not with a careful or prepared response, but by a determined grasp of power on the part of the Oligarchs and a retreat into religious dogmatism and clerical authority by the frightened and disenfranchised populace.

It was quickly obvious to me why this volume had not received the Stamp of Approval, and I moved to replace it on the shelf, but not before Calyxa, returning from the kitchen with a cup of tea in each hand, saw me handling it. "Do you read, Adam Hazzard?" She seemed surprised.

"I do—as often as I can."

"Really! Have you read Parmentier?"

I confessed I hadn't had the pleasure. Political Philosophy was not a subject I had pursued, I told her.

"Too bad. Parmentier is ruthless on Aristocracy. All my friends read him. Who do you read, then?"

"I admire the work of Mr. Charles Curtis Easton."

"I don't know the name."

"He's a novelist. Perhaps I can introduce you to his work sometime."

"Perhaps," Calyxa said, and we sat down on the sofa. She took a sip of tea, and seemed more or less at ease, considering that she had just seen her homicidal brother shot in the head, and had spent the evening leaping about the rooftops of Montreal. Then she put down her cup and said, "Look at your feet—you're bleeding all over the carpet."

I apologized.

"It's not the carpet I'm concerned about! Here, lie back and put your feet on this towel."

I did so, and she fetched a medicine for me—an ointment that smelled of alcohol and camphor, and burned on application, but soon began to feel soothing. She examined my feet closely, then wrapped them in a linty bandage. "And you left your boots behind," she said.

"Yes."

"That wasn't wise. Army-issue boots. Job will recognize them for what they are. He'll know I was with an American soldier, and it won't improve his temper."

Shooting his brother in the head had probably angered him right up to the hilt, I thought, and the boots wouldn't add much of a fillip to it; but I took Calyxa's concern seriously. "I'm sorry to say this, Calyxa, and I don't mean to insult your family, but I begin to wish I had shot both of them."

"I wish you had, too, but the opportunity failed to present itself. Your poor feet! We'll fix them up a little more, come morning, and replace your boots with something better before you have to march back to your regiment."

I hadn't thought that far ahead, and the prospect was daunting, but she didn't dwell on it. "Adam Hazzard, I thank you for all you've done for me today. I was afraid of your motives at first, but Evangelica was right—you're just as simple as you look. I want to reward you," and here she put her arm around my shoulder, and drew my head closer to hers, and kissed me lightly on the cheek, "and I want to reward you *in the best possible way,* but it's not practical right at the moment—"

My skin still tingled where her lips had been. "You don't need to explain! I would never question your virtue, or make any claim on it, just because I helped you fend off your brothers!" (And I readjusted my Chinese robe to disguise any testimony to the contrary on the part of my masculine nature.)

"It isn't that. I do *want* to thank you, Adam. It would be my pleasure, as well as yours. Do you understand me? But *the time is not propitious.*"

"Of course it isn't, with the gunplay and all."

"What I mean is—"

"It's enough that I can sit and talk with you. I wanted your friendship, and now I have it—that's my reward."

"*J'ai mes règles, espèce de bouseaux ignorant!*" she said, a little impatiently, and I took this to be another testimonial to her gratitude to me, which was irrepressible. I expected nothing from her, but I hinted that a second kiss would not be unwelcome . . . and she gave me that, and I returned it, and I was as happy as I had ever been, despite all the rooftop calisthenics and bloody violence. Such is Love in a time of War.

I slept on the sofa, and she woke me in the morning. She examined my feet again, and said the injuries inflicted by the sharp tiles of the Montreal roofs were not as bad as they might have been, and she re-wrapped the bandages, and added a layer of leather, one for each foot, to function as soles, and more bandages, so that I could walk out of doors without re-injuring myself. "That ought to get you where we're going," she said.

She wanted to replace my boots with something better than bandages, and she wanted to find out what the ultimate outcome of the events at the tavern had been. She said she knew a place where both those needs might be addressed.

She put on a large sun-hat, to conceal her face if she crossed paths with a Blake brother, and I took her arm, and we stepped out into the sunny morning.

Last night's tempest had washed the air clean, and the ferocious wind had been domesticated into a pleasant breeze. If not for the danger, and the pain in my feet, our stroll would have been entirely enjoyable. But it was brief, and it ended at the door of a basement shop on a street I didn't recognize. The shop, a tannery and bootery, was closed—by law, because it was Sunday. Nevertheless Calyxa knocked loudly. "I know the owner," she said.

The owner turned out to be a bearded and irritable man who would not have been out of place at the table she had occupied in the tavern last night, except that his attention to his clothing was more particular. He looked at Calyxa curiously, and at me with an undisguised mixture of loathing and distaste. "Let us in, Emil, I don't want to dawdle here," she said; and he waved us inside reluctantly.

His shop was a cellar, rank with the smell of tannin and glue, but he had some very nice boots on display. "Can you fit my friend?" Calyxa asked.

"Anything for you," Emil said slowly, "you know that, but surely—"

"He needs something supple and sturdy on his feet. He lost his boots doing me a favor."

"Don't his army masters give him boots? *Tu es folle d'amener un soldat américain ici!*"

"*Il m'a sauvé la vie. On peut lui faire confiance. En plus, il n'est pas très intelligent. S'il te plaît, ne le tue pas—fais-le pour moi!*"

This exchange, whatever it meant, mollified Emil a little, and he agreed to measure my feet, and when he had done that he searched among his stock of pre-made boots, and showed me a fine pair of deerskins, calf-high and golden-brown. I was sure I couldn't afford them.

"This has to do with your savage brothers," Emil said to Calyxa. "I heard about what happened at the tavern last night."

Calyxa became more attentive. "What do you know about Job and Utty?"

"Job was badly creased by a bullet. He lost a lot of blood, but his skull wasn't cracked, and the story I heard is that he'll survive it. Utty threatened to shoot a few people just for show, but Job's wound distracted him. They left the tavern for the charity clinic—I expect Job's still there, unless he had the grace to die during the night. That's all I know, except that the military police took notice, and they're holding a warrant on both men."

Calyxa smiled as if this were welcome news, and I suppose it was; but sooner or later, it seemed to me, the Blake brothers would be back, angrier than ever, and I was afraid for her.

The boots were expensive even at Emil's grudging discount. I was reluctant to spend the money—I was saving for a typewriter—but I didn't want to appear tight in front of Calyxa, and I did need boots; so I paid the proprietor his ransom.

And I was not sorry. Even to my injured feet the deerhide boots felt like an upholstered corner of Heaven. I had never owned boots that fit me so neatly. The men of my company would be envious, I thought, and they would mock my vanity, and call me dainty; but I decided I would endure all that without complaint, for the boots comforted my feet and reminded me of Calyxa.

She and I walked a little farther, but the day was passing quickly, and I couldn't stay away from camp much longer. We parted at the great iron bridge. Calyxa asked whether I might be back next weekend, and I promised I would try to see her, if the military situation allowed, and that I would think of her constantly in the meantime.

"I hope you do come back."

"I will," I vowed.

"Don't forget to bring your pistol," she said; then she kissed me and kissed me again.

7

I kept my promise, and returned many times to the City of Montreal that summer, and became better acquainted with Calyxa and with the city in which she lived. I won't weary the reader with a description of all our encounters (some were too intimate to record, in any case), but I will say that we were not further troubled by the Blake Brothers—not that season, anyhow.

Camp life was easy for a time. My feet healed quickly, thanks to light work and those supple deerhide boots. The Dutch sallies became less frequent, and the only fighting for a while (locally, I mean) was between our scouting parties and a few enemy pickets. Contradictory rumors continued to emerge from the Saguenay campaign, however: a great victory—a great defeat—many Mitteleuropans killed—scores of Americans sent to early graves—but none of that could be confirmed, due to the slow pace of communications and the unwillingness of high staff to share intelligence with soldiers of the line. But around Thanksgiving we had a substantial hint that things had not gone well. A new regiment of draftees and recruits—soft, naive lease-boys, as I now saw them, mostly drawn from the estates and freehold farms of Maine and Vermont—arrived in camp. They were quickly trained in the business of garrisoning Montreal City and maintaining its defenses, which freed up those of us with battle experience for that most dreaded of military maneuvers: a Winter Campaign.

"Galligasken would never have approved of this," Sam said when our regimental orders were finally cut. "The orders must have come down from the Executive Palace itself. This smells of Deklan Comstock's meddling and impatience. The news of some defeat nettled him, so he ordered all his forces into a strategically absurd retaliation—I'd bet money on it."

But there was no arguing with orders. We packed our ditty-bags and slung our Pittsburgh rifles, a whole division of us, and we were carted to the docks and loaded into steam-driven boats for the journey down the St. Lawrence to the Saguenay. There wasn't time to say goodbye to Calyxa, so I wrote a hasty letter, and posted it from the quayside, telling her I would be away at the front for an undisclosed time, and that I loved her and thought of her constantly, and that I hoped the Blake Brothers wouldn't hunt her down and kill her while I was gone.

The boats on which we rode burned wood rather than coal, and their smudge hung over the river and followed us in the wind, a poignant, earthy smell.

I had never been out on a boat before. The River Pine back in Williams

Ford was too swift and shallow for navigation. I had *seen* boats, of course, especially since our arrival in Montreal, and they had fascinated me with their elephantine grace and their negotiations with the unpredictable and oft-stormy St. Lawrence. Consequently I spent much time at the rail of this little vessel as it traveled, experiencing what Julian called the "Relativistic Illusion" that the boat itself was stationary, and that it was the land around it that had gone into motion, writhing to the west like a snake with a war in its tail.

We had been issued woolen coats to protect us from the weather, but the day was fine and sunny, though autumn had the countryside in its final grip. We approached and passed the great fortifications at Quebec City, and followed the North Channel beyond Ile d'Orleans, where the river grew much wider and began to carry the tang of salt. The foliage along the north bank was umber and scarlet where it had not already abandoned itself to the wind. Denuded branches cast skeletal silhouettes against a dusty blue sky, and crows swept the forest-top in wheeling masses. Autumn is the only season with a hook in the human heart, Julian had once said (or quoted). This fanciful figure of speech ran through my mind right then—*the only season with a hook in the heart*—and because it was autumn, and because the land was vast and empty, and the air was chill and smelled of woodsmoke, the poetic words seemed to make sense, and were apt.

About then Julian came to stand beside me at the rail, while the other soldiers milled about on deck or went below to try their luck at mess. "Last night I dreamed I was on a ship," he said, the long light falling on his face as the wind tousled the hair that flowed out beneath his cap.

"A ship like this one?"

"A better one, Adam. A three-masted schooner, like the ones that sail up the Narrows to Manhattan. When I was a child my mother used to take me to the foot of Forty-second Street to see those ships. I liked the idea that the ships came from faraway places—the Mediterranean Republics, or Nippon, or Ecuador, as it might be—and I liked to pretend some spirit of those places still clung to them—I convinced myself I could smell it, a whiff of spice above the stink of creosote and rotting fish."

"Those must be very fine ships," I said.

"But in my dream the ship was leaving New York Harbor, not arriving. She had just caught the wind in her sails—'took the bone in her teeth,' as sailors say; and she was passing under the old Verrazano Bridge. I knew I was being carried away somewhere . . . not to a safe place, exactly, but to a different place than I was accustomed to, where I might change into someone else." He smiled sheepishly, though there was a haunted look in his eye. "I don't suppose that makes sense."

I said I guessed it didn't, and I didn't believe in prophetic dreams any more than Julian believed in Heaven; but something about the melancholy way he spoke made me think his dream must be another Poetic Metaphor, like that figure of speech involving hooks and hearts—the kind of riddle that cuts close to the tear ducts in its nonsense.

Around dusk we sailed past the Dutch fort at Tadoussac. It had been taken by American forces, and among the soldiers on deck a cheer went up at the sight of the Thirteen Stripes and Sixty Stars flying above those battle-scarred and broken walls on the high headland. What did not please us so much was the litter of broken ships clinging to that stark shore. Half-sunken hulls gutted by artillery fire stood sentinel over islands of charred debris trapped by the whorl of the river. Here there had been fighting of the fiercest kind, both ashore and afloat; and it was a dire and oppressive place by the fading light of day.

We reached the craggy mouth of the Saguenay shortly thereafter, and our flotilla of troop-ships, their wood-fired engines straining, sailed up that "fjord,"* making a scant few knots against the current. Most of us tried to sleep in the narrow bunks that had been assigned to us. But we kept our arms close, and come morning we could hear the distant sounds of war.

They landed us at the Siege of Chicoutimi, and we spent three weeks in the trenches.

The companies of our Regiment were kept close together, to prevent our morale from being deflated by the long-term infantrymen who had fought their way here from Tadoussac over the course of the summer, and whose losses had been staggering. It had been a badly-planned and deadly campaign, and the Staff had not been spared the effects of its winnowing. It was rare to see an officer at Chicoutimi even as old as Sam Godwin. High rank and hasty promotions had been handed out to boys no older than myself, and commanders' tents had become kindergartens from which one graduated to the grave.

The "siege," in fact, was a stalemate. *Our* entrenchments had encountered *their* entrenchments, and it was all we could do to keep the daily killing at an equitable level—no grander goal could be imagined. We controlled the Saguenay right up to River-of-Rats, but the Mitteleuropans held Chicoutimi in a firm grip, and their supply lines were secure all the way to the railhead at Lake Saint John, where the *Stadhouders* had established farms, mills, mines, refineries, shipworks, and a flourishing community of workers and owners. No matter what artillery we dragged upriver to attack them, they could float some equivalent weapon downstream to repulse us. And because of their greater numbers, we were in constant danger of being outflanked.

On top of all that, winter was coming fast. Cold weather had already driven off the Black Flies, but that was the only good thing about it. Our lines

* As I believe the Dutch called it.

were a wasteland devoid of trees or vegetation. We had dug our trenches and redans out of the soil, which in this neighborhood was thick with the debris of the Efflorescence of Oil—bricks, broken foundation-stones, and that tarry crumble with which the ancients paved their roads. Our entrenching tools turned up human bones from time to time. The bones were not useful to us,[*] but the bricks were largely sound, and we worked them into our defenses. Some of the more ambitious men made entire brick fortifications, with mud for mortar, but these barricades were a two-edged sword: fine against rifle fire but dangerously unstable when artillery shells exploded nearby. Craftsmanship was everything, and men with bricklaying experience were in high demand for their advice, at least until the ground froze over, making it impossible to dig bricks or mortar them. These are the subtler arts of war.

We had nothing to eat but trail rations, and little enough of that. It was difficult even to keep warm. There were days when all we had to burn were fragments of rotted wood and asphalt. And there was no relief by night, for the Dutch loved to shell us during the hours of darkness, and our artillery companies were obliged to return fire. By the end of three weeks the lack of sleep, constant cold, and inadequate rations had turned us all into automatons, shuffling through frozen or muddy trenches according to orders given by distant madmen or local commanders no older than ourselves. Major Lampret was with us—the stories of his cowardice and self-regard had made it mandatory that he travel to the front lines, or lose all credibility with the men—and he conducted Sunday services on three occasions, each event less well-attended than the one before. His rivalry with Julian still simmered, and I expect Lampret wished he had demoted or even imprisoned "Private Commongold" when the opportunity presented itself; but Julian was well-liked, and Lampret could not do anything against him. Sam knew that Lampret had a spy among us, and he had concluded that the informer was most likely Private Langers, our entrepreneurial colporteur, who had been seen conferring with Lampret on several occasions; and certainly there was nothing about Langers's moral character that would make the charge implausible. But Langers was careful, and no money or favors were seen to change hands.

The last Camp Meeting held by Major Lampret drew a larger audience, but that was because we were ordered to it. We stood in a circle on cleared ground, under cloudy skies, in a spitting snow, as grim news was announced. General Galligasken had been injured by shrapnel from an enemy shell, even though his headquarters had been set up out of the range of conventional artillery—perhaps a Chinese Cannon was responsible. The General still lived, but he had been taken down to Tadoussac for emergency treatment, and he would probably lose an arm, if he survived. His replacement was a new

---

[*] Though some of the men carved scrimshaw out of venerable ankles, or employed knobby old forearms as hooks on which to hang blankets to dry.

General from New York City named Reddick. A pawn of the Executive, Sam whispered, and a lackey of the Dominion as well. This was bad news indeed.

There was worse to come. Reddick in his enthusiasm had ordered an all-out dawn attack. We were to sleep on our arms, and be prepared for heavy action come morning.

The quartermaster issued us double rations—a welcome change, though as a "last supper" it did little to dispel the gloom—and fresh rounds of ammunition. We were more convincingly cheered by the arrival of a new division of cavalry, men armed with Trench Sweepers of the type that had proved so effective in the Battle of Mascouche. Perhaps we were not doomed after all. That faint hope sustained us.

The sky was red with dawn when all the bugles sounded and all our artillery fired at once, announcing the attack.

We deployed by regiments, and ours was in the vanguard. I asked Sam what the strategy might be, but he couldn't tell: the armies were too large for one man to survey them, and this battle was being coordinated by staff in the rear. Telegraph cables had been laid to help Reddick communicate with field commanders, and there were messengers and horsemen to carry intelligence back and forth. But this was a clumsy way to manage something as fluid as a massive battle, Sam said, so most of the initiative would be in the hands of regimental captains. Julian asked pointedly, and loudly, whether Major Lampret would deign to involve himself in the attack, or whether he would supervise, in a spiritual sense, from behind. Lampret overheard this comment—as he was no doubt meant to—and announced to the assembly that he would take up a rifle if there was one to spare. This won him a few scattered hurrahs; though his face, when he made the offer, was chalk-white, and he gave Julian a long daggered stare.

Then we were in the thick of it. I will spare the reader the ghastly minutiae of that awful morning, except to say that our company was reduced to half its numbers before an hour had passed; and I saw so much of what ought to have remained *inside* the human body, but *hadn't,* that I passed beyond revulsion into a kind of emotionless efficiency. The roar of battle was all but deafening, and if not for the organizing genius of flags and bugles I suppose we would have abandoned all order and fought for our lives, individually.

Here, as in Mascouche, it was the Trench Sweeper that made the difference. I had learned to recognize the sound of those heavy rifles—a sort of deadly, prolonged cough—and so had the Dutch troops, who dreaded it. The Army of the Laurentians began to make a striking advance as soon as those weapons were brought to bear, though I was still not sure what our ultimate objective might be. But General Reddick ordered a pursuit of the fleeing enemy, and we had no choice but to oblige.

The battle passed out of the cratered no-man's-land of trenches and abandoned redoubts as the Mitteleuropans fell back to prepared positions on forested, hilly land. The order for pursuit rang out from all quarters, and Sam (who had been slightly wounded in the thigh, but stanched the bleeding with a cotton handkerchief) guessed that Reddick intended to destroy the Dutch army in detail, if our cavalry could flank them and get in their rear. To this end our regiment was ordered into the trees, to keep the enemy moving, and acquire any loose supplies or animals they left behind, and capture or kill any stragglers.

It was a bold plan, and we might have been a useful part of it, except for the consequences of a single bullet.

Our company commander was Captain Paley Glasswood, formerly a New York City counter clerk, who was at least ten years younger than Sam Godwin—perhaps about Major Lampret's age—but senior in rank to most of us. Today he led us through a volley of fierce but (as it then seemed) ineffective sniper fire, into the woods, and across a stream, and along the bow of a gentle ridge, then down into a forested valley, never encountering the enemy even once; and we marched for more than two hours in this fashion, patient but puzzled, before the Captain stopped and said in a ringing voice:

"I'm tired, boys, and the stars are awfully bright."

Then he sat down on a log, sighing and mumbling.

We were hours from darkness, though the day was gloomy, with little squirts of snow now and again, so his comment about the stars surprised everyone. Sam went up to Captain Glasswood to ask him what was the matter, but got no response. Then he examined the left side of the Captain's head and grimaced. "Oh, Hell! Here, Adam—help me lay him down."

Captain Glasswood made no protest as we stretched him out on the cold forest floor under a canopy of creaking pines. The Captain's gaze was distant, and the pupil of one eye had grown as large as a Comstock dollar. He looked at me solemnly as I cradled him down to the ground. "Oh, now, Maria, don't cry," he said in a petulant voice. "I haven't been to Lucille's since Tuesday."

"What's the matter with him?" I asked.

Sam, who had been holding the Captain's head, lifted up his palm and showed me streaks of clotted red. "Apparently he was shot," he said with disgust.

"Shot where?"

"In the skull. Through the ear, by the look of it."

That was a dreadful thing, I thought, to be shot in the ear. The idea of it made me shudder, despite all I had seen today. "I didn't hear any rifle fire."

"It must have happened during the battle, or just after. Perhaps one of those sharpshooters got him."

"That long ago! Didn't he notice?"

"The wound didn't bleed much, externally. And he has a bullet in his brain, Adam. People with bullets in their brains lose all kinds of sensibility, and sometimes they don't even know they're hurt. I expect he still doesn't know he's wounded. And never will. He's dying. That's a certainty."

I was afraid that Captain Glasswood might overhear this unhappy diagnosis and be upset by it, but Sam was right; the news, if he understood it, didn't trouble him at all. The Captain just closed his eyes and curled on his side like a man making himself comfortable on a feather bed. "Can't you get a blanket from the cedar chest?" he asked wistfully. "I'm cold, Lucille."

Then he screamed once and stopped breathing.

There were not quite twenty of us left in the company, and we had lost our only commanding officer. There was Lampret, of course, who was accompanying us. But Lampret was a Dominion man, not a seasoned combatant. And at the moment he was no more useful than a stick of wood, staring at Captain Glasswood's corpse as if it had popped up from the ground like a poisonous mushroom. The men of the company, by some unspoken mutual instinct, looked to Julian for leadership. And Julian looked to Sam, and by so doing bequeathed on him the respect and obedience of the common soldiers.

"Post a guard," Sam said, when he realized the burden of command had fallen on him. "But I guess we're far enough from the battle that we can bury Captain Glasswood without attracting enemy fire. We can't carry him back, at any rate, and it doesn't seem right to abandon him."

It was, of course, impossible to truly bury him in the frozen ground; so we scraped a shallow trench out of pine-needle duff, and rolled Captain Glasswood into it, and covered him over. This would not protect his body from wild animals for very long, but it was a Christian gesture; and after a little prodding we even got a funeral prayer out of Major Lampret, though he delivered it in a small and quaking voice. Julian seemed moved by the death, and he did not make any disparaging remarks about God. All of us were badly taken by the Captain's death—as peculiar as that might seem, given how much death we had already witnessed and absorbed today. It might have been the loneliness of the woods that made the difference, or the clouds leaking frigid grains of snow, or the conspicuous absence of banners and bugle-calls.

The problem we confronted now, though Sam did not say so explicitly, was that Captain Glasswood had led us, according to what we all imagined was some clever strategy, deep into the wilderness, and away from the field of battle. But the only *strategy* at work had sprung from the Captain's damaged mind, and it was no longer available to us, if it ever existed.

In other words—words I was reluctant to pronounce even in the privacy of my own thoughts—we were lost in the wilds of the upper Saguenay.

The sound of battle had faded behind us long ago. Either the Dutch had been chased from their trenches, stragglers and all, and the war had entered

another pause, or we had simply passed out of hearing of it. The latter possibility was undeniable, for we had crossed many wooded ridges, which baffle or
amplify sounds in unpredictable ways. The best plan now, Sam told the company after we had finished prayers for Captain Glasswood, would be to return
to our own lines. But that return might not be direct, he said, "until we get
firm bearings," and in the meantime we must act as a scouting party, and note
the position and defenses of the Dutch, should we stumble across any. Sam
said he would try to backtrack us. Whether he truly possessed this skill or was
only saying so to buoy our spirits, I couldn't tell.

We walked for hours more, and by nightfall we seemed to be no closer to
our lines. Sam remained mute on the subject. We dared not make a fire. We
carried only minimal rations, and we ate sparingly, and made what shelter
we could, and wrapped ourselves in blankets in order to sleep . . . which I suppose some of us were able to do, though the bare limbs of the trees creaked
like the timbers of a ghostly ship, and the wind made a sound like the sea.

"It seems to me," Lymon Pugh said, "that we're sunk pretty deep in a vinegar
brine of trouble," and that truth was impossible to deny.

Lymon Pugh was as emaciated as the rest of us after all our time in the
trenches, but his muscular forearms, sliced by flensing knives and tattooed by
beef blood, were still impressive, even buried under the sleeves of his thick
woolen jacket; and he made a reassuring companion. We walked behind Sam,
who was scouting a path. We had come a good distance up a wooded hill, all
of us sweating despite the frosty air.

The day, though cold, was fortunately not overcast, and the position of the
sun gave us some clue as to the cardinal points of the compass. We knew we
were east of the Saguenay, and probably well north of our own lines. It was fortunate for us that this part of the country was not much inhabited, or we might
have been taken captive long ago. But we could not avoid civilization for long,
unless we set up housekeeping in the woods, and that would have been a tall order, since there was nothing much to eat—even small game had been chased
away by warfare or scoured up by hungry Dutch soldiers. So we continued to
climb this increasingly steep bluff until, as we reached the top, Sam held up a
hand, signaling us to stop, and whispered that we should not make any noise.

We came up singly or in twos, crouching.

From the height of this ridge we could see a long declining counterslope,
gentle enough that a railroad (of the narrow gauge the Dutch prefer) as-
cended it at an angle, passing close to where we stood. This was presumably
the line between Chicoutimi to the Mitteleuropan estates at Lake St. John, or
perhaps it ran all the way to the rocky Atlantic—the Dutch had built skeins
of railroads across occupied Labrador in the decades during which they controlled this land.

The most important fact about this railroad was its connection to the town of Chicoutimi, which we could also see, though dimly, across a misty expanse of winter wilderness, attached like a smudged appendix to the blue ribbon of the Saguenay. And that meant we were no longer lost—though we were still a great distance from where we wanted to be. The way ahead was clear and obvious: we need only follow the railroad until we could veer off toward more friendly territory. And our hearts were light, for that did not appear to be an insurmountable task. We might even be back with our old regiment in time for a hot meal before bed.

But the journey had to be postponed a few moments more. Sam urged us to keep silent. He had seen a train approaching from the east—he pointed out a trail of smoke hovering over the eastern passes. "Stay hidden until it goes by, every one of you."

We were only a few yards from the track where it crossed the peak of the ridge to begin its descent into Chicoutimi, and soon the train would be just adjacent to us. "Shouldn't we fire on it, or do something soldierly such as that?" asked Lymon Pugh.

"It may not be a military train," said Sam. "I don't see any great advantage in shooting unarmed civilians, even among the Dutch. And gunfire would draw attention on us, in any case, and probably get us killed."

No one was inclined to argue the point. We were low on ammunition, anyhow, for we had wasted some of it shooting unproductively into empty squirrels' nests in hopes of bringing down a little fresh meat. We sat tight among the rocks and spindly winter bushes until we could hear the train's Dutch engine straining against the slope, and feel the rumble of it. I had not seen a Mitteleuropan train before, and I wondered what it would look like.

It hove into view, finally, and it was not much different from an American train, in so far as *function* dictates *form* in these matters, though it did look very smoothly-built, and the engine was painted an unusual blue-gray color. What was alarming was not the design of the train but its speed, which was slow, and, worse, slowing. In fact it seemed as if the train was coming to a stop.

We raised our heads despite Sam's warning. The train was a military one. That much was patently obvious. The engine was drawing only a pair of cars, both of which bore the sinister cross-and-laurel insigne of the Mitteleuropan army. "We ought to have pulled up the track," Lymon Pugh whispered to me, "to keep that thing from reaching Chicoutimi with whatever it's carrying."

"There wasn't time," I said, "even if we had thought of it. Perhaps we can tear up the tracks later; but keep your wits about you, Lymon, I believe that train isn't going any farther than right here."

We had no plan for this unexpected contingency. Sam hastily motioned at us to move a little ways up along the ridge, though still keeping the mysterious Dutch train within sight. Why had it come to this hilltop near

Chicoutimi, and why had it paused right near us? No simple explanation sprang to mind.

Sam halted us in a stand of naked birches where the hummocky ground made it easy to disguise ourselves against accidental discovery. We watched the train in breathless anticipation. Someone wondered aloud whether the train might not have been sent explicitly to hunt for us; but one misplaced American infantry company was not significant to the Dutch, Sam said.

Major Lampret stirred from his funk and said, "We ought to get as far from that thing as possible. We endanger ourselves by sitting here—why don't we retreat?"

"We're as safe here as anywhere," Sam said coolly, "as long as we're not seen. Stay put."

"Don't presume to give me orders," said Lampret.

Evidently Major Lampret had regrown his spine; but he had chosen a poor time to enter into an argument over rank, I thought. The men of the company thought so, too, for they hissed at him to keep quiet. "I suppose we could all *fly* home, if we had Angel's Wings," one man muttered.

Lampret gave way, fearing mutiny; but he said to Sam, in a low tone, "We'll talk about insubordination when we get back to camp."

"That would be a more convenient time to discuss it," Sam agreed; and Lampret lapsed back into his sullen silence.

In the meantime the Dutch train had halted altogether, noisily bleeding steam from its valves, and a few Mitteleuropan soldiers clambered off the rear car. What appeared to interest them was a little clearing just at the western side of the train—a granite shoulder covered with pebbles and tufts of brittle weeds. The Dutch soldiers scouted out that flat space meticulously, and shaded their eyes, and peered off toward the distant Saguenay, and spoke their unintelligible language to one another. Then they returned to the train, and rolled back the door on one of the twin boxcars.

The open door admitted a shaft of sunlight and revealed the car's contents, at which we all gasped: for the train was carrying a Chinese Cannon.

Sam detailed a pair of men to count the enemy soldiers as they disembarked and prepared to assemble the Cannon. I asked Julian what he thought was going on.

"Isn't it obvious, Adam? They mean to set up an artillery battery."

"What—here? It's a long way from the fight."

"You forget the extraordinary range of the Chinese Cannon. That's the advantage of it: it can be placed far from the active lines, and still be an effective weapon. The drawback is that it's bulky and has to be carried by a whole convoy of wagons, or by a train, for instance in those two cars."

Both boxcars had been opened now, and we could see that the assembly and activation of the Cannon would not be a simple task for the gunners. Its great Rotary Base occupied one car, and the Barrel of the thing, broken into telescoping pieces, occupied the other. The cargo of the train also included a couple of mules, to assist in haulage and enstationment, and winches and levers and other necessary tools. There was also a number of crates marked BOMBE, a word even Lymon Pugh was able to translate from the Dutch.*

We counted fifteen artillerymen, give or take, plus whatever crew remained aboard the engine.

"We outnumber them," Julian remarked.

"Perhaps," Sam said. "But they're conspicuously better-armed."

"But we have the element of surprise."

"Are you suggesting we engage the Dutch artillery?"

"I'm suggesting we have a duty not to let those shells fall on American soldiers, if we can help it."

That was a bold but bracing declaration, and it pleased some in our company who were anxious to make the Dutch pay a price for inconveniencing us with their war, and for the cowardly act of shooting Captain Glasswood through the ear. Sam smiled. "Well said. But we have to be clever about it, Julian, not just belligerent. What would you do, if it was your command?"

"Capture the train," Julian said.

The company of us had all gathered around, and some grinned at this, though Major Lampret scowled and shook his head.

"That's an objective," Sam said patiently, "not a plan. Tell me your plan."

Julian took a moment to assess the situation, peering at the train and the surrounding landscape. "Post most of our company on that lip overlooking the ridge where the tall trees are—do you see? We can conceal ourselves and make every shot count, which is important, given our limited munitions; and from there we can range in on anyone who hasn't deliberately taken cover."

"Thus employing the element of surprise," Sam said.

"Surprise and distraction. We could leave a couple of men here, to make some sort of demonstration, and draw the attention of the Dutch in exactly the wrong direction."

The two of them discussed the idea at length, with others in the company chiming in with suggestions. Then Sam said: "It might work. I think it *will* work, if we execute it correctly. But that would leave us in possession of a train containing a Chinese Cannon—what do we do with it once we have it?"

"Drive it down toward Chicoutimi," said Julian.

"For what purpose?"

"It depends on the state of the fighting. If the rail happens to cross into territory held by our forces, we can deliver the Cannon to them—and be feted

---

* Or Deutsche, in this case, I'm told.

as heroes, no doubt. Failing that, we can destroy the Cannon and render it useless to the Dutch."

"Destroy it how?"

"Put some sort of fuse on those shell-casings and blow it all up, I suppose. We might even turn the entire train into a sort of bomb—set it on fire and send it hurtling into Chicoutimi."

"Hard on *us*, though, that scenario."

"We can leap off at the closest approach to our lines, and make our way home." Julian smiled. "If nothing else, it might save us a few miles walking."

It was that humble suggestion that clinched the issue. We were all tired of walking, and the idea of riding a captured enemy train even halfway home was a pleasant one to contemplate.

All of us agreed to the plan, at least tacitly, except Major Lampret, who insisted that we were lunatics and mutineers for undertaking this battle without his consent, and that there would be "consequences" if we carried it out, assuming we weren't all killed by our own foolishness. But Lampret's credibility had been so thoroughly undercut that he was easy to ignore.

I was in favor of the attack, and my only disappointment when it was approved was that Lymon Pugh and I were assigned to provide the "useful distraction."

I asked Sam what he wanted us to do.

"Wait here until the rest of us are in place. I'll signal you when it's time to begin the proceedings."

"Begin them how, though?"

"Just make a noise of some kind—nothing too belligerent, just something that will draw all eyes. It needn't be anything fancy—the firing will commence at once."

The Dutchmen were beginning to harness up their mules, so we had to move quickly. Lymon and I watched the other men of the company scuttle away, backs bent and weapons ready, to their hiding places a few hundred yards to the east.

Lymon said, "You'd better orchestrate this thing, Adam. I don't know how to distract a Dutch soldier, except by shooting at him. Maybe you can call out to them in their own language."

"Perhaps I would, except I don't speak it."

"You have that letter you bought from Langers's Lucky Mug. I've seen you reading it over and over."

"But not for the sense of it. And I can only guess at the pronunciation, based on what I've heard from Dutch prisoners. They wouldn't believe me for a second."

"They don't have to *believe* you—Sam's instruction was only that we should obtain their *attention.* Look there!—Sam is already waving his hand—I believe the time is ripe—go on, Adam, *call out to them!*"

I was flustered by the rapid progression of events, and I could think of nothing to do except to adopt Lymon Pugh's suggestion.

I cleared my throat.

"Louder!" Lymon said. "Make yourself heard!"

I cupped my hands around my mouth and cried out, *"Lieftse Hannie!"*

"What's that mean?" Lymon asked.

"I don't know!"

"They can't hear you. Wasn't there something about Americans being no better than dogs?"

I racked my brain. *"Fikkie mis ik ook!"* I shouted, so loudly that the obdurate syllables pricked my throat like thorns. *"Lieftse Hannie! Fikkie mis ik ook!"*

That did the trick. For one fragile moment—a fraction of time as motionless as a bug in amber—every Dutch soldier looked in my direction, and each one wore an identical expression, of *confusion* bordering on *bewilderment*.

Then a barrage of rifle fire began to cut them down.

At the end of the ambush we had taken a two-car train, a Chinese Cannon, and three prisoners, and left a score of dead Mitteleuropan soldiers scattered about. The prisoners consisted of an artilleryman and two civilian engineers. They were not cooperative, and had to be bound and tied.

Everything that had been taken from the train we put back in place. (None of the heavy parts of the Chinese Cannon had yet been unhitched.) This was indeed a fine haul, if we could get it into American hands. Fortunately one of the men of our company—a long-haired mechanic named Penniman, from Lake Champlain—had studied trains, and understood the theory of steam-driven engines well enough that he could discern the use of the controls even though they were labeled in a foreign language. While he got up pressure in the boilers the rest of us policed the area, collecting Dutch rifles and pistols from their former owners. Then Julian and I went to join Sam in the cab of the engine, while the rest of the company found room for themselves in the heavily loaded boxcars.*

This had all gone very smoothly, and would have been a complete triumph except that, as it turned out, one of the Dutch soldiers had been "playing dead," and had secreted his rifle beneath his apparently lifeless body. Just as soon as Penniman released the brake and the train began to move, this troublesome Mitteleuropan grabbed up his weapon and fired on us. Bullets flew through the cab, and Penniman was lightly injured. Sam cursed and took up his own rifle. He leaned around the coal hopper and fired three shots. I thrust out my head long enough to see the Dutch rifleman retreat into a thicket of skeletal, leafless trees.

* We were forced to evict the mules.

We would have kept on rolling without further incident, I suppose, since the artilleryman could hardly have followed us, except that the door on the rear boxcar rolled open and Major Lampret popped out of it, shooting his own rifle wildly. "Brake up!" Sam cried disgustedly, and Penniman did so. The train vented steam-clouds into the cold air.

I managed to discern more of the action despite the veils of mist that obscured it. Apparently Major Lampret had decided to demonstrate his courage, which had been so severely questioned in recent days, and to restore himself to command. Perhaps he deemed the odds respectable—himself against one desperate Dutchman. Or it may be that his motives were sincere and patriotic, if misguided. In any case, his act of bravery or stupidity produced no good result. The Dutch infantryman fired back, and his defense was more calculated than Lampret's attack. Major Lampret took a bullet and slumped to the ground.

At this point Julian astonished me by leaping out of the engine-cabin and running toward the place where Major Lampret had fallen.

Sam was equally astonished; but he kept his wits, and shouted, "Fire on the enemy! Give cover!"—while doing so himself. Other men of our company began to follow his example, though none of us was willing to make himself as vulnerable to the Dutchman's bullets as had Julian.

I fired my rifle, too, though part of me felt frozen in the event, watching Julian dodge and dash toward an injured a man who had once threatened to imprison him. When Julian reached the Major he didn't hesitate, but thrust his hands under Lampret's inert arms and began to drag him back to the train. Geysers of icy dirt flew up around Julian and the Major—these were the impacts of hostile bullets, each one coming closer to its mark. Then the Dutchman gave out an audible cry from the thicket where he was hidden, and threw up his arms and fell forward; and on this occasion his death was not feigned, but entirely authentic.

Several of our men jumped from the train to help Julian with his burden. Soon the Major was safely aboard. Major Lampret had been badly hurt—the artilleryman's bullet had passed through his shoulder, leaving ugly wounds on the front and back of him—but he was breathing freely, and there seemed to be a decent chance that he might recover if he received prompt medical attention.

If Major Lampret had meant to establish his courage by this act, the attempt was a failure. I supposed it was brave of him to go after the Dutch soldier the way he had. But Julian's bravery in the rescue was more conspicuous, especially as it was aimed at saving the life of a man he despised; and this was what drew admiration from the other men, while Lampret received only the most cursory attention in his suffering.

Lampret remained unconscious, and just as well, or his jealousy might have killed him on the spot.

The gunfire and the damage to Major Lampret made our journey down the hill-side more eerie than triumphal. It was a feeling exacerbated by the land around us, for our captive train soon passed out of the winter forest into a Stygian realm of churned and frozen craters, cutwire fences festooned with corpses, and the blackened frames of burned-down farmhouses. The fighting had been fierce in our absence.

We began to calculate our options. From here the railroad ran straight to the embattled town of Chicoutimi. As far as we knew, that locality remained in the hands of the Mitteleuropans. But Julian found a Swiss spyglass among the articles left behind in the engine cabin, and he pointed it ahead of us, look-ing very distinguished, it seemed to me, in his battle-scarred uniform, with his long hair flowing out behind him. After a time he began to smile. The smile broadened. Then Julian handed the spyglass to Sam. "Look ahead, Sam—focus on the church tower on the hill."

"Hard to see in this mist." The valley through which we traveled was foggy in places, and a leaden overcast had blunted the blue sky. "But that must be the church tower—riddled with artillery impacts—it's not very clear . . ."

"Turn the side-wheel with your thumb," Julian said, "to bring it into focus."

Sam fiddled with the adjustment, cursing. "The Swiss are too clever by half—too clever for their own good. I don't think—ah! *There.*"

Then Sam smiled, too.

"What do you see?" I demanded. "Don't make a secret of it!"

"Only a flag on the church tower."

"Well, why shouldn't there be a flag on the church tower?"

"No reason at all. What distinguishes this flag is that it has thirteen Stripes and sixty Stars." He put down the spyglass and said more gently, "Our forces have taken Chicoutimi."

Thus it was only a matter of slowing the train and rumbling into Chicoutimi with our prize.

A Dutch military train arriving from the east might not be the most welcome sight among American troops, Sam reminded us. We had already passed a couple of pickets, who had taken hasty shots at us. What we needed was some convincing signal of our amity.

"Major Lampret is a Dominion Officer," Julian said. "Don't they carry American flags with them at all times, for funerals and prayers?"

We stopped in an isolated place long enough for Julian to visit the men in the boxcars, who gave a spontaneous hurrah when he told them Chicoutimi had fallen, and to procure a flag from Major Lampret, who carried one folded inside his shirt.

Julian came back to the engine of the Dutch train, but he didn't enter the cab. Instead he tied the flag to a charred tree-branch, which he found on the ground, and clambered onto the front of the engine, perching himself on an iron shelf just below the lantern-lens.

"Go in slowly," he called back to Penniman.

The train lurched forward as Penniman released the brake, almost tumbling Julian onto the tracks, then proceeded more smoothly.

And that was how we arrived in the newly-captured town of Chicoutimi. A fine snow had begun to fall, and the afternoon was theatrical in its shifting scrims of sun and cloud. We rode all the way into the depot with Julian up front like a patriotic ornament. His uniform was ragged and dirty, and his face was alabaster with the cold, but he grinned irrepressibly and waved the Sixty Stars and Thirteen Stripes before the hundreds of infantrymen and cavalrymen who assembled at the sight of our smoke. The engine passed down a corridor of these astonished soldiers before it finally hissed to a stop. Then the doors of the boxcars were thrown open, and a great and jubilant outcry rose up, for it was obvious to every spectator that we had captured a Chinese Cannon all intact.

8

The scourge of cholera caught up with us later that month. Many brave men who had survived injury and starvation all the way up the bloody Saguenay were taken to their graves by the disorder. The stench, inconvenience, and tragedy of the disease made life unpleasant for all of us, sick or not, and eventually most of us did get sick, though we did not necessarily die. I did not, for example—and I was as sick as anyone.

The human mind edits from memory its feverish interludes, and I can recollect very little of January or February of 2174. When I came to myself, what astonished me most—apart from my emaciation and general weakness—was that I had been transported without my knowledge from Chicoutimi to a field hospital in Tadoussac, and from there to the Soldier's Rest, a recuperation-house in the City of Montreal. I learned that many men I knew and liked had died in the outbreak, and that saddened me. But there was good news, too. Sam, Julian, and Lymon Pugh had survived the disease, though they were sickened by it; and all three of them were here in the Soldier's Rest, also recuperating. Out of all of our small circle the sickest had been Julian; the doctors said he had come close to dying; but he was well enough now that he could sit up, and take medicinal soups and such. Sam and Lymon were in even better mettle, and would be leaving the Rest within days.

And there was another bright light on the horizon, which served to improve my mood. That was the prospect of our release from the Army of the Laurentians. The Draft Act of 2172 specified a single year of involuntary service (though an Aristo could contribute an indentured man "for the duration"); and although we were strenuously canvassed to re-enlist we resisted that temptation (except for Lymon Pugh, who felt the Army, despite its manifest dangers, was a more attractive option than the meat-packing trade). This meant that as early as Easter I would be able to leave here with Sam and Julian, and we would be bound for New York City—as civilians!—just as we had intended when we fled Williams Ford, though with a heightened sense of the injustices and opportunities of life.

During my enforced idleness I did a great deal of reading and writing. I wrote to my mother in Williams Ford, as I had written several times before, being careful not to disclose any dangerous information about Julian or our precise whereabouts, since there was always a chance the mail might be intercepted by some perfervid Dominion or Government agent still hunting the President's nephew. That meant that I could not receive any letters from my mother in return, a sore trial for me; but I was careful to write as regularly as possible, and to reassure her about my health and welfare.

I also wrote to Calyxa Blake, confessing my continued love and my desire to see her again. She responded with letters of her own, but these were curiously brief, though friendly enough. Something in the tone of them worried me, and I vowed to seek her out as soon as I could convince the doctors to release me.

That did not happen immediately, however; so I pursued other kinds of writing. I wrote an account of the events of the winter—of our voyage up the Saguenay, the Siege of Chicoutimi, the fall of that town, and the capture of the Chinese Cannon. I tried to hew to the principles the correspondent Theodore Dornwood had taught me, that is, to remain within the borders of the truth but to veer, where there was latitude, toward Drama. I worked at the piece over several days, reading what I had written and re-writing it, until I was satisfied with the result. Then I pondered how to get the pages to Mr. Dornwood, if he was still anywhere near Montreal. Mr. Dornwood had praised my previous efforts, and—if the truth be told—I had grown somewhat addicted to his flattery, coming as it did from a professional War Correspondent.

In the end it was Lymon Pugh who offered to be my intermediary.

He was the healthiest of us, and he came to the ward-room the day he was due to be released. We talked idly at first. Then he saw what I was reading, and asked me about it.

It was *A History of Mankind in Space.* I had kept this tattered and very ancient volume with me all through my military career, tucked into the bottom of my ditty-bag. It wasn't heavy—the formidable stiff covers of the book had fallen off months ago. Really it was only a bundle of pages held together with a binding of threads which I had sewn myself (clumsily). "An old book," I said to Lymon.

"How old?"

"More than a century. It's from the last days of the Secular Ancients."

Lymon's eyes widened. "That old! Did they write in English back then, or did they have some language of their own?"

"It's English, though some of the words and usages are peculiar. Here, look."

Lymon had lately taken an interest in books, since he was now able to puzzle out enough words to make them intriguing to him—books, which had been mute lumps in prior times, were suddenly full of voices, all clamoring for attention. In the course of Lymon's instruction I had read him chapters of Mr. Charles Curtis Easton's *Against the Brazilians,* which had also survived intact in my ditty-bag, and I had even allowed Lymon to borrow the volume and read ahead, once he was captivated by the plot.*

---

* Lymon, though not experienced in reading, endorsed my opinion that Mr. Easton was probably the greatest of our living authors. He could not imagine a better one, at any rate. It was a miracle that anyone wrote books at all, Lymon said, much less good ones; and he was impressed by Mr. Easton's formidable knowledge of foreign places, historic battles, pirates, and such interesting subjects.

But the *History of Mankind in Space* seemed to oppress him as he leafed through its pages and inspected its photographs. His features knotted into a spindled emblem of perplexity. "It seems to say here that people went to the moon," he uttered in a low voice.

"That's exactly what it says."

"And this is not a work of fiction?"

"It claims not to be. I don't know whether folks walked on the moon or not. But the Secular Ancients clearly believed it, and so does Julian."

It was a poorly-ordered world we lived in, Lymon said, if moon-visiting was deemed to be "non-fiction" while Mr. Easton's straightforward narratives about wars and pirates were excoriated (as they had been, Julian once told me, in some quarters) as crude storytelling. "This isn't a Dominion book, is it?"

"No. When it was written, there *was* no Dominion."

"Keep your voice down—you'll get us in trouble with that kind of talk."

"It's not 'talk,' only history. Even the Dominion admits that it came into being with the False Tribulation. Before that all the churches were independent, and disorganized, and had little sway with the government, or any way of fulfilling the ideal of a Christian World under the direct administration of Heaven."

"That's what the Dominion means to set up?"

"That's its ultimate purpose—to unite the world in advance of the rule of Jesus Christ." Which he would have known, if he had not slept through so many Sunday services.

"I'm not well-churched," said Lymon, rubbing his left hand over his scarred right forearm. "Do you suppose that's about to happen, with the fall of Chicoutimi and all?"

"The Dominion must conquer a great deal more of the world than just Labrador before the end of all worldly strife. I doubt we'll see the Global Reign of Christianity in our lifetime."

Lymon nodded with obvious relief. He said he didn't mind the prospect of Christian government—he was willing to be ruled by Heaven—what troubled him was that Heaven might employ men like Major Lampret as intermediaries.

I asked whether the Major had recovered from the wounds he received during the capture of the Chinese Cannon.

"He did, and he even survived the cholera; but he's gone back to Colorado Springs for the time being. The events up the Saguenay were an embarrassment to him, and he needs to improve his morale and reputation as much his health."

"Good news for Julian, at least," I said. "Lymon, since you're leaving here shortly, and I'm still confined to bed, would you do me a favor?"

"Yes, certainly—what?"

"I have two packages I need delivered in Montreal." I took these out from where I had stashed them beneath the bed. "The smaller one is a letter, to be delivered personally to Calyxa Blake. I've written her address on the envelope—can you read it adequately well?"

"I think so."

"This bigger bundle of papers is meant for Mr. Theodore Dornwood, if he's still around, and if you can find him."

"Dornwood the newspaper writer? That might be difficult. Rumor is that he left the regiment when we went up-river, and that he sits in some cheap rental and posts lies to Manhattan, between bouts of drunkenness and debauchery. But I'll try to find him, for your sake, if you want me to, Adam."

The reader may imagine with what impatience and anxiety I awaited Lymon's return, for each of the missives I had entrusted to him was greatly significant to me. The package for Theodore Dornwood contained my whole account of the Saguenay Expedition. The smaller letter, meant for Calyxa, was even more momentous. In it, I expressed my intention to propose marriage to her, should she find the time to visit me in the hospital.

But Lymon did not return that afternoon, nor in the evening. To forestall my uneasiness I talked with the two other patients with whom I shared the ward. One was a lease-boy like myself, but from a Southern estate, where he had been worked cruelly in the tropical heat; he had been wounded north of Quebec, and his whole right arm, though intact, was a useless appendage. My other companion was a cavalryman with a generous mustache and his head shaved bald, who wouldn't say how he had acquired the injury that was hidden by a layer of bandages wrapping his belly. Neither of these men were scintillating conversationalists, since both were in constant pain; but the cavalryman owned a box of dominoes, and we passed an hour or two playing Estates. After that I asked the nurse whether the hospital had any fresh reading material, since I had memorized nearly every page of the *History of Mankind in Space* and *Against the Brazilians*. "I think there might be something," she said. But all she could scare up was a slender volume of stories by Mrs. Eckerson. Mrs. Eckerson was one of the classic authors of the nineteenth century, suitable for modern tastes, and preserved from extinction by the Dominion press; but she wrote mainly for young girls, and the book provoked memories of my sister Flaxie. Nevertheless I read until my eyes tired of it; and my bedside lamp, by the time I blew it out, was the last one burning.

In the morning I was treated to one of the hospital's Hygienic Baths—a mandatory ordeal, overseen by nurses, and damaging to male dignity—and when I returned to my bed I found Lymon Pugh waiting in the visitor's chair. He was alone.

"Well?" I said. "Did you deliver the messages I gave you?"

"Yes," he said, with an apparent uneasiness.

"Well, don't make a mystery of it! Tell me what happened."

He cleared his throat. "I found that Theodore Dornwood for you. The stories about him are true, Adam. He's living by the docks, in a shack not much better than a stable. He lies in a yellow bed and drinks whiskey and smokes hempen cigarettes all day long. He still possesses that 'typewriter' you always talk about, but he don't seem to employ it much."

"His bad habits don't concern me. Did he accept my account of the Saguenay Expedition?"

"At first he didn't want to see me at all—he's surly when he's drunk, and he called me a poxy hallucination, and said I was absurd, and things of that nature. Ordinarily I wouldn't take that from anyone, but I took it from him, Adam, on your behalf, and he mellowed somewhat when I mentioned your name. 'My Western Muse,' he called you, whatever that means. And when I showed him that bundle of papers his eyes lit right up."

The praise tickled my vanity, and I asked whether Mr. Dornwood had said anything more on the subject.

"Well, he took the papers out and began to read them, and then he looked at the last few pages and grinned. He said it was excellent work."

"That's all?"

"If he said anything else, it wasn't to me—he shooed me away without a thank-you. But the package must have improved his mood, because I heard a great deal of clacking and tapping from his machine as I walked off."

"I'll seek him out when I'm released," I said, pleased by the report of Mr. Dornwood's enthusiasm, though it had lacked any flattering specifics. A vastly more important question loomed. "And did you deliver my letter to Miss Blake?"

"Well, I went to the address you gave me."

"Wasn't she home?"

"No, and hadn't been for quite a while, according to the neighbors. So I asked after her down at the Thirsty Boot. It took some effort, because those people are not universally well-disposed toward American soldiers, but I finally found out what had become of her."

He paused at this critical juncture, as if considering his words; and I said, "Go on! Whatever you learned, tell me!"

"Well, I—I found her, at the place where she's now residing; and I gave her your letter—that's the bones of the story."

"Flesh it out, then! Didn't she have any response?"

"She was thoughtful about it. She read it a couple of times over. Then she said, 'Tell Adam I find his suggestion interesting—'"

"Interesting!"

It wasn't an acceptance of my proposal, but neither was it a rejection—I held that small hope close to my heart.

"'Interesting,' she said, 'but unfortunately not practical right at the moment.'"

"Not practical!"

"I expect she meant, because of where she lives."

I could not help remembering that her villainous brothers had threatened to sell her into a brothel, and I was terrorized by the notion that they might have succeeded. "Lymon, I'm strong enough for the truth—what terrible place has she gone to, that prevents her from coming to see me?"

Lymon blushed and looked at his feet. "Well—"

"Oh, say it!"

"She's in—and don't take this too hard, Adam—she's in prison."

I set up a meeting between myself, Sam, Julian, and Lymon Pugh, in order to plan strategy, and in defiance of the rules of the Soldier's Rest. We convened in the ward where Julian was recovering, ignoring the protests of the nurses, and it was quickly agreed that we ought to rescue Calyxa, although my proposal—that we leave immediately and storm the prison—was rejected. It was unwise strategy, Sam said, to attack a target before acquiring reliable intelligence about its strengths, its weaknesses, and the mood of its defenders. I was forced to admit the truth of this; though sitting in idleness while Calyxa endured confinement was not a comfortable chore.

Sam was as healthy by now as Lymon Pugh, and he agreed to leave the hospital for the purpose of scouting out the prison. I would stay here, in the meantime, with Julian, who was less recovered, though he took a keen interest in the subject.

I shook hands with all parties at the conclusion of the meeting, and I was profoundly moved, and struggled to control my emotions. "It's more than I ever expected to have such friends as would risk themselves on my behalf—despite the difference in our stations in life—and I want you all to know that I would do the same for each one of you, if the boot were on the other leg."

"Don't be so eager to thank us," Sam said, "until we actually accomplish something."

But I could tell that he was moved, as well.

I sat with Julian a while longer after Sam and Lymon left. Julian appeared more frail than I liked to see him. His skin was very white, and it cleaved to the bones of his cheeks, for he had lost considerable weight, and Julian had never been stout. Something about his eyes had changed, too, I thought, as if they had absorbed an unpleasant wisdom, which dulled their color. That might have been due to the cholera, or to war in general and all the death he had seen. It made me nervous, and I thanked him again for his kindness, addressing him as if he were an Aristo, and I was a lease-boy . . . which of course we *were*; but it had never seemed so, between us.

"Settle down, Adam," he said. "I know how fond you are of this Montreal woman."

"More than fond!" I confided in him, and shared my secret, that I hoped to marry her.

He grinned at the news. "In that case we must certainly have her released from jail! It would never do to have my best friend wedded to a prisoner."

"Don't make light of it, Julian—I can't bear it. I love her more dearly than I can describe without blushing."

He said, more gently, "It must be wonderful to feel that way about a woman."

"It is; though it has its distressing aspects. I know one day you'll meet a suitable woman, and feel about her as I do about Calyxa."

I think he appreciated this kindness on my part, for he looked away, and smiled to himself. "I suppose anything is possible," he said.

What was not possible was for us to converse much longer, for the hour of lamps-out was approaching, and the nurses had rallied and were preparing to descend on us in force. I told Julian he needed his sleep. "You must sleep as well, Adam," he said, "though it might be hard to keep from worrying all night long. Sleep confidently—that's an order."

"An order from a fellow Private?"

"But I'm not a Private anymore—didn't Sam tell you? Both Sam and I were given promotions while we were unconscious."

I expect it was an attempt on the part of the Staff to induce them to re-enlist, or else a result of the terrible casualties the Army of the Laurentians had suffered during the Saguenay Expedition; but, for whatever reason, Sam was now officially a Colonel; and Julian was a Captain—Captain Commongold— just as Theodore Dornwood had predicted.

I stood up and essayed a salute, but Julian waved it off: "Don't, Adam—I need a friend far more than I need a subordinate. And we'll all be out of the Army soon, and on an even footing once again."

I supposed that was true, in the sense he intended it; but in another sense we would never be "even" again—if we ever had been—for, whatever else we were, we were no longer boys. We had survived a War; and we were Men.

Sam and Lymon returned in the morning with their scouting report.

The good news was that Calyxa was being held in a military prison, not a civilian jail. That was a boon because the rules applying to military prisons were more flexible than civil law—she hadn't been convicted of anything, and was serving no fixed term, but was being held "on suspicion," which meant that it required only an official adjudgment to have her released.

"What was her crime?" I asked.

"She was hauled in," Sam said, "as part of a gang of troublemakers who call themselves *Parmentierists,* after some European philosopher, when they were marching down the street with signs reading ALL SOLDIERS OUT OF MONTREAL and such slogans as that."

"Surely it's not illegal to carry a sign, even under military occupation."

"It wasn't the sign-carrying that got them arrested. The mob she was with ran into a pair of backwoods ruffians who had some grievance against them, and gunfire was exchanged. She was found to be carrying a small pistol, which she had fired."

The backwoodsmen, I suspected, were none other than Job and Utty Blake, her murderous siblings; but Sam couldn't confirm it, since he had confined his inquiries to Calyxa's particular circumstances. "Will they let her out, then?"

"Not without orders from headquarters . . . which is a problem, since the leadership of the Army of the Laurentians is in a state of flux, and trivial matters are being ignored. It could be months before the situation returns to normal."

"Months!"

"Obviously we need to retrieve her sooner than that. But it might take delicate maneuvering, and perhaps some forgivable chicanery. May I suggest a plan?"

He did so—and it was an admirable plan, which I will describe in its enactment—but it required that we function as a group, and some question remained about Julian's health and fitness. The nurses refused to discharge him, but they couldn't physically prevent him from leaving . . . which is what he did, standing up, a little shakily, and demanding his uniform, which was presently delivered to him. He was pale and perilously thin, but seemed to improve as soon as we stepped into the sunshine. The season was young yet, with Easter still a week in the future, but Montreal was pleasantly warm under a cloudless, breezy sky. We proceeded to a tavern, where we rented a room to store our possessions; and we waited there while Lymon Pugh went off to seek Theodore Dornwood once again.

It wasn't Dornwood we needed but the use of his typewriter. Mr. Dornwood had been reluctant to allow it, Lymon said on his return; but Lymon had cited urgent necessity, and flexed his enormous arm muscles in a conspicuous fashion, until the journalist relented.

"It was lucky I caught him when I did," Lymon said. "He was packing up. Says he's been called back to Manhattan by his newspaper. Another hour and he'd have been gone by train."

"But you got what we needed from him?" asked Sam.

"Here it is."

Lymon Pugh unfolded a piece of paper, and placed it on the table before us.

"This isn't exactly the text I requested," Sam said.

"Dornwood wouldn't consent to type it—I had to pick it out myself. And I couldn't remember quite everything, at least not the way you said it."

The message as printed said:

HEADquaRTERS ARMy of the LORENSHENS
tO THE ARMY JAIL MONTReALL

PleASE RELEASE to the BARER OF this NOTE
one PRISONER
of the naME OF Calixa BLAKE
Bein a Female Person of Athletic Build
Curly blacK Hair &
ThiCK ANKELS

BY ORder of Colonel SAM SAmSON, signed.

"Is it all right?" Lymon asked anxiously. "I wrote 'Colonel' as you wanted me to, Sam, though the spelling seems irregular to me. That machine is a menace, Adam, I don't know why you crave it so—it took me most of an hour to peck out the letters on it. Writers must suffer as badly as beef-boners, if they're attached to such a device all day."

"The spelling's not important," said Sam. "The night guards at the prison are almost certainly illiterate. The printed letters are what will impress them, along with my rank, or so I hope." In order to further impress them Sam had purchased a bottle of blue ink, which he spilled onto a cloth napkin; then he took a Comstock dollar from his pocket and pressed the side of it bearing the image of Julian's uncle into the ink, and used the coin on the paper as a sort of stamp or imprimatur, which indeed looked very official, and would have fooled me if I had been less schooled in reading.

After that it was only a matter of waiting. We ordered meals of cut pork and kidney beans all around, to brace us for the evening, and to advance the cause of Julian's improving health. Those of us who drank spirits took beer or wine. I took plain water, as usual, though I added a small amount of red wine to the cup at Sam's insistence, to discourage any microscopic disease germs flourishing therein (for the cholera had not spared Montreal). It was a medicinal, hygienic precaution; and it did not make me drunk, or even count as a sin, as far as I could see, though perhaps the angels account it differently.

We waited until well after sunset, and then until the evening crowds had abandoned the streets and all but the overnight torches had been extinguished. Then we left the tavern and walked as a group to the prison where Calyxa was unjustly confined.

The prison was a building with thick, ancient stone walls. It had been divided into a habitation for the guards and staff, on the top floor, and cells for the inmates, on the ground floor and in a basement below. Perhaps the building had served a civic purpose at one time; but the Army of the Laurentians had made the building their own, and draped it with military banners, and posted guards at the rusty iron doors. Our sole advantage, Sam said, would be in our confident bearing. We had to present ourselves as men assigned a necessary but unexciting duty; so we were not to speak furtively, or cast around nervous glances, but to play the role "to the hilt." Colonel Sam led the way, of course, his bar of command freshly sewn to the shoulder-strap of his overcoat (useful now that the day's heat had evaporated), while "Captain Commongold" acted as his adjutant, and Lymon and I as ordinary soldiers.

The guards at the door glanced at Sam's insignia of rank, and briefly at our counterfeit note, before allowing us inside. We came into a kind of ante-room, where a sleepy-looking officer of the guard regarded us from behind a desk.

He was surprised to have visitors at this late hour, and his expression wasn't welcoming. "You have some business to conduct?" he asked.

Sam nodded regally and presented him with the certificate Lymon Pugh had printed on the typewriter of Mr. Dornwood.

The guard looked it over. He was a skinny man not much older than myself, aspiring to a beard. He gave the note back to Sam and said, "I have misplaced my eyeglasses, Colonel—best if you read it to me."

Sam did so.

"This is an irregular hour for a prisoner transfer," the guard said.

"I don't care that it's regular or irregular," said Sam. "I'm here to do a job, and if you have to wake your commanding officer before I can do it, then wake him, please, and do it promptly."

"I don't know as that's necessary . . . as long as you'll sign for the prisoner."

"Of course I'll sign for her! Where is she?"

The head man did not bestir himself, but called one of his underlings from door duty. "Packard, show these men to the cellar. Take the keys."

We followed Packard down a set of stairs into a dimly-lit and stinking arrangement of iron-barred cells—a man-made Hell, I might even say, except that it was rather more cold than warm at the moment. I looked around this awful place for any sign of Calyxa, but what I saw was something much worse: the unhappy faces of Job and Utty Blake.

The two villains jointly occupied a single cell. Our passage had waked them up, and they gazed at us with sleepy suspicion. I did not doubt they were the Blake brothers, though I had only seen one of them before, and then only the top of his head. That one was Job; and if he recognized me by the dim light of the guard's lantern he showed no sign of it.

Both brothers possessed the family signature, which was a crown of

bushy, curly hair; but Job's incarnation of it had been altered by my prior encounter with him. At the top of his forehead a wide swatch of hair was gone,
replaced by a conspicuously scarred and wrinkled divot where my pistol shot
had creased his skull. I cannot say I took pride in the sight of the wound I had
inflicted on this terrible man . . . but it didn't entirely displease me.

I was careful to betray no reaction, however, for it would have been awkward had he known me. We proceeded on to a much larger cell, as big as a
room, in which several people had been confined together—the "Parmentierists," of whom Calyxa was one. She sprang to her feet at the sight of me;
but I made a cautioning gesture, and she spoke not a word.

"That's her there," the guard said, pointing.

"Let her out, then," Sam demanded.

Packard fumbled with a ring of keys by the dim glow of the lantern.
While he was doing that Calyxa stepped forward and stood where she could
whisper to me without being overheard.

"What do you want, Adam?" she asked with unexpected coolness.

"What do I want! Didn't you get my letter?"

The other inmates—I recognized some of them from her circle of
friends at the Thirsty Boot—were frankly curious about this midnight visit;
but they kept their distance from us, once Calyxa had given them a fierce
glare.

"Yes," she said. "I got it and read it. You said you want to marry me."

I did, of course, but I hadn't thought to discuss it so baldly, or through the
bars of a prison cell. "I want to marry you above all other Earthly things," I
said. "If you consent to be my wife, Calyxa, the world won't hold a happier
specimen of a man. Once you're free of this place—"

"But if I *don't* consent?"

"Don't consent!" That bewildered me. "Well—that's your decision—all I
can do, Calyxa, is ask."

"I won't consent to any such arrangement until I know the details of it.
There's a suspicion of you among my friends, who aren't inclined to trust a
soldier of any breed or nationality."

"What am I suspected of?"

"Bargaining my freedom in exchange for my betrothal."

"I don't understand!"

"I can't make it any plainer. Am I free to go, whether I marry you or not?
Or am I to rot in this prison unless I consent?"

I was astonished that she could suspect me of such blackmail, and I put it
down to the bad influence of her political companions. At least, I thought, the
expression on her face was more hopeful than despairing. I said, "I love you,
Calyxa Blake, and I won't let you linger here an hour longer even if you despise me with all the passion in your body. To see you set free is all I care about
right now—we can discuss the rest of it another time."

I said this loudly enough to be heard by the cynical Parmentierists, who responded by giving me a cheer, perhaps not altogether ironical in intent; and they started up an impudent chorus of *Piston, Loom, and Anvil,* as Calyxa shot them a vindictive look that said, in essence, *I told you so!*

Unfortunately I was also overheard by the slack-jawed guard, Packard, who looked alarmed, and pulled back his key from the key-hole. "What's this about?" he asked, and he persisted in his questioning until Lymon Pugh was forced to silence the poor man.* Sam retrieved the keys from Packard's limp hand and opened the door, and said to all those it contained, "You might as well take the opportunity, you boys—there are only two guards in the outer office, and if you handle them fast they won't have time to raise an alarm."

The Parmentierists seemed impressed by this act of generosity on the part of an American soldier, and I hoped it would make their political views more nuanced in the future. They crowded out quickly, eager to overwhelm the remaining guards, and Calyxa came into my arms.

"Well, will you?" I asked, once we had breath enough to speak.

"Will I what?"

"Marry me!"

"I suppose I will," she said, sounding surprised at her own answer.

My joy was unconquerable, though it ebbed as we passed the cage where Job and Utty Blake were confined.

Utty sat at the back of the cell, scowling and muttering. But Job, whom I had shot, came up to the bars, and rattled them as savagely as a gorilla, and spat out curses in the French language.

"I don't guess we'll set these two free," Sam said, the keys still jingling in his hand.

"No," said Calyxa, "*please don't*—they're murderers, bush runners, and spies for the Dutch when the money is good—they've already been convicted and sentenced to hang."

She explained that in the melee between the Blake Brothers and the Parmentierists several shots had been fired, but only Job and Utty had struck targets. Job had killed a young Parmentierist, and Utty had gunned down a luckless bystander. Some Colonel or Major of the local garrison had promptly appointed himself a court and sentenced the pair to public hanging . . . perhaps not a wholly legal procedure even under the rules of military occupation; but no one, apart from the Blake Brothers, had taken exception to it.

Job had heard all about Calyxa's dalliance with a soldier, and he had

---

* Lymon had amused himself during his hospital confinement by making himself a Knocker—a very fine one, consisting of a lead egg in a hempcloth sack, just as he had once described to me—and it was this device he employed to relieve the guard of his senses.

deduced by the events of this evening that I was that person, the one who had come within an inch of blowing out his brains. He directed more curses and not a little saliva at me, before turning his vulture's gaze on Calyxa.

"*Tu nous sers à rien, mais pire . . . tu nous déshonores! Dommage que tu sois pas mort dans l'utérus de ta mère!*"

"What's he saying?" I asked.

"He says he regrets that I was ever born."

I looked Job Blake hard in the eye. "We all have regrets in this life," I said, philosophically. "Tell him I regret I didn't aim lower."

9

The wedding was arranged to take place on the Saturday after Easter, by which time Sam, Julian, and I would be civilians again; and after the ceremony we would all board the train for New York City, and begin our lives afresh.

I won't strain the reader's attention by narrating every detail of our mustering-out. Suffice to say that we rejoined our Regiment and concluded our business there. Sam performed one duty enabled by his new rank, which was to rebuke Private Langers, whom he suspected of having acted as a spy for Major Lampret. Langers had survived the Saguenay Campaign, and was running his "Lucky Mug" business whenever a skirmish with the Dutch provided fresh corpses to loot. Sam waited until a crowd had gathered around Langers's tent. Then he demanded to see the entire contents of the Lucky Mug, which he proceeded to inventory, demonstrating to the assembled soldiers that the numbers on the slips corresponded to the worthless trinkets, but never to the valuable goods. This revelation so incensed the Private's customers than no further discipline on Sam's part was necessary. I learned later that Langers survived his chastisement.

We signed ourselves out of the Army of the Laurentians and were given documents testifying to our discharge, along with something called a "recall number" which would summon us back to active duty in case of an emergency—but we gave that prospect scant thought. Sam, Julian, and I said goodbye to Lymon Pugh, who had re-enlisted, and vows of friendship were exchanged, and Lymon promised to write occasionally, now that he was able to do so. Then we rode a wagon to the City of Montreal, where Calyxa was waiting for me.

A few days remained before the wedding. Sam used the time to say goodbye to friends he had made among the Jews of Montreal, though they were not satisfied with his degree of orthodoxy. Sam was firmly a Jew, in his own estimate, and had been born such, but he never adopted the refined and intricate doctrines and habits that characterize that faith, such as not working on Saturday (a day the Jews had apparently mistaken for the Sabbath), or attending "shool" on a regular basis, or following every commandment of the Torah (which was some sort of cylindrical Bible, as Sam described it). "I was taken from those things too early," he lamented to me, "and they don't come naturally at my age. I never underwent a Bar-Mitz-Va. I don't read or speak Hebrew. I'm lucky to have had a bris, come to that."*

---

* A custom that can't be described outside of a medical textbook; though by Sam's account of it I was astonished that he would consider himself "lucky."

"Don't the Jews of Montreal understand your limitations?"

"They do, but they're impatient with my apostasy. Properly so, it may be."
He shook his head. "I'm not one thing or the other, Adam. There's no suitable
faith for people like me."

I told him not to feel sad, and that he was not the only person daunted
by the complexities of religion, even under the generous rule of the Dominion of Jesus Christ. For instance, there was no congregation of the Church
of Signs in Montreal, which meant I couldn't marry Calyxa in the faith of
my father (had I wanted to—I confess I did not). We had settled on an in-
terdenominational Dominion marriage, to be performed by the local Dominion man who licensed dioceses and collected tithes on behalf of Colorado
Springs. We would at least be married in a church, albeit a nominally
Catholic one. The church charged fees for its use by those who confess to
other faiths, and the going rate was steep, and it used up much of the money
I had saved toward the purchase of a typewriter; but Calyxa was worth it, I
thought.

Julian had also made friends in Montreal, and he used the time before
the wedding to take his leave of them. These were the Philosophers and
Aesthetes who gathered at the coffee-shop called Dorothy's. Julian had
not introduced me to any of them, and they seemed exactly as loose-limbed
and pallid as Lymon Pugh had described them, when I saw them from a
distance; but I was no judge of Philosophers. At least they did not parade around with unpatriotic signs, or get themselves locked up in military
prison.*

As for me, I spent my time with Calyxa. Part of this devotion was practical, since there were arrangements to be made and invitations to be delivered. But it was an indulgence, too; for we were at that stage of betrothal in
which we craved each other's company in all ways and at all hours. If we
"anticipated our vows," perhaps the reader can forgive us for our eagerness;
and I'll say no more on the subject, except to repeat that it was a very happy
time for me.

Of course I wrote to my mother to announce the occasion, and to apologize for not being able to bring Calyxa to meet her, though I assured her I
would do my best to make that happen, preferably sooner rather than later.
Calyxa had no family except Job and Utty, who had a prior engagement—they
were to be hanged on the day of the wedding—but all the Parmentierists
would be there, and the staff of the Thirsty Boot, and assorted street musicians and sundry revolutionaries; and "my side of the aisle" would be full up
with survivors of the Saguenay Campaign, and perhaps a few Philosophers,
Jews, and Aesthetes, at the invitation of Sam and Julian.

---

* They were sometimes locked up for other reasons, Julian said; but he changed the subject when I
asked him to explain.

In the end it was a wedding like any other—familiar enough in its trappings to subdue the need for description. In short: we were wed; we kissed; there were cheers; refreshments were served.

A carriage had been hired for our trip to the train station. It was not quite a "wedding carriage," for Sam and Julian shared the transportation with us. All of us had purchased tickets for the New York Express, which was due to leave Montreal at sundown. I rode with my arm around Calyxa, and we cooed at each other, and uttered pleasant trivialities, while Sam and Julian blushed, or coughed into their hands, or made a point of staring out the curtained windows even though the city was dull in the fading light and decorated only with gray banners announcing BOIL ALL WATER or similar hygienic instructions.

There was one stop Calyxa insisted on, however, before we reached the train station, and that was the public square where the Army of the Laurentians conducted its hangings.

Job and Utty had already met their fate, at about the time Calyxa and I solemnized our vows. I suggested she might not want to sully the memory of the day by visiting a gallows; but she needed reassurance that her brothers were truly dead, she told me, and that they wouldn't spring back to life at some inconvenient time in the future.

So I told the hired driver to stop where the hangings had taken place. It was the policy of the Army of the Laurentians to leave corpses dangling from the gallows until a day or two had passed, so the dead would serve as a useful advertisement of the wages of vice and rebellion. This custom had been but partially honored in the case of Job and Utty. Two ropes dangled from the elaborate scaffold, but only one was occupied. I asked a bystander about this, and the man explained that Utty Blake had been hanged first, but that the scaffold had been built too high, or the rope made too long, and at the critical moment Utty's head had been "nipped off," as the man put it, so that the body no longer depended from the rope, but slipped through at the neck and had to be hauled away in two pieces. Stains on the ground attested to the truth of this.

But Job was still "on duty." He looked much smaller in death. His face was purple, and not pleasant to contemplate, though I had seen uglier corpses during my military career. A chill wind had come up, and it flapped the banners adorning the nearest buildings and turned Job's corpse like a pendulum at the end of his mournfully creaking rope. Ponderous clouds swept through the darkening sky, and the mood of the place was altogether dour and unhappy.

Nevertheless Calyxa sprang from the wedding carriage energetically, and walked right up to the unkempt and frankly foul body of her brother. His bootless feet dangled at about the level of her shoulders.

I let her stand alone on that dusty, windy square, in contemplation of the ephemerality of life and all worldly things, for many long minutes. Then I joined her, and put a consoling arm around her waist.

"As awful as your brothers were," I said, "this must be hard to endure."

"Not very hard," she whispered.

"Say your goodbyes, then, Calyxa—we have a train to catch."

I was moved by her somber expression, which implied a soul less hardened than she liked to pretend; and I was even more moved when she found the Christian charity to utter a quick prayer* for the soul of poor dead Job.

Then we climbed back into the carriage, and I instructed the driver to take us on to the train station. The atmosphere had cooled somewhat, and there was no more post-nuptial cooing. Instead, Calyxa attempted to make conversation.

She didn't know Sam or Julian very well just yet. In a sense she didn't know them at all: despite the confidences we shared, I had avoided telling her that Julian was actually Julian Comstock, the President's nephew, or that Sam had been the best friend of Julian's murdered father. I had promised Sam and Julian that I wouldn't mention these awkward truths, and I had been true to my promise.

But I had told her other things about my friends and my adventures with them. She looked squarely at Julian and said, "You like to tell Bible stories."

Julian was uncomfortable—as he often was in the presence of women—and seemed not to know how to respond. He swallowed repeatedly, his Adam's apple bobbing in his throat. "Ah, well . . . do I?"

"According to Adam. Bible stories of your own invention. Most of them blasphemous."

"Perhaps Adam exaggerates."

"Tell me one," Calyxa said, as the carriage rattled down the gloomy, windy street, and a small rain began to fall. Her gaze drifted to the window of the carriage. "Tell me an Easter story, if you know one."

I didn't like the trend of this conversation. Julian's apostasies were often shocking to the uninitiated, and I had hoped Calyxa would get to know him better before he trained the cannon of his Agnosticism on her at close range. But Julian liked a challenge; and I think he was charmed by Calyxa's boldness and directness.

He cleared his throat. "Well, let me see." The overhead lantern teetered on its gimbals. Rain drummed on the carriage-roof, and Julian's breath hung visibly in the chill air. "God created the world—"

"That's starting a long way back," Calyxa said.

"Perhaps it is; but do you want to hear this story or not?"

"I beg your pardon. Continue."

"In the beginning God created the world," Julian said, "and set it turning;

* *"Passe mon bonjour au Diable quand tu le verras."*

and let events transpire without much in the way of personal intervention. He stage-managed a few tribal disputes, and arranged a misguided Flood that cost many lives and solved very few problems; but in the end He decided the human race was too corrupt to be salvaged, and too pathetic to destroy, and so He stopped tinkering with it, and left it alone.

"But humanity, on the whole, was conscious of its fallen condition, and went on petitioning God for unearned gifts or the redress of grievances. All this badgering, in God's eyes, amounted to a lament for lost innocence—a nostalgia for the abandoned paradise that was Eden. 'Make us innocent again,' humanity cried out, 'or at least send innocence among us, to serve as an example.'

"God was skeptical. 'You wouldn't recognize Innocence if it handed you a calling card,' He said to humanity, 'and Goodness exceeds your grasp with the regularity of clockwork. Look for these things where you find them, and leave Me alone.'

"But the prayers never ceased, and God couldn't indefinitely ignore all that grief and lamentation, which lapped at the walls of Heaven like a noxious tide. 'All right,' He said at last, 'I've heard your noise, and I'll give you what you want.' So He fathered a child by a virgin—in fact a *married* virgin, for God was fond of miracles, and for a woman to be simultaneously a wife, a virgin, and a mother seemed like a miracle with compound interest accrued. And so in the fullness of time a child was born—innocent, bereft of sin, invulnerable to temptation, and good-hearted down to the very marrow of him. 'Make of him what you will,' God said grimly, and stood back with His arms folded."

(I tried to evaluate Calyxa's reaction to these blasphemies. She kept her face motionless, but her eyes were attentive and unblinking. The rain came down stiffly, and the wheels of passing carts made a muted sound in the dusk.)

"A quarter-century or so went by," Julian continued. "And eventually that child of God was returned to his Creator—scorned, insulted, beaten, humiliated, and finally nailed to a splintery cross and suspended in the Galilean sunshine until he died of his wounds both physical and spiritual.

"God received this much-abused gift by return mail, as it were, and He was ferociously scornful, and said to humanity, 'See what you do with Innocence? See what you make of Love and Goodwill when it looks you in the eye?' And so saying He turned His back on Mankind, and determined never to speak to the human race again, or have any other dealings with it.

"And even this," Julian said, "might have been a useful lesson, taken as such; but Man misunderstood his own chastening, and imagined that his sins had been forgiven, and put up effigies of the tortured demigod and the instrument on which he had been broken, and marked the event every Easter with a church service and a colorful hat. And as God made Himself deaf to Man, so Man became deaf to God; and our prayers languished in the dead air of our cavernous churches, and do so to this day."

The carriage was silent in the aftermath of this cruel and frankly blasphemous narrative. Sam sighed and stared out into the rain. The vehicle's
springs creaked as we bounced over wet cobblestones, a sound that reminded
me of the creaking rope where Job Blake had been hung. Julian looked at
Calyxa boldly, if a little apprehensively, while she pondered her response.

"That's a fine story," she said finally. "I like that story very much—thank
you, Julian. I hope you'll tell me another one some day." She essayed a smile.
"Perhaps I'll make up one of my own, now that you've shown me how."

It was Julian's turn to gawk in astonishment. He slowly took the measure
of Calyxa's sincerity. Then he grinned—perhaps the first genuine grin I had
seen on him since the Saguenay Campaign.

"You're welcome!" he said. Then he turned his grin on me. "You married
well, Adam! Congratulations!"

"Oy," said Sam, in the cryptic language of the Jews.

10

The future defied our expectations. The future always does, as I'm sure Julian would say. "There's no predicting Evolution," he used to say, "either in the long or the short term."

Still, the shock of our arrival in New York City can hardly be overestimated.

This is what happened.

Our train, although an Express, slowed at every switch yard, and the journey lasted all night. Calyxa and I had a stateroom to ourselves. We were awake until the early hours, and consequently slept past sunrise. We did not see anything of the City of New York until the porter knocked at the door to announce our imminent arrival.

We dressed quickly, and joined Sam and Julian in the passenger car.

I was sorry I hadn't arisen earlier, for we were already well within the boundary of Manhattan. I will not detail its wonders here—those will emerge in the later course of the story. But I knew something exceptional was going on as soon as we rolled into the columned interior of the great Central Train Station. Visible through the rain-streaked windows of the passenger car were many bays and depots where trains could embark or dispense passengers, and the one we approached was crowded with people in all kinds of colorful dress, many of them carrying signs or banners. A wooden stage had been erected, and a band played patriotic songs. The exact details were hard to distinguish through the smudged and grimy glass, but the mood of excitement was unmistakable.

We asked a passing porter what the occasion was, but he didn't know. "Someone famous in from the battle-front," he said, "probably."

Someone famous! It would be ironic, I thought, if we had come all this way with General Galligasken for a fellow traveler; but there was no hint that such was the case. We didn't know which passenger was being honored until we stepped out onto the platform. Then a ticket-taker pointed at us—at Julian, specifically—and the band promptly struck up a march.

"Dear God!" Sam said, paling, as he read the signs and banners held aloft by the crowd—and I read them, too, and my expression must have been equally gap-jawed.

WELCOME THE HERO OF THE SAGUENAY CAMPAIGN! said one.

NYC POLICE & FIREFIGHTERS SALUTE THE CAPTOR OF THE CHINESE CANNON!—another.

And a third said, simply,

HURRAY FOR CAPTAIN COMMONGOLD!

Sam trembled as violently as if he had looked at the jubilant crowd and seen, in its place, a firing squad.

Julian was even more bewildered. He opened his mouth and couldn't muster the strength to close it.

At that moment a white-haired woman came to the fore of the crowd. She was not young, nor especially thin, but her manner was vigorous and purposeful. She was clearly an Aristo—she was dressed expensively and gaudily, as if she had marched through a milliner's shop and a tropical aviary and emerged with bits of both places adhering to her. She carried a wreath of flowers on which was laid a paper banner bearing the words WOMEN'S PATRIOTIC UNION OF NEW YORK WELCOMES CAPTAIN COMMONGOLD. The wreath was so extravagant that her face was all but concealed by it, until she lifted it up with the intent of settling it around Julian's neck.

Then she got a good look at the intended object of all this adoration, and froze as if she had been struck by a bullet.

"Julian?" she whispered.

"Mother!" cried Julian.

The wreath dropped to the floor. Julian's mother embraced him. The photographers in the crowd grew interested, and hoisted their cameras, and the reporters took their pencils from behind their ears.

ACT THREE

EVENTS PATRIOTIC AND OTHERWISE

CULMINATING IN INDEPENDENCE DAY, 2174

Keep thy peaceful watch-fires burning,
Angels stand at all thy doors,
Washing from thy homes dissension
As the oceans wash thy shores.

—"A HYMN FOR AMERICA"

1

I was hastily introduced to Julian's mother as a friend from the Army, and Calyxa as my wife, and then we adjourned (at Mrs. Comstock's insistence) to a luxurious carriage, big enough to contain all five of us. A team of fine white horses carried us away from the noise and confusion of the rail station.

The upholstery of the carriage was lush, the city outside was astonishing . . . but I was hardly conscious of any of those things. In fact I was in a stricken state. I did not yet fully understand the mechanism by which this unwelcome Welcome had worked out; but I was already convinced that I had upset the plans, and perhaps hastened the doom, of my friend Julian.

Calyxa was even more bewildered by this turn of events, for which her experience supplied no antecedent or explanation. The carriage might have been silent, each of us dwelling on private thoughts and fears, but for Calyxa's periodic demands to be "let in on the joke."

"I wish I could oblige you, Mrs. Hazzard," said Julian's mother, who had succeeded in committing our names to memory despite the chaotic conditions under which we were introduced. "But I'm not sure I understand it myself."

In fact Mrs. Comstock was exhibiting an admirable degree of level-headedness, as I saw it. She was a solidly-built woman of middle age, her coifed brown hair streaked at the temples with white. She occupied a central carriage-seat. Julian brooded to her left, while Sam on her right looked pale and stricken (except when he glanced at Mrs. Comstock, which action caused a ferocious blush to rise to his cheeks).

"Excuse me," Calyxa said, "and probably this question violates some etiquette I haven't been warned about, but *who are you exactly?*"

"Emily Baines Comstock," the older woman said gamely. "Julian's female parent, if you haven't inferred that fact already."

"The name 'Comstock' comes as a surprise," Calyxa said, casting me a sour glance.

I immediately confessed that I had deceived her about Julian's pedigree. I apologized but cited my promise to Julian and Sam.

"I thought you were a Western lease-boy, Adam."

"I am! Nothing less, nothing more! I was befriended by Julian Comstock when he was sent to Williams Ford to protect him from possible conspiracies."

"Comstock," Calyxa repeated. "Conspiracies."

Julian roused from his brooding silence and said, "It's true, Calyxa, and it isn't Adam's fault he didn't tell you before now. I had hoped to remain a 'Commongold' for many more years to come. But the pretense is all blown up. The President's my uncle, yes, and he isn't charitably disposed toward me."

"And now that your identity has been revealed?"

"News of the scene at the rail station is bound to circulate quickly, the city being what it is . . ."

"And will your uncle try to kill you, then?"

Mrs. Comstock stiffened at these blunt words, but Julian just smiled sadly.

"I expect so," he said.

"Murderous relatives are a curse," nodded Calyxa, who considered herself knowledgeable in these matters. "You have my sympathy, Julian."

The plush carriage followed a street I would later learn to call Broadway, then turned aside into a fashionable district of antique houses with stone facades, either original or built up from authentic remains. I looked about as we dismounted, and everything I saw—a tree-lined street, gardens blooming with spring flowers, glass windows of gemlike clarity, etc.—spoke of Aristocracy and Ownership, and not timidly, but boastfully. Up a flight of stairs into the reception-room of the great house, then, where a small army of servants greeted the returning Mrs. Comstock and gaped at her son. Mrs. Comstock clapped her hands and said brusquely, "We have guests—rooms for Mr. and Mrs. Hazzard and Mr. Godwin, please, and if Julian's quarters are not in order they must be brought up to acceptable conditions. But only for the night. Tomorrow we remove to Edenvale."

I looked questioningly at Julian, who told me in a low voice that Edenvale was the family's country Estate, located up the Hudson River.

Some of the servants began to welcome Julian personally. They seemed to remember him warmly from earlier times, and were astonished at his arrival, since (as I later learned) rumors of his death had been circulating freely. Julian smiled to see these old acquaintances; but Mrs. Comstock was impatient, and clapped the servants to their chores, and we adjourned to an enormous parlor. A girl in a white apron brought us iced drinks. I supposed this sort of hospitality was common among Aristos, and I tried to accept it as if I were accustomed to it, though such luxury exceeded anything in my experience, including what I had seen in the houses of the Duncan and Crowley families at Williams Ford—rustic retreats by comparison with the excesses and indulgences of Manhattan, if this was an example.

Calyxa, meanwhile, regarded it all with a painfully visible skepticism, and looked at the servant girl as if she wanted to indoctrinate her into Parmentierism, a project I hoped she would not undertake.

"I think I understand the outline of the misfortune," Julian said as we settled into the depths of our prodigiously-upholstered chairs. "Somehow the story of my experience in the war has been circulated in the city . . . though I don't know how that could have come about."

I gritted my teeth but said nothing. I couldn't, until my suspicions were confirmed.

"You've been in the papers," Mrs. Comstock acknowledged. "Under your assumed name."

"Have I?"

Mrs. Comstock summoned the servant girl again. "Barbara, you know I banned cheap journals from the house. . . ."

"Oh, yes," said Barbara.

"And I know that the ban isn't universally observed. Please don't deny it—we don't have time. Go down to the kitchen and see if you can find anything sufficiently degraded on the subject of 'Julian Commongold.' Do you know what I mean?"

"Yes! The cook reads them out loud to us," Barbara said, then blushed at the admission, and hurried off to find the papers.

She came back with a weeks-old copy of the *Spark* and a crudely bound pamphlet. These specimens of urban journalism were passed among us to inspect.

The *Spark* contained "the latest intelligence from the Saguenay front, including the capture of a Chinese Cannon!" This proved to be a truncated account of Julian's bravery at Chicoutimi, printed under the byline of Theodore Dornwood, "the *Spark*'s famous front-line correspondent in the Saguenay Campaign."

Worse than this was the pamphlet, nearly a small book, which had been printed as a compilation of Mr. Dornwood's reporting, under the title *The Adventures of Captain Commongold, Youthful Hero of the Saguenay*. It was selling briskly on all the better street-corners, the servant girl said.

Julian and Sam explained to Mrs. Comstock that Dornwood was a scoundrel who had debauched himself in Montreal all during the Campaign, and who made up his stories out of rumor and whole cloth.

But I looked into the pamphlet with careful attention, and my humiliation was complete. I confessed at once—I could do nothing else. "It's Dornwood's signature," I said haltingly. "But the words . . . well . . . the words are mainly my own."

They say it's a pleasant experience for any aspiring writer to see his work set in print for the first time. This occasion was an exception to that rule.

The pamphlet's paper cover featured an engraved illustration of "Julian Commongold" (rendered as an iron-jawed youth with a piercing gaze and immaculate uniform) astride the fender of a Dutch train-engine, waving an American flag several times larger than the version he had actually employed for the purpose, while a crowd of soldiers cheered at the capture of a supposed Chinese Cannon the size of an iron-mill smokestack. Apparently artists as well as journalists were expected to err on the side of drama, and this one had not stinted in the effort. Mrs. Comstock took the pamphlet from me and held it at arm's length, an expression of distaste playing about her features.

"Did you actually *do* these things, Julian?" she asked.

"Some less florid version of them."

She turned to Sam. "And is this your idea of protecting him from harm?"

Sam looked stricken; but he said, "Julian is a young man with a will of his own, Emily—I mean, Mrs. Comstock—and he doesn't always yield to suggestion."

"He could have been killed."

"He nearly was—several times. If you regard this as a failure on my part, I can hardly contradict you." He explained the circumstances of our departure from Williams Ford and our unwilling enlistment in the Army of the Laurentians. "I did my best to keep him safe, and here he is intact, despite his recklessness and mine—I say no more."

"You may continue to call me 'Emily,' Sam—we never stood on ceremony. I'm not unhappy with you, only confused and surprised." She added, "You shaved. You used to wear an admirable beard."

"I can grow another just as admirable . . . Emily."

"Please do so." She refocused her attention. "Julian, did you have to indulge in such theatrics simply because you found yourself in the Army?"

"I felt as if I did. I was performing my duty, in my mind."

"But did you have to be so *thorough* about it? And you, Mr. Hazzard, you claim to have written the words published by this Theodore Dornwood?"

"They were never meant for publication," I said, blushing down to my hair-roots. "This is as shocking to me as it must be to you. Dornwood pretended to tutor me in the literary art, and I showed him what I imagined were exercises in narrative. He said nothing about publishing them, much less publishing them under his own name. I would have forbidden it, of course."

"Which of course is why he didn't ask. Are you really that naive, Mr. Hazzard?"

I could not frame an answer to this humiliating question, though I saw Calyxa nodding vigorously.

"None of this would be a problem," Sam reminded her, "if the connection between Commongold and Comstock hadn't been made. What were you doing at the depot, Emily?"

"A favor for the Patriotic Women's Union. We often greet returning veterans who distinguish themselves on the field of battle. Such ceremonies improve morale among civilians, and the name 'Comstock' lends a certain *éclat*. I wouldn't have reacted the way I did, but . . . well, a great deal of time has passed since you and Julian disappeared from the Duncan and Crowley Estate. There was the implication that you might have been killed. I didn't adopt that repulsive idea, but neither could I completely discount it. When I saw Julian again—well." She dabbed a tear from the corner of her eye.

"Wholly understandable!" Sam exclaimed. "Don't blame yourself!"

"Luck was against us. The vulgar papers will be full of this tomorrow. And of course . . . *he'll* hear of it."

The emphatic pronoun referred to President Deklan Comstock—Deklan Conqueror, as he was also known. A grim silence fell over the gathering.

"At least," Mrs. Comstock said finally, "we can put some distance between ourselves and the Executive Palace. Edenvale won't protect us, but it will make things less convenient for Deklan if he decides to act rashly. More than that I cannot do. But let's not be gloomy. My son is home safely—that's something to celebrate. Mr. and Mrs. Hazzard, will you join us at our Estate for the next few days?"

I was humbled by Mrs. Comstock's offer, since I had done nothing to deserve her hospitality and everything to deserve her opprobrium. I was about to decline, when Julian answered for me: "Of course Adam will come. We can hardly set him loose on the streets of the city. He'd be eaten alive."

Mrs. Comstock nodded. "You've been a loyal friend to my son, Adam Hazzard, and it would please me if you traveled with us, especially if Julian can locate some more appropriate clothing for you and your lovely wife. Consider it settled."

She clapped her hands again. A dozen servants appeared as if from thin air, and the household became a whirlwind of preparation for the journey to the countryside.

Calyxa and I spent a night in one of the guest bedrooms of the Comstock brownstone—as sybaritic an apartment as I had ever inhabited, fitted with a mattress so plush and downy that lying *on* it was equivalent to lying *in* it. This might have presented unique opportunities for marital intimacy,* except that Calyxa was conscious of the movements of servants in the hallway and adjoining rooms, which awareness of interfered with her sense of privacy.

She did note that the bedroom, like the other rooms we had seen, contained a framed photograph of Julian's father, Bryce Comstock, in a neatly-tailored Major General's uniform. "He doesn't much resemble the reigning President," she observed, "at least the face on the coin."

The resemblance existed but it was entirely structural: the high cheekbones, the thin lips. In that which *animates* a face—that is to say, the

---

* I beg the reader's pardon.

spectrum of human emotion, apparent even in a photograph—Bryce was the opposite of Deklan. In fact there was much of Julian in him: the same brightness of eye and readiness of smile. "He was the better brother," I told Calyxa. "Genuinely brave, and not inclined to casual assassination. He was a hero of the Isthmian War before Deklan had him hanged."

"Heroism is a dangerous profession," Calyxa observed, correctly.

I slept restlessly and woke as the rest of the household began to stir in the morning. The stars were just disappearing and the air was cool as we assembled ourselves and our luggage into another of Mrs. Comstock's capacious carriages, and set off with a train of servants for the docks.

Manhattan in a spring dawn! I would have been in awe, if not for the dangers overhanging us. I won't test the reader's patience by dwelling on all the wonders that passed my eye that morning; but there were brick buildings four and five stories tall, painted gaudy colors—amazing in their height but dwarfed by the skeletal steel towers for which the city is famed, some of which leaned like tipsy giants where their foundations had been undercut by water. There were wide canals on which freight barges and trash scows were drawn by teams of muscular canal-side horses. There were splendid avenues where wealthy Aristos and ragged wage workers crowded together on wooden sidewalks, next to fetid alleys strewn with waste and the occasional dead animal. There were the combined pungencies of frying food, decaying fish, and open sewers; and all of it was clad in a haze of coal smoke, made roseate by the rising sun. As we approached the docks I saw the masts and stacks of schooners and steamers bobbing against the sky. Our company traveled along a wharf until we came to a steam launch, the *Sylvania*, which belonged to Mrs. Comstock. It was a small, trim, impeccably whitewashed vessel, gilded in places, and its captain and crew had already brought the boiler up to pressure and were ready to sail.

Before we went on board Mrs. Comstock sent a dock-boy to procure copies of the morning *Spark*. The boy returned with a bundle of these journals, and as soon as we had been assigned staterooms and stored our possessions we gathered in the fore-cabin to inspect them.

Our worst fears were quickly confirmed. The front-page headline announced:

COMMONGOLD A *COMSTOCK!*
HEROIC "BOY CAPTAIN" REVEALED AS NEPHEW OF PRESIDENT.

The byline this time wasn't Theodore Dornwood's, but there were several mentions of his *Adventures of Captain Commongold*, the sales of which would no doubt be redoubled by the news. The story itself was a reasonably accurate account of Julian's arrival in Manhattan and the warm greeting he received from his mother, not much embroidered with spurious drama. Most disconcerting was a brief note in the tail of the piece to the effect that the Executive Palace had been approached for comment "but has not yet issued a public statement."

Julian, Sam, and Mrs. Comstock began to discuss the possible ramifications of all this, while Calyxa and I went to the foredeck in a gloomy mood, to distract ourselves with the passing sights. Manhattan with its skeletal towers and relentless commerce had already fallen behind us, but there was evidence of the work of the Secular Ancients on every shore—scavenged ruins as far as the eye could reach, a reminder that human beings in inconceivable numbers had swarmed here during the Efflorescence of Oil. What they had left behind was essentially a Tip of monumental proportions, so expansive that even a century of scavenging had skimmed off only the most accessible deposits of copper, steel, and antiquities. There was testimony to this continuing work on the New Jersey shore, where re-rolling mills and iron foundries vented black smoke into the air. We passed beneath two monstrous bridges—one half-fallen and choked with goosegrass, one still in repair and busy with industrial traffic—while the river itself was alive with barges, steamers, and those oddly-rigged little boats called *dahabees* which the numerous Egyptian immigrants liked to sail.

Calyxa had dressed herself, under Mrs. Comstock's tutelage, in the blouse and skirt of a modest Aristo. She wore the clothes unwillingly, but they were becoming to her, although she picked at the belt that cinched her waist as if it were some medieval implement of torture. "This is not exactly how I expected to spend my honeymoon," she remarked.

I began to apologize, but she waved it off. "It's all very interesting, Adam, if slightly terrifying. Is Julian really in mortal danger?"

"Almost certainly. His father was killed by Deklan Conqueror as punishment for achieving exactly the sort of notoriety Julian has just acquired. There are limits to what even a President can do, of course—the contending forces of the Army and the Dominion are practical constraints, Sam says—but Deklan is devious and may bide his time until some scheme occurs to him."

"Is there anything we can do to help?"

"In *strategizing*, no—that's best left to the Aristos, who understand how these things work. In practical matters, Julian knows he can count on us."

"Much of the blame, of course, lies with this Theodore Dornwood."

"If there's any justice he'll be made to pay for his thievery and lies."

"Is there, though? Any justice, I mean?"

I took this as a practical rather than a philosophical question. "There will be, if I can help it."

"You mean you intend to punish him yourself?"

"Yes," I said, and meant it, though I hadn't given the prospect much thought. Perhaps Deklan Comstock couldn't be brought to justice, unless at the Final Judgment; but Theodore Dornwood was no Aristo, and he didn't live in a walled palace, and it might be within my power to extract some sort of payment from him.

I vowed that I would do so, sooner or later.

2

"Any outdoor game or sport," Julian said, "to *be* a sport, ought to have three essential qualities. It should be difficult, it should be impractical, and it should be slightly silly." His father had taught him that interesting truth, he said.

It was our second week at Edenvale. There had been no word or signal from Deklan Comstock, and the furor in the press had begun to die down for lack of supplemental fuel. Perhaps that engendered a premature sense of security among us.

Certainly Edenvale was a soothing locality. I had never summered at an Aristo's country Estate, unless you count tending stable for the Duncans and the Crowleys, and I was appalled and seduced by the luxury and laziness of it. Edenvale's properties were not cultivated, but kept in the wild condition. Trails were maintained for Scenic Strolling or Riding, and the vast acreage of wilderness invited hunting and exploration.

Edenvale House itself sat on an immaculately-tailored lawn bordered with flower gardens. During pleasant weather we took breakfast outdoors, the meal catered to us by servants while we sat at dainty whitewashed tables. On rainy days Calyxa and I explored the seemingly endless rooms of the House, or perched in its library, which was stocked with nineteenth-century classics and Dominion-approved novels of light romance. In the evenings Sam broke out a deck of cards, and we pursued the diversions of Euchre or Red Rose until bedtime; or we adjourned to the music room, where Mrs. Comstock was teaching herself to play *Las Ojos Criollos* on the piano.* In palmier days, Julian explained, the house might have been crowded with visiting Aristos and Owners and Senators and such. But the hanging of Bryce Comstock had cast a shadow over the family, and Mrs. Comstock had been shut out from the elite social circuit. Since then her companions had been drawn from the Manhattan show business crowd, or from the lower ranks of rising wealth; and Edenvale was not the social magnet it once had been.

After two weeks these small entertainments began to pall, and Julian proposed taking me on a tour of the wilder parts of the Estate—the Estate as he had known it as a child, before he was sent to Williams Ford. I readily agreed, and we set out from the house on a sunny, cool morning. Julian carried an unusual piece of luggage with him: a canvas bag, narrow, and about three feet

---

* She played earnestly but haltingly, and Calyxa and I often excused ourselves from these sessions. Sam, on the other hand, was made rapturous by her performances, and claimed he could listen to her all night without tiring, though even he seemed grateful when she moved on to such simpler compositions as *Ladies of Cairo* or *Where the Sauquoit Meets the Mohawk.*

long. I asked him about it; and that was when he quoted his father's remark about the nature of sport.

"Is it sporting equipment of some kind, then?"

"Yes, but I'll keep the nature of it to myself for now—I think you'll be pleasantly surprised."

We had dressed in clothes not much grander than what we had worn in Williams Ford when we hunted squirrels in the forest; and this was a relief after the complex and constraining Aristo fashions into which we had recently been belted and braced. A breeze turned the leaves of the ailanthus and the birch trees as we walked beneath their overarching branches, and it was as if we had become young again, for a few hours, at least.

In Williams Ford such expeditions always put Julian in a philosophical mood. That hadn't changed. We paused in a grove of cork trees to refresh ourselves from the canteens we had packed, and Julian said, "This is where I learned to love the past, Adam—as a boy, this was my private Tip."

"More trees than treasure, as far as I can tell."

"So it was meant to be. But all this forest has grown up over layers of scuttle from the days of the Secular Ancients. Dig anywhere and you're bound to unearth an old spoon or button or bone. Over that way"—he pointed at a hillside lush with birch and blackberry—"over that way there are foundations cut into the slope, and the remains of tumble-down houses. Do you know what I found there, as a boy?"

"Beetles? Spiders? Poison ivy?"

"All those; but more importantly—books!"

"You loved books so early, did you?"

"Even when I didn't know what they meant. The books I found were mostly foul and water-damaged, but here and there a readable page was preserved. I didn't just read those fragments, Adam, I nearly memorized them. It was a peculiar delicious feeling just to hold them in my hand—as if I'd found a way to eavesdrop on a conversation that faded into the air a hundred years ago."

"What sort of books were they?"

He shrugged. "Novels, mostly. Stories of intimate relations, or murder, or fantasies of flying to the stars or traveling in time."

"Not Dominion-approved, of course."

"No, and therein lay half the pleasure. The fruit was forbidden but it was sweet, even when it surpassed my understanding. What it told me was that the history the Dominion teaches is partial at best. The Dominion's truth is built on a cracked foundation, and buried in the cracks are things of immense interest and great beauty."

"Dangerous things," I said, though I was intrigued by the idea of stories about traveling in time and other such abominations.

"Truth is a perilous commodity," Julian admitted, "but so is ignorance, Adam—more so."

"Are we going to see those ruined buildings, then?"

"Everything valuable I took away from them long ago. No," Julian said, "today we're going fishing."

So saying, he led me another half-mile through a stand of birch and ailanthus to a lake—a glass-flat blue oval in the woods, its banks choked with goosegrass and purple loosestrife. Julian began to unroll his bundle, which I assumed would contain the rods and reels necessary for fly-fishing. But it did not.

We fished from kites, instead.

The kites—a pair of them—were of a design I hadn't seen before: a wedge of silk with stubby "wings" and a vent in the lower quadrant, supported by three parallel sticks of supple lathing. The kite thus conformed was not rigid, but was what Julian called a "parafoil." When lofted into the wind it opened like a sail, and was very stable in the air, and did not dip and bob like the crude kites I had made as a child, or fly upside-down, or plummet to the earth without warning. Julian sent his kite aloft first, to give me the idea, though the business wasn't complicated. Left to itself, the kite was stable enough that it hung in the sky as if riveted there by the gentle breeze. By tugging the string or running the reel Julian could make the kite rise or descend, or travel left and right, according to his will.

But that wasn't the end of the story. Attached to the bridle of each kite was a second string, which carried a cork float and a hook with a tied fly. Thus "kite-fishing." The kite carried the bait farther from shore than even an expert fly-fisher could have cast it, and fish grew plentifully in those deep and undisturbed waters.

I told Julian the invention was ingenious, but I wasn't absolutely certain the fish would cooperate in this novel means of persuading them to undertake the journey from their watery home to the frying pan. He nodded and smiled. "You're right, of course. Which is as it should be. Remember my father's maxim? A sport, to *be* a sport, must be difficult, impractical, and slightly silly."

"I guess this qualifies on all counts, then."

"But you're enjoying yourself, aren't you?" He stretched out on the mossy bank of the pond, his spine braced against a tree trunk and the kite reel cradled in his lap. Clouds of midges circled lazily over the sunlit lake, while a turtle sunned itself on a nearby rock. "Which is the entire purpose of a sport."

"These kites are unusual. Where did you learn how to make them?"

"From an antique book—where else?"

"Did the Secular Ancients really bother about such trivial things as kites?"

"Astonishing as it may seem, Adam, the Secular Ancients didn't spend all their time fornicating outside of wedlock, afflicting the faithful, marrying individuals of the same sex, or terrorizing schoolchildren with the Theory of Evolution. They had their innocent amusements just as we do."

They were people, that is, as human as Julian or I—a commonplace truth, but one that slips too easily from the mind. "They seem to have been very powerful, and very smart about kites and engines and such things. It's a surprise to me that they declined so rapidly during the False Tribulation."

"The False Tribulation—so called, and what an impudence on the part of the Dominion, to name a disaster after their own misinterpretation of it!— wasn't one event but many. The End of Oil, or more precisely the end of *cheaply acquired* oil, crippled the Ancients' top-heavy economic regime. But there were similar crises involving water and arable land. Wars for essential resources expanded, while machine agriculture became more expensive and finally impractical. Hunger stressed national economies to the breaking point, and disease and plague overcame all the hygienic barriers the Ancients had erected against them. Cities that couldn't support their own populations were inundated by starving peasants and eventually looted by angry mobs. With the Fall of the Cities came the establishment of the first rural Estates and the sale of able-bodied men into indenture. All of this was complicated by the Plague of Infertility that reduced the world's population so drastically, and from which we're only now recovering."

"And so the Ancients were punished for their arrogance. I know—I've read the histories, Julian; it's an old sermon."

"Punished for the crime of attempted prosperity. Punished for the crime of free intellectual inquiry. Or so the Dominion would have us believe."

"Perhaps the Dominion histories exaggerate; but surely the Secular Ancients weren't entirely innocent."

"Of course they weren't. Who is? The Ancients suffered under an economic system that resembled nothing so much as a complex elaboration of Private Langers's Lucky Mug. They were beset by greedy Aristocrats, belligerent Dictators, and ignorant Religionists . . . as are we, if you haven't noticed."

"But aren't we making progress of our own? Our cities are larger and busier than they have been since the Efflorescence of Oil."

"Yes, and it might be that we're on the cusp of a change in our traditional arrangements. The workers are discontented—even some of the indentured are learning to read and to express their grievances. The Dominion still keeps a tight grip in the west, but fights to stifle the Unaffiliated Churches in the east. In politics, the Presidency confronts an increasingly restive Senate, peopled by new-money Owners who distrust the old order or want a bigger piece of it. The Army of the Laurentians and the Army of the Californias function as independent powers, only nominally under the control of the Executive. And so on. The entire system wobbles on its axis, Adam. All it needs is a push in the right direction, and it would collapse."

"Would that be a good thing?"

"Increasingly, I think it would."

"People would suffer, though."

He waved his hand dismissively. "Don't people always suffer? Suffering is unavoidable."

Perhaps he was right about that. But his nonchalance frightened me. Sam had once accused Julian of "behaving like a Comstock," in a sense not complimentary to him. This was something worse, it seemed to me. Now he was thinking like a President.

For the rest of the afternoon we set aside Political Philosophy and attended strictly to fishing. The day was as sweet as the sight of two kites bobbing over a sunny blue lake could make it, and if the dividends were unimpressive—Julian snagged a single fish; I did not snag any—we wouldn't starve for our failures. It was a day that, as boys, we would have enjoyed wholeheartedly. But we weren't boys, and the pleasant illusion was impossible to sustain. Eventually the sun approached the hilltops of the Hudson highlands, the air grew calm, the long light silvered the leaves of the birches, and we packed up our kites and catch and started back to the Country House.

Edenvale was melancholy in the gloaming. Whether or not it was ever an Eden, just now it seemed more like Eden after the Fall: untenanted, possibly haunted. I found myself wondering whether Julian had disturbed the dead with his loose talk; and I pictured our indignant ancestors emerging from their wormy basements, all charged up with Electricity and Atheism. Despite the absurdity of the idea I was grateful when we passed out of the shadows of the forest and onto the wide lawn of the Estate. Lamplight soft as butter seeped from the windows of the Country House, a welcome sight.

There was also the faint and reassuring sound of music. We reached the house and entered the back hall quietly, so as not to make a disturbance, then followed the sound to the parlor, where Mrs. Comstock sat at the piano striking the familiar chords of *Where the Sauquoit Meets the Mohawk*. Sam gazed at her as if lost in admiration; while Calyxa, her coiled hair shimmering in the lamplight, stood with clasped hands, singing:

> *Though the years have fled*
> *Since we were wed*
> *Where the Sauquoit meets the Mohawk,*
> *Still the fields are green*
> *Down in between*
> *Where the Sauquoit meets the Mohawk* (etc., etc.).

Sentimental though the song undeniably was—it had been popular in Mrs. Comstock's youth—its virtue was its melody, which clambered up and down a minor scale as if in sympathy with human hope and mortal resignation. Calyxa seemed to know this, and she gave the melody an appropriate voice, so that the song became a wholehearted lament, sweet as summer love reconsidered in an autumn dusk. It made me think of the fallen condition of Edenvale, and of all the losses Mrs. Comstock had suffered since the death of her husband, and of the threat that hung over her son.

Calyxa performed the song in its entirety. Mrs. Comstock banged out the final chords of the last chorus and sat away from the piano, drained . . . but Calyxa, to the astonishment of us all, carried on for another two verses without accompaniment. Her fine voice expanded into the dusky stillness, singing:

> *In a tender year*
> *You kissed me here,*
> *Two hearts joined in one beating;*
> *But lovers met*
> *May suffer yet,*
> *And love, like time, is fleeting.*
> *But if your heart*
> *From mine must part*
> *Where the Sauquoit meets the Mohawk,*
> *Still the rolling sea*
> *Keeps the memory*
> *Of the Sauquoit and the Mohawk.*

Long moments passed after the last syllable faded into the air. Mrs. Comstock, obviously moved, wiped her eyes. When she had controlled her emotions, she gave Calyxa a curious look.

"Those verse aren't in the song-sheet," she said.

Calyxa nodded and seemed embarrassed. "No, I'm sorry—I added them myself—impulsively."

"The lyrics are your own?"

"It's a trick I picked up singing in taverns. Make up a fresh verse, surprise the audience."

"You invented these lyrics beforehand, or on the fly?"

"They were an improvisation," she admitted.

"What a remarkable talent! I'm increasingly impressed with you, Calyxa."

"Likewise, Mrs. Comstock," Calyxa said. She very nearly blushed—something I had seldom seen her do.

Then Mrs. Comstock cleared her throat. "In any event, the men are back from the woods. Julian, Adam, please sit down. We've had a communication from the Executive Palace, and I need to tell you about it."

Julian whitened, in so far as his naturally pale complexion made that possible. We did as we were told, and seated ourselves.

"Well?" Julian asked. "Which is it—a death sentence or a reprieve?"

Mrs. Comstock was somber but didn't seem unduly alarmed. "Perhaps a little of both. We've been invited to the Independence Day celebration on the Palace grounds. Deklan sent a note claiming he wants to honor the heroism of 'Captain Commongold,' now that the Captain is revealed as his nephew."

"My notoriety protects me," Julian said in a sneering tone. "At least until the Fourth."

"I doubt he'll make an attempt on your life before that date, in any case, and he can hardly slaughter you at the height of the celebration. In the meantime you should issue a statement to the newspapers acknowledging your patrimony and giving credit for your achievements to the Comstock bloodline."

"And abase myself before that butcher? Shall I defile my father's grave while I'm at it?"

Mrs. Comstock flinched. Sam said harshly, "These are measures to protect your life, Julian."

"For what it's worth."

"It's worth a great deal," Mrs. Comstock said tartly. "To me, Julian, if not to you."

Julian accepted his mother's rebuke, and his expression softened. "Very well. We have a few weeks until Independence Day, in any case. And if I'm to live that long, I want to live as a human being, and not a fugitive."

"What do you mean?"

"I mean that tomorrow I'm going back to Manhattan."

Our nervous idyll had ended.

We went aboard the *Sylvania* the next day. A storm had blown up overnight, and the morning was a cool and rainy one. I spent some time in the *Sylvania*'s pilot house, satisfying my curiosity about the principles and techniques of steam navigation. Then I went to the warmer cabin below, where Julian was sitting with a book in his lap.

"The future is on my mind," I said.

"Should we prove lucky enough to have one, you mean?"

"Don't joke, Julian. I know the risks we face. But I'm a married man—I have obligations, and I need a plan of my own. Calyxa and I can't impose on your hospitality forever. When we reach Manhattan I mean to find myself a job—anything short of the meat-packing industry*—and then locate a place where Calyxa and I can live on our own."

"Well, the thought is nobly intended. But don't you think you should wait until after Independence Day? You can certainly stay with us until then. You're no burden on the household, believe me."

"Thank you, Julian, but why wait? I might miss an opportunity."

"Or undertake an engagement you won't be able to keep. Adam . . .

---

* I had taken to heart Lymon Pugh's many sermons on that subject.

perhaps my mother wasn't sufficiently explicit about Deklan Comstock's invitation. When she said *we* were invited to the Executive Palace, the pronoun included *you*."

"What!"

"And Calyxa as well."

I was appalled, and not a little weak about the knees. "How's that possible? What does the President want with me? For that matter, how could he know anything about me at all?"

"The President's men no doubt bribe or threaten the household servants. Walls are transparent to them. Your name and Calyxa's were explicitly mentioned in the invitation."

"Julian, I'm just a lease-boy—I don't know how to behave in the company of a President, much less a murderous one!"

"Probably he won't have you killed. But he must have learned that you were the true chronicler of my so-called 'adventures,' and I suppose he wants to have a look at you. As for your behavior—" He shrugged. "Be yourself. You have nothing to gain by posing, and nothing to lose by revealing your origins. If the President wants to mock me for associating with lease-boys and tavern singers, let him do so."

This was not a pleasing prospect; but I bit my lip and said nothing.

"Meanwhile," Julian said, "I owe you a favor."

"Surely you don't."

"I do, though. You befriended me in Williams Ford, and showed me all you knew about that Estate and how to hunt it."

"And you've shown me Edenvale."

"Edenvale is nothing. *Manhattan,* Adam! My town is Manhattan, and I want to instruct you in the perils and the pleasures of it, before you begin life as a working man."

Perhaps this was meant as a distraction, but I was willing to abandon myself to it, considering how perilous our existence seemed to have become. "Maybe I can learn some of the ways of the Aristos before I'm thrust into their company at the Presidential Palace."

"That's right. And the first lesson is not to use the word 'Aristos.'"

"*Aristocrats,* then."

"Nor even that. Among ourselves, we're 'the Eupatridian Community.'"

A label big enough to strangle a man, I thought; but I practiced it dutifully, and after a while it ceased to stick in the throat.

3

The reader, if not versed in recent history, may be anxious to discover whether or not Julian and I were killed on Independence Day. I do not mean to protract the answer to that important question, but the events of the Fourth will make more sense once I have described some of what happened prior to that date.

It was a nervous time for Calyxa and me, though we were newlyweds and tempted to believe in our own immortality. President Comstock was hardly concerned with us, Calyxa said, and in any event we were not locked up in the fine rooms of the Aristocracy. We could pack up our belongings at any time, and travel to Boston or Buffalo, and live there anonymously, beyond the reach of any maddened Chief Executive. I would write books under an assumed name (in this scenario), and Calyxa would sing in respectable cafés. We went so far as to price railway tickets and scrutinize timetables, though I was distressed at the prospect of abandoning Julian to his fate.

"It's his own fate," Calyxa said, "and he could shed himself of it if he chose to. He ran away once—can't he run away again? Ask him to come with us."

But when I proposed this option to Julian he shook his head. "No, Adam. That's no longer possible. It was a miracle that I escaped from Williams Ford. Here, I'm under much closer scrutiny."

"What scrutiny? I don't see it. New York City is a big locality—big enough to get lost in, it seems to me."

"My uncle has eyes everywhere. If I so much as packed a bag he'd hear of it. This house is watched, though very discreetly. If I go for a walk, the President's men aren't far behind. If I drink to excess in some Broadway tavern, a report will find its way to Deklan Conqueror."

"And are Calyxa and I also under this observation?"

"Probably, but the surveillance isn't so strict." He cast a glance to make sure no servant could overhear us. "If you want to escape, you're well advised to do so. I won't stop you or blame you. But it must be a *clean* escape, or else the President's men will haul you back and use you against me. To be honest, given your trivial position in Deklan's eyes, you might be safer here than elsewhere. But the decision is yours, of course." He added, "I'm sorry you find yourself mixed up in it, Adam. I never meant for it to be so, and I'll do anything I can to help."

So Calyxa and I went on studying our railroad timetables, and made airy plans, but failed to pursue them. We continued living in the brownstone house as the days and weeks passed. Mrs. Comstock kept on with her charitable work, and held occasional gatherings of the Manhattan artistic circle, events which Julian enjoyed very much. Sam was often absent during this time, pursuing contacts in the upper echelons of the military—for he was no longer "Sam Samson" but Sam Godwin once again, restored to his reputation as a veteran of the Isthmian War; and I imagined he was performing his own kind of intelligence-gathering, with the aim of discovering the President's ultimate intentions.

There was no such useful work for me, but I spent many pleasant hours with Calyxa as we adjusted to wedded life. Calyxa in her own way was as philosophically-inclined as Julian, and liked to discuss the flaws and short-coming of the system of Aristocracy, of which she disapproved. When that palled, we took walks around the city. She enjoyed exploring the shops and restaurants on Broadway or Fifth Avenue; and on fine days we ventured as far as the great stone walls of the Presidential Palace Grounds.* The walls were immensely tall and thick, and made of granite fragments salvaged from city ruins. The huge Broadway Gate at 59th Street, with its stone and steel guard-house, was a work of architecture nearly as impressive as the Montreal Cathedral where I had first spied Calyxa in her surplice, and twice as monolithic. I couldn't imagine what lay within those moated and forbidding walls (though I was destined to find out).

The month of June was unusually fine and sunny, and we took such walks often. To avoid monotony we varied our route; and we were returning from Broadway by way of Hudson Street when we passed a Manhattan book-store. The sunlight fell aslant through the window glass, revealing the illustrated cover of a book by Mr. Charles Curtis Easton—a volume I hadn't seen before, called *American Sailors Afloat*.

Needless to say, I hurried inside.

I had never been in a book-store before. All the books I had read had been borrowed from the Estate library at Williams Ford, or (in the case of *A History of Mankind in Space*) dug moldering from ancient Tips. Of course I had known such stores existed, and that Manhattan must include more than a few of them. But I had not gathered up the courage to seek one out. I suppose I had imagined a book-store to be an intimidating place, as airy and marble-pillared as a Greek temple. This store was not such a sacral establishment. Grogan's Books Music and Cheap Publications was the name of it, and it was no more or less grand than the shoe store to the left of it or the vaccination shop to the right.

Even the smell of the air inside the shop was inviting, a perfume of paper and ink. The books on sale were many and various, and all unfamiliar to me; but I made my way by some instinct to the section where Mr. Easton's novels were on display—a great plethora of them, fresh and bright in their stamped and colored boards.

---

* The grounds of the Executive Palace had once been a great Park, according to Julian, and open to the public; but that had changed when the federal government moved north from Washington.

"Close your mouth," Calyxa said, "or you'll begin to drool."

"This must be near everything Mr. Easton has published!"

"I hope it is. He seems to have written far too many books already."

I had been hoarding my back pay from the Army of the Laurentians, grudging every expense—the hope of one day owning a typewriter was still at the back of my mind—but I could not resist buying a volume or two* of Mr. Easton's recent work. Calyxa browsed among the sheet music while I counted out Comstock dollars to the cashier.

When we left the store Calyxa lingered a few moments in front of the vaccination shop next door. Calyxa, for all her contempt of the Aristocracy, was not immune to certain aspects of Manhattan fashion. The window of the vaccination shop advertised a newly-arrived Yellow Fever serum, popular with the sort of stylish young city women who sport vaccination scars as if they were jewelry. A single dose of this serum cost more than a dozen novels, however; and Julian had already warned us against such shops, which tended to dispense more diseases than they ever prevented.

In any case my attention was absorbed by the prospect of new Easton books to read. I confessed to Calyxa, as we walked home, how inspiring Mr. Easton's work had been to me, and how it had formed my ambition to become a professional writer, and how distant that prospect now seemed.

"Nonsense," Calyxa said. "Adam, you *are* a professional writer."

"Not professional—not even published."

"You've written a popular pamphlet already. *The Adventures of Captain Commongold* was on sale in Grogan's, if you didn't notice. Selling briskly, it appeared to me."

"That abomination! The piece that imperiled Julian's life. Horribly mangled by Theodore Dornwood, on top of it all. He murdered half my commas, and misplaced the rest."

"Punctuation aside, it's your work, and professional enough that a surprising number of literate Manhattanites are willing to part with a dollar and fifty cents to read it."

That was true, though I had not thought of it in such a light. My indignation at Mr. Dornwood was rekindled. I escorted Calyxa to the brownstone house of Mrs. Comstock, and said no more about the question, though I privately determined to visit the offices of the *Spark* and express my grievances there.

I would have preferred to spend that evening reading, for the books I had bought were a novelty to me, and I could not help admiring the crisp pages and unsmudged letters of the freshly-purchased volumes, and the clean white string that bound the signatures snugly together; but Julian insisted on taking

---

* Four, actually.

Calyxa and me to see a movie—an invitation that was difficult to resist after everything Julian had said about movies back in Williams Ford.

We rode a taxi to the Broadway theater where Julian had reserved our seats, and we mingled in the lobby with a crowd of well-dressed Eupatridians of both sexes. It was clear even before we entered the auditorium that this would be a performance infinitely grander than the recruiting film I had seen in the Dominion Hall in Williams Ford. The movie to be shown here, which was called *Eula's Choice,* was advertised with colorful Lobby Posters, which portrayed a female in antiquated dress, and a man with a pistol; also a horse and an American flag. Julian explained that *Eula's Choice* was a patriotic story, its debut timed to coincide with the Independence season. He didn't expect much in the way of refined drama, he said, but the movie had been produced by a local crew known for its extravagant camera-work and lavish stage effects. "It ought to be a fine spectacle," he said, "if nothing else."

Calyxa was ill-at-ease among the haughty Eupatridians, and she seemed relieved when a team of ushers appeared to shoo us into the auditorium, where we took our assigned seats. "All the money that changes hands here," she said, "could feed a thousand orphans."*

"That's not the way to think of it," Julian reproved her. "By that reasoning there would be no art at all, nor philosophy, nor books. This is an independent theater, not a Eupatridian institution. The profits pay the salaries of working actors and singers, who would otherwise go hungry."

"Singers as well as actors? In that case I withdraw the remark."

The entire theater was powered by an in-house dynamo which thrummed from the basement like a snoring Leviathan. The lights were electric, and they dimmed in unison as the orchestra—a full brass band, with strings—struck up the overture. The curtain rose, revealing a huge white Screen and the veiled booths in which the Voice-Actors and Sound Effects persons worked. As soon as the darkness was complete the beam of the projector threw an ornate title on the screen:

THE NEW YORK STAGE AND SCREEN ALLIANCE

presents

EULA'S CHOICE

A Musical Story of Antiquity

accompanied by the Dominion Stamp of Approval.

"This ought to be rich," remarked Calyxa, who had seen movies under less elaborate circumstances in Montreal; but Julian shushed her, and the music swelled and subsided as the story began.

---

* Orphans were a common sight on Manhattan streets, where they begged for coins in ingenious and aggressive ways. There was also a generous supply of limbless veterans, their competition.

I won't describe my astonishment—the reader can take it for granted. I will say that, for once, Julian's pride in Eastern culture seemed justified and wholly excusable. This was Art, I thought; and on a grand scale!

The story took place at some unspecified time during the Fall of the Cities. The main characters were Boone, the beleaguered pastor of an urban Church; Eula, his fiancé; and Foster, a thrifty industrialist.

The show was divided into three Acts, itemized in a Program Book the ushers had distributed. Each Act featured three songs, or "Arias."

There was no singing at first, however—only Spectacle, as the audience was treated to flickering scenes of a City of the Secular Ancients in the last stage of its decline. We saw many impossibly tall buildings, artfully constructed of paper and wood, but fully real to the eye; we saw streets crowded with Business Men, Atheists, Harlots, and Automobiles.* Boone and Eula appeared, working together in Boone's small pious church, and bantering in a way that suggested their approaching nuptials; but they were interrupted by a troop of Secular Policemen who barged in and accused Boone of speaking such forbidden words as "faith" and "heaven." These thugs led Boone away to prison, while Eula wept piteously. Boone, as he was dragged through the street in chains, sang the first song, which according to the program was:

Aria: The hand of God, not gentle.

The filmed actor was expressive, and he was voiced by a masculine tenor who lent fire and discipline to the lyrics. (*The hand of God, not gentle but just / Descends upon the wicked by and by*, and so forth).

If the Secular Policemen by this brutish behavior had earned themselves a place in Hell, their city was already halfway there. We witnessed a montage of strikes, rioting, and fires, the tall buildings beginning to burn as if they had been built of kindling. Now the audience was introduced to Foster, the industrialist, who labored mightily to subdue a fire in his iron mill, which had been set ablaze by unruly workers; but he was forced back by the heat and fallen timbers. Against this backdrop of destruction Foster wiped his sooty brow and sang in resignation the

Aria: Gone, all that I have built.

All this was sorrowful enough to melt the hardest cynic's heart, but it wasn't finished. Eula appeared once more. She had left the scene of Boone's

---

* The Automobiles were perhaps a less successful artistic effect, as they seemed unusually one-dimensional, and bobbed unconvincingly as they moved; but the dedicated crew of Sound-Makers compensated for this with engine noises created by a baritone growling into a speaking-tube. How these automobiles had survived so long into the End of Oil was a question the film-makers did not address.

cruel arrest, only to find her family home engulfed in flame, and her mother and father crying out from a window from which they could not be rescued. The flames consumed them. Overwhelmed with grief, Eula stumbled on to the jail where she believed Boone had been taken; but that building, too, had burned to the ground.

Several of the Eupatridian ladies in the audience were moved by this tragic scene, and they dabbed their eyes and blew their noses in a manner that distracted from Eula's excellently performed

Aria: Lost and alone among the ruins,

which was the conclusion of Act I.

The lights came up for an intermission. Many of the Eupatridians adjourned at once to the lobby; but Calyxa and Julian and I were young and staunch of bladder, and we kept our seats. Images from the film were still vivid in my mind's eye, and I began to think about the lost wonders of the Secular Ancients. I said to Julian, "The Secular Ancients made movies, didn't they?—you told me so, I think."

"Movies too numerous to count, though none survive, unless they've been locked away in the Dominion Archives." The Dominion's Cultural Committee kept a large stone building in New York City, Julian explained, where it preserved antique texts and documents and other items too blasphemous to be seen by the public. No one outside the licensed clergy knew what treasures it contained.

"And their movies had recorded sound, and color photography?"

"They did."

"Then why can't we have such movies? Or at least a larger number of the ones we do make? I don't understand it, Julian. The simpler technologies of the past are no mystery to us. We may not have bountiful supplies of oil, but we can burn coal to much the same effect."

"We *could* make movies with recorded sound," Julian said, "but the resources haven't been allotted that way. The same is true of that typewriter by which Theodore Dornwood seduced your services. We could build a typewriter for every human being in Manhattan if we liked; but it would be a reckless expenditure of iron or rubber or whatever they make typewriters out of—materials the Senate assigns to Eupatridian manufacturers, who in turn supply the military with weapons and other necessities."

I had not thought of it in those terms. I supposed every Trench Sweeper in Labrador could be considered a typewriter not manufactured or a movie not produced. A painful bargain, but what patriot could disagree with it?

"An artist," Julian said, "or a small manufacturer or shopkeeper, has to make do with whatever resources trickle down as surplus from above, or with second-pickings from some local Tip. The justice of this is debatable, of course." He turned to Calyxa. "What do you think of the film so far?"

"As drama?" She rolled her eyes scornfully. "And the songs—excuse me, the *arias*—are simple-minded. The female singer is good, though. A little flat in the upper registers, but bold and fluent overall."

I politely disagreed with her about the quality of the drama; but what she said about the music amounted to high praise, for Calyxa dispensed her approval grudgingly at the best of times.

Now the audience filed back into the auditorium and the lights were extinguished for Act II. The production resumed with yet another Spectacle: hundreds of ragged men and women fleeing the Fall of the Cities, set to a mournful trumpet eulogy and the rhythm of tramping feet. Among these individuals was the convicted pastor Boone, who (unknown to Eula) had escaped ahead of the flames. In one touching scene he came across his former captors, the brutal Secular Policemen, now starving and suffering from burns; and despite their sins against him he helped them renounce their apostasy, and led them to redemption in the moment of their deaths. Rising tear-streaked from this sacred task, Boone spotted a distant Banner of the Cross among the plodding refugees. He recognized it as a symbol of the nascent Dominion of Jesus Christ on Earth—a union of all the Persecuted Churches—and he marked the event by singing his

Aria: In the wilderness, a flag.

Eula, unknown to Boone, was part of the same mass of vagrant urbanites. When hunger threatened to overcome her she was forced to beg help from Foster, the former industrialist. Foster, traveling in a wagon, explained that he was aiming to reach a certain rural plantation he owned. His behavior toward Eula was impeccably kind and chaste, and although she still loved Boone she believed the pastor had been killed in the fire; so she accepted Foster's gifts with a relatively free heart. Eula's plaintive second-act song, accompanied by piano rather than full orchestra, was

Aria: I will take this offered hand.

Then Foster and Eula—growing ever closer—traveled in Foster's horse-drawn wagon through a montage of scenes of the degraded world of the False Tribulation. There were ruined houses, dust-blown farms, starved cattle, fallen Airplanes, rusted Automobiles, and so forth. Eventually, and after arduous adventures, they came to a hilltop town not far from the rural property Foster owned. This town had survived the Fall of the Cities intact, and was protected by the steadfast Christianity of its population. The inhabitants had erected a huge symbol of their faith at the highest point of land, prompting Foster's

Aria: What shines on that far hill? A cross!

The Act concluded with Eula's astonished glimpse of one of the many clerics who had assembled in this virtuous town to join in the work of defending its piety: none other than Boone, her former intended husband.

The curtain closed on this breathless discovery.

This time the three of us adjourned to the lobby during the intermission. While attending to human necessity I discovered yet another of the unanticipated luxuries of the Eupatridian class: indoor plumbing so immaculate that the enameled receptacles for gentlemen gleamed as if freshly polished, and were scented with lemon. Amazing, what subtle easements human ingenuity can contrive!

I made my way back to my seat in time for Act III.

Act III was that portion of the movie in which a Choice, prominent in the title, was set before poor Eula. That would provide great opportunities for the actresses portraying her (both voice and on film) to exert themselves; but first we saw Foster facing a dilemma of his own. His plantation, not far from the pious town where he and Eula had taken refuge, was in a shambles. The wheat crop had been trampled by hungry refugees, and what remained could not be harvested for lack of help. Meanwhile refugees crowded into town on a daily basis, hoping to be fed. Clearly the solution was to use landless vagrants as field-hands—but he couldn't *hire* any, in the classic sense, because he had no money with which to pay them. In any case farm work (which guaranteed a daily meal) was so desirable that the mob would have fought for it. Therefore Foster worked out an ingenious solution:

Aria: All that may be sold generosity may buy,

he sang, accepting pledges of lifelong indenture from men willing to forego daily wages.* To enforce the arrangement, and to make a success of it, he required the assistance of the clergy in general, and Pastor Boone in particular.

Thus Eula was treated to the sight of her contending suitors united in the creation of that new and more pious America which would grow from the ruins of the old. Foster was ignorant of Boone's prior relation to Eula; but Boone was introduced to Eula at a social gathering and recognized her at once. Quickly discerning the nature of her intimacy with Foster, Boone pretended ignorance,† and Eula played along. This culminated in a walk by Boone through a moonlit meadow, where he performed his melancholy

Aria: I give to God that which the Earth denies,

---

* *A pledge alone secures the deed / Your labor's mine, while I fulfill your need,* etc. If there was any haggling over this bargain, the film did not depict it.
† Though only an idiot could have misinterpreted his facial grimaces, which the screen actor portrayed in a broad manner.

renouncing terrestrial love in favor of the more dependable heavenly variety. Eula, listening from a place among the trees, wept almost as copiously as the ladies in the theater.*

Foster proposed to her in a scene of the following day. Eula did not accept his proposal at once, but went to see Boone for advice. She approached him as a penitent to a pastor—neither of them acknowledging their prior acquaintance, though both were painfully conscious of it—and told him the story of everything that had happened to her since the Fall of the Cities, culminating in Foster's proposal. She had seen her former betrothed, she said, whom she had believed dead; and she still loved him authentically; but she loved Foster as well, and her mind was all in a confusion.

Boone, overcome with feeling, eventually spoke. "Many things have changed since the end of the old world," he said, the voice actor giving this speech all the quirks and quavers of suppressed emotion while synchronizing his words precisely with the vocal movements of the actor on the screen. "We're embarked on a new relationship with the sacred. It's the twilight of an old way of life, and the dawn of a new. Vows from prior times are not broken but annulled. Your marriage if you make it will surely be blessed—[a long choked pause]—despite, despite what came before."

Eula turned her brimming eyes to his. "Thank you, Pastor," she said; and if she said anything else it was drowned out by the sniffling in the audience.

Eula's return to Foster was bittersweet. She accepted his attentions with an

Aria: I pledge to thee,

followed by scenes of a spectacular Wedding, with many poignant glances cast between Eula and the noble Pastor, and at last a lengthy

Ensemble/ Medley:
The hand of God, not gentle
What shines on that far hill?
I pledge to thee,

the cast being joined by a Chorus, with much ringing of bells, and exclamations by the trumpet section, and a triumphant final refrain over a distant image of that Christian town, its wheatfields plowed by contented indentured folk, and the Sixty Stars and Thirteen Stripes waving optimistically over it all.†

---

* The ladies were not pleased with certain Broadway sophisticates also present, whose cries of "That's right—keep single if you can help it!" were quickly suppressed.

† An error of history, since the northern states had not yet been acquired at the time of the Fall of the Cities; but forgivable in the name of Art and Patriotism.

There was protracted applause as the curtain fell. I applauded at least as vigorously as anyone else—perhaps more so. I had not known that the Cinematic Illusion could exist on such an exalted scale, sustained by the painstaking efforts of so many skilled performers working in close concert. It was as much a revelation to me as the plumbing in the Gentlemen's Room.

We followed the crowd outside. The movie had generated in my mind a sort of Patriotic Glow, which was compounded by the glow of the city. It was the last quarter of the nightly four-hour Illumination of Manhattan, and artificial lights glittered along Broadway like legions of fireflies all in harness. Even the skeletal remains of the antique Sky-Scrapers seemed infused with an electric liveliness. Coaches and taxis passed in great profusion, and scarlet Banners of the Cross, draped from eaves and lintels in anticipation of Independence Day, fluttered in the pleasant breeze. I told Julian how impressed I was, and asked him to forgive me for doubting all his boasts about New York City and the movies.

"Yes, it was a tolerably good show," he said, "a very pleasant evening out, all in all."

"Tolerably good! Are there better?"

"I've seen a few that topped it."

"Good?" Calyxa asked skeptically. "And you notorious for your agnosticism? Pretty as it might be, isn't *Eula* an insult to your profoundest beliefs?"

"Thank you for asking," Julian said, "but no, I don't feel particularly insulted by it. If I am an *agnostic*, Calyxa, it's because I'm also a *realist*."

"There was no realism in the film that I could discern—just a simpleminded version of what they print in the Dominion readers."

"Well, yes—considered as history it was feeble and propagandistic—but it could hardly be anything else. You saw the Dominion stamp at the beginning of it. No film-maker can proceed without submitting his script to the Dominion's cultural committees. *Realistically,* these matters are exempted from art, since they're beyond the artist's control. But in structure, pacing, dialogue, photography, harmony between the screen and the voice performances—everything over which the film-makers *did* exercise a shaping influence—it was above reproach."

"Above reproach, then," Calyxa said, "in everything except what matters."

"Do you mean to say the singing didn't matter?"

"Well . . . the singing was fine, admittedly . . . and the singers didn't write the script. . . ."

"My point exactly."

"So it was a beautiful, stupid thing. Wouldn't it be even more beautiful if it were slightly less stupid?"

"I don't disagree. I would love to make a movie that wasn't just beautiful but also thoughtful and true. I've thought about it often. But the world isn't rigged to allow such a thing. I doubt anyone on Earth has the power to overrule the

Dominion in these matters, except possibly the President himself." Then Julian, as if startled by his own thought, blinked and smiled. "Of course that's not something we can expect of Deklan Comstock."

"No," Calyxa said, searching his face. "No, certainly not of *Deklan* Comstock."

Come morning I let Calyxa sleep late, and took myself off to visit the publisher of the *Spark* and of *The Adventures of Captain Commongold, Youthful Hero of the Saguenay.*

I was equipped with nothing more lethal than my smoldering indignation, fueled by the scenes of courage and sacrifice I had witnessed in the movie the night before. I would confront the thieves, I thought, and the self-evident justice of my case would cause them to crumble before me. I don't know why I expected such extravagant results from the application of mere justice. That kind of calculation is seldom borne out by worldly events.

My first trial was in finding the office I wanted. I had no trouble locating the building in which the *Spark* was published, since its address was printed in every issue: it turned out to be a vast stonepile near the Lexington Canal. Most of its huge space was devoted to printing, binding, warehousing, and distributing the company's papers and pamphlets, however, and I was reduced to asking my way of a grimy press-operator who told me, "Oh, you want Editorial."

"Editorial" was a suite of rooms at the top of a flight of stairs on the fourth floor. All the heat of the building (and it was a warm June day) had collected in that airless warren, and so had the smells of ink and solvent and machine oil. I did not know precisely to whom I ought to speak, but further inquiries led me to the door of the Editor and Publisher, a man named John Hungerford. Apparently Mr. Hungerford wasn't accustomed to meeting visitors who hadn't scheduled appointments; but I was firm in my entreaties to his secretary, and eventually I was allowed into his office.

Hungerford sat behind an oaken desk, in one of the few rooms on the floor that possessed an open window, though it looked out on a brick wall. He was a man of fifty years or thereabout, stern and peremptory in his manner. He asked without preamble what I wanted from him.

I said I was a writer. I had hardly pronounced that word when he interrupted me: "I can't give you a job, if that's what you want. We have all the writers we need—they're thick on the ground at the moment."

"It's not a job I want, it's justice! I'm a sorry to say that a man connected with your firm has robbed me, and he has done it with your collaboration."

That silenced him for a moment. His eyebrows inched up, and he looked me over. "What's your name, son?"

"Adam Hazzard."

"Means nothing to me."

"I don't expect it would. But the thief is Mr. Theodore Dornwood—maybe you know *that* name."

He evinced less surprise than I expected. "And what do you claim Dornwood stole from you? A watch, a wallet, a woman's affections?"

"Words. Twenty thousand of them, roughly." I had made an estimate of the length in words of *The Adventures of Julian Commongold*. A word is a small thing; but twenty thousand of anything is a ponderable number. "May I explain?"

"Be my guest."

I told him the story of the work I had done for Dornwood in Montreal, and what Dornwood in turn had done with my work.

Mr. Hungerford said nothing but asked his secretary to send for Dornwood, who apparently had an office in the building. In a moment or two that villain arrived.

Dornwood in Manhattan was not quite the hemp-scented drunkard I had last espied near Montreal. The success of *Captain Commongold* had improved his clothing, his tonsure, and his skin tone. Unfortunately it also seemed to have damaged his memory. He looked at me blankly, or pretended to, until Mr. Hungerford made an introduction.

"Oh, yes!—Mr. Hazzard—*Private* Hazzard, wasn't it? I'm pleased to see you survived your tour of duty. I'm sorry I didn't know you out of uniform."

"Well, I know you," I said, "uniform or not."

"This young man has a grievance against you," Hungerford said, and he proceeded to repeat in fair detail what I had told him. "What do you have to say for yourself?"

Theodore Dornwood shrugged and looked vaguely hurt. "Well, what *can* I say? I suppose there's some truth in it. I do recall Private Hazzard coming to me for lessons in writing. And I did agree to peruse a few pages for him."

"You admit it!" I cried.

"Admit to *consulting* you, yes. I think you misunderstand the nature of journalism, Private Hazzard. But I don't blame you, for a boreal lease-boy could hardly know any better. A journalist draws on many sources. You and I talked about Julian Commongold, yes—you may even have shown me some written notes—but I discussed the subject with a great number of infantrymen and officers, of which you were only one. In so far as I did employ your notes as a partial source (and I admit I may have), it was in exchange for my advice on writing . . . such advice as I could supply to a poorly-schooled Westerner. No formal bargain existed, of course; but if ever there was an *informal* one, surely it was fulfilled."

I stared at him. "I made no bargain at all!"

Mr. Hungerford looked up sharply from his desk. "If you made no bargain, Mr. Hazzard, then there was no bargain to be broken, was there? I'm afraid Mr. Dornwood has the better of you on all counts."

"Except that every word printed in *Captain Commongold* is mine, exactly as I wrote it!—apart from the misplacement of the commas."

Dornwood, who was proving to be a smooth and efficient liar, threw his hands up and gave his employer a beseeching look. "He accuses me of plagiarism. Must I stoop to deny it?"

"Look, Mr. Hazzard," Hungerford said, "you're not the first individual to blow in here claiming some pamphlet was based on an idea of his, somehow 'stolen.' It happens with every successful piece we publish. I don't mean to call you a liar—and Dornwood generously admits that he used you as one source among hundreds—but you present no evidence that what you say is true, and every indication that it's simply a painful misunderstanding on your part."

"I'm glad you don't mean to call me a liar, for I'm not one—though you might find one close to hand!"

"See here," said Dornwood.

"The discussion is closed," Hungerford said, abruptly standing. "And I want to go to lunch. I'm sorry we can't do anything to accommodate you, Mr. Hazzard."

"I don't want to be accommodated, I want to be paid! I'll have you before a court, if necessary!"

"So you say. For your sake I hope you won't pursue the matter. If you insist, you can come back this afternoon and speak to me in the presence of my lawyer. He stops by the office about three o'clock. Perhaps he can convince you the case is hopeless, if I can't. Goodbye, Mr. Hazzard—you know where the door is."

Dornwood smiled at me, maddeningly.

I went home disconsolate. Calyxa, as it turned out, had gone off with Mrs. Comstock to buy clothing for the Independence Day celebration at the Executive Palace. Julian—who had stayed out late after the movie, meeting friends among the showpeople and aesthetes of Broadway—had just rolled out of bed. I passed him on the way to the kitchen; he asked me if I had had my breakfast yet.

"Breakfast hours ago, and it's already late for lunch," I said irritably.

"Fine—I'd rather eat lunch than breakfast. Why don't we go out and have a decent meal? No offense to the kitchen staff."

"I'm not sure but that I wouldn't rather spend the afternoon reading."

"Not on a day as fine as this!"

"How would you know what sort of day it is? I'm sure you haven't even looked out a window yet."

"The fineness of it seeps under the doors. I smell sunshine. Don't be a fossil, Adam. Join me for lunch."

I could hardly resist his invitation without citing the morning's events, which I preferred to keep to myself. We dined at a restaurant not far distant, which served ox-tongue cobblers and lozenged pork of a refined quality, and I tried to smile and make small talk. But I hardly tasted the food; and I was such glum company that Julian repeatedly asked about my state of mind.

"It's nothing," I said. "Maybe indigestion."

"Maybe nothing of the kind. Have you had an argument with Calyxa?"

"No—"

"Are you worried about Independence Day?"

"No—"

"What, then? Come on, Adam, confess."

He refused to be put off the scent; so I relented, and described my visit to the *Spark*.

Julian listened to my account without interrupting. Coffee and cakes were produced by an attentive waiter. I ignored them. I could hardly meet Julian's eyes. But when I finally fell silent and Julian spoke, it was only to say, "The cakes really are excellent, Adam. Try one."

"I'm not concerned with cakes," I exclaimed. "Aren't you going to chide me for my naïveté, or some such thing?"

"Not at all. I admire what you did. Standing up for yourself, I mean. The justice is all on your side—no doubt about that. The problem lies in your methodology."

"I don't know that I have any."

"Clearly you don't. I'll tell you what: Why don't we go back to Hungerford's offices this very afternoon, as he suggested?"

I was astonished at the suggestion. "What for? So that he can have his lawyer hang me up and beat the dust out of me?" My threat to take Hungerford to court had been empty. I couldn't produce any evidence to support my side, and the New York courts had no reputation for impartiality. "I would sooner not, I thank you."

"This time the outcome might be different."

"I don't see how. Hungerford is determined not to admit liability, and Dornwood is a professional liar."

"Trust me," Julian said.

This was all very embarrassing, but I could not see my way out of it; and so I made the journey back to Hungerford's office with Julian at my side.

If Mr. Hungerford was surprised to see me back again, he didn't let on. He had told the truth about his lawyer. The three of them were sitting together in Hungerford's office—Hungerford, Theodore Dornwood, and a fat man with greased hair, soon introduced as Buck Lingley, Attorney at Law—when I entered.

Julian, dismayingly, chose to wait in the outer office. He had instructed me to summon him if the publisher didn't relent.

That seemed an inescapable outcome.

Mr. Hungerford invited me to sit down. Before I could say anything Hungerford's lawyer asked whether I had proceeded with legal action—filed a complaint, or anything of that sort.

I said I had not.

"Better for you, then," Lingley said. "You're swimming in rough waters, Mr. Hazzard. Do you know anything about the legal system?"

"Very little," I confessed.*

"Do you understand what it would cost you to bring a legal action against this business, or against Mr. Dornwood as an individual? And do you understand that it would cost double that once the case was thrown out of court, as I assure you it would be? It's not a trifling thing to impugn the integrity of such men as these."

"They impugn themselves, it seems to me. But I'm sure you're right."

Lawyer Lingley looked briefly puzzled. "You mean to say you'll quit your claim?"

"I expect that phrase has some legalistic significance of which I'm not aware. What happened, happened—neither you nor I can change that, Mr. Lingley. And if the courts don't judge in this matter, Heaven might not be so lax."

"Heaven isn't within my jurisdiction. If you're willing to be reasonable, I've prepared a paper for you to sign."

"A paper saying what?"

"That you have no fiscal claim on this company or Mr. Dornwood, no matter whether some small amount of material you wrote found its way into Dornwood's published accounts."

"It was not a 'small amount,' Mr. Lingley. We're talking about an act of thievery bold enough to make a vulture blush."

"Make up your mind," Lingley said. "Do you want to settle the matter, or are you going to persist in these libels?"

I looked at the paper. It was, in so far as I could decipher the whereases, a renunciation of all my prior complaints. In exchange, it said, the company would not pursue me for "defamation."

There was a space prepared for my signature.

"If I sign this," I said slowly, "I suppose I'll need a witness?"

"My secretary will witness it."

"No need—I've brought a witness of my own," and I gestured through the door for Julian to enter.

Hungerford and the lawyer blinked at this unexpected development. If they did not recognize Julian Comstock, Theodore Dornwood certainly did. He sat bolt upright, and an unprintable word escaped his lips.

---

* I felt I had nothing to lose by honesty—nor much to gain, come down to it.

"What's this about?" Hungerford demanded. "Who is this man?"

"Julian Comstock," I said. "Julian, this is Mr. Hungerford, the publisher of the *Spark*."

Julian offered his hand. Hungerford took it, though every other part of him seemed frozen in shock.

"And this is Mr. Hungerford's lawyer, Mr. Buck Lingley."

"Hello, Mr. Lingley," said Julian in an amiable tone.

Lingley's complexion, which up to that moment had been florid, turned the color of an eggshell, and his tendentious manner went the way of the morning dew. He did not speak. Instead he reached across the desk and picked up the paper I was meant to sign. He folded it in thirds and tore it in two pieces. Then he pursed his lips in a sickly imitation of a smile. "I'm delighted—no—honored—to meet you, Captain Comstock. Unfortunately an urgent appointment calls me away—I cannot linger." He turned to Hungerford. "I think our business is finished for today, John," he said, and left the room in such a hurry that I was surprised the breeze didn't pull the door shut after him.

Mr. Hungerford had yet to close his slackened jaw.

"And I recognize Theodore Dornwood," Julian said, "our regiment's civilian scribe. I've read some of your work, Mr. Dornwood. Or at least the work that was published under your name."

"Yes!" Dornwood said in a strangled voice, which was not helpful. "No!"

"Shut up, Theo," Mr. Hungerford said. "Captain Comstock, do you have a contribution to make to this discussion?"

"Not at all. It was only that my friend Adam seems to be having a hard time making himself understood."

"I think we've overcome that difficulty," Hungerford said. "As a responsible publisher I mean to correct any mistake that finds its way into print. Naturally I'm astonished to discover that Mr. Dornwood borrowed another man's work without attribution. That error will be corrected."

"Corrected in what way?" Julian inquired, before Dornwood could stammer out some version of the same question.

"We'll print a notice in tomorrow's *Spark*."

"A notice! Excellent," said Julian. "Still, there's the matter of the thousands of pamphlets that have already been distributed under Mr. Dornwood's name. If some profit or royalty has been paid to Mr. Dornwood by mistake—"

"Sir, there's no problem in that department. I'll have our accountants calculate the full amount and pay it to you directly."

"To Mr. Hazzard, you mean."

"I mean, of course, to Mr. Hazzard."

"Well, that shows a Christian spirit," said Julian. "Doesn't it, Adam?"

"It's almost contrite," I said, not a little astonished myself.

"But it seems to me," Julian went on, "though I'm no expert on the publishing business, you might be missing an opportunity, Mr. Hungerford, and a lucrative one, at that."

"Please explain," Hungerford said warily, while Dornwood cringed in his chair like a spanked child.

"We've established that Adam was the true author of *The Adventures of Captain Commongold*. Was it well-written, do you think?"

"The public has taken to it in a big way. We've gone into a third printing. That makes it well-written, by my definition. You say it was all your work, Mr. Hazzard?"

"All but the punctuation," I said, glaring at Dornwood.

"Does that suggest anything to you, as a publisher?" Julian asked. "Adam is too modest to mention it, but he's written more than just these matter-of-fact *Adventures*. He has a novel in progress. Your press prints novels as well as newspapers, doesn't it, Mr. Hungerford?"

"We have a modest line of bound thrillers."

Julian asked me if my novel could be considered "thrilling."

"It has pirates in it," I said.

"There you are, then! Adam is a proven best-seller, and he's writing a book with pirates and other exciting persons in it—and here he is standing in your office!"

"I'll have a contract drawn up," Hungerford murmured.

"Mr. Hungerford is a canny businessman, Adam. He wants to publish your novel. Will the terms be generous, Mr. Hungerford?"

Hungerford quoted a colossal number, which he said was his standard rate for first-time novelists. I was quite taken aback, and probably turned as white in the face as Lawyer Lingley had when he recognized the President's nephew. I could not speak. My toes and fingers were numb.

"Good," Julian said. "But is Adam really a first-time novelist?—given the success of his previous work, I mean."

Hungerford nodded woodenly and announced a number twice as cosmic. I might have fainted, if I had not had the desk to lean on.

"Is the number acceptable, Adam?"

I allowed that it was.

"As for Mr. Dornwood—" Julian began.

"He'll be fired immediately," Hungerford said.

"Please don't do that! I'm sure Adam doesn't want to punish Mr. Dornwood any further, now that the error had been corrected."

"I guess that's right," I managed to say. "I won't hold a grudge against any man. You can keep your job, Dornwood, for all of me. Although—"

Dornwood gave me a pleading look. He was no longer the smug Manhattanite. He might have been some condemned slave kneeling before a Pharaoh for clemency. It was an unusual sensation to hold another man's fate in my hands. I could ask for his apology, I supposed. I supposed I could ask for his head, too, and Hungerford would have it delivered it to me on a china plate. But I'm not a vindictive person.

"I want your typewriter," I said.

They say the typewriter was invented in 1870 or thereabouts. It has had many incarnations in the centuries since. It went out of production even before the End of Oil, and was re-introduced only recently. Modern typewriters are made by hand, by craftsmen who have studied innumerable rusty remains rescued from various Tips. They are expensive to buy, and costly to maintain. They're also very heavy. Julian and I took turns carrying Dornwood's type-writer down the street to a taxi stand.

"Say something," Julian suggested, "or I'll think you've lost your tongue."

"I'm out of words entirely."

"Unfortunate condition for a writer to be in."

That brought me up short. *Was* I a writer, in the professional sense? I guessed I was. Hungerford and his lawyer had meant for me to sign a quit-claim this afternoon. Instead I had signed a contract to write a novel, and inked my name on a receipt for Theodore Dornwood's writing machine. Probably those two items, the contract and the typewriter, were acceptable *bona fides* in the author's trade.

I said to Julian, "I didn't know you could do that."

"Do what?"

"What you did at the *Spark*. Command obedience. Hungerford practi-cally bowed to you."

As long as I had known Julian I had known he was an Aristo. And I knew Aristos were meant to be respected and obeyed. But we had ignored that dic-tum as boys, and been forced to ignore it as soldiers, and agreed to ignore it as friends, and it was seldom topmost in my mind. I reminded myself that to a stranger, even a highly-placed businessman such as Mr. Hungerford, Julian was no more or less than a member of the family of the reigning President. No doubt Hungerford imagined that a word from Julian to his uncle would cause the *Spark* to be shut down and placed under a permanent Dominion sanction. That was the kind of power Deklan Conqueror was able to exercise.

By implication—at least in the mind of Hungerford and his lawyer—it was Julian's power as well.

"It's a handy thing," Julian said as we maneuvered first the typewriter and then ourselves into an available cab, "to invoke the family name now and then."

"It must be daunting to possess such power, and to wield it."

"The power is all Deklan's, I'm afraid."

"Perhaps not all. You borrowed a little of it just now."

"I don't want it. The thought of it sickens me. The power to do good—that's the power I'd like to wield," said Julian.

"Anyone can do good in the world, Julian, to some degree." Or so my mother had often told me, and the *Dominion Reader for Young Persons* concurred.

"The kind of good I want to do requires the kind of power few men possess."

"What kind of good is it, that wants such muscle?"

But Julian wouldn't answer.

Calyxa wasn't impressed by the typewriter. She pointed out all its dents and scars—which were many, for the machine had been carried to Labrador and back at least once, and had seen hard service under Dornwood. It still smelled a little of liquor and burnt hemp. But it was serviceable and well-oiled, and did its job uncomplainingly.

Calyxa also reminded me that I didn't know how to type. There was a skill associated with it. I could find letters and poke them, but this was a relatively laborious way to conduct business. She told me she had seen a booklet at Grogan's called *Typewriting Self-Taught,* and I promised her I would buy myself a copy, even if it cost as much as a Charles Curtis Easton novel.

If she was cynical about the typewriter, she was genuinely pleased by the news that I had signed a contract for my novel, and that Dornwood's royalties for *Julian Commongold* had been consigned to me. We would have money of our own, in other words, and there was the solid promise of more to come.

"So we won't be running off to Buffalo," she said.

"We can support ourselves in New York City. You can sing in cafés or not, as the mood suits you."

"Assuming we survive the Independence Day festivities at the Executive Palace."

I wished she hadn't mentioned it. "Julian's almost certain no harm will come to us there."

"Almost certain," she said. "That's almost reassuring."

There was a sound like gunfire in the street that night.

I rose and went to the bedroom window. The window had been left open in order to soften the heat in the upper stories of the house, though barely a breeze was blowing.

I put my head outside. Manhattan lay quiet in the midnight darkness. I could hear the rustling of draped flags and the creek of insects. The bones of Sky-Scrapers cut angular silhouettes out of the stars, and here and there the fulgent glow of distant foundries smoldered. Down below, in the stables attached to the house, a sleepless horse snuffled and tapped its shod hoof on the ground.

More explosions followed, and the sound of stifled laughter. A crew of five or six boys dashed out between two of the row houses, lit punks glowing in their hands. Offended voices hailed them from other windows.

What I had taken for gunshots was only the sound of exploding fire-crackers, tossed about by mischievous children in anticipation of the Fourth of July. Julian and I had played the same kind of tricks back in Williams Ford in our younger days. The dairymen had despised us for it, and claimed our concussions dried up the milk in the udders of their cows.

I couldn't bring myself to be angry.

The smell of black powder came in with the night air. Calyxa stirred and asked sleepily whether something was burning. "Smells like the whole town's on fire," she murmured.

"Just mischief," I told her.

I shivered, though the night was warm. Then I shuttered the window and went back to bed.

4

In the days before the Fourth of July I wrote up a special Introduction to the revised edition of *The Adventures of Captain Commongold (Now Revealed as Julian Comstock), the Youthful Hero of the Saguenay,* and replaced all the commas Mr. Theodore Dornwood had deleted or misplaced. In the matter of the Introduction I accepted the tutelage of Sam Godwin, who said it was very important that I should not insult the reigning President, but rather say something to praise him.

I didn't like to do this. After everything Julian had said about his uncle, it felt like hypocrisy. I told Sam so.

"It *is* hypocrisy. A lie, frankly. But it's for Julian's sake. It may save his life, or at least prolong it."

I could hardly refuse, then, for this was the same document that had imperiled Julian in the first place, and I was not sorry if it could be made to serve the opposite purpose. So I wrote down that Julian had joined the Army of the Laurentians under an assumed name "so that he would not receive any special treatment that might otherwise accrue to a President's nephew, but would be treated as an ordinary soldier of the line." Not that Deklan Comstock would ever stoop to influencing the military to obtain a better position for Julian: "The President no doubt believes, as Julian does, that a man must distinguish himself on his own hook, and for his own behavior, and no one else's. It was Julian's fear that some commissioned officer might attempt to curry favor through favoritism; and his pride and patriotism would not allow him to accept any such unearned privilege." Julian, I wrote, wanted to achieve the condition of heroism, if he achieved it at all, "as Deklan Conqueror had: on his own behalf, and without any softening help."

Julian winced when he read this, and told me I ought to work for the Dominion, since I was so facile with a flattering lie; but Sam rebuked him and explained that I had included the passage at his insistence.

"I've been spending time with Army officers on leave from the Laurentians," Sam said. "In the high ranks, particularly the men around General Galligasken, there is considerable discontent with Deklan Comstock. The President attempts to rule the Army like a tyrant, and orders peculiar attacks and strategies of his own contriving; and when these fail—as they almost inevitably do—he punishes some hapless Major General, or appoints a more servile one in his place. Unfortunately our success at Chicoutimi isn't typical of the general progress of the War. The Army of the Laurentians can't continue to sustain losses at the current rate—the President will have to recall veterans, or whip up a new draft, if he wants to prevent a complete collapse.

I tell you this in utmost confidence: if we can placate Deklan Conqueror, even temporarily, we may also outlast him."

That was unsettling news, even if it had a bright side, but there was nothing I could do about it. Julian accepted it with a nod and a frown.

Later that day I asked Sam whether he had been in contact with any of the Jews of New York City, for there were many of them—I had seen them walking black-suited to their Saturday services, in an enclave near the Egyptian part of town.*

"In Montreal I could afford such associations," he said. "As Sam Godwin I'm too well known to risk it."

"What would the risk be? Judaism is legal in this state, isn't it?"

"Legal but hardly respectable," said Sam. We were strolling down Broadway, not for the exercise but in order to have a conversation that wouldn't be overheard by servants. The rattle of carriage wheels, the clatter of horses' hooves, and the flapping of Independence Day banners made it impossible for anyone to eavesdrop on us—we could barely understand each other.

"What does respectability matter?" Having very little of my own, I was inclined to devalue the commodity.

"It matters not at all to me personally, but a great deal to certain people I deal with. The military, of course. The Dominion, it goes without saying. I can't do what I have been doing on behalf of Julian if I become known as a practicing Jew. And even in my private life—"

"Do you have one, Sam?" I asked, and immediately regretted the impertinence. He gave me a sour look.

"I hesitate to talk about it. But as a newly married man perhaps you can understand. Years ago—even before the death of Julian's father—I had the misfortune of falling in love with Mrs. Emily Baines Comstock."

It wasn't earth-shaking news. I had seen him blush whenever Mrs. Comstock entered a room; and I had seen her blush, too, in a way that suggested the possibility of mutual affection. Sam was nearly fifty years old, and Mrs. Comstock the same, but I had learned that love can blossom even in the elderly. Still it was shocking to hear him speak of it aloud.

"I know what you're thinking, Adam—the barriers are insurmountable."

It wasn't exactly what I had been thinking, but it would do.

"Nevertheless," Sam said, "I've confided some of my feelings to Emily, and she has hinted that those feelings might be in some measure returned."

"She told you to grow your beard back," I observed, "and you did it."

"Beards don't come into the matter. This is serious. When Bryce Comstock was alive I kept my affections to myself, and Emily was a devoted wife to a brave soldier, a man for whom my respect was immeasurable and my

---

* At first I thought the immigrant Egyptians might also be Jews, since they worshipped at unusual temples of their own; but this was not the case, Sam said.

friendship absolute. But Bryce is gone these several years, and Emily is a widow, and in social eclipse on top of that. The day may come when I can propose a wedding to her. Not until political matters are settled, however—and not at all, if I'm revealed as a Jew." The Dominion forbade such marriages, and called them unnatural.

"That would make you Julian's step-father," I said.

"What else have I been, since Julian was a child, except a second father to him?—though he thinks of me more as a servant, I'm afraid."

"He's fonder of you than he can say. He trusts your advice."

"I don't deny that I'm of value to him—only that he values me as a useful servant might be valued."

"More than that!"

"Well, maybe so," said Sam. "The situation's murky."

That was the third day of the month of July, the eve of our visit to the Executive Palace.

Independence Day! What cherished memories of Williams Ford that date provoked, despite all my present anxieties.

It had always been the least solemn of the four Universal Christian Holidays, second only to Christmas in my childish calculations. It was, of course, a profoundly sacred occasion, marked by innumerable services at the Dominion Hall. There had been many public lectures by Ben Kreel about the Christian Nation in which we lived, and the valuable role of the Dominion in all our lives, and such weighty matters as that. But Independence Day also marked the true beginning of summer—summer in its maturity, July and August populating the world with perfume and insects. The creeks that fed the River Pine, though still cold, were available for swimming; squirrels begged to be stalked and shot; peddlers came up from Connaught with fireworks to sell. Best of all, Independence Day drew the Aristos out of their Estate for picnics and celebrations, which meant that my mother, in her role as a seamstress, could sneak into the Estate library and fetch out a book or two for me to read. (These volumes were usually, but not always, returned in good order.)

I was prompted by this sentiment to compose a letter to my mother in Williams Ford. Because Julian's identity had been revealed I could finally write to her openly, and receive mail in return, and I had already sent her several notes—though no response had been received. I sat by the window in the room I shared with Calyxa; there was a small desk there, and I took a sheet of paper from its topmost drawer.

Dear Mother, I wrote.

If my last letter reached you, you will already know that I have survived a year in Labrador—that I did not embarrass myself in battle—that I have married a good woman in a legal Dominion service—and that your daughter-in-law is Calyxa Hazzard (formerly Blake) of Montreal.

Well, all that must be news enough! I have not got any reply just yet, but I hope you will write soon, and communicate your thoughts and Father's on this exciting subject. Naturally, I hope for and expect your blessing. If Father is disappointed that I did not marry in the Church of Signs, please tell him I'm sorry but that there was no suitable Pastor available.

We are well and doing fine in New York City. In fact I have recently published a Pamphlet (I enclose a copy), and I have been commissioned to write an entire Novel for the same publisher. I seem to have become an author, that is to say, after the style of Mr. Charles Curtis Easton! It is a more lucrative profession than I had expected; and I will send you some money if you tell me how to address it so that it won't be stolen.

As I write it is the morning of Independence Day, very sunny and pleasant all around, and all over Manhattan church bells are ringing. How is it back in Williams Ford? Does Ben Kreel still talk in the Dominion Hall until nightfall, and are the fireworks still reflected in the waters of the River Pine?

I have said we are well, and that's true. In fact, because of my friendship with Julian Comstock, Calyxa and I have been invited to the Executive Palace this evening for the annual celebration there! I know you have told me not to mix with Aristos if I can help it—"tempt not contagion by proximity," as you used to quote to me from the Dominion Reader—but an invitation from the President carries a certain weight, and can't safely be refused.

In all likelihood nothing untoward will happen at the Palace. The chance that I will be beheaded or disemboweled or any such unpleasant thing is really very slight, although Julian is at a somewhat greater risk. Please do not assume that I have been killed if you do not hear from me—you know how unreliable the mails are!

That is about all for now. Please give my love to Father. Many troubles have come my way since I left Williams Ford, but I am less a child than you remember me, and able to carry myself virtuously through even the most venomous garden, while keeping my eye on the straight and narrow path, and looking neither left nor right, except as necessary to keep from tripping over things.

I signed it, *Your loving son, Adam.*

In the late afternoon we boarded a carriage—Calyxa, Mrs. Comstock, Sam, Julian, and myself—and set out for the Presidential Palace. It was a nervous journey; but we were brave, and did not speak about the risks and hazards.

The long light cast a golden patina on Broadway, which was dressed up for the occasion with banners and bunting. I was dressed up, too, in a tailored Aristo costume that pinched various tender parts of me, and so was Calyxa, whose elegant mauve-colored dress took up all the space not already filled by Mrs. Comstock's even bulkier outfit. I was glad to have a seat by the window of the carriage, where I could see past these mounds of compressed silk to the outside world.

We entered the Palace grounds by the Broadway Gate at 59th Street. Our carriage and our invitations were inspected by a black-uniformed member of the President's private security force, which is called the Republican Guard. Once approved by that dour individual, and carefully watched by a dozen just like him, we passed over the moat and through two heavy iron doors into the manicured grounds of what had once been, according to Julian, a vast Central Park.

Very little remained of the original version of that Park, Julian said, except the great Reservoir in the middle of it. All the wooded areas had been burned over during the False Tribulation, and what did not burn had been cut down for fuel by starved and freezing urbanites. Both the Sheep Meadow and the Ramble had been plowed and planted in the years that followed—a quixotic enterprise, for the soil was not suited to agriculture. Then, after the fall of Washington, the entire Park from north to south had been donated to the Executive Branch under President Otis. It was Otis who had caused to be built the huge enclosing walls of brick, marble, and stone recovered from the ruins of Manhattan; it was Otis who had designed the Hunting Grounds and stocked them with game; it was Otis who had erected the Executive Palace overlooking the Great Lawn.

Our path wound northward past ailanthus groves and broad meadows of mown grass to something called the Statuary Lawn, where large examples of sculpture dating from the Efflorescence of Oil had been preserved. Here to the left of us was a statue of a man on horseback, named Bolivar, and a stone spike called the Needle of Cleopatra. To the right, a huge metallic Arm held a verdigrised Torch as tall as an Athabaska pine, and a fractured Crowned Head adjoined it.* These items (and others like them) looked both bold and melancholy, casting shadows like the gnomons of monstrous sun-dials as we rode among them in the last light of the day.

We were not the only coach on the path. There was a regular circus of carriages, coaches, and mounted horsemen making their way toward the Executive Palace from each of the Park's four Gates. The coaches had gilded fittings, the horsemen were formally dressed, and the carriage lanterns were lit and had begun to glimmer in the gathering dusk. All the finest and richest men and women of Manhattan had received an invitation to this annual fete. Those who did not, considered themselves slighted. The failure to receive an invitation was often a sign that some unlucky high Eupatridian had fallen

* The Head and Arm were fragments of the Colossus of Liberty, Julian said. According to legend the Colossus used to stand astride the Verrazano Narrows, while boats and barges passed between her feet. A cursory inspection shows that the scale is off, and Liberty would not have been able to span the distance even with her legs splayed at an unflattering angle. Still, she must once have been a very large and prominently visible Statue—I don't mean to diminish her grandeur.

from favor with the Executive; and the uninvited person, if he was a Senator, might begin to watch his back for knives.

Calyxa, of course, was not impressed with all this gaudiness and show, on account of her Parmentierist principles. I had hoped she would conceal her disdain for the Eupatridians, at least for the duration of the Independence Day event. But that was not to be the case.

We arrived near the vast stables of the Executive Palace, where boys in livery were accepting the carriages of the many guests. We dismounted and had begun to walk toward the entranceway of the Palace when we came across an angry Aristo beating his driver with a cane.

The Aristo in question was a stout man of middle age. His carriage had thrown a wheel, and the owner apparently blamed his driver for the accident. The driver was a man at least as old as his master, with hollow cheeks and a sort of doggish resignation about his eyes. He bore the beating stoically, while the Aristo cursed him in words I can't repeat.

"What the hell!" exclaimed Calyxa, coming upon this scene.

"Hush," Sam whispered to her. "That man is Nelson Wieland. He owns half the re-rolling mills in New Jersey, and holds a Senate seat."

"I don't care if he's Croesus on a bicycle," Calyxa declared. "He ought not to use his cane that way."

"It's none of our business," Mrs. Comstock put in.

But Calyxa would not be dissuaded from walking right up to Mr. Wieland and interrupting him in the strenuous work of beating his employee.

"What has this man done?" she asked.

Wieland looked at her, blinking. He didn't recognize Calyxa, of course, and he seemed to be confused about her status. By evidence of dress, if not deportment, she was a wealthy Aristo herself—she had, after all, been invited to a Presidential reception—and he decided at last to humor her.

"I'm sorry to trouble you with an unpleasant sight," he said. "This man's carelessness cost me a wheel—and not just the wheel but the axle, hence the carriage."

"How was he careless?"

"Oh, I don't know exactly—he claims the rig struck a stone—that the suspension of the vehicle was not well-maintained—in other words he offers every excuse that would relieve him of responsibility. Of course I know better. The man shirks—it's habitual with him."

"And so you beat him bloody?"

This was not an exaggeration, for the blows had caused wounds which stained the fabric of the driver's starched white shirt.

"It's the only way he'll mark the event in his memory. He's an indentured man, and slow."

"*De toute évidence, non seulement vous êtes un tyran, mais en plus, vous êtes bête,*" said Calyxa.

Mr. Wieland was brought up short by the unfamiliar language. He gave Calyxa another perplexed look, as if she were some exotic form of life, a crawfish perhaps, that had emerged unexpectedly from its native element. Perhaps he thought she was the wife of an ambassador.

"Thank you," he said finally, "you flatter me, I'm sure; but I don't speak the language, and I'm afraid of being late for the reception." He took up his cane and hurried away.

Calyxa lingered a while longer with the beaten driver, conversing with him in a tone too low for me to overhear. They spoke until Sam called her back to us.

"Was that necessary?" he asked.

"That man you call Wieland is a thug, however much he owns."

Julian asked what the injured driver had had to say for himself.

"He's been working for Wieland most of his life. He's a blacksmith's son from some little town in Pennsylvania. His father sold him into Wieland's mill when the smithy business failed. He spent years casting hubs, until the coal fumes made him stupid. That was when Wieland took him for a personal driver."

"Then Wieland's entitled to beat him if he chooses. The man is chattel."

"Entitled by the law, maybe," Calyxa said.

"The law is the law," said Sam.

The Executive Palace was so expansive and grand that it might have done double-duty as a museum or a train station. We entered through a Portico, where marble pillars supported a cathedral-like ceiling, and passed into an immense Receiving Room, where Aristos clustered in conversation and waiters circulated with carts of drink and plates of small food items. Some of these* were impaled on toothpicks. I thought it was a skimpy selection for a Presidential Dinner, until Julian explained that the morsels were not the main course but only "appetizers," designed to provoke hunger rather than slake it. We picked at these trifles and tried to appreciate the elaborate wainscoting, which was painted with images from the history of the Pious Presidents, and the sheer scale of the architecture.

Julian's fame had preceded him. In fact the story of his career as a soldier and his sudden re-appearance in Manhattan had circulated widely. Several Senators approached to congratulate him for his bravery, once his presence was noted, and many young Aristo women made a point of flattering him with their attention, though he was merely courteous in return.

Calyxa regarded these fashionable young women skeptically. I suppose they seemed unserious to her. They wore sleeveless gowns, in order to display

---

* The food items, not the waiters.

the number and prominence of the vaccination scars on their upper arms. Mrs. Comstock said that such scars were a vain self-decoration: expensive, largely useless against disease, and a danger to the recipient. This might have been true, for several of the vaccinated women were pale, or seemed feverish or unsteady in their gait. But I suppose the pursuit of fashion has always carried a price, monetary or otherwise.

Julian did not stint his introductions as he passed through the crowd. He called me an "author" or a "scribe," and Calyxa was "Mrs. Hazzard, a vocal artist." Those of the elite to whom we spoke were unfailingly if briefly polite toward us. We were circulating a little uneasily among this mob of cheerful Eupatridians when the President of the United States made his first appearance.

He did not enter the Receiving Room, but greeted us from a sort of balcony at the top of a staircase. Stern and well-armed Republican Guardsmen were arrayed at his back, their demeanor suggesting that they might have preferred to aim their pistols at the crowd if etiquette had not precluded that hostile act. Silence fell over the room, until every face was turned toward Deklan Conqueror.

The coins didn't do him justice, I thought. Or perhaps it was the other way around. He was less handsome than his graven image, but somehow more imposing. It was true that he looked a little like Julian, minus the feathery yellow beard. In fact he looked the way I imagined Julian might look if he were years older and not entirely sane.

I don't say this to demean the President. Probably he couldn't help the way he looked. His features were not irregular; but there was something about his narrow eyes, his hawk nose, and his fixed, ingratiating grin that suggested madness. Not out-and-out lunacy, mind you, but the kind of subtle madness that dallies alongside sanity, and bides its time.

I saw Julian wince at the sight of his uncle. Mrs. Comstock drew a choked breath beside me.

The President wore a suit of formal black that suggested a uniform without actually being one. The medals pinned to his breast accentuated the effect. He saluted the crowd, smiling all the while. He expressed his greetings to his guests, and thanked them all for coming, and regretted that he couldn't visit with them more personally, but encouraged them to enjoy themselves with refreshments. Dinner would be served before long, he said, followed by Independence Day festivities in the Main Hall, and further refreshments, and fireworks on the Great Lawn, and then he would deliver a speech. It was a proud day for the Nation, he said, and he hoped we would celebrate it vigorously and sincerely. Then he disappeared behind a purple curtain.

He wasn't seen again until after dinner.

When we filed into the dining hall we discovered that our seats at the long tables had been assigned to us, and marked with small ornaments bearing our names. Calyxa and I sat together, but nowhere near the other members of our party. Directly across from us—an unfortunate coincidence—was Nelson Wieland, the brutal industrialist who had made such a poor impression on Calyxa outside the stables. Seated beside him was a similarly aged gentleman in silk and wool, introduced to us as Mr. Billy Palumbo. It emerged in conversation over the soup course that Mr. Palumbo was an agriculturalist. He owned several vast domains in upper New York State, where his indentured people grew pea-beans and corn for the city market.

Mr. Wieland criticized the gourd soup, which he claimed was too thick.

"Seems all right to me," Mr. Palumbo rejoined. "I like a substantial broth. Do you care for it at all, Mrs. Hazzard?"

"I suppose it's fine," Calyxa said in an indifferent tone.

"More than fine," I added. "I didn't know a common gourd could be made so palatable, or even harvested this time of year."

"I've tasted better," said Wieland.

The discussion continued in this culinary vein throughout the meal. Boiled onions were served—undercooked, or over; we debated them. Medallions of lamb—Palumbo considered the cut too rare. Potatoes: picked young. Coffee, too strong for Mr. Wieland's constitution. And so on.

By the time dessert was served—wintergreen ice-cream, a novelty to me—Calyxa seemed prepared to throw her portion across the table, if Palumbo and Wieland didn't leave off the topic of food. Instead she lobbed a different kind of missile. "Do your indentured people eat this well, Mr. Palumbo?" she asked abruptly.

The question took Palumbo by surprise. "Well, hardly," he said. He smiled. "Imagine serving them ice-cream! They'd soon grow too stout to work."[*]

"Or perhaps they might work harder, if they had such a thing to look forward to at the end of the day."

"I doubt it very much. Are you a radical, Mrs. Hazzard?"

"I don't call myself that."

"I'm glad to hear it. Compassion is a fine thing, but dangerous when it's misplaced. What I've learned in many years of overseeing the indentured is that they have to be treated very strictly at all times. They mistake kindness for weakness. And if they see a weakness in an Owner they'll take advantage of it. They're notorious for their laziness, and inventive in finding ways to pursue it."

"I agree," Mr. Wieland put in. "For instance, that servant you saw me discipline earlier tonight. 'Only a broken wheel,' you might think. But let it slide, and tomorrow there would be two broken wheels, or a dozen."

---

[*] As Palumbo had, long since, though I do not hold a man's girth against him.

"Yes, that's the logic of it," Palumbo said.

"Logic," Calyxa said, "if you carry it to its conclusion, might imply that men working against their will are not the most efficient laborers."

"Mrs. Hazzard! Good grief!" exclaimed Palumbo. "If the indentured are sullen, it's only because they fail to appreciate their own good fortune. Have you seen the popular film *Eula's Choice*?"

"Yes, but I don't see what that has to do with it."

"It explains the origins of the indenture system very succinctly. A bargain was struck sometime around the end of the False Tribulation, and the same terms obtain today."

"You believe in the theory of Heritable Debt, Mr. Palumbo?"

"'Heritable Debt' is the radical's term for it. You ought to be more careful in your reading, Mrs. Hazzard."

"It's a question of property," Wieland interjected.

"Yes," Calyxa said, "for the indentured don't have any—in fact they *are* property."

"Not at all. You defame the people you mean to defend. Of course the indentured have property. They own their bodies, their skills, if any, and their capacity for labor. If they don't *seem* to own these things, it's only because the commodity has already been sold. It happened as in the film Mr. Palumbo mentions. Refugees from the Fall of the Cities traded the only goods they possessed—their hands, their hearts, and their votes—for food and shelter in a difficult time."

"A person ought not to be able to sell himself," Calyxa said, "much less his vote."

"If a person *owns* himself then he must be able to *sell* himself. Else what meaning does property have? As for the vote, he isn't deprived of it—it still exists—he has only signed it over to his landed employer, who votes it for him."

"Yes, so the Owners can control that sorry excuse for a Senate—"

This was perhaps too much to say. Nearby heads turned toward us, and Calyxa blushed and lowered her voice. "I mean, these are opinions that I have read. In any case, the bargain you describe was made more than a century ago, if it was made at all. Nowadays people are born into indenture."

"A debt is a debt, Mrs. Hazzard. The commitment doesn't vanish simply because a man has had the bad luck to die. If a man's possessions pass by right to his survivors, so do his obligations. What have you been reading that left you laboring under such misapprehensions?"

"A man named . . . oh I think Parmentier," Calyxa said, pretending innocence.

"Parmentier! That European terrorist! Good God, Mrs. Hazzard, you do need some direction in your studies!" Wieland cast an accusing glance at me.

"I have recommended the novels of Mr. Charles Curtis Easton," I said.

"The spread of literacy is the problem here," said Palumbo. "Oh, I'm all in favor of a sensible degree of literacy—as you must be, Mr. Hazzard, given your career as a journalist. But it has an infectious tendency. It spreads, and discontent spreads along with it. Admit one literate man to a coffle and he'll teach the others the skill; and what they read won't be Dominion-approved works, but pornography, or the lowest kind of cheap publications, or fomentive political tracts. Parmentier! Why, Mrs. Hazzard, just a week ago I purchased a string of three hundred men from a planter in Utica, at what appeared to be a bargain price. I kept them apart from my other stock for a time, a sort of quarantine period, and I'm glad I did, for it turned out reading was endemic among them, and Parmentierist pamphlets were circulating freely. That kind of thing can ruin an entire Estate, if it flourishes unchecked."

Calyxa didn't ask what Mr. Palumbo had done to check the flourishing of literacy among his "stock," perhaps because she feared the answer. But her face betrayed her feelings. She tensed, and I worried that she was about to fling some new accusation across the table, or perhaps a fork. It was at this moment, fortunately, that the dessert plates were cleared away.

Intoxicating drinks circulated freely after the meal, including such expensive abominations as Champagne and Red Wine. I did not partake, though the Eupatridians went at it like horses at a trough.

Deklan Comstock briefly appeared from another indoor balcony—he preferred a commanding height, Julian said—and invited us to step into the ballroom adjoining, where the band would play patriotic tunes. We followed at the President's bidding. The music struck up at once, and some of the Aristos, well lubricated with fiery fluids, began to dance. I didn't dance, and Calyxa didn't want to; so we looked for genial company instead, well distant from Mr. Wieland and Mr. Palumbo.

We found company—or it found us—but it was not congenial, in the long run.

"Mr. Hazzard," said a booming voice.

I turned, and saw a man in clerical garb.

I gathered he was some high functionary of the Dominion, for he wore a broad-rimmed felt hat with silver trimming, a sober black jacket, and a formal cotton shirt on which the legend *John 3:16* was stitched in golden thread. I didn't recognize his face, which was florid and round. He carried a glass in his hand, and the glass was half-filled with an amber fluid, and his breath smelled like the copper-coil stills Ben Kreel used to discover and destroy in the indentured men's quarters back in Williams Ford. His eyes glittered with intrigue or drink.

"You know me, but I don't know you," I said.

"On the contrary, I don't know you at all, but I've read your pamphlet on the subject of Julian Comstock, and someone was kind enough to point you out to me." He extended the hand which was not holding a drink. "My name is Simon Hollingshead, and I'm a Deacon of the Diocese of Colorado Springs."

He said that as if it was a trivial thing. It wasn't. The simple title belied a powerful position in the Dominion hierarchy. In fact the only clergymen more elevated than the Deacons of Colorado Springs were the seventy members of the Dominion High Council itself.

Pastor Hollingshead's hand was hot and moist, and I let go of it as soon as I could do so without offending him.

"What brings you to the east?" Calyxa asked warily.

"Ecclesiastical duties, Mrs. Hazzard—nothing you would understand."

"On the contrary, it sounds fascinating."

"Well, I can't speak as freely as I would like. But the eastern cities have to be taken in hand from time to time. They tend to drift away from orthodoxy, left to their own devices. Unaffiliated Churches spring up like fungal growths. The mixing of classes and nationalities has a well-known degenerative influence."

"Perhaps the Easterners drink too freely," I couldn't help saying.

"'Wine that gladdens the heart of man,'" quoted the Deacon, though it appeared to be something more powerful than wine in his glass.* "It's sacred doctrine I've come to protect, not personal sobriety. Drinking isn't a sin, though drunkenness is. Do I seem drunk to you, Mr. Hazzard?"

"No, sir, not noticeably. What sacred doctrines are in danger?"

"The ones that prohibit laxness in administering a flock. Eastern clergy will overlook the damnedest things, pardon me. Lubriciousness, licentiousness, lust—"

"The alliterative sins," Calyxa said quietly.

"But enough of my problems. I meant only to congratulate you on your history of Julian Comstock's military adventures."

I thanked him kindly, and pretended to be modest.

"Young people have very little in the way of uplifting literature available to them. Your work is exemplary, Mr. Hazzard. I see it hasn't yet received the Dominion Stamp. But that can be changed."

It was a generous offer, which might result in an increase of sales, and for that reason I thought we shouldn't offend Deacon Hollingshead unnecessarily. Calyxa, however, was in a sharp mood, and unimpressed with Hollingshead's ecclesiastical rank and powers.

"Colorado Springs is a big town," she said. "Doesn't it have problems of its own you could be looking after?"

"Surely it does! Corruption can creep in anywhere. Colorado Springs is

---

* The quotation from Psalms is authentic, although it would never have been allowed into *The Dominion Reader for Young Persons.*

the very heart and soul of the Dominion, but you're right, Mrs. Hazzard, vice breeds there as well as anywhere else. Even in my own family—"

He hesitated then, as if unsure whether he ought to proceed. Perhaps the liquor had made him distrust his tongue. To my dismay, Calyxa wouldn't let the matter drop. "Vice, in a Deacon's family?"

"My own daughter has been a victim of it." He lowered his voice. "I wouldn't ordinarily discuss this. But you seem to be a thoughtful young woman. You don't bare your arms like so many of the ladies present, nor cover your skin with ugly vaccination marks."

"My modesty is well-known," Calyxa said, though she had lobbied to wear just such a sleeveless costume—Mrs. Comstock had overruled her.

"Then I won't offend you by mentioning, um—"

"Unpleasant vices are offensive to me, Deacon Hollingshead, but the words describing them are not. How can we eradicate a problem unless we're allowed to name it?"

She was baiting him; but Hollingshead was too virtuous or drunk to understand. *"Homosexuality,"* he whispered. "Do you know *that* word, Mrs. Hazzard?"

"The rumor of such behavior has occasionally reached my ears. Is your daughter a—?"

"God forbid! No, Marcy is a model child. She's twenty-one now. But because she has yet to marry, she drew the attention of a league of degenerate women."

"In Colorado Springs!"

"Yes! Such a thing exists! And it continues to exist, despite all my efforts to eradicate it."

"What efforts have you made?"

"Both the Municipal Police and the investigatory arm of the Dominion have been put on the case. Needless to say, I don't let Marcy go anywhere unobserved. There are eyes on her at all times, though she doesn't know it."

"Is it really a wise thing to spy on your own daughter?"

"Certainly, if it protects her."

"*Does* it protect her?"

"Several times it has saved her from absolute ruin. Marcy seems hardly able to leave the house without wandering by accident into some depraved tavern or other. Naturally, when we discover such establishments we shut them down. More than one degenerate woman has attempted to make Marcy a special friend. Those women were arrested and interrogated."

"Interrogated!—why?"

"Because there's more than coincidence at work," the bibulous Deacon said. "Clearly, some group of deviants has *targeted* my daughter. We interrogated these women in order to find out the connection between them."

"Has the effort succeeded?"

"Unfortunately no. Even under extreme duress, none of these women will admit that their interest in Marcy was planned in advance, and they deny all knowledge of any conspiracy."

"Interrogations aren't generally so fruitless, I take it," said Calyxa, and I could tell by the reddening of her face that she didn't approve of the Deacon's enthusiastic approach to the knotty issues of vice and torture.

"No, they're not. Our investigators are skilled at extracting information from the unwilling—the Dominion trains them in it."

"How do you explain the failure in this case, then?"

"Vice has unsuspected depths and profundities—it hides by instinct from the light," the Deacon said grimly.

"And it occurs so close to home," Calyxa said, adding, in a low tone, *"On aurait peut-être dû torturer votre fille, aussi."*

I expected Deacon Hollingshead to ignore this incomprehensible remark. He did not. Instead he drew himself up in a rigid posture. His features hardened abruptly.

"Je ne suis ni idiot ni inculte, Mrs. Hazzard," he said. *"Si vous vous moquez de moi, je me verrai dans l'obligation de lancer un mandat d'arrêt contre vous."*

I didn't know what this exchange meant, but Calyxa paled and took a step backward.

Hollingshead faced me. His put his smile back on, though it seemed forced. "I congratulate you again on your success, Mr. Hazzard. Your work does you credit. You have a fine career ahead of you. I hope nothing interferes with it." He took a noisy sip from his glass and walked away.

I don't mean to leave the reader with the impression that all the Eupatridians we met at the Presidential Reception were boors or tyrants. Many, perhaps most, were entirely pleasant, taken as individuals. Several of the men were yachtsmen, and I enjoyed listening to their spirited discourse on nautical subjects, though I couldn't reef a mainsail if my life depended on it.

Mrs. Comstock knew a number of the wives. Many of them were astonished to see her here, so long after the death of her husband; but they were accustomed to the caprices of Presidential favor and quickly accepted her back into their ranks.

Sam spent his time with the military contingent, including a handful of notable Generals and Major Generals. I suppose Sam was gauging their attitude toward the Commander in Chief, or trying to pick up clues about the President's intentions toward Julian. But all that was beyond my ken. Julian himself was deep in conversation with what he described to me as a genuine Philosopher: a Professor of Cosmology from the newly-reformed New York University. This man had many interesting theories, Julian said, about the Speed of Light, and the Origin of Stars, and other such refined subjects. But he was under the thumb of the Dominion, and could not discourse as freely as he might have liked. Nevertheless the man had enjoyed some access to the Dominion Archives, and hinted at the artistic and scientific treasures concealed there.

The general hilarity occasioned by the drinking of Grape Wine, etc., soon reached fresh heights. The musical band had adjourned for a short while—they were out behind the stables, Calyxa suggested, smoking hempen cigarettes—but they returned in relatively good order, and better spirits, just as Deklan Comstock made a third appearance on one of his marbled balconies.

This time the President called out recognition to the most elevated members of the crowd, including the Speaker of the Senate, Deacon Hollingshead, several prominent Landowners, the Surgeon General, the Chinese and Nipponese Ambassadors (who had been eyeing each other uneasily from opposite ends of the room), and other dignitaries. Then he smiled his unwholesome smile and said, "Also present, and home from his adventures defending the Union in Labrador, is my beloved nephew, Julian Comstock, as well as his celebrated Scribe, Mr. Adam Hazzard, and his former tutor, Sam Godwin."

Hearing my name pronounced by this man was unnerving, and caused a shiver to rush up my spine.

"Mr. Hazzard," the President continued, "has a very great and subtle literary talent, and I've recently learned that his wife is talented as well. Mrs. Hazzard is a singer, and it occurs to me to wonder whether she might favor us with a ballad or such, now that the band is warmed up. Mrs. Hazzard!" He feigned shielding his eyes against the light. "Mrs. Hazzard, are you willing to entertain these ladies and gentlemen?"

Calyxa's jaw was grimly set—clearly this was Deklan Comstock's attempt to humiliate her, and indirectly Julian, by exposing her as a cabaret singer—but at the same time it was an invitation she dared not refuse. "Hold my drink, Adam," she said flatly;* then she climbed up onto the bandstand where the musicians were arrayed.

This turn of events had taken the bandleader by surprise as well. He looked at her blankly, perhaps expecting her to call out a familiar song-title— *Where the Sauquoit Meets the Mohawk*, or some respectable piece like that.

But Calyxa was never one to do the expected, especially at the beck of a tyrant like Deklan Comstock. She looked out at the sea of Eupatridian faces confronting her. It was an awkward moment. She didn't speak, or even smile, but lifted her cumbersome skirt and began to stomp her right foot. This activity amused some of the Aristos, and it didn't display her ankles to her best advantage; but it established a terse martial beat, which the drummer soon picked up.

---

* Calyxa had not refused the Champagne as consistently as I had.

Then, without prelude, she began to sing:

> *By Piston, Loom, and Anvil, boys,*
> *We clothe and arm the nation,*
> *And sweat all day for a pauper's pay*
> *And half a soldier's ration. . . .*

There was shock at first. Many of the Eupatridians in the room knew this song, or had heard rebellious servants singing it from kitchens and cellars. If they didn't know it intimately, they knew it by reputation. In any case the lyrics were explicit in their sympathy for the common man.

The silence and gasps from her audience did not discourage Calyxa, though even the drummer faltered for a beat or two. She finished the chorus and ran right through the first verse, which—like every other verse in this long and encyclopedic song—decried the suffering of some class of laborer at the hands of an Industrialist or Owner.

Heads turned toward President Deklan Comstock as if to gauge his reaction. Was he enraged? Insulted? Would the Republican Guard bring out their pistols and end the show abruptly?

But Deklan Conqueror didn't appear to be angry. He raised his hand, instead, in a kind of mock salute.

That small gesture broadcast a signal among the Eupatridians that for tonight, at least, the usual proprieties had been suspended. They drew the inference that Calyxa's performance was not a Protest but a kind of Show, ironically intended. *Piston, Loom, and Anvil* sung at the Executive Palace! It had the deliciously inverted logic of a bacchanal. A few of the more astute Aristos began to clap in time.

That caused the orchestra to take courage and join in. The musicians were all familiar with the tune, and began to work little trills and arpeggios around Calyxa's powerful voice. Calyxa herself carried on as if none of these nuances mattered: it was the song she meant to sing, and she was singing it.

"Bless her," said Julian, who had come to stand beside me.

Some in the room still didn't appreciate the incongruous performance. Mr. Wieland, Mr. Palumbo, and Deacon Hollingshead stood in a single dour knot, arms crossed. Because they worked directly with indentured men, Wieland and Palumbo knew the song for what it was: a dagger aimed at their livelihoods. Deacon Hollingshead had no such direct interest, though he was a stalwart supporter of the status quo, and perhaps had tortured men who dared such verses in his presence. Even the President's indulgence could not persuade these worthies to relax their vigilance.

In fact I began to worry about their health. Wieland's already ruddy complexion deepened, until his head came to resemble a beet embedded in a shirt collar, and Palumbo wasn't far behind in this competition.

Julian had once told me a story about deep-sea divers. In recent times it had become possible for Tipmen in sealed rubber suits, supported by air pumped to them from the surface, to descend into the murky waters around the ruins of seaside cities. This was an occasionally lucrative but wildly dangerous pursuit. It often yielded fresh treasure from sites that had, on land, been picked clean. But for every valuable antiquity thus obtained, a man's life was put at risk.

It is a peculiar quality of the oceans that the pressure of the water increases with depth. There was a legend among these undersea Tipmen, Julian had said, that a diver, if he came untethered in deep enough water, might sink so far that the fist of the sea would squeeze him to death. Worse, the water pressure would literally *roll him up like a tube of tooth-paste*. His body, encased in rubber, would be crushed and then forced into his enclosing helmet, so that the whole of him would at last be concentrated in that steel shell like a bloody stew in an inverted bowl—until even the helmet itself exploded!

This was, of course, usually fatal.

I thought about that legend (which, for all I know, may be true) as I looked at Wieland, Palumbo, and Hollingshead. With every succeeding verse—the one about the buried coal-miner, the one about the seamstress reduced to penury and prostitution by her employer, the one about the railway porter bisected by a runaway train—yet more blood rushed to the crania of these indignant gentlemen, until I wondered whether they would simply drop dead or whether their skulls would burst like pressed grapes.

Calyxa, if anything, was slightly miffed by the genial reception she was now receiving. She cranked out even more radical verses, which named Owners as Tyrants and Senators as Fools. "I'm not sure this is especially decorous," said Mrs. Comstock from beside me. But the President continued to grin (though his grin was far from mirthful), and the Eupatridians, by and large, continued to mistake insult for irony, and smirked at the joke of it.

I began to think Calyxa's inventive powers had been exhausted—which might have been a good thing—when she stepped to the very edge of the bandstand. Aiming her gaze directly and unmistakably at the industrialist Nelson Wieland, and still pounding the stage with her foot, she sang:

> I know someone, a blacksmith's son,
> Who learned to mill old steel—
> He cast the parts
> For rich men's carts,
> But the heat took a toll,
> And the fumes of the coal—
> He was broken at the wheel, oh!
> Broken at the wheel!
> By Piston, Loom, and Anvil, boys,
> We clothe and arm the nation . . .

If there was any doubt whether she had improvised this verse for the specific benefit of Mr. Wieland, he didn't share it. His eyes started from their sockets. He clenched his fists—in fact his entire body seemed to clench. It was as if the deep ocean had taken him in its grip.

Then, apparently satisfied with the reaction she had produced, Calyxa finished the chorus and addressed the agriculturalist Billy Palumbo, singing:

> *The indentured men in the Owner's pen*
> *Are bought and sold like cattle;*
> *But a man's got a mind,*
> *And an Owner might find*
> *That all he bought*
> *Is an awful lot*
> *Of Revolutionary Chattel, oh!*
> *Revolutionary Chattel . . .*

Mr. Palumbo was not accustomed to this kind of insolence any more than Mr. Wieland was. I watched with profound apprehension as the veins in and around his face stood forth. The legend of the explosive Diving Tipmen came once more to my mind.

Then, inevitably, it was Deacon Hollingshead's turn. As she repeated the chorus the Deacon glared viciously. But Calyxa had faced down Job and Utty Blake, and she was not to be intimidated by a mere Dominion cleric, no matter how powerful. Her voice was her cudgel, and she meant to use it. She sang—*con brio*, as the composers say—

> *The Colorado maid was not afraid*
> *When the Deacon's henchmen caught her,*
> *She suffered in her pride,*
> *But they beat her till she cried,*
> *And when her courage grew thin*
> *She confessed her sin:*
> *"I was kissed by the Deacon's daughter! Oh!*
> *Kissed by the Deacon's daughter!"*
> *By Piston, Loom, and Anvil, boys . . .*

There was a sudden flash of light, and a thunderous report—I looked apprehensively at Deacon Hollingshead—but the Deacon was intact—it was only that the fireworks had begun out on the Great Lawn. The band abruptly ceased playing, and we all adjourned outside with a certain sense of relief.

Calyxa sat next to me, breathless from her exertions, and I was very proud of her, though very worried, as the Independence Day fireworks crackled through the hot night air above the Executive Palace.

She had probably just scotched any possibility that my Commongold pamphlet would receive the Dominion Stamp of Approval. But that didn't matter much—the pamphlet was doing well enough without it. In any case, if it had been Deklan Comstock's intention to humiliate Calyxa, I believed he had gotten more than he bargained for.

For the duration of the fireworks display we sat on wooden bleachers. There was a special box reserved for the President and a few close allies, including, I was dismayed to see, Deacon Hollingshead. Calyxa and I sat with Julian and Sam and Mrs. Comstock among the lesser Eupatridians.

"There are portents to be read at any event like this," Sam said in a low voice. "Who attends, who doesn't—who speaks to whom—who smiles, who frowns—it can all be read, the way a fortune-teller reads a deck of cards."

"What fortune do you divine?" I asked.

"The Admiral of the Navy isn't here. That's unusual. There are no representatives from the Army of the Californias—ominous indeed. The Dominion is favored. The Senate is ignored."

"I don't know that I can parse such signs."

"We'll learn more when the President speaks. That's when the axe will fall, Adam—if it does fall."

"Is the axe literal or metaphorical?" I inquired anxiously.

"Remains to be seen," said Sam.

That was alarming; but the matter was out of my control, and I tried to enjoy the fireworks while they lasted. The Chinese Ambassador had arranged for the importation of some incendiaries from his own Republic, as a gift to the President. The Chinese are experts in armaments and gunpowder. In fact the presence of that Ambassador, and his obvious largesse, propelled a rumor that Deklan Comstock was attempting to buy advanced weapons from China as a sort of riposte to the Chinese Cannon of the Dutch.*

Certainly the celestial fire was an excellent advertisement for Chinese workmanship. I had never seen such a display. Oh, we had had fireworks in Williams Ford—fine ones, and they had impressed me in my youth. But this event was altogether more spectacular. The warm summer air was alive with the smell of cordite, and the sky crackled with Occult Starbursts, Blue Fire, Whirling Salamanders, Keg-Breakers, and other such exotic devices. It was almost as noisy as an artillery duel, and I had to restrain myself from flinching when the bangs and stinks provoked unhappy memories of the War. But I reminded myself that this was Independence Day in Manhattan, not winter in Chicoutimi; and Calyxa put a soothing arm around me when she saw that I was shaking.

The spectacle concluded after a good half-hour with a Cross of Fire that

---

* The Chinese were officially neutral in the War in Labrador, thereby doubling their supply of potential customers.

hung over Lower Manhattan like the benediction of an incendiary Angel. The band played *The Star-spangled Banner*. The assembled Eupatridians applauded vigorously; and then it was time for Deklan Comstock to make the final speech of the evening.

The Executive Palace was fully electrified, powered by dynamos designed and operated by the Union's most cunning engineers. A fierce artificial light drenched the stage that was set up for the President.* He stepped up on the makeshift wooden platform and braced his hands on both sides of the podium. Then he began to speak.

He began with homilies and platitudes appropriate to the occasion. He spoke about the Nation and how it was formed in an act of rebellion against the godless British Empire. He quoted the great Patriotic Philosopher of the nineteenth century, Mr. John C. Calhoun. He described how the original Nation had been debased by oil and atheism, until the Reconstruction that followed on the heels of the False Tribulation. He spoke of the two great Generals who had served as Presidents in times of national crisis, Washington and Otis, and flung about their names as if they were personal friends of his.

That eventually got him onto the subject of war. Here his voice became more animated, and his gestures bespoke a personal urgency.

"Perpetual peace is a dream," he said, "as much as we may yearn for it— but war! War is an integral part of God's ordering of the universe, without which the world would be swamped in selfishness and materialism. War is the very vessel of honor, and who of us could endure a world without the divine folly of honor? That faith is especially true and adorable which leads a soldier to throw away his life in obedience to a blindly accepted duty, in a cause he little understands, during a campaign of which he has little notion, under tactics of which he does not see the use.† On the field of battle, where a man lives or dies by the caprice of a bullet or the verdict of a bayonet, life is at its best and healthiest."

"That's a novel definition of health," said Julian, but Sam hushed him.

"To date," Deklan Conqueror declared, "we have had some notable successes in Labrador and some regrettable failures. Failure is inevitable in any war, I need not add. Not every campaign will be brought to a successful conclusion. But the number of failures in recent months points to a dismaying possibility. I mean the possibility that *treason* rather than *fortune* is at work in the Army of the Laurentians." The President's countenance became abruptly grim and judicial, and his audience cringed. "For that reason I have today taken bold steps to consolidate and improve our armed forces. Several Major Generals—I will not name them—have been taken into custody as I speak.

---

* This light attracted flying insects in brigade strength, and they swooped back and forth as if bathing in it. Before long a number of bats joined in, drawn by the plentiful prey. It was as if another Feast was being conducted in the air, now that our own dinner had concluded.

† A fairly succinct description of the situation in Labrador as I remembered it.

They will undergo public trials, and be given every opportunity to acknowl-edge and recant their plotting with the Dutch."

Sam groaned quietly, for the unnamed Major Generals probably included men he knew and respected.

"The places of these traitors," Deklan Conqueror continued, "will be filled from the ranks of enlisted men who have distinguished themselves in battle. Because of this we can look forward to renewed success in our effort to establish control over this sacred continent as a whole and the strategically important waterway to the north of it."

He paused to sip from a glass of water. Absent fireworks, the night seemed very dark.

"But not all the news is bad. Far from it! We have had our share of suc-cesses. I need only cite the example of the Saguenay Campaign and the rescue of the town of Chicoutimi from its Mitteleuropan occupiers. And let me re-peat, acknowledging a certain familial pride, that a key role in that battle was played by my own nephew Julian."

Here the President smiled once more, and paused in the way that invites applause, which the nervous Eupatridians hastened to give him.

"Come up here, Julian," the President called out, "and stand beside me!"

This was the humiliation Deklan Comstock had been storing up all eve-ning. Putting Calyxa on show as a singer was only the prelude to it. He would have the son of the man he had murdered stand beside him as an ornament, helpless to protest.

Julian at first didn't move. It was as if the command had scarcely regis-tered on his senses. It was Sam who urged him out of the bleachers. "Just do as he says," Sam whispered in a mournful voice. "Swallow your pride, Julian, this once, and do as he says—go on, or he'll have us all killed."

Julian gave Sam a vacant look, but he stood up. His journey to the Presi-dential Podium was visibly reluctant. He mounted the steps to the stage as if he were mounting a scaffold to be hanged, which was perhaps not far from the truth.

"Dear Julian," the President said, and embraced him just as if he were a true and loving uncle.

Julian didn't return the embrace. He kept his hands stiffly at his sides. I could see that any physical contact with the fratricidal Chief Executive was nauseating to him.

"You've seen more of war than most of us, though you're still a very young man. What was your impression of the Saguenay Campaign?"

Julian blinked at the question.

"It was a bloody business," he mumbled.

But Deklan Comstock didn't mean to give his nephew the freedom of the podium. "Bloody indeed," the President said. "But we're not a nation that flinches at blood, nor are we a people constrained by feminine delicacy. To us all is permitted—even cruelty, yes, even ruthlessness—for we're the first in the world to raise the sword not in the name of enslaving and oppressing anyone, but in the name of freeing them from bondage. We must not be miserly with blood! Let there be blood, if blood alone can drown the old secular world. Let there be pain, and let there be death, if pain and death will save us from the twin tyrannies of Atheism and Europe."

Some cheering erupted, though not from our part of the bleachers.

"Julian knows first-hand the price and preciousness of liberty. He has already risked his life anonymously as a soldier of the line. Sacrifice enough for any man, you might say, and in normal times I would agree. But these aren't normal times. The enemy presses. Barbarous weapons are deployed against our soldiers. The Northeastern wilds swarm with foreign encampments, and the precincts of Newfoundland are once again in jeopardy. Therefore we are called upon to make sacrifices." He paused at that ominous word. "We are *all* called upon to make sacrifices. I don't exclude myself! I, as much as any citizen, have to forego my own happiness, if it contradicts the greater national purpose. And as pleased as I am to have my brother's son back in the bosom of my family, a soldier with Julian's skill can't be spared at this critical hour. For that reason I have already relieved from duty Major General Griffin of the Northern Division of the Army of the Laurentians, and I intend to replace him with my own beloved nephew."

The audience gasped at the boldness of the proclamation. It was a great benevolence on the part of the President, or so he wanted us to think. The Eupatridians burst into another round of applause. Encouraging shouts of "Julian! Julian Comstock!" went up into the gunpowder-scented night.

But Julian's mother didn't join in the bellowing. She seemed to grow weak, and put her head on Calyxa's shoulder.

"First Bryce," she whispered. "Now Julian."

"This is the axe I spoke of," said Sam.

A SEASON IN THE LAND
GOD GAVE TO CAIN

THANKSGIVING, 2174

God has chosen the weak things of the world,
to confound the things that are mighty.

—First Corinthians 1:27

1

I will not exhaust the reader by narrating every incident that attended on our dispatch to Labrador, prior to the triumphant and tragic events surrounding the Thanksgiving season of 2174. *Our* departure, that is, and not just Julian's; because the recalled-to-battle order proclaimed by Deklan Conqueror also included Sam Godwin and myself.

In short I was compelled to leave my wife of a few months, and my brief career as a New York City writer, and to sail off to Labrador as part of the staff of Major General Julian Comstock—and not to one of the pleasanter sections of Labrador, such as the Saguenay River, but to an even more inhospitable and unwelcoming region of that disputed State, on a mission the true purpose of which was to turn Julian from an awkward potential heir into a silent and untroublesome martyr.

In mid-October we left New York Harbor on a Navy clipper and sailed north. This was a weathery time of year in the Atlantic, and we survived a ferocious storm in which our vessel was tossed about like a flea on the rump of an irritable stallion, before we rendezvoused with a fleet of ships under Admiral Fairfield off the port of Belle Isle (now in American hands).

The Union Navy is not as powerful a political entity as the nation's two great Armies, to which it is attached as a nautical wing; but just lately it had harassed the Mitteleuropans more effectively than had our land-based forces. Deklan Comstock, in one of his few genuinely useful strategic initiatives, had declared a comprehensive blockade of European shipping in the waters off Newfoundland and Labrador. This had been attempted before, with disappointing results. But today's Navy was larger that it used to be, and better equipped to conduct such an ambitious project.

I was aboard the flag-ship of the armada, the *Basilisk,* during the famous Battle of Hamilton Inlet. The Dutch had been aware of our movements, for an enormous battle-fleet is a difficult thing to disguise; but they had mistakenly assumed that we meant to attack them near Voisey Bay, from which they export the nickel, copper, and cobalt ores that are mined so abundantly in Labrador. (The many small islands and waterways in that region make Voisey Bay a haven for blockade runners even when it's under heavy surveillance.) But we had been given a bolder objective than that. We put in for Hamilton Inlet instead; and while the Dutch were hunting us farther north our guns silenced their fortress at the Narrows, and we quickly reduced their artillery emplacements at Rigolet and Eskimo Island. Because the Dutch defenses weren't braced for us, we suffered relatively minor casualties. Of the twenty gunships in our flotilla only one, the *Griffin,* was altogether lost. Five others suffered damage the ship's carpenters were able to repair; and our ship was altogether untouched, even though we had been in the vanguard of the battle.

A detachment of the First Northern Division was sent ashore to occupy and restore the captured forts. It was a grand day (and sunny, though chill) when we saw the Sixty Stars and Thirteen Stripes rise above the Narrows, signifying our command of all shipping through that mile-wide bottleneck.

Ahead of us lay the immense body of water called Lake Melville, which was fed by the Naskaupi and Churchill River watersheds. To the south rose the gray, blunt-toothed Mealy Mountains—a daunting sight when not obscured by cloud. Invisibly distant were our true objectives: the Dutch-held towns of Shesh and Striver, and the all-important railhead at Goose Bay.

Julian and Sam were occupied during much of this time with military planning and consultations with Admiral Fairfield. But on this particular afternoon Julian came up to where I was "planking the deck"* and joined me.

It was the antique explorer Jacques Cartier, Julian said, who had called Labrador "the land God gave to Cain."† "Though it was colder then, of course," he added. "It's not as barren as all that nowadays—though I would dislike to be a farmer here."

"No wonder Cain was so sullen," I said, pulling my duffle coat more snugly around me, for the wind was harsh and cutting, and the sailors on watch had hunkered down among the rope coils where they could swear freely and smoke pipes. In fact the land was not literally barren: it produced rich crops of black spruce and white birch, balsam fir and trembling aspen; and in the chilly shadows of those trees lived caribou, and such hardy creatures as that. Waterfowl were plentiful, I had heard, in the warmer months. But Labrador's forests were bleak, and the land in general was not a welcoming place for the Race of Man. "At least we've cut back the Dutch, and lived to tell about it," I said.

The three of us—Sam, Julian, and I—understood that this expedition wasn't meant to be survived, at least not by Major General Comstock. But Julian argued that any campaign, even the most apparently hopeless, might turn on a small contingency and produce unexpected results. Usually this observation worked to buoy my spirits. But today, despite our recent naval victory, a little of November had crept into my soul. I was a long way from home, and apprehensive.

If I expected Julian to repeat his reassurances, on this occasion he did not. "The worst is ahead of us," he admitted. "Admiral Fairfield has orders to land

---

* I had made it a point to befriend some of the sailors, and I picked up a little of their "salt slang," which I thought would lend verisimilitude to the novels I planned to write.
† "And Cain went out from the presence of the Lord, to dwell in the Land of Nod, in the eastern part of Eden." Genesis 4:16—it doesn't mention anything about Lake Melville or Goose Bay.

the infantry at Striver for an attack on Goose Bay—and Goose Bay won't be easy pickings. They'll know we're coming—their telegraphs must already be chattering."

I looked out across the windy gray waters abaft of us. "It's not myself I'm afraid for so much as Calyxa. She's alone in New York City, she's already earned the enmity of Deacon Hollingshead, and for all I know she may have offended other authorities in the meantime."

"She has my mother to defend her," Julian said.

"I thank your mother, but I wish I could do the job myself."

"You'll be back at Calyxa's side soon enough, if I have anything to do with it."

Deklan Conqueror had banked on Julian's youth and lack of experience to make him an easy target for the Dutch. But the President had almost certainly underestimated his nephew. Julian was young, and many of the troops he commanded had initially balked at taking orders from a yellow-bearded boy. But Julian had covertly arranged for copies of my pamphlet to circulate among the literate soldiers, who read it aloud or summarized its contents for the non-readers, and his reputation had grown accordingly. Nor was Julian as ignorant as Deklan Comstock might have hoped. Under Sam's tutelage he had long studied war in the abstract, and during the Saguenay Campaign he had been able to compare theory with practice. "Perhaps we'll return to Manhattan in triumph," I said.

"Yes, and force my uncle to find a more prosaic way of killing me."

"We'll outlast old Deklan Conqueror," I said, keeping my voice low. "Sam believes we will."

"I hope he's right. In the meantime, Adam, look at you, you're shivering—shouldn't you be in your cabin recording the heroism of the hour?"

My cabin was close enough to the bilge that fresh air was often desirable, no matter how cold it might be. But Julian was right. I had agreed to keep a narrative of events for publication in the *Spark*. The Fall of Eskimo Island would make an exciting episode, with little need for dramatic exaggeration. "I will," I said. I had already produced many thousands of words. I hoped they would be in some sense useful. But none of them would float the *Basilisk* if she were holed below the waterline, or deflect for a moment the enemy's missiles.

I left Julian on deck. He continued to stand at the taffrail, gazing back toward the Narrows as if lost in his thoughts. His eyes were shadowed by the brim of his Major General's hat, and his blue and yellow jacket flapped in the chill wind off the Mealy Mountains.

Once the Narrows had been secured we sailed for Striver, a town on the north shore of Lake Melville.

We found a handful of Dutch warships anchored there. They were formidable craft, heavily armored and heavily armed; but we came hard at them in the first light of dawn, and before their anchors were well up we had already sheered their masts with cannonfire and put a few dents in their armored flanks.

The *Basilisk* took heavy fire that day. I sheltered with the infantrymen belowdecks, while the sailors fought above; and I was present when a solid shot struck us amidships. Such a projectile could not penetrate the plating that protected the *Basilisk's* engine room and boilers, but it could and did pierce the wooden hull just where we sat. I wasn't injured in the explosion, but huge splinters speared several men who were situated near the bulkhead, and a freshly-drafted Kentucky lease-boy suffered a crushed skull, which spilled his brains out on the deck, and was fatal.

After that I could hear nothing but the sound of the artillery battle and the screaming of the wounded. The *Basilisk* fired one cannonade after another, both shot and shell, from its big guns. At one point I risked a look through the newly-created "window" in the side of the ship, but I could see nothing save the hull of a Dutch vessel very close by—and I ducked back hastily when the business end of a Dutch cannon, still smoking, hove into view. Several times our vessel shook in the water like a palsied dog, until I was certain we must have lost our engines; and I fully expected the deadly waters of Lake Melville to rush over us in an icy flood at any moment.

But that was only the stink of the blood and the gunpowder making me giddy. Eventually the battle ended. Then Julian himself came down to the hold where the infantrymen were huddled, to tell us that we had conquered the enemy and taken control of the harbor.

I went up with him to survey the results.

Smoke still hovered over the lake, for there was no wind to dispel it. The sky was overcast. One of the *Basilisk's* masts was down, and a gang of sailors was busy casting the remnants of it overboard. The damage we had sustained was not critical, but other ships in our small armada had been more severely hurt. The *Christabel* was burning steadily, and the *Beatrice* rode perilously low in the water.

The Dutch had had the worst of it, however. Of the eight ships defending the town of Striver fully six had sunk, with only fractions of them showing where their hulls rested on the stony lake-bottom. The two still afloat were mastless and gouting black smoke. We sent out boats to pick up survivors.

Basilisk and her sister vessels had also placed a few strategic shots among the buildings and warehouses at the foot the town's main thoroughfare, an action that caused white flags to be sent up where the defiant Mitteleuropan banner had lately flown, signifying a wholesale surrender. "We've reclaimed a little piece of America, Adam," Julian said. "The homeland is enlarged by a few square miles."

"I don't know how you can be cynical, after winning such a battle."

"I'm not cynical. The victory was tremendous, but it's Admiral Fairfield's, not mine. I've done nothing useful on this expedition except drill my men on the quarterdeck. But that's about to change. This is where we land the infantry."

He explained that all the footsoldiers in our flotilla would go ashore this day. Two entire divisions would soon follow, if the troop-ships were on schedule and our garrisons continued to hold the Narrows. When the army was landed and assembled Julian would lead it to Goose Bay by road, while the Admiral and his flotilla shelled that town from a distance and kept the Dutch defenders busy.

I promised I wouldn't get in his way, if I could help it.

"You're not in my way. Don't you know you're one of my most trusted advisors?"

"I don't recall giving any *advice*, as such."

"It's not your advice I value so much as your sensibility."

"You give me too much credit."

"And you're my friend. That's a scarce commodity in the circles we've moved in lately."

"My friendship at least you can rely on. And my Pittsburgh rifle, when it comes to fighting on solid ground."

"It'll come to fighting soon enough," said Julian, turning his face away as from an ugly truth.

More than two thousand additional infantrymen were landed at Striver over the next several days, ferried in from bases in Newfoundland under the Admiral's protection. All the Dutch soldiers in Striver were taken captive, and sent back in the emptied troop-ships to the War-Prisoner encampments on the Gaspé Peninsula. Harmless citizens of Striver were advised to stay indoors, if possible, and a strict curfew was imposed. On our part, discipline was stern enough to prevent the sort of large-scale theft, rape, pillage, and arson that local citizens invariably find distressing. We didn't lack for provisions, since the rail line had been recently extended from Goose Bay, with Striver acting as an alternative off-loading point for European goods bound for the interior of Labrador. The *Stadhouders* like their luxuries: dockside warehouses yielded slabs of smoked fish, barrels of uninfested wheat flour, huge wheels of odorous cheese, and similar interesting items.

I walked with Julian among the newly-arrived troops a few days after we landed. I had been assigned the rank of Colonel for the duration of my re-enlistment, mainly to justify my presence on Julian's immediate staff; and I was just another faceless officer to most of these men, though several of them had read my *Adventures of Captain Commongold* and might have recognized my name had I announced it. Julian himself, of course, was famously recognizable by his rank, his youth, his yellow beard, and his immaculate uniform. Men saluted him or attempted to shake his hand as we walked down a rank of bunks that had been installed in an empty stable. Daylight came through a gap in the roof made by an artillery shell, and Julian stood in that shaft of cold illumination like a saint in a painting. He had mastered the art not only of *appearing* confident but of *generating* confidence, as if courage were heat and Julian was a hard-coal stove. It made his men better and more loyal soldiers, because they had come to believe in him as a military prodigy. I expect they would have tugged his beard for luck if that impertinence had been allowed.

I looked about the sea of faces surrounding him, hoping to catch sight of someone from our old Montreal regiment. Lymon Pugh would have been a welcome presence, but I didn't see him. The only face I *did* recognize was, perhaps unfortunately, that of the larcenous Private Langers, who had not advanced in rank since our last meeting. When I approached him he turned his cadaverously thin body away and tried to escape; but the crowd was too thick for that maneuver to succeed.

"Private Langers!" I called out.

He stopped short and turned back. At first he was intimidated by my new rank and station, and tried to pretend I had mistaken him for someone else; but he relented at last and said, "Is that Sam Samson around somewhere? I hope not. You were always decent to me, Adam Hazzard, but that old man had me pummeled for being a crook—he seems to have no faith in me at all."

"His name is Godwin now, not Samson, and he's on Julian's staff; but I doubt you have anything to fear from either one of them. Neither Sam nor Julian are disposed to hold grudges. I expect you'll do fine, if you keep quiet and don't shirk from battle. In any case you seem to be in excellent health." Though his nose sat a little more crookedly than I remembered it. "Are you still selling battlefield trinkets?"

He blushed at the question and said, "None to sell right at the moment . . . don't mean to rule anything out, of course . . ."

"I hope you don't continue to rob the dead and swindle the living!"

"I'm a reformed man," Private Langers said. "Not that I'm averse to a dollar here and there, honestly extracted."

"I'm glad to hear it," I said. "About being reformed, I mean. I'll pass that on to Sam and Julian."

"Thank you very kindly, but please don't bother them on my behalf . . . I'd just as soon remain anonymous. Tell me, Adam—I mean, Colonel Hazzard—is it true what they say about this expedition?"

"Hard to say, since I don't know who 'they' are, or what it is they're supposed to be saying."

"That we have a secret weapon to use against the Dutch—something deadly and Chinese and unexpected."

I told him I knew nothing about it, if so; but I'm not sure he believed my disclaimers.

Later, in the command quarters we had established in upstairs chambers of the house of the former mayor of Striver, Julian was philosophical when I told him Private Langers was among us. "If Langers is a reformed man then my uncle is a Philosopher. But as long as Langers can carry a rifle he's as good as the next soldier. I'm more interested in this notion of a secret Chinese weapon."

"Is there such a thing?" I asked hopefully.

"No. Of course there isn't. But it might be useful to morale if the army believes there is. Don't spread that particular rumor, Adam . . . but don't discourage it, if you hear it."

The next day I walked through camp once more. I found Private Langers and a number of other infantrymen gambling at dice in an alley behind a looted tavern. They didn't notice me, and I didn't disturb them. Perhaps it didn't matter if they wasted their money, I reasoned. They might be dead before much longer, and wouldn't be able to collect their back pay, much less spend it sensibly.

Of course gambling is a sin as well as a vice. But they could make their own reckoning with Heaven. If a man arrived at the Last Judgment with bullet holes in him, acquired in the defense of his country, would he really be dismissed on account of a habit of dice or cards?

I didn't think so. Julian had made at least that much of an Agnostic of me.

Next morning the troop-ships stopped arriving at Striver.

That was an ominous sign. The ships had been coming down the Narrows like clockwork prior to this time, bringing men and goods and articles of war; but we were still not up to the full strength allotted us in the general military planning. It wasn't that the army already assembled was insignificant. The Navy had delivered two full divisions of three thousand men apiece, including a detachment of cavalry, along with their mounts; also a fully-equipped field hospital, and an artillery brigade with brand-new field-pieces and ample supplies of ammunition.

On paper it was a formidable force, although several hundred of those men were already suffering from complaints ranging from seasickness to contagious fevers, rendering them unsuited for battle. But we had hoped to face the enemy with ten thousand able-bodied soldiers altogether—because that was roughly the number of Dutch troops believed to be defending Goose Bay, a force that would be reinforced by rail very soon, if it hadn't been already.

Julian spent most of the day at the docks, peering across the troubled waters of Lake Melville with the intensity of a sailor's widow. I had gone out to summon him back to a hot dinner and a conference with his sub-commanders when a sail at last hove into view . . . but it was only the *Basilisk,* which had been across the lake at the town of Shesh, a smaller locality than Striver, now also in American hands. The Admiral came ashore in one of the *Basilisk*'s boats and joined us for the evening meal.

I haven't described Admiral Fairfield before. Suffice to say that he was even older than Sam Godwin, but active and alert, a veteran of many sea battles, and with the political indifference common among Navy men; for the Navy, unlike the two armies, was seldom called upon to settle arguments over the ascension to power of Commanders in Chief. The Navy, in short, never marched to New York City for the purpose of making kings. It simply fought the enemy at sea, and took pride in that tradition; and that was the way Admiral Fairfield liked it.

He wore a gray beard, its great length commensurate with his age and station, and tonight he frowned through his whiskers, even though the beefsteak set before him was excellent, the best the commissary could come up with.

"Where are my men?" was the first thing Julian asked of the Admiral, as soon as we were seated.

"The ships don't come through the narrows," the Admiral said bluntly.

"Do we still hold the Dutch forts?"

"Securely. Melville is an American lake now, as far as naval power goes. Something must be interfering with the transit between Newfoundland and Hamilton Inlet. For all I know there might have been an ambuscade at sea, or something of that nature. But the news hasn't reached Rigolet or Eskimo Island, if so."

"I'm not sure I can postpone the march to Goose Bay any longer. We lose out advantage, if we have any, with every hour that passes."

"I understand your concern," the Admiral said. "I wouldn't wait, if I were you. March with the thousands you have, is my advice."

Julian forced a smile, though he clearly didn't like the way events were trending. "As long as the Navy is there to support us with her guns, I suppose the risk might be acceptable."

Admiral Fairfield said with all the gravity that was in him, which was very much, "You have my word, Major General Comstock, that the *Basilisk* will be off-shore when you and your army arrive at Goose Bay. The Dutch might sink every other vessel in the flotilla, but you won't be abandoned if I have anything to say about it."

"I thank you," said Julian.

"This is a bold campaign. Some might say foolish. Certainly the odds are long. But a strike at the Dutch vitals in Labrador is overdue."

"Then we won't let it wait any longer." Julian turned to Sam. "We'll march in the morning," he said.

"We're still low on horses and mules."

"Don't short the cavalry if you can help it, but make sure the field-pieces aren't left behind."

"Very well. Shall I give the news to the men?"

"No, I'll do it," said Julian. "After dinner."

The news of an imminent march quelled many appetites among the regimental commanders, but Julian ate heartily. Arrangements were made to bed down the Admiral until morning; then Julian and his subordinates set out to communicate orders to the men. I tagged along for journalistic purposes.

We went to each of the buildings that had been set aside as shelters for the infantrymen, and to the cavalry quarters, and finally to the general camp established in the town square. The meetings were mostly uneventful, and the men accepted the news cheerfully, for they were eager for a fight.

We entered one structure, formerly a sports arena, in which five hundred veteran soldiers were sheltering from the cold. Night came early in the northern parts of the world at that time of year, and November in Labrador would pass for January in a more hospitable section of the country. A number of coal stoves had been installed in the building, and the men had gathered around these, and they were singing *Piston, Loom, and Anvil* in loud and imperfect harmony when we entered. A Colonel named Abijah, who had dined with us, was embarrassed by their behavior, and he shouted out orders to cease singing and stand to attention.

As soon as the men became aware of us they fell silent.* Julian stood up on a barrelhead and addressed them.

"Tomorrow the caissons roll for Goose Bay," he said simply. "It's a day's march, and we may see action by the end of it. Are all of you prepared?"

They shouted "Yes!" in unison, or cried out "Hoo-ah!" or made similar martial exclamations, for their spirits were high.

"Good," Julian said. He looked hardly more than a child in the lantern light—more like a boy playing soldier than a grizzled general—but that just suited the infantry, who had grown fond of the idea of being led by the Youthful Hero of the Saguenay. "I believe you were singing when I came in. Please don't let me stop you."

There was some uneasiness over this. These were men who had worked in industry before they were drafted, or had herded horses on rural Estates, or were the living donations of landowners who held them in indenture. For all their loyalty they remained conscious of Julian's status as an Aristo, and some

---

* They were perhaps a little slow in their thinking, for among the other luxuries imported by the Dutch had been a few bales of cultivated Indian Hemp, some of which had begun to circulate among the troops, until Sam had the contraband placed under guard.

of them were ashamed of what they had been singing, as if it were an insult to his class (which in a real sense it was). But Julian clapped his hands and began it for them—"By Piston, Loom, and Anvil, boys," in his reedy but heartfelt tenor. And before the chorus was finished the whole group had joined in; and at the end of a few verses they cheered lustily, and called out *"General Julian!"* or *"Julian Comstock!"* or—the first time I had heard this formulation—*"Julian Conqueror!"*

For reasons I couldn't fathom, the sound of hundreds of men shouting "Julian Conqueror" caused a melancholy shiver to run up my spine, and the night seemed colder for it. But Julian only smiled, and accepted the men's regard as if it were his due.

2

The Battle of Goose Bay has been much described elsewhere, and I will not weary the reader with details of our maneuvers, nor tease out the minutiae of those tragic days.

I rode near Julian in the forefront of our army. In the cold, low sunlight of the morning we were by all appearances a formidable body of men. Julian rode a muscular gray-and-white stallion at the very forefront of the troops, with the Campaign Flag carried by a mounted adjutant just behind him.* The road from Striver to Goose Bay was a fine one, paved in the Dutch manner, so that our carts and caissons were not bogged down even though the land around us was all icy fens and jagged rock and stands of spruce. Whenever we marched over a slight rise I made a point of looking back at the chain of men, mules, ammunition carts, hospital wagons, etc., strung out behind us. It was a heartening sight; and if we felt invincible that morning perhaps the error was understandable.

The cavalry scouted ahead of us, and every so often a man on horseback would report all-clear ahead. We made good time until the afternoon, when the cavalry began to encounter pickets, and there was some mild skirmishing.

Almost simultaneously we came under attack from small groups of Dutch riders who knew these woods and string bogs intimately and used them to their advantage. None of this amounted to much—a few shots fired from cover, a few horses frightened, a few men nicked with lead. One regiment or another would make quick work of the attackers, or at least chase them away. But if such flea-bites did not damage us materially, they did succeed in slowing us down.

Julian and his subordinate commanders did their best to keep the army in good order. Our objective was a line of low ridges where he believed the bulk of the Dutch army was encamped. Soon enough our scouts confirmed that suspicion. The Dutch entrenchments straddled the road on the outskirts of the town of Goose Bay. Their positions were well-chosen, and dislodging them would not be simple.

We camped for the night just out of range of these enemy emplacements. The infantrymen dug holes where the ground was yielding; and after dark, by subtle moonlight, the artillerymen hauled their guns to forward positions.

---

* The flag of the Goose Bay Campaign had been designed by Julian himself. It showed a red boot against a yellow orb on a starry black background, and carried the legend "WE HAVE STEPPED UPON THE MOON." Most of the troops understood the story of Americans on the Moon as a fable, rather than historical fact; but it was a bracing boast, and implied to the enemy that we were experienced at treading on things, and that they might be next.

Once the moon was down, a tenuous blue aurora shivered in the sky. The temperature dropped, and the breath of sleeping men rose up like luminous smoke. In the morning the battle began.

Julian had studied the way armies maneuver in the field, and he had made sure his regimental commanders were up to the task of understanding and enacting his orders. Although he remained at a command tent in the rear of the action—and Sam and I with him—he pored over maps all the while, and messengers transited in and out of his headquarters as busily as ants at a picnic.

All morning the artillery roared relentlessly, theirs and ours.

We were outnumbered; but the Dutch had not positioned themselves to their best advantage. Not knowing which way Julian would attack, they had reinforced their flanks and neglected their middle. Julian abetted their confusion by feinting left and right, but stored up his big guns for a frontal charge. This began about noon, and was bloody. We lost nearly a thousand men in the battle that came to be called Goose Gap, and five hundred more were trucked away in Dominion wagons with missing limbs or other disabling injuries. By nightfall the battlefield resembled the waste-bin of a remedial school for inept butchers. I will not describe the odors that began to arise from it.

The Mitteleuropans fled their positions as soon as we were close enough to bring our Trench Sweepers to bear. We captured dozens of prisoners, and after some "mopping up" of stray pockets of resistance the day was ours. We had taken the low ridge that was the gateway to Goose Bay, and we hastily occupied and strengthened the former Dutch defenses there. The Dutch commander arranged under a flag of truce to remove his dead and injured from the battlefield. That was a mournful sight—foreign soldiers stumbling with carts among the corpses, accompanied by the terrible groans of the dying—and no doubt disappointing to Private Langers, who would be denied the luxury of looting the enemy dead.

Julian relocated his headquarters and the Campaign Flag to an elevated position from which we could see the town and the harbor of Goose Bay, as well as the surviving Dutch forces, who were hastily rolling out cutwire and building abatisses in anticipation of a siege. Julian used this perspective to mark his maps, and he was still examining those maps by lamplight as midnight approached. My typewriter had been brought up in a wagon along with other supplies appropriate to a mobile headquarters, and I sat in a corner of the same huge tent recording the events of that notable day. At last fatigue overcame me; but before I departed for my own cot I told Julian we had won a great victory, and that he ought to rest now that it had been achieved.

"I can't afford to rest," he said, rubbing his eyes.

He looked gaunt and distracted, and I pitied him. It might seem unjust to feel sympathy for a Major General who had not lifted a rifle, on a day when

thousands of men had sacrificed lives and limbs on his behalf. But it seemed
to me that Julian had lived the struggle of every soldier under his command,
at least in his imagination, and suffered each loss as though the bullets had
pierced his own body. He identified closely with his men, and always took
pains to see that they were fed and rested, and this had helped to make him
popular among them; but he paid for it now, in stress and in grief.

"Of course you can afford to rest," I said gently. "You'll be a better officer
for it."

He rose from his camp table, stretching, and together we stepped outside.
Away from the portable stove the air was very cold, and the fires of the enemy
smoldered like coals in the flatlands ahead of us.

"See all that we've won," I said.

"I'm content with what I see," said Julian. "Apart from the number of the
dead. What worries me is what I *don't* see."

"Well, it's dark, after all . . . *what* don't you see?"

"The cavalry detachment I sent to tear up tracks behind the enemy's lines,
for one. Not a man of them has reported back. If the rail connection to Goose
Bay remains intact, reinforcements will begin to arrive, and keep on arriving."

"It's no easy job, bending rails and blowing up bridges. Probably the cavalry was just detained in its work."

"And the harbor at Goose Bay. What do you make out by this light,
Adam?"

"It seems peaceful." There was a glow in the sky—a dusty patch of the
Northern Lights, which waxed and waned—and I saw a few masts and ships
at anchor—Dutch commercial shipping, I supposed. "They threw all their
gunboats against us at Striver, and lost them."

"I see the same. What I *don't* see is any American ship of war. I had hoped
Admiral Fairfield would be shelling Goose Bay by now, or at least positioning
his vessels."

That was true . . . and the absence seemed ominous, now that he pointed
it out to me.

"Perhaps they'll arrive in the morning," I said.

"Perhaps," said Julian wearily.

I have not yet said very much about Sam Godwin and his role in these events.

That's not because his part was insignificant, but because it was performed in intimate consultation with Julian, and I didn't participate directly
in battle-planning.* But Sam pored over the maps just as intently as did Ju-

---

* I had learned all my strategy and tactics from the war narratives of Mr. Charles Curtis Easton, in
which every attack is fierce and bold, and nearly fails, but finally succeeds by some combination of
luck and American ingenuity. These circumstances are more easily arranged on the printed page than
on the field of battle.

lian, and brought his greater experience into play. He did not attempt to take command, but made himself sympathetic to Julian's suggestions, and seldom contradicted them, but only offered nuance in their refinement. I supposed this was the role he had played with Julian's father Bryce during the successful Isthmian War, and at times, when the two of them put their heads together, I could imagine that twenty years of history had been rolled back, and that this was the command tent of the Army of the Californias . . . though Julian's unusual yellow beard belied the daydream, as did the cold November weather.

Julian, in any case, succeeded in maintaining a fragile optimism about the campaign; while Sam, though he tried not to show it, was obviously less hopeful. Ever since we sailed from Manhattan, all humor had fled from him. He didn't joke, or laugh at jokes. He scowled, instead . . . and there was a glitter in his eye that might have been fear, sternly suppressed. I expect Sam had concluded that he might not see New York City, or more importantly Emily Baines Comstock, ever again in this earthly life; and it was my fervent wish that Julian might succeed in proving him wrong. But the events of the next day were not encouraging.

The Dutch counter-attacked at dawn.

Perhaps they had done some scouting of their own, and calculated that our army, while intimidating, was not as large as they feared; or perhaps reinforcements had arrived by rail during the night. Whatever the case, their resolve had grown firm and their courage was not lacking.

Though the defenders of Goose Bay lacked a Chinese Cannon, their field artillery outranged ours by several hundred yards. They had figured that difference finely, and used it to their advantage. Shot and shell pummeled our forward ranks and masked their first advance. Our men soon brought their own weapons to bear, including the formidable Trench Sweeper; but the Dutch had come ahead too quickly for our field-pieces to be of much use against them, and an important hill, along with an entire artillery battery, was captured before Julian or his lieutenants could react.

All that morning I heard the unceasing roar of cannonry and the cries of wounded men as they were carried back from the front. Dutch and American regiments went at one another like clashing sabers, shooting off sparks of blood and mayhem. Messengers arrived and departed with desperation in their eyes, and each one seemed more exhausted than the last. An entire battalion collapsed on our right flank, driven back by cannonade, although reinforcements held the position—barely.

Noon passed, and the smoke of the battle continued to rise like a crow-colored obelisk into the wan and windless sky. "Panic is our greatest enemy now," Sam said grimly.

Julian stepped away from his map-table, throwing down a pencil in frustration. "Where is the Navy? There's nothing happening here the shelling of Goose Bay wouldn't correct!"

"Admiral Fairfield promised us his armada," Sam said, "and I believe he meant it. Whatever keeps him, it must be dire. We can't count on him arriving."

"Do you suppose this was my uncle's plan all along—to plant us here among the Dutch, and then withdraw the Navy?"

"I wouldn't put it past him. The point is that we don't have the Navy, and we can't *expect* to have the Navy. And without the Navy we can't hold our position much longer."

"We will hold them," Julian said flatly.

"If the Dutch flank us and take the road we won't be able to retreat to Striver—and that'll be the end of us."

"We'll hold," Julian said, "until we know for a fact that Fairfield isn't coming. He doesn't strike me as a man who would abandon a promise."

"He wouldn't, though he might be unable to fulfill it, for any number of reasons."

But Julian refused to be swayed. To the rear of the fighting there was a hill with an old spruce tree on it, and Julian posted an agile man atop this tree as if it were a mizzenmast on an ocean-going vessel, and gave him a sailor's chore: to watch Lake Melville for ships. Thus any hint of Admiral Fairfield's tardy arrival would be relayed directly to Julian's headquarters as soon as it was perceived.

In the meantime he bowed to Sam's suggestion and gathered his subordinates to plan an orderly retreat, should it become necessary. If we must withdraw, Julian said, then it ought to be a fighting withdrawal, making the enemy pay for every yard of mossy soil he gained. Julian described how troops could be placed along ridges and behind the humped earth of the railway embankment, so that Dutch soldiers in pursuit of a retreating regiment might be drawn into an ambush and killed. Messages were quickly sent out to battalion commanders to coordinate this strategy, and to keep the planned fall-back from turning into a general rout.

The scheme was successful, in so far as it went. Our front buckled—or so it was made to seem—and Mitteleuropan forces poured into the gap. The Dutch infantry were hooting and firing their rifles in triumph just as rows of hidden men turned Trench Sweepers on them and artillery shells began to burst in their midst. Their cross-and-laurel flag, which had been coming ahead at full speed, was suddenly thrown down, along with its bearer and dozens of common soldiers. Dutch troops continued to pour into the line of fire from the rear, but they roiled over their dead comrades uncertainly and were slaughtered in turn.

It was a hideously costly advance for the Dutch . . . but in the end it *was* an advance, hard-won or not. Sam argued that we should strike our headquarters immediately and get the wagons rolling back toward Striver, where we could at least supply ourselves in the event of a siege.

Then Julian's crow's-nest observer dashed into the tent and told us he had seen smoke across the water.

Julian stepped outside, taking a pair of captured field glasses with him. His position was more exposed than it would have been even an hour ago—Dutch shells burst dismayingly nearby—but he stood unmoved in his bright Major General's uniform, looking out over the leaden waters of Lake Melville.

"Smoke," he confirmed, when Sam and I joined him. "A vessel approaching under steam. Burning anthracite, by the look of it, which makes it likely one of ours." And after a moment's pause: "A mast. A flag. *Our* flag." He turned to Sam with a kind of fierce satisfaction in his eyes. "Tell the men to hold their positions at all costs."

"Julian—" Sam said.

"None of your pessimism right now, Sam, please!"

"But we don't know for certain—"

"We don't know *anything* for certain—battle is risk. Give the order!"

And Sam, like a dutiful servant, did so.

Ten minutes later the whole ship was visible, and it was the familiar *Basilisk*, Admiral Fairfield's vessel. We expected the rest of the American armada to follow in its wake.

But we were mistaken in that hope.

Soon it became obvious that there was the *Basilisk*—and there was *only* the *Basilisk*.

I cannot describe Julian's appearance as this unwelcome truth sank home. His skin took on an additional pallor. His eyes grew haggard. His bright blue and yellow garb, which he had worn so boldly, clung to his slumped shoulders like an admonition.

Admiral Fairfield did what he could with his single ship. The *Basilisk* was one of the finest vessels of the Navy, and he worked it ingeniously. He came in under full steam, all sails reefed, the ship's stacks gouting smoke as if half the coal in all the world were burning belowdecks. He slid obliquely past the Dutch wharves at Goose Bay, strafing the town with well-placed cannon shots. Then he came up the shoreline and attempted to shell the Mitteleuropan positions where we fought. That bombardment would have helped us enormously, had it succeeded. But the Dutch shore batteries were well-manned and well-entrenched. They raked the *Basilisk* in return. She withstood the barrage for many minutes, trying to work in close enough to be of some use to us. But the closer she got, the more vulnerable she became. Her masts were nearly chewed away, and flames had broken out on her forecastle by the time she finally gave up the attempt. She could do nothing but limp away while her engines were still capable of turning her screws. She seemed to be headed for Striver, or some other protected place up-lake.

Julian watched until she was nearly out of sight. Then he turned and ordered Sam to call a general retreat. His voice sounded as chill and eerie as if it emanated from a gap in some old hollow log. Sam was glum as well, and walked off speechlessly, shaking his head.

A retreat is not as glamorous a thing as an attack, but it can be accomplished either well or badly, and Julian deserves credit for a careful withdrawal from the disaster Goose Bay had become.

Still it was a costly and humiliating maneuver. By the time we were in acceptable form for a forced march to Striver, the Dutch were swarming at our backs. Julian assigned fresh troops (in so far as we had any) to the rear, and their careful feint-and-fall-back operations helped protect the bulk of the army.

Much of our cavalry had been lost in the futile foray behind the Mitteleuropan lines, so we were vulnerable to sniping from Dutch horsemen. Their detachments came at us from oblique angles, attempting to cut away companies of American troops and "take them in detail." More than a few infantrymen were scooped up in this fashion. But whenever such a firefight erupted Julian would ride to the place like a human battle-flag, to shore up morale; and we fought these battles with a ferocity that appeared to startle and unnerve our opponents.

By sundown we were within sight of the outskirts of Striver. Messengers had warned the garrison that we would be arriving under Dutch harassment, and a defensive perimeter, with abattises and lunettes and clean lines of fire, had already been established. These were a welcome sight for battered survivors. The Dominion wagons went in ahead of us, so that their cargo of wounded men could be received by the field hospital.

Julian and Sam, and I along with them, helped fight the rear-guard action while the bulk of our men sought the safety of the captive town. This went well enough for a time, for the Dutch had straggled in their pursuit and couldn't put together a formal assault. But as soon as their artillery came up we were in a ticklish situation.

Explosive shells landing in a tight mass of men, all of whom are within sprinting distance of safety, are a perfect recipe for death and panic. That's what happened. In terms of actual losses it wasn't too bad—Striver's defenders silenced the Dutch cannons as soon they could range in on them—but the mossy ground in front of our entrenchments was quickly watered with a great deal of patriotic blood, and festooned with other patriotic body parts, during that long cold and terrible dusk.

Julian on his horse was a conspicuous target, and I was astonished that he was not picked off immediately by some far-sighted Dutch rifleman. But—as in the Battle of Mascouche outside of Montreal—he seemed wrapped in some cloak of invulnerability, which warded off hot lead.

The miraculous protection didn't extend to those beside him. Our battle-flag went down when a staff officer's horse was killed by shrapnel from an exploding shell. Sam dismounted at once and stooped to retrieve the banner. But he had barely raised it again when a Dutch bullet took him, and he toppled to the ground.

I don't remember exactly the events that followed, except that I rallied two men who helped me carry Sam to a Dominion wagon, where he was stacked with a dozen other wounded soldiers awaiting treatment. The ambulance driver flogged his mules when I told him he had one of Julian's staff aboard; and I rode along with him to the makeshift hospital in that wide street in Striver called Portage.

Sam's wound was in his left arm, below the elbow. I couldn't tell whether it was a bullet or shrapnel that had struck him. Whatever it was, it had broken the narrow bones above the wrist and torn away so much flesh that what remained was little more than tags and tatters. His entire left hand was nearly severed, and kept its association with his body only by the merest hinge of bloody gristle.

He was conscious, though groggy and pale, and he told me to tie a tourniquet about his arm to staunch the prodigious bleeding. I did so. I was glad to be helpful, and did not mind the blood which spattered across my already torn uniform, so much of it that when we arrived at the hospital an attendant looked at me wide-eyed and asked me where I was hurt.

The hospital was already crowded, and quickly becoming more so as cartloads of injured men were unloaded at the door. Three medics were in attendance, but two of them were already engaged in operations that couldn't be interrupted. Luckily there was a kind of triage-by-rank being practiced, and the third doctor came promptly at the announcement of Sam's high position.

The doctor made a hasty inspection of Sam's injury and announced that it wanted an amputation. Sam did not like this idea, and began a feeble protest, until the medic doused a cloth with liquid from a brown bottle and held it against Sam's mouth, which caused the patient's eyes to close and his struggles to abate. It looked more like murder than mercy; but the physician, rolling up one of Sam's eyelids to inspect his pupils, seemed satisfied with the result.

"How does inhaling through that rag cure his wound?" I asked.

The doctor took notice of my presence for the first time. "It doesn't," he said. "It only makes it easier for me to do my work. What are you to this man?"

"His adjutant," I said; and added, "His friend."

"Well, now you're an assistant surgeon."

"I beg your pardon, but I'm not."

"Yes you are. My name is Dr. Linch. You—?"

"Colonel Adam Hazzard."

He grabbed a cotton smock from a nearby shelf and threw it at me. "Cover yourself with this, Colonel Hazzard. Have you washed your hands lately?"

"Yes, just a couple of days ago."

"Dip them in that bucket on the table."

The bucket contained an astringent chemical of some kind, which burned the small cuts I had acquired over the course of the retreat from Goose Bay, but it dissolved away most of the dirt. It had been used for this purpose before me, I deduced, for the liquid was discolored with oily scum and old blood.

"And rinse a bone saw there while you're at it," Linch said, pointing at a nasty-looking bladed thing, which I dipped in the same bucket, and dried on the cleanest part of an old towel. "Now steady his arm while I cut."

Dr. Linch was a brusque man, and didn't brook debate.

I had never witnessed an amputation before, at least at close range. Linch was not a young man, but his hands were remarkably steady, and I admired his quickness even as I suppressed an urge to flee. I was fascinated (in the least pleasant sense of that word) by the efficiency of his bone-cutting. He was very neat about sealing the blood vessels which extended from the stump of Sam's forearm once the grisly surgery was complete. Linch kept a number of sewing needles in the lapel of his white jacket, and each needle was fitted with a length of silk thread. At intervals the doctor would pluck one of these needles and use it to stitch a leaking vein, his hands moving with a brisk familiarity that made me think of a fisherman baiting a hook with a pulsing blue worm— leaving a few inches loose so the thread could be pulled out again once the stump had healed. He insisted on explaining these procedures as he worked, even though the thought of it made me queasy; and I resolved that I would never undertake a medical career even if the job of writing fiction failed to pan out. It was as bad as boning beef, it seemed to me—worse, in some ways, since beef carcasses don't wake up screaming as they're flensed, and need to be sedated a second time.

I couldn't watch the surgery too closely without experiencing a degree of nausea; and whenever possible I looked away, though the room was full of beds occupied by men just as badly injured as Sam, if not worse, and the sight of them offered little relief. Amputation was the chief cure being applied by the medics. The grating sound of the bone saws never altogether ceased. A blood-drenched orderly came through the room at intervals to collect severed limbs for disposal. When he took what remained of Sam's left hand from the floor where Dr. Linch had dropped it, this unusual act brought home the horror of the occasion in a way the surgery itself had not. I wanted to retrieve the hand—carrying it off so casually seemed disrespectful, and I couldn't silence the thought that Sam might want it again in the future. I had to clench my teeth to steady my nerves.

During one of these unsuccessful attempts to distract myself I caught sight of a face I recognized, in a novel context. A tall, gaunt individual wearing a Dominion hat moved among the wounded and the dying, offering solace and words from the Bible. He recognized me, too, and tried but failed to keep his face averted—this individual was none other than Private Langers!

I was outraged, but said nothing until Sam's stump had had its skin-flaps sewn together, for fear of distracting Dr. Linch from that important work. As soon as he had wrapped the last bandage, however, I said, "Dr. Linch, there's an impostor here," and pointed out Langers to him. "That man is no Dominion officer."

"I know all about it," Dr. Linch said indifferently.

"You do! Why don't you throw him out, then?"

"Because he serves a purpose. There are no genuine Dominion officers to be had. Julian Conqueror barred them from the expedition, and for the most part that's not a bad thing, since we haven't had to endure their Sunday scoldings. But a dying soldier generally wants a godly man beside him, and seldom inquires into the Pastor's pedigree. When I asked for a volunteer among the troops—someone, anyone, even if his only religious office was passing the plate at church—this man Langers raised his hand. The rest were afraid of missing the action, or of appearing cowardly."

"I'm sure those concerns weren't foremost in Private Langers's mind. What religious experience does he claim to have?"

"He says he used to be a colporteur, distributing pamphlets on sacred subjects."

I explained that Langers's pamphlets had been little more than pornographic guides to behavior not approved of by Biblical authorities, and that Langers himself was a fraud and a habitual liar.

"Has a Dominion officer ever been disqualified on those grounds? Don't bother about him, Colonel Hazzard—he may be a cracked vessel, but we don't own a better one just now."

I took Dr. Linch's advice. Perhaps it wasn't as cynical as it sounded. As I left the surgical ward I overheard Langers giving solace to a man who had suffered a ghastly head injury. The victim's one good eye was fixed on Langers, while the larcenous Private misquoted what were perhaps the only Bible verses he had ever learned verbatim, from the Song of Solomon, mingled with passages from the banned poet Whitman.

How much better is love than wine! he intoned in a soothing voice, one hand poised in a benediction and a sly, sweet smile on his lips. *Divine am I inside and out, and I make holy whatever I touch or am touched from. In the faces of men and women I see God, and in my own face in the glass. Awake, oh north wind, and come thou south, and blow through this garden so that the spice of it might flow out! Deep waters cannot quench love, nor a flood drown it. Set me as a seal on your heart, for love is as strong as death, and jealousy is as cruel as the grave.*

These words were not the standard consolation, but they were pleasant to hear at any time; and in the privacy of my thoughts I forgave Private Langers for uttering them under false pretenses, for the tear that formed in the single whole eye of the dying man was unquestionably a grateful and authentic one.

3

Sam was awake the next day, although the doses of watered opium that kept his pain at bay also interfered with his clarity of thought.

Julian didn't visit him, for he was too busy securing Striver to withstand what might be a long siege. We were well protected—our defensive perimeter was anchored against Lake Melville and the Northwest River, so we could not easily be outflanked; and it would have been outrageously costly for the Dutch to mount a frontal attack. But they could starve us out, given time; and that was probably what they intended to do. This meant that food and medical supplies had to be itemized, guarded, and rationed—and that was some of the business Julian was about.

I sat by Sam's bed in his place. For the most part Sam was silent, when he was not sleeping; but occasionally he spoke, and I tried to be an encouraging audience. He mentioned his father once or twice—his Judaic rather than his adopted father—and I attempted to draw him out on the subject when he seemed to need distraction.

"What work did your father do?" I asked him.

Sam was very gaunt beneath the blankets that covered him. It was a cold day outside, and a small snow was falling. We had to be chary with coal because of the siege, and the stoves in the hospital did little to dispel the chill. Whenever Sam spoke his words became visible as mist, as if he were emitting his immortal spirit directly from his mortal lungs. "He was a scrapper," Sam said.

"He fought for a living?"

"No, Adam—a scrap-collector. He prospected in the Houston Ship Canal, down in Texas. That's the territory where I was born."

"Is it a good place, Sam?"

"The Canal? The Canal is hell on earth. It's a poisonous trench as large as a city, rich in copper and aluminum, made not for human beings but for Oil and Machines back in the days of the Secular Ancients. In the Canal a prospector can make good money in a short time, if he's smart and lucky. But the risks are terrible. The waters are vile and breed disease. When I was very small I saw scrappers come back from the Canal with blood running freely from their noses, or with their skin turned black and shriveled by contamination. My father was always careful to protect himself with boots and gloves and leather aprons. There were days when he carted out copper or aluminum very nearly by the ton, or soil that could be treated to recover arsenic, cobalt, lead, and other valuable elements, which sell for a premium at the Galveston Exchange. By the time he was thirty he had saved enough money to take his family east. But the

Canal killed him the way it killed so many others, only more slowly. He died a year later, in Philadelphia, choked on tumors that filled his chest and neck. My mother was already frail and consumptive—she survived him by less than a month."

"And you were adopted by a Christian family?"

"By a kind but aloof man who was a friend of my father. He and his wife provided for me until I was old enough to be sent for military training, on the stipend my father left for my education."

"But you had to renounce your religion."

"Rather to pretend it had never existed. Which had been my father's strategy all along. In my family, Adam, all we had of piety was the lighting of candles on certain winter days and the pronunciation of a few incomprehensible prayers. The family that adopted me knew nothing of it, nor ever would."

That was a melancholy confession, and I blushed at the memory of how I had mistaken his prayers for sorcery back in Williams Ford, when I was younger and less worldly. "Would you like me to pray for you, Sam? I can say a Jewish prayer, if you teach me the words."

"No prayers, please, neither Jewish nor Christian—they won't do. I'm not one thing or the other."

I told him I understood his predicament, for I was equally a mixed creature, neither a handler of serpents like my father nor as ecumenically pious as my mother. I was east of Skepticism and north of Faith, with an unsettled compass and variable winds. But I could offer up a prayer as well as the next man, and leave it to Heaven to judge the result.

"I hope I don't need praying over just yet," said Sam, his voice losing some of its momentary clarity. "I wish I had my hand back, though. I seem to feel it there still—clenched and burning. Adam!" he called out suddenly, his eyes gone watery and vague. "Where's Julian? Where's Admiral Fairfield? We need to repulse the damned Dutchmen!"

"Calm down—you'll aggravate your wound."

"Damn my wound! Julian will want to send me away—*don't let him do it!* He needs my advice more than I ever needed my lost left hand! Tell him that, Adam—tell him—!"

Sam's agitation attracted the attention of Dr. Linch, who forced a preparation of opium down Sam's throat, and not long after that Sam's anxiety yielded to silence, and he fell asleep again.

"Is he recovering?" I asked the doctor.

"His fever is increased. That's not a good sign. There may be some putrefaction in the wound, judging by the smell."

"He'll get better soon, though?"

"This is a poor excuse for a hospital, Colonel Hazzard, and bound to deteriorate as supplies run low. Nothing is certain."

I wanted more reassurance than that, but Dr. Linch was stubborn, and wouldn't yield it up.

I did not expect that Julian would really send Sam away, but in fact that's what happened.

Admiral Fairfield's battered *Basilisk* anchored a little away from the harbor at Striver, and the Admiral came ashore in a launch. We still controlled the harbor, which was beyond the reach of the Dutch artillery, and we would have welcomed the American fleet had it arrived. But, as at Goose Bay, there was only Admiral Fairfield's ship. The *Basilisk,* although a noble craft, looked small and forlorn against the chilly waters of Lake Melville and the distant spine of the Mealy Mountains, as sailors swarmed over her rigging repairing the damage she had taken in battle. The Admiral arrived at the dock in a bitter mood, and he was silent as I accompanied him to Julian's headquarters.

In the privacy of that building, which had once housed the Dutch Mayor of Striver, in the upstairs bedroom Julian had commandeered for his office, Admiral Fairfield—whose initial skepticism of Julian's abilities as a commander had yielded to grudging and finally enthusiastic approval—explained that his entire fleet had been ordered out of Lake Melville.

"*Ordered* out!" Julian exclaimed. "Why?"

"The command came without explanation," Admiral Fairfield said with patent disgust. "From New York."

"From my uncle, you mean."

"I suspect so, though I can't say for certain."

"And all obeyed it but you?"

"Officially, the *Basilisk* is covering our retreat against any Dutch attack. That was my excuse for remaining behind long enough to contribute what I could at Goose Bay—which was little enough—and to come here to consult you."

"But you'll have to leave shortly," Julian surmised. "And, obviously, you can't deliver reinforcements."

"I cannot, though it pains me to say so. All I can do is offload what extra provisions the *Basilisk* is carrying, and take away those of the wounded who need better treatment than a field hospital can supply."

"Leaving us here," Julian said, "besieged, until the day comes when we yield to starvation, or surrender ourselves to the Mitteleuropan forces . . . which is no doubt what my mad uncle intends."

"My oath of loyalty prevents me from acknowledging the truth of it. In extremis, General Comstock, you might attempt to break out to the east. A road runs through to the Narrows, though it's unimproved, and the fortifications there ought to remain in American hands long enough to receive you. But it would be a desperate attempt at best."

"Desperate indeed, since we're considerably outnumbered."

"The decision is yours, of course." Admiral Fairfield stood up. "Leaving you in these circumstances is inexcusable, but I've already stretched my written orders past the limits of interpretation."

"I understand," Julian said, taking the Admiral's gnarled hand in his own with a touching sense of occasion. "I hold no grudge against you, Admiral, and I thank the Navy for everything it's done on our behalf."

"I hope the gratitude is not misplaced," the Admiral said grimly.

Julian and I went down to the docks, where Sam and dozens of other seriously wounded men were carried to boats for removal to the *Basilisk*. I delivered several typewritten sheets to that vessel's Quartermaster—my war dispatches to the *Spark*, which the Quartermaster promised to post from Newfoundland.

We caught up with Dr. Linch, who was supervising the proceedings, and he led us to Sam, who rested in a litter with a woolly blanket wrapped around him and the fitful snow collecting in his beard. His eyes were closed, and fever-roses flourished on his weathered cheeks. "Sam," said Julian, laying a gentle hand on his mentor's shoulder.

Sam's eyelids peeled back, and he gazed up into the rolling clouds a moment before his gaze fixed on Julian.

"Don't let them take me," he said in a shockingly frail voice.

"It's a question of need, not wish," said Julian. "Do as the doctor tells you, Sam, and soon you'll be well enough to resume the fight."

Sam wasn't soothed by these homilies, however, and he reached up from the blankets with his good right arm and took Julian by the collar. "You need my advice!"

"I can hardly do without it; but if you have any advice, Sam, give it to me now, for the boats are preparing to cast off."

"*Use it,*" Sam said, cryptically but insistently.

"Use it? Use what? I don't understand."

"The weapon! The *Chinese* weapon."

Julian's eyes grew wide and his expression mournful. "Sam . . . there *is* no Chinese weapon."

"I know that, you young fool! Use it anyway."

Perhaps he was the victim of a febrile delusion. In any case, if he had more to say, we didn't hear it; for the litter-bearers carried him off, and before long he was tucked aboard the *Basilisk* and bound for the Naval hospital at St. John's.

I think I had never felt quite so alone as I did when the *Basilisk* weighed anchor and sailed east—not even on the snowy plains of Athabaska, with Williams Ford and all my childhood standing behind me like a closed door.

Then, at least, I had been in the familiar company of Sam and Julian. Now Sam was gone . . . and Julian, in his blue and yellow uniform (slightly tattered), seemed hardly a ghost of the Julian I had once known.

Among the goods Admiral Fairfield left us was a bag of mail. These packages and letters were distributed to the troops the same day. One of Julian's adjutants brought me an envelope with my name written on it in Calyxa's hand.

Night had fallen; so I took the letter close to a lamp, and opened it with trembling hands.

Calyxa had never been much of a correspondent—no one would call her wordy. The letter consisted of a salutation and three terse sentences:

Dear Adam,
    The Dominion threatens me. Please come home soon, preferably alive.
Also, I am pregnant.

                                                          Yrs, Calyxa.

4

Much could be said about the days leading up to Thanksgiving, as I experienced them. But I won't belabor the reader with trivialities. Those were dark and hungry times. I kept a careful record, sitting down each night with lamp and typewriter before I permitted myself the luxury of sleep. The pages are still in my possession, and in the interest of brevity I'll confine myself to quoting passages from them, *viz*:

THURSDAY, NOVEMBER 10, 2174

It has become necessary to exclude what remains of the civilian population of Striver from the town, in order to conserve supplies.

The residents of Striver were no more or less hostile to us than might be expected of any group of otherwise comfortable men and women subjected to occupation and forced from their homes at gunpoint. Many were relieved to be handed back into Mitteleuropan custody, for that's their preference, irrational though it might seem to a sane American.* I stood on the roof of our headquarters this afternoon and watched the men, women, and children of Striver trudge across a frosty no-man's-land between the opposing trenches, protected by nothing more than a flag of truce. Their hunched figures, limned in an early twilight, tumbling now and then by accident into artillery craters, made me feel sympathetic, and I could almost imagine myself among them. Perhaps any man is potentially a mirror of any other—perhaps that's what Julian means by "cultural relativism," though the term is reviled by the clergy.

At least in the hands of the Dutch these unfortunates will be guaranteed a daily meal. We are not. Rationing is in effect. Dutch luxuries taken from the dockside warehouses are counted as carefully as the salt beef and cornmeal, and apportioned along with those familiar foods, strange as it seems for American soldiers to be dining on calculated portions of Edam cheese, sturgeon roe, and mashy goose-liver along with their trail-cake and bacon. In any case, these delicacies serve only to postpone the day when our hunger becomes absolute. Given our numbers, and the accounted supplies, Julian calculates that we'll be tightening our belts by mid-month, and thoroughly starved by December.

The men still speculate about a Chinese weapon, and expect Julian to deploy it soon. He refuses to dispel these rumors, and smiles with a sort of mad recklessness whenever I mention the subject.

My mind, of course, is generally on Calyxa, and her troubles with the

---

* Despite the well-known cruelty and Atheism of Mitteleuropa, that principality nevertheless inspires in its subjects a kind of "patriotism" which resembles in almost every particular the real thing.

Dominion, and the other astonishing news contained in her letter. I am to be a father!—*will be* a father, assuming Calyxa carries the child to term, even if I'm killed in this desolate corner of Labrador. For even a dead man can be a father. That's a small but real comfort to me, though I can't hold back from worrying.

TUESDAY, NOVEMBER 15, 2174

The wind blows steadily from the west, and is very cold, though the sky remains clear. Dusk comes early. We burn few lamps, to conserve fuel. Tonight the Aurora Borealis does a chill and stately dance with the North Star. It's not, unfortunately, a *silent* night, for the Dutch have brought up their heavy artillery, and shells fall into the town at irregular intervals. Half the buildings of Striver are already blown up or burned down, it seems. Chimney-stacks stand like upraised fingers along empty, shattered streets.

Julian is moody and strange without Sam to guide and advise him. He insists on compiling a list of goods—not food, but dry goods—contained in the dockside warehouses. Today I assisted at one such inventory, and brought the list to Julian at the mayor's house.

The Dutch and their luxuries! The *Stadhouders* are not just gluttons; they insist on all the subtler fineries of life, it seems. Julian carefully perused the lengthy catalog of textiles, tortoise shells, pharmaceutical compounds, cattle horns, musical instruments, horseshoes, ginseng, plumbing supplies, *et alia*, ours by right of pillage. His expression as he examined the list was thoughtful, even calculating.

"You don't itemize these bolts of silk," he remarked.

"There was too much of them," I told him. "The silk is all crated and stacked high—I expect it had only just arrived when we took the town. But you can't eat silk, Julian."

"I don't propose to eat it. Inspect it again tomorrow, Adam, and report back about the quality of it, especially the closeness of the weave."

"Surely my time could be better spent than by counting threads?"

"Think of it as *following orders*," Julian said sharply. Then he looked up from his lists, and his expression softened. "I'm sorry, Adam. Humor me in this. But keep quiet about it, please—I don't want the troops thinking I've lost my mind."

"I'll knit you a Chinese robe, Julian, if you think it might help us survive the siege."

"That's exactly my plan—to survive, I mean—no *knitting* will be required—though a little *sewing*, perhaps."

He wouldn't discuss it further.

WEDNESDAY, NOVEMBER 16, 2174

It occurs to me that Thanksgiving is coming. We have not given very much thought to that Universal Christian Holiday, perhaps because we can find so little to be thankful for in our current situation. We're more likely to pity ourselves than to count our blessings.

But that is shortsighted, my mother would surely say. In fact I'm thankful for many things.

I'm thankful that I have Calyxa's letter, however terse and brief, folded in my pocket next to my heart.

I'm thankful that I might be blessed with a child, the product of our possibly hasty but blessed and bountiful marriage.

I'm thankful that I'm still alive, and that Julian is still alive, though our condition is provisional and subject to change. (Of course no mortal creature "knows the hour or the day," but we're unusual in being surrounded by Dutch infantrymen eager to hasten the unwelcome terminal event.)

I'm thankful that despite my absence life goes on much as it always has in Williams Ford and in every other such simple place within the broad borders of the American Union. I'm even grateful for the cynical Philosophers, grimy Tipmen, pale Aesthetes, corrupt Owners, and feckless Eupatridians who throng the streets of the great City of New York—or anyway grateful that I had the chance to see them at close proximity.

I'm thankful for my daily ration, though it shrinks from day to day.

THURSDAY, NOVEMBER 17, 2174

Today our troops overran a Mitteleuropan trench which had been dug too close to our lines. Five captives were taken, and in an act of Christian charity they were allowed to live, though it will diminish our own supplies to feed them. Julian hopes they might be traded for American prisoners already in Dutch hands—he has sent that suggestion by flag-of-truce to the Dutch commander, but as yet no reply has been received.

I went to see the captives as they were being interrogated, in part to satisfy my curiosity about the enemy, whom I know only as faceless combatants and as the authors of incomprehensible letters. Only one of the men spoke English; the other four were questioned by a Lieutenant who has some Dutch and German.

The enemy soldiers are gaunt, stubborn men. They offer little more than their own names, even under duress. The exception to this is the single English-speaker—a former British merchant sailor, conscripted out of a barroom in Brussels while he was insensible with drink. His loyalties are mixed, and he doesn't mind giving estimates of the enemy's strength and positions.

He said the Dutchmen were confident that they would prevail in the siege. They were cautious about initiating any attack, however, for rumors of the (unfortunately imaginary) Chinese weapon have reached them. The prisoner said there was no detailed information concerning this weapon,* but speculation about its nature suggested something profoundly deadly and unusual.

---

* Nor could there have been.

I carried that news to Julian tonight.

He greeted it with grim amusement. "Just what I hoped the Dutch were thinking. Good! Maybe we can find a way to *deepen* their fears."

Again, he wouldn't explain what he had in mind. But he has sequestered one of the warehouses by the docks (out of range of enemy artillery), and is converting it into some sort of workshop. Men have been recruited and sworn to secrecy. He has requisitioned countless bolts of black silk; also sewing machines, hooks and eyes, strips of lathing from damaged houses, bottles of caustic soda, and other peculiar items.

"Maybe it's good for the Dutch to believe in this imaginary weapon," I said, "but unfortunately our own troops believe in it too. In fact they imagine you're preparing to activate it."

"Perhaps I am."

"There *is* no Chinese weapon, and you know that as well as I do, Julian, unless hunger has driven you entirely mad."

"Of course I know it. I'm a firm believer in its non-existence. All it means is that we're forced back on our ingenuity."

"You mean to build a weapon out of silk and fish-hooks?"

"Please keep that thought to yourself. The rest will become clear in time."

SATURDAY, NOVEMBER 19, 2174

The pace of activity in Julian's sealed warehouse increases. The "secret weapon" is now so commonly spoken-of that I fear the men will be bitter or even vindictive in their disappointment, when the truth is finally revealed.

More shells fell today, causing heavy casualties among one particular regiment. I volunteered at the field hospital in the afternoon, assisting Dr. Linch in the chopping, paring, and stitching of shattered limbs. The work is almost unbearable for anyone of a sensitive nature (and I count myself among that number), but necessity knows no excuse.

Our gravest enemy, Dr. Linch says, is less shrapnel than dysentery. At least a quarter of our soldiers are down with it, and it spreads with the infectiousness of a fire in a kindling-yard.

Corn-cake and salt cod for dinner, in small servings.

SUNDAY, NOVEMBER 20, 2174

Extraordinary events! I mean to set them down before I sleep, though it is already very late.

After the evening meal Julian summoned me to his quarters and asked me to bring along my typewriter. I carried the machine (no small task, in my weakened and hungry condition) to the upstairs study of the former mayor's house, and Julian instructed me to keep it ready, for there was a message he wished to dictate.

Then, to my astonishment, he summoned an adjutant and ordered Private Langers to be brought into his presence.

"Langers!" I exclaimed as soon as the adjutant had gone out. "What do you want with Langers? Has he committed some fresh outrage? I saw him at the hospital, perpetrating his clerical fraud; but I don't suppose that's what this is all about."

"It isn't—or only in part. And please, Adam—you might be startled by some of what I have to say to him; but it's essential to the success of my plans that you don't interrupt or correct me while Langers is in the room with us."

This was a sterner tone than Julian usually took in my presence; but I reminded myself that we were at war, and under siege, and that he was a Major General, and I was not. I promised not to speak out of turn. Of course my curiosity was profoundly aroused.

We shivered for most of half an hour—Julian heated his quarters parsimoniously, to conserve the supply of coal—before Langers arrived. Langers was shivering, too, as he stumbled into the room, perhaps not entirely from the cold. He looked at Julian apprehensively. "Sir?" he said.

Julian put on his most imperial manner.* "Please sit down, Private."

Langers inserted himself into a chair by the stove. "You called for me, sir?"

"Obviously I did, and here you are. I've received a complaint about you."

Langers—no doubt recalling what had happened to him when Sam gave out the truth about his Lucky Mug during the Saguenay Campaign—seemed almost to shrivel with dismay, and his expression grew even more furtive and wary. "It's ungrounded," he muttered.

"You haven't heard the charge yet."

"I know it's unjustified because my conduct has been above reproach. These past weeks I've labored exclusively at the field hospital, sir, consoling the sick and the dying."

"I know all about that," said Julian, "and I would commend you for it, but for one thing."

"What *thing*?" Langers demanded, feigning indignation, not very successfully.

"One of my regimental commanders discovered several suspicious items hidden under your bedroll. These included a large number of gold rings and leather billfolds."

"Well?" Langers said, though he reddened. "A man can harbor a few keepsakes, can't he?"

---

* A skill every Eupatridian of Julian's class has mastered: it consists of regarding the world and all its inhabitants as if they emitted a faint offensive odor.

"No, he may not, not if the same items have been reported as missing from the mortally wounded. I have a corroborating statement from one of the doctors who saw you at the field hospital, your right hand raised over an injured man in a benediction while the left hand stripped a wallet from the victim's pocket. As for the rings, ordinarily such ornaments are sent to grieving widows, not squirreled away under the bedrolls of counterfeit Deacons."

"Well, I—" Langers began, but he faltered. The evidence against him was shocking, and he had lost the opportunity to mount a defense. His naturally long and equine face seemed to grow even longer. "Sir—the hospital is an awful place—it affects a man's mind, over time—perhaps the circumstances drove me to irrational acts—"

"Perhaps they did, or perhaps it was just your acquisitive nature. But don't worry, Private. I didn't call you here to scold you or punish you. I mean to give you an opportunity to redeem yourself."

Langers was not so naive as to grasp that straw without squinting at it first. "I'm sure I thank you—redeem myself how exactly?"

"Be patient. Before we go on, I need to dictate a letter. Adam, will you write it down on that machine of yours?"

I suppressed my astonishment at these unfolding events and said, "Yes, certainly, Julian—I mean, General Comstock."

"Good. Are you ready?" (I applied paper to platen, hastily.) "Put in a top line with the date and mark it as from my headquarters, Army of the Laurentians, Northern Division, Town of Striver, Lake Melville, Eastern Labrador, etc." I clacked away at this task. My typewriting skills had improved since I first acquired the machine, and I was proud of my speed, though it set no records. "Address it to Major Walton, General Headquarters, Newfoundland."

I did so. Then Julian dictated the body of the text, which I will set down here while it remains fresh in my mind, including the unusual capitalizations which Julian demanded:

This is to let you know that, after much solemn deliberation, and in the face of continuing enemy encirclement and bombardment, I have resolved to deploy the MECHANISM we earnestly hoped would never be used in civilized warfare.

I do not take this decision lightly. It is no easy thing to enter into a war as brutal as this one, and to make it yet more inhuman by the employment of such a cruel DEVICE. It is not the prospect of the IMMEDIATE death of countless enemy soldiers which pangs me, for that is the nature of war, so much as the knowledge of the LINGERING EFFECTS, in which death comes only after hours or even days of intolerable suffering. You know that in councils of war I have argued against the deployment of this WEAPON, which is so vicious in its workings that any Christian trembles at the mention of it.

But I find myself in a position that allows no other outcome. My army has been besieged, and we are sent no SUPPLIES or REINFORCEMENTS.

Thousands of loyal men confront starvation, and I dare not surrender them to the mercies of the Mitteleuropan Army. Therefore I have resolved to do everything in my power to deliver the troops, or some fraction of them, to safety, even if the conduct of this war is made that much more HELLISH and SATANIC.

You may pass this information to the General Staff and to the Chief Executive.

God help me for taking this decision. PRAY FOR US, Major Walton! We act within days.

"Add the usual salutations," Julian said, ignoring my gap-jawed amazement not only at the contents of the letter but at the unusually ecclesiastical tone of it, "and give it to me to sign. Thank you, Adam."

I did as he asked, though I could hardly contain my questions and anxieties.

"What does this business have to do with me?" Private Langers demanded. "I don't know anything about these dreadful things!"

"Of course you don't; but a message, to be useful, has to be delivered. That's *your* task, Private Langers. The letter will be sewn into a satchel. You will carry the satchel past the Dutch lines to the American fortifications at the Narrows, and personally hand it to the ranking officer there."

"Across enemy lines!" The Private's eyes were as wide as Comstock dollars.

"That's correct."

Impossible!" Langers exclaimed; and I was inclined to agree with him, though I kept my silence, as instructed.

"Perhaps it is," Julian said, "but I need someone to make the attempt. You're healthy enough, and it seems to me you have a powerful motive for succeeding at it. The choice is stark, Private Langers. You can accept the assignment, or you can stay here and face exposure for robbing wounded men."

"You wouldn't tell the infantry about my indiscretion!"

"I would—at the next Sunday meeting! The men don't like to think of a tract-peddler stealing from them in their most vulnerable moment."

"But they'll kill me if they find out—they're prudish about things like that!"

"I don't doubt that they'll be unhappy. The choice is yours."

"I object! It's blackmail—face certain death here, or be shot by the enemy!"

"You might not be shot, if luck is with you. You'll have to be very quiet and move by moonlight. If I thought your capture was a certainty I wouldn't send you out at all."

Langers hung his head morosely, an acknowledgment that he could see no way out of the trap Julian had sprung on him.

"Let me add," Julian said, "that if you do accept the task you must not under any circumstances allow the document to fall into the hands of the Dutch. It would nullify our purpose entirely if they learned of our plans. And the enemy are sly—even if they capture you, even if they attempt to bribe you with promises of protection or great rewards, you must not succumb."

This was precisely the wrong thing to say to Langers, I thought. It was no use appealing to Langers's conscience—which, if it existed at all, must be a particularly feeble and anemic specimen—and I longed to correct Julian's mistake. But I remembered his instructions, and bit my tongue.

Langers seemed to brighten a little after Julian's admonition. I don't doubt that he was calculating the angles of the situation in which he suddenly found himself, attempting to discover a geometry more suitable to his goals. He made a few more small objections, just to keep up the seeming of the thing, but finally agreed to expiate "the potential stain on his military record" caused by stealing from the not-quite-dead. Yes, he agreed, he would brave the Mitteleuropan lines and make a run for the Narrows, if that was what duty demanded. "But if I'm killed," he said, "and if that news reaches you, General Comstock, I ask you to make sure I'm listed among the honorable dead, so as not to bring shame to my family."

"*What* family?" I couldn't help exclaiming. "You always said you were an orphan!"

"Those who are *as close to me as family*, I mean," Langers said. (And Julian gave me a poisonous look, which reminded me to keep silent.)

"I promise," Julian said. Incredibly, he extended his hand to the larcenous Private. "Your reputation is safe, Mr. Langers. In my eyes you redeem yourself simply by accepting the commission."

"I thank you for your confidence. You're a generous commander, sir, and a Christian gentleman—I have always said so."

(If this did not cease, I thought, I would soon shred my tongue entirely, from the biting of it.)

"It's essential that you leave at once. One of my adjutants will conduct you to the forward trenches and give you your final instructions. You'll be provided with an overcoat and a fresh pair of boots, along with a pistol and ammunition."

Julian summoned a young Lieutenant, who tucked the message into the lining of a leather satchel and escorted Langers away.

I looked at Julian aghast, now that we were alone.

"Well?" he asked, with an insouciant note in his voice. "You have something to say, Adam?"

"I hardly know where to begin, but—Julian! Is there really a Chinese weapon?"

"Can you think of some other reason I might send that note to Major Walton?"

"But that's just the absurdity of it! Using Langers as a messenger, and then telling him that the Dutch would reward him for betraying us! You accuse *me* of naïveté from time to time, but this tops it all—you might as well have invited him to defect!"

"Do you really think he might succumb to the temptation?"

"I think he could hardly do anything else!"

"Then we share the same opinion."

"You mean you *expect* him to betray us to the enemy?"

"I mean that if my plan is to succeed, it will be better if he does."

I was naturally confused, and I suppose my expression showed it, for Julian took pity on me, and put an arm about my shoulders. "I'm sorry if I seem to trifle with you, Adam. If I haven't been entirely frank, it's only for the purpose of preserving absolute secrecy. Report to me in the morning and I'll make it all clear."

That dubious promise was the most I could extract from him, and I left his headquarters in a whirling state of mind.

Now I must stop writing, if I want to sleep at all before reveille.

The air is cold but clear tonight, the wind as sharp as scissors. I find myself thinking of Calyxa, but she is awfully far away.

MONDAY, NOVEMBER 21, 2174

Julian has explained his plan. Tonight we perform an essential test. I can confide the truth in no one—not even in these Notes, which I keep for myself.

It's a thin chance, but we have no other.

(Here the Diary concludes, and I resume the narrative in the customary style.)

5

Julian took me into his confidence at last, and during the afternoon of the 21st of November he conducted me on a tour of the warehouse where the "weapon" was being prepared.

It soon became obvious that what I had overlooked about Julian was his persistent and unconquerable *love of theater*. That aspect of his personality had not been much manifest during his tenure as Major General Comstock . . . but neither, apparently, had it been wholly suppressed. The interior of the warehouse (illuminated by freshly-scrubbed skylights and a generous number of lanterns) resembled nothing so much as the backstage shambles at some colossal production of *Lucia di Lammermoor*,* with Julian as the property-master.

Men in uniform had been made into seamstresses, working bolts of black silk at feverish speed, often while cutters slashed at the same cloth. Carpenters had busied themselves sawing wooden poles or lathing into supple strips as tall as a man. Cordage from a wholesale spool the size of a millwheel was carefully measured out, and segments of it rewound onto smaller hubs. This was only a sample of the vigorous business taking place.

The huge room stank of various chemical substances, including caustic soda and what Julian claimed was liquid phosphorous (in several pitted metal barrels). My eyes began to water as soon as the door was closed behind me, and I wondered whether some of what I had mistaken for fatigue in Julian's countenance was simply the result of long hours spent in this unpleasant atmosphere. I was impressed by the industriousness and scale of the work, which filled the enclosed space with a fearsome noise, but I confessed I could not make sense of it.

"Come on, Adam, can't you guess?"

"Is it a game, then? I assume you're assembling some weapon—or at least the *seeming* of one."

"A little of each," said Julian, smiling mischievously.

A soldier came past carrying a wrapped assemblage of lathes and black silk, which Julian briefly inspected. I told Julian the bundle resembled one of the fishing-kites he had got up at Edenvale, though much enlarged.

"Very good!" said Julian. "Well observed."

"But what is it really?"

"Just what you imagine it is."

"A kite?" The soldier in question stood the object upright among many

* A revival of which had been popular in Manhattan the summer past. I know it only by reputation.

others similar to it. Folded, they resembled so many sinister umbrellas, fashioned for the use of a fastidious giant. "But there must be a hundred of them!"

"At least."

"What use are *kites*, though, Julian?"

"Any explanation I could give you would be beggared by the truth. Tonight we test the product. When you see the result, perhaps you'll understand."

His coyness was aggravating, but I supposed it was another manifestation of the showman in him, not wanting to describe a stage effect for fear of diminishing its impact. He said he wanted me as "an unbiased observer." I told that I had no bias but impatience; and I went to the field hospital in a mixed humor, and made myself useful there until after dark.

When night had fully fallen, and after our meager evening rations had been doled out, Julian and I once more made our way toward the docks. The warehouse, though still heavily guarded, was less busy at this hour. The men Julian had chosen as his workforce had been sworn to secrecy, and they slept apart from the other soldiers so as not to risk unwise conversation. Most of the recruits, Julian said, knew only the particular task assigned them, and had been kept ignorant of the whole outline of the business. But there were a hundred or so men who had been made to understand our ultimate objective, and this elite group was in the warehouse tonight—or rather *on top* of the warehouse, for we climbed an iron stairway to the roof of the building, which was securely tiled and only gently sloped. The "Kite Brigade," as Julian called them, awaited him there.

The night was moonless, the stars obscured by high fast-running clouds. Apart from a few campfires, and lanterns in odd windows, the town of Striver was entirely dark. The huge kites I had seen before had been brought up here. They were still furled, but their bridles had been attached to reels of hempen twine which were nailed to wooden bases and equipped with hand cranks. Each kite also had a bucket tied to its bridle with a short string, and as we arrived a man was just finishing the work of pouring a measured amount of sand into each of these buckets.

"What's that for?" I asked Julian—quietly, since the eerie atmosphere of the rooftop seemed to discourage anything beyond a hushed whisper.

"I've calculated how much weight each parafoil can carry," Julian said. "Tonight we discover whether my calculations were correct."

I didn't ask how one estimated the lifting power of a "parafoil," or with what kind of arithmetic—no doubt it was something else Julian had learned from one of his antique books. If it depended on the wind, we were in luck; the breeze was brisk; but it was very cold, and I kept my hands in the pockets of my overcoat, and wished I had my old packle hat on top of my head, instead of the thin Army cap I was wearing.

Everything seemed ready for the "test flight," as Julian called it, except for the darkness. "How can you see whether they fly, when the moon is down and even the Northern Lights aren't operating?"

Julian didn't answer, but beckoned to a man nearby. This soldier carried a bin with some liquid in it, and a brush.

The liquid, as it turned out, was a compound of phosphorous which radiated an unearthly green light.* The soldier employed his brush to splash a little of this on each bucket, until they had all been so marked, and glowed like demonic jack-o'-lanterns in the darkness.

"Stringmen prepare!" Julian called out abruptly.

Dozens of men jumped to their stations at the anchored kite-reels.

"Furlers stand ready!"

An equal number of men, positioned downwind along the rim of the roof, grasped the huge furled kites and held them at present-arms, ready to be unrolled so that their wings might catch the wind.

"Launch!" cried Julian.

The reader should understand that a black silk kite taller than a man, lofted into the Stygian darkness of a Labrador night, while the wind comes skirling from the arctic regions like a madman with a knife in his teeth, is not the same beast as a child's kite bobbing in the sunlight of a summer day. The immense black kites, though not easily visible, made their presence known as soon as the first one caught the icy breeze and opened with a concussive bang as loud as a gunshot.

Each kite, as the wind filled it, made the same deafening report (which reminded me of the popping of sails aboard the *Basilisk* when that vessel began to trim for heavy weather), until it sounded as if an artillery duel was under way and we were in the middle of it. Then the kites rose to the limit of the strings which bound them to the buckets they were meant to carry, each with its weighed portion of sand and its glowing green insigne.

Evidently Julian's calculations had been correct. With only a moment's hesitation, and an encouraging tug from the Stringmen, the buckets soared aloft. Mere words cannot convey how unusual and strange this looked: all that was visible from any distance was the phosphorescent paint that marked each rising container. These unearthly Lights (as they seemed) rose and bobbed and rose again, like angels or demons sailing in close formation. I was suffused with awe, even though I knew the explanation for what I was seeing. An unenlightened observer might easily have been terrified.

"Not every American soldier in town is asleep," I said. "Might not someone see this, and alert others?"

"I hope so. It will brace up the men, to think that this is a sample of what we've been preparing."

"They'll take it for supernatural."

---

* The Dutch use it for military signaling, but it also serves in theatrical effects.

"Let them take it according to their beliefs—it makes no difference."

"But—as impressive as this is—a kite isn't a *weapon*, Julian, even if it flies at night and glitters like an owl's eye."

"Sometimes seeming is as good as being." Julian busied himself with a sort of sextant, performing an act he called "triangulation." By this time the kites had come to the end of their measured lengths of tether. The tether-lines were taut; in fact the Stringmen had to struggle to keep the reels in place, so powerful was the force generated by the wind upon the parafoils. The hempen lines strained ferociously, and made a singing noise, eerie in the darkness.

Julian spent some time instructing the Stringmen on how to buck and lax their lines so that the kites could be made to drop and rise again. They performed the task crudely, but Julian reckoned that even a little experience was better than none. Then the Stringmen began the slow and laborious task of reeling the kites back from the sky.

An impressive display, but it wasn't finished—Julian had one more theatrical effect he wished to test.

"Tubemen ready!" he shouted.

Another group of soldiers, who had previously been huddled at the chimney-brace for warmth, suddenly separated and formed into a row. Each of them carried a length of rubber tubing, perhaps originally intended to transport water in some Dutch governor's mansion. When they had room enough—much to my amazement—they began to *whirl the tubes above their heads,* the way a cattle-herder might whirl a rope, though less elegantly. The result was that each tube (and they had been cut to various lengths) began to sing, much the way an organ-pipe sings when wind is blasted through it. What the performance yielded in this circumstance was not music, however, but a kind of unearthly, dissonant hooting—the sound a chorus of loons might make, if they were inflated to the size of elephants.

I had to clap my hands over my ears. "Julian, the whole town will be awake—you'll wake up the Dutch infantry, though their trenches are miles away!"

"Good!" said Julian; or at least that's what he appeared to say; the keening of the rubber tubes drowned him out somewhat. But he smiled contentedly, and after a time made a hand signal that caused the Tubemen to cease their whirling. By this time the black kites were almost reeled in, and before long the whole production was over.

No more than an hour had passed.

My astonishment was boundless, but I told Julian I still could not see the point of it. The Dutch troops, if we tried this trick on them, would no doubt be *impressed*—quite possibly *frightened*—but it didn't seem to me they would be materially *damaged* in any way.

"Wait and find out," said Julian.

The next day, rather than attack the Mitteleuropan forces, we exchanged prisoners with them.

Julian went to the trenches to oversee the exchange, which took place under a flag of truce, and I went with him. The Dutchmen scurried across noman's-land with their white flag fluttering, and an equal number of our men passed them going the other way. There was no ceremony, only a brief ceasefire; and when the business was complete the Dutch snipers resumed their deadly practice and the Dutch artillery geared up for more pointless volleys.

"The prisoners we returned," I said to Julian, as we stood shivering in a rear trench, "are they aware of last night's test?"

"I made sure their quarters faced the right direction. They would have had a fine view."

"And your objective is to add their narrative to the rumors already circulating among the Dutch—including that note you dictated, assuming Private Langers has yielded to temptation?"

"That's the goal exactly."

"Well, this is all fine *theater*, Julian—"

"Psychological warfare."

"All right, if that's the name of it. But sooner or later the *psychological* has to yield to the *actual*."

"It will. I've given the order to prepare for battle. We sleep in forward positions tonight. The attack will begin before dawn. We have to strike while the Dutch panic is still fresh."

I grasped the sleeve of Julian's tattered blue and yellow jacket, to make sure I had his full attention. It was cold in that trench, and despite the cutting wind the air stank of blood and human waste, and desolation was all that I could see in every direction. "Tell me the truth—will any of this charade make a difference, or is it only a show to bolster the courage of the men?"

Julian hesitated before he answered.

"Morale is also a weapon," he said. "And I like to think I've increased our arsenal at least in that insubstantial way. We have an advantage we lacked before. Any advantage we can take, we sorely need. Are you thinking of home, Adam?"

"I'm thinking of Calyxa," I admitted. And the child she was carrying, though I had not mentioned that news to Julian.

"I can't promise anything, of course."

"But there's hope?"

"Certainly there is," Julian said. "Hope, yes—hope, always—hope, if nothing else."

I wrote another letter to Calyxa that afternoon, and buttoned it into the pocket of my jacket so that it might be found on my person if I died in battle. Perhaps it would eventually reach her, or perhaps it would be buried along with me, or become the souvenir of some Mitteleuropan infantryman—the calculation wasn't mine to make.

I thought about praying for success, but I wasn't sure God could be coaxed to intervene in such a remote and desolate land.* In any case I doubted my prayers would be altogether well-received, given my ambiguous denominational status. I was not in an easy state of mind, and wished I did not have to face death quite so soon.

Because it was almost Thanksgiving Julian ordered extra rations for everyone, including the last of our meat (strips of salt beef, plus whatever we could spare of horse—the mules had already been eaten). It wasn't a proper Thanksgiving dinner as my mother would have prepared it back in Williams Ford, with a baked goose, perhaps, and cranberries purloined from the Duncan and Crowley kitchen, and raisin pie with stiff cream. But it was more than we had had for many days. The feast depleted our larder: all it left was hardtack, and we would need that for the march if we succeeded in breaking the siege of Striver.

The field hospital was a gloomy place when I visited it that evening. A group of orderlies sang sacred songs, in keeping with the spirit of the season, though somewhat halfheartedly. Many of the wounded men were unable to travel, and Dr. Linch said they might have to be abandoned to the mercies of the Mitteleuropan army. The choice of who would be hauled off and who left behind rested in his hands; and he disliked the obligation, and was in a sour mood about it.

"At least," Dr. Linch said, "the men are a little warmer tonight—that intolerable cold wind has finally stopped blowing."

It took a moment for the significance of what he had said to register on my mind. Then I ran outside to see for myself.

Dr. Linch was entirely correct. The wind, which had been keening steadily for almost a month, had suddenly ceased to blow, and the air was as still as ice.

We are becalmed! I wrote in my journal.

No food but trail food, and we must be parsimonious with that. Julian can't tell the men why the attack has been delayed, without betraying the secret of the Black Kites (which of course cannot fly without wind). The troops are restive, and grumble constantly. Thanksgiving Day, 2174—bitter and disappointing.

---

* If I were Him I might be tempted to suppress My power of omniscience when it came to Labrador, and focus My attention on the world's warmer and greener places.

Another cold and windless day. Julian frets over the question, and is constantly scanning the horizon for meteorological clues and auguries.

None are perceived, though tonight the Aurora shimmers like a cloth of gold just north of the zenith.

Dutch shelling increases, and we have had to put out a number of fires in the eastern section of town. Fortunately the fires do not spread—no wind.

No wind.

We are in danger of losing any advantage Julian's plan might have given us. He suspects the Mitteleuropans have already been reinforced. We're greatly outnumbered, and the "Chinese Weapon" begins to seem like an empty threat, if it was ever anything more.

Nevertheless Julian has dreamed up another addition to the charade: his "male seamstresses" have hastily produced nearly two hundred protective masks for the men at the vanguard of our envisioned advance on the Dutch. These are essentially black silk sacks, with holes cut for the eyes, large enough to drape over a man's head. The eyeholes are circled in white paint, and they present a fearful appearance from a distance—up close they seem slightly clownish. But a phalanx of armed men in such garb would surely be intimidating to a wary enemy.

Still the wind does not blow.

No wind, but snow. It falls gently, and softens the gaps and angles of this broken town.

A few gusts today, not sufficient for our advance.

Wind!—but the snow obscures all. We cannot march.

Clear skies this morning. Gusts fitful but freshening as the afternoon wears on. Will it last until dawn?

Julian says it will. He says it must. We advance in the morning, he says, wind or no.

6

At last, after a dark midnight, and much surreptitious preparation, I stood with Julian and the rest of the general staff in an earthen breastwork near the front lines. We sat at a crude table where two lamps burned while Julian read a letter from the Dutch commander—received that afternoon—offering terms of surrender, "given your present unsustainable occupation of a town the jurisdiction of which is bound to pass to us sooner or later." The Mitteleuropan general, whose name was Vierheller,* said that we would all be well-treated, and eventually exchanged back to American territory "at the cessation of hostilities,"† so long as our surrender was not conditional.

"They grew back their spine," a regimental commander commented.

Julian had been forced to brief his staff on the nature of the "Chinese weapon," though he kept some details to himself. They understood that it would terrify the Dutch, but that any weakness or confusion it excited would have to be quickly and efficiently exploited. For most of these commanders the attack would be purely conventional, conducted along traditional military lines.

"They still fear us a little, I think," said Julian. "Perhaps we can remind them why they should."

Thus there was a small overture to the drama he had planned. An hour after midnight he sent his crew of Tubemen as close to the front as they could safely go. The Dutch army was encamped on the plain beyond the hills where we had built our defenses. We had seen their fires burning like countless stars in the darkness, and heard the sound of their threatening maneuvers. Tonight they slept; but Julian meant to wake them. He ordered the Tubemen to begin their ruckus, orchestrating them as if they were a musical act. The eerie noise did not commence abruptly, but started with a lone man generating a single hollow note, soon joined by others, and others still, and so on, until the whole blended chorus, which suggested the cries of unquiet souls hired out for temporary labor by entrepreneurial demons, was carried to the ears of the enemy infantry, who no doubt stirred from their sleep in profound consternation. All across the lowlands the Dutch soldiers must have startled awake and grasped their rifles and peered anxiously into the wintry darkness, though there was nothing to see but a few chill stars in a moonless sky.

"Let that keep them for a while," Julian said with some satisfaction, when the noise at last faded.

---

* Perhaps the Mitteleuropans know how to pronounce this jaw-cracker—I do not.
† Hostilities which had not ceased for decades, and showed no sign of doing so now, which weakened the argument somewhat.

"What do you suppose they'll make of it?"

"Something dire. I mean to play on their imaginations. What do you suppose a Dutch infantryman pictures when he contemplates the rumor of a secret Chinese weapon?"

"I'm sure I don't know."

"Nor do I; but I expect his imagination will have been shaped by stories of ancient European wars, which were fought with all sorts of fanciful and terrifying weapons, including aircraft and poison gas. I hope the sound of the Tubemen gives some vague inspiration to these nightmares, and that the Black Kites will confirm them. We'll know soon enough, in any case."

I cleaned and oiled my Pittsburgh rifle by lamplight while we waited, and I kept a generous supply of ammunition handy, for even the Major General's staff would not be exempted from the coming battle—every able-bodied American soldier in the vicinity would be pressed into action before the day was done.

Julian could not give orders from the rear echelons. The kites were to be launched from behind a low rill, set about with earthen lunettes and perilously close to the Dutch lines. The effect would be most useful coming in utter darkness, so we had to launch well before dawn, even before the false glow that precedes the rising sun; and our regiments were prepared to advance at first light. Julian stood in our frozen trench, or paced back and forth in it, consulting his Army watch and an almanac for the precise hour of sunrise. He muttered to himself at length; and with the collar of his coat turned up, and his yellow beard flecked with motes of ice, he looked far older than his years.

His adjutants and sub-commanders waited impatiently for Julian to read the auspices. At last he looked up from his watch and gave a pallid smile. "All right," he said. "Better too early than too late."

With that he went up to the very edge of the battlements and ordered the Stringmen to stand by their reels and the Furlers to "loft up."

The effort proceeded much as it had on the rooftop in Striver, though with certain important variations. At the warehouse the kites had been loaded with buckets of sand. Tonight there were heavy skin bags attached to their bridles. I asked Julian what the bags contained.

"Anything noxious we could find," he said. "Some contain pure caustic soda or industrial solvents. Some are filled with liquid bleach, some with waste from the tannery or the field hospital. Some have lice powder in them, and others are stuffed with ground glass."

The bags had been broadly daubed with luminous paint, just as the buckets had been. Otherwise there would have been nothing to see, nor any way to judge the kites' ascent. I had worried about the wind, which was capricious; but just lately it had picked up speed and was blowing gustily. The kites unfurled with loud, crisp bangs. They rose, tested their luggage, hesitated. Then the glowing cargo swept skyward with terrifying speed.

Julian quickly called on the Tubemen to begin their whirling again, to make sure the Dutch were on alert.

I cannot say to what height the kites flew, but their clever design kept them level with one another and stable in flight. They appeared as a hundred and more eerie, bobbing green lights, risen above the crowded Mitteleuropan army camp like rogue stars. To an enemy infantryman it would have been impossible to gauge the true size or proximity of the phenomenon—which was why Julian had worked so hard to fertilize the Dutch imagination with hints and legends.

Certainly the kites didn't go unnoticed. Almost immediately enemy trumpets began to sound, loudly enough that the howling of the Tubemen did not entirely drown them out. Peeking through an embrasure in the earthen embankment where we sheltered, I saw lanterns flicker in the staff tents of the Mitteleuropan camp. A few stray shots were fired in haste. I cupped my mouth in my hands and leaned toward Julian's ear. "Won't they shoot down the kites, Julian?"

"Not yet—they're too high. And when they *do* shoot, Adam, they won't aim at the *kites,* which are more or less invisible, but at their *cargo.*"

The chief Stringman called out numbers from his immense twine-reel, which had been calibrated to gauge the amount of line paid out. The other Stringmen presumably kept pace, while Julian worked numbers with a pencil and a paper pad,* and the hempen twine bucked and sang at the anchored reels.

At last Julian reached the conclusion of his figuring and sent out the order to "lax line." The Stringmen let their cord play out freely a moment longer, then braked the reels with wooden chocks.

The luminous, toxic cargo glided closer to the enemy infantry, and fresh rifle shots rang out.

These increased in volume and intensity. Peering across the flat expanse of darkness where the Dutch were encamped I could see the flash of rifle fire as if it were the play of lightning inside a thunder-cloud—a vast, wide *crackling* of rifle fire, shockingly intense.

The Tubemen increased their hooting to a high unholy pitch. I expect all this show intimidated the Mitteleuropans—in fact it was beginning to intimidate me. Those Dutch rifles, though aimed at the kites, were pointed roughly in our direction, and bullets began to drop out of the sky around us, not entirely harmlessly. Hails of them fell against the earthen embankments.

---

* To this day I don't understand how Julian was able to estimate the kites' position by noting their apparent height above the horizon and the amount of string paid out. It seemed like black magic; though it involved numbers, not spells or toad's-feet or any such occult contrivances.

In the sky to the east of us, the luminous floating targets jerked and danced as they were struck and struck again.

I pictured in my mind what must be happening on the field of battle. I reminded myself that the Dutch had intercepted the letter Julian entrusted to Private Langers, and that what they perceived was not a theatrical effect but the actions of (in Julian's words as I had transcribed them) a HELLISH and SATANIC DEVICE, insidious in its LINGERING EFFECTS. As the skin bags were perforated and finally obliterated by volleys of bullets they released into the night air their unpleasant contents, which descended onto the fearful infantrymen like a ghastly dew.

"Light on the eastern horizon, sir," an adjutant soon reported to Julian. I looked and detected a brightening there, the air-glow of the coming dawn.

"Reel in!" Julian ordered.

Even such feeble first light soon made the battlefield more visible. A few of the Black Kites had been battered beyond utility, or had their strings cut by rifle fire, and these had fallen like enormous wounded bats among the Dutch. But the Mitteleuropan troops weren't paying much attention to the fallen kites—in fact they were running aimlessly, many of them.

I tried to put myself in the shoes of one of those soldiers and imagine it from his point of view. Woken from a troubled sleep by an unearthly keening, he's called out into the darkness and finds a great number of peculiar Flying Lights descending on his encampment. All manner of fears and fancies compete for his attention. He's grateful when the order to fire freely rings out, and he lifts his Dutch rifle—let's say he's a marksman—and discharges round after round at the eerie targets above him. If his aim isn't accurate, it doesn't matter; a thousand men like him are doing just the same thing.

The shooting bolsters his courage. But before long he perceives a certain rank *scent,* unpleasant but unidentifiable, composed (though he doesn't know it) of all the poisons Julian's men have sent aloft: powders for killing rats, solvents for paint, lye for soap, offal from the field hospital. . . . A drop of *something* touches his exposed skin, and tingles or burns there. He squints once more into the night sky; his eyes are doused with caustic agents; he weeps involuntarily, and cannot see. . . .

There was not enough of toxins and poisons in those bags to kill an army of Dutchmen, perhaps not enough to kill even *one* Dutchman, barring a lucky chance. But our hypothetical soldier chokes, he sweats, he fancies himself murdered or at least mortally tainted. It's not a threat he can contain or confront. It comes out of the night like a supernatural visitation. All he can do, in the end, is run from it.

He's not alone in reaching this conclusion.

I looked out on the Dutch encampments and saw chaos. First light could do nothing to dispel the fears Julian had so adroitly conjured. And Julian's conjuring wasn't finished. "Fire canister!" he cried, and the order was swiftly conveyed to our artillery emplacements. Evidently Julian had ordered certain canister shells to be filled with (as he later described it to me) a combination of *flea powder* and *red dye*. These exploded in huge clouds of amber dust, which the wind carried among the Dutch infantry in swirling clouds—harmlessly; but the Dutch reckoned the shells to be full of potent poison, and they fled from them the way they would never have fled a conventional artillery barrage.

The Mitteleuropan commanders rode among the men on horses, trying to rally their troops; but it was soon clear that the Dutch middle had collapsed, creating an opening for an American advance.

Julian ordered the attack at once. Moments later an entire regiment of American infantry, wearing black silken hoods over their heads, stormed out of our trenches and lunettes, hooting ferociously and wielding Pittsburgh rifles and a few invaluable Trench Sweepers.

The Dutch commander panicked and threw all his forces against us in an attempt to hold the center. Julian had anticipated this, and quickly directed our cavalry to ride against the Dutch flanks. The American cavalry were hungry men on hungry horses, but their charge was effective. More Trench Sweepers were brought to bear. The watery sun, when it finally broached the horizon, peered down on bloody carnage.

Our entire army was poised to break out, the infantry and cavalry in front, supply wagons and the portable wounded behind them, more infantry and cavalry at the rear for protection. "Ride with me, Adam!" Julian cried; and two slat-ribbed stallions were brought up, with saddles and provisions and ammunition bags; and we galloped eastward behind a brave flourish of regimental flags.

I had seen desperate battles before, of course, but there was something especially gaudy and terrible about this one.

We came down behind the advance regiments into a tumbled and ravaged land. The Dutch emplacements, now abandoned, were a hazard to us, and many horses stumbled into trenches or craters and died of their injuries. The aftermath of that first advance, along with the residue of Julian's Black Kites, had created a charnel-ground abandoned by all but the dead. Dutch troops cut down by Trench Sweepers lay in place, their bodies contorted by their dying exertions. The colored-powder canister barrage had painted the trampled snow with scarlet plumes, and the stink of the various aerial emoluments combined into one acrid, excremental, chemical vapor which even in its dissipated state caused our own eyes to water freely.

Julian rode past companies of foot-soldiers toward the front, pausing at one point to take up the Battle Flag of the Goose Bay Campaign. This was an ennobling sight, in spite of (or *because of*) the tattered condition of the flag.

WE HAVE WALKED UPON THE MOON, the banner declared, and we might have been marching on the Moon right now for all the desolation around us; though the Moon, I suppose, is not pockmarked with crude abattises and open latrines. Every infantry company we passed took pleasure in the sight of the banner, and cries of "Julian Conqueror!" were commonplace.

We came into a lightly forested, complex terrain. The wind, for which we had prayed so fervently and which we had so eagerly welcomed, became a nuisance as the day progressed. Low clouds raced across the sky in gusts and gales, scouring old snow into the air and bringing fresh squalls. The Dutch army had fled before us, but we didn't pursue them; our objective was escape, not confrontation, and for a time the only fighting was sporadic, as we encountered straggling Mitteleuropan infantrymen and overwhelmed them.

But the Mitteleuropan commander was no fool, and as the snow impeded our progress he was busy rallying his troops in their fall-back positions. Our first hint of this was the sound of gunfire in the snowy haze to the east of us—I took it for just another skirmish, though Julian frowned and pressed his mount to greater speed.

In our eagerness to escape Striver we had allowed our forces to disperse somewhat, and now it seemed our vanguard had fallen into a trap. The sound of rifle fire swelled rapidly, and as we galloped toward it we began to see casualties flowing back on us in limping lines. Full battle ahead, one soldier warned us, "and the Dutch aren't running anymore, sir—they're standing fast!"

Julian established a rough command headquarters near the fighting and quickly organized his staff. Scouts reported that the American vanguard had marched into a declivity on the road and come under sustained fire from protected positions; before they could entrench or retreat, shells exploded in their midst. They were falling back by companies, in a state of confusion.

Julian did what he could. He ordered his artillery up. He consulted his maps, and tried to anchor his lines securely, though the terrain was flat and unsuitable. Before long one of his adjutants announced that the sparse American right wing had entirely collapsed and the Mitteleuropans were rolling it up.

I could hear the artillery and the rifle fire—it was noticeably closer now. Dutch shells began to fall perilously near to us. We were in danger of being overrun by our own troops, should the battle become a rout.

Julian barked ferociously at the Lieutenant who first counseled retreat. It was not at all certain that we could return to Striver safely—and then we would only be under siege again, with our numbers depleted and our provisions exhausted. Striver was a prison, and our whole purpose had been to break out of it. But more messengers arrived with increasingly bad news, and when a shell knocked down the crude shelter around us Julian finally admitted the impossibility of sustaining the advance. The Dutch had regained all their courage, and had checked us effectively, and there were no more pantomime weapons to throw at them.

The realization that his plan had failed drove Julian to his lowest ebb. He had been fed no more generously than the rest of us, and several times I had to stand beside him as he consulted with his adjutants, and take his arm to support him when his physical weakness crested. There was in Julian a fierce, almost supernatural strength; I had seen it sustain him through terrible battles before this one; but even that strength had its limit, which he seemed to have just about reached. "I'm cold, Adam," he whispered to me as the day advanced, "and the dead are all around—so many dead!"

"We have to extract all the survivors we can," I told him.

"So they can have the privilege of dying *later* rather than *sooner*," he muttered; but the admonition worked to brace him. He reached down into the deepest part of himself, as it seemed, and discovered there a last reserve of courage.

"Bring me the campaign flag," he told the nearest adjutant, "and my horse, and sound a general retreat."

I wish I could paint a word-picture vivid enough to convey the nightmare of our Retreat to Striver. I have neither the skill or the stomach for it, however. It isn't that these images are lost to me, for they return, on a regular basis in my sleep, and I often awake sweating or shouting from their thrall. But I cannot bear to set them down on the page with minute fidelity.

Suffice to say that we rode through Tartarus with the Devil at our backs, fighting all the way.

Days were short in Labrador at that time of year. The light we had greeted so optimistically at dawn grew thin and watery. Julian, still drawing on his deepest wells of strength, carried the battle pennon high and fought alongside the rear-guard. I fought beside him, on horseback, as we gave up land that hours earlier we had won and watered with American blood. Dutch bullets flew around us like lethal insects, and—as at the Battle of Mascouche, so long ago—Julian seemed, at first, invulnerable to them.

But only at first. He could not remain wholly unperforated, in a flurry of lead that made his campaign banner a tattered and illegible rag.

I was next to him when a bullet pierced the cloth of his uniform coat about the shoulder. The wound was not grave, but it numbed the arm; and the banner with its proud boast slipped from his grasp. The faded image of the Moon was trodden on by his horse's hooves as he slumped in the saddle.

"Julian!" I called out.

He turned to the sound of my voice, an apologetic expression on his face. Then a second bullet struck him, and his mouth filled with blood.

7

After dark, the Dutch were in no hurry to chase us—they knew where we were going, and would be content to "mop us up" at their leisure. Thus some fraction of the army that had marched out of Striver arrived back by moonlight, battered and hungry, and took up positions along their old defensive lines. And in the town itself, Dr. Linch—the only one of our physicians to have survived the attempted break-out—set up a diminished version of his old field hospital. His only supplies were a handful of knives and saws, a few bottles of medicinal brandy and liquid opium, and some needles and thread scavenged from the ruin of a tailor's shop. He boiled water over a stove in which he burned scraps of broken furniture.

He looked at me vaguely when I brought Julian to him. His own exhaustion had just about overcome him. I had to remind him of the urgency of his work, and of the necessity of saving Julian's life.

He hesitated, then nodded. I carried Julian into the shell of the old field hospital, past corpses piled like cords for a bonfire. Linch examined Julian's wounds by lantern light.

"The shoulder is only a flesh wound," he said. "The wound to his face is more serious. The bullet tore away a part of his cheek, and two of his molars are shattered. At that, he's lucky it wasn't worse." He paused and smiled—it was a mirthless, bitter smile, such as I hoped never to see again. "I'd say he might recover, if we had food to give him, or real warmth, or shelter."

"Will you sew his cheek, in any case?"

"No," said Dr. Linch. "There are men whose suffering is more intense, and they deserve my attention—and don't mention the name Comstock, as if *that* had any claim on my sympathies. If you want him sewn up, Adam Hazzard, do it yourself. You've assisted me often enough. You know how it's done."

He gave me a needle and thread and left a lantern for me.

Julian remained insensible with shock as I worked on him, though he moaned once or twice. It was not pleasant to press a threaded needle through his lacerated skin—to dab the blood away in order to judge my own work—and then do it again—and yet again—until a rough seam drew the tissues together, effectively if not handsomely. I could do nothing about his cracked and shattered teeth except, at Dr. Linch's suggestion, to pack the damaged area with cotton. Much blood was spilled during this exercise. It covered my clothing; and the loss of it left Julian breathless.

Dr. Linch, returning, gave him a weak preparation of opium. I sat with Julian through the dark hours, and stoked the stove when the night wind cut too close.

In the morning the shelling resumed with fresh vigor, as if the Dutch meant to punish us for the impudence of our attempted escape. Or perhaps they were just anxious to finish the work of killing us, and get on with their regular business.

Julian spat clotted blood until noon. His distress was palpable, but he couldn't speak. Eventually he gestured for a paper and pencil.

I kept these items with me habitually, as a writer should,[*] and handed them to him.

He wrote, in quavering capitals, a demand for

MORE OPIUM.

I went and canvassed Dr. Linch, but the news I carried back to my friend's bedside wasn't good. "There's very little opium left, Julian. The doctor is reserving it for the worst cases."

MORE,

wrote Julian.

"There *is* no more—can't you hear me?"

He was an awful sight, twig-thin, linen-white, his injuries brown with stale blood, blood congealed on his dusty yellow beard. His eyes rolled in their sockets.

I SHOULD HAVE DIED,

he wrote.

But after a while he slept.

The next day our surviving troops retreated to their final defensive position, in a close perimeter around the town. The noose had fully tightened on us, in other words. The word "surrender" was mooted about; but it had not yet come to that . . . not while there were still trail-crackers to eat . . . but those wouldn't last long.

---

[*] Even one who owns a typewriter, for those machines are not convenient to carry in one's pocket.

I softened hardtack in water until it was soggy and dropped small morsels of it into Julian's mouth, which was the only way he could eat in his present condition. He took some nourishment that way, but refused it when the pain became intolerable.

I asked him whether he had any orders for the men.

NO ORDERS (he wrote)
NOTHING LEFT
WHY WOULD THEY WANT MY ORDERS?

"Because you're their commander, Julian. Even if our attack didn't succeed, the men recognize it as a noble attempt—better than they could have made without you."

FAILURE

"The Dutch were reinforced. It's no one's fault we couldn't overwhelm them. It was a glorious effort—it will be remembered as such."

FOOLISH
NO ONE TO REMEMBER
WE WON'T LEAVE HERE ALIVE

"Don't say so!" I pleaded with him. "We will go home—we must! Calyxa needs me—she's having problems with the Dominion. Perhaps that Deacon from Colorado wants to torture her. Also, she's—that is—I haven't told anyone yet, Julian, but—she's going to have a child!"

He stared at me. Then he took up the pencil and paper again.

YOUR CHILD?

"Of course my child!—what else would it be?"
He wrote, after another pause,

GOOD NEWS
CONGRATULATIONS
WOULD SMILE IF I COULD
OF COURSE YOU'LL GO HOME

"Thank you, Julian. You'll come home with me, and we'll see that baby born. You'll be its uncle, in effect; and you can hold it on your knee and feed it mashy apples if you like."

GODFATHER?

"Yes, if you'll accept the nomination!"

CLOSE TO GOD AS I'LL GET,

he wrote, and then laid back against the wooden slats that served him as a bed. His eyes closed, and his wounds seeped pinkish fluids.

8

The next day looked to be our last, despite the optimism I had tried to impress upon Julian. The shelling of Striver intensified. The Dutch barrages reached every part of the town, and I was often bathed in plaster shaken from the ceiling while I tended to Julian's needs.

His adjutants and junior colonels had stopped begging him for orders—he was too badly hurt to lead, and anyway there were no useful orders to give. The Army of the Laurentians, Northern Division, had become a sort of automaton, firing reflexively whenever a target presented itself. That couldn't continue—our last supplies of ammunition had been tapped.

It was a cold day, clear and windless. Julian slept fitfully whenever the cannonade permitted; and I slept, often enough, on the chair beside him.

I was awake, however, and Julian was asleep, when a freshly-promoted Lieutenant rushed into the room. "General Comstock!" the man exclaimed.

"Quiet, Lieutenant—the General's napping, and he needs his rest—what's the matter?"

"Sorry, Colonel Hazzard, but I was sent to report—that is, we've seen—"

"What? Some new Dutch outrage? If our defenses have collapsed there's no need to trouble Julian Comstock about it. He's in no position to help, though he would, if he could."

"It's not that, sir. *Sails!*"

"I beg your pardon?"

"*Sails*, sir! We've sighted *sails*, coming down Lake Melville from the east!"

"Dutch sails?"

"Sir, it's hard to be sure, but the lookouts think not—in fact it looks like Admiral Fairfield's fleet! The Navy has come for us at last, sir!"

I found I couldn't speak. There is a species of *release from fear* that in its effect is as unmanning as fear itself. I covered my face with my hands to conceal my emotion.

"Sir?" the Lieutenant said. "Aren't you going to tell the General?"

"As soon as it's confirmed," I managed to say. "I wouldn't like to disappoint him."

But I couldn't wait for an adjutant's word. I left Julian sleeping and climbed up to the top of the hospital.

The hospital, in better days, had been a Dutch shop, with apartments overhead, located at the shoreward end of Portage Street. It had lost its roof in the battle, and the second story had become an open platform, exposed to the elements. It afforded a good view of the harbor. I stood in the empty casing of a shattered window, gazing off across the lake.

The sails hove into view soon enough. Without a spyglass I couldn't discern the colors they were flying, and I feared some new Mitteleuropan attack despite the Lieutenant's encouraging words. Then the outline of the nearest vessel began to seem familiar to me, and my heart fluttered a little.

She was the *Basilisk*—the beloved *Basilisk*—Admiral Fairfield's flagship.

I was grateful, and I addressed my prayerful thanks to the slate-gray sky and the surging clouds, or whatever lay beyond them.

Lake Melville was too salt to freeze entirely, but fringes of ice had formed at the edges of it, and the Navy couldn't anchor as close to shore as they might have liked; but there were gaps of open water where her boats could freely move. An advance party quickly gauged the extremity of our situation, and communicated details to the *Basilisk* by signal-flags; and before long that ship, along with the others of the fleet, began to fire shells which flew above Striver and dropped into the Dutch lines with telling accuracy. The bombardment was continuous; it drove the Mitteleuropans back a mile or more from their forward entrenchments; and the sound of it was what finally woke Julian from his profound sleep.

He was afraid we were about to be assaulted by the enemy, and I soothed him by giving him the good news.

He was less cheered by it than I expected. He took up pencil and paper and wrote:

ARE WE SAVED?

"Yes, Julian, that's what I've been trying to tell you! The men are coming into the streets, cheering!"

USELESS THEN I MEAN OUR ATTEMPT TO BREAK THROUGH

"Well, but how could we have known—?"

HOW MANY DEAD FOR NO PURPOSE
HUNDREDS THOUSANDS
STILL ALIVE IF ONLY I HAD WAITED

"That's not the way to think of it, Julian!"

BLOOD ON MY HANDS

"No—you were magnificent!"

He refused to be convinced.

An adjutant arrived with word that the Admiral wanted to see Julian, in order to begin to plan the evacuation of our troops from Striver.

TELL HIM I'M NOT IN,

Julian wrote; but he didn't mean it—it was only his injuries speaking.

The Admiral was promptly admitted.

It was so heartening to see the old naval officer again that I nearly wept. His uniform was so bright and bold, compared to our tattered rags, that he seemed to have descended from a distant Valhalla well-supplied with patriotic tailors. He looked at Julian with the knowledgeable sympathy of a man who had seen injured men, and worse, many times before. "Don't rise," he said, as Julian struggled to sit straight up and essay a salute. "And don't try to speak, if your wounds make it difficult."

I CAN WRITE,

Julian hastily set down, and I read the message to Admiral Fairfield on his behalf.

"Well," said Fairfield, "there is not much to say that can't wait a short while. The important thing is that your men have been rescued—the siege is lifted."

TOO LATE,

wrote Julian, but I couldn't communicate anything so pessimistic to the Admiral. "Julian thanks you," I said, ignoring the looks he shot in my direction. The expression was all in his eyes, since Julian's jaw was too badly hurt to move—even a frown would have wounded him.

"No thanks are called for. In fact I apologize for delaying as long as we have."

DEKLAN MEANT FOR ME TO DIE HERE
A WELL-LAID PLAN
WHAT CHANGED?

"Julian says he can hardly accept your apology. He does wonder what circumstances made this rescue possible."

"Of course—I forget you've been cut off from all news," the Admiral said. "The order that kept us out of Lake Melville was rescinded."

DEKLAN MUST BE DEAD

"Julian asks about the health of his uncle."

"That's the key to it," Admiral Fairfield said, nodding. "The plain fact is, Deklan Conqueror has been deposed. In part it was because of the reports of the Goose Bay campaign you sent out when the *Basilisk* last saw these shores, Colonel Hazzard. The *Spark* published them in the ignorant belief that Deklan Conqueror would want Julian's heroism widely publicized. But it was obvious enough, reading between the lines, that Julian had been betrayed by the Executive Branch. The Army of the Laurentians was already profoundly unhappy about Deklan's misrule and arrogance—the balance was finally tipped."

DID THEY KILL HIM?

"Was Deklan Conqueror's abdication wholly voluntary?" I asked.

"It wasn't voluntary at all. A brigade came down from the Laurentians and marched on the Presidential Palace. The Republican Guard chose not to resist—their opinion of Deklan Comstock is no higher than anyone else's."

DOES THE MURDERER YET LIVE?

"Was Julian's uncle injured in the process?"

"He's a prisoner in the Palace for the time being."

WHO TAKES COMMAND OF THE PRESIDENCY?

"Has a successor been named?"

Here Admiral Fairfield looked somewhat abashed. "I wish I had a more ceremonial way to convey the information," he said, "and a venue for it grander than this ruined building, but—yes," he said, looking Julian hard in the eye, "*a successor has been named,* pending my confirmation that he has survived. That successor is *you,* General Comstock. Or I should say *President* Comstock. Or *Julian Conqueror,* as the infantry like to style you."

Julian sank back into his rude bed, his eyes clenched shut. All color fled from his face. I expect Admiral Fairfield took this as an expression of pain or shock due to his injury. There was an embarrassed silence. Then Julian gestured for the pad and pencil again.

THIS IS WORSE THAN DEATH (he wrote)
I WISH THE DUTCH HAD KILLED ME
OH GOD NO
TELL HIM GO TO HELL
ALL OF THEM GO TO HELL
I WILL NOT SERVE

"Julian is too feverish to express his astonishment," I said. "He's humbled by the honor so unexpectedly bestowed upon him, and hopes he'll prove worthy of it. But he's tired now, and needs to rest."

"Thank you," the Admiral said to me, and "Thank you, Mr. President," to Julian.

ACT FIVE

JULIAN CONQUEROR,
including
"THE LIFE AND ADVENTURES OF THE GREAT NATURALIST CHARLES DARWIN"

CHRISTMAS, 2174–CHRISTMAS, 2175

Ever the Virtues blush to find
The Vices wearing their badge behind,
And Graces and Charities feel the fire
Wherein the sins of the age expire.

—WHITTIER

1

It falls to me now to write the final chapter of my story, which is an account of the reign of Julian Conqueror, Commander in Chief of the Armed Forces and President of the United States, as I experienced it, with all its attendant tragedies and conciliatory joys.

Those events are still close to my heart, though considerable time has passed since their conclusion. My hand trembles at the task of describing them. But the reader and I have come this far, which is no small distance, and I mean to bring the project to completion, whatever the cost.

It occurs to me that one virtue of the Typewriter as a literary invention is that tears shed during the act of composition are less likely to fall upon the paper and blot the ink. A certain clarity is preserved, not otherwise obtainable.

2

Manhattan was all got up for the celebration of the Nativity when we arrived at the docks, and such a frenzy of decoration I had never seen, as if the city were a Christmas tree decked with candles and colored tinsel, with the Sacred Day less than forty-eight hours distant—but all of that meant little or nothing to me, for I was anxious to discover the fate of Calyxa.

Julian and I, along with the other survivors of the Goose Bay Campaign, had recuperated for three weeks at the American hospital in St. John's. Fresh food, clean linen, and boiled water restored us to health as effectively as any medicine could; and Julian's facial wound, though my stitching of it was inexpert, had nearly healed. Evidence of my inadequacy as a physician would persist in the form of a scar that curved between Julian's jaw-hinge and his right nostril like a second mouth, primly and permanently shut. But that was little enough, as war wounds go, and Julian had never been vain about his appearance.

His mood had also improved, or at least he had wrestled down his pessimism. Whatever the reason, he had given up his initial resistance and submitted to all the plans the Army of the Laurentians had laid for him. He was willing, he had told me, to assume the Office of the Presidency, at least for a time, if only to undo a fraction of the wickedness his uncle had committed.

The appointment to the Executive was none of his doing, of course. It had come about in his absence, and his name had been put up as a compromise. My early dispatches to the *Spark,* carried out of Striver on board the *Basilisk* after the Battle of Goose Bay, may have played a role in these developments. No doubt Deklan Comstock would have preferred to have the news of Julian's survival suppressed; but the editors of the *Spark* didn't know that, and assumed they were doing the President a favor by publicizing his nephew's heroism and hard times.

Those news items were widely reprinted. The American public, at least in the eastern half of the country, had become enamored of Julian Comstock as a youthful National Hero; and his reputation was equally golden among the forces of the Army of the Laurentians. Meanwhile, in the higher echelons of the military, resentment of Deklan's war policies had heated up to the boiling point. Deklan had mismanaged so many audacious but ill-designed Campaigns, and jailed so many loyal and spotless Generals, that the Army had resolved to unseat him and replace him with someone more sympathetic to their goals. The publication of my reports helped stoke that smoldering fire to a white-hot intensity.*

All that stood in the way of a military overthrow of Julian's uncle was the choice of a plausible successor, always a ticklish business. An acceptable candidate can be difficult to procure. A tyrant's overthrow by military action doesn't admit of any formal democratic choice, and important contesting interests—the Eupatridians, the Senate, the Dominion of Jesus Christ on Earth, even in some sense the general public—have to be addressed and mollified.

The Army of the Laurentians could not meet all these conditions, nor could it readily obtain the consent of its distant partner, the Army of the Californias, which was much more a creature of the Dominion than the Eastern army. But the necessity of replacing Deklan Conqueror was admitted by all. The solution eventually reached was a temporary one. Succession by dynastic inheritance was allowed under the 52nd Amendment to the Constitution;† and since Deklan was childless, that mantle could be construed as falling to his heroic nephew Julian—who at the time was caught up in the Siege of Striver, and wouldn't complicate matters either by accepting or by declining. Thus Julian had become a *figurehead*, almost an *abstraction*, and acceptable in that form, until the tyrant was hauled out of his throne room by soldiers and clapped into a basement prison.

Now that Julian had survived the siege, however, and since he had been rescued by the single-minded efforts of Admiral Fairfield, the *abstract* threatened to become uncomfortably *real*. Had Julian been killed, some other arrangement would have been made, perhaps to everyone's greater satisfaction. But Julian Conqueror lived—and the public sentiment on his behalf had grown so clamorous that it would have been impossible *not* to install him in the Presidency, for fear of triggering riots.

For that reason he had been surrounded, both during his recovery and on the voyage back to New York City, by a phalanx of military advisors, civilian consultants, clerical toadies, and a thousand other brands of manipulators and office-seekers. My opportunities to speak to him privately had been few, and when we arrived in Manhattan he was quickly enclosed in a mob of Senators and beribboned soldiers, and borne away toward the Presidential Palace; and I could not even say goodbye, or arrange a time to meet once more.

---

* I did not, in my dispatches, condemn Deklan Conqueror by name, or even mention him; but it was possible to infer from what I wrote that the Lake Melville campaign had been mismanaged from New York. I did record a few cynical comments of Julian's directed toward "those who cut orders without considering them first, and would make history without having read any." I thought this barb at the President would be blunted by its obscurity—I may have been mistaken.

† Not the 53rd—that's a common mistake. It was the 52nd Amendment that allowed succession by inheritance; the 53rd was the one that abolished the Supreme Court.

But that wasn't a pressing problem—it was Calyxa who was foremost on my mind. I had written her several letters from the hospital in St. John's, and even telegraphed her once, but she hadn't responded, and I feared the worst.

I made my way from the docks to the luxurious brown-stone house of Emily Baines Comstock, where I had left Calyxa in the care of Julian's mother. It was heartening to see that familiar building, apparently unchanged, bathed in the glow of a Manhattan dusk, as sturdy a habitation as it had ever been, with lantern light glinting sweetly at the curtained windows.

But as I approached the walk a soldier stepped out of the shadows and raised his hand. "No admittance, sir," he said.

That was astonishing; and I was outraged, as soon as I was sure I had understood the man correctly. "Get out of my way. That's an order," I added, since my Colonel's stripes were intact and plainly visible.

The soldier blanched but didn't stand down. He was a young man, probably a fresh draftee, a lease-boy hauled out of some southern Estate, judging by the accent in his voice. "Sorry, Colonel, but I have my orders—very strict—no one to be admitted without authorization."

"My wife is in this house, or was, or ought to be—what under heaven are *you* doing here?"

"Preventing exit or entry, sir."

"By what authority?"

"Writ of Ecclesiastical Quarantine."

"That's a mouthful! What's it signify?"

"Don't precisely know, sir," the soldier confessed. "I'm new at this."

"Well, where do these orders emanate from?"

"My superior officer down at the Fifth Avenue headquarters, most directly; but I think it has something to do with the Dominion. 'Ecclesiastical' means 'church,' don't it?"

"I expect it does. . . . Who is inside, that you're guarding so adamantly?"

"Only a couple of women."

My heart beat twice, but I pretended to keep aloof. "Your dangerous prisoners are women?"

"I deliver food parcels to them now and again . . . women, sir, yes, sir, a young one and an old one. I don't know anything about their crimes. They don't seem hateful, or especially dangerous, though they're a little short-tempered now and then, especially the younger female—she hardly speaks but it bites."

"They're in there now?"

"Yes, sir; but as I said, no admittance."

I couldn't contain myself any longer. I shouted Calyxa's name, at the greatest volume I could muster.

The guard cringed, and I saw his hand stray to the pistol on his hip. "I don't think that's allowed, sir!"

"Do your orders say anything about preventing a uniformed officer from shouting in the street?"

"I guess they don't, specifically, but—"

"Then, *specifically*, follow your orders as they were written—guard the door, if you have to, but don't improvise, and don't pay any attention to what's going on the sidewalk; the sidewalks of New York are not your kingdom right at the moment."

"Sir," the young man said, blushing; but he didn't contradict me, and I called out Calyxa's name several more times, until the head of my beloved wife at last appeared at an upstairs window.

I could hardly contain my happiness at the sight of her. How often I had imagined seeing her again, during the long Goose Bay Campaign! Calyxa's form, recalled in the interlude between waking and sleep, had become a deity to which I inclined as predictably as any Mohammedan to Mecca. Framed in the upstairs window of Mrs. Comstock's stone house she looked at least as lovely as any of my visions of her, though a little more impatient, which was not surprising.

I called out her name once more, just to feel the throb of it in my throat.

"Yes, it's me," she called back.

"I'm home from the war!"

"I see that! Can't you come in?"

"There's a guard on the door!"

"Well, that's the problem!" Calyxa turned away for a moment, then reappeared. "Mrs. Comstock is here also, though she doesn't like to shout at the window—she sends her regards."

"Why are you locked up? Is it the trouble with the Dominion you wrote to me about?"

"It's too long a story to bellow into the street, but Deacon Hollingshead is in back of it."

"Julian won't let this go on!"

"I hope he hears about it quickly, then."

The soldier on guard, during this exchange, peered at me with a frank curiosity, his jaw agape. I didn't enjoy his close attention. I wanted to ask Calyxa about our child—I wanted to proclaim my love for her—but the draftee's blunt stare, and the public circumstances in general, made me feel awkward about it. "Calyxa!" I called out. "I have to tell you—my affectionate feelings are not diminished—"

"Can't hear you!"

"Undiminished! Affection! Mine, for you!"

"Please don't waste time, Adam!"

She left her place at the window.

I turned to the guard, my cheeks burning. "Are you enjoying the show, soldier?"

But he was immune to irony, or had been raised somewhere outside its orbit. "Yes, sir," he said, "thank you for asking. It's quite a distraction. This is tedious work, as a rule."

"I'm sure it is. You look cold. Wouldn't you rather go someplace warm, take a meal perhaps, this close to Christmas?"

"I surely would; but my relief isn't due for two hours."

"Why don't I relieve you? I know I can't go inside—that would violate regulations—but I believe a ranking officer can assume an enlisted man's duties for a short period of time, as a kindness on a cold December night."

"Thank you, Colonel, but that dodge won't work. I can't afford to eat at my own expense. I haven't been paid since last month, with the turbulence in the government and all."

"There's a place around the corner that serves beef tongue and lozenged pork, piping hot. Here," I said, pulling a pair of Comstock dollars out of my pocket and pressing them into his palm, "go on, enjoy yourself, and Merry Christmas to you."

The recruit looked at the money with wide eyes, then clapped the coins into the pocket of his duffel coat. "I suppose I could leave the ladies in your custody for an hour or so—no more than that, though."

"I appreciate it, and I'll make sure they're safe when you get back."

Delicacy prevents me from recounting every detail of my reunion with Calyxa, but it was a warm and at times tearful meeting, and I made many demonstrations of my affection, and perceived with amazement and a melting pride the way her feminine form had softened and enlarged. Mrs. Comstock watched these displays with uncomplaining indulgence, until our intimacies began to embarrass her; then she said, "There are important subjects we need to discuss, Adam Hazzard, unless you mean to carry Calyxa off to the bridal chamber instantaneously."

I might have liked very much to do just that; but I submitted to the implied suggestion, and left off kissing my wife for a time.

"I've bribed the guard away," I said. "We can escape now, if you like."

"If it were a matter of bribery," said Mrs. Comstock, "we would have been away long ago—but where do you imagine we would go? We're not criminals, and I at least don't propose to behave like one."

"This is confusing to me," I confessed. "I'm less than two hours off the boat from Newfoundland, and I've had no answer to the letters I sent."

"They didn't arrive, or were turned back. And Julian is here as well?"

"That's what the ringing of the city bells was all about. He was carried off to the Executive Palace to be inaugurated, or whatever they do with new Presidents."

Mrs. Comstock was relieved to hear the news, so much so that she had to sit down and compose herself. It was a long moment until she took notice of me again. "I'm sorry, Adam," she said. "Take a chair and keep still while I explain the situation. Then we can discuss the important question of what to *do* about it."

Her explanation was discursive, with much back-tracking, and heated interjections from Calyxa, but the gist of it was this:

Since Deacon Hollingshead's arrival in town last July the Dominion had been hard at work, cleansing New York City of moral corruption.

"Corruption" is a popular word with the enthusiasts of the Dominion, usually uttered as a prelude to the knife, the docket, or the noose. In the present case it referred to the growing number of non-tithing churches in this city—churches, that is, which were not just unrecognized by the Dominion but disdained that recognition; for they regarded the Dominion as a worldly institution, feeding on forced donations while it suppressed genuine apostolic brotherhood and individual salvation in Christ.

I had heard of these renegade churches. They existed in all the large cities, but were especially common in Manhattan, where several varieties of them catered to the poor and malcontent, to the lowest echelons of mechanical workers, or to the Egyptians and other newly-arrived immigrants. But I could make no connection between these institutions and the confinement of Calyxa and Mrs. Comstock.

"We were *found in*," Calyxa said bluntly, interrupting Mrs. Comstock's more nuanced narrative.

"What do you mean, *found in*? Found in *what*?"

"It's a legal term," Mrs. Comstock said. "We were arrested with a dozen other people when one of these institutions was raided by Hollingshead and his clerical police—'found in attendance,' in other words."

"You were attending a renegade church?" That surprised me, since Mrs. Comstock's religious devotions in the past had been wholly conventional; and Calyxa, who was educated in a Catholic institution, often told me she had garnered from that experience just as much religion as she expected to need, and then some.

"Not for religious purposes," Calyxa said. "The church allowed its premises to be used for political meetings. I had been telling Mrs. Comstock about the idea of the Parmentierists, and she was interested, and we went there so she could take a sample."

"Isn't that an extenuating circumstance?"

"Not in Deacon Hollingshead's eyes," said Mrs. Comstock. "*Parmentierism* hardly constitutes an *alibi*, under the current regime. I almost suspect the Deacon pursued us for the explicit purpose of incriminating us. It may have been part of some scheme he worked up with the Executive before Deklan was deposed."

"But Deklan *is* deposed, and you're still confined to the house."

"Deacon Hollingshead is as powerful as ever, and a Writ of Ecclesiastical Quarantine isn't so easily suborned. Once issued, it tends to stick. We're only here, and not in jail along with all the other Found-Ins, because I am a Comstock, and Calyxa is pregnant."*

"Julian will fix it," I said.

"I expect he will," Mrs. Comstock said, "once he learns about it. He won't be easily reached, however, now that he's installed in the Executive Palace."

"I can find a way to him."

"I expect it won't be necessary. Julian has never failed to join me for Christmas, if he was in Manhattan, and I'm sure he'll send for me this year. In any case Calyxa isn't due until April, which means Hollingshead can't act until then. No, Adam, I have another commission for you, if you'll accept it."

I could hardly refuse, though this was all a surprise to me, and disorienting in its effects.

"My commission," Mrs. Comstock said, "involves Sam Godwin."

"Sam! I haven't seen Sam since Labrador. He was sent home with an injury. We asked after him at the military hospital in St. John's, but he had already passed through, bound for New York. He must have arrived long since—have you seen him? I would like to shake his hand again." *His remaining hand,* I thought, but did not say.

"I made similar inquiries," Mrs. Comstock told me, "and I know he arrived safely in the city, and spent some days at the Soldier's Rest, but he was released—and promptly vanished, or at least hasn't bothered to contact me. This isn't like him, Adam."

I agreed that it was not. "Perhaps I can find him, and solve the mystery."

"I hoped you would say so." She beamed. "Thank you, Adam Hazzard."

"You don't need to thank me. But what about the guard on the door? He'll be back before long, and I can't stay."

"Never mind the guard—he's harmless, and as prisons go this one is comfortable enough."

"Once I'm out of the house it might be difficult to get back in," I said. I didn't like the idea that I might be barred from my marital chamber for some indefinite time. It was cruel, if not unusual.

---

* The law preventing pregnant women from being jailed on suspicion, or prosecuted for proven crimes, dates from the era of the Plague of Infertility. For many years after the Fall of the Cities it seemed as if our human numbers might drop below some critical level—that we would become an extinct species, as so many other species had become extinct during the Efflorescence of Oil. That threat has receded, of course—our numbers are steadily increasing—but the law, along with a host of other laws and customs protecting female virtue and fertility, remains firmly in effect.

"Stay at the Soldier's Rest, if you have to, and say your goodbyes to Calyxa for the time being. We'll be together again on Christmas Day, I'm sure of it."

"Welcome home, Adam," Calyxa added, and she embraced me again; and we exchanged intimacies once more, until Mrs. Comstock indicated by the clearing of her throat and the rolling of her eyes that the time had come for me to leave—too soon!

The guard was returning as I came down the steps into the damp December air. "Thank you, Colonel," he said. "That was a fine meal, much appreciated, and Merry Christmas to you."

"Keep a firm watch on the house," I told him. "Be sure you don't let any villains in."

I passed the night at the Soldier's Rest near the docks. My rank entitled me to better accommodations than a common soldier would have received, though in practice this was just a cubicle containing a yellow mattress and a threadbare blanket. The bed and the blanket were infested with fleas, who took the opportunity to cavort at will and dine at leisure; and I slept fretfully, and hurried out as soon as the sky grew light.

Sam Godwin was in New York, or recently had been. That much was an established fact. I went to the Regimental headquarters, and the clerk there showed me a ledger which said Sam had been discharged as a wounded veteran. It listed a New York address where mail could be forwarded.

The address was in a disreputable neighborhood, not far from the Immigrant District. I went there directly. The houses in that location were mainly wooden frame structures crowded shoulder-to-shoulder, most of them divided up into rooms for rent, with here and there a tavern or hemp shop or gambling den in which degraded men could indulge their vices without traveling very far out of their way. Smoke poured from every chimney, for the day was cold. The thought of all those coal-grates and wood-stoves made me wary of fire, for these buildings were little more than tinder and brown paper, putting on airs of architecture.

I knocked at a ramshackle door, and after a while an elderly woman with pox scars on her face answered. When I asked for Sam Godwin she said, "I don't know any." But I pressed her with a description, and proclaimed him as my friend; and she relented and showed me to an upstairs room at the end of a lightless corridor.

The door was a little ajar. I pushed it and entered, calling out Sam's name.

He was asleep on a narrow bed no better than the one I had occupied during the night. He wore a ragged shirt, and he had pulled an old overcoat around himself to serve as a blanket. His face was drawn and haggard even in repose. His hair was thinner than I remembered it, his beard unkempt and almost entirely white. His left arm was curled under him and pressed against his belly as if to shelter his missing hand.

There was a bottle on the floor beside him, and on the battered night-table a long-stemmed pipe, and a wooden box with a few crumbs of dried hemp flowers in it.

I sat on the bed beside him. "Sam," I said. "Sam, wake up if you can hear me. It's me—it's Adam Hazzard."

A few repetitions of this and he began to stir. He groaned, and turned on his back, and sighed, and opened one eye warily, as if he anticipated bad news. At last the light of sensibility seemed to penetrate all the way to his inward parts, and he struggled to sit up. "Adam?" he mumbled in a hoarse voice.

"Yes, Sam, it's me."

"Adam—oh! I thought for a moment we were back in Labrador—is that the sound of *shelling*?"

"No, Sam. This is New York City, though not a very attractive neighbor-hood of it. The sound is just freight wagons out on the street."

He stared at me afresh as comprehension dawned. "Adam! But I left you at Striver. You and Julian. The *Basilisk* carried me away. . . ."

"It carried us away, too, Sam, a few weeks later, and after considerable tragedy and fuss."

"I thought—"

"What?"

"The situation was hopeless. Striver was meant to be a slaughterhouse, and seemed to serve the purpose. I thought—"

"That we had been killed?"

"That you had been killed, yes, and that I had failed in my commission of protecting Julian."

"Is that why you're living in these circumstances? But we're alive, Sam!—I'm alive, and Julian is alive. Have you looked at a newspaper lately?"

He shook his head. "Not for . . . weeks, I suppose. You mean to say Admiral Fairfield reinforced the divisions at Striver?"

"I mean to say that Deklan Comstock is no longer President! If you had poked your head out of this ugly den you might have seen the Army of the Laurentians marching to depose him!"

Sam, in his amazement, stood up suddenly, and then blushed, as he didn't have his trousers on. He took a crumpled pair from the floor and buttoned himself into respectability with a shaking hand. "Damn me for my inattention! *Deklan Comstock deposed!* And have they installed a new President?"

"Yes, Sam, they have . . . but perhaps you had better sit down again before I tell you about it."

I helped Sam dress himself, and comb his hair, and when he was relatively pre-sentable I took him to a nearby tavern, where we ordered eggs and toast from the kitchen. It wasn't gourmet fare—the butter was maggoty—but it was filling. Sam admitted that he had been alone since his return to Manhattan. It wasn't just his grief over Julian's presumed death that had caused him to hide himself away; it was the loss of his left hand, or the sense of wholeness and manliness that went with it. He ate efficiently with his right hand but kept his left forearm immobile in his lap, and he was careful at all times not to show the stump. He kept his chin down and avoided the eyes of other customers. I didn't mention his condition to him, or act as if I noticed it, and I thought by that strategy to distract him.

While he ate I shared the story of my adventures with Julian in Striver, and Julian's unexpected ascension to the Presidency. Sam was greatly interested, and thanked me repeatedly for relieving his mind about Julian. "Not that the Presidency is any kind of safe haven, God knows. I'm glad you came to me, Adam, and I thank you for the meal, but you had better leave me alone after this. I don't care to see people, as things stand. I'm not what I used to be. I'm of no value to Julian anymore. I'm a useless appendage."

"The problem is more pressing than that, Sam. Deacon Hollingshead has been making trouble for Calyxa. She and Julian's mother are both confined under guard, pending prosecution."

Sam's eyes, which until now had worn a moist, narcotized glaze, narrowed to a fine point. "Emily is in danger?"

"Potentially, yes—and Calyxa. It was Mrs. Comstock who asked me to find you."

"Emily!" He spoke the word in a tormented voice. "I don't want her to see me like this."

"Understandably; but we can buy you a bath and a haircut as soon as you finish your breakfast."

"I don't mean that!"

"But it might be a good idea in any case. Mrs. Comstock is particular about the odors of things."

"What I'm ashamed of, Adam, is nothing I can bathe away!"

He was talking about the stump of his arm, of course. "Emily Comstock doesn't care about that, Sam."

"Perhaps she doesn't—*I do*." He lowered his voice, though the pain in it was impossible to disguise. "There was a time after I left Striver when I prayed for the infection to kill me."

"That kind of prayer isn't welcome in Heaven, and I'm not surprised it wasn't answered."

"I'm less than a whole man."

"Did you feel that way about One-Leg Willy Bass, back when he was chasing us through the wilds of Athabaska? Seems to me you had considerable respect for him, though he lost more of his leg than you did of your arm."

The comparison appeared to startle him. "Willy Bass was nobody's cripple. But is that what you imagine I want, Adam—a career in the Reserves?"

"I don't pretend to guess what you want as a *career*, but don't you want to help Mrs. Comstock, when she needs you? That's the issue right now."

"Of course I want to help her! But what use is a drunken cripple?"

"None—so you must stop drinking, and you certainly must stop thinking of yourself as a cripple. Show me your injury."

He bristled, and kept his arm below the table, and refused to speak.

"I worked alongside Dr. Linch at the field hospital in Striver," I said. "I've seen amputations before, and worse things than amputations. You have always been a kind of second father to me, but it seems the role is reversed. Don't be a child, Sam. Show me."

His cheeks burned crimson, and for a long moment he sat stiff in his chair. I hoped he would not take offense and strike me with his good right hand, for he was still a powerful man despite his recent debauches. But he relented. Averting his eyes, he raised his arm until it was just visible above the rim of the table.

"Well, that's nothing," I said, though in fact it was an unsettling sight, the stump of his forearm terminating in an old bandage rusty with stains.

"It still weeps from time to time," he whispered.

"We all do. Well, Sam, I suppose you have to decide which you value more—your wounded pride, or Emily Baines Comstock. If the former, go back to your hovel and drink yourself to death. If the latter, come to a barber with me, and have a bath, and let me change that bandage; and then we'll get our women out of the trouble they're in, or die trying."

There was a risk in saying this. He might have walked away. But I had never known Sam to refuse a challenge, bluntly presented.

"I suppose a bath won't kill me," he muttered, though the look he gave me was vicious and ungrateful.

The town's barbers and bath-houses had already begun to close for Christmas Eve, but we managed to find one of each still willing to serve us. We also visited a clothing shop, and exchanged Sam's military rags for a more presentable civilian outfit. These purchases just about exhausted the pay I carried with me, and Sam had only pennies in his pockets.

But he wouldn't go to Emily Comstock's house right away. He wanted to recover from his debauches first; so we spent a night at the Soldier's Rest. He slept soundly, while I fought a series of skirmishes with the invertebrates gamboling among the bedclothes.

Christmas morning came. We woke about dawn, and refused the offer of a charitable breakfast. "We should go directly to Mrs. Comstock's," I said, "if you're ready."

"I'm far from ready," he said, "but I won't get any readier by waiting."

There was a carriage at the brown-stone house when we arrived there. It was a fine full carriage, with three horses to pull it, and gilt embellishments, and the crest of the Presidential Palace on the doors. It was accompanied by a number of Republican Guards, who had overpowered the single posted sentry (not the same man I had treated to a meal), and who were escorting Mrs. Comstock and Calyxa to the vehicle.

Calyxa and Mrs. Comstock caught sight of us as we approached. They beckoned us aboard the carriage. The Republican Guards initially resisted this suggestion—it wasn't part of their detail—but relented after a tongue-lashing from Julian's mother. As quick as that, the four of us were confined together in the cabin of the conveyance.

Sam looked at Mrs. Comstock, and she looked at him, and there was a protracted and uncomfortable silence.

Then Mrs. Comstock spoke up. "You lost your left hand," she said.

I blanched, and Calyxa winced, and Sam turned red.

"Emily—" he said in a husky voice.

"Was it a war injury, or just carelessness?"

"Lost in battle."

"Can't be helped, then, I suppose. Your beard is whiter than I remember it. I suppose that can't be helped, either. And you look frail—sit up!"

He straightened. "Emily . . . it's good to see you again. I'm sorry it had to be under such circumstances."

"The circumstances are about to be altered. We're off to the Executive Palace at Julian's request. Is that your best shirt?"

"My only shirt."

"I don't think the war has done you very much good, Sam."

"I guess it hasn't."

"Or *you,* Adam—is that a flea on your trouser-leg?"

"Speck of dirt," I said, as it leapt away.

"I hope there are no photographers at the Palace," Mrs. Comstock said grimly.

We were escorted through the main public chambers of the Executive Palace, past the wainscoted rooms where we had been entertained during the Presidential Reception of the previous Independence Day, to a series of cozier rooms in which lamps glowed on polished tabletops and fires burned in ventilated iron stoves, and at last to a spacious but windowless sitting room in which a fir tree had been set up and decorated with colored glass bulbs of intricate design. Julian was waiting for us there, and he dismissed the guards at once.

It was an emotional Christmas morning all around, considering half of us had nearly given up hope of seeing the other half alive. Julian embraced his mother tearfully; Sam's haggard face regained some of its former animation

whenever he gazed at Emily Baines Comstock; and Calyxa and I were inseparable on a settee near the fire.

Hasty narratives and explanations were delivered by all hands. Julian had
only just learned of his mother's confinement at the hands of Deacon
Hollingshead, and he was seething with anger; but he suppressed those feelings for the sake of the holy occasion, and tried to focus his conversation on
pleasanter things.

But it was impossible to ignore the changes in Julian's manner and appearance since the last time we had all gathered together. Both Calyxa and Mrs.
Comstock gave him troubled glances. It wasn't just the scar on his cheek, or the
immobility of his mouth on that side of his face, though those things lent him
a new and uncharacteristically sinister expression. There was a coolness about
him—a deliberation that appeared to mask great turbulence, the way a calm
sea conceals the peregrinations of the whale and the appetites of the shark.

Julian asked about his mother's confinement to the brown-stone house,
and what sort of case Deacon Hollingshead had made against her and Calyxa.
He was startled to learn that they had been Found In at an Unaffiliated Church,
and he asked his mother whether she had given up Methodism for incense
and prophecy.

"We were there for a political meeting of Parmentierists—"

"Even worse!"

"—but the Church of the Apostles Etc. is not that kind of institution, in
any case. I spoke at length with the pastor, a Mr. Stepney. He's a thoughtful
young man, not entirely a fanatic, and very presentable and handsome."*

"What does he preach? Death to the Aristocracy, like his Parmentierist
friends?"

"Pastor Stepney isn't a fire-breather, Julian. I don't know all the details of
his doctrine, except that it has to do with Evolution, and the Bible being written backward, or something like that."

"Evolution in what sense?"

"He talks about an Evolving God—I don't understand it, to be honest."

"I think I might like to meet Pastor Stepney one day, and debate theology
with him," Julian said.

It was a genial remark, not seriously intended, though it turned out to be
prophetic.

In view of the continuing harassment of Mrs. Comstock and Calyxa by
Deacon Hollingshead it was sensibly resolved that they could not return to the
brown-stone house. There were a number of luxurious guest-houses on the
property of the Executive Palace, not currently in use; and Julian designated
one of those for his mother, and another for Calyxa and me. We would be safe
there, he said, until he could settle this row with the Dominion.

---

* Sam frowned at this description but said nothing.

For the rest of the day, and well into the evening, Julian turned aside any courtiers who came calling, and devoted all his attention to his old friends and family; until, at last, full of good food from the Palace kitchen, we retired.

It was a blessing to lie down on a bed that was soft, and not an invertebrate playground, and to share it with Calyxa for the first time in many months. We celebrated Christmas in our own fashion, once we were alone— I'll say no more about it.

Julian was busy, too, though we didn't know it. I had only just finished breakfast the following morning when he summoned me to attend a meeting he had arranged with Deacon Hollingshead.

Christmas had fallen on a Sunday that year, a sort of double Sabbath, which accounted for some of the unusual calm at the Executive Palace. Monday marked a return to the customary bustle. Servants and bureaucrats were everywhere, as well as a number of high-ranking military men. They brushed past me as I went to keep my appointment with the President, alternately ignoring me or eyeing me with suspicion.

But Julian was alone in the office where he was scheduled to meet the Deacon. "Any conference between the Executive Branch and the Dominion," he explained, "is closed to the bureaucracy."

"Then what am I doing here?"

"Hollingshead is bringing a scribe, presumably to write down anything I say that might be turned against me. I insisted on the same privilege."

"I'm not much of a scribe, Julian. The politics of the situation are opaque to me."

"I understand, and all I expect you to do is sit quietly with a pad and pencil. If at any point Deacon Hollingshead begins to seem uncomfortable, write something down—or at least *pretend* to write something down, so as to compound his discomfort."

"I'm not sure I can remain complacent, if he begins to talk about Calyxa."

"You don't have to be *complacent*, Adam, just *silent*."

It wasn't much longer before the Deacon arrived. He came with a cortege of Ecclesiastical Police, which he parked in the anteroom. He was dressed very formally in his Dominion vestments, and he bowed his way into Julian's presence with all the pomp of an Oriental king. He nodded at Julian, and shook his hand, and smiled unctuously, and congratulated him on his swearing-in as Deklan's successor. He could not have been sincere in this, but his acting was first-rate, entirely suitable for the Broadway stage. Apart from a single glance he ignored me altogether, and I wasn't sure whether he recognized me as Calyxa's husband.

His own "scribe" was a mean-looking little man with gimlet eyes and a fixed scowl. This creature set himself down in a chair opposite the chair where I sat. He glared at me, and I glared back. We did not speak.

The formalities and pleasantries continued for a time between Julian and Deacon Hollingshead. They spoke not as Princes but as Principalities, each of them "we," alluding to the separate fiefdoms they represented, the Executive Branch and the Dominion.

They didn't launch immediately into a discussion of the difficult subject at hand, but warmed up with generalities. Julian talked about his plan for greater cooperation between the Navy and the Army of the Laurentians in the conduct of the War in Labrador. Deacon Hollingshead talked about the need for a pious and prayerful foreign and domestic policy, and about the Dominion's role in fostering that happy outcome. Commonplace as these sentiments might seem, they were, at bottom, disguised assertions of power. Julian was boasting that he controlled the military, and Hollingshead was reminding him that the Dominion held a sort of veto power, exercisable through the nation's pulpits. They were like two tomcats, each one puffed up to make himself seem larger in the eyes of the other. Though they smiled, they growled; and the growls were an invitation to combat.

It was Julian who finally raised the subject of Mrs. Comstock's house arrest. The Deacon responded with a conciliatory smile. "Mr. President, you're talking about the incident at the so-called Church of the Apostles Etc. in the Immigrant District. You know, I'm sure, that the raid captured a whole school of Parmentierists and radical apostates. It was the result of a collaborative investigation between civil authorities and the Ecclesiastical Police, and we're proud of the success of it. Because of that raid there are now people in jail who would otherwise be spreading sedition—not just against the Dominion but against the Senate and the Presidency."

"And there are others suffering under forced confinement, who are guilty of nothing at all," said Julian.

"I don't mean to be disingenuous, sir. I know your mother was caught up in the matter—"

"Yes, and I had to send the Republican Guards to wrench her out of your grasp, just so we could be together on Christmas."

"And I apologize for that. I'm happy to say, the Writ against her has been annulled. She's free to come and go as she likes."

That took some of the wind from Julian's sails, though he remained wary. "I think I'll keep her on the Palace grounds for now, Deacon Hollingshead. I'm not sure she's entirely safe, elsewhere."

"That's up to you, of course."

"And I thank you for the annulment. But she's not the only one under arrest as a result of the affair."

"Ah—well, that raises a different and more troublesome question. Your beloved mother could hardly have been part of any conspiracy, could she?—

either ecclesiastical or political. That's self-evident. As for any *other* persons, they'll have to undergo the customary trial if they want to establish their innocence."

"I'm talking about a woman who is currently my guest on the Palace grounds."

Here Deacon Hollingshead looked directly at me—the first and last glance he gave me during this entire encounter. I expected to find either open hatred or concealed shame in his face, but his features were entirely relaxed and indifferent. It was the look an alligator might give to a rabbit who stopped to drink from his pool, if the alligator had recently dined and didn't consider another meal worth taking.

He turned back to Julian, frowning. "Mr. President, don't misunderstand me," he said. "Mistakes happen. I know that—I freely admit it. We made a mistake in the case of your mother, and we corrected it as soon as it was brought to our attention. But the Dominion is a rock—immovable—when it comes to matters of principle."

"I think we both know better than that, Deacon Hollingshead."

"Excuse me, no. If you and I were ordinary men with a worldly disagreement, some compromise might be worked out. But this is an ecclesiastical matter above all else. The threat of the Unaffiliated Churches isn't trivial or ephemeral. We take it very seriously, and I'm speaking here for the entire Dominion Council."

"In other words you can find a way to excuse a high Eupatridian, but not a common person."

Hollingshead was silent for a moment.

"I hope you don't doubt my loyalty," he said at last, in a flat and uninflected voice. "My loyalty to the Nation is tempered only by my faith. Eventually the whole world will come under the government of the Dominion of Jesus Christ, and after a thousand years of Christian rule the Savior Himself will return to make His Kingdom on Earth.* I believe that revealed truth as wholeheartedly as a man believes in his own existence. I hope you believe it, too. I know you've made statements in the past that could be interpreted as skeptical, even blasphemous—"

"I doubt that you know any such thing," said Julian.

"Well, sir, I have sworn affidavits from a Dominion Officer, a Major Lampret, who was attached to your unit during the Saguenay Campaign, and he testifies to that charge."

"It's a *charge,* is it? But I don't think you ought to take Major Lampret so seriously. He did a lamentable job of discharging his duties in battle."

"Perhaps he did; or perhaps he was defamed by jealous officers. What I'm telling you, sir, is that your faith has been impugned in some circles, and it

---

* This is the core doctrine of the Dominion, to which every participating Church must commit itself.

328 ROBERT CHARLES WILSON

might be a good idea to publicly demonstrate your confidence and trust in the Dominion."

"And if I do that, if I make some fawning statement to the press, will Mrs. Calyxa Hazzard be redeemed from her Ecclesiastical Writ?"

"That remains to be seen. I believe the chances are good."

"But the Writ remains in effect until I make such a gesture?"

Deacon Hollingshead was wise enough not to affirm a positive threat. "Mrs. Hazzard can remain on the Palace grounds, as far as we're concerned, until her child is brought to term and a trial can be arranged."

"You insist on a trial!"

"The evidence against her is substantial—it warrants an airing."

"A *trial,* and then what? Do you really propose to imprison her?"

"According to the records we've obtained," Hollingshead said, "it wouldn't be the woman's first time in prison."

The rest of the session was a blank to me—all I could think about was Calyxa, and it took a profound exercise of personal will to restrain myself from leaping at the Deacon and taking his throat in my hands. Hollingshead was a large man, and I might not have succeeded in choking him to death; but it would have been very satisfying to make the attempt, and I gave it much thought.

Julian cut the meeting short and asked a Republican Guard to escort Deacon Hollingshead and his man off the grounds. Then he told me to take a deep breath, or else I might explode like a diving Tipman.

"He means to keep the Writ on Calyxa!" I said.

"So he says. But she's safe for now, Adam, and we have enough time to work up a strategy."

"Strategy—that sounds too flimsy! It's as if he's holding her hostage!"

"That's exactly what he's doing. He means her to be a hostage, and even if I capitulate I expect she'll remain a hostage, as a check on my behavior."

"What good is *strategy,* if that's the case?"

"Clearly," said Julian, tugging his yellow beard, which made the scar on his cheek dance to the motion, "what we need to do is to take a hostage of our own."

I didn't know what he meant by that, and he wouldn't explain. He asked me to keep the details of the meeting secret (especially from Calyxa) until he had worked out certain notions about how to proceed. He said he was determined that the Writ would not stand, and he assured me Calyxa would be safe.

I tried very hard to believe him.

On January 1st, 2175, a detachment of Republican Guards surrounded the ancient building on Fifth Avenue that served as the Dominion's warehouse of forbidden secular books and documents. They forcibly evicted the Dominion curator and his staff and took possession of the building. In an official decree published in that day's *Spark* and other city newspapers, Julian announced that "security concerns" had made it necessary to "federalize" the Dominion Archives. "The Dominion's effort to protect the public from the errors of the Secular Ancients by barring the doors of this great Library, while laudable, has become unproductive in the modern era, when knowledge itself is a weapon of war," he wrote. "And so I have ordered the Army to secure that institution, and in time to make it accessible to both military and civilian scholars, in order to ensure the continued success and prosperity of these United States."

We had our counter-hostage, in other words; only it was a building, not a person.

Hollingshead sent Julian a fiery protest on Dominion letterhead, which arrived by courier the following day. Julian read it, smiling. Then he crumpled it and tossed it over his shoulder.

3

The months between Christmas and Easter, though I spent them mainly on the grounds of the Executive Palace and under unnerving circumstances, were nevertheless happy ones in many ways.

Mainly this was because I could be close to Calyxa. She remained under the Ecclesiastical Writ, and could not leave the enclosure, but her pregnancy would have kept her largely confined in any case; and we had Julian's assurances that he would shelter her from the Deacon's henchmen, and that she would receive the best medical attention doctors of the Eupatridian class could provide.

At the same time I was working on the novel I had promised to Mr. John Hungerford, the publisher of the *Spark*. The title I settled on was *A Western Boy at Sea; or, Lost and Found in the Pacific*. In part I had taken the advice Theodore Dornwood gave me after the Battle of Mascouche, to "write what you know," and I had made the hero a young man much like myself, if somewhat more innocent and trusting. Much of the narrative, however, concerned Pacific islands, and pirates, and sea adventures in general. For these passages I employed what I had learned of sailing from my time aboard the *Basilisk*, along with some generous borrowing from the work of Charles Curtis Easton, whose stories had taught me all I knew about the business of Asiatic piracy.

The book was a pleasure to write, and I thought it both original and good, though what was original about it was not necessarily good, and what was good about it was not always original. The chapters I showed to Mr. Hungerford pleased him, and he declared that the finished product would probably sell briskly, "given the popular taste in such things."

Most mornings I wrote until noon, and then took lunch with Calyxa. During the afternoon I would walk for exercise, sometimes in the streets of Manhattan but more often, as the weather improved, on the Palace grounds. The ancient "Park," as some of the groundsmen still called it, was full of peculiarities to interest the casual stroller. There was, for instance, an elderly male Giraffe—last descendant of a family of those unlikely creatures, donated by an African prime minister during the days of the Pious Presidents—who was allowed to wander freely, eating leaves from trees and hay from the lofts of the horse-barns. It was best not to approach the animal too closely, for he was evil-tempered and would stampede anyone who annoyed him. But he was beautiful when apprehended from a distance, where his shabbiness and bile were less distinct. He especially liked to pass time on the Statuary Lawn, and it was fascinating to see him taking the shade of Cleopatra's Needle, or standing next to the copper torch of the Colossus of Liberty as if he expected it to sprout green and edible shoots, which of course it never did.

On rainy days he sheltered in the ailanthus grove near the Pond. There were fences to keep him out of the Hunting Grounds, so he wouldn't be accidentally shot. His name, the grounds-keepers told me, was Otis. He was a noble bachelor Giraffe, and I admired him.

There were occasions that winter when Julian, weary of the distractions of the Presidency, came to the guest house and asked me to go rambling with him. We spent several sunny, chilly afternoons walking the preserve with rifles, pretending to hunt but really just reliving the simple pleasures we had shared in Williams Ford. Julian continued to talk about Philosophy, and the Fate of the Universe, and such things—interests which had been rekindled by his exploration of the Dominion Archive and deepened by the tragedies he had experienced at war. A certain tone entered his conversation—melancholy, almost elegiac—which I had not heard before, and I put this down to his experiences during the Goose Bay Campaign, which had hardened him considerably.

He visited the liberated Archive often. One Saturday in March I went with him to that contested building, at his invitation. The building's marbled facade, one of the oldest standing structures in the city, was still ringed with armed guards, to prevent any attempt at re-occupation by the Ecclesiastical Police. We arrived under the careful escort of the Republican Guard, but once inside we were able to roam unaccompanied in what Julian called "the Stacks"—room after room of tightly-packed and closely-arranged shelves, on which books from the days of the Secular Ancients were arrayed in startling numbers.

"It's a good thing for us the Ancients were so prolific in their publishing," Julian said, his voice echoing among the dusty casements. "During the Fall of the Cities books were often burned for fuel. Millions of them must have been lost in that way—and millions more to neglect, mildew, floods, and so on. But they were produced in such numbers that many still survive, as you can see. The Dominion did us a noble service by preserving them, and committed a heinous crime by keeping them hidden."

The titles I inspected seemed random, and the books, long neglected by their Dominion caretakers, had not been arranged according to any rational scheme, though Julian had initiated the work of having them catalogued and itemized. "Here," Julian said, drawing my attention to a particular shelf which his small army of clerks and scholars had begun to arrange, labeled *Scientific Subjects*. It held not one but three copies of the *History of Mankind in Space*, all of them pristine, covers and bindings intact.

He took one down and handed it to me. "Keep it, Adam—your old copy must be getting ragged by now, and there are duplicates. It won't be missed."

This book, unlike the one recovered from the Tip at Williams Ford, possessed a brightly colored paper wrapper, with a picture of what I recognized from previous study as the Plains of Mars, dusty under a pinkish sky. The printed image was so crisp and clear it made me shiver, as if the ethereal winds of that distant planet were blowing out of it. "But it must be very valuable," I said.

"There are things in this building far more valuable than that. Authors and texts from the Efflorescence of Oil and before. Think about the Dominion-approved literature we were raised on, Adam, all that nineteenth-century piety the clergy admire so—Susan Warner and Mrs. Eckerson and Elijah Kellog and that crew—but the Dominion readers don't include Hawthorne from that era, or Melville, or Southworth, just to begin with. And as for the twentieth century, there's a whole world we haven't been allowed to see— scientific and engineering documents, works of unbiased history, novels in which people curse like sailors and fly in airplanes. . . . Do you know what we found locked away in the cellar, Adam?"

"I'm sure I don't."

"Movies!" He grinned. "At least a dozen of them—movies on celluloid film, in metal canisters, from the days of the Secular Ancients!"

"I thought none had survived."

"I thought so too, until we uncovered these."

"Have you seen any of them?"

"Not yet. They're fragile, and they don't run in the simple projection machines we use. But I assigned a group of mechanics to study them and work on the problem of duplicating them for posterity, or at least rendering them into a form more easily viewed."

This was all wonderful and daunting. I took books from the shelves and handled them reverently, fully conscious that they had not been regarded by sympathetic eyes since before the Fall of the Cities. Later Julian would give me another book he had culled from among the Archival duplicates, a short novel called *The Time Machine* by Mr. H. G. Wells, about a marvelous but apparently imaginary cart which carried a man into the future—and it fascinated me—but the Archive itself was a Time Machine in everything but name. Here were voices preserved on browning paper like pressed flowers, whispering apostasies into the ear of a new century.

It was dark by the time we left, and I was dazed by what I had seen. We were silent for a time as the carriage and its military escort passed along Broadway and into the grounds of the Presidential Palace. But I had been thinking about what Julian had said regarding movies, and I was reminded of that project he used to talk about so passionately, namely *The Life and Adventures of the Great Naturalist Charles Darwin.* "What about *your* movie, Julian?" I asked. "Have you made any advancement on that front?" Julian was busy these days with matters of State; but in his spare time, he had admitted to me, he still contemplated the project, which might now be within practical reach; and he had begun writing a script for it.

On this occasion he was evasive. "Certain things are difficult to work out. Details of plot and so forth. The script is like a horse with a nail in its hoof—it isn't dead, but it won't move forward."

"What are the problems exactly?"

"I make Darwin the hero of it, and we see his fascination with beetles, as a child, and he talks about the relationship of all living things, and then he gets on a boat and goes looking at finches—"

"Finches?"

"For the shape of their beaks and such, which leads him to certain conclusions about heredity and environment. All this is important and true, but it lacks . . ."

"Drama," I suggested.

"Drama, possibly."

"Well, the boat is a good touch. You can't go wrong with a boat."

"The heart of the thing eludes me. It won't settle down on paper the way I want it to."

"Perhaps I can help you with it."

"Thank you, Adam, but no. I would rather keep the business to myself, at least for now."

If Julian's cinematic work-in-progress lacked drama, the incidents of daily life did not, especially regarding his increasingly hostile relations with the Dominion of Jesus Christ in general and Deacon Hollingshead in particular.

Sam told me he feared Julian was involving himself in a battle he could never win. The Dominion had a devious history and deep pockets, he said, and Julian's best bet would be to ingratiate himself with the Senate, and be sure to keep the Army on his side, which would give him greater leverage in any political wrestling match with Colorado Springs.

But that was strategy for the long run; in the short term it was the threat to Calyxa that concerned us. Julian's capture of the Dominion Archive did not result in the withdrawal of the Writ against Calyxa . . . nor did it seem that Julian would be willing to surrender his prize, now that he had it in his possession, even if such a bargain had been offered. But he continued to insist that Calyxa was safe; and I could hardly believe otherwise, since it would require a wholesale revolution before the Dominion could march onto the grounds of the Executive Palace and take her into their custody. In all likelihood, Julian said, Deacon Hollingshead wouldn't even issue a summons to court; if he did, Julian would see that it was quashed.

In light of all this he began to take a greater interest in the events that had resulted in the Writ of Ecclesiastical Quarantine in the first place. "This

Church where you were Found In," he asked Calyxa, "is it still in operation or did Hollingshead shut it down completely?"

The Parmentierist friends Calyxa had made in the city continued to keep her informed of developments. She sat on a sofa in the guest-house (this was late in March, on a windy night), her swollen belly prominent under a maternity dress Mrs. Comstock had obtained for her. She looked beatific, I thought, with her coiled hair for a halo; and I could not so much as glance at her without smiling to myself.*

"Its former location has been seized and put up for auction," she said. "But Pastor Stepney managed to avoid arrest. The Church of the Apostles Etc. continues to meet, at a new location . . . and with a different congregation, since the first batch are still in prison."

"I'm curious about this church. We might do ourselves a favor by learning more about the case, as a way of anticipating any new move Hollingshead might make."

"Stepney seems like a good man," Mrs. Comstock remarked, "though I only saw him from a distance. I was impressed with him, despite his radical doctrines."

(She said this even though she knew the words would make Sam, who was also visiting us that evening, shudder and scowl. She gave him sidelong glances to gauge his reaction, which I suspect she found entertaining.)

"I could take you there," Calyxa said, "if I were allowed to travel freely in the city."

She was far too close to her term to entertain any such idea, and Julian quickly demurred. Then Mrs. Comstock said, "Well, I for one would like a chance to speak to Pastor Stepney, and get to know him. Perhaps I could go with you, Julian, if Calyxa will tell us the current address."

"The last thing we need," Sam growled, "if for you to be 'Found In' a second time. I won't sanction it."

"I didn't ask for your *sanction*," Mrs. Comstock said stiffly.

Julian forestalled the argument with a wave of his hand. "I'm the one who's curious," he said. "And I'm the one Deacon Hollingshead wouldn't dare to arrest. Perhaps Adam and I can go to this man's church, with enough Republican Guards to warn us if the Dominion tries some trick."

"It would be dangerous even so," said Sam.

"Is it Hollingshead you're afraid of, Sam, or the charismatic Mr. Stepney?"

Sam didn't respond to Julian's impertinent question, but lapsed into a brooding silence.

"It might be a fascinating Expedition," Julian repeated. "Will you come with me, Adam? Tomorrow, say?"

---

* The glances she returned were not always equally warm, for carrying a child to term is a cumbersome job, which can wear down a person's good spirits.

I said I would. In fact I wasn't much interested in Pastor Stepney's apostate church. But I was interested in Julian's interest in it.

Stepney is just the type to intrigue Julian," Calyxa said as I climbed into bed beside her that night. March breezes rattled the big bedroom windows, and it was pleasant to huddle under the thick blankets with my arm around my wife. "Probably a fraud, like most of these unaffiliated pastors, and his doctrines don't interest me. But he was generous to the Parmentierists who met at his church, and he talked a good line, whenever I happened to overhear him. Not the usual small-church fanaticism. Much about Time and Evolution and such topics, the sort of thing Julian likes to babble about, and he's as eloquent as any Aristo."

"Julian thinks of it as Philosophy more than Babble," I said.

"Maybe so. Either way, it's thin gruel for a working woman or a mechanic with a grievance. Here, fold yourself around me, Adam—I'm cold."

I did as she asked, and we grew warm together.

Pastor Stepney's former church in the Immigrant District having been seized and sold, he had moved his enterprise to the loft of a crumbling warehouse alongside one of the canals of Lower Manhattan. Julian disguised himself in the clothing of an ordinary working man, and I wore the same, and we walked up the wooden steps to the loft by ourselves, though there were Republican Guards in plain clothes outside, ready to warn us if the Dominion's men arrived in any force.

A sign had been tacked to the door at the top of the stairs, engraved in an ornate script with the words:

CHURCH OF THE APOSTLES ETC.
GOD IS CONSCIENCE
—HAVE NO OTHER—
LOVE YOUR NEIGHBOR AS YOUR BROTHER

"That's a noble sentiment," I said.

"I suppose it is. More often honored in the breach, though, I imagine. We'll see." Julian knocked at the door.

It was answered by a woman in a tight red dress and a heavy shawl. In appearance she resembled one of the less virtuous women who frequented the neighborhood, perhaps a few years past her peak of desirability; but I don't meant to insult her character, only to offer a description. "Yes?" she said.

"We would like to meet Pastor Stepney," said Julian.

"There's no service on at the moment."

"That's all right. We don't require one."

"Well, come in." The woman admitted us into a small, barely-furnished room. "I'll tell him you're here, if you tell me who you are."

"Pilgrims in search of enlightenment," Julian said, smiling.

"We get five or six of those a day," the woman said. "Pilgrims are cheap as fleas around here. Sit down, I'll find out if he has time for you."

She vanished through another door, and we perched ourselves on the small bench that was the only available seat. A few pamphlets had been left on the rough pine table in front of us. *The Evolving God* was the title of one. "He takes an interest in Evolution," I said. "That's unusual for a clergyman."

"I doubt he knows what he's talking about. These impostors seldom do."

"But perhaps he's sincere."

"Even worse," said Julian.

Then the adjoining door opened, and Pastor Stepney himself came into the room.

He was a handsome man. Mrs. Comstock and Calyxa had already testified to that effect, and I could not say they were wrong. Stepney was a tall, slender youth—he looked no older than Julian—with lustrously dark skin and wiry hair. But his most arresting feature was his eyes, which were penetrating, opulent, and of a shade so dark it was almost umber. He gave us a benevolent smile and said in a soothing voice, "How can I help you boys? Come for some spiritual wisdom, have you? I'm at your service, as long as you don't forget the donation-box on the way out."

Julian stood up at once. His demeanor had utterly changed. His eyes grew wide with astonishment. "My God!" he exclaimed. "Of all the Stepneys in New York City—is that *you*, Magnus?"

"Magnus Stepney, yes," the pastor said, backing off warily.

"Don't you know me, Magnus? Though we're both years older now!"

The young pastor frowned a moment more; then his own eyes expanded in astonishment. "Julian!" he cried, a grin breaking out on his face. "Julian Comstock, by the grace of God! But aren't you *President* now?"

It took me a while to sort out this unexpected development, but I won't compel the reader to share my own confusion. It was obvious that Julian and Stepney had met before, and from listening to their conversation I garnered a few salient facts.

Stepney invited us into his sanctuary—which was the greater part of the warehouse loft, fixed up with benches and a makeshift altar—so that we could talk more comfortably. I use the collective "we," but in fact it was Julian and the pastor who talked—I kept out of it. They had embarked on a series of reminiscences even before Julian remembered to introduce me.

"This is Magnus Stepney, an old acquaintance of mine," he said eventually. "Magnus, this is Adam Hazzard, another friend."

Pastor Stepney shook my hand, and his grip was strong and genial. "Pleased to meet you, Adam. Are you also some high functionary in the Executive Branch, operating in disguise?"

"No, just a writer," I said.

Julian explained that he had gone to school with this man (boy, in those days) before he was sent to Williams Ford to protect him from his uncle. The school they had attended was a Eupatridian institution in which bright Aristo children were taught whatever it was considered decorous to know about arithmetic and literature. Julian and Magnus had been fast friends, I gathered, and a continual terror to their overseers. Both had been intelligent in advance of their years and impudent in their relations with authority. The friendship had been prematurely severed by Julian's evacuation to Athabaska, and Julian had lost track of his former acquaintance. "How on earth did you come to be a pastor of a scofflaw Church?" Julian asked.

"My father wouldn't toady to the Senate in some conflict over a dockside property," Stepney said, "and he was punished for it, and forced to flee to Mediterranean France for his own safety. My mother and I would have followed after a prudent time, but his ship was lost at sea. My mother was all the family I had after that, and smallpox took her in '72. I was reduced to accepting any work I could find, or making it for myself."

"And this is the result?" Julian asked. "The Church of the Apostles Etc.?"

"By a long and winding road, yes," said Stepney.

He gave Julian an abbreviated account of those difficult years, while I listened with half an ear. I supposed all this meant that Pastor Stepney was a fraud, and his Church nothing more than a vehicle for extracting cash donations from gullible parishioners. But Stepney spoke modestly and apparently sincerely about his religious beliefs, and how they had moved him to create the apostate sect of which he was the master.

This caused Julian and Stepney to launch into a vigorous discussion of Theology, the Existence of God, Evolution by Natural Selection, and such topics as that, which I inferred had been the subject of their childhood conversations as well. I was necessarily left out of such talk, and I passed the time by looking over the crudely-printed pamphlets Pastor Stepney had left scattered about the place.

Between the pamphlets and the conversation I began to assemble an outline of Magnus Stepney's unusual doctrines. He was a true apostate, in that he denied the legitimacy of the Dominion of Jesus Christ as a worldly power, and his ideas about God were profoundly unorthodox. God, he asserted, was not contained in any Book, but was a Voice, which every human being could hear (and which most of us chose to ignore). The common name of that voice was Conscience; but it was a God by any reasonable definition, Stepney claimed. What else could you call an Invisible Entity who said the same thing to members of every diverse branch of humanity, regardless of class, geography, or language? Because that Voice was not contained in any *single* mind, but experienced consistently by *all* sane minds, it must be more than merely human, and therefore a God.

Gods, the pamphlets asserted, were not supernatural beings, but tenuously living things, like ethereal plants, that evolved in concert with the human species. We were simply their medium—our brains and flesh the soil in which they sprouted and grew. There were other Gods beside Conscience; but Conscience was the one worth worshipping, because its commandments, if universally obeyed, would usher us into a veritable Eden of mutual trust and universal charity.

(I don't offer these notions to the reader with my endorsement, but only as a sample of Magnus Stepney's peculiar doctrines. At first encounter the ideas seemed to me both eccentric and alarming.)

Julian's discussion with Stepney covered much of the same ground, though at greater length. Julian was obviously entertained by these airy abstractions, and enjoyed pressing the pastor with logical objections, which Stepney, for his part, equally enjoyed parrying.

"But you're a Philosopher!" Julian exclaimed at one point. "This is Philosophy, not Religion, since you rule out supernatural beings—you know that as well as I do!"

"I suppose it *is* Philosophy, looked at from one angle," Stepney conceded. "But there's no money in Philosophy, Julian. Religion is far more lucrative as a career."

"Yes, until the Dominion takes your Church away. My mother and Adam's wife were caught up in that trouble, you know."

"Were they? Are they all right?" Stepney asked, with a concern that did not seem feigned.

"Yes; but only because I took them under my wing."

"The President's wing must be a reasonably reliable shelter."

"Not as sturdy as it could be. Don't you fear the Dominion at all, Magnus? You'd be in prison yourself, if you hadn't escaped the raid."

Pastor Stepney shrugged his broad shoulders. "I'm not the only unaffiliated church in town. The business is only dangerous when the Dominion is in a vindictive mood, and the Deacons take up these crusades just once or twice in a decade. A few weeks or months will pass; then they'll declare the city sanctified, and the rogue Churches will spring up again like mushrooms after a rain."

The chapel of the Church of the Apostles Etc. contained one single high window, and through it I could see the daylight beginning to ebb. I pointed this out to Julian, and reminded him that I had promised to be back with Calyxa by nightfall (as she preferred during the nervous last weeks of her pregnancy).

Julian seemed reluctant to leave—he was enjoying the pastor's company, and sat so close to him that their knees touched—but he looked at the window and nodded. Julian stood up, and Pastor Stepney stood up, and they embraced as two old friends.

"You ought to come to the Palace," Julian said. "My mother would be pleased to see you."

"Do you think that would be wise?"

"I think it might be fascinating," said Julian. "I'll send you a note, discreetly."

Pastor Magnus Stepney did come to the Executive Palace, more than once in the ensuing months, often for overnight visits. And Julian's renewed acquaintance with his old friend produced two immediate and unanticipated results.

One was that Julian was moved to meddle even further in the relations between the civil authority and the Dominion. He summoned lawyers, and made himself knowledgeable about ecclesiastical law, and came to certain conclusions. The fact was, he said, the Dominion had no real jurisdiction over the non-affiliated churches, except to deny them membership in its organization. What gave the Deacons their power was the *legal consequence* of that denial. A rogue church could not be a registered charity, nor were its tithes and properties tax-exempt. In fact its possessions were taxed at a punitive rate, forcing such institutions into bankruptcy if they attempted to comply with the law, or into an outlaw existence if they did not. Those regulations had been put in place by a compliant Senate, and they were enforced by civil, not religious, authorities.

Julian objected to such laws, believing they conferred an undue power on the Dominion. To remedy the injustice he composed a Bill to moderate the levies on such churches and place the burden of proof of "apostasy" on the complainant Deacons. He felt he had enough popularity to shepherd the bill through the Senate, though he knew the Dominion would oppose it bitterly, for it constituted nothing less than an assault on their long-standing Clerical Monopoly. Sam didn't approve of this maneuver—it was sure to rake up another fight—but Julian would not yield to argument, and tasked his subordinates with introducing the measure before the Senate as soon as possible.

The second visible result worked indirectly by the visits of Pastor Stepney was a change in Sam's relationship to Emily Baines Comstock. Mrs. Comstock was attentive to Magnus Stepney during his visits (although he was only a fraction of her age), complimenting his appearance within the hearing of others, and saying she was not surprised that he came of Eupatridian stock, and making other such flattering comments as that. This effusive praise wore on Sam like a saw-blade on a piece of rough lumber. Sam did not care to see Mrs. Comstock so patently charmed by another and younger man. Her affections ought to be channeled more in his direction, he believed. Therefore, after what must have been much deliberation, he summoned up his courage, and suppressed his embarrassment, and barged into her presence one night while she was dining with Calyxa and me.

He arrived trembling and sweating. Mrs. Comstock stared at him as if he were a strange apparition, and asked what was wrong with him.

"Conditions," he began—then he hesitated, shaking his head as if he was appalled at his own effrontery.

"Conditions?" Mrs. Comstock prompted him. "What conditions, and what about them?"

"Conditions have changed . . ."

"Be specific, if it's within your power."

"Before Julian assumed the Presidency I could never—that is, it wasn't within my compass to ask—although I've always admired you, Emily—you know I've admired you—our stations in life are different—I don't have to tell you so—me a soldier, and you high-born—but with the recent changes in all our fortunes—I can only hope that my feelings are reciprocated—I don't mean to presume to speak for you—only to ask—to ask hopefully—to ask *humbly*—"

"Ask *what*? Arrive at a point, Sam, or give it up. You're incoherent, and we're ready for dessert."

"Ask for your hand," he finished in an uncharacteristically meek and breathless voice.

"My hand!"

"In marriage."

"Good Lord!" said Mrs. Comstock, standing up from her chair.

"Will you give it to me, Emily?"

"What an awkward proposal!"

"But will you give me your hand?"

She reached out to him, frowning. "I expect I'll have to," she said, "since you've gone and lost one of your own."

Sam and Emily set their wedding date for mid-May, and it was to be a quiet ceremony, since she was a widow and he was of uncertain lineage (as the Eupatridians would say). I would forever mark that ceremony as the end of a brief "golden era" in the reign of Julian Conqueror—but not before the advent of some events even more historical, at least from my point of view. On Tuesday, April 11th, two days after we celebrated Easter, I finished writing *A Western Boy at Sea; or, Lost and Found in the Pacific.* I presented the typewritten manuscript in person to Mr. Hungerford at the offices of the *Spark.* He thanked me and told me he would bring the book to press quickly, to capitalize on the recent success of *The Adventures of Captain Commongold.* It might see print by mid-summer, he said.

Even more significantly, Calyxa went into labor on the 21st—a Friday afternoon, as sunny and pleasant as any day that season, with a high blue sky and a warm wind blowing.

The doctor who attended Calyxa was a man named Cassius Polk. Dr. Polk was a white-haired venerable of the highest respectability, who carried himself with immense dignity and didn't smoke or drink. Toward the end of Calyxa's term he began to spend much of his time at the guest-house, even sleeping there on occasion. Julian had enrolled him to attend exclusively to Calyxa, and paid him generously for his time.

On that particular afternoon he was sitting with me at a table in the kitchen of the house. Calyxa was resting upstairs, as she did most days. We knew her hour was near. Her belly was drum-taut, and when I held her at night I could feel the child kicking and moving about inside her with surprising vigor and determination. Its entrance into the world seemed, if anything, slightly overdue.

Dr. Polk sipped a glass of water I had given him. He was a discursive man, and liked to talk about his work. He specialized in obstetrics and female problems, and kept an office in a desirable section of Manhattan when he was not attending the births of high Eupatridians. Many of his clients, he told me, were young women of wealth, "the kind who insist on daring the devil by patronizing vaccination shops. I give them my advice on the subject, but of course they ignore it."

I told him I knew very little about the business of vaccination.

"Oh, it's fine in principle. Vaccination has been a useful preventative for certain diseases since before the Efflorescence of Oil. But it has to be scientifically applied, you see. The problem with *fashionable* vaccination is precisely that it *is* fashionable. A scar on the arm is imagined to make a woman more attractive to suitors, and it advertises her wealth, in addition, since the shops charge absurd amounts of money for their services."

"Still, if it's an effective treatment—"

"Sometimes it is—more often it's fraudulent. A syringe full of creek water and a sharpened knitting needle. The field is rife with profitable fraud, and more likely to spread disease than prevent it. Just this month a new Pox has broken out, especially severe among the high-born, probably as a result of just such unhygienic practices."

"Can't the Senate make a law against it?"

"Against vaccination shops? I suppose it could; but the Senators are wedded to the idea of Free Trade, and the Invisible Hand of the Marketplace, and all those shibboleths. Of course they feel the consequences too—or will, when their daughters begin to sicken. Fifteen cases this week alone. Ten the week before. Not a Pox that's familiar to me, either. A little like Dog Pox, a little like Denver Pox in its signs and indications."

"Is it very deadly?"

"Fewer than half my patients have recovered."

That was alarming. "Do you fear an epidemic, then?"

"I've seen Pox sweep through this city half a dozen times in my career. I fear an outbreak of it every day of my life, Mr. Hazzard. We don't know where epidemics come from and we don't know how to stop them. If it were up to me—"

But I never learned what the doctor would do, if it were up to him, for Calyxa called out anxiously from upstairs. Her labor had begun, and Polk dashed off to attend her.

I didn't follow him. He had told me to keep clear during the delivery. It wasn't a difficult promise to make. All I knew of the act of birth was what I had learned as a stable-boy in Williams Ford. I understood, *abstractly*, that Calyxa would be enduring the same trials the brood mares in the Duncan-Crowley barns suffered when they foaled; but I could not juxtapose those memories with my intimate knowledge of Calyxa—the resulting image was distasteful, at best.

The sound of Calyxa's cries came down from the bedroom at increasingly frequent intervals. Dr. Polk had sent for a female accoucheur (as the Eupatridians called their midwives) as soon as the labor began, and when this nurse arrived she took note of my anxiety and tried to ameliorate it by giving me a tincture of hemp oil and opium in a glass of water.

I wasn't accustomed to the medication. It took effect within the hour, and the result was not altogether calming. I lost direction of my thoughts; and before long I had invested all my attention in a survey of the doors of the kitchen cupboards. The oiled oaken doors became a kind of Movie Screen, to my eyes, on which the grain of the wood evolved into images of animals, steam engines, tropical forests, scenes of war, etc. These impressions were elastic, and each one flowed into the next like water in a rocky stream. I laughed at some of the visions, and recoiled at others—an observer might have mistaken me for feeble-minded. And while the effect was distracting, it was less than reassuring.

Dr. Polk and his nurse passed in and out of the kitchen like wraiths during this interval, drawing pans of water or rinsing out towels. Hours passed, though they might have been minutes or months, in so far as I could calculate time in my intoxicated state. I did not entirely wake from my reveries until I heard a prodigious scream from the upstairs bedroom—a deep, *masculine* scream, in the voice of Dr. Polk.

I stood up shakily. I hadn't forgotten my promise to keep out of the doctor's way. But this seemed like an exceptional circumstance. Had Dr. Polk really cried out in terror, or had I imagined it? Uncertainty retarded my step. Then there was another cry, neither Calyxa's nor the doctor's—the nurse had joined the chorus. A cold dread came over me, and I rushed to the stairs.

Dire fantasies played about my imagination. Monstrous births and miscarriages had been common during the Plague of Infertility, and they still occurred from time to time, even in the second half of the twenty-second century. I refused to permit myself the thought that Calyxa might have given birth to some creature so unusual that even a hardened physician would cry out and recoil from it. But the possibility haunted me. The stairs seemed absurdly steep, and I was breathless by the time I reached the landing. I found the bedroom ajar. Unsteadily, I lunged for it.

The cause of the excitement was immediately obvious, though at first I doubted what I was seeing.

Dr. Polk and his nurse stood with their backs to the wall, expressions of stark terror distorting their faces. They were staring at the bedroom's large double window. Earlier in the day Dr. Polk had thrown open the shutters, as he often did, in the belief that fresh air is an invalid's best friend. Just now that same window was filled with an enormous, foul-smelling, bestial Head.

I was not so intoxicated that I didn't grasp what had happened. The Head belonged to Otis. Otis, being a bachelor Giraffe, must have been attracted by the unusual sounds and smells of childbirth. Wandering close to the house, he had put his head inside the open window as a natural means of satisfying his curiosity. But Dr. Polk didn't know that an adult Giraffe was allowed to roam the Palace grounds, and he was understandably startled by such a development. His nurse shared his astonishment and terror.

Calyxa was well enough acquainted with Otis not to be frightened, but his arrival had unfortunately coincided with the penultimate moments of her labor. Her face was red and dewed with perspiration, and she shouted *"Virez-moi cette girafe d'ici!"* in a fierce and desperate voice.

I went as close to the window as I dared and made remonstrances with Otis by shouting and waving my arms. This annoyed him enough that he eventually obliged me by withdrawing. I quickly closed the windows and latched the shutters. Otis bumped his nose against these barriers once or twice, then abandoned his inquiries in disgust.

"Only a Giraffe," I said to Dr. Polk—apologetically, though I was not responsible for Otis.

"Keep it away, please," he said, struggling to recover his dignity.

"Otis is his name. He won't bother you any more, if you keep the window shut."

"I wasn't warned about Giraffes," the doctor growled. Then he regained a degree of composure, and told me I was the father of a baby girl.

4

Readers hoping for a political chronology of Julian's career as President of the United States, with all the minutiae and details of his legislation, will be disappointed by my narrative.* The weeks between Easter and Independence Day of 2174—as important as they were in the evolution of the Executive Power—were consumed, for me, by the considerable work and fuss attendant on fatherhood.

Authors who discuss the period generally portray Julian as a haughty and implacable enemy of religion, or as a broad-minded and indulgent friend of liberty, as their convictions dictate. Perhaps both characterizations contain some element of truth, for Julian—especially in the Presidency—was more than one man.

It's true that during this time his hostile relations with the Dominion reached the boiling point, with consequences familiar to historians. It's also true that his relations with the Unaffiliated Churches were warm and generous, uncharacteristically so for one who has been labeled "the Agnostic" or "the Atheist." These were not contradictions of policy so much as contradictions of character. Julian loathed Power, but couldn't resist the urge to use it for what he considered benevolent ends. He had disdained the scepter; but now it was in his hands, and he made a tool of it. His vision expanded, and his perspective narrowed.

I saw him often during these months, though not in any official capacity. He stopped by the guest-house often, and he was always delighted to see and handle Flaxie.† Flaxie, a good-natured baby, enjoyed his attentions, and it pleased me to watch them together. He was equally attentive to Calyxa, and made sure she had all she wanted of luxuries and kindnesses during her recovery. "The only thing he hasn't given me," Calyxa remarked at one point, "is an exemption from that damned Ecclesiastical Writ"—but he would have done so, had it been in his power; and he continued to vex Deacon Hollingshead about it, among other weighty issues.

Sam was equally absorbed in the domestic business of his marriage to Emily Baines Comstock (now Godwin), and I was afraid that Julian would grow lonely without the kind of close companionship Sam and I had formerly

---

* There are several such accounts in print, by various authors. Some of these are quite accurate, and others have received the Dominion Stamp of Approval.

† We had named the child Flaxie in honor of my lost sister, but also because of her crop of fine wheat-colored hair. By the time she reached her first birthday Flaxie had lost that baby hair, and wore an ebony crown just as lush and tightly-curled as her mother's. We kept the name, however, despite the apparent contradiction.

offered him. For that reason I was glad of his burgeoning friendship with Pastor Magnus Stepney of the Church of the Apostles Etc. The two of them had lately become inseparable, and their amiable arguments over God and Destiny and such topics were, for Julian, a welcome relief, and a distraction from the burdens of the Presidency.

In the military realm Julian won accolades for consolidating the few gains his uncle had made, for withholding further ground initiatives until the Army of the Laurentians had been restored in strength and spirit, and for pursuing the battle with the Dutch at sea rather than on land. Admiral Fairfield conducted several successful naval maneuvers during this time, and the strategic Mitteleuropan coaling station at Iqaluit was shelled into submission. If it wasn't "the final crushing blow to European aggression" so many had expected of Julian Conqueror, it was at least enough to satisfy patriotic sentiment.

In truth, that spring and summer season, I gave little thought to the future, except on those nights when Flaxie slept soundly in her crib, and Calyxa and I lay in bed together, talking.

"We'll have to leave, you know," Calyxa said on one such night in June. A warm breeze came through the bedroom window, which we had equipped with sturdy screens to discourage insects and Giraffes. "We can't stay here."

"I know," I said, "though it's been pleasant enough." I would miss the Preserve, the Statuary Lawn, the respite from urban noise and clutter; but we couldn't make the Palace grounds a permanent home. "We can find a place in the city as soon as Julian has that Writ annulled."

She shook her head. "The Dominion won't annul it, Adam. It's time we admitted the truth of the thing. The Writ is a point of honor with Deacon Hollingshead. He won't relinquish it until he's in his grave, and he has the whole weight of the Dominion behind him. Institutions like the Dominion of Jesus Christ on Earth don't surrender power willingly."

"That's pessimistic. Unless the Writ is annulled, we *can't* leave the Palace grounds."

Calyxa turned her head away, and the moonlight made a reflection in her pensive eyes. "How long do you think Julian will keep the Executive, if he insists on picking fights with Senators and Deacons?"

"He's only just become President."

"What guarantee is that? Presidents have had shorter terms."

It was true that, in the course of history, certain Presidents had been removed or murdered after a brief term of office. But only under unusual circumstances. Most famously, young Varnum Bayard had been deposed after less than a week when he inherited the Executive in 2106; but that was because he was twelve years old, and not experienced enough to defend himself against a coup. I said that Julian seemed safe enough for now.

"That's an illusion. Sooner or later, Adam, we'll have to leave, if we want to live out our lives in safety. Six months from now—a year, maybe—almost certainly not more than that."

"Well, but where would we go? We would hardly be more anonymous in the city, with my career as a book-writer. And the city isn't a safe place either, given the new Pox that's going around."

"In the worst case, Adam, we might have to leave the city altogether. Maybe even the country."

"The country!"

"To keep Flaxie away from harm, wouldn't it be worthwhile?"

"Of course it would, if that was the only practical way to protect her, but I hardly think it is—certainly not yet!"

"Not yet," Calyxa agreed; but her mouth was pursed in a frown, and her eyes seemed focused on some point well beyond the encompassing walls of the Guest House. "No, not yet; but time passes, Adam. Things change. Julian is on a dangerous path. I don't mind him tackling the Dominion—he's brave to do it—but I don't mean to let anything happen to Flaxie, no matter the politics of it."

"Of course we won't let anything happen to Flaxie."

"Tell me again. Say it again, Adam, and then I might be able to sleep."

"Nothing will happen to Flaxie," I promised her.

"Thank you," she said, sighing.

She did sleep then. I couldn't; for the same conversation that settled her fears had aggravated mine. After an hour of restlessness I put on a robe and went to sit on the porch of the guest-house. The broad swathes of lawn and forest that comprised the Palace grounds lay dark under a clear and moonless sky. The appointed hours of the Illumination of Manhattan had passed, and the city cast no special glow. Summer constellations performed their calendrical marches overhead, and I reminded myself that the same stars had shone indifferently over this island back when it was inhabited by Secular Businessmen, or Unchurched Aborigines before that, or even Mammoths and Giant Sloths (if Julian's evolutionary narratives were to be believed). Because my wife and child were sleeping in the house behind me, away from immediate danger, I prayed that this particular moment of time would linger indefinitely, and that nothing would happen to change it.

But the world *would* change, one way or another—it couldn't be stopped from changing. Julian had preached that homily to me in Williams Ford, long ago; and events since then had only driven home the truth of it.

The stars set, the stars rose. I went back to my summer bed.

Mr. Hungerford had wanted *A Western Boy at Sea* published by the Fourth of July, in the belief that the patriotic emotions of that Universal Holiday might boost its sales. His printers achieved the goal he set for them: the book was impressed and available for purchase by the first of that month. I attended a small event at the offices of the *Spark* to celebrate the release.

Apart from Mr. Hungerford, I hardly knew any of the persons present in the room. Some were authors of other books in Hungerford's line—generally a seedy bunch (the authors, I mean, not necessarily their novels), many displaying the visible effects of dissipative living. Present as well were certain Manhattan businessmen who distributed books, or shopkeepers who sold them—also a roguish crew, but less hopelessly inebriated than the writers, and more genuinely enthusiastic about my work. I said polite things to all these people, and reminded myself to smile whenever I detected a witticism.

Copies of *A Western Boy* had been stacked on a table. They were the first I had seen in finished form. I remember to this day the nervous pleasure of holding one of these specimens in my hand and inspecting the two-color blind-stamped illustration on the front of it. The illustration showed my protagonist, the Western boy Isaiah Compass, with a sword in his right hand and a pistol in his left, battling a Pirate beneath a sketchy Palm Tree, while an Octopus—inexplicably out of his native element—looked on menacingly. I had not included an Octopus in my story, and I hoped the general reader, his interest aroused by this illustration, would not be disappointed by its absence from the text. I mentioned my concern to Mr. Hungerford, who said it didn't matter; there were better things than Octopuses in the novel, he said; the Octopus was only there to snag the attention of potential customers, in which role it admittedly performed a useful service. Still, I wondered if I ought to put an Octopus, or some other exciting and deadly form of oceanic life, into my next book, in order to compensate readers who might feel cheated by this one.

One New York City writer who was not present at the event (nor expected to be, since Hungerford wasn't his publisher) was Mr. Charles Curtis Easton. I asked Mr. Hungerford whether he had ever met that famous author.

"Charles Easton? Met him in passing once or twice. He's a decent enough old man, not at all haughty about his success. He lives in a house off 82nd Street."

"I have always admired his work."

"Why don't you go see him, if you're curious? I hear he's willing to entertain fellow writers if they don't take up too much of his time."

I was intrigued and dismayed by the suggestion. "I'm a complete stranger to him . . ."

Hungerford dismissed this objection as trivial. He took out one of his personal cards, and wrote on the back of it an introduction to me and my work. "Take this with you when you visit—it'll get you in the door."

"I wouldn't like to disturb him."

"Do or don't—suit yourself," John Hungerford said.

Of course I wanted to meet Charles Curtis Easton. But I was also afraid that I might embarrass myself by fawning, or exhibit my greenness in some other way. I could not visit him, I decided, without some better pretext than a first novel and a scribbled introduction on a calling card.

As it happened, it was Julian who provided that pretext.

Julian was visiting Calyxa when I arrived back at the guest-house. Flaxie sat in his lap, flailing at his beard with her tiny fist. Flaxie was tremendously interested in Julian's beard, which depended from his chin like a hank of yellow twine. On the occasions when she managed to get hold of it she yanked it as enthusiastically as a boat-captain sounding a steam whistle, and laughed at the screeches Julian inevitably gave out. It was a game they both seemed to enjoy, though it left Julian's eyes watering.

I showed off my new book, and gave copies to Julian and Calyxa. They admired it and praised it, though uncomfortable questions arose about the illustration on the cover. Eventually Flaxie grew restive, and Calyxa carried her off for a feeding.

Julian took advantage of her absence to confide in me that his work on *The Life and Adventures of the Great Naturalist Charles Darwin* remained stalled and incomplete. "I always meant to make this movie," he said. "Now I have the means within my grasp—who knows for how much longer?—and it still won't settle on the page. I'm serious about this, Adam. I need help—I admit it. And since you're the author of a novel, and have some understanding of these things, I want to beg your assistance."

He had brought the manuscript with him. It was a thin stack of pages, battered and dog-eared from his constant handling of it. He seemed abashed when he handed it to me.

"Will you look at it?" he asked with genuine humility. "And give me any advice that occurs to you?"

"I'm only a novice," I said. "I'm not sure I'll be able to help."

But I could think of someone who might.

I waited until Monday, the third day of July, to ride out to 82nd Street to find the residence of Mr. Charles Curtis Easton. The house where he lived was clearly numbered, and easy enough to identify in the summer sunlight; but I passed it once, and passed it twice, and passed it yet again, working up the courage to knock at the door.

When I finally knocked, however tentatively, the door was opened by a woman with a young child tugging at her skirt. I showed her Hungerford's card with its referral. She looked at it and smiled. "My father generally naps between three and five. But I'll see if he's available. Step in, please, Mr. Hazzard."

Thus I entered the Easton house, that Temple of Story, which enclosed a cheerful din, and where the air was rich with the odors created by good food and perhaps less good children. After a brief interval, during which three of those same children stared at me with relentless interest, Mr. Easton's daughter returned down a flight of stairs, dodging wheeled toys and other impediments, and invited me up to her father's study. "He would be happy to meet you. Go on in, Mr. Hazzard," she said, indicating the open door. "Don't be shy!"

Charles Curtis Easton was inside. I recognized him instantly from the portrait which was embossed on the backs of all his books. He sat at a crowded desk, under a bright window dappled with ailanthus shade, the very picture of a working writer. He wasn't a young man. His hair was snowy white, and it had retreated from his forehead and taken up a defensive position at the back of his skull. He wore a full beard, also white; and his eyes, which were embedded in networks of amiable wrinkles, gazed out from under ivory brows. He wasn't fat, exactly, but he had the physique of a man who works sitting down and dines to his own satisfaction.

"Come in, Mr. Hazzard," he said, glancing at the card his daughter had given him. "I'm always happy to meet a young writer. *The Adventures of Captain Commongold*: that was yours, wasn't it?"

"Yes," I said, pleased that he had heard of it.

"A fine book, although the punctuation was somewhat eccentric. And you have a new one?"

It was in my hand. I had brought an inscribed copy as a gift. Stammering out my purpose, I passed it over.

"*A Western Boy at Sea*," he read, examining the boards. "And it has an Octopus in it!"

"Well, no . . . the Octopus was the illustrator's conceit."

"Oh? Too bad. But the sword and the pistol?"

"They make several appearances." My embarrassment was almost painful. Why *hadn't* I put an Octopus in the story? It wouldn't have been hard to do. I ought to have thought of it in advance.

"That's fine," said Mr. Charles Curtis Easton, concealing any disappointment he might have felt. He put the book aside. "Sit down. You met my daughter? And my grandchildren?"

I fitted myself into an upholstered chair. "We weren't fully introduced, but they seem very nice."

He beamed at this modest compliment. "Tell me about yourself, then, Mr. Hazzard. You don't appear to be one of the high Eupatridians—no insult intended—and yet you're associated with the current President, isn't that right?"

I told him as briefly as possible about my origins in the boreal west and about the unexpected events that had led to my residing on the Palace grounds. I told him how much his work had meant to me when I was a young lease-boy eager for books, and how I remained loyal to his writing and frequently recommended it to others. He accepted the praise gracefully, and asked more questions about the war, and Labrador, and such topics. He seemed genuinely interested in my answers; and by the time half an hour had passed we were "old friends."

But it was not my intention just to flatter him, much as he may have deserved the flattery. Before long I mentioned Julian Comstock's interest in the theater, and his intention of developing a movie script on a subject close to his heart.

"That's an unusual ambition for a President," Mr. Easton observed.

"It is, sir; but Julian is an unusual President. His love of cinema is genuine and earnest. He's hit a snag, though, which his storytelling skills can't surmount." I went on to describe in general *The Life and Adventures of the Great Naturalist Charles Darwin.*

"Darwin and biological evolution are difficult topics to dramatize," Mr. Easton said, "and isn't he worried that the result won't receive the Dominion's approval? Very religious persons aren't keen on Mr. Charles Darwin, if I remember my lessons."

"You remember them correctly. Julian is no admirer of the worldly power of the Dominion, however, and he intends to overrule their objections in this case."

"Can he do such a thing?"

"He says he can. But the problem is with the script. It won't spring to life the way he wants it to. He asked my advice, but I'm only a beginning writer. I thought—of course I don't mean to presume on your generosity—"

"I wouldn't ordinarily look at a novice's screen-play. A commission from a sitting President of the United States is a different matter, however. I've worked on a few cinematic translations of my own stories in the past. I suppose I could examine President Comstock's material, and offer some advice, if it's wanted."

"It's very much wanted, sir, and I'm sure Julian will be grateful for anything you can tell him, as will I."

"Have you brought the script?"

"Yes," I said, drawing the folded pages out of my vest pocket. "Handwritten, I'm afraid," for I saw that Mr. Easton owned a typewriter even more sleek than the machine I had obtained from Theodore Dornwood, "but Julian's cursive is legible, mostly."

"I'd like to read it. Will you wait downstairs while I do so?"

"You mean to read it right now, sir?"

"If you'll oblige me."

I assured him I would. Then I went downstairs and spoke for a while with his daughter, who was named Mrs. Robson. She shared the house with her father while her husband was up in Quebec City commanding a regiment. During this conversation Mrs. Robson's four children (if I counted correctly) bounded through the room at irregular intervals, shouting for attention and wiping their noses on things. Whenever they passed I favored them with a smile, though they mainly grimaced in return, or emitted disrespectful noises.

Then Mr. Easton himself came hobbling down the stairs, a cane in one hand and *Charles Darwin* in the other. His age had made him slightly infirm, and Mrs. Robson hurried to his side and scolded him for attempting the staircase without help.

"Don't fuss," he told his daughter. "I'm on Presidential business. Mr. Hazzard, your evaluation of your friend's work was exactly correct. It's obviously sincere and well-researched, but it lacks certain elements indispensable to any truly successful cinematic production."

"What elements are those?" I asked.

"Songs," he said decisively. "And a villain. And, ideally, *pirates*."

I was eager to communicate this news to Julian—that the famous writer Mr. Charles Curtis Easton had agreed to help him develop his script—but there was a telegram waiting for me when I came home to Calyxa.

I had not received a telegram before. I was alarmed when I saw it, and guessed in advance that it contained bad news.

That intuition was correct. The telegram was from Williams Ford. It had been sent by my mother.

Dear Adam, it said. *Your father gravely ill. Snakebit. Come if you can.*

I made the arrangements at once, and secured a ticket on an express train; but he died before I reached Athabaska.

5

The train rolled over half of America that Fourth of July, it seemed to me, past small towns thriving and many abandoned, past vast Estates worked by shirtless indentured men, past countless Tips and Tills and ruins, into a sunset that burned like slow coal on the horizon, and on into the prairie night. There were no fireworks that evening, though there was some impromptu merry-making in the dinner car—I didn't join in. I was asleep by moonrise. Late the next day the train entered the State of Athabaska, its border marked by a landscape of enormous pits where the Secular Ancients had once strained the tarry earth for oil. I saw the ruins of a Machine the size of a Cathedral, its rusted treadwork embedded in scabs of calcified mud. Wherever there was open water, geese and crows flocked up to salute the passing train.

Julian had wired the Duncan-Crowley Estate to tell them I was coming. That presented a social difficulty to the Aristos there. Seen from one angle, I was a recreant lease-boy of no account come home to visit his illiterate father's grave; from another, I was the scribe and confidant of the new President, the nearest thing to an emissary from the Executive Power that Williams Ford was ever likely to receive. The Duncans and the Crowleys, whose fortune was all in Ohio farmland and Nevada mines, and whose New York connections were tenuous, had resolved their dilemma by sending Ben Kreel to meet me. He came down to Connaught in the Estate's best rig, drawn by two high-stepping horses.

The train had arrived with the dawn. I hadn't slept well; but Ben Kreel was an early riser by habit, and he shook my hand as cheerfully as the occasion permitted. "Adam Hazzard! Or should I call you *Colonel* Hazzard?"

He had not changed much, though I had new eyes (it seemed) to see him with. He was still bluff, stout, red-cheeked, and utterly in control of himself. "I'm out of the Army now—plain Adam will do," I said.

"Not so plain as when you left us," he said. "We all thought you and Julian must have been running from conscription. But you distinguished yourselves in battle—and in other ways—didn't you?"

"What a person runs run *from* and what a person runs *to* aren't always as different as we hope."

"And you're an Author now, and speak like one."

"I don't mean to put on any airs, sir."

"A justified pride is never out of place. Very sorry about your father."

"Thank you, sir."

"The Estate physician did what he could; but it was a bad bite, and your father wasn't a young man."

The carriage moved away from the clutter and noise of the train depot, past wood-frame hostels and the many bar-rooms and hemp-dens my mother used to call "the curse of Connaught," onto the pressed-earth road leading north to Williams Ford. It was a warm and windless morning, and the rising sun picked out the peaks of the distant mountains. Devil's Paint-Brush grew in colorful thickets along the verge of the road, and the sparsely-wooded land gave out its old familiar summer odors.

"The Duncans and the Crowleys," Ben Kreel said, "are prepared to welcome you to town, and no doubt would have put on some sort of public reception if the circumstances were less unhappy. As it is, they've set aside a room for you in one of the Great Houses."

"I thank them kindly; but I was never uncomfortable in my mother's house, and I expect she would like me to stay there, and that's what I mean to do."

"Probably that's wise," Ben Kreel said, with something that might have been a suppressed sigh of relief.

When at last we came through the fields where the indentured men worked, into the low rolling hills near the River Pine, and reached the outskirts of Williams Ford, I mentioned that the Independence Day fireworks must have been extravagant this year.

"They were," Ben Kreel said. "A peddler brought in a handful of Chinese rockets from Seattle for the event. Blue Fire-Wheels and some very colorful Salamanders . . . how did you know?"

"The air still smells of gunpowder," I said. It was a sensitivity I had picked up in the war.

I won't dwell on the details of my grief. The reader understands the delicacy of these painful emotions.*

I put in a brief appearance at the Estate, for the sake of politeness, and I was politely received by the Duncans and the Crowleys, but I didn't stay long. It was more important for me to see my mother. I passed the stables on the way from the Estate to the lease-holds, and I was tempted to find out whether my old tormentors still worked there, and whether my new rank had made them afraid of me; but that was a petty urge, not worth indulging.

The cottage where I had grown up stood just where I had left it. The creek behind it still ran dappled and cheerful toward the Pine, and my sister Flaxie's grave was where it had always been, modestly marked. But there was another grave beside it now, a fresh one, with a white wooden cross above it on which my father's name had been burned. Though he was illiterate, he had

---

* Or if the reader doesn't understand it right now, he will before very long. That's the contract Life makes with Nature and Time; and we're all bound by it, though none of us consented to the bargain.

learned to recognize his written name and could even produce a plausible signature—he would be able to read his own gravepost, I supposed, if his ghost sat up and craned its neck.

Graves are best visited by sunlight. The warm July weather was soothing, and the bird sounds and the faint chuckling of the creek made the idea of death more bearable. I hated to think of next year's snows weighing down this fresh-turned sod, or the January winds blowing over it. But my father was next to Flaxie now, so she wouldn't be alone; and I didn't suppose the dead suffered very badly from the cold. The dead are immune to seasonal discomforts—there is at least that much of Heaven in the world.

My mother saw me standing by the grave and came out from the back door of the cottage. She took me by the arm, wordlessly. Then we went indoors and wept together.

I stayed five days. My mother was in a fragile condition, both because of her grief and because of her age. Her eyes were poor now, and she was no longer useful to the Aristos as a seamstress; but because she was of the leasing class, and had served faithfully all her life, she continued to receive chits with which to buy food at the lease-store, and she would not be forced out of her home.

Her eyesight had not dimmed so much that she wasn't eager to see a copy of *A Western Boy at Sea,* and of course I had brought one for her. She handled it with exaggerated care, smiling a little; then she put it on a high shelf next to *The Adventures of Captain Commongold,* which I had also sent her. She would read it, she said, chapter by chapter, in the afternoons, when the light and her eyes were at their best.

I told her that I couldn't have written either of these books if she had not been so determined about teaching me to read—teaching me the love of reading, that is, and not just the names of the letters, as most lease-boys were taught on Sundays.

"I learned to read from my own mother," she said. "And she learned from her mother before her, all the way back to the Secular Ancients, according to family legend. There was a school-teacher in our family, long ago. Perhaps another writer, too—who knows? Your father's greatest shame was his illiteracy. He felt it deeply, though he didn't show it."

"You could have taught him the art of it."

"I offered to. He wouldn't try. Too old and set for that, he always said. I expect he was afraid of failing."

"I taught a man to read," I said, "when I was in the Army." That made her smile again.

She was keen for news about Calyxa and the baby. By a fortunate coincidence Julian had arranged to have a photograph of us taken shortly before Independence Day, and I showed it off. Here was Calyxa in a chair, her coiled hair shining. Flaxie sat in her lap, slightly lopsided, baby dress askew, goggling at the camera. I stood behind the chair with one hand on Calyxa's shoulder.

"She has a forceful look," my mother observed, "your Calyxa. Good strong legs. The baby is pretty. My eyes aren't what they used to be, but I can still spot a pretty baby, and that's one."

"Your grand-daughter," I said.

"Yes. And *she'll* learn to read, too, won't she? When she's ready?"

"No doubt of it," I said.

Eventually we talked about my father's death—not just the fact but the circumstances of it. I asked whether he had been bitten during a Signs service.

"There aren't any services of that kind anymore, Adam. Church of Signs was never popular except among a few of the indentured, and not long after you left the Duncans and Crowleys decided it was a 'cult,' and ought to be suppressed. Ben Kreel began preaching against the sect, and the most enthusiastic members of the congregation were sold off or sent away. Your father was the only lease-man among them, so he stayed; but there was no congregation to preach to anymore."

"But he kept the snakes." I had seen them in their cages out back, writhing unpleasantly.

"They were pets to him. He couldn't bear to stop feeding them, or destroy them any other way, and it wouldn't have been safe to set them loose. I'm not sure I can bring myself to kill them, either. Although I despise them." She said this was a vehemence that startled me. "I do despise them very much. I always have. I loved your father dearly. But I never loved those snakes. They haven't been fed since he died. Something has to be done about them."

We didn't discuss the matter any further. That night, however, after she had served a modest stew and dumplings and gone to bed, I left the house very quietly, and went out to the cages.

A bright moon hung above the distant mountains. It cast a steady pale light on my father's family of Massasauga Rattlers. The serpents were in a bitter mood, no doubt from hunger. There was a slashing impatience in their motions. Nor would they have been milked of their venom recently. (This was something my father used to do secretly, before services, especially if he thought children might participate in the handling. He would stretch a bit of thin leather over the mouth of an old jar, and let the serpents bite it. It took the poison out of them for a period of time. That was his own private apostasy, I suppose—an insurance policy against any momentary lapse of attention on the part of higher powers.) The snakes were aware of my presence. They twined and curled restlessly, and I imagined I could feel a cold fury in their blank and bloodless eyes.

A man who submits himself wholeheartedly to God might handle them and not be harmed. That was the faith my father had professed. Certainly he trusted God, in his own case, and believed God manifested Himself in the rolled eyes of his congregants and in their babble of incomprehensible tongues. Trust and be saved, was his philosophy. And yet in the end it was the snakes that killed him. I wondered which element of the calculation had ultimately failed him—human faith or divine patience.

I was not a faithful man by most definitions. I wasn't a devotee of the Church of Signs, and I had never adopted its doctrines as my own. Nevertheless I lifted the latch and opened the door of the nearest cage. I didn't wear gloves or any such protection. My hands and arms were exposed and vulnerable. I reached inside.

I had entered some wordless principality of grief and anger. There was no logic to the act, only the memory of the advice my father had given me, years ago, when I watched him feed living mice to his snakes while dodging their strikes and lunges. *It shouldn't be necessary to kill a serpent,* he said, *in the ordinary course of things, if you know what you're doing. But unexpected events happen. Perhaps a stray viper threatens some innocent man or animal. Then you have to be decisive. You have to be quick. Don't fear the creature, Adam. Grasp it where its neck ought to be, behind the head; ignore the tail, however it may thrash; and crack its skull, hard and often enough to subdue it.*

And that is what I did—repetitively, mechanically—until a dozen serpentine corpses lay stiffening at my feet.

Then I turned back to my familiar old home, and went to the bed that had comforted me through many winters, and slept for hours without dreaming.

In the morning the wire cages were bright with beads of dew, and the carcasses I had left behind were gone—some hungry animal had carried them off, I supposed.

The day before I left Williams Ford I asked my mother whether she believed in God, and Heaven, and Angels, and that sort of thing.

It was a bold question, and it took her by surprise. "That's not the sort of thing a polite person ought to ask," she said, "outside of church."

"Perhaps not; but it's the kind of question Julian Comstock enjoys asking, almost every chance he can get."

"And it gets him in trouble, I expect?"

"Often enough."

"You can take a lesson from that. And you know the answer, in any case. Haven't I read to you from the Dominion books, and told you all the stories in the Bible?"

"As a parent to a child. Not as one adult to another."

"You never stop being a parent, Adam, no matter how old or wise your child becomes—you'll see."

"I'm sure you're right. Do you, though? Believe in God, I mean?"

She looked at me as if to gauge my earnestness. "I believe in all sorts of things," she said, "though I don't necessarily understand them. I believe in the moon and the stars, though I can't tell you what they're made of, or where they come from. I suppose God falls into that category—real enough to be felt from time to time, but mysterious in His nature, and often confusing."

"That's a subtle answer."

"I wish I had a better one."

"What about Heaven, though? Do you think we go to Heaven when we die?"

"Heaven is generally regarded as having strict admission requirements, though no two faiths agree on the details. I don't know. I expect it's like China—a place everyone acknowledges as real, but which few ever visit."

"There are Chinamen in New York City," I volunteered. "And a great many Egyptians, besides."

"But hardly any *angels*, I expect."

"Next to none."

That was as much Theology as she would tolerate, so we dropped the subject, and spent our last day together discussing more cheerful matters; and in the morning I said goodbye to her, and left Williams Ford behind me for the second and last time.

"**In** your many travels since we last met," Ben Kreel said to me as we drove back down the Wire Road to Connaught, "did you ever get as far as Colorado Springs?"

"No, sir," I said. It was another sunlit day. The telegraph wires hummed in a warm breeze. The train that would take me away from my childhood home and all its memories was due in just three hours. "Mostly I was in various parts of Labrador, well north and east of Colorado."

"I've been to Colorado Springs five times," Ben Kreel said, "for ecclesiastical training. It isn't at all like the pictures in the Dominion readers. You know what I mean—the Dominion Academy is all they show, with its white pillars, and those big paintings of the Fall of the Cities."

"It's very impressive, and worth a photograph."

"Certainly it is; but Colorado Springs is more than just the Academy, and so is the Dominion."

"I'm sure they are, sir."

"Colorado Springs is a town full of pious, prosperous men and women who are loyal to the Union and to their faith; and the Dominion isn't strictly a *building*, nor even an *organization*, but an *idea*. A very bold and ambitious idea, an idea about taking the battered and imperfect world we live in and making it over fresh and new—making a Heavenly Kingdom of it, pure enough that the angels themselves wouldn't be reluctant to tread there."

Unlike Manhattan, I thought to myself. "It seems as if we're a long way from that. We haven't taken Labrador yet, much less the world."

"It's a chore for more than one lifetime. But we can't commune directly with Heaven until we perfect the world, and we can't perfect the world until we perfect ourselves. That's the job of the Dominion, Adam: to make us all more perfect. It's a stern duty, but it arises out of the common instincts of charity and good will. Those who chafe under it are generally too attached to some imperfection of their own, which they love with a sinful stubbornness."

"Yes, sir, that's as you used to tell us at holiday services."

"I'm pleased you remember. Our enemy is anyone who rebels against God—perhaps you remember that aphorism, too."

"I do."

"What form do you suppose that rebellion generally takes, Adam?"

"Sin," I guessed.

"Sin, yes, certainly, and plenty of that to go around. But most sin only sabotages the sinner. Some sin is more insidious, and aims directly at impeding the Dominion in its work."

"I'm not sure I know what you mean." Though I had my suspicions.

"Don't you? When you were in the Army, did your regiment have a Dominion officer in it?"

"Yes."

"And was he universally loved?"

"It wasn't a unanimous sentiment, no."

"Nor could it have been, since it was his job to elevate virtue and excoriate wrong-doing. Thieves do not love prisons, and sinners don't love the Church. My point is that the Dominion stands in relation to the United States as that pastor stood to his troops. His purpose wasn't to be loved for *himself*, but to coax and herd a recreant population into the corral of *divine* love."

For some reason I had a recollection of Lymon Pugh and his description of the meat-packing industry.

"The Dominion takes a profound interest in the destiny of this nation, and every nation," Ben Kreel said. "Compared with that *institutional* interest, the whims of Presidents are fleeting."

"This conversation is too cryptic," I complained. "Is it about Julian? If that's what you mean, just say so."

"Who am I to stand in judgment of the Chief Executive? I'm just a country pastor. But the Dominion watches, the Dominion judges; and the Dominion is older than Julian Comstock, and ultimately more powerful."

"Julian has nothing against the Dominion, except in some particulars."

"I hope that's true, Adam; but, if so, why would he attempt to sever the ancient and beneficial connection between the Dominion and the Armies?"

"What! Did he?"

Ben Kreel smiled unpleasantly. For many years this man had seemed to me a minor deity, above reproach. He was a kindly voice, a useful teacher, and a sturdy peacemaker when there was conflict in the community. But looking at him now I detected something sour and triumphant in his nature, as if he delighted in having stolen a march on an upstart lease-boy. "Why, that's exactly what he did, Adam; don't you know? The news came by wire from Colorado Springs this morning. Julian Conqueror, so-called, has ordered the Dominion to withdraw its representatives from the nation's Armies and cease participating in military counsels."

"That's a bold step," I said, wincing.

"It's more than a *bold step*, Adam. It's very nearly a declaration of war." He leaned close to me and said in an oily and confiding tone, "A war he cannot win. If he doesn't understand that, you ought to enlighten him."

"I'll be sure to tell him what you said."

"Yes, thank you," said Ben Kreel. "You're a good friend to Julian Comstock."

"I try to be."

"But you shouldn't walk in the footsteps even of your best friend, Adam Hazzard, if the road he's following leads to Hell."

I was tempted to tell Ben Kreel that my belief in Hell was even shakier, these days, than my confidence in Paradise. Or I might have said that I had met a man in New York who claimed the only God was Conscience ("have no other"), under which standard the whole Dominion was an Apostasy, if not something worse; but I didn't want to engage him in any further discussion, and I sat sullenly the rest of the way to Connaught.

Shortly thereafter I boarded the train that would take me back to Manhattan. It was a more comfortable ride than the Caribou-Horn Train had been, the first time I left Williams Ford. But I felt no less afraid as I traveled in it.

6

After I had arrived back home, and made my reunion with Calyxa and Flaxie, and bathed away the grime of travel, and slept a night, I went to the Palace to see Julian.

The Executive Palace was still, in the main, a mystery to me. It was an immense structure, finely divided into labyrinthine rooms and chambers. It housed servants, bureaucrats, and a small army of Republican Guards, in addition to the President himself. It rose three stories above the ground, and sheltered extensive basements and cellars beneath. It was the most wainscoted, draped, sashed, carpeted, and furbeloved building I had ever been inside; and I was never comfortable in it. The minor officials I passed regarded me with a disdain bordering on contempt, while the Republican Guards scowled and fingered their pistols at the sight of me.

Julian did not "inhabit" this entire space—surely no one man could have done so—but spent most of his time in the Library Wing. The Library Wing contained not just the Presidential Library (which was extensive, though mainly Dominion-approved, and to which Julian had added many items culled from the liberated Archives) but a large reading room with high, sunny windows and an enormous oaken desk. It was this room Julian had made particularly his own, and that was where I visited him.

Magnus Stepney, the rogue Pastor of the Church of the Apostles Etc., was also present, lounging in a stuffed chair and reading a book while Julian sat at the desk applying pen to paper. Pastor Stepney had been Julian's close companion for many weeks now, and both of them smiled when I entered. They asked about Williams Ford, and my father and mother, and I told them a little about that sad business; but not much time had passed before Julian once more raised the question of his Movie Script.

I mentioned to him that I had discussed the script with Mr. Charles Curtis Easton. I was afraid Julian might be unhappy that I had taken the matter "out of the family," and gone to a stranger with it. He did seem a little nonplused; but Magnus Stepney—who was as much an Aesthete and devoted follower of Drama as Julian was*—clapped his hands and said I had done exactly the right thing: "That's what we need, Julian, a *professional* opinion."

"Possibly so. Did Mr. Easton *render* an opinion?" Julian asked me.

"He did, in fact."

---

* Stepney, though sincere about his pastoral duties, made no secret of the fact that he might like to play the part of Charles Darwin when the production eventually began. This was not as vain as it sounds, for he was handsome, and had a talent for striking poses and putting on amusing voices.

"Would you care to mention what it was?"

"He agreed that the story lacked some essential ingredients."

"Such as?"

I cleared my throat. "Three acts—memorable songs—attractive women—pirates—a battle at sea—a despicable villain—a duel of honor—"

"But none of those things actually *happened* to Mr. Darwin, or had any connection with him."

"Well, I suppose that's the point. Do you want to tell the truth, or do you want to tell a story? The trick," I said, remembering Theodore Dornwood's commentary on my own writing, "is to steer a course between Scylla and Charybdis—"

"Fine talk for a lease-boy," Magnus Stepney said, laughing.

"—where Scylla is *truth*, and Charybdis is *drama*—or the other way around; I don't remember exactly."

Julian sighed, and rolled his eyes; but Stepney gave a little cheer and cried out, "That's just what I've been telling you, Julian! It was good advice from me, and it's good advice from Adam Hazzard and Mr. Charles Curtis Easton!"

Julian said nothing more about it that day. Initially, of course, he was skeptical. But he didn't resist the idea for long, for it appealed to his sense of Theater; and by the end of the week he had adopted it as his own.

The rest of July was devoted to producing a final script. Some scholars have suggested that Julian "fiddled" with cinema, while his Presidency was collapsing around his head. But that's not how it seemed in the summer of 2175. I think Julian saw the possibility of redemption in Art, after all the horrors he had experienced in War, though War is more customarily the business of the Commander in Chief. And I think there was a deeper reason why Julian ignored the protocols and entanglements of political supremacy. I believe he had genuinely expected to die in Labrador—had accepted it as his fate, once the Black Kite maneuver failed—and was shocked to find himself still alive, after he had led so many others to their deaths.

His order to sever all formal connections between the Dominion and the Military had sent shock-waves through both Armies. Colorado Springs was in a state of virtual rebellion, and Deacon Hollingshead had ceased to visit the Executive Palace, or to acknowledge Julian in any way. The Dominion still kept a firm grip on its affiliated Churches, however, and "Julian the Atheist" was denounced from pulpits all over the country, which made the Eupatridians and the Senate uneasy in their support of him.

But if Deacon Hollingshead did not pay us any visits, he was welcomely replaced by Mr. Charles Curtis Easton, who was invited to the Palace to meet Julian and discuss modifications to the *Darwin* script. Julian was charmed by

Mr. Easton ("This is what you might become, Adam, if you live to a ripe old age, and grow a beard"), and delegated him to work alongside me as a Screen-Play Committee. We met on scheduled occasions, and Julian or Magnus Stepney often joined us, and within weeks we had sketched out a completely new outline of *The Life and Adventures of the Great Naturalist Charles Darwin*, which I will briefly describe.

Act One was called *Homology*, and it dealt with Darwin's youth. In this Act young Darwin meets the girl with whom he is destined to fall in love—his beautiful cousin Emma Wedgwood—and discovers he has a rival for her affections in the form of a young divinity student named Samuel Wilberforce. The two boys enter into a Beetle-Collecting and Interpreting Competition sponsored by the local University, which is called Oxford, and Miss Wedgwood in a coy moment mentions that she'll save a kiss for the winner. Wilberforce then sings a song about Bugs as Specimens of the Divine Ordination of Species, while Darwin retorts with musical observations on Homology (that is, the physical similarities shared by Insects of different species). Wilberforce, a ruthless and cunning conspirator, tries and fails to have Darwin disqualified from the contest on the grounds of Blasphemy. But Oxford is deaf to his pleadings. Darwin wins the contest; Wilberforce comes in a bitter second; Emma kisses Darwin chastely on the cheek; Darwin blushes; and a simmering Wilberforce vows ultimate vengeance.

Act Two was entitled *Diversity; or, An English Boy at Sea,** and it covered Charles Darwin's exciting voyages around South America aboard the exploratory vessel *Beagle*. This is where Darwin makes some of his many observations about Turtles and Finches' Beaks and such things, though we kept the scientific matter to a minimum so as not to strain the audience's attention, and enlivened it with a scene involving a ferocious Lion. Out of all these unusual experiences Darwin begins to formulate his grand idea of the Diversity of Life, and how it arises from the effects of time and circumstance on animal reproduction. He resolves to communicate that insight to the world, though he knows it won't be welcome in ecclesiastical circles. Back home, however, Wilberforce—now a junior Bishop at Oxford, and grimly determined to achieve even greater ecclesiastical power—has drawn on his family fortune and hired a gang of nautical pirates to hunt down the *Beagle* and sink her at sea. The Act culminates in a closely-fought Nautical Battle in which young Darwin, flailing about on the fore-deck with sword and pistol, speculates musically on the role of chance and "fitness" in determining the ultimate outcome of the conflict. The battle is bloody but (as in nature) the fittest survive—Darwin, happily, is one of them.

By the beginning of Act Three, called *The Descent of Man*, all England is caught up in a fierce religious controversy over Darwin's theories. Darwin has

* My suggestion.

published a book about the Origin of Species; and Wilberforce, now Oxford's head Bishop, has made a point of denouncing that work and ridiculing the author. He hopes by this strategy to create a conflict between Darwin and Emma Wedgwood, who have postponed their marriage (under pressure from Emma's family) until Darwin's respectability is more firmly established in the public mind. It seems a distant goal, at a time when English churches resound with anti-Darwinian rhetoric, torch-bearing mobs threaten Oxford, and Emma herself is torn by the conflict between Romantic Love and Religious Duty. The tempest culminates in a public Debate in a crowded London hall, where Darwin and Wilberforce argue over the ancestral relations of Ape and Man. Darwin expounds (*sings*, that is) his doctrine eloquently, with gentle humor; while Wilberforce, under the fierce lamp of logic, is revealed as a jealous poseur. "Darwin a True Scholar!" a headline in the next morning's London *Times* proclaims, calming the general excitement and smoothing the way for Emma and Darwin to marry. But Wilberforce won't suffer himself to be humiliated in such a manner. He accuses Darwin of blasphemy and personal insult, and challenges him to a duel. Darwin reluctantly accepts, seeing this as his only chance to rid himself of the meddlesome Bishop; and both men climb to a craggy meadow high in the wild and windblown mountains that loom over Oxford University.

The climax of the movie is essentially that duel, with ruses and low tricks attempted by Wilberforce, and thwarted by Darwin. There is singing, and pistol-shooting, and some lively screaming from Emma, and more pistol-shooting, and wrestling about on cliff-edges, until Darwin stands wounded but victorious over the cooling corpse of his ruthless enemy.

Followed by a wedding ceremony, bells rung, cheerful noises, and so forth.

Julian gave his approval to this outline, though he took a certain pleasure in pointing out the distance between our dramatic liberties and historical truth in the strictest sense. ("If Oxford has Alps," he liked to say, "then perhaps New York City has a Volcano, geography being so flexible a science.") But these were amicable objections, not serious ones; and he understood our motives in remodeling the obstinate clay of history.

As for the songs and their lyrics—so important to the success of any such enterprise—what could we do but recruit Calyxa's formidable talents? Julian supplied her with a biography of Darwin recovered from the Dominion Archives, along with works discussing the taxonomy of beetles, the geography of South America, the habitat and life-cycle of Pirates, and such subjects. Calyxa undertook her assignment very seriously, and read all these books with close attention. Several times, when the household help was absent, I was delegated to attend to Flaxie's infant requirements (which were numerous and urgent) while Calyxa continued her creative work at the desk or the piano.

In a few days she had sketched out Arias and melodies for all three Acts of *Charles Darwin*. She presented these to Julian on a night when he arrived along with Pastor Stepney for our weekly Script Conference. Julian leafed through the music and lyric sheets with deepening appreciation, judging by the expression on his face. Then he turned to Calyxa and said, "You ought to sing some of it for us. Magnus doesn't read music, but I want him to hear it."

"Most of the Arias are male parts," Calyxa said, "though Emma Wedgwood has a song or two."

"That's understood. Here," Julian said, handing over one of the first sections, in which the young Charles Darwin, during a beetling expedition outside Oxford, spots his cousin Emma in the woods.* Calyxa sat down at the piano and picked up the song at the point where Darwin is inspecting the contents of his bug-net, singing:

> *These creatures yet are all alike in*
> *Several ways that I find striking:*
> *Six legs fixed on a tripart body;*
> *External shells, some plain, some gaudy;*
> *Some have wings, or hooks, or hair*
> *—distinctions, yes, eight, ten, a dozen—*
> *And yet in General Structure they're*
> *As like as I am to my cousin.*
> *Here comes my cousin now! And as she*
> *Pauses in the shady hedge-wood*
> *I hope she'll turn her eyes to me,*
> *That young and pious Emma Wedgwood!*
> *White summer dress, blue summer bonnet,*
> *A red coccinellid clinging on it—*

"Stop!" cried Julian. "What's a *coccinellid*?"

"Ladybug," said Calyxa, tersely.

"Very good! Carry on."

> *All life intrigues me, without doubt,*
> *And yet in truth (for truth will out),*
> *I find Miss Emma's pretty legs*
> *More interesting than Skate-Leech Eggs. . . .*

There were a few more interruptions from Julian, when he needed some point clarified, but for the most part Calyxa sang without interruption—the whole score, except for one duet (which she couldn't manage by herself) and the final choral Medley. She sang the male parts with gusto and the female parts in a fine contralto, and banged the piano with great enthusiasm and skill. Little Flaxie could not sleep through all this noise, of course, and her nurse

---

* The English, in those days, were not particular about wooing and marrying cousins. It was a practice as acceptable to them as it is to our own Eupatridians.

eventually brought her down to join us. In the end we had nearly an hour of Calyxa's wonderfully entertaining performance, at the end of which she sat back from the piano with a satisfied smile on her face. She undid the scarf she was wearing, "and down her slender form there spread / Black ringlets rich and rare," while Julian clapped his applause, and the rest of us joined him for a long ovation. Even Flaxie attempted to clap, though she was inexpert at it, and her flailing hands passed in mid-air more often than they collided.

It was altogether the finest time we had had for quite a while, and we might have been some large family, joined together after a long absence, taking delight in one another's company, and never heeding the griefs and dangers that circled about us like carrion birds over a tubercular mule.

7

It was late that summer when an assassin crept into the Executive Palace and hid himself in the Library Wing, for the purpose of putting a pistol to Julian Conqueror's head and killing him.

August had just given way to September, and the production of *The Life and Adventures of the Great Naturalist Charles Darwin* was well under way. Julian had not been idle during the preparation of the book and music. All the power of the Presidency and much of the wealth he controlled as a Comstock had been devoted to it. He had renovated a set of unused stables at the West 110th Street end of the Palace grounds, turning them into a "movie studio" as modern as anything in Manhattan; and he had recruited the talents of the city's finest Production Company, which was called the New York Stage and Screen Alliance. This combination of players, singers, noisemakers, camera-operators, film-copiers, *et alia,* had been responsible for many well-regarded movies, including *Eula's Choice,* previously described. In the past, however, they had always been bound by the rules of the trade and the strictures of the Dominion. In this case Julian had taken charge of them directly; and they were bound to his instructions, and no one else's.

On this particular day I was down at the "studio" watching some incidental photography not involving the major actors. It was a day off for Magnus Stepney, who was playing Darwin; and Julinda Pique, the screen actress representing Emma Wedgwood, had gone to visit relatives in New Jersey. But the players interested me less than the technical work of the business, which continued without them. I had befriended the Camera Operator In Charge of Illusions, or *Effects Shooter,* as he was called for short, and I was helping him arrange "shots" for the South American montage in Act Two. He had set up a painting the size of a wall, of jungles and mountains, uncanny in its realism, and he had placed in front of it some very convincing paper imitations of tropical plants and bushes, as well as wildlife in the form of tame dogs dressed as tigers, and a number of armadillos sent by mail from Texas, mainly living. Julian had instructed him not to keep the camera still, but to move it around some, giving a more lively impression; and he was doing so as I watched, trying to keep the restive animals in the frame without inadvertently revealing the artificiality of the backdrop. This was warm work on a sultry September day, and it called forth some unusual curses before he achieved the result he aspired to.

He was just "wrapping up" this business when an Executive Page in green livery came hurrying toward us. The man was obviously agitated, and he had to recover his breath before he could gasp out, "There's been shooting, Major Hazzard! Shooting at the Palace, sir!"

I rushed there without waiting to hear more. It wasn't easy getting past the Republican Guards who had cordoned off the Library Wing, and I was alarmed when I saw the court physician hurried in ahead of me. I remonstrated with the Guards until Sam Godwin appeared; then we both proceeded together.

I feared the worst. Julian's position as President had become increasingly insecure as his battles with the Dominion escalated. Just last week he had declared all Ecclesiastical Writs of Replevin null and void, pending new legislation. This meant that the authorities could no longer claim, seize, or imprison fugitives on complaints issued solely by the Church. It had the effect of releasing Calyxa from her confinement, but it also set free countless jailed apostates, the congregations of various Unaffiliated Churches, a number of Parmentierist radicals who had been scooped up on ecclesiastical charges, and a few of those unfortunate lunatics who insist on proclaiming their personal divinity.

The voiding of that law, added to his ongoing attempt to separate the Church from the Military, amounted to an emasculation of the Dominion. The Dominion could still collect tithes from affiliates, and could pronounce anathema on dissenters, but without legal traction it would soon begin to lose ground—or so Julian hoped.

In response, it seemed they had sent an assassin into our midst: for I did not doubt that the Dominion was behind this treachery. "Is Julian killed?" I asked Sam as we pressed through the crowd in the Library Wing.

"Don't know," said Sam. "Has the physician been called for?"

"Yes, I saw him go in—"

But Julian wasn't killed. Once we attained the Reading Room we found him sitting in a chair, upright and alert, although a bandage had been wrapped around his head. He called us over as soon as he spotted us.

"How badly are you hurt?" Sam demanded.

Julian's expression was grim. "Not badly, or so the doctor tells me—the bullet took a piece of my ear."

"How did it happen?"

"The assassin hid behind a chair and came out at me unexpectedly. He would have killed me completely, except that Magnus caught sight of him and called out a warning."

"I see," said Sam. "Where is Magnus now?"

"Lying down. The event was alarming for him—he has a sensitive nature."

"I guess an attempted murder would alarm most anyone. What about the assassin—where's *he*?"

"Mauled by the Republican Guards," said Julian, "and taken into confinement in the basement."

The "basement" of the Executive Palace included a set of cells in which prisoners could be detained.* "Has he said anything useful?" Sam asked.

"Apparently his tongue was cut out years ago, and he can't or won't write. The Dominion chooses its assassins carefully—it knows how to break men, and tries to make its men unbreakable."

"You don't know for certain it was the Dominion that sent him."

"Is there any evidence to the contrary? I don't need *certainty* in order to act on a well-grounded suspicion."

Sam said nothing to this, but shook his head unhappily; for he believed, and often said, that Julian in his argument with the Dominion had set himself on a course for destruction just as certainly as if he had plunged into the rushing waters above Niagara.

"In any case," Julian said, "the man's motivation is plain enough. He was carrying a crudely-printed leaflet demanding the restoration of Deklan Conqueror to the Executive."

"But if he can't read or write—"

"I expect the leaflet was a prop, meant to draw suspicion away from the clergy, though who but the clergy would want my murderous uncle back in the Executive seat? Still, I don't like to have Deklan used as a nail on which assassins pin their hopes. I'll have to do something about him."

There was a cold glint in his eye as he said this, and neither Sam nor I dared to pursue the matter, though Julian's manner filled us with foreboding.

"And there's the question of the Republican Guards," Julian continued.

"What about them? It seems as if they acted as soon as the assassin revealed himself."

"But they *ought* to have acted *before* the assassin revealed himself; otherwise what purpose do they serve? It was luck and Magnus Stepney that saved my life, not the Guardsmen. I don't see how the man could have got this far without a collaborator among them. I inherited those men from the previous regime, and I don't trust them."

"Again," Sam said in a conciliatory tone, "you don't know—"

"I'm the *President*, Sam, isn't that clear to you yet? I'm not required to *know*; only to *act*."

"How do you propose to *act*, then?"

Julian shrugged. If he wanted advice from us, he didn't ask for it.

Sam eventually went off to attend to ancillary business, once the atmosphere of crisis began to cool. I stayed to keep Julian company while the doctor removed the temporary bandage in order to dab the wounded ear with iodine and stitch what remained of its ragged edges. The court physician was

---

* The cells were installed during the reign of the very first Comstock, and had been used by every Comstock since, including Julian: Julian's uncle Deklan, since his deposition, had been languishing in that same internal prison.

as smoothly professional as Dr. Linch had been back in Striver, but there would still be a scar when the injury healed. "My head has been pared more often than a pie-apple," Julian complained. "It gets tiresome, Adam."

"I'm sure it does. You ought to rest now."

"Not just yet. I have business to take care of."

"What business?"

He gave me a look that was almost metallic in its indifference.

"Presidential business," he said.

No mention was made of the attempted assassination in the city press, for it was a delicate subject; but Julian arranged to make public his response to it, as I discovered the following morning when I left the Palace grounds for a walk down Broadway.

A crowd of pedestrians thronged the street beyond the 59th Street Gate, gazing upward with wide eyes. It was not until I reached the sidewalk outside the great walls that I could see what had attracted all their attention.

High on the iron spikes that surmount the stone wall two Severed Heads had been mounted, one to the left of the Gate and one to the right.

This was as gruesome a sight as anything I had seen in Labrador, more shocking for its presence in an otherwise peaceful city. However, it was not without precedent. The heads of traitors had been displayed here in earlier years and other conflicts, though seldom since the turbulent 2130s. From ground-level it was difficult to discern the identity of the victims, since the heads were contorted by death and had been pecked at by pigeons. But some of the curious onlookers had fetched opera-glasses in order to satisfy their curiosity, and a consensus had emerged among the crowd. The head on the left was not familiar to anyone present (nor could have been, for it belonged to the assassin captured in the Library Wing). The head on the right, however, was the one that had recently rested on the shoulders of Deklan Conqueror, the former President, who had once feared his nephew as a usurper, and had nothing to fear now but the judgment of a righteous God.

The unpleasant trophies remained there most of a week, rotting. Small boys gathered every day to toss pebbles at them, until the ghastly ornaments at last came loose from their spikes and tumbled back onto the Palace grounds.

Julian wouldn't speak of the beheadings, saying only that justice had been done and that the event was finished. I hoped he had not *ordered* the executions, but had only *sanctioned* them—though that was bad enough. I did not, of course, feel any sympathy for Julian's uncle or the anonymous assassin, since the former had committed many murders and the latter had attempted at least one. But the cutting off of their heads without benefit of trial did not seem to me entirely civilized; and I could not help thinking that the public display of their remains served no better purpose than to make Julian appear brutal and imperious.

During that same week, in another imperious act, Julian dismissed every serving member of the Republican Guard—some five hundred altogether—and replaced them with members of the Army of the Laurentians, selected by Julian personally from a list of those who had fought by his side at Mascouche, Chicoutimi, and Goose Bay. Many of these men were my comrades as well, and it was startling to walk down the halls of the Executive Palace and find myself greeted not with the malign stares and suspicion to which I had become accustomed, but by hearty hails from old friends and acquaintances.

That feeling was compounded one Friday evening when I went to join Julian and Magnus Stepney to plan out the next week's efforts on *Charles Darwin.* The new Captain of the Republican Guards, whom I had not met, was standing watch over the Library Wing when I turned a corner in one of that building's long halls and nearly collided with him.

"Watch out," the new man cried, "I'm not a door you can swing wide and walk through—state your business, mister—but—*be damned if it isn't Adam Hazzard!* Adam, you bookworm! I'll shake your hand or know why not!"

He did shake my hand, and it was a bruising experience, for the new Captain of the Guard was Mr. Lymon Pugh.

Perhaps I shouldn't have been so glad to see him, but at that moment he seemed like an envoy from a simpler and easier world. I told him I hadn't expected to meet him again, and that I hoped the Palace was a good place in which to find himself employed.

"Better than a slaughterhouse," he said. "And you! Last time I saw you, Adam, you had just married that tavern singer from the Thirsty Boot."

"I did, and we have a daughter now—I'll introduce you!"

"You wrote a book, too, somebody told me."

"A pamphlet about 'Captain Commongold,' and a novel which is selling adequately well; and I've met Mr. Charles Curtis Easton, and worked beside him. But you must have accomplished things just as significant!"

He shrugged. "I lived to my present age without dying," he said. "That's enough to boast about, by my lights."

Calyxa kept her distance from *The Life and Adventures of the Great Naturalist Charles Darwin,* as well as from Julian himself. Having supplied the score and lyrics, she felt no need to involve herself in the minutiae of movie-making, especially during a time when she was instructing Flaxie in the fundamentals of eating, and standing upright, and such useful skills as that.

She continued to meet with Parmentierist friends from the city, however, and Mrs. Comstock (or Mrs. Godwin, as I could not get accustomed to calling her) pursued certain of her contacts among the lesser Eupatridians. More importantly, the two women consulted one another and formulated plans to deal with any crisis that might arise out of Julian's political situation.

"Do you know very much about Mediterranean France?" Calyxa asked me with a certain affected casualness, one September night as we lay in bed.

"Only that Mitteleuropa claims it as a Territory, while it insists it's an Independent Republic."

"The weather there is very clement, and Mediterranean France has cordial relations with other parts of the world."

"I expect that's so . . . what about it?"

"Nothing at all, except that we may have to live there one day."

I didn't dismiss her assertion out of hand. In fact we had discussed the possibility several times before. In the event of a disaster, such as the collapse of Julian's presidency and the ascension to the Executive of hostile agencies, all of us (including Julian) might need to flee the country.

But I fervently hoped those conditions would not arise; or, if they did, that it would happen far in the future, when Flaxie was older and better able to travel. I didn't like to think of taking an infant on a trans-Atlantic journey. I was not even willing to let Flaxie be taken for rides in the streets of Manhattan, especially not now, with a new Pox circulating and half the citizens going about with paper masks over their noses.

"You can't leave these arrangements to the last hour," Calyxa said. "Things need to be set up in advance. We decided on Mediterranean France—"

"Wait—*who* decided?"

"Emily and I, between us. I consulted the local Parmentierists, and they say it's an ideal refuge. Emily has connections with people in the shipping business—right now she would have no trouble arranging passage for us, though that might change, with a changing situation."

"I still hope to spend my life in America and write books," I said.

"You wouldn't be the only American author in Marseilles. You can send manuscripts by mail."

"I'm not sure my publisher would agree to that."

"If things get much worse in Manhattan, Adam, you may not have a publisher."

Perhaps that observation was true. But it didn't cheer me up, or help me sleep.

All the filming of *The Life and Adventures of the Great Naturalist Charles Darwin* was finished by Thanksgiving of 2175. That wasn't the end of it, of course. What had been captured on film was only the visual portion of the show; to be presented in a theater it still needed voice-actors, noise-makers, intensive rehearsals, and a suitable venue. But a large part of the hardest work was done, especially for the technicians and screen-actors, and Julian thought it would be appropriate to commemorate the moment by hosting what he called a "wrap party."

The grounds of the Executive Palace had not been a social magnet during Julian's reign, especially so after the unannounced beheadings. Julian was not discomfited by this, since he didn't much care for the companionship of high Eupatridians, including even members of the Senate. Although the Senate had been generous toward his regime in the beginning, there had been friction with that branch of the government as well as with the Dominion. Julian did not enact any radical labor legislation,* but he had refused to dispatch troops during the servile insurrection in the thread trades.† His implied sympathy for the rebels enraged those Senators who had connections with the trade, and strongly-worded protests had been issued from that body.

So we did not have friendly Eupatridians to invite to our Wrap Party; but that wasn't a drawback, in Julian's opinion. Increasingly Julian had chosen to surround himself with a crowd of Aesthetes and Philosophers—not just the movie crew, but a motley assortment of well-born radicals, religious reformers, musicians, Parmentierist tract-writers, artists with more ambition than income, and people of that stripe.

The party took place on the last warm evening of the year. The temperature was nearly tropical, though Thanksgiving was almost on us, and after dark the celebration spilled out onto the great lawn of the Executive Palace. The efficiency of the New York City Hydroelectric Dynamo had lately been improved, and Julian had extended the hours of the Illumination of Manhattan, so that the cumulative light shed by the city's electric lamps gave the clouds overhead an eerie glow. The Pond and the Hunting Grounds were wrapped in shadow and looked very mysterious and romantic, and the guests and film crew were soon giddy with champagne. They strolled or capered about on the lawn, or shared hempen cigarettes in secluded places, and as the evening wore on their behavior became more flagrant and less discreet.

I sat on the marble steps of the Palace watching the revelry from a safe distance. After a time Pastor Magnus Stepney came and joined me. "It's a cheerful event, Adam," he said, settling his lanky frame onto the step just to the left of me.

"It's a spectacle, anyhow," I said.

"Don't you like to see people enjoy themselves?"

That was a subtler question than he seemed to realize. I had come to be friendly with many of these revelers, especially the crew who had worked on the filming of *Charles Darwin*, and I knew them to be good-souled and

---

* Much to Calyxa's disappointment and disgust.
† In July of 2175 a rebellion among indentured laborers at an Ohio broad-silk mill had spread to neighboring ribbon factories and dye shops. Over one hundred men died in the resulting siege.

well-intentioned people, for the most part. But the event was beginning to surpass anything I would have recognized as civilized celebration back in Williams Ford. Men and women not related by marriage were dancing to lewd songs, or chasing one another amidst gales of laughter, or indulging in intimate caresses regardless of the observation of those around them. Some of the crew were so intoxicated that they began to press such intimacies even on members of their own sex; and often enough these attentions were willingly received.*

"Well," I said, "that depends. I don't disapprove of anybody having a good time. And I don't like to set myself up in judgment. But what about you, Magnus? You being a church pastor and all, even if your church is an eccentric one. Is this how you encourage your congregation to behave?"

"My only God is Conscience, Adam. I put that statement up on a sign, to warn the unwary."

"Your conscience is happy to sit here and watch your friends debauch by moonlight?"

"The moon's not up quite yet."

"That's a dodge, Pastor."

"You misunderstand my doctrine. Perhaps I can give you a pamphlet. I encourage people to obey their conscience, and follow the Golden Rule, and so forth. But Conscience isn't the mean-spirited overseer so many people seem to think it is. Genuine Conscience speaks to all people in all tongues, and it can do so because it has just a few simple things to say. 'Love your neighbor as your brother,' and do all that that entails—visit the sick, refrain from beating wives and children, don't murder people for profit, etc. You know how I think of Conscience, Adam? I think of Conscience as a great green God—literally green, the color of spring leaves. With a garland of laurels, perhaps, or some leafy underwear, as in the Greek paintings. He says: Trust one another, even if you aren't trusted. He says: Do as I tell you, and you'll be back in Eden in no time. Do you know anything about Game Theory, Adam Hazzard?"

I said I did not. Magnus Stepney explained that it was an obscure Science of the Secular Ancients, and that it dealt with the mathematics of bargains, and mutually beneficial exchanges, and such matters. "Basically, Adam, Game Theory suggests that there are two ways for human beings to operate. You can be trustworthy and trust others, or you can be untrustworthy to your own advantage. The trustworthy man makes a deal and keeps it; the untrustworthy man makes the same deal but absconds with the cash. Conscience tells us, 'Be the trustworthy man.' That's a tall order, for the trustworthy man is often cheated and exploited; while the untrustworthy man often occupies thrones and pulpits, and revels in his riches. But the untrustworthy man, if we all

---

* To be fair, many of these same individuals defied expectations in matters of Masculine and Feminine Deportment even when fully sober. It's a common failing among theater people, I have found.

emulated him, would hasten us into an eternal Hell of mutual predation; while the trustworthy man, if his behavior became general, would throw open the gates of Heaven. That's what Heaven *is*, Adam, if it's anything at all—a place where you can trust others without hesitation, and they can trust you."

I asked Pastor Stepney if he had been drinking. He said he had not.

"Well," I said, "is this a sample of Paradise, then—this raucous party?"

"Conscience isn't a brutal taskmaster. Conscience has no argument with kisses in the dark, if they're freely given and freely received. Conscience offers no cavils to our taste in music, clothing, literature, or amative behavior. It smiles on intimacy and banishes hatred. It doesn't scourge the reckless lover."

That was an interesting doctrine, and it seemed sensible, if heretical.

"So, then, yes," he said, waving his hand at the champagne- and hemp-fueled festivities proceeding about us, "you can think of all this as a rehearsal for Paradise."

I meant to ask him what Conscience in his leafy underwear might have to say about Julian's conflict with the Dominion, or the posting of severed heads on iron spikes. But Pastor Stepney rose and went off to pursue his own unspecified pleasures before I could pose the question. So I took his advice, and tried to look at the revelries unfolding before me as if they were a foretaste of that Reward to which we all aspire; and I had some success at this effort, until a drunken camera-man stumbling up the Palace stairs paused and vomited at my feet, which diminished the illusion considerably.

Conspicuous by his absence from these revels was Julian himself. He had appeared briefly at the opening of the Wrap Party, waving at us from one of the indoor balconies where his murderous uncle used to address Independence Day gatherings—but he had absented himself shortly thereafter, and I hadn't seen him since. That was not unusual, for his moods were mercurial, and he was increasingly inclined to brood alone in the Library Wing or in some other part of the labyrinthine Executive Palace. In truth I didn't give it much thought, until Lymon Pugh came down the marble stairs, sparing a disgusted glance for the gamboling Aesthetes, and said I ought to come see to Julian.

"Why, where is he?"

"In the Throne Room with Sam Godwin. They've been shouting at each other for most of an hour, ferociously. You might need to interfere, if it comes to blows—if you can walk straight."

"I'm completely sober."

"That makes one of you, then."

"Do you find this shocking, Lymon?"

He shrugged. "I've seen drunker parties. Though where I come from they usually end in a murder or a mass arrest."

I followed him to the Executive Office, which Lymon and other members of the Republican Guard called the Throne Room. Perhaps they can be pardoned for the exaggeration. The Executive Office was a vast square tiled room at the very heart of the Palace, windowless but forever ablaze with electric lamps. Its high ceiling was painted with a panoramic picture of Otis* on his gunboat fighting the Battle of the Potomac long ago. This was the room in which Presidents signed their Proclamations, or met with foreign consuls or Senatorial delegations on formal occasions. As such, it was set up to emphasize the dignity and power of the Presidency. The Presidential Chair wasn't quite a "throne," but approached that description as closely (or more closely) than any respectable republican chair really ought to have: it was carved from the heart of some noble oak, upholstered in purple cloth and plastered with gold leaf, and raised on a marble dais. Just now Julian sat sidelong on it, while Sam paced before him in short angry strides.

"All yours," Lymon Pugh whispered, ducking out of the room before I could announce myself. Neither Sam nor Julian took any notice of my presence, for they were too busy arguing. Their voices echoed from the ornamental tile floor and bounced back from the high ceiling.

I didn't like to see the unhappiness so obviously written on Julian's face, nor was it pleasant to hear Sam berating him. The argument concerned some decision Julian had given out without Sam's knowledge or approval.

"Do you have any conception," Sam was asking, "of what you've done—of what the *consequences* of this will be?"

"The consequence I'm hoping for," said Julian, "is the extinction of an old and ugly tyranny."

"What you'll get is a civil war!"

"The Dominion is a noose around the neck of the nation, and I mean to cut the rope."

"A noose is what *you're* staring at, if you don't desist! You act as if you can proclaim any doctrine you like, and enforce it with soldiers—"

"Can't I? Isn't that exactly what my uncle did?"

"And where is your uncle now?"

Julian looked away.

"The enemies of a President hold daggers in their hands," Sam went on. "The more enemies, the more daggers. You offended the Dominion—well, that can't be undone. You've defied the Senate, which doubles your danger. And if these orders reach the Army of the Californias—"

"The orders have been dispatched. They can't be withdrawn."

"You mean you *won't* withdraw them!"

"No," Julian said, in a softer but no less hostile tone. "No, I won't."

There were smaller chairs arrayed before the Throne, presumably for

* The former President, not the Giraffe which was named after him.

lesser dignitaries to sit in. Sam kicked one of these chairs with his foot and sent it screeching across the tiled floor. *"I will not let you commit suicide!"*

"You'll do as you're told, and be quiet about it! The fact that you married my mother doesn't make you my master! I had but one father, and he was killed by Deklan Conqueror."

"If I protected you all these years, Julian, it was out of my loyalty to your father, and my affection for you, and for no other reason! I don't have any ambition to sit on a throne, or meddle with the man who does so!"

"But you *didn't* protect me, Sam, and you *do* meddle! By all rights I should have died in the Goose Bay Campaign! Everything that's happened since then is just a ridiculously prolonged *last gasp*—can't you see that?"

"That's not the sort of thing your father would ever have said, or allowed you to say."

"Your debt to my father is your own business. Mine was paid in full, with Deklan's head."

"You can't salve your conscience with an execution! Bryce Comstock would tell you the same thing, if he was here."

Julian had ceased shouting, but his anger had not abated. It had run underground, instead, and glittered in his eyes like a rushing torrent glimpsed through the crevice of a glacier. "Thank you for your advice. But there's nothing more to discuss. You're dismissed."

Sam looked as if he might kick over another chair. But he didn't. His shoulders slumped, and he turned to the door, defeated.

"Talk to him if you can," he whispered to me on his way out. "I can't."

"I'm sorry you had to hear that," Julian said as Sam's footsteps faded down the corridor.

I advanced to the foot of the Throne. "Lymon Pugh tipped me off. He was afraid it might come to blows."

"Not quite."

"What did you do, Julian, that offended Sam so much?"

"Declared a sort of war, in his view."

"Haven't you had enough of war yet?"

"It's nothing to do with the Dutch. There's been a rebellion in Colorado Springs. Yesterday the Council of the Dominion told their parish Deacons to disobey any Presidential mandate that conflicts with ecclesiastical regulations."

"Is that what you call a rebellion? It sounds more like a lawyer's brief."

"It amounts to an expressed wish to overthrow me!"

"And I suppose you can't tolerate that."

"Tonight I declared the City of Colorado Springs a treasonous territory, and I ordered the Army of the Californias to capture it and establish military law."

"A whole Army to occupy one city?"

"An Army and more, if that's what it takes to overthrow the Council and burn the Dominion Academy to the ground. Traitorous Deacons, should any survive, can be tried in court for their crimes."

"Colorado Springs is an *American* city, Julian. The Army might not like to raze it."

"The Army has many opinions, but only one Commander in Chief."

"Won't innocent civilians get killed in the fighting, though?"

"What fight ever spared the innocent?" Julian scowled and glared. "Do you think I can sit in this chair and not imagine *blood*, Adam Hazzard? Blood, yes; blood, granted! Blood on all sides! Blood past, present, and future! I didn't ask for this job, but I don't deceive myself about the nature of it."

"Well," I said, not wanting to provoke him into another outburst, "I expect it'll work out all right in the end, if you say so."

He stared at me as if I had contradicted him. "There are rules about entering this room—do you know that, Adam? I don't suppose you do. Visitors customarily bow when they cross the threshold. Senators bow, ambassadors from distant nations bow, even the clergy is obliged to bow. The rule doesn't exempt Athabaska lease-boys, to my knowledge."

"No? Well, it's a fine room, but I'm not sure it requires any genuflection on my part. I didn't bow down to you when we were shooting squirrels by the River Pine, and I don't think I could get in the habit of doing it now. I'll leave, if you like."

Perhaps I sounded sharp. Julian's face was immobile for a long moment. Then his expression changed yet again.

Incredibly, he smiled. He looked, for a moment, years younger. "Adam, Adam . . . I would be more insulted if you bowed than if you didn't. You're right, and I'm sorry I mentioned it."

"No offense given or taken, in that case."

"I'm tired, and I'm tired of quarreling."

"You ought to go to bed, then."

"No—it wouldn't work. It's been days since I was able to sleep. But at least we can put Colorado Springs out of our minds. Would you like to see something unusual, Adam? Something from the days of the Secular Ancients?"

"I suppose so . . . if you want to show it to me."

If anything had lately alarmed me about Julian's behavior it was the way his moods and whims darted about as unpredictably as minnows in a fish-pool. The tendency had first become obvious when he was producing *The Life and Adventures of the Great Naturalist Charles Darwin*. He would appear on the set unannounced, and stalk around like an Oriental tyrant, demanding petty changes to the scenery or harassing the actors. Then the intemperance would pass from his mind as quickly as a cloud shadow crosses a prairie meadow, and he would smile sheepishly and offer apologies and praise. "Sometimes he wears the crown," Magnus Stepney once remarked, "and sometimes, by the grace of God, he takes the damned thing off."

I wished he wouldn't wear the crown at all; for it plagued him, and made him imperious, and confused his mind.

He came down from his high chair and put his arm across my shoulder. "A fresh discovery from the Dominion Archives. Do you remember when I told you there were ancient Movies hidden there?"

"Yes—but not in any form we could see, you said."

"And I said I would assign a Technician to work on the problem. Well, there's been some success in the project. Come downstairs, Adam, and I'll a show you a Movie that hasn't been seen for two hundred years—part of one, at least."

It turned out Julian had established a Cinema Room in the lower section of the Palace, useful for work on *Darwin* as well as the restoration of ancient moving pictures. I didn't like to go into the basement of the Palace, as a rule, for it was a cold place even in warm weather, and I had heard of the prison cells and interrogation chambers located there. But the Cinema Room was a new installation, wholly modern and tolerably warm. Unusual machines and chemical baths had been installed there, along with a pristine white Movie Screen at one end and an elaborate Mechanical Projector at the other.

"Most of the films we found were crudely stored and eroded beyond repair," said Julian. "Even the best of them were only partially recoverable, but what a treasure nonetheless," and I heard in his voice an echo of the Julian Comstock who had pawed through books in the Tip outside Williams Ford with just such rapt fascination. "Lately I like to come down here at night, when it's still and quiet, and watch these fragments. Here," he said, picking up a can the size of a pie-plate, "this is a film called *On the Beach,* from the twentieth century—about half an hour of it. The original was longer, of course, and had recorded sound and such refinements."

I took a chair as he threaded the ancient Movie, which had been copied onto modern celluloid, into the projecting machine. Midnight had come and gone, and Calyxa would be expecting me home, but I sensed that Julian needed my company just now; and I was afraid that if I left him he might fall into a deeper funk, or declare yet another war. "What's it about?"

The projector, driven by the Palace's unsleeping electrical generators, hummed and clattered to life. "Boats and things. You'll see." He dimmed the lights.

I confess that I didn't understand most of what played out on the screen before me. It was riddled with gaps and lacunae. Many of the scenes were terribly faded, almost ghostly. Our inability to reproduce recorded sound interfered with the intelligibility of the film, since much of it consisted of people talking to one another. But there were many striking and unusual things in it.

There was an Underwater Boat, for instance, which Julian said was called a Submarine Boat. The interior of it looked like the engine room of a modern steamer, but more complex, decorated with countless clocks, levers, pipes, buttons, blinking lights, etc.; and the ship's crew wore uniforms that were perpetually clean and starched.

But only a few of the scenes were nautical. Some took place in a city of the Secular Ancients. There were automobiles in the streets, at least in the earlier portion of the film, though not as many as I might have expected, and then none at all. The people of the city behaved in ways that suggested great wealth but even greater eccentricity.

There was also, as the title suggested, a beach scene, in which men and women socialized in clothing so abbreviated as to approach blatant nudity. A glimpse of this, I thought to myself, would have confirmed Deacon Hollingshead in all his prejudices about our ancestors.

Inexplicable events happened. There was an automobile race, with casualties. The city was evacuated, and a newspaper blew down an empty street.* Julian paid close attention to the fragmentary film, though he had watched it many times before; but it seemed very sad and elegiac to me, and I wondered if Julian's repeated viewing of it had not further depressed his mood.

It ended abruptly. Julian shook his head like a man recovering from a trance, and stopped the projector and turned up the lights. "Well?"

"I don't know what to say, Julian. I wish there had been more scenes of that underwater boat in operation. I suppose it's a good movie. I'm surprised the people in it seemed so unhappy, though, since they lived in a world full of automobiles and submarine boats."

"It's a drama—people in dramas are seldom happy."

"It didn't end with a wedding, or any uplifting thing such as that."

"Well, it's incomplete. We don't know what the whole of it was like."

"Certainly it's a rare glimpse into the lives of the Secular Ancients. They don't seem as bad as the Dominion histories make them out to be. Though clearly they were imperfect."

"I don't deny that they were imperfect," Julian said in a distant voice. "I'm not uncritical of the Secular Ancients, Adam. They had all sorts of vices, and they committed one sin for which I can never bring myself to entirely forgive them."

"What sin is that?"

"They evolved into us," he said.

Clearly it was past time for me to go home. The sun would be up before very many more hours passed. I told Julian he ought to try to sleep, and see if the Presidency wasn't more tolerable to a rested mind.

---

* I asked Julian whether this was about the False Tribulation, but Julian said no; *On the Beach* had been produced nearly a century before the End of Oil. The events it dramatized must have been purely local in nature, or purely imaginary.

"I will," he said, unconvincingly. "But before you go, Adam, I want to ask a favor of you."

"Anything, if I'm able to grant it."

"My mother has been making plans for all of us to leave the country. I've told her repeatedly we won't be forced into such a drastic retreat. But I may be wrong. It's true that I've made enemies. I've gambled with History, and I can't guarantee the result. Adam, do you see those three film canisters on the table by the door?"

"Hard to miss them. What are they, some fresh discovery from the Archives?"

"No. That's *The Life and Adventures of the Great Naturalist Charles Darwin*. All three acts, a master print of it, plus the performance script. Perhaps it's childish, but I don't like to think of it being permanently destroyed. If the political situation gets worse, or if anything unpleasant happens to me, I want you to take *Darwin* out of the country with you."

"Of course I will!—I give you my word—but you'll come to Mediterranean France along with us, if the necessity arises, and you can bring the canisters yourself."

"Yes, Adam; but it would please me to know I'm not the only one thinking of it. I put all the best part of myself into that film. It deserves to be seen."

"All Manhattan will see it. The debut is only a few weeks away."

"Of course. But you promise to do as I ask?"

It was an easy guarantee to make. I gave him my hand on it. Then I left the room, without bowing.

As I walked off, I heard the projector start up again.

The enclosed grounds of the Palace make up a rectangle two and a half miles long by half a mile wide, carved out of Manhattan by a man named Olmsted in ancient times. Pleasant and rustic by day, in the small hours of the night it was a lonely place. It hosted a large permanent population of bureaucrats, servants, and Republican Guards; but the majority of them had been asleep since midnight. Now even the revelries of the Wrap Party had ceased. Little evidence remained of what had taken place earlier in the evening, apart from a pair of Aesthetes snoring in wicker chairs along the Palace's great piazza.

Not every member of the Republican Guard was allowed to sleep, however. They kept the watch in shifts, like sailors. They manned the four great Gates at all times, and patrolled the high walls for intruders. Lymon Pugh was one of them, and he met me as I was leaving the Palace. "On duty still?" I asked him.

"Just coming off it. Felt like walking a little before going to bed, the night air being so warm."

The moon was up. A mist rose from the nearby Pond and put its pale fingers into the ailanthus groves edging the lawn. "This weather seems strange to me," I said. "In Athabaska we often had snow by Thanksgiving. And in Labrador, too, of course. Not here, though . . . not this year."

"Let me walk a little way with you, Adam. I have no other business, and I doubt I could sleep, to be honest."

"Sleep is an elusive quarry some nights," I agreed. "Do you enjoy doing this work for Julian?"

"I guess I don't mind it. It was kind of him to select me, and there's no heavy lifting involved. I don't expect it to last, though. No offense to Julian Commongold—Comstock, I mean—but I'm not sure he's altogether suited to the Presidency."

"Why do you say so?"

"From what I've seen, it's one of those jobs like being a line overseer at a packing factory—it rewards ruthlessness, and it kills whatever goodness a man might have in him. I knew a Seattle man who was hired up to be a line over-seer at the factory where I worked. A generous man, saintly to his children, well-liked all around; but they made him a line boss, and after a week in that job I heard him threaten to cut a man's throat for slowness. He meant it, too. Began to carry a razor in his hip pocket. Flaunted it from time to time."

"That's how you see Julian?"

"It's not that he's bad by nature. He isn't. That's just the problem. A truly bad man would have an easier time as President, and probably make a greater success of it."

"Must a President be *bad*, then?"

"It seems so to me. But I don't know much history—maybe it hasn't al-ways been that way." We walked a little farther, listening to the soft sound our shoes made on the gravel path. "My point, though," Lymon Pugh said, "is that Julian's not succeeding in the Presidency, whatever the reason for it. I know you and your family are planning your get-away—"

"Who told you that?"

"Nobody told me anything, but I hear things. I don't *repeat* what I hear, if that's on your mind."

"No—what you say is true. I hope it isn't necessary to flee the country. But it never hurts to know where the back door is. Come with us, Lymon, if the worst happens, God forbid. Calyxa has good things to say about Mediter-ranean France."

"Thank you for asking, Adam. That's very flattering to me. But I wouldn't know what to do in a foreign country. I don't know France from Canaan. If it comes to that I mean to steal a horse and head west, maybe as far as the Willamette Valley."

We came to the guest-house where Calyxa and Flaxie and I had made our temporary home. I felt unaccountably sad; but I didn't want Lymon Pugh to see that emotion, or hear it in my voice, so I did not speak.

"You have a fine family, Adam Hazzard," he said. "You make sure nothing unpleasant happens to them. That's your task, if you don't mind taking advice from a plain Republican Guardsman. And now I'm off to bed." He turned away. "Goodnight!"

"Goodnight," I managed.

I paused at the door as Lymon Pugh headed back toward the Palace.

The night had that unusual calm which marks the hour before the dawn, "silence brooding like a gentle spirit / O'er all the still and pulseless world." Off in the darkness I saw a huge silhouette lumbering among the trees—that was Otis, who seemed well on the way to becoming a nocturnal Giraffe. Perhaps he especially enjoyed the lonely hours of the morning. Or perhaps he couldn't sleep any better than the rest of us.

I looked into the darkness for a good long while. Then I went indoors, and crept into bed with Calyxa just as the sky was lightening, and curled into the warmth of her sleeping body.

8

Less than a month passed between the night of the Wrap Party, which marked the end of the filming and editing of *The Life and Adventures of the Great Naturalist Charles Darwin,* and its debut in a plush Broadway theater. A short time by ordinary reckoning; but it was a dire eternity in Julian's reign as President.

Sam Godwin, who maintained close contact with the military, had taken on the thankless duty of conveying bad news to Julian—a role he was forced to play increasingly often. It was Sam who told Julian that the Army of the Californias had been met with fierce resistance by ecclesiastical forces at Colorado Springs. It was Sam who told him how the Rocky Mountain Division of that Army had rebelled, and swung its support from the Executive Power to the Dominion of Jesus Christ on Earth. It was Sam (and I envied him this task least of all) who was obliged to tell Julian that, after extensive but ineffectual shelling and burning, Army commanders had worked out a truce with the Dominion Council and declared a unilateral cease-fire—all in violation of Julian's direct orders.

Sam emerged from that session ashen-faced and shaking his head. "At times, Adam," he confided in me, "I don't know whether Julian even understands what I say to him. He acts as if these reverses were inconsequential, or too distant to matter. Or else he storms and rages at me, as if I were the author of his defeats. Then he hides away in that Projection Room of his, mesmerizing himself with moving pictures."

There was worse to come. A mere three days before the debut of *Charles Darwin,* news reached us that the joint leaders of the Army of the Laurentians had declared solidarity with their comrades in California and had raised the possibility of a march on New York for the purpose of unseating Julian Conqueror. The name of Admiral Fairfield (who had been so successful at sea) was mooted as a possible successor. That might have been the keenest cut of all, for Julian admired the Admiral, and they had got along well during the Goose Bay Campaign.

These small and large insurrections shook the foundations of his Presidency; but Julian continued to make plans for the Broadway opening of his film. Local churches had begun calling for a boycott of it, and it would be necessary to cordon the theater with Republican Guards to prevent riots. Nevertheless Julian invited us all to the premiere, and made sure the finest carriages were available, and told us to dress in our best clothes, and make a grand occasion of it; and we did so, because we loved him, and because we might not have another chance to pay him such an honor.

A phalanx of gilded carriages, surrounded and preceded by armed Guardsmen on horseback, made its way out of the Palace grounds on the appointed afternoon.

Calyxa and I rode in one of the central carriages, following the vehicle that carried Julian and Magnus Stepney, with Sam and Julian's mother in a third conveyance behind us. It was near Christmas, but the streets of Manhattan were not merry. Banners of the Cross had been pulled down in order to clear a line of sight for the sharpshooters Julian had placed on all the rooftops between Tenth and Madison Avenue. But the streets weren't crowded in any case, in part because of the new Pox—the same Pox Dr. Polk had worried about last summer—which had been communicated by fraudulent vaccination shops to young Eupatridian ladies, and which had spread from there into all walks of life in the great City of New York.

It was not an especially virulent disease—not more than one in forty or fifty New Yorkers had come down with it—but it was unpleasant and deadly. It began with fevers and confusions, followed by the appearance of yellow pustules all over the body (especially the neck and groin), and culminated in bleeding lesions and a rapid decline into death. As a result many people chose to keep at home despite the season, and many of the pedestrians we passed wore paper masks over their noses and mouths.

All that, plus a chill wind blowing from the north, lent a certain bleakness to the city's Christmas.

Fear of Pox had not altogether prevented public gatherings, however, since the disease seemed to be transmitted by something more than casual contact. The theater as we approached it was brightly-lit, its sidewalks swarming with patrons and curiosity-seekers, and the roast-chestnut vendor was doing a roaring business.

The theater's grand marquee proclaimed the title of the movie, and added a banner announcing THE WORLD DEBUT OF JULIAN CONQUEROR'S BRILLIANT AND STARTLING CINEMATIC MASTERPIECE!* A cordon of Republican Guards kept out would-be troublemakers, mobs of whom had been dispatched by church committees as an obeisance to the Dominion. The film, of course, was not attractive to especially pious or conservative people; but there were more than enough Aesthetes, Philosophers, Agnostics, and Parmentierists in Manhattan to make up the deficit. These people were Julian's constituency, if he could be said to have one, and they had turned out in force.

Julian left his carriage just as ours was pulling up. He would watch the movie from a protected box above the gallery, along with Magnus Stepney, who

---

* A bold boast, but that's how show-business operates.

was accorded that privilege as the star of the film. Sam and Julian's mother had a similar box assigned to them, while Calyxa and I held reserved seats in the orchestra section. We were only halfway through the enormous lobby, however, when a man I recognized as the Theater Director came up to us in a rush.

"Mrs. Hazzard!" he cried, recognizing her, for she had had some dealing with him in her role as lyricist and composer.

"What is it?" Calyxa asked.

"I've been trying to reach you! We have an unexpected and serious problem, Mrs. Hazzard. As you know, Candita Bentley* vocalizes the role of Emma. But Candita is ill—a sudden attack—*Pox*," he confided in a scandalized tone. "Her understudy is down with it, too."

"The show is canceled?"

"Don't even whisper it! No, certainly not; but we need a new Emma, at least for the songs. I can call up someone from the chorus; but I thought—since you wrote the score, and since everyone says you have the voice for it—I know this is absurdly short notice, and I know you haven't rehearsed—"

Calyxa took the startling invitation very calmly. "I don't need to rehearse. Just show me where to stand."

"You'll sing the role, then?"

"Yes. Better me than some chorister."

"But that's wonderful! I can't thank you enough!"

"You don't have to. Adam, do you mind me voicing Emma?"

"No—but are you confident you can do this?"

"They're my songs, and I can sing them as well as any of these Broadway women. Better, I expect."

Calyxa had been offered the vocal part of Emma early in the planning of the production, but she had reluctantly refused it, since she was preoccupied with Flaxie and the ceaseless duties of motherhood. Tonight's unexpected opportunity obviously pleased her. Stage fright wasn't one of her faults.

I wished her well, and she hurried off to prepare. There was a general announcement that the curtain-time had been postponed by fifteen minutes. I milled in the lobby in the meantime, until Sam Godwin approached me.

His expression was somber. "Where's your wife?" he asked.

"Recruited into the show. Where's yours?"

"Gone back to the Palace."

"Back to the Palace! Why? She'll miss the movie!"

"It can't be helped. There have been fresh developments, Adam. She's packing for France," Sam said in a very low voice, adding, "*We leave tonight.*"

"Tonight!"

"Keep your voice down! It can't be that great a shock to you. The Army of the Laurentians is moving on the city, the Senate is in open revolt—"

---

* A Broadway voice-actress, famous for her silvery voice and impressive girth.

386 ROBERT CHARLES WILSON

"All that was true before this evening."

"And now a fire has broken out in the Egyptian district. From what I've heard, most of Houston Street is in flames and the burning threatens to cross the Ninth Street Canal. The wind spreads it quickly, and if the flames reach the docks our only avenue of escape may be cut off."

"But—Sam! I'm not sure I'm ready—"

"You're as ready as you need to be, even if you have to sail with just the shoes on your feet and the shirt on your back. Our hand has been forced."

"But Flaxie—"

"Emily will make sure the baby gets to the boat. She and Calyxa calculated everything well in advance. They've been ready a week now. Listen: our ship is the *Goldwing*, docked at the foot of 42nd Street. She sails at dawn."

"What about Julian, though? Have you told him about the fire?"

"Not yet. He's sealed himself in that box above the balcony and ringed himself with guards. But I'll speak to him before the movie is finished, if I have to knock heads together to get at him."

"I don't expect he would be willing to leave before the end of the show." Nor would Calyxa be, now that she had been recruited into the business.

"Probably not," Sam said grimly. "But as soon as the curtain rings down we must all leave at once. Look for me in the lobby between acts. If you don't see me, or if we're separated—remember! The *Goldwing*, at dawn."

A bell rang, signaling us to take our seats.

Of course my head was whirling with these plans as the curtain rose on *Charles Darwin*; but (apart from the fire in the Egyptian quarter) none of it was entirely unexpected, though I had hoped the need for flight would not arise so soon. There was no immediate active role I could take, however, so I tried to focus my attention on the event at hand.

The orchestra played a lively overture combining the film's major musical themes. The excitement in the audience was palpable. Then the lights went down and the projection began. A grandly ornate title card announced:

THE LIFE AND ADVENTURES OF
THE GREAT NATURALIST CHARLES DARWIN
(*FAMOUS FOR HIS THEORY OF EVOLUTION, ETC.*)
Produced by Mr. Julian Comstock and Company
WITH THE ASSISTANCE OF THE
NEW YORK STAGE AND SCREEN ALLIANCE
featuring
Julinda Pique as Emma Wedgwood
and introducing
Magnus Stepney in the Title Role

That faded to a simpler card reading:

OXFORD
IN THE COUNTRY OF ENGLAND
Long before the Fall of the Cities

Thus the scene was set; and now young Darwin appeared for the first time, strolling through the Oxford countryside, which was really the game preserve of the Executive Palace dressed up with signs reading FORTY MILES TO LONDON and WATCH OUT FOR FOX HUNTS and such, to create a general impression of Englishness.

I had not seen any of the finished footage of the movie before tonight, and I had entertained some doubts about Pastor Stepney's acting skills. But he performed a respectable Darwin, somewhat to my surprise. Perhaps a career in the pulpit is acceptable training for an actor. In any case he made a handsome naturalist; and the famous Julinda Pique, though nearly twice his age, portrayed a suitably attractive Emma, with make-up to conceal any cosmetic imperfections.

I have already given the outline of the story, and I won't repeat it here, except to mention certain highlights. Act I held the audience's attention in a merciless grip. Darwin sang his Aria about the resemblance between insects of disparate species, voiced by a powerful tenor. The Oxford Bug Collecting Tournament was portrayed, with Emma cheering from the sidelines. I was unfailingly aware that, while it was Julinda Pique's form and figure on screen, the voice that seemed to issue from her mouth was in fact produced by Calyxa in a side-booth. I had been afraid that Calyxa's inexperience would betray her; but from her first refrain* she sounded strong and straightforward; and there were murmurs of appreciation from the audience.

Of course the audience was disposed to be sympathetic, being composed mainly of apostates and rebels. Still, it was shocking to hear heresies so openly proclaimed. When the villainous Wilberforce sang *Only God can make a beetle* he was repeating exactly the orthodoxy I had learned in Dominion school; and Darwin's riposte (*I see the world always changing / unforced, unfixed, and re-arranging*) would have earned me a stern lecture, or worse, if I had offered it up to Ben Kreel in my youth. But was Darwin wrong? I had seen too much of the unfixed world to deny it.

The insect tournament concluded with victory and a kiss for Charles Darwin. Darwin's subsequent vow to travel the world in search of the secret of life, and Wilberforce's jealous pledge of vengeance, formed the subject

---

* *I had not entertained the thought*
 That I could love a scholar,
 For they read from books an awful lot
 And seldom spend a dollar. . . .

of a rousing Duet, which rang down the curtain on Act I, to riotous applause.

A dry December wind blew steadily from the north that night, fanning the flames in the Egyptian quarter. The *Spark* had hurried out a special edition, and newsboys were already hawking copies of it outside the theater doors. BIG BLAZE HITS GYPTOWN was the vulgar but accurate headline.

This was dismaying news, for an uncontrolled fire in a modern city can quickly become a general disaster; but the theater was far from the flames, and there was no panic in the crowded lobby, only some excited conversation.

I looked for Sam, and found him coming down a stairway from one of the high balconies.

"Damn Julian!" he said as I came up beside him. "He won't open that theater-box to anyone, including me—sits in there with Magnus Stepney and armed guards on the doors—no exceptions!"

"I expect he's nervous about the success of his film."

"I expect he's half mad—he's certainly been acting that way—but it's no excuse!"

"He'll have to come out eventually. You can speak to him at the conclusion of the last act, perhaps."

"I'll speak to him before that, if I have to pull a gun to do it! Adam, listen: I've had a report from the Guardsmen I sent along with Emily to the Palace. They say she had two wagons ready to go, and that she set off for the docks along with Flaxie and several nurses and servants and a fresh contingent of Guards. It was all very neatly and efficiently done."

I didn't like the idea of Flaxie being spirited through the streets of Manhattan on a perilous night like this, without me to protect her; but I knew Julian's mother loved the baby as if it were her own and would take every possible precaution. "And they're safe, as far as you know?"

"I'm certain they're safe. Probably snug aboard the *Goldwing* by now. But there's trouble at the Palace—that's the bad news. The servants and Guard troops saw her drive away with all her possessions, and they're bright enough to divine the reason for it. Lymon Pugh is doing his best to preserve order and prevent looting. But the news will get around quickly that Julian Conqueror has abdicated the Office of the Executive—and he *has,* whether he knows it or not—and the Palace grounds might yet be invaded by rioters or a rogue Army detachment."

"What does that mean?"

"It means the hounds are at our heels, and I hope this damned Movie comes to an end soon!"

With that, the bell rang for Act II.

Act II was the story of Darwin's travels at sea, a stark contrast to the rural idyll of Act I. As such, it mirrored the tempests and turmoil taking place in my own mind.

Here was the *Beagle* (actually an old schooner hired by Julian for the production, anchored off Long Island), bound for South America with its crew of hardy sailors. Here was Emma Wedgwood back in England, refusing the courtship of the increasingly bitter (and wealthy) Wilberforce. Here was Wilberforce in a low dive by the sea, paying a drunken pirate captain to pursue and sink the *Beagle*.

Here, too, was South America with all its peculiar tropical beauty. Here was Darwin discovering sea-shells in cliff-sides and prying up the bones of extinct mammals from ancient marl, all the while singing a meditation on the age of the Earth and fleeing from unusually aggressive armadillos. Here he was on the Galapagos Islands, collecting mockingbirds and confronting a ferocious Lion (really a mastiff dressed up in a carpet and a wig, but very convincing for all that). Jungles (mostly paper) stretched to distant mountains (painted), and a Giraffe appeared fleetingly.*

The *Beagle* encountered Wilberforce's cut-throats on the return voyage to England. The *Beagle* was boarded, and the ensuing battle was very realistic. For pirates Julian had recruited a number of men from New York waterfront dives, who suited the part in perhaps too many ways. They had been told how to strike blows and wield swords without killing anyone; but their grasp of the technique was often uncertain or impatient, and some of the blood in the scene was more authentic than the professional actors might have liked.

Darwin proved to be a surprisingly skilled swordsman, for a Naturalist. He leapt up on the *Beagle*'s windlass, and defended the forecastle against dozens of assailants, singing:

> *Now we see in miniature the force that shapes Creation:*
> *I'll slay a Pirate—this one, here—and stop the generation*
> *Of all his heirs, and all their heirs, and all the heirs that follow,*
> *Just as the Long-Beaked bird outlives the starving Short-Beaked Swallow.*
> *Some pious men may find this truth unorthodox and bitter:*
> *But Nature, Chance, and Time ensure survival of the fitter!*

It was as good a scene of fighting as had ever been filmed, at least in my limited experience. The attending crowd of Aesthetes and Apostates was not easily impressed, but cheering broke out among them, and triumphant shouts when Darwin pierced the Pirate Captain with his sword.

The *Beagle* reached London battered but unbowed—watched from the

---

* Giraffes, strictly speaking, are not native to South America; but we had a Giraffe, and we used it.

shore by Emma, and from the shadows by Wilberforce, now a Bishop, who gritted his teeth and sang a reprise of his murderous intentions.

In the lobby, waiting for the third and final act to begin, I moved through the crowd to the great glass doors of the theater. I could see that the wind had gained strength, for it tore at the awnings and banners along Broadway, and the taxi-men at the curb were huddled together, struggling to keep their pipes alight. A two-horse fire wagon came rattling by, its brass bell ringing, no doubt headed for the Immigrant quarter.

Messengers in Republican Guard uniforms came and went in flurries, shouldering past the ushers and ascending and descending the stars to the high balcony where Julian kept his box. Sam did not appear in the lobby, however, and I went back into the auditorium for Act III without being further enlightened.

It was during this final act, as Darwin and Bishop Wilberforce sang at one another relentlessly during their great Debate, that the truth of my situation began to sink in. Even as the audience showed its appreciation for the drama—with cheers and whistles for Darwin, boos and catcalls for Wilberforce—my spirit was weighed down by the knowledge that I would soon be leaving my native country, perhaps forever.

I considered myself to be a patriot, or at least as patriotic as the next man. That didn't mean I would bow down to just any individual who assumed the Presidency, or to the Senate, for that matter, or even to the Dominion. I had seen too much of the imperfection and shortsightedness of such people and institutions. I loved the land, however—even Labrador, as much of it as I had seen, though with a tempered love; and certainly New York City; but above all the west, with its sundered badlands, open prairie, lush foothills, and purpled mountains. The boreal west was not rich or greatly inhabited, but its people were kind and gentle, and—

No, that's not what I mean. I don't suppose westerners are humbler or nobler than anyone else. I knew for a fact there were crooks and bullies among them; though fewer, perhaps, head for head, than in Manhattan. No: what I mean is that I had grown up in the west and learned the world from it. From its wideness I learned the measure of a man; from its summer afternoons I learned the art and science of repose; from its winter nights I learned the bittersweet flavor of melancholy. All of us learn these things one way or another; but I learned them from the west, and I was loyal to it, in my fashion.

And now I was leaving it all behind.

These feelings gave a particular edge to Darwin's Aria on the subject of Time and the Age of the Earth, though the sermon was not a new one to me, for I had heard these sentiments from Julian often enough. The mountains I admired were not eternal, the wheat I fed on grew from the bed of a primeval ocean, and ages of ice and fire had passed before the first human beings approached the Rocky Mountains and discovered Williams Ford. "Everything flows," in the words of some philosopher Julian liked to quote; and you would be able to watch it do so, if you could hold still for an eon or so.

That idea was as disturbing to me, this night, as it was to Bishop Wilberforce, up on the screen. I did not approve of Wilberforce, for he was a villain to Charles Darwin and a menace to poor Emma; but I felt an unexpected sympathy for him as he climbed the crags of Mount Oxford (actually some headland up the Hudson), hoping to gun down Evolution and murder Uncertainty into the bargain.

It was Calyxa's voice that brought me out of my funk. Emma Wedgwood sang,

> It's difficult to marry a man
> Who won't admit the master plan
> In nature's long exfoliation,
> But finds a better explanation
> In Natural Law and Chance Mutation—
> His theories shocked a Christian nation—
> But I love him nonetheless!
> Yes, I love him, nonetheless!

and she sang it so wholeheartedly, and in such a winsome voice, that I forgot that it was Julinda Pique's image on the screen, and saw Calyxa in my mind's eye; and I became Darwin, battling for his bride. It wasn't a trivial analogy, for Calyxa was in as much danger from the collapse of Julian's Presidency as Emma Wedgwood ever was from the Bishop's bullets and schemes.

Those bullets and schemes were cunningly portrayed, and the audience gasped and cheered at each turn and reversal, and it seemed to me that Julian's *Life and Adventures of the Great Naturalist Charles Darwin* was a great success, and that it would play to packed houses wherever it was allowed to be seen, if it *was* allowed to be seen. But by the end of it I was so wrought up with anxiety over current events that I didn't wait for the end-credits to finish showing, but jumped the orchestra and cut around the screen to the hidden booths where the voice-actors and noise-makers did their work.

That might not have been a wise act, for rumors of fire and abdication had already made the audience nervous. Ticket-holders were startled by the sight of me dodging in such a hurry past the screen, and casting awkward shadows on it; and when I tripped over a snare drum of the sort used to mimic the sound of gunshots, causing a racket that might have been the opening cannonade of a military attack, the audience finally gave up applauding and cleared the auditorium, endangering an usher in the process.

Calyxa was surprised to see me, and a little miffed that I cut short the curtain-calls. But I caught her by the arm, and told her we were forced to leave Manhattan this very evening, and that Flaxie and Mrs. Godwin were already aboard the *Goldwing.* She took the news stoically and accepted a few compliments from her fellow players; then we left by a stage door at the rear.

The crowd in front of the theater was already well-dispersed, but a cordon had been kept for members of the Presidential party, and we were admitted through those lines.

Sam hailed us as soon as he saw us, but his expression was grim.

"Where is Julian?" I asked.

"Gone," he said.

"Gone to the docks, you mean?"

"No, I mean gone, plain gone—gone in the general sense. He sneaked out of the theater with Magnus Stepney during Act III, and left this note with my name on it."

With a disgusted expression Sam passed Julian's note to me, and I unfolded the paper and read it. It had been written with obvious haste in an unsteady hand, but the penmanship was recognizably Julian's. The note said:

Dear Sam,

Thank you for your repeated attempts to reach me with news of the imminent departure of the *Goldwing* for foreign waters. Please tell my mother and Calyxa that I admire their extensive and thoughtful planning for this eventuality. I regret that I cannot join them, and you, and Adam and all, for the voyage. I would not be safe in Europe, nor would those I love be safe as long as I was among them. And there are more personal and pressing reasons why I must stay behind.

As unsatisfactory as this explanation is, it will have to do. Please don't attempt to seek me out, for nothing can change my decision, and I would only be endangered by the attempt.

I thank you all for the kindnesses you have shown me over so many years, and I apologize for the hardships those kindnesses too often caused you. Thank you, especially, Sam, for acting in the place of my father, and for guiding me usefully even when I defied your guidance. Your lessons were not wasted, and never more than briefly resented. Please be kind to my mother, as I know she will be upset by my absence, and please emphasize my love for her, which is everlasting, if anything is.

Also thank Adam for his boundless friendship and many indulgences, and remind him of the promise he made to me.

Yours,
Julian Comstock (never really a Conqueror)

"Do you know what he means, Adam?"

"I think I understand it," I said in a small voice.

"That's more than I do! *Damn* Julian! It's just like him to throw a shoe into the works! But about the promise he mentions—"

"It's nothing much."

"Do you care to tell me about it?"

"It's only an errand. Escort Calyxa to the *Goldwing*, and I'll join you there."

Calyxa made some objection to this, but I was adamant, and she knew me well enough to hear the steel in my voice, and she yielded to it, though not gracefully. I kissed her and told her to kiss Flaxie on my behalf. I would have said more, but I didn't want to increase her anxiety.

"Only an errand," Sam repeated, once Calyxa was settled in the carriage.

"It won't keep me long."

"It had better not. They say the fire is spreading quickly—you can smell the smoke on the wind even here. If the docks are threatened we sail at once, with you or without you."

"I understand."

"I hope so. I might have lost Julian—I can't do anything about that—but I don't want to lose you as well."

His statement made me feel very emotional, and I had to turn my head away so as not to embarrass myself. Sam took my hand in his good right hand and gave it a sturdy shake. Then he followed Calyxa into the carriage; and when I turned back they were gone.

All the crowd had gone away before them. Except for a few Republican Guards still keeping a vigil, the street was nearly empty. Only a single horse cart remained at the curb. It bore the insigne of the Executive Branch.

Lymon Pugh was holding the reins. "Drive you somewhere, Adam Hazzard?" he asked.

A few trucks and carriages passed us as we rode up Broadway, all of them headed away from the burning Egyptian quarter. A brisk wind blew steadily along the empty sidewalks, lofting up loose pages from the special edition of the *Spark* and inconveniencing beggars in the darkened alleys where they slept.

Sam's parting words had touched me, and I have to admit that Julian's unexpected letter caused some turmoil as well. I supposed he had his reasons for doing as he did. Or at least imagined he had good reasons. But it was hurtful that he hadn't lingered long enough to say goodbye face-to-face. We had survived so many harrowing turns together, that I thought I was owed at least a handshake.

But Julian had not been himself lately—far from it—and I tried to excuse him on those grounds.

"He was probably just in a big hurry," Lymon Pugh said, divining something of my thoughts.

"You saw the note?"

"I carried it to Sam myself."

"How did Julian seem when he passed it to you?"

"Can't say. It was handed out from behind that curtained box of his. All I saw was a gloved hand, and all I heard was his voice, which said, 'See that this gets to Sam Godwin.' Well, I did. If I unfolded it on the way, and had a quick read of it, I guess that's your fault."

"My fault!"

"For teaching me my letters, I mean."

Perhaps it was true, as the Eupatridians believed, that the skill of reading shouldn't be too widely distributed, if this was the general result. But I passed over his indictment without comment. "What do you make of it?"

"I'm sure I don't know. It's all above my station."

"But you said he might be in a hurry."

"Perhaps because of Deacon Hollingshead."

"What about Deacon Hollingshead?"

"Rumor among the Guard is that Hollingshead holds a personal grudge against Julian, and is hunting him all over the city, with a body of Ecclesiastical Police to help him."

"I know the Deacon is hostile to Julian, but what do you mean by a *personal* grudge?"

"Well, because of his daughter."

"The Deacon's daughter? The one who famously shares intimacies with females of her own sex?"

"That's more delicate than I've heard it put, but yes. The girl was an embarrassment to Hollingshead, and he locked her up in his fancy house in Colorado Springs to keep her out of trouble. But Deacon Hollingshead's house was blown up during the trouble with the Army of the Californias. The Deacon was safe here in New York, of course. But he blames Julian for his daughter's death, and means to take his revenge on Julian directly. A noose or a bullet, it don't matter to the Deacon, as long as Julian dies."

"How do you know these things?"

"No offense, Adam, but news that circulates in the Guard barracks don't always reach the upper echelons. All of us that Julian hired to be Republican Guards are fresh from the Army of the Laurentians. Some of us have friends in the New York garrison. And talk goes back and forth."

"You told Julian about this?"

"No, I never had an opportunity; but I think the rogue pastor Magnus Stepney might have said something. Stepney has contacts among the political agitators, who pay attention to questions like this."

Or it might all be hearsay and exaggeration. I remembered how, back in Williams Ford, a head-cold among the Duncans or the Crowleys became the Red Plague by the time the grooms and stable-boys told the story. Still, that was unhappy news about Hollingshead's daughter. I had always felt sympathy for the girl, though all I knew of the situation was what I had learned from Calyxa's pointed verses at the Independence Day ball a year and a half gone.

"Any particular reason we're heading back to the Palace?" Lymon Pugh asked, for that was the destination I had given him.

"A few things I want to pick up."

"Then off to South France, I suppose, or somewhere foreign like that?"

"You can still come with us, Lymon—the offer stands. I'm not sure what your prospects are in Manhattan just now. You might have a hard time drawing your wages after tonight."

"No, thank you. I mean to take my wages in the form of a breed horse from the Palace stables, and ride the animal west. If any horses remain, that is. The Republican Guards are fond of Julian, and remember him as Conqueror, but they can read the writing on the wall as well as the next man. Many of them have pulled out already. Probably some of the Presidential silverware has gone with them, though I name no names."

We call people rats, who desert a sinking ship; but in some cases the rat has the wisdom of the situation. Lymon Pugh was correct about the looting and the reasons for it. Ordinarily the Republican Guard is a non-partisan group, and survives these flurries of Regime Change without much trouble simply by transferring its loyalty to the next man in the chair. But Julian had made the current Guard his own animal, and it would sink or swim along with his administration.

We came to the 59th Street Gate. Apparently some members of the local chapter of the Army of the Laurentians had heard about the sacking of the Palace, and felt they ought to be allowed to join in, since their northern comrades would be marching on Manhattan any day now. A group of these vultures had gathered at the Gate, and were clamoring for admittance and firing pistols into the air. Enough Guardsmen remained on the wall to act as warders, however, and they kept out the mob; and the mob retained enough respect for the Presidential Seal to allow us to pass through, though they did so grudgingly and with some shouted sarcasm.

I asked Lymon Pugh to make two stops on the grounds of the Executive Palace. One was at the guest-house where, until this evening, I had lived. Calyxa had packed up our most treasured possessions days earlier, in anticipation of the necessity of flight, and these had already gone to the docks. Only a few odds and ends remained behind. One such was a box of souvenirs and mementos, which I had put together without Calyxa's knowledge, and I took it out of the sadly empty building with me.

From there we went to the Palace itself. Lymon Pugh had been correct in his description of the Republican Guard's paradoxical behavior. Some men still occupied their traditional places at the portico, stubbornly "on duty," while others sallied freely up the marble stairs, and down again, burdened with cutlery, vases, tableware, tapestries, and every other portable object. I didn't blame them for it, however. As of tonight they were effectively unemployed, with poor prospects, and entitled to back pay in whatever form they could get it.

I hoped no one had already taken what I had come to retrieve. In that regard I was lucky. Few of these men (some of whom gave me a sheepish salute as I passed them) had ventured into the underground section of the Palace, which still had an unsavory reputation. They had not breached the Projection Room, and the master copy of *The Life and Adventures of the Great Naturalist Charles Darwin* was just where Julian had left it, divided among three pie-tins, along with the score, script, stage instructions, etc.

I didn't linger once I had retrieved these things. I suppose, if there had been a prisoner in the Palace's underground jail, I might have paused to release him. But there weren't any prisoners to release. The only prisoner Julian had kept was the one he had inherited—that is, his murderous uncle Deklan—and Deklan had since taken up a new residence: in Hell, or atop an iron post, depending on how you look at it.

Lymon Pugh was waiting when I emerged from the Palace. He had made good on his word, and taken a pedigreed horse from the Palace stables, and fitted it up with a fine leather saddle and saddlebags; and I could hardly rebuke him for the theft, for he had brought along a second horse just like the first, and similarly equipped, for me.

"Even if you're only riding as far as the docks, you ought to ride in style," he said.

The saddlebags were a convenient way to transport the three reels of *Charles Darwin*, as well as my other souvenirs, and I packed these things carefully. "But I'm not going straight to the docks," I said.

"No? Where first, then?"

"Down to the rough part of town—a certain address."

He was interested in this plan. "Won't that be near the fire?"

"Very near—perilously near—but still accessible, I hope."

"What's there?"

I shrugged. I wasn't ready to confide my awkward hopes in him.

"Well, let me ride with you at least that far, whatever your purpose is."

"You'd be putting yourself in danger."

"It wouldn't be the first time. If I get nervous I'll shy away—I promise."

It was a welcome offer, and I accepted it.

Just before we remounted I fetched from among my own goods a spare copy of *A Western Boy at Sea* (I had packed half a dozen) and gave it to Lymon to keep. He marveled at it by the light that leaked from the Palace doors. "This is the one you wrote?"

"It has my name on the front. Just up from the Octopus. The Octopus doesn't appear in the book."

He seemed genuinely moved by the gift. "I'll read it, Adam, I promise, just as soon as I come to a slow spot in my life. Here," he said, reaching into his pocket, "here's something for you, in return. Something to remember me by. Call it a Christmas present."

I accepted his gift, which he had made himself, and solemnly thanked him for it.

We nearly had a disastrous adventure even before we left the Palace grounds. On the way to the 59th Street Gate we rode through the Statuary Lawn, where sculptures and relics from the days of the Secular Ancients were preserved. It was an eerie place even by daylight, and eerier still in the diffuse night-glow of the city, with the copper head of the Colossus of Liberty listing perpetually to the south, the Angel of the Waters gazing in solemn pity at Christopher Columbus, and Simon Bolivar frozen in a cavalry raid on the Needle of Cleopatra. The road twined among these bronze enigmas from ancient times as through a maze. We seemed to be alone in it.

But we were not. A small group of men on horseback, who must have forced their way through one or another of the Gates, was lurking among the statues, perhaps on the theory that they could rob any Eupatridians or unaccompanied Guardsmen departing the property with loot; and I suppose they imagined they could get away with this outrage, in the general atmosphere of chaos and abandonment.

Whatever their plan, they saw us coming and rode at us from their hiding place in a tight group. I counted six of them. The lead man did not disguise his intentions, but pulled a rifle from his saddle-holster. "This way!" Lymon Pugh cried, and we spurred our mounts; but the thieves had calculated their attack very finely. They were about to cut off our escape route, and probably kill us for our modest treasure, when the rifleman suddenly looked past us, his eyes wide, and shouted an obscenity, as his horse reared up under him.

I turned in my saddle to see what had frightened him so.

It was nothing hostile. It was only Otis, the elderly bachelor Giraffe, who liked to spend his evenings among the statues. All the night-time activity at the Palace had made him nervous, I suppose, and when Otis was nervous he was apt to charge, which was just what he did—he came out from behind Liberty's battered diadem with his long neck swaying majestically, and galloped straight at the bandits. I think he would have roared, if nature had blessed him with such a talent.

The thieves scattered in several directions. Lymon and I took the opportunity and fled the scene without looking back, not slowing until we saw the lights of 59th Street.

I heard some gunfire as we passed out of the Gate. I don't know whether Otis was injured in his confrontation with the bandits. I believe he was not, though I can't produce evidence. Giraffes are as mortal as any other creature, of course, and entirely vulnerable to bullets. But I didn't think Otis would let himself be killed by such low men as those—it wasn't in his nature.

9

I didn't tell Lymon Pugh our destination until we were much closer to it, for I was constantly unsure of the wisdom of going there; but I thought Julian deserved a final opportunity to change his mind about staying in Manhattan, especially now that the city was burning down; and if I found him (or so I reasoned) I could ask him why he had not offered his farewell by some means less impersonal than a short, scrawled note.

I wasn't entirely sure I *could* find him; but I had a firm hunch as to his whereabouts, and I calculated there was enough time left to pursue the matter, if only just.

If anything would stymie us it would be the fire in the Immigrant District, depending on how it had spread. As we crossed Ninth Street we were nearly borne back by a tide of fleeing Egyptians. They were a troubled people, despised by the majority. Many of them had left their native country to escape the poverty and warfare of Suez and the sickness that haunts the terrible ruins of Cairo. They had seen destruction before, and they didn't seem surprised by this fresh catastrophe, but were resigned to it, and trudged along with their packs on their shoulders and their carts dragged behind them as if it were not the first apocalypse they had witnessed or the last they expected to see. They paid us no attention; but we were riding against a human avalanche, and it slowed our progress.

Soon we could see the fire itself, leaping above nearby rooftops. The flames had already consumed most of the Immigrant District, where the flimsy houses, often appended to old concrete ruins and built from whatever debris could be dug out from makeshift excavations, burned like tinder. All Manhattan's fire-wagons and water-engines had been brought to bear on the problem, or so it seemed. The pumpers took their water from the Houston Canal, a freight canal, and from the Delancey Canal, a sewage canal—though in practice there was little to choose between them. Debris of the most noxious sort often plugged the firemen's hoses; and the stench of smoke, char, and boiling human waste nearly turned us back. Fortunately Lymon Pugh had brought along an assortment of paper plague masks (some dipped, as was the Eupatridian custom, in oil of opoponax); and we each donned one of these, and they were modestly useful in impeding the unwelcome odor of the conflagration.

The wind was fierce, and carried sparks and embers with it. At least so far, however, the water-engines had succeeded in keeping the Houston Canal as a sort of fire-break, and the flames had not spread beyond it. That was fortunate, for the address I was seeking was just this side of that Canal.

"You might as well break down and tell me where we're going," Lymon Pugh said.

"The Church of the Apostles Etc."

"What—Magnus Stepney's old barn? It was raided last year, I thought."

"He keeps a smaller version of it in the loft of a building on Ninth Street."

"You think Julian went there, despite the fire?"

"It's an intuition," I muttered, and it was, and probably a mistaken one; but the idea that they had come here, once fixed in my mind, had been impossible to dislodge.

"Maybe more than that," Lymon said suddenly, reining up his horse and gesturing to me to follow him into an alley. *"Look there."*

We kept to the shadows as a group of horsemen rode by, not away from but *toward* the fire, the same direction we were going. Shortly I realized what had alarmed Lymon about them: the man at the head was Deacon Hollingshead himself, with a body of Ecclesiastical Police in gilded uniforms trailing behind. I was sure it was the Deacon, for he was close enough to be easily recognized, and I could not forget the hateful face of the man who had attempted to put Calyxa on trial.

He glanced at us as he passed; but the plague masks served to disguise us, and he was too intent on his business to spare us any closer attention.

His destination was ours. By the time we reached the warehouse which contained the attic Church of Magnus Stepney, Hollingshead and his men were dismounted in front of it. The half-dozen Ecclesiastical Police quickly surrounded the building, blocking every entrance. Lymon and I watched from a safe distance as they performed their evolutions.

There were no fire-fighters nearby—in fact the street was deserted; its residents had long since fled. The street had changed some since my last visit, mainly due to Julian's lifting of the ban on apostate churches. Just a year ago it had been a furtive neighborhood of hemp-shops and boarding houses and other low businesses. It still was; but newly-established Temples and Mosques and Places of Worship had sprung up among the taverns and slatternly hotels, many of them painted in gaudy colors, or decorated with fanciful symbols and slogans, as if a Carnival of Faith had arrived in town.

The fire-wagons were all down at the Canal itself, behind and to the west of us. The Immigrant District burned freely, and wind-blown embers floated down, but neither the warehouse containing the Church of the Apostles Etc. nor any of the nearby structures was actually burning yet.

"Julian must be inside, as you guessed," said Lymon Pugh, "or else the Deacon wouldn't be here. Look how they cover the entrances—very professional, for Dominion men, though any Army patrol would do it better."

"And they're well-armed," I added, for the ecclesiastical troopers carried gleaming Pittsburgh rifles in their hands. "If only we had got here first!"

"No, Adam, you're wrong about that. If we had got here first we'd be inside with Julian, and subject to the Deacon's whims. As it stands we have a chance of taking the enemy by surprise."

"Just the two of us?"

"Calls for stealth," Lymon Pugh admitted, "but it can be done."

"I don't have even a pistol to use against their weapons."

"Leave that part to me. They divide their forces, Adam, see? Six men plus the Deacon, and he just sent three of them around the back to cover the exits."

"Even three armed men—"

"Dominion police! Why, I could have brought down a dozen such men even before I joined the Army. Often did."

Despite what Lymon had told me about his street-fighting and beef-boning days, it struck me as a risky proposition. But he was firm about it. He told me to stay where I was, and soothe the horses, while he circled around back of the warehouse. Once the rear guards were out of action he would commandeer their rifles, and when we were both armed we could assault the front—if I thought it was worth doing. I told him I had come this far, and might as well finish the journey, so long as we had a reasonable chance of escaping death.

He smiled and dashed off into the darkness, keeping to the shadows and circling wide.

The horses were made nervous by the fire across the Canal, and they wanted to whinny and stomp. I tethered them to an alley post, and spent considerable time calming them down. The flames were so high in the sky that they cast a red twilight over everything, and the smoke was so thick that even my plague mask couldn't keep it out, and it was all I could do to keep from coughing explosively.

Then there was the sound of a gunshot, followed by a second stuttering volley of rifle fire. All my work calming the horses was instantly undone. I looked across the street to the warehouse. The ecclesiastical thugs remaining there took up their weapons and hurried around the side of the building to find out what had happened, leaving the Deacon by himself.

The Deacon didn't linger, however. He entered the warehouse by the front door, alone, and seeming very determined, and with a pistol gripped tightly in his hand.

Lymon's plan was not developing as expected, and I was forced to act on my own recognizance. I hurried across the empty street, past overturned trash-barrels and flakes of ash newly-fallen from the sooty sky, and followed Deacon Hollingshead into the building, treading very lightly so he would not be aware of my presence.

It took me a while to make my way up the stairs, for the only illumination was the glare of the fire as it came through the landing windows. At every moment I feared hearing another gunshot, and expected to arrive at the upstairs chapel to find Julian dead at the Deacon's hands. But no such shot was fired; and when I came to the sign at the top of the stairs—

CHURCH OF THE APOSTLES ETC.
GOD IS CONSCIENCE
—HAVE NO OTHER—
LOVE YOUR NEIGHBOR AS YOUR BROTHER

I was able to hear the sound of voices.

A few more steps brought me to the door of the large attic room which Magnus used for a chapel, with its benches for parishioners and its high round window under a peaked roof. There were no parishioners inside, however, as I discovered when I put my head around the door. What I saw was Deacon Hollingshead with his back to me, aiming a pistol at Julian Comstock and Magnus Stepney, who sat side-by-side on the nearest bench.

This was about all I could make out, for the only light was from the high window facing the Egyptian district. Everything was bathed in shades of umber, orange, and smoldering red; and this light was not steady, but trembled and wavered and waxed and waned.

I had not yet been seen, and I stopped where I was.

"Of all the crimes you committed," Hollingshead was saying, "and they're too numerous to account, the one that 'brings me here,' since you ask, is the murder of my daughter."

Magnus and Julian leaned into one another on their bench. Their faces were shadowed and obscure, and Julian's voice, when he spoke, was hardly a whisper.

"Then you're here on a useless mission," he said. "Whatever else I may have done, I haven't harmed your daughter in any way."

The Deacon gave a wild laugh. "Haven't harmed her! You ordered the attack on Colorado Springs, didn't you?"

Julian nodded slowly.

"Then you killed her as surely as if you had driven a dagger into her breast! Her house, *my* house, was demolished by artillery fire. It burned to the ground, *Mr. President*. No one survived."

"I'm sorry for the destruction of your property—"

"My property!"

"—and for all the lives that were lost in the attack—pointlessly, I suppose— though history will have the final word on that. The Dominion could have yielded, you know, and all that bloodshed would have been prevented. But as far as your daughter is concerned—your daughter is alive, Deacon Hollingshead."

The Deacon had probably expected some fumbling denial or perhaps a plea for mercy. But this mild retort took him by surprise. He lowered his pistol a few degrees, and I thought about tackling him and fighting him for it, but the risk seemed too great just now.

"Do you mean something particular by that," he asked, "or are you completely mad?"

"The story of your daughter's troubles circulated widely—"

"Thanks in part to that vulgar song your friend's whorish wife performed at last year's Independence Day celebrations—"

"And I admit I took an interest in her. I investigated her situation very carefully. Not long before the attack on Colorado Springs I sent two of my Republican Guards to interview her."

"To interview her! Is this true?"

"My men apprised her of the pending military action and offered her a means of escape."

Hollingshead took a step closer to his captives. "Lies, no doubt; but I swear to you, Julian Comstock, if in fact you took my daughter as a hostage, tell me where she is—*tell me,* and I might let you live a while yet."

"Your daughter's not a hostage. I said she was offered a means of escape. By that I mean relocation to another city—far from the heart of the Dominion, and far from *you,* Deacon Hollingshead—where she can live under an assumed name, and associate freely with anyone she likes."

"*Sin* freely, you mean! If that's true, you might as well have killed her! You've murdered her immortal soul, which is just the same thing!"

"Just the same to you. The young lady has a different opinion."

That cranked up the Deacon's rage another notch. He took a menacing step forward, and so did I, coming up behind him. By this time Julian and Magnus had seen me. But they were wise enough to give no sign.

"If you imagine you've achieved some sort of victory," the Deacon said, "think again. President Comstock! *Julian Conqueror!* Hah! Where's Julian Conqueror now, when you think about it? Hiding in an apostate church, with his Presidency down around his head and the city burning not a hundred yards away!"

"What I did for your daughter I did for her sake, not on account of you. Your daughter carries scars from the whippings you gave her. If I hadn't intervened I doubt she would have lived to see thirty years of age, under your tutelage."

I wondered if Julian was trying to get himself killed, he vexed the Deacon so. I took another quiet step forward.

"I'll have her back before long," the Deacon said.

"I expect you won't. She's pretty carefully hidden. She'll live to curse your name. She's cursed it more than once already."

"I should kill you for that alone."

"Do so, then—it won't make any difference."

"It makes every difference. You're a failure, Julian Comstock, and your Presidency is a failure, and your rebellion against the Dominion is a failure."

"I guess the Dominion will stagger on a while longer. But it's doomed in the long run, you know. Such institutions don't last. Look at history. There have been a thousand Dominions. They fall and are forgotten, or they change beyond recognition."

"The history of the world is written in Scripture, and it ends in a Kingdom."

"The history of the world is written in sand, and it evolves as the wind blows."

"Tell me where my daughter is."

"I won't."

"I'll kill your sodomitic friend first, in that case, and then—"

But he didn't finish his speech. I took from my pocket the Christmas gift Lymon Pugh had given me. It was a Knocker, of course. Lymon had continually improved his technique in the art of Knocker-making, and had honored me with one of his best. The hempen sack was stitched and beaded in a cunning pattern, and the lead slug inside it might have been forged in an Ostrich egg.

I lunged forward, and employed this useful gift in knocking the pistol out of the Deacon's hand.

He got off a shot in the process, but the bullet went wild and lodged in the floor. Hollingshead whirled around, gripping his injured hand, and stared. First he stared at me (I suppose he recognized me as Calyxa's husband), and then he stared at the device in my hand.

"What is that thing?" he demanded.

"It's called a Knocker," I said, and I gave him a brisk demonstration of its uses, and before long he was lying at my feet, inert.

Lymon Pugh came up the stairs just then. "I had some trouble," he began, "but I put away all the Ecclesiastical Police, one by one—but I heard a shot from up here—say, is that the Deacon? He looks all caved in."

"Keep a guard on the door, please, Lymon," I said, for I wanted to hold a private conversation with Julian. Lymon took the hint and left the room.

Julian didn't stand, or otherwise alter his position. He sat propped against Magnus Stepney, who was likewise propped against him, and they looked like a pair of rag dolls tossed aside by an impatient child. I stepped around the fallen Deacon and walked toward them.

"Not too close," Julian said.

I hesitated. "What do you mean?"

Magnus Stepney answered this time, instead of Julian: "I nearly failed to recognize you in that plague mask. But you had better keep it on, Adam Hazzard."

"Because of the smoke, you mean?"

"No."

Magnus reached down to pick up a lantern, which was at his feet. He lit it with a match, and held it high, so that the light fell over him and Julian.

I understood instantly what the problem was, and I admit that I gasped and fell back a step.

Julian was pale, and his eyes were half-lidded, and fever-spots burned on both cheeks. But that wasn't the telling symptom. The telling symptom was the crop of pale yellow pustules, like snowdrops in a winter garden, that rose above his collar and descended down his arms.

"Oh," I said. "Oh."

"The Pox," Julian said. "I wasn't sure until tonight that I was infected, but when the lesions appeared I couldn't fool myself any longer. That's why I kept myself separate in my box at the theater—that's why I left without warning. And that's why I can't join you aboard the *Goldwing*, in case you were about to ask. I might infect the whole crew and passengers. Kill half the people I love, and die myself, into the bargain."

"So you came here?"

"It's as good a place to die as any, I think."

"The fire will kill you before the plague does."

He only shrugged at that.

"What about you, Magnus?" I asked. "You're sitting there right next to him—aren't you afraid of getting sick?"

"In all likelihood I already am," he said, "but thank you for asking, Adam. I mean to stay with Julian as long as I have the strength in me."

It was a saintly thing to say. Julian took the hand of Magnus, and stretched himself out on the pew, moaning a little at the pressure on his sores, and rested his head in Magnus's lap.

I had always hoped Julian would find a woman who loved him, so he could experience some of the pleasures in life that had been granted to me and denied to him. That didn't happen; but I was consoled that he would at least have his friend Magnus beside him in his extremity. He might not have a wife to give him solace, or to smooth his dying pillow; but he had Magnus, and perhaps in Julian's eyes that was just as good.

"I missed the third act curtain," Julian said wistfully—I think his mind had begun to wander. "Was there applause?"

"Applause, and cheering, and plenty of it."

It was hard to tell in the dim light, but I think he smiled.

"It was a good show, wasn't it, Adam?"

"A fine show. None better."

"And I'll be remembered for it, do you think?"

"Of course you will."

He nodded and closed his eyes.

"Is it true," I asked him, "what you told the Deacon about his daughter?"

"She's safe in Montreal on my orders."

"That was a noble act."

"It offsets the stink of war and death. My own small offering to Conscience. Do you suppose it's good enough?" he asked, turning his feverish eyes to Magnus.

"Conscience isn't particular," Magnus said. "He accepts most any offering, and you made a generous one."

"Thank you for coming, Adam," Julian said, and I could see that he was tiring quickly. "But you had better make for the docks now. The *Goldwing* won't wait, and the flames are spreading, I expect."

"The wind carries embers over the canal. This very building will be on fire soon, if it isn't already."

"I expect you're right," said Julian.

But neither of them moved, and I couldn't turn away.

"I'm afraid I wasn't a very good President," Julian whispered.

"But you were a good friend."

"See to that baby of yours, Adam Hazzard. Do I hear her crying? I think I'd like to sleep just now."

He closed his eyes and paid me no more attention. I thanked Magnus for his kindness and left without turning back.

In the hot and cindery air outside the building I said my goodbyes to Lymon Pugh. Lymon took my hand a final time, and said he was sorry about Julian, and wished me well in "foreign places." Then he rode away uptown, a lone horseman on a vacant street all strewn with windblown embers.

I made the docks by midnight. I took the saddlebags from my breedhorse and donated the animal to a passing family of Egyptians, to whom it probably represented the wealth of Croesus. The *Goldwing* had not sailed. I came aboard and found my cabin. Calyxa was there, tending Flaxie in her crib. Calyxa was impatient over my absence, and wanted to know where I had been; but I didn't explain myself, only took her in my arms and wept against her shoulder.

10

The *Goldwing* left harbor at dawn, ahead of the flames. She came through the Narrows and anchored in the Lower Bay to wait for a favorable breeze. A bright December sun was shining.

We could see the smoke rising from the city. The fire took lower Manhattan almost up to the Palace grounds before the wind turned the blaze back on itself. The smoke rose in a wide canted column, up to where the upper air caught it and fanned it over the ocean. I had the macabre idea that this cloud of ash and soot contained—*must* have contained, by scientific reasoning—particles of what had once been my friend Julian. His own atoms, I mean, transfigured by fire, and cleansed of disease, and finally allowed to rain down over an indifferent ocean.

The thought was painful; but I supposed Julian would have approved of it, for it was Philosophical in nature, or as close as I could come.

By mid-day the captain of the vessel elected to get under way. This was not a single act, but involved the raising of anchors and the setting of sails and the rotating of winches and several such actions as that. (The *Goldwing* had only a small boiler-engine, for close navigation. At sea she was a schooner and at the mercy of the wind.) Calyxa and I left Flaxie with a nurse and came up on the aft deck to watch the sails loft, and we found Sam and Julian's mother already there, and the four of us fell together in a group—not saying much, for we shared a grief that was literally unspeakable.

The captain's orders were shouted down the chain of command in serial echoes, and the results reported back in reverse order. *"Ship the capstan bars!"* dinned about our ears, and *"Heave in the cable to a short stay!"* as the anchor was brought apeak. Sunlight heated the planked deck and made it steam.

Sam went to the taffrail to look back at the burning city. We joined him there, keeping out of the way of the busy sailors. The topsails were shaken out, sheeted home, and neatly hoisted. The *Goldwing* gave a little stir, like an animal turning in its sleep.

Sam turned to Emily. "Do you think it would be all right," he asked, "—*appropriate*, I mean—if I said—well, a prayer—?"

"Of course," she said, taking his good hand in hers.

"One of my prayers, I mean."

"Yes, Sam," she said. "There's no Dominion here to punish you for it, and I imagine the crew have heard stranger things—half of them are European heathens."

Sam nodded, and began to speak the prayer for Julian, which he must have preserved in memory from distant childhood. The nautical shouting continued over his solemn chant. Saltwater slapped the vessel's wooden cladding, and gulls cried out above us.

He lowered his head. *"Yit gid-all,"* he began, *"va-yit ka-dash—"*

"Man the jib and flying halyards!" came the next command relayed from the captain by the mate. Sailors swarmed the high rigging.

"—Smay ra-bah balma div-ray—"

"Hoist away! Avast, and pawl the capstan! Cat and fish the anchor there!"

"—Hero-tay ve-am-lik mal ha-tay—"

"Port the helm now!"

The *Goldwing* began to move through the water, briskly.

"—Bu-chaw yay honey vi-ormy chon—"

"Man the outhaul! Cast off the brails and loose the vangs!"

"—Of chay-yed whole bate yis-royal by agula you viz man ka-reef —"

"Man the fore and main braces! Let go and haul! Haul, now, haul hard, HAUL!"

"—vim roo ah-main," said Sam; and "Amen," said Emily; and Calyxa said "Amen"; and so did I.

Then we stood at the rail and watched America slip away over the western horizon.

EPILOGUE

Doubts of all things earthly, and intuitions of some things
heavenly; this combination makes neither believer nor infidel,
but makes a man who regards them both with equal eye.

—MR. HERMAN MELVILLE,
in a book rescued from the Dominion Archives
by Julian Comstock

I t has been my purpose in this book to give the reader a true and authentic portrait of the life and career of Julian Comstock—or, where truth was in doubt or unobtainable, to err on the side of drama. To the best of my ability that is what I have done; and I lay down my pen with mixed feelings of pride and shame, love and guilt.

Sixteen years have passed since these events. The *Goldwing* anchored safely at Marseilles in the new year of 2176, and although we were strangers in Mediterranean France, and of the bunch of us only Calyxa spoke the language, and that in an accent which made the natives wince and curl their lips—nevertheless, we have prospered here. The weather is generally pleasant. The local population is mixed but peaceful—the Moslems and the Christians maintain a rivalry, but they haven't killed one another for decades, at least not in large numbers.

When we first arrived we lived at the expense of Emily Godwin, who had imported enough of the Comstock fortune to pay for a villa in a small town by the sea. But neither Sam nor I was content to be "kept" in that fashion. Sam eventually found his way into the horse business: he borrowed enough of Emily's money to import a selection of brood mares from east of the Caspian Sea, and with these he built up a brisk local trade, and made a considerable reputation for himself.

Calyxa regularly sings at the local taverns, and is sometimes called upon to perform in the port of Marseilles. Her accent, which provokes such contempt in ordinary conversation, is considered "charming" when she applies it to music; and out of this paradox she has forged a respectable income. She also finds occasional work voicing American women in French movies, for the movie industry has a strong presence in Mediterranean France. It has no Dominion to quash its originality (though the government interferes from time to time), and recorded sound is becoming commonplace. Lately Calyxa provided the voice for a French translation of Julian's *Life and Adventures of the Great Naturalist Charles Darwin*, which was mechanically recorded; and copies of the film were smuggled into the Mitteleuropan mandates north of Lyon, where it reportedly played to enthusiastic audiences. News came just yesterday of a riotously popular exhibition in Brussels.

Flaxie is a young woman now. She was taught to read at an early age, in English and in French, and she's a master of both languages, and popular among the village boys, none of whom are suitable for her, in my opinion, although she disagrees. She loves books and music, and her hair is as glossy and dark and tightly coiled as her mother's was before the gray set in. She assists

Sam at his stables out of a fondness for horses, not inherited from me, and she also enjoys long rides in the hills north of town.* We are very proud of her.

As for me, I earn my bread by means of my pen (*typewriter*, literally, though Mr. Dornwood's machine is old and well-traveled, and missing some of its parts). The presses of New York City survived the fire, and the American book trade thrives under President Fairfield despite the edicts of an enfeebled Dominion. I am a mainstay of that trade, I'm told, though my manuscripts are delivered by Atlantic mail, and frequently lost at sea.

My last book (before this one) was *American Boys on the Moon*, which sold well even without a Dominion Stamp.[†] The book was praised by Mr. Charles Curtis Easton, who also survived the fire, though he is even older than my venerable typewriter, and is drawing his career to a close. I took inspiration for *American Boys on the Moon* from my copy of the *History of Mankind in Space*. That antique book sits on my desk now, along with a number of other mementos salvaged from the Palace grounds—a faded letter which begins *Lieftse Hannie*; a train ticket, validated from Montreal to New York City; a Comstock dollar with Deklan Conqueror's face on it (Julian didn't last long enough to mint his own coins); a play-bill from the Broadway debut of *Darwin*; a decorative Knocker (badly stained); and other such items as that. Tomorrow I'll pack them away again.

As if in silent commentary the breeze flaps the pages of a calendar hanging on the wall. Hard to believe that in only eight years we'll be entering the twenty-third century! Time is mysterious to me—I can't get accustomed to how it passes. Perhaps I've become old-fashioned, forever a Twenty-Second Century Man.

Now Calyxa comes through my study on her way to the garden. Our villa sits on a high bluff, and the property grows little more than sea-grass and sand, but Calyxa has long since walled off a square of good soil, and she plants it every year with lavender, mimosa, and sunflowers. She has been an invaluable resource in the writing of my Julian memoir—filling out exact French phrases from my memory of a few dim words, and copying the sentences for me with accents *grave* and *aigu* and such frills.

Today she pauses and gives me a cryptic smile. "*Tu es l'homme le plus gentil et le plus innocent que je connaisse,*" she says. "*Tu rends les laideurs de la vie supportables. Sans toi, elles seraient insoutenables.*"

No doubt this is some mild joke at my expense, for Calyxa is skeptical by nature, and often couches her ironies in French, which after sixteen years in

---

* But not for the purpose of carrying supplies to the Parmentierist rebels who hide out in the caves there—she was cleared of that charge.

† Sam had a few criticisms of that work. He argued that a Space Rocket, buried for a century and a half under the sands of Florida, could not be put into working order by a mere band of boys, even if some of them were students of the mechanical arts. Perhaps not; but they could hardly have got to the moon by any other means, and I let the improbability stand.

this country I still do not confidently understand. "That's what you think," I tell her; and she laughs as she walks away, her white skirt swirling about her ankles.

I mean to leave my typewriter and follow her. The afternoon is too tempting to be denied. It isn't Paradise here, or even close, but the mimosa is in bloom and the air from the sea is cool and pleasant. On days like this I think of poor old Magnus Stepney's evolving Green God, harking us all up to Eden. The Green God's voice is faint enough that few of us hear it clearly, and that's our tragedy, I suppose, as a species—but I hear it very distinctly just now. It asks me to step into the sunshine, and I mean to do its bidding.

ACKNOWLEDGMENTS

Julian Comstock could not have been written without the generosity and support of people too numerous to list (including, once again, my endlessly patient wife, Sharry). Of the legions of used-book dealers I consulted in the course of my research, two deserve special mention: Jeffrey Pickell, at Kaleidoscope Books & Collectibles in Ann Arbor, who first drew my attention to the work of "Oliver Optic" (William Taylor Adams), and Terry Grogan, at BMV Books in Toronto, who has an absolutely uncanny talent for finding the right book at the right time. Many thanks also to Mischa Hautvast, Peter Hohenstein, Mark Goodwin, and Claire-Gabriel Robert for help with the Dutch and French passages—any errors are, of course, all mine. And, not least, my sincere thanks to Peter Crowther, of PS Publishing, whose handsome chapbook edition of "Julian: A Christmas Story" opened the door for this much larger work.